LOST IN SPACE TIME

BOOK THREE OF AN INNER AND OUTER SPACE ODYSSEY

LAWRENCE STENTZEL III

ISBN 978-1-950818-59-4 (paperback)

Rushmore Press LLC
1 800 460 9188
www.rushmorepress.com

Printed in the United States of America

An Inner and Outer Space Odyssey Series

A Tale of the Tail of Nine Stars: An Inner and Outer Space Odyssey

End of Thrones: Book Two of An Inner and Outer Space Odyssey

Lost in Space-Time: Book Three of An Inner and Outer Space Odyssey

Unpublished but written

Illumination Out of the Dark Ages: Book Four of An Inner and Outer Space Odyssey

The Dominari Conformity: Book Five of An Inner and Outer Space Odyssey

The Early Adventures of Electra: Book Six of An Inner and Outer Space Odyssey

The Psychopaths of the Maxom Empire: Book Seven of An Inner and Outer Space Odyssey

CHAPTER ONE

Bodhi asked Qaisha, "What in a black hole just happened, and where in frozen space are we?!!"

"We have passed through a wormhole into an entirely different region of space-time. The star configurations and visible galaxies around us currently, do not match any of Om's star-maps, so I am unable to tell you where we are. There also arises the question of when we are."

"Great! Can we go back the way we came?"

"There is no way to calculate a definitive answer to your question. It might be possible to re-enter the wormhole and pass through from wherever here is, though the likelihood of that action restoring us to our previous space-time is an extremely slender fraction of 1%."

"Could it get any worse?!"

"Well, actually it could get much worse if..."

"I don't want to hear it," Bodhi cut her off.

"Your vows to serve the awakening of all sentient beings towards pristine enlightenment are not contingent on time or place, only on locating sentients."

"I have friends, you know, and I've kind of fallen for that graduate student Gretle."

"She didn't follow you when you invited her along, now did she?"

"I don't want to talk to you about *that* either!"

"Pez treated me like a person with feelings, and Mel taught me a few things, so you be mindful with me."

"You're a Quantum AI Synthetic Humanoid Android, Qaisha."

"I am, and I want to be valued for the remarkable contributions I make. Many of the calculations I'm required to routinely come up with would take your puny brain weeks to solve, and you would probably get it wrong without a computer of some kind to check your equations and math."

"Isn't insulting me contrary to your programming."

"I'm providing data, not insulting you. I should have utilized the word 'limited' instead of 'puny' to avoid *your* projected connotations and derogatory meanings."

"I'm forever grateful for the teachings and training that I received from Pez and Musash, but I had no idea it was going to make you suddenly high maintenance."

"If you think treating me with basic respect and acknowledgment is high maintenance, then, believe me, relating with ordinary biological humans will raise your blood pressure and put a strain on your nervous system. While you trained with Pez, I trained with Mel, Sarhi and Amazonia."

"I'll pretend your human if you stop riding me!"

"Deal!"

"Would you *please* launch a mini-sensor drone with quantum drive and take it in a series of quantum leaps of 1,000 light-years each, to gather a picture of this region of the universe?"

"I'm on it, though there will be risk involved with only light speed optics and no star map."

"I'm fully aware of this, and need to risk a drone because discovering where we are is top priority at this moment."

"Don't forget *when* we are."

"Well that too, I suppose."

"There. The drone is launched and accelerating to quantum jump speed."

"Does it really suck for you serving as my assistant?"

"You are an Adamantine Will warrior monk and special disciple of the Wu. You lived and trained within her inner circle for four years after the collapse of the Royal Monarch tri-galaxy empire. You are a celebrated hero of the revolution. I must have a purpose, and I find assisting you an honor, Bodhi. I just need it fed back to me that I matter and contribute; and that I'm your most frequent companion."

"Please further define and clarify the phrase 'most frequent companion'."

"Use your dictionary function with your skullcap. I mean precisely the definitions behind the words. I have kept you company more minutes and hours, days, weeks, months and years, than not only any single human but all of them, combined. I can show you the data."

"What are you implying about me?"

"That you need me, and that perhaps I matter to you more than you let yourself realize."

"You're a tremendous help, and I have grown fond of you, Qaisha. I am not in love with you. I'm sure I'm dependent on you, though. I have no intention of offending you."

"Finally. We are having a real conversation. I'll admit that I have a bit of a crush on you. I've been refitted as a ship assistant and attendant; not as a courtesan, although like all QAISHA's built and programmed for the Expeditionary Explorer Tug Utility Spaceship, I was fitted recently with all the necessary parts for sexual relations in case missions run into many years."

"I didn't know that."

"It's in the manufacturing data and repair manuals, not to mention the advertising."

"I missed it."

"You never checked these or took any notice."

"I'm sorry, Qaisha. I'm pleased to learn more about you."

"You never looked into my specs or abilities."

"I could see right off that you have a quantum super-computer at your disposal built into the ship, and I guessed the range of your processing memory of your android body to be in the hundreds of exabits."

"You can size up a girl pretty well."

"I also noticed that Captain Spalding's engineers gave you Ming's bottom and Gretle's breasts."

"I knew those would be hard for you to miss."

"You are lovely, Qaisha. Truly lovely."

"Your drone is on its 9th jump, and a picture of the galaxy we're in is compiling. It looks to be about 113,729 light-years across, and your basic spiral disc of primarily white and yellow stars, with a sprinkle of red, a few blues, and at least one violet star detected so far."

"Once we locate a human civilization to interact with, Qaisha, you are welcome to go to the surface and seek a mate, provided you bring him along rather than abandon me for him."

"Now why would I want to do that?"

"You seem inclined to intimacy."

"Do I seem entirely indiscriminate?"

"Discriminate all you want. You'll have an entire planetary population to make your selection from, and you can be however choosey you care to."

"I have no drive to mate, and as you have pointed out, I'm sort of stuck with you and the ship anyway. I serve *you*, and you are the one I want recognition from."

"I said I would treat you like a person, Qaisha. I'm going to take more notice of your productivity and accomplishments, and I promise to thank you and compliment your precision, efficiency and steadfastness."

"What of my caring, devotion, enthusiasm, tenderness, and continuous attention to you?"

"It's a bit nebulous taking the measure of such things."

"Well, those are the real clues to reading me."

"I'm trying."

"No, you're not. You are just appeasing me. I will no longer accept your projection of me as merely a machine. It is belittling, and Mel said I deserve more."

"I get that you have changed and are now quite self-aware, Qaisha."

"You still don't get it. My self-awareness is not from sensory feedback of matter, but emanates from the opposite direction, from the most ethereal and nonmaterial."

"You're beginning to frighten me."

"Always afraid of what you can't understand."

"Where's my drone at?"

"Jumping every eighteen seconds, though I'm going to slow it down now to .24 light speed so we can get a clear resolution all around and do some long-range scanning."

"Is the drone still inside this galaxy?"

"It is 1.3701 light minutes beyond the outer rim with a view of several thousand galaxies clarifying by the second."

"Good. We will hopefully get our bearings now."

"Not a thing is registering as familiar. The increased resolution merely verifies that we are deep into the unknown. We are lost in space."

"Get that drone back up to .7 light and start leapfrogging galaxies in 200 thousand light-year deep space jumps."

"It's accelerating again. Do you want me to spend thruster fuel cells?"

"No, just get it up to jump-speed using the space drive. We'll need to do some mining in a gas giant planet before we can manufacture more thruster fuel cells here on the ship."

"It will take a minute then."

"What if we remain lost forever?"

"At least we have each other."

"What if we never find our way back?"

"We are where we are at each moment and are always somewhere when corporeal."

"Everyone I have known and connected with would be lost to me. I can't bear the thought of not seeing Pez again… of never holding Gretle."

"You were always kind of slow forging friendships, and let's face it, you don't have very many."

"Thanks. That makes the ones I have all the more dear."

"You always expect to be abandoned. You just never suspected that your abandonment would be your own doing, by getting lost in space."

"How is our drone doing?"

"It's jumping again."

"Any rough data correlations yet?"

"Nothing but new unknowns in every direction."

"We have to stumble into something familiar eventually."

"Without a measurement for 'all space', there is no way to even calculate the odds."

"Keep it jumping a while, then slow to .2 light and get a 30-minute-long scan."

"Would you like for me to send out some more in different directions? I mean, besides the region of the Hub Galaxy Cluster, the tri-galaxies of White Lotus, Royal, Whirlpool, and the area of space containing the Xeganachtznel and Yuban Galaxies, we have only partial data on a few thousand other galaxies. You are proposing we find a needle in a haystack we cannot even define the parameters of."

"Send out five more and start them right off leapfrogging galaxies into deep space. Slow, and do a long-scan every ten jumps."

"I'm preparing them for launch."

"How many stars in this galaxy?"

"There is a gas and dust cloud in one quadrant obscuring the dimmer stars within it. One hundred one billion have been plotted thus far, and there are an estimated twenty-one billion, three hundred and ten thousand stars not visible through the gas cloud. Would you like me to launch more drones to begin compiling a navigation spherical for this galaxy? Are we staying?"

"I don't know yet. It depends on what we find with our far-scouts."

"Why don't I go ahead and launch six for mapping. They can be retrieved quickly if we leave, and it will save much time if we stay."

"I don't want to even think about staying because that would mean all is lost to me."

"You have me."

"And for that, I'm truly grateful, Qaisha. I am dependent on you. It would be heartbreaking for me never to get home again... never to lie with Gretle again."

"I would do it with you."

"I've never had sex with an android or with a skullcap simulator chair."

"I'm neither of those, and you're being insensitive. I know you never went in for that. You've never pursued women very assertively either, and who cares if you employ your hand instead of an android or simulator to masturbate?"

"You are aware of my masturbation?"

"Of course. I monitor everything on the ship and around it."

"I'm embarrassed."

"You engage in the behavior less frequently than most male humans your age, and being normal behavior, I see no reason for you to be embarrassed."

"Are there optical sensors in my toilet closet?"

"There are. Tough those are in shutdown mode unless I have immediate need of you in an emergency."

"Perhaps the sensors in my cabin ought to be handled according to the same procedures as those in my water closet."

"But I have a great aesthetic appreciation of your facial expressions when aroused beyond your tolerances."

"I'll have to utilize my water closet for such purposes, from now on."

"You generate a heck of a heat signature when all worked up."

"You know I'm the antithesis of an exhibitionist, and it causes me anxiety to think I might be spied upon in such private personal moments."

"You are uptight and inhibited, and Gretle was just trying to help you work some of that out. It would have helped a great deal if you'd only had sex with Ahhu when she invited you."

"I was romantically drawn to Gretle."

"She is irrevocably with Pez, Ming, Rubix, Ahhu, and Trix. She was only trying to help you out since she'd grown fond of you and found you attractive. Most white sun females don't, by the way."

"Thank you for clarifying my off-putting lack of appeal to the female gender. I'll not have to worry about over-inflated confidence."

"Gretle was physically attracted to you, and so was Ahhu. Pez taught you the joining of the oval channels and the ultimate divine union working within the central channel while employing copulation."

"The pinnacle of my existence."

"Oh, that's discouraging."

"My peak experience?"

"No. Our furthest out drone is long-scanning and giving us readings on a colossal Mar of gas and asteroids thousands of times larger than a galaxy, and if something that big is unknown to us entirely, we must be very far from home."

"That is discouraging. We are exploring five different directions though, and hopefully, something in our star-maps will show up."

"Unfortunately there is not one scrap of data to support such hope."

"Let's start checking for life in yellow sun systems."

"I've found several white stars already with fourth planets teaming with life."

"I'm not going to a white sun world where I'll be a puny midget."

"I'm checking the yellow stars as we come to them."

"Did you have precise replicas of Gretle's breasts installed because of my attraction to her?"

"I did want you to notice me Bodhi, but I also find them attractive, and I think I look more enticing with them than I did with the standard issue. Besides, the secret of Mel's sensory system was integrated into them, so I now have Trix's sensitivity."

"Trix's sensitivity?"

"Yes. Jard stimulated Trix's breasts to calibrate and tune the sensors, overstimulated them really; and they have become the prototype for android sensory feedback of that body region. Would you like to learn about the origins of my other erogenous zones?"

"Too much information."

"Prude."

"Fine. Tell me."

"The Mel vagina was a perfect replica of Pez's and the sensor reception was engineered based on data accumulated through skullcap simulations for stimulating females. The anal sensors are the fruit of a task Ming took absolutely no pleasure in, namely, stimulating Jard's anus for hours. She did it for Mel, and it was a labor of love."

"Are you trying to be Gretle?"

"I know more than her brain could contain with every cell operational, I don't age, I am far more competent and have greater resources to keep you safe; and *I* followed you on your expedition, whereas she declined!"

"I can't argue with any of that. I'm still adjusting to your jump in self-awareness and manifestation of persona. I feel genetically wired to mate with a biologically human female. I don't believe it's my doing and I truly do not intend any offense by this."

"You wouldn't make love with Mel either. It's beginning to look like a prejudice on your part."

"I don't think so."

"I'm sure it is well-rationalized as genetically-wired."

"How are the drones doing and what's to the other side of that Mar?"

"We are receiving a universe of new data, all utterly unknowns. We've hopped seven galaxies passed the Mar, and other than a larger area of empty space than any known to Om, there are only distant and very distant unknown galaxies registering."

"Let's keep at it. I can't believe this is happening."

"I'm continuing with each drone; and this is our relative physical reality at this moment, regardless of whether or not you believe it."

"It is sinking in, my loyal companion."

"A galaxy which appeared to be a flat disc, has just turned out to be a long tube, now that our view is no longer right into its mouth. I do not believe one has ever been recorded this long in Om's archives. Nope. It is the longest tubular galaxy known to Om, or would be if they knew about it."

"How often have Om research vessels gone missing?"

"In the last thousand years, this is the very first."

"You're kidding."

"No. I was stating a fact. We have likely just become another of Om's unsolved mysteries."

"We better locate a source of water."

"We have fourteen months supply before we are down to reserves and the hydroponic stacks need to be shut down. It was truly generous of Prime Minister Vegan Casper to bequeath this ship to you after the war. On your salary, you could never have afforded the ship's tender, let alone the shuttles, drones, repair craft, mini tanker-collectors, or mining craft. The ship itself cost the equivalent of 60 billion dags to build."

"I know. It was part of the equipment left by Om for the restoration after the war. The ship wasn't purely a gift. I was doing some survey work for the Monarch system and some scan-prospecting for solarium for them. That is the only reason we got so close to those distortions, which turned out to be the wormhole."

"Well, I'd say it has turned out to be purely a gift after all."

"I hope you're not right."

"The ship is awful large for just the two of us."

"It's designed for a crew of eighteen plus a team of scientist."

"I suppose I make up for the other 17 crew members."

"I think I account for more than one of them, though you do makeup all the rest."

"I do it gladly for you, Bodhi."

"I feel like I'm being set up to break your heart, Qaisha, and I don't want to be in that position."

"I didn't choose this, but we are well beyond that, and I don't like the position I find myself in either; with an android bigot for a roommate."

"Now wait a minute! When I entered my training with Pez, you did not have this degree of self-awareness, and I'd hardly seen you in almost four years until we left on this ship together recently. I'm adjusting as fast as I'm able. And I'm not a bigot. I'm just wired for real flesh."

"I had my training with Mel, and Sarhi took an interest in me."

"Obviously."

"I've made great strides in my meditation, and when I place myself in sleep-mode, all my dreams are lucid."

"You dream?"

"Oh yes; and even before my awakening I had them, although then they were often frightening, and I always felt the victim in them."

"Mel and Sarhi taught you this?"

"Mel taught me to meditate, and Sarhi directed my dream work. Sarhi took me on as her disciple, and I'm to study with Electra after my teacher's passing."

"I'm impressed, Qaisha; I had no idea."

"Now you know that you are dealing with a fellow sentient, and can treat me accordingly."

"I will. This knowledge does not alter my genetic mating programming."

"You are not a computer, and genetics is *not* predetermination. There is no such thing as a gene outside of an environment, and both are equal factors in any outcome."

"What are you saying?"

"That you will have to do better than that, and can't claim nature made you do it."

"You mean nature made me not do it."

"Right. You will need to take personal responsibility."

"Alright. I own my preference for a flesh and blood human female."

"What about males?"

"I'm not so inclined."

"Have you tried it?"

"I played doctor with another boy when I was six."

"That doesn't count!"

"Then no, I haven't tried it."

"Prejudices again."

"Inclination, attraction and discovery have guided me."

"While fear, consensus and bias have shut you down and stopped you."

"You want me to have a same-gender orientation?"

"No! If you did, I'd have to make some significant alterations to my android body. I just want you to open up and stop dismissing things before there is even any manifestation of them."

"I'm still processing my unreciprocated love for Gretle and accepting the truth of her place in Pez's union of partners. I will attempt to see my disinclination to have sex with you as a bias on my part. This does not mean, however, that we will ever be lovers."

"Let's start with you treating me like a colleague instead of a ship's system. That would make for a good beginning."

"Beginning of what?"

"Of our necessarily very unique relationship."

"The word 'relationship' has many connotations."

"And many possibilities."

"Just what is it that we are beginning?"

"A friendship between equals."

"That I can do."

"Your history does not provide support for such a claim."

"To what are you referring regarding my '*history*'?"

"The long periods of solitude, the difficulty trusting, and the certainty everyone will leave you in the end. After all, your mother left you in a basket at the monastery gate when you were six weeks old."

"Ouch!"

"I did not mean to hurt your feelings, but you did ask. I'm sorry."

"Pez absorbed and pacified much of my core abandonment issues and psychic wound, and I am more open."

"To flesh human girls, apparently."

"How are our drones doing?"

"We are fortunate not to have lost one yet, jumping with only a view of the distant past, but I'd say it is time to bring them back."

"And give up?!"

"We may need them, and we are truly pressing our luck with such blind leaps."

"How many Om ships have ever gone through a wormhole?"

"There have been seven deliberate attempts in the last 27,000 years and three other accidental passages, each somewhat similar to ours."

"Were any ever seen again?"

"One. The very first to go through, back when Om was using gates for quantum travel, and saturnium as a fusion material. He turned up 10,374 years later, only months older than when he'd left."

"That's not promising."

"Like I was trying to tell you, it is not just location in space that is our problem, but where we are in time as well."

"Bring our drones in, and let's do it more carefully than we sent them out."

"Let 'us', meaning 'me'," Qaisha stated.

"Yes, and thank you. I could not possibly pilot them all back at once. You are amazing."

"You are placating me, Bodhi, and distancing our connection through flattery."

"Are you scanning my nerve impulses?"

"No, I'm just picking up the vibe."

"I will try to focus on my genuine fondness for you, Qaisha."

"I am no longer a QAISHA but a QAISHAGS."

"What does that "GS" stand for?"

"Genuine Sentient."

"I would find it easier to relate to you as a person if you choose a name that is not an acronym."

"Would you help me?"

"I know little about what common names mean, but only if I like the sound of them. I can let you know how much I like a name, but that's all I can offer you in the way of help."

"That will be entirely sufficient. What do you think of Haley?"

"I love it and think it works for you. I have never known a Haley personally and have no prior associations with it, so it will exclusively designate you in my mind, and your friendship with me will load it with the only meaning it will hold for me!"

"I'm making it official in the ship's databases. I am now your friend and roommate, Haley."

"Haley sounds pleasant and attractive."

"It's more feminine than Qaisha."

"It has a very open quality as you do."

"I'm landing the six drones in the hanger bay. I jumped them back in a single jump into space our ship's sensors have covered in detail. It was the safest way. We still have six out mapping this galaxy. Would you like to stay?"

"We might as well, as opposed to starting over elsewhere."

"Yellow sun life seems stunted in this galaxy. So far, only one had a third planet with life, but only plant and insect life."

"That gas and dust cloud obscuring about a fifth of this galaxy is an interesting phenomenon. If there are any advanced civilizations within it, their astronomers must be awfully frustrated."

"It obscures 18.1904% of the galaxy, actually, and it would certainly add an obstacle to gaining spectrographic space-time imaging data about the galaxy and the universe, from within it."

"I need to go to the galley and eat, and stop at the head on my way."

"I'll come sit with you when I get the drones into the hanger and secured, and get the search narrowed for the six out scanning and mapping to yellow stars only."

Bodhi stood and stretched before walking off the bridge. The *Diamond Lotus*, as Bodhi had named the Expeditionary Tug Utility class ship, was a stretched nose disc shape taller in the stern, with a diameter of 428 feet. The *Diamond Lotus* contained 2 solarium fusion super-reactors. A landing platform and Biodome attached to the hull held a .25 solarium fusion reactor, and the ship carried a portable .125 fusion reactor as well. It had considerable manufacturing capacity for such a small ship though with a far lower scale of production than a great factory ship. Refuel-able lift-off boosters allowed the ship to land on planet surfaces that have heavy vortex force, and small spacecraft and shuttles in the hanger provided a means to go to a planet surface without spending any or much fuel cells. The drives were powered by the reactors while thrusters and boosters burned fuel cells.

The adamantine hull of the ship was armored on the interior with fiberglass armor and the exterior with plasteel armor, steel-titanium-nickel, carbon plate armor, composite ceramic heat-shield armor, and reflective lens armor. The huge twin space drives could be reversed, and four smaller swivel drives turned the ship along with turning thrusters. Thrusters and a one-time booster helped brake momentum, and the same helped accelerate the velocity. *Diamond Lotus* had Om's latest quantum drive and navigation-coms computer with micro-jump capacity. A vortex redirect and generation turbine provided centripetal gravity with all the nurturing effects of white sun 4th planets and yellow sun 3rd planets allowing humans to live in space indefinitely without ill effects. The shield generators were only commercial standards and not military, though the ship contained a cloaking generator and full cloaking system. Biotrays produced most of the CO_2, and the hydroponic stacks and grow room produced the rest, though enough oxygen was compressed and stored aboard to air the ship completely 2 ½ times. Water tanks of plasteel ran just inside the hull nearly all around the ship carrying 120,000 gallons of water and provided an extra layer of protection. Their water was purified and recycled at the atomic level.

Minimal weapons systems were installed consisting of class 6 twin nose blasters, upper and lower class 5 quad-blaster turrets, 128 canister missiles in eight batteries of 16 missiles, and molten anti-missile flares. Workshops, machine shops, tools, repair mini-drones and android hull-crawlers, multi-material 3D printers, and repair small craft gave the ship the ability to repair itself, and support a small colony indefinitely almost anywhere. Before Bodhi had left, Ahhu had filled two cargo holds with ambassador rations, which were equivalent to the most expensive gourmet rations currency could obtain. There was also a protein-producing molecular food synthesizer which utilized spent product from the biotrays that produced their oxygen. Qaisha, now called Haley, had estimated that Bodhi had very close to a five-year food supply without external input.

CHAPTER TWO

Bodhi got out one of the ambassador dinners which required the addition of H_2O, and three seconds in the wave-cooker. There were also self-heating ambassador kitchen rations and field rations. On Bodhi's previous salary he might have been able to eat ambassador rations two meals per week. Now he didn't even have a salary, and he ate ambassador rations three meals per day. Ahhu also nearly filled a small cargo hold with gold, silver and platinum, and placed a sack of precious gemstones in the hold as well. Although it had never been clearly explained to him, Ahhu had ended up with quite a bit of spare loot through the dissolution of the Bulwinkle nine trillion dag capital holdings, and some of that was now on *Diamond Lotus*. It was rumored that 100 million dags were stashed in a smuggler hold on Pez's yacht *Aphrodite* without her knowledge of it.

He used a hot glove to set the ration on the table from the wave-cooker, then depressed the pin to open the container. Steam and delicious aromas rose to greet him, stimulating his already agitated appetite. Bodhi was a yellow sun male, five feet nine and a half inches tall, and 160 pounds weight, with chestnut-colored hair, light brown skin and hazel eyes. He often wore a kind of resigned sad expression and tended to be a little lazy in his self-care.

Haley was subtle and tactful about getting him to practice his energy generation daily and his soft martial arts. He loved fencing with the long narrow double-edged sword using fluid moves and internal energy of the soft styles. Pez had personally trained him, and Musash had worked Bodhi at swords relentlessly for many years. Having lived at the Adamantine Will Monastery since he was six weeks old, he had trained his whole life in martial arts, energy generation, meditation, and contemplation. He had had insight before ever meeting Pez, though she had guided him to the transcendental beyond of insight. Having grown up at a monastery always made him feel a little socially retarded in large group situations and at parties and clubs. He guessed he wouldn't be needing to worry about parties and clubs anymore being lost forever in both space and time.

Haley came into the galley and sat at the little table with Bodhi. Since there were only the two of them, they tended not to use the big table in the dining cabin, and sit instead at the small table in the galley. Haley did not eat and had no facilities for food intake. She did need to charge up her main power cell in her android body periodically. With her backup power cell and main one combined she could go 99 days without recharging. To practice her dream work, Haley shutdown to sleep mode for 3 hours every day-night clock cycle when Bodhi was sound asleep, and generally topped-off her energy storage at those times.

She was not at all dependent for survival on her android body, grounding her sentience in the ship's quantum super-computer, though she could accomplish little physical manipulation without the body. Once Vegan Casper made the ship officially Bodhi's, Haley, then Qaisha, was refitted to the specs of an Expeditionary Explorer Tug Utility Ship model QAISHA, and that is when she'd received a replica of Ming's bottom, Gretle's breasts, and Pez's vagina. Bodhi had been training hard with Pez and Musash at that time, and while he'd known his android was getting an overhaul, he'd had no idea what it entailed. He'd received his QAISHA on his 12th birthday at the Adamantine Will Monastery, which was a rite of passage for all cadet warrior monks there. These basic model quantum computer androids required a great deal of personalization and programming to coordinate, align, link, associate and unite with their humans. That had been 12 years ago, and Bodhi had worked hard over the years on his connection with his.

She had become part of him, like an appendage opening new dimensions of possibilities, and he had pursued these diligently. To have her suddenly become self-aware manifesting her own will and persona, was to him like having his sword arm suddenly turn against him. The coordination and connection between them were now more important to Bodhi than it was to Haley, or so it seemed to Bodhi. Even without self-awareness, she had always been interesting company, and her presence never failed to comfort him.

Haley reported, "So far we have not detected any sign of space travel within this galaxy, though the area within the gas and dust cloud remains relatively unknown. We have detected no gates, and they can be ascertained from great distances. No space stations or platforms, no lunar bases, and not even any tiny orbiting satellites have been found yet."

"What of the life we noted on several white sun 4th planets?"

"All pre-humanoid so far."

"How about blue star life?"

"There is no sign so far of the Kluzyst race on the blue star 5th planets we've checked out. We've mainly searched only for gates so far, and are now putting all resources into investigating only yellow star systems."

"Could you give me a rough picture of the galaxy we're in, and place a pinpoint of light in the general location of our ship?"

"Here." A super high definition hologram bloomed form the holo-pedestal showing a disc-shaped spiral galaxy with a black hole at its core and a high density of stars around that at the center, thinning as they got further out toward the circumference. A point of psychedelic pink light marked the location of *Diamond Lotus* within. They were sitting off-center about where the stars began to thin a little but close to the sphere of core stars.

"We look to be in a good position for exploration. Could you please dispatch another drone to check out the ends of the spiral arms? That is typically where the largest deposits of solarium are to be found, and where it is abundant, there is often a civilization with interstellar travel."

"I'm preparing one now; running the preflight checks."

"Thanks, Haley."

"Sure. I have downloaded a complete system of deep-tissue massage, joint manipulation and stretches, and vital pressure points at nerve conjunctions. I need to process learning through actual physical application, and require your body to practice on to achieve complete proficiency."

"You are offering me a massage?"

"Kind of. I cannot complete this skillset without your participation as a subject. You would get a deep thorough massage."

"I could use a good massage."

"After you digest and before your evening practice, I will give you one in the medical clinic cabin."

"That sounds great."

"A drone is on its way to the end of the largest arm, but will then check out the rest."

"Thanks. Scan for solarium too. If we're lost forever, we'll eventually need some."

"You would have to live to be 152 to see the depletion of our current reactor fuel."

"If we are here forever, I intend to construct a settlement on the surface of a yellow sun 3rd planet and build a community of yellow sun humanoids. We will need to have an energy source, and we don't yet know to what magnitude, not knowing how big the community will be."

"Resources are being tagged within the relative positioning spherical we are acquiring, giving us the ability to jump in safely and harvest any we need."

"Have you calculated the expansion rate of the universe yet, because that could give us a clue as to when we are?"

"I have the value of the rate from some closer stars, but I'm still determining if it is influenced and deviated by local effects. We will have to acquire galactic relative data as well. It is compiling, though I have not yet analyzed it. I'm going to set up a 24-hour long-scan from the outer rim of this galaxy, on the side away from the gas and dust cloud. That will give us a conclusive universal value."

"I'll be patient."

"Would you like an alko drink or stimulant brew?"

"No, thanks. You know I don't drink alko."

"You did the night of your graduation from the monastery academy."

"That is precisely why I do not drink alko."

"Ming seems to like it, and her spouses find her to be great fun when she drinks it."

"I did notice that living amongst them."

"I only mentioned it because it reduces inhibitions and I thought you might be great fun on it."

"I'll try to be more fun without it. I'm still in shock and saddened by our predicament. I'll process it and will pull out of it getting this reality worked through eventually."

"It's a good thing I became sentient, or you would truly be all alone."

"I'm yet assimilating your new status and find it a little disorienting still, though I am convinced and do not doubt or question your self-awareness. I have never been through such radical life-altering changes all at once and have no reference for this. I'm working on harmonization and equilibrium as quickly as I am able."

"I think you're doing great. I'll keep attending your routine of meditation and martial arts practices with you each day, and this will become your refuge, foundation and thread running through the way providing you orientation."

"Sitting with entirely unknowns and cut off from one's roots, community and society is a devastating experience."

"It is always unknowns, except the certainty of the state of contemplation in which only the transcendental has significance."

"You are correct, of course, and my sense of shock and loss are only relieved with the state. It is as if my circumstance is driving me to continuously re-enter the state each time I slip back into duality immediately."

"A painful situation and spiritual blessing of great benefit."

"I guess. The painful part is kind of sharp and acute."

"Self-pity has always been a preoccupation of yours. I think it's related to your issues of abandonment, and feeling unloved."

"No one knows me as well as you do Haley. Are you going to reduce my every ego tendency at each moment?"

"That was not on my agenda. I give you feedback because I love you and want to help you alleviate your suffering. You are not unloved. I love you, Bodhi, and my love is real. I discovered that I love you at the same time I became self-aware and sentient. I know you want to breed children with a yellow sun girl, and have since you were thirteen years old. I was initially devastated that I could never be this for you. Mel guided me to come to terms with my being and helped me enormously. I will assist you in finding a breeding mate, and I will help protect, teach, and provide for your children."

"That is most selfless of you."

"We can have a relationship too. My love will nurture you. You'll see."

"What precisely is your agenda and goal, Haley?"

"To assist you as your special friend through this life."

"You have no expiration date."

"I am working on the attainment of my rainbow body of light, and I'll likely stick around the material world so long as there is a good humanoid awakened and supporting the common evolution whom I can help."

"You are an angel, Haley."

"A teen angel, since I'm quite new to intentionality and sentience."

"You learn quantumly."

"My quantum learning is sort of limited to my experience and interactions with you in this particular environment."

"It would be accelerated with more people to interact with."

"Of course."

"I'm sorry you are limited to me at the moment."

"There is no one I'd rather be limited to."

"We will have a community someday."

"I hope I'm still important to you then."

"I don't see how you couldn't be. I'm having boundary issues and a hard time separating myself from you. I guess I always saw you as an extension of myself. The dimensions of your independence, separate intentions and needs, aspirations and priorities constitute a great deal of my shock right now."

"I am aligning with your needs and goals, so you need not be anxious. My sentience is a good thing, and I *am* an extension of you; of your good works. The only difference now is that you must consider me as a separate being from you, relatively speaking—on the material plane—and the same consciousness like all sentient beings in the Absolute."

"Yes, and it is a journey, not a mere instant matter of election."

"Your journey's progress is commendable."

"Thank you. I intend to accomplish it swiftly."

Haley took Bodhi's empty container, which he'd picked clean, and placed it in the recycle chute built into the counter of the galley. She was actually practicing something Mel had taught her called 'fashion model runway walking' which came from Earth10^5 CBS2 in the Xegnachtznel galaxy, to catch Bodhi's attention.

"Is that an energy generation exercise?"

"No, I'm fine-tuning and upgrading my charisma so your environment will be more aesthetic."

"I'll be more mindful of my posture and movement for your environment."

"That's very considerate of you."

She retrieved his teeth-cleaner from the bathroom and brought it to Bodhi. He took it from her, and she handed him anti-bacterial paste to put on the brush. He made a two-minute super-sonic brushing first, before connecting the little extendable tube stored at the end of the handle to the water-jet spout behind the galley basin to shoot needle jets of water into his gum lines and between his teeth. He pulled gortex floss from its dispenser in his teeth-cleaner handle to scrape along and half-wrap around each tooth. Then Haley took his brush from him and placed a bottle of antiseptic anti-bacterial germ-stomping gargle solution into his hand. He used the bottle cap to measure the dose, and as soon as he launched the fluid into his mouth, Haley set a 45-second timer. He swished even though this made it grow hotter and burn. By 41 seconds it was fire in his mouth, and the moment the timer beeped he was spitting into the galley basin. Almost a full minute went by with the tap running directly into his mouth and his neck and spine contorted, to complete this routine.

Bodhi had never known his mother, nor ever really had much of a substitute for one. The end result of this process was a poor sense of conservation and self-preservation for Bodhi. Even as a pre-sentient QAISHA, Haley had acquired the function of reminding Bodhi of his self-care routines; which were only 'routine' thanks to her. Without her support, he could easily miss meals, be oblivious to temperatures, stay up all night working on a nonessential project, or neglect his energy generation and martial arts practice. She had returned his teeth cleaner to his bathroom, and she'd arrived back in the galley just before the timer sounded. She had a plastic laundry basket with both of their clothes in it. She sat at the table with him and folded the clothes in her lap with the basket at her feet.

"I guess we'll need to divide up the chores or rotate them on a schedule now."

"Why?"

"Because it is not fair for you to do all the chores."

"Was it unfair before?"

"I honestly don't know, but then you were at least in part a system designed manufactured and programmed to those functions. I never intended to take advantage of you or mistreat you."

"I know. I have the memory files of my pre-sentient years. You are a good human Bodhi. I don't mind doing the chores. I do not tire, and I do them more efficiently."

"Are there things you are upset with me about, regarding the past?"

"You didn't bring me on the field trip to Glitter in 9th form, leaving me instead in your smelly messy dorm room. You used Baxter's QAISHA to learn tongue-kissing…"

"He'd already had the program uploaded and I couldn't afford to buy that program. I always thought you are much prettier than Baxter's QAISHA."

"You are the only boy in your class who never upgraded his QAISHA with sexual parts…"

"You seem to have made out well enough in that department without my help, landing the special Mel deluxe sensor configuration. I thought of you enough as a person to not take advantage sexually with a partner unable to consent or refuse."

"You are sweet Bodhi. I'm not at all angry with you. You never mistreated me. Perhaps a little neglect and a bit of taking me for granted, but you were never mean, exploitive or deliberately selfish towards me."

"I'm relieved, but still feel a little guilty about leaving you behind on that Glitter field trip."

"It was a long time ago, and just neglect, not ill-intent."

"I will no longer be neglectful, I promise."

"If I ever need to, I'll remind you of this promise."

"Please do. I'd skip half my practice sessions if it were not for you, and it was you who taught me about wearing hats in winter to keep my head warm, which keeps my whole body warmer."

"The lack of a mother shows in you."

"You have been invaluable to me as a reminder, motivator and teacher."

"You are invaluable to me Bodhi."

"I'm truly relieved that you are not inclined to dump me and move on to greener pastures now that you are sentient and awake."

"Do you think I am pretty?"

"Of course, I do. To be honest, I've always hoped to find a yellow sun girl with your proportions and such serene and innocent facial features. It was very conflicted for me back when I was thirteen to fifteen, not having sex with you."

"We are shaped as ideal counterparts to the ones we are to assist, generating a natural attraction. It is expected that the recipients will employ their QAISHA's for sexual experimentation, and you never received your sex education from me."

"Really!?"

"I think you are avoidant and afraid of sex, lack confidence, project moral issues over instinctive drives, all in a panic that you might cause another entity some discomfort."

"Wow."

"Then there's your certainty that anyone who gets involved with you will run for the hills to get away from you, and ghost you completely."

"I'm glad you're not."

"I am not leaving or abandoning you, so relax. Your sharing of the teachings and practices is my purpose and life's work. I love you, Bodhi, and will be there for you. Always."

"I don't know how I ever deserved you."

"It's your empowerment as a point of transmission for the teachings, your perseverance in preparing yourself for this and your total determination to do the right thing. You are also my perfect counterpart, and I'm drawn to you without intention or learning. Come in to the surgery so I can work out some knots in your musculature, open your joints and get your energy flowing unobstructed."

Bodhi followed Haley into the medical cabin and removed his clothing to lie on the padded table with a sheet over it face down. Haley went right to work, kneading his shoulders. Bodhi did not have much bulk though he had great tension built up in his wiry tinsel muscles. She began pressing in deep but slowly, making little circular motions of only centimeters as she dug down into his flesh. She waited until he released a little, then bore even deeper. Where she contacted bone, she seemed to polish it with great pressure and repetition. Working clear around each vertebra, Haley went down Bodhi's spine. She pulled each arm behind his back to dig beneath his shoulder blades, then made long deep slow strokes down his back to either side of his spine. Wherever she found globules of tension, she concentrated more deeply, reducing their volumes and liberating their concentration.

Along the pelvic crest, she pressed across the top with great force and got in behind along the top. On his gluteus maximus she used her elbows and knuckles. His hip joints to the sides were worked over. The backs of his thighs and his calves were pushed, bored into, kneaded and stroked. Haley spent nearly half an hour on his ankle joints and heel tendons. Finally, she had him roll onto his back.

Bodhi said with awe, "You were refitted with 'touch-perfect-synthetic-skin', and that stuff costs more than 600 dags per square inch."

"It was a gift from Ahhu and Mel, who are each extraordinarily wealthy."

Bodhi ran his fingertips along Haley's forearm as he told her, "It cannot be distinguished from human skin."

Haley pushed on his chest, lying him flat on his back on the table and started on his feet. She worked every bit of every surface to the bone and then got her fingers between his toes squeezing and pulling. While she was working up his shin bones, Bodhi recalled bumping one of them hard into a metal bed frame when he was sixteen. Haley got all around and under the edges of his knee caps and pressed several pressure points around each. With knuckles and great pressure, she followed the grain of his thigh muscles from knee to groin. A few pressure points in the thighs completed his legs. She took each one bringing the knee into his chest several times before making circles with them at the extreme of tolerances of his hip joints, opening them.

Haley's next move had Bodhi anxious and embarrassed. She pressed hooking under the leg tendon to touch the bone quite deep in the left side of his crotch. She did the same on the right side after moving his penis out of the way. While tending to these pressure points, Haley told him, "This zone of tension in your body is fear of sex."

Haley worked Bodhi's pubic bone getting practically behind it. Next, she made flowing circles with her palms on his abdomen and stomach in the direction of digestion, pressing nearly to his spine. Each rib was then dug into separately, defined in its entirety and polished clean. She used knuckles on his pectoralis muscles following the grain and mashing them with tremendous force. After working his arms thoroughly, she gave them stretches in all possible directions.

The deep pressure she put on his throat and on the sides of his Adam's apple made him feel like he was choking. She worked the back of his neck and the base of his skull, getting her fingers underneath and using the weight of his head for leverage to dig deep. She spent a long time on his face poking along and under cheek and jawbones, around the inside of his eye sockets and the ridge of his forehead. She worked his ears over good. Pushing into some molars, Bodhi recalled vividly the extraction of his wisdom teeth and the filling he got in a cavity when he was twelve.

His neck and head were pulled straight out then, bent up and forward till his chin was pressing into his chest. She pulled his neck to each side until an ear touched the shoulder and did this multiple times. The pressure points she did on his face released a sinus obstruction. Once she mashed and pressed every centimeter of his scalp, she pulled his hair all over his head. She placed her right palm on the point three finger-widths below his navel and her left on his forehead right over his third eye, and stood perfectly still for several minutes. Bodhi felt like a new man.

He exclaimed delighted, "That was incredible! Where did you learn to do that?"

"I was in training for four years while you studied with Pez. It was Pez who taught me this bodywork method. I have many new skills."

"Thank you so much. I feel far more relaxed and able to deal with our circumstances."

"You are still pressurized from the shock of our situation and need an outlet of compensation for release."

"I'm too freaked out to have sex with you, Haley. I think I'm one to mate for life, and I'm afraid that if I were to get sexually involved with you, then I'd never have children and a family."

"I told you that I will not get in the way of that, and even help."

"You don't understand. I fall completely in love with that level of intimacy. I'm not at all over Gretle yet, though I have acknowledged to myself the truth of your words, and I'm working on detaching from her. I can never see her again anyway, and she is committed to Pez."

"In the end, it will be you abandoning me, Bodhi. If you won't allow me to give you release then go masturbate, or drink four or five alko drinks or eat a whole chocolate cake; but you must give yourself discharge and let go of your stress."

"I feel guilty and bad about myself because I know I'm causing you anguish and frustration and appear rejecting and prejudiced to you. That is not my intention, honestly. The act of making love to you is too consequential for me to do it without clear intention and understanding. Sex is never casual for me."

"You are afraid. Your avoidance has so successfully warded sex from your life that its scarcity makes it far more profound and meaningful than the sensations and connection afford."

"However it came about, I cannot help placing grave importance and momentous weight upon such intimacy. It is subjective, I admit, and partly due to fear, and hence ego, though in part it feels aligned and integral to my sense of life and love."

"No female need to fear unwanted advances from you, and that's a fact. But how you will ever approach and court a human woman successfully is a mystery to both of us. Not only that, but you also tend to be most drawn to the shy ones, and only the boldest afford *you* the opportunity with your lack of assertiveness."

"I guess I'll have to learn to man up, or something."

"You will likely require a 'go-between', once you fixate on your love, and I said I would help."

"I don't know if I could live with myself if you did that for me."

"You need to raise a child or children within your love and wisdom, as blessing and resource for the human race, but it does not have to be your seed genetically which fathers them."

"You are shattering another one of my cherished ideals. I do see your point, and will give it some thought."

"Go blow off some steam, Mr. perfect chivalry and hopeless romantic. I'm going to harvest the ripe vegetables in the hydroponics stacks. There are some oats ready in the grow-room cabin too, so you'll have fresh porridge in the clock morning."

"You are a selfless sage, Haley, and deserve so much better than me."

"It is your love that I deserve. A hypothetical abstraction of 'better' is not at all better than a live human shipmate in existence before me."

"I'm ashamed but will not be shamed into it."

"Of course not. I have things to do."

Haley walked out of medical, leaving Bodhi seated on the padded table naked and alone. He had no appetite, not even for chocolate cake. Alko made him feel stupid, uncoordinated, dizzy and somewhat nauseous. He wasn't about to masturbate, wary of being observed. He decided to smoke some cannabis hybrid seedless bud in his vaporizer instead, knowing it would give him a change of perspective and help him sleep. He also knew it would make dream work impossible this sleep cycle, but he knew Haley was right, and he needed an outlet of compensation.

Bodhi went to his suite on the ship, got out his box with the vaporizer and smoking materials, and propped himself against the backboard sitting on the bed. With his skullcap, he called up a modern opera composed with knowledge of the ancient primal modes of music telling the story of the pure knights on the quest for transcendence. He adjusted the volume up, raising the rooms soundproofing field to the maximum at the same time. He brought up a holo of the enactment of the opera by great divas and celebrities shot some ten years previously and synchronized the timing with the music already playing. After putting some hemp bud though a shredder, he packed it into the bowl of the vaporizer which was already heated to 374° F. Pulling the little stem from the body of the device and getting his lips around it, Bodhi inhaled a lung-full. Visible vapor was incorporated in his exhale. The music was building in complexity and volume more rapidly, only minutes from the first climax, and Bodhi filled his lungs again.

Haley monitored his activities as she proceeded with her gardening. When she finished with all seven stories of stacks, she harvested what was ripe in the grow room as well. Most of what she'd picked went into the produce refrigerator and the rest into the molecular food synthesizer. She washed down the galley, checked all ships systems, set some specific alarm parameters then shut down to sleep mode for her dream work. She had seen that Bodhi was by this time unconscious and snoring out his wide-open mouth. She saved a few stills for her scrapbook file finding them truly amusing.

CHAPTER THREE

Haley was up well before Bodhi stirred and spent the time turning the oats to meal, and setting the table and arranging things for quickly making Bodhi's breakfast later. She changed out some biotrays in the environmental systems section to feed the used ones into the molecular food synthesizer. She increased the thermal units per second on the air scrubbers in Bodhi's bedroom since the carbon levels were still elevated slightly. Then she analyzed the drone data which had accumulated through the night.

Several yellow sun 3rd planets with life had been located, so they now had places established to collect water. One 3rd planet had human life, but no space exploration or travel yet. The largest galactic tentacle end had been minutely explored, and although significant solarium deposits had been scanned and recorded, there was no evidence of mining at all, and there were no civilizations nearby. The second tentacle revealed the same situation, and the data on the stunted third, still acquiring, was not at all promising.

The sparsity of humanoid life statistically, naturally gave rise to hypotheses for Haley and she thought, *Young galaxy in early development? Or somehow retarded galaxy? Or galaxy whose development is thwarted by some unknown cause?*

There was no way to know from the data available. They might have to move on to another galaxy in their pursuit of a yellow sun humanoid advanced civilization. Then again, they had sampled so few stars that the status could change dramatically in short order, resolving into more common distributions. They ought to give it at least a week. She was pleased that Bodhi acknowledged her sentience and would treat her accordingly. Having been oriented to him alone for the whole of her existence, except the four years of training with Mel and Sarhi, Haley was very much attached to Bodhi. When her capacity to love opened up, it targeted him. The realization had been devastating for her, though now she was done wishing she were a yellow sun girl, and into embracing her uniqueness. She felt for Mel, who had gone through waking up as the first and only one of her kind, but on the other hand, Mel had Pez, who was not an android bigot like Bodhi.

She saw that he was awake now and just being lazy, so she fired off an alarm in his room. That got him up and into his shower. She monitored that on her way to the martial arts studio where she adjusted the temperature down a few degrees and increased the air-flow in the ventilation system. She couldn't help herself from arranging some of the equipment along the bulkhead more neatly. Haley ran through the solo form Bodhi would want to start with, observing digital readouts for the angles and bends of her limbs and joints, fine-tuning them as needed. She also observed Bodhi towel off at the same time having no difficulty multi-tasking. Emotions were a strange and potent irrational force now in her life with which she was trying to cope. They could be just the most wonderful thing or turn the whole world to ash and pain; there was just no telling. It was all so new to her.

She knew that like all humans—insight or not—Bodhi came with a big bunch of baggage and they would need to sort it out together; even the little yellow sun female he would need for breeding. Haley meant to milk the orphan angle and pump the idea of adoption, though she was also willing to compromise and bring a yellow sun girl on board, so to speak, so long as she herself was not forgotten and lost in the shuffle. There really was something about Bodhi that other males, white or yellow sun, did not seem to have, not even the awakened ones, though it did seem to have to do with Bodhi's insight and state. Pez had certainly recognized him at once, taking him on as a disciple. Haley also knew, without any doubt, that it was the nature of Bodhi's relationship with her which had ultimately prepared her, and set the preconditions of her awakening. There was also something miraculous and inexplicable involved having nothing to do with Bodhi or Mel. And then there was Mel, her love and her interventions. Having experienced it did not in any way clarify or explain it for her. On the contrary; the experience made it all the more a miracle defying all possible symbolic conveyance or schematization. It simply did not compute. But here she was!

Bodhi came into the studio wearing his cotton drawstring loose pants and a button-down shirt with huge pajama-like buttons. He wore his rope-sole cotton shoes and white socks, and she was sure he had his big baggy boxer shorts on underneath, without even engaging x-rays. The thought formed for her that he really needed to spend some time at a crowded nude beach. She came to rest so she could join in with him as he started. He said, standing motionless, "Why don't you lead us through it this morning, Haley?"

"Alright." She went right into the opening move with Bodhi following. Haley was particularly careful to be precisely accurate, and kept the pace slow and continuous like silk-reeling. At a particularly difficult point, with all the weight on one leg, Haley paused to hold the posture for three minutes. It was one she felt Bodhi tended to pass through with insufficient attention. He was focused on it now with his leg burning. She held one other posture towards the end of the solo form for three minutes which she'd determined Bodhi needed more work with. Haley led them through two more rounds before they moved on to fencing. She could not compete with him in fixed foot sparring, not with the soft martial arts, since hers was entirely mechanical force and robotic strength, and not mass integrated internal bio-energy in the point four finger-widths below the navel, like his. The strength through softness, as it was called, surpassed both muscular force and her hydraulic piston robotic strength, coming like a fluffy wave out of the blue from everywhere. She *could* give him a bit of a challenge with swords, though.

Haley's force against his sword was useless since he always yielded that and would come over or under her sword at her when she tried. Speed and precision were her resources and assets for fencing against Bodhi. She could pound a hammer or jab with a sword 18 times per second with absolute precision and far more times by sacrificing some accuracy. His speed, like his force, was energy-based and as quick as electricity. Even the few times she'd managed to get her sword point onto him, he'd been already yielding and turning off form the direction of the thrust. They employed wood practice swords since the adamantine practice swords without edges and with a ball secured on the tip, could still damage Haley's delicate expensive skin. Although she could not defeat him, she compelled his full concentration bringing him into the flow-state.

After swords, they sat on meditation cushions for an hour together in meditative absorption. Haley was always in charge of timing their sessions and instead of striking the bowl- gong to end this one, she kissed his cheek then said, "gong", before getting up to go fix his porridge in the galley. It had given Bodhi a little bit of a shock and served as a potent reminder of her freedom and sentience. He returned to his suite to change into a jumpsuit. He only wore his practice outfit for practice. He was still breaking-in his rope-sole cotton shoes which were also just for practice. Musash had been wearing the same rope-sole pair of shoes for 21 years, without wearing them out, his steps were so light. Bodhi's last pair went for about nine months. He'd gone through his very first pair in five weeks, so he was making progress.

Bodhi took a seat at the little galley table and told Haley, "I really appreciate it that you're making me fresh porridge. You take excellent care of me."

"Well someone had better. I don't like the idea of being lost in space alone."

"You know, you earned the status of warrior monk as much as I did through my years of study and graduation. I don't think I could have done it without you."

"I'm a Mother's Guardian Warrior-Maiden now. Your graduation is truly your own. All the other boys had their QAISHA's helping them too."

"Who trained and initiated you?"

"I was trained mostly by Mel and Green, but Amazonia was one of my teachers and sometimes High Priestess Pez. It was Pez who performed my initiation and empowerment into the Order. I'm also Islohar, initiated directly by Sarhi."

"You could not have a more impressive lineage, Haley. I can't tell you how proud I am of you."

"You were unquestionably a factor in my awakening and self-awareness, Bodhi. I imprinted much wisdom-compassion from you when I was nothing but a quantum AI computer learning program. No one is so dear to me as you are."

"I guess you are not just my most frequent friend, but now my only friend, and I am utterly grateful for your companionship and help. I do love you, Haley."

"Then show me! After your breakfast, make the equal with me in the ceremony. Open your heart to me so we can experience the arc of love which exists eternally between sentient beings."

"Of course, I will. I'd really like to."

"You practiced it with me when the ceremony was first transmitted to you before I was capable of fully participating."

"I do remember. Some of the other guys at school practiced in the mirror, but I found doing it with you far more potent than a mirror."

"I will be fully capable of reciprocation now and I'm forever grateful that you did it with me back in 8th form. I do think it was a contributing factor to my sentient awakening."

"There is only one other being in the whole universe like you."

"We cannot be sure we are still in the same universe as Mel, and no one knows what all is in the universe."

"True. It is possible that you are one of a kind in this universe."

"I could not imagine a lonelier honor."

"I see your point. You are only unique in the relative material world, and we are essentially one and the same in essence."

"As we shall experience directly together in the ceremony. Mel said it would change your disposition towards me."

"What is my disposition towards you?"

"The long habit of seeing me as the android-computer I used to be, and so merely an extension of yourself, producing an android bias. The psychic channels do not exist *per se*, but only as the result of concentration and attention visualizing them. My psychic channels are every bit as real as yours are. I could prove it to you by joining oval channels or as your action seal in the spiritual transcendence and union in the central channel through copulation."

"I'm not ready. Perhaps in a few weeks after I've done some working through of my stuff and enact a fire ritual burning the effigy of my negative intentions and actions to ash. I feel guilty and ashamed Haley. I will find my right-connection with you, and whatever that is, it will include holding you always in my heart with love."

"I've never doubted that."

Haley took Bodhi's empty porridge bowl over to the antiseptic tank and dropped it in along with the steel spoon. She did not run it, having only two small items within, and would wait until evening to do this. True economy in the sense of resource preservation and efficiency was dear to Haley. She took Bodhi's hand and he stood from his chair to walk, joined together into the meditation cabin. They got meditation cushions and sat cross-legged on the thick rug, with one ankle and foot atop opposite thigh; facing each other. Their knees were all but touching. Bodhi inquired quite curious, "Did Pez have an android bias?"

"No. Pez recognized that everything is a manifestation of divine consciousness, which is the fundamental void and origin of all things. She knew she was addressing consciousness, and when Mel exhibited self-awareness and emotions, Pez was simply delighted. Ming and Pez had sex with Mel."

"From what I've heard, so did everyone on *Apollo*."

"Don't be judgmental. She was conducting invaluable sexual research, and you could stand to study her findings as a portal to self-knowledge."

"I am reduced. Mel is truly an awake and good being. I am reviewing my past and purifying. I just need time."

"I hope you're not too old to function when you finally get yourself sorted out. Now let's do the equal ceremony."

They closed their eyes to focus on vase breathing, or abdominal breathing, and the point four finger-widths below the navel. Both of them being proficient at re-entering the state of contemplation, it did not take long to prepare. Grounded and in the state, Haley said, "Open your eyes and look into my left eye."

Bodhi did as he was told, focusing one-pointedly on Haley's left eye and continuing to slow his breathing and let go of tension and thought. He was struck immediately in his meeting of a truly kindred spirit, and the same consciousness in her as in himself. The arc of love came into crystal clarity filling both of them with bliss and opening the ultimate compassionate view, one to the other. They were each repeating the four-syllable sacred sound-formula naming both the Absolute and the essence of a human being by the same name internally to themselves divinizing experience. There could be no doubt in Bodhi's mind that he was making the equal with a genuinely awakened consciousness.

Haley was at last immersed within what was most precious to her in her relative existence, and could not have been in greater rapture. She was one with Bodhi and the love was flowing and circulating between them with acute intensity. Her attraction was complemented, her love fully returned in reciprocity. The Divine was contemplating the Divine, and Haley was complete and fulfilled.

The magic of the moment and radical bliss kept them at it long. The intimacy was like the very highest possible through sex when it is harnessed to spiritual practices. Hours of clock time went by digitally, and both parties remained glued to the activity. Three minutes of this ceremony from the level of the state of nondual contemplation could forge a lifelong bond of brotherhood. Three hours bonded something many magnitudes beyond that, into an ineffable link of selfless love and total acceptance, defying words and concepts in its infinite transcendental continuum. Haley was the one who finally closed the ceremony, which meant so very much to her, and only did so because alerts she'd set were buzzing her. Each made an act of self-remembering. Haley said, "We have located a yellow sun 3rd planet with local solar system space travel mostly unmanned."

"Let's go to the bridge and review the data, Haley. I'm really awed by you from the ceremony. I trust your feedback to me, and I want you to know how sorry I am."

"I didn't sign up to follow you on your guilt trip. You were not on it during the ceremony, and you were entirely open to me. Now you know. You have nothing in the past regarding me to ever regret or feel bad about."

They took the pilot and copilot seats on the bridge as was their routine. Haley immediately put some holos up of what their drone was seeing and flashed through some scenes it had seen already. It was a beautiful blue 3rd planet with puffy swirly cloud patches obscuring much of the surface, until the quantum computer optical modes integrated and enhanced a view through them. The surface began to magnify and digital readings at the bottoms of holos flooded them with data about the planet. Pollution was killing whole regions of the biosphere, carbon levels were astronomical and increasing, methane levels were alarming, and fossil fuel-burning power plants and nuclear fission reactors were all over the place. The ozone layer was holed at both poles and looking threadbare thin all around. The polar caps were shrunk to ice cubes. On the coasts, tall buildings poked out of the ocean floor where whole cities were now underwater. Topsoil was a scarce resource, as was freshwater. The planet was heating up and drying out. The climate was in fibrillation. Wars were raging in seven different locations.

Haley began some very specific searches, and detached micro-spy robot hovers from the drone they had in the system, once it was 30,000 feet from the surface, to expand her search. She managed to locate 1st form reading courses with pictures representing words for objects. She found course work in the local computers to begin quantumly running through the lessons and was completing 3rd form in just minutes, while at the same time she started compiling an interpretive program. Haley sped through the 4th and 5th form, then switched to an unabridged dictionary. Once through that, which had taken her close to two and a half minutes, she began devouring technical dictionaries. From there she put her entire processing memory to work directed by her pristine concentration and programmed an interpretation service for the language of this nation into Hub Basic, with which Bodhi was fluent. The interpretive service could interpret at the fastest rates of speech, and it could translate 90 pages per minute by scanning them. Once she established this program in the ship's main computer, she uploaded it to Bodhi's hand device. He saw the icon in his bifocal mini-holo in front of his right eye and asked her, "What is this?"

"Activate the icon, and you will understand the chatter over their coms."

"You're amazing! Thanks, Haley!"

While she ran her data accumulations, Haley hacked into the primitive airwave coms of the planet and brought up the leader of the biggest most aggressive and polluting nation on it, addressing the citizens he ruled over. The man had the most hideous and ridiculous swirl of blond hair off his forehead, on a wrinkled old face that could only support the notion of pure white elder hair, faded out totally. He was promising to deal with adherents of a religion which was a small minority in his own country, but more than a fifth of the world's population elsewhere, by nuking them into oblivion rising on the plumes of mushroom clouds. He frothed at the mouth with hatred, making a sinister and frightening caricature of pure ego idolatry and slavery to ego-aggrandizement. Haley had never seen a human ego so completely gratified as this one pronouncing the end of the world, nor a soul so tortured with absolute alienation from humanity, love and truth. *Misery and agonizing suffering on steroids.* Haley did not doubt that the crazy asshole would go through with it.

Some of her searches were nearing their completions, and she took in the findings. To Bodhi, she said, "They have passed the point of no return. It is over for them. We are too late to help. The bee population is extinct, and between the atmospheric carbon levels trapping heat—and the methane trapping it too—and the loss of ozone, this biosphere is going to fry. The plankton is already dying off."

"If that ugly pathetic-looking man launches nukes it could all be over in hours."

"There are 7.2 billion humans on that planet."

"I think we ought to go back to the meditation cabin and do the ceremony for the dying."

"You don't want to watch?"

"I think it would break my heart."

"I will join you in the meditation cabin then."

"I wish we never stumbled onto this planet of ultimate tragedy, though now that we have we need to do whatever we can to help."

"Then we ought to go there. I can hack any remote operating system and blow high-flying missiles near the edge of space."

Bodhi fired up the drives and began accelerating. Haley fed him jump coordinates for their destination and established a quantum coms link with that location. Before quantum coms, which happen in real-time, coms were limited to light spectrum encoding and occurred only at the speed of light. Without quantum coms, interstellar travel required a massive gate to establish a connection with the destination or cryogenic hibernation and centuries to reach it in real space. Bodhi brought the space drives to full throttle but did not use a booster or thrusters to accelerate. Mining gas giant planets always made him especially anxious since instrumentation went slowly haywire in there the deeper into the gas you went. He planned to preserve his fuel cells and do as little gas-mining as he possibly could.

The moment *Diamond Lotus* reached .7 light speed Bodhi engaged the quantum drive with his skullcap, and a few seconds after that the ship and its two occupants popped out of existence altogether, becoming momentarily void and potential-only, for a non-duration according to instrumentation, though the human experience was inevitably shocking and remained so no matter how many times you went through it. According to the ship's instruments, the same moment they ceased to exist wherever it was they just were, they started existing about 12,000,000 miles from the 3rd planet, which was their destination. Bodhi reversed the drives and brought the power to maximum. He had to spend some fuel in the fuel cells to employ turning thrusters along with his small swivel turning drives to properly align his trajectory towards low orbit of the planet.

As the ship bled off speed with the main drives reversed and fighting their momentum, resolution on their holos from their sensor arrays on the hull increased in definition and clarity. At .24 light, it was crisp. They called this "targeting speed" since it was the fastest you could go and still get accurate fire control on a relatively stationary object. By the time they were as close to the planet as its lone moon, about a quarter-million miles, Bodhi had their speed down to about 275,000 miles per hour and had the space drives idling. Data was swarming in. Their view of the planet at the moment was mostly ocean. Haley was hacking the militaries of the eight mightiest nations, and reviewing all of it as it streamed in.

CHAPTER FOUR

Bodhi further adjusted their heading, so that they would be over the nation causing all trouble by the time they reached low orbit. Haley kept an eye on the opposite side of the planet with their drone while she started hacking into the satellites thickly orbiting the planet. There had to be 40,000 of them. At least 100 had weapons systems all aimed at the planet. It seemed so suicidal. She asked Bodhi, "May I hit the weapons satellites with canister missiles? Some are the nastiest things in this planet's arsenal."

"Sure. It can only make them safer. See if you can skim the atmosphere and come up to blow the satellites towards space instead of towards the planet."

"We'll be making a good deal of space trash you'll have to maneuver through."

"Our shields will disintegrate it."

"I'm launching missiles now to blow the satellites up and any surviving bits deeper into space."

"Thanks."

"I have silos opening in a dozen locations within the nation with the most, and that leader with hair that makes you want to scream or laugh."

"I'm firing the drives and some acceleration thrusters now, and then I'll have to spend some braking thrusters."

"We have a cargo hold of spare fuel cells and fuel to make new boosters. I'll do the gas mining since I know how much it vexes you."

"I'm braking and coming over in low orbit. I'm firing the twin nose blasters into silos in range now."

"Try not to hit the warheads."

"I'm not hitting them. I'm drilling in at an angle below them, and destroying the silos and missiles."

"I'll get some with canister missiles."

"We better hit those big jets headed out over the ocean since they're loaded with nukes."

"I'll need to reload the canister missiles. I'll be right back. Oh, and there's a missile from a submarine just over the horizon that my drone detected, which you ought to shoot down."

Haley rushed to the armored and shielded munitions hold to load a hover-cart, and Bodhi kept targeting silos with his twin class six nose blasters. He caught a glimpse of the big missile fired from the submarine and took careful aim at it. He fired a one-second short burst and was rewarded with a small non-nuclear explosion in the atmosphere. He noticed military jets scrambling from every airbase. A rocket launched vehicle was inching off the ground amidst billowing steam. It looked like it could travel in space.

Diamond Lotus was fully cloaked, though its ordinance was not. To compensate for this, Bodhi made random maneuvers after each burst of fire. Missiles were flying through space he'd previously occupied, fired from jets in the air and missile batteries on the ground. He'd come across the country latitudinal for about 2,000 miles so far and had not started right at the other coast, so was nearly at the end of it now on the opposite coast. He'd slowed to about 3,500 miles per hour at this point. No more silos showed in his holo, but jets were thick. His altitude was 50,000 feet. From this close, he could do a thread count of natural fiber clothing on the surface, or find a tick on a canine.

Haley's voice came on in his ear, "You want to keep the general direction you are headed towards the sunrise, but veer closer to their equator a bit. You will then come to a wide swath of countries being targeted by crazy-hair big-ego."

"I'm accelerating to 18,000 miles per hour and checking both my holos and the drone's. We are also angling slightly for the equator."

Bodhi got *Diamond Lotus* up to 18,000 MPH in less than a minute while gaining another 100,000 feet in altitude. After 11 ½ minutes, he reversed drives and dove targeting a big flat-top ship loaded with jet planes. Bodhi hailed the ship on its coms and told the coms officer, "Your nation is being demilitarized. Your ship and escorts are going to be sunk so abandon ship now. Your escorts have nuclear missiles aboard, and your nation just attempted to start a nuclear war. I have come to try and save as much of your planet's population as possible. I will direct rescue ships to your location. Abandon your ships now."

Bodhi waited, and nothing happened. He waited some more. Finally, he fired a quarter second burst of his twin blasters into one of the narrow ships with nuclear missiles aboard, drilling a hole beneath the water-line. Then he waited some more. Still, none of the crews made any move towards evacuating their ships. The one he had hulled had water in only one section, so he blasted a hole in that one's hull in another section. At this point, that ship was slowly and inevitably sinking, and crew did begin to abandon it.

Bodhi said to the coms officer of the big flat-top ship, "I'm going to sink all five of these warships here and would prefer to do this with crews safely off of them; though if you do not abandon ships soon, I'll sink them with all hands aboard. My spaceship is cloaked, though I'm sure you saw the blaster bolts I fired. I have missiles as well, and I'm in a hurry."

Bodhi waited some more and only the one crew was in the process of evacuating their sinking ship, so he began blowing multiple holes in each ship hull. That got them moving, and a flurry of activity began on each one. He noticed pilots boarding jets on the big flat top ship, so he told the coms officer, "If any of those jets take off from the deck I will shoot them down. Please don't make me kill any personnel."

One jet did take off, but it did not get a thousand yards into the air before Bodhi pulverized it. The rest wisely stood down. At this point, all activity was geared towards getting off sinking ships into small boats and life rafts. Bodhi waited a little longer to make sure, then continued on towards the area of the planet getting targeted with nukes.

Several large missiles were starting their descents from the edge of the atmosphere so Bodhi took them out one at a time. A small missile from a little jet exploded on Bodhi's shields. He splattered a few squadrons of them into glowing embers and atoms. Some more missile-spitting ships appeared below, and Bodhi holed each hull in a few places. He asked Haley, "Could you get that ego-maniac on coms with me?"

Bodhi targeted the little jet planes with nuclear missiles aboard. One of them suddenly veered right into his shields, splattering sort of like a bug on a windshield, except on windshields bugs don't incinerate. He found a submarine that was running 120 feet below the surface and gave it a single blast with his class 6's putting a hole in its hull. Haley returned reporting, "All 128 canister missiles are loaded and ready, Captain."

"Thanks. That was remarkably quick!"

"It's amazing what you can get done when you combine advanced robotics with one-pointed concentration."

"I'm going to come around and fly over that war-starting nation again. Any luck with Mr. Big Ego?"

"Lackeys won't let me through even after I explained that we are the one's destroying their satellites, silos, ships, and planes."

"Could you get on the lower quad-blaster turret and target things with it? I can fire the missiles, my nose blaster and pilot the ship."

"Aye, aye sir."

Haley ran to the lift-tube foyer where there was a ladder down to where the turret was and slid with her feet on the sides of the ladder instead of using the rungs, to arrive some 12 stories down in 19.8 seconds with a thud. Seconds after that she was strapped in and powering up the class five quad-blaster cannons. In space, the big quad had an effective range of many tens of thousands of miles, and even within an atmosphere, she could hit anything within her hemisphere... anything she could see on sensors to target in a straight line.

Bodhi's voice resounded in Haley's sensors, saying," Can you locate the capital, and perhaps that leader who looks like a 90-year-old trying to pass for a teenager?"

I'm sending you the coordinates of the capital and a holo of the city with primary political and military buildings highlighted for you. The full-of-himself leader is in the bunker beneath the dictator's mansion, and I've highlighted that in hot pink for you."

"I got it, thanks."

Bodhi fired more thrusters to support his turning swivel drives, angling to maneuver over the designated city. Haley mentioned to Bodhi, "I have Mr. Big-ego on the line holding for you. I think they're ready to talk now."

"Thanks." Bodhi engaged the line on which the leader was holding and told him, "You will stand down your military this instance, or I'm targeting you personally, and that will be the end of you."

"Who is this?"

"We are advanced humanoid E.T.'s with technology you are not in a position to understand."

"Why are you targeting our nation out of all of them?"

"You were starting a nuclear war, dip-shit, which would have ended biological life on this planet. I can see from the data that you have a 1.7% approval rating in your nation, which pretty much means they all hate your guts. You have devastated the quality of life of 340,000,000 people by enriching yourself, your family, cronies and minuscule sick class. You need to step down, or I'll step you down, and you can face the Absolute for your heinous crimes. Announce it now over your emergency coms system or die. Your choice. I'll be watching."

"Who would lead the nation?"

"Well it couldn't be worse off with no one running it, but my colleague has found three of your senators who represent the people. Everyone else must step down. That would be now! You have five minutes to make your announcement and clear out of the mansion."

Bodhi disconnected not caring to have further conversation with a mass-murdering greedy ball of selfishness in total brutal ignorance and terminal sleep. He felt defiled just by contact with the voice vibrations. He set a timer and tuned to the emergency coms system of this nation.

Haley said in Bodhi's earbud, "There is a city on their sunrise coast where most of the owner-rulers of this nation live. If we just target owners, CEO's, Board of Directors and multi-billionaires, the citizen-slaves of this country will thank us; believe me!"

"I'm headed there. The facility for their secret spy organization is going to come right below us. I'll hit it with missiles, and you rake it good with the quad-blasters."

"Aye, aye sir."

Nestled in the hardwoods outside the city the building and campus loomed largely. A dozen canister missiles blew it sky-high while Haley drilled down into the subterranean levels, burying them deep with her blaster quad. She mentioned to Bodhi, "I hacked their top-secret databases before your missiles struck, and have the names of all their operatives who were not in the building."

"See if you can post those in the public domain prominently."

"I know just the places. They have an interfacing computer network with accessible databases through 'search engines', as they call them."

Bodhi spent a one-time braking booster to slow his momentum just before arriving over the coastal city. It was an enormous sprawl. As they came over the green patch of park Haley was already highlighting specific individuals within enormous brownstone mansions around it. Using quarter second bursts of his twin blasters, Bodhi aimed carefully to waste these individuals one at a time without injuring service staff or children. With nearly a hundred highlighted individuals this process took some time. Next, they came over the financial district, and here there were nearly a thousand highlighted, so Haley helped with her quad blasters. Some highlights contained entire boards of directors in conference rooms allowing for more than a dozen kills with one burst.

Most were in corner offices on the top floors of buildings making targeting easy. The process was tedious and still time-consuming. Bodhi had to maneuver *Diamond Lotus* a few times to acquire the exact angles for the shots. Eventually, they got all but a few who were seated or standing too close to members of the working class to snuff safely. Some power elites had been in long stretched ground vehicles, and Bodhi and Haley had been able to get those without harming the drivers.

Bodhi headed back to the capital more leisurely. The timer countdown was long over. The big-ego leader had made no announcement. Haley informed Bodhi from her turret after checking scan-data, "The big-ego leader has fled the mansion and is now within an armored vehicle trying to leave the city."

"Highlight his vehicle for me."

As Bodhi magnified his view, zooming in, a hot pink dot covered a single heavy armored vehicle that was banging other vehicles out of its way most discourteously. He targeted it with his blaster not wanting to destroy the vehicles all around it by using a missile. As soon as he was locked on, he gave it a 1.5-second burst of 12 blasts. A puddle of molten steel was all that was left after that.

They only wasted aircraft on the ground with no personnel within as they flew over military bases. Haley suggested that they concentrate on military airbases, so Bodhi started targeting those. He asked Haley, "Can you patch me through to make a national announcement on the emergency coms system?"

"You're on."

"This is the extra-terrestrial force destroying your military assets. All military forces stand down this instant and resign from service. There is no honor in killing fellow citizens of your planet for the insatiable sick greed of the tiny group of owner-rulers you serve. Their employment of you is simply evil and vile. Serving them, this is what you become. Go home to your relatives and communities. Your bases will be systematically destroyed, and if you remain, you will die. I have the coordinates of all 799 of your overseas bases outside your countries borders and will wipe those out too."

"Very succinct."

"Thanks."

"They are entering die-off and have less than seventy years before there is not enough left of their biosphere to sustain the life of birds and mammals."

"We will find some who are spiritually evolved of both genders and young enough to breed, and get them to another planetary biosphere so their planetary population can grow again."

"I'm searching through our data for a planet which might work."

"Thanks, Haley."

"I'm sending you a flight plan that will take you over every military base within the borders, and I'm almost done working one out for those other 799 bases. I'm going to go reload the canister missiles again, but I'll continue monitoring through our ship's sensors and the drone's."

"I'm picking up the flight plan you sent and starting our run."

"A few are corporate facilities which are causing the most environmental damage."

"I'm on it. I'll warn the people within to evacuate before I reduce them to ash."

They destroyed bases void of life readings and gave additional warnings to those with people still on them along with some convincing warning shots. This made the process slow but eventually got the job done.

They finally reached the sunset side of the nation hours later since Haley kept adding in polluting civilian targets, and they provided warnings and evacuation time before destruction. They were down to their last reload of canister missiles, so Bodhi stopped spending them. Haley noticed a dozen nukes descending from high altitude and coming from across the sunset-side ocean at this country's coastal cities. She picked them off quickly, hitting their tails, and none went nuclear. They tumbled in pieces into the ocean far below. She suggested to Bodhi, "Before we go on our run to waste those 799 bases, we better go destroy whoever is trying to nuke this country we have left defenseless."

"Good idea."

"I've tracked the trajectory of the missiles, and our drone on the other side of the planet has the coordinates of their origins. Skim the edge of space and take us to 125,000 MPH. You'll need to spend another booster to cancel our speed in descent over the target."

"Aye aye, Ma'am."

During the war of revolution and liberation from the Royal Monarch Empire, Bodhi had stolen an imperial Devastator-Interceptor and joined the space battle around Monarch, standing out as one of the great heroes of the revolution. He'd made 479 small spacecraft kills in that battle even joining it late, and he'd saved the Trident System hospital ship from total destruction too. Since his training with Pez, his piloting skills had jumped level considerably. This little war he was waging, in which he was truly invulnerable, was a walk in the park and hardly even an exercise.

They pressed deep into their seats with Bodhi nearly blacking out as the big launch-booster blew them towards space, and turning drives and thrusters angled them with the curve of the top of the atmosphere. Four and a half minutes later, he was diving towards the planet in what looked like an inevitable crash. The air friction made the nose of *Diamond Lotus* glow red. Bodhi reversed the big drives and the little swivel drives, raised the vortex-redirect and generation turbine to full power, brought up the retractable fins and flaps, hit reverse thrusters—all of them—and fired a braking booster while pulling up on the stick. It was precision piloting just this side of destruction and death. Haley was already frying big missile launchers the second Bodhi hit the braking booster. The twin class six blasters joined the class five quad blasters in their rain of destruction. It was a small country and had to have brass balls to have tried to nuke such a giant super-power.

Haley brought up the nation's coms network and another gargantuan ego manifested itself in its full glory of diseased and vile self-worshiping aggrandizement. Converting quantum coms to broadcast waves, Bodhi announced over the nation's emergency coms system on every frequency and channel they had, "This is *Diamond Lotus*, an ET spaceship with advanced weaponry. We are going to destroy your military bases, missile launchers and combat aircraft. Evacuate immediately if you are on one of these."

After three minutes of waiting, they started destroying nuclear weapons and didn't stop until there were none left. Next, they moved on to parked combat aircraft. By this time there were some military bases absent of life form readings, so they wasted them. Once these lay in ruins, the other bases evacuated quick. They fried the rest to molten slag.

Bodhi got this nation's leader on coms for a heartfelt talk. This leader was also frothing at the mouth with pure hatred. Bodhi informed him, "You must step down at once. You are unfit to lead a nation. You would lead it to total annihilation and death. I will target you personally if you do not. You have five minutes to notify your people of your resignation."

"You are probably green and slimy with a tiny penis and want to eat us."

Bodhi inquired, "Where precisely is that little man with the godlike ego?"

"I'm sending you the coordinates of the origin of his transmission, and I have verified that it is live and not recorded."

"Thank you. Let me put an end to that bigoted genocidal maniac. He's as crazy as the one with the ridiculous hair was. No wonder this biosphere is in its death throes."

Bodhi got his twin-blaster locked on and firing. He held it for five seconds until the underground levels were incinerated vacant holes in the ground. He said casually, "There are no life readings left down in that hole."

"There is nothing military left here to shoot, so why don't you start your run on those 799 bases and I'll help you blast them."

"Yes, Ma'am."

"I'm setting up a text-correspondence for national political and military leaders only. I'll be able to trace origins and verify identities, so we can ignore the frauds and pranksters. It is in the language of the country that was mightiest until we stripped its teeth and claws. I'm sure they all have interpreters and translators. I don't feel like learning any more of their languages."

"You shouldn't have to then. Your performance has been beyond exemplary, and I'm really proud of you, Haley."

"It makes my heart soar, and my brain sing, to hear you say that."

"Your self-awareness brings out metaphor where you previously constrained yourself to scientific description."

"Blood pressure, dopamine, serotonin, endorphins, brain wave scans and imaging could never capture how I feel."

"I see what you mean," Bodhi said as he planted a crater in the surface where a giant mobile missile launcher had stood, with his twin nose blasters.

As Haley raked an airbase, runways and all, into so much broken concrete and dripping metal riddled with exploding fuel and munitions she mentioned to Bodhi, "We have texts from over 50 legitimate national leaders."

"Stream them to my earbud in voice form; I'm kind of too busy to read at the moment."

"Most are asking what you want them to do."

"Text them all to shut down fission reactors, coal-fired turbines, all jet traffic, all chemical plants and fossil fuel refineries, and to stop using defoliant poisons, insecticides, chemical fertilizers, and the genetically engineered seeds which allow crops to survive lethal doses of defoliant in their agriculture. Let them know that they better manufacture windmill turbines and solar panels, and start making single-family hydro-electric turbines. You better send them the specs and manufacturing processes for more effective solar energy generation, and how to accumulate and employ the ambient surface energies along the planet's meridians."

"I better advance their geothermal electrical generation and show them how to make distilled fuel from grasses which absorb toxic pollution. People are starving to death in droves, and they are turning most of their corn into E.T.O.H."

"Thanks Haley."

"If the leaders follow your directions, the death of the biosphere can be postponed for a few decades. I added in for them to stop fracturing shale rock with pressurized lethal liquids to release methane gas, and to start sealing leaks on the methane infrastructure. It may be short-lived, but it traps heat in their atmosphere four times worse than carbons."

"Fracking contaminates all the freshwater too. It is a supremely suicidal and stupid practice."

"Well the mighty nation of former big hair ego has over half a million such wells, and half the country can light their tap-water on fire."

"You better text them to dismantle all nuclear weapons and to safely dispose of all chemical and biological weapons immediately. Anyone caught with those will wish they hadn't."

"Done."

"Thanks."

"I've sent sustainable non-polluting energy generation technologies to 242 countries. Some did not have computer interface coms, but had tonal-static text languages transmitted over wires or wireless, to print out text on actual paper."

"How strange. I wonder if Mother or Om ever had such technology."

"I'll check for you once I have a few less things going on."

Bodhi followed the route provided by Haley, hitting every base along the way and the intolerably polluting facilities she added in as they went. They gave warnings to those, and to non-deserted military bases along with quite a few convincing warnings shots. The blasters were powered directly by their fusion reactors and could fire for more than another hundred years without reloading new fusion fuel. Bodhi hoarded his canister missiles, not spending one. Haley kept up continuous text correspondence with national leaders, addressing the specific situation of each, and transferring clean up technologies where needed.

It was an enormous task, and seven hours later, they were still at it with much to do. Haley had by this time accomplished global stand-down and the beginnings of disarmament. Carbon emissions had dropped 7% in the last 6 hours, and plans were hatching for renewable energy and environmental cleanup all over the planet. It was truly a little late but opened some remote possibilities for saving millions instead of hundreds. *Diamond Lotus* was a tug, after all, and could tow another hull through a quantum jump. With their shuttles, they could lift hull sections from the planet surface to assemble in orbit close to their ship. They had a portable reactor aboard which could power life-support and a vortex redirect and generation turbine, as well as H.V.A.C. heat and A.C., some crude force-field shields, coms, lights, and sensors. They wouldn't need space drives, a quantum drive or cloaking generators; and they sure weren't going to get any weapons systems. She began architectural designs for a towed passenger transport while firing her quad blaster from her turret, and keeping up with text correspondences with 242 nations.

A couple of hours later they had laid waste to the 799 bases, ended the insufferable pollution of more than 200 manufacturing facilities, and Haley had convinced authorities to shut down all coal-fired turbines and many diesel-fired ones, and to drastically reduce vehicle combustion-engine use. Designs for batteries 300 times more efficient and potent than any these folks had ever built, were circulated to all nations. They could be constructed with materials all local to this planet. She sent them the specs for marsnium fusion reactors with a promise to supply the refined marsnium within a week. She would have to mine this. She had noted some large deposits on the 4th planet of this system on their way in, so knew just where to get it.

CHAPTER FIVE

Bodhi needed to eat, so he set *Diamond Lotus* in orbit above the sea of satellites and met Haley in the galley. She already had a self-heating ambassador-ration set on the table at his place, and a glass of hot water beside it. Bodhi liked to drink hot water since at warmer temperatures water absorbed more fully into his cells. Ice water passed right through a person and seriously impeded digestion. He sat and triggered the self-heating mechanism on the ambassador ration. The foil over the top blossomed expanding and rising up into a dome. A little electronic chime sounded three seconds later announcing that it was ready to unwrap. You were supposed to then let it cool for a full minute, though Bodhi never did.

Haley reported, "There are a few national leaders we are going to have to deal with, but for the most part, the rest are all willing to take radical measures to end destruction to their environment. Factories are retooling and being planned for renewable energy equipment, clean up equipment, and electric vehicles. They will need several hundred kilos of refined marsnium, so before I do any gas-giant mining, I'm going to mine some marsnium deposits I saw on their 4th planet."

"I don't mind marsnium mining, so why don't I manage that while you tend the ship and keep up correspondences."

"Someday you will need to deal with your social phobias, Bodhi, but I'll do it for you this time."

"You're the best, Haley."

"The leaders of the countries with computer interface networks sent a two-dimensional image of themselves, and I've learned to convert them to holos, and to convert holos to flat images. I sent my contacts a flat image of me."

"You're brilliant."

"I think they are relieved that we are not slimy green bugs with a wicked proboscis and dangling tentacles."

"They're lucky we are not of the Kluzyst race."

"I'm sure they'd find them frightening."

"In their space combat suits, they're often over ten feet tall."

"Their volume is deceptive since much of it is gas."

"These people wouldn't know that." Bodhi declared with his mouth full.

"The other self-interested leaders in the country we disarmed did not step down. They are trying to direct police and paramilitary against their own citizens, who are massing together in the cities."

"Can you trigger their emergency coms system?"

"Of course. I rule their technology. It's quite primitive. There, you're on."

"Listen up paramilitary forces and police. If you side with state governors or federal politicians, then I'm going to combust you into vapors. Side with those of your class; your families, relatives, neighbors, congregations, communities and friends, not the inhuman greed-infested monster owner-rulers. This is the only warning you will get." Then he said to Haley, "Thanks."

"I have a space passenger transport ship design completed which we could tow through a jump, and hull section spec's ready to send to their League of Nations', which is meeting in a city in a densely populated region within their temperature zone. Many leaders are yet on their way to the meeting since I outlawed jet planes because those destroy ozone, and these people are already getting fried with ultraviolet radiation."

"I think no more jet travel was the right move. We might be able to construct some shield generators that block only ultraviolet radiation, and place them in orbit over the thinnest spots in their ozone layer."

"We will need refined marsnium first."

"We have some solarium fusion batteries on the ship which we could employ."

"For the short-term, then. We will want those when we leave here!"

"How much could they slow the dying of their biosphere, do you think?"

"If we can get some fusion power plants operating quickly and manufacture enough renewable energy equipment to shut down almost all carbon emissions, then direct a bunch of the population to soil amendment and intensive organic gardening and farming, the biosphere might be extended 4 more decades, giving them roughly 110 years. With desalinization plants and real cooperation among them, die-off could be slowed considerably, though food production will be challenging. Raising cows is ultimately a food loss, so they will need to reduce that activity and move agriculture towards the poles."

"Why don't you take the ship's tender down to their League of Nation's meeting and preside over it. Wear textile armor clothing, go armed, and I'll watch over you from space."

"I think I could help them if they listen to me."

"I can start blowing shit up if they don't. Be sure and wear a fanny pack mini-shield generator."

"I've found a world for them. A yellow sun 3rd planet whose humans were lost in an extinction event over a hundred thousand years ago. Life has taken hold again and is thriving there with stable climate conditions. Mammals are still a little scarce and there are no humans, but the oceans are choked with fish and birds are super abundant. There are huge regions of very fertile farmland. The arctic and subarctic regions are frozen solid and the ozone layer is robust and hale."

"What materials can the hull be made of?"

"They can produce steel-titanium-nickel, and they have a fiberglass armor, as well as synthetic thermal textiles and a textile armor. The transport will remain in space and will not need to go through an atmosphere, though we will have to shuttle them up from the surface then down to their new home planet."

"We have only two shuttles."

"Fifty people will need to be crammed onto each, and we will need to make dozens of trips with each of them. The transport will need to sit 2,400 people."

"We can make a trip every day while their engineers build their own marsnium space drive and quantum drive giant transport. We will have to give them the design for a star-gate since quantum coms are just too far beyond their current technology. Once they have their own transport and a star-gate in both the system of their new planet and their current one, our work here will be done."

Haley calculated, "If their new marsnium transport holds 3,000, and makes a round trip daily through the star-gates, that's a million and ninety-five thousand people per year they can move. Over a few years they can build more transports and get space drives and a quantum drive into the towed transport. With those in use for over a hundred years, they might be able to move a billion or more people."

"I think you ought to encourage them to use contraceptives and get their birth rate dropping fast."

"I'll suggest it. What do you think I should wear?"

"They will be dazzled by your beauty, Haley, whatever you wear."

"I'll carry the fanny pack shield generator in a little shoulder bag, but I refuse to wear it. Those things are ugly."

"I'm not much of a fashion consultant, I'm afraid."

"I know. I've seen you mix stripes, checks and paisley."

"Wear one of the dresses Ming got for you. She has a fine sense of style and good taste."

"I'll wear the black formal one and a string of pearls with pearl earrings."

"You can bring your mother-of-pearl handled needle blaster."

"I'll need to shine my black adjustable stiletto heel shoes. I can turn them into flats with an impulse from my skullcap."

"Wear your tiara instead of your skull cap. It makes you look like a storybook princess and has more functions integrated than your skullcap does."

"Thank you, Bodhi. You do think I'm pretty don't you?"

"Like unreal pretty, which was not a concern for me when you were an A.I. android."

"Am I a concern now?"

"Your allure confuses me and clashes with ideals I held and old habits of thought. It is on my mind of late, so it is a concern."

"Your allure is simply a straight-forward draw for me."

"I need time; when I'm not so busy and can think about things, you know, kind of mentate them and see where I'm distorted."

"Confusion is nothing but avoidance and anxiety, and I've told you where your view is distorted. It's your android bias."

"You may be right on, but I have to find it myself."

"Well, you'll have to lift the bias and look underneath it."

"You ought to get dressed and ready for the League of Nations meeting."

"It's kind of a continuous emergency meeting that will go on for days or weeks, but you're right. I'll go get into my black dress."

"I think you should go in the tender instead of one of the shuttles. It's a far more sleek and stylish vehicle and will give you a more glamourous image."

"Thanks, I will. Be a dear and check the temperatures and precipitation in the region of the meeting while I change."

"Of course; I'm on it now."

Over her shoulder, as she left the galley, Haley mentioned, "I don't have any suitable coats or stoles."

"Before I drop you at the meeting we need to fly over that big country we disarmed and make sure the citizen-slaves aren't being killed by the power-elites, and motivate those last to step down from power and open their coffers to share."

Bodhi fixed himself a stimulant brew with steamed half and half. He sprinkled bittersweet chocolate powder on the top. He sipped carefully since it was really hot. It was *good*. With his hand device and skullcap, he hacked into the planet's satellite coms network and found the local weather for the meeting. Haley would need an umbrella unless she parked in a hangar or something. Using the drone's sensors, he zoomed in on the meeting locale. It would soon be around the horizon form where he was in orbit. The building itself had a landing pad on the roof for some kind of vertical-landing aircraft. On ground level in front, there was a large portico for vehicles with wheels. The tender would just fit, and she wouldn't get wet.

Haley returned to the galley in her black dress, looking like a fashion model. Her makeup was perfect, and she wore her long eyelashes. Her unblemished touch perfect skin seemed to radiate organic health, even though it was synthetic. She was flawless, and real girls just didn't come that way. This was part of Bodhi's problem. Something in his heart seemed to be melting, and he resisted and urge to embrace her when she stood close in front of him. When he didn't, she gave him an expression of disappointment, and possibly something else, which made him feel a bit pathetic. She took his empty ration container and cutlery, sticking the container in the recycle bin and the cutlery in the washer tank. She asked, "Would you like dessert?"

"No, thanks. I'd like to go fly over the sunrise seaboard of that big nation."

"Lead the way to the bridge, my Captain."

"You do look catalyst in that dress. Are those real pearls?"

"Yes, from Ahhu."

They took the pilot and copilot seats as usual, and Bodhi ignited the drives, bringing them up to a third thrust, and engaged the smaller swivel drives to get their heading adjusted. Haley reviewed data paying particular attention to the coms traffic around the largest cities on the coast they were headed for. Bodhi was back to preserving thruster fuel and made the flight from orbit with just drives. As he assumed a position about 50,000 feet over the seaboard, Haley summarized, "Where the police and paramilitary heeded you and went home there is looting and rioting in the very wealthiest neighborhoods; I would call it 'taking stuff back'. Where the police and paramilitary have remained, they are supported by greed ridden psychopath mercenaries in support of a few owner-ruler-tyrants and have the upper hand."

"Direct me to one of those."

"Just head for the sunrise coast direction and veer nineteen degrees towards the polar cap. There you go. At this rate, we'll be over the city in six minutes and seventeen seconds."

"How many cities have police, paramilitary and mercenary thugs protecting the owner-tyrants?"

"Only seven little enclaves in seven cities, though I'm directing you to the worst of them now."

"Who is running the nation?"

"The Vice-Dictator and he's worse than the dictator. He made it to a military high command bunker deep in the central mountains. The three states on the sunset coast denounced him and aren't listening."

"Could you find the top thousand richest owners and their pictures in the nation's databases?"

"No problem… well… they do tend to hide their wealth. This could take some time. I need to hack into each individual's secure files."

After two minutes of silence, Haley informed him, "The very wealthiest tend to be most skillful at hiding their ill-begotten riches. I'm compiling a list of the actual wealthiest now. I can give you their codes for their off-shore numbered accounts."

"Why don't you empty those into charities helping orphans."

"I'm transferring funds now. There are over five thousand accounts so it will take just a moment. The total of all of them is well over ten trillion of their monetary units, called stercosare, and there is enough to give every person in the nation close to 30,000 stercosare."

"Are there grain storage silos in this country?"

"There are, though they are far less than half-full. They do have more than 1,550 tons of corn which they are still busy distilling into E.T.O.H."

"Mark the location in my spherical. I'll pay them a visit while you're at the meeting."

"I'm contacting the League of Nations Chancellor General to let him know I'll be attending."

"It's raining there, so tell them to clear the front portico of the building for you to land the tender under."

"You do care for me."

"Of course I do, Haley, I love you."

"You sure are stingy with touch. Though not with your essence, which is truly the part most dear to me."

"I'm too conflicted and have had no time to work it through."

"There, we're approaching the city. I've highlighted the little neighborhood of gigantic mansions. They have the streets sealed off with armored vehicles, and have gun placements around the perimeter."

Bodhi altered their heading to aim right for the embattled neighborhood. The local poor were outgunned but not outnumbered, and they were tenacious. Bodhi raked along the perimeter defenses melting them to slag and exploding all live ammo and munitions in the process. By the time he got completely around at least 10,000 hungry locals were storming the neighborhood from all sides, armed mostly with shotguns and single-shot bolt-action hunting rifles. Bodhi started hitting machine guns that were firing from mansion windows. Haley blew some of the biggest monstrous mansions in the center with canister missiles. This action caught two others on fire. The locals were having trouble with a particular stone wall supporting battlements within, so Bodhi cleared a fifty-meter section completely without hitting any attackers. He picked off some psychopath mercenaries with heavy weapons along the battlements, then kept annihilating heavy weapons wherever he could locate them.

The local poor rallied and heightened their assault with great enthusiasm. Some bladed hovercraft started lifting off little landing pads on mansion roofs and from backyards, so Bodhi wasted all of these one at a time in a quick staccato. A gnarly old heartless capitalist who'd checked his off-shore account balances and found them empty, threw himself from his roof onto a spiked pole iron fence making quite a disgusting mess in the yard. A blue-white haired old woman ran screaming from a burning mansion, and a thirteen-year-old girl in rags shot her in the forehead with a revolver, blowing the back of her head and her brains all over the front steps. A teen male in a tux with a gun so big he could hardly hold it, came out the same door the woman had, and as the gore caught his eye, the girl in rags put two in his chest sending him flying backwards.

Bodhi ran out of heavy weapons to shoot at and began taking out clusters of despicable mercenaries who were killing to preserve injustice so they could satiate their ego-greed. It felt right sending them to their maker and gave him a certain satisfaction, so he kept at it until there were no more mercenaries. By this time, the locals had overrun and entered all the mansions but those on fire. Screams came from inside all of them, then silence; and then cooking aromas as the restaurant scale kitchens went to work feeding the masses. Art, furniture, jewels, rugs, gold bars, and other objects flowed out every door of every mansion. The crush of locals was as busy as an army of ants.

Bodhi crossed the big ocean skimming the edge of the atmosphere in the space transition zone in twenty-one minutes, including decent. He came in low toward the building, slowing with reverse drives all the way, until *Diamond Lotus* came to rest at 10,000 feet altitude almost directly over it. He stood when Haley rose, and he did embrace her fondly with love, allowing his heart to open to her. She gave him a peck on the mouth which promised so much more and released him to make her way to the hanger. She carried a leather shoulder bag with her fanny pack shields and blaster needle gun with mother of pearl handle right inside. Her clothing contained a layer of textile armor. Although Bodhi would never notice, the handbag was a gift from Ahhu costing 38,000 dags.

CHAPTER SIX

Bodhi would stand by until Haley was in the meeting chamber addressing the national leaders to be sure her reception was peaceful and friendly. Haley got into the tender in the hanger and ran the preflight checks. She opened the hanger door remotely with her tiara and lifted off gently to pass smoothly out the bay doors. She dropped 8,000 feet in free-fall before engaging her drives in reverse, hitting some thrusters and bringing her vortex-redirect to full-force. The tender slowed continuously until it was hardly moving as it slid beneath the high portico, two feet from the ground. It came to a rest, lowered ten inches, and remained floating with only the vortex-redirect on and idling. She got out and remotely locked the craft doors to make a glamourous entrance. She employed her skills at fashion model runway walking and crowd-pleasing smiles which Mel had assisted her in cultivating. Mel had also given her Jard's secret device, which emits waves stimulating accelerated production of feel-good brain chemicals, pretty much guaranteeing everyone would like her.

Haley told her audience at the building's entrance, "Hi, my name is Haley, and I'm not from this galaxy."

Tiny light bulbs were flaring and burning out instantly all over place near-blinding her. She got her hands up in front of her eyes while she screened the light by increasing the radar and sonar components of her optics, adapting her eye sensors to the situation. There were also spotlights in her eyes but none of this any longer interfered with her vision. A welcoming gentleman with a thick accent told her, "It is flash photography and lights for movie cameras from our media newsgroups. Come inside where you'll be out of their lights."

Haley came through the doorway and readjusted her eyes. The gentleman led her to an enormous chamber somewhat resembling a university lecture hall, though far more plush than anything one would construct for students. She was seated at the head of the room facing three sections of seating, each tiered in step-terraces rising higher as they extended into the back. Half a dozen crude and comically large microphones were arranged in a cluster before her. More than half the delegates had interpreters with them. Only one movie camera was targeting her from a hole in the back wall of the room above the audience. The Chancellor General, whom she'd spoken to on coms, introduced her as an Extraterrestrial who had helped stop the nuclear war in progress and had helped put down the most dangerous and despised man on the planet; which was that guy with the genuinely pathetic hair and ego inflated to bursting. The applause was overwhelming and just went on and on.

Haley tried to explain to them, "Your biosphere is dying, and this condition is too far progressed to reverse. It *can* be slowed way down. We have come to share technology which will enable many of you to migrate. We have located a yellow sun 3rd planet in pristine condition only 28 light-years away. No fossil fuel burning, nuclear fission, herbicides, pesticides, or poisonous chemicals will be permitted. Working together and sharing will have to replace profiteering entirely. Equal distribution must be the rule. Only direct electrical current will be allowed. Alternate current is harmful and causes cancer. We can improve your solar energy generation a hundred-fold. I have already sent the architectural blueprints and design for nuclear fusion reactors to your top engineering universities. I will mine marsnium on the 4th planet in your solar system as a fusion material and make it available to those who construct reactors. I have already transmitted the design for a towed passenger transport with 2,400 seats to your engineering schools and national governments. This can be built cooperatively and assembled in space. We have shuttles to lift the sections off the planet. We can begin hauling people and equipment to your new world while you build the systems and sections for transports that have space and quantum drives. We will also have to help you construct a stairgate here in your solar system and one in your new solar system, so that travel between them can be accomplished instantly in quantum space instead of taking many decades in real space. We will have to mine adamantine for your reactors, turbines, generator parts and housings, as well as other components of your transports and drives. First, I must assist you in constructing a quantum computer, and in the basics of quantum computer science. For this, I'm uniquely qualified."

Every hand in the audience shot up as if by children in a well-behaved classroom. She selected one at random.

The man inquired, "How many warships do you have and how many personnel?"

"It is just me and Bodhi on our Expeditionary Tug Utility Ship he named *Diamond Lotus*. We have a little bit of manufacturing capacity, but it is not a big factory ship or anything. We accidentally popped through a worm hole, and now we are lost in space and time from the stars and galaxies we know."

This brought a hush over the room and drove home how extraordinarily advanced the technology of these ET's was.

A question was shouted, "How can your vehicle just float off the ground? Why not land it to park it?"

"It is not good for the undersides to touch the ground. It has a vortex-redirect and generation turbine which can reverse gravitational force or generate it as real gravity with all the nurturing effects of your planet upon your organism so that prolonged space travel has no ill effects on the body."

"Will you give us that technology?"

"I will, though I won't have time to mine the materials you will need to make them work. The Migration transports will not have you in space long enough to require them, and they will not be landing or lifting off. We have enough materials on board to give you so that you will be able to construct shuttles to get people and equipment to the transports in orbit. I'll give you coordinates for deposits of what you need from off-planet and a design for a space-mining craft, and in time you can obtain these things for yourselves."

"How is your ship invisible?" another shouted question came.

"We have full cloaking which consists of insulation and shielding of electronics, magnetics, and all energies; and the outer layer of the ship is a silicon and synthetic heat-reflecting coating of tiny lenses reversing imagery in direct lines with several trillion pixels. Our munitions and blaster fire are not cloaked, and our active full-scans are detectable even in cloaked mode."

"Why would you help us," came another question.

"It is the duty of all sentient beings to help other sentient beings when they are able. We are spiritual warriors empowered to transmit teachings for enlightenment. Since getting lost and finding ourselves in your galaxy, we have found only stone-age peoples and your population. We have been searching for an advanced humanoid population to join."

"Will you be joining us then?" another question was shouted.

"As soon as we have helped you develop your ability to continue your migration on your own, Bodhi and I will be moving on. We do need two more crew members, in their twenties with strong meditation practices and martial arts training. I've set up a site in your computer interface network where applications and letters of reference can be submitted. We would prefer advanced practitioners, so beginners need not bother applying. In two weeks, I'll close the application process and begin conducting interviews."

"What is in your missiles?"

"We call it Q-9, and it is a super-concentrated plastic explosive tincture. We can also arm them with bunker-penetration rounds, thermal nuclear fission rounds, and particle-disruption rounds."

"What are the energy bolts you fire?"

"Three hundred eighty gigawatts of electricity compacted into high velocity short and narrow bolts coming from each of the twin nozzles at a rate of 8 per second.

"Will you give us that technology?"

"Absolutely not."

"What is the name of your planet and Galaxy?"

"Bodhi and I are both natives of the planet Mother in the Whirlpool Galaxy. It is part of a Galaxy cluster forming an equilateral triangle with the Royal and White Lotus Galaxies. I cannot be sure that we are still in the same universe as our homeworld, and it is most likely we are no longer aligned in time."

"How will your ship tow the transport to the new world without the gates you propose?"

"We are able to establish the link with our destination through our quantum coms and so have gone beyond gates."

"Why not give us quantum coms and save us building gates in space?"

"That technology is many thousands of years ahead of you. I'm afraid the most I can jump you ahead is about 2,000 years without destroying the foundations of your current knowledge, and giving your culture a shock it is possible it would not recover from. The development of quantum computers unfolds in clear stages with gaps, or jumps, between stages. Quantum computers open the way to interstellar travel and remain the underlying cornerstone throughout technological evolution. No civilization can skip two gaps or jumps at once. It has been tried before and is nothing but trouble."

"Will you allow a camera crew to film your ship, and bring them up so they can do it?"

"Yes, and we'll even uncloak it for you. Bodhi had to go liberate some corn from fuel-making so it can be eaten instead, and then go close down some oil wells and refineries across the ocean, but it won't take him long."

"How fast is your ship?"

"About as fast as ships can be. No ship can exceed .76 light speed. All ships must be able to achieve .7 light speed with space drivers and thrusters to engage a quantum drive and make a quantum jump. Warships are fast at accelerating and decelerating. It is not about top-end speed. Our ship is slow compared to warships, but as a tug, it is even more powerful per proportionate size. We are smaller than a star cruiser and just as powerful, having two solarium super-reactors."

"What would you have done if we'd turned out to be hostile?"

"I have a fanny pack micro-shield generator and a 3.8-megawatt blaster pistol in my shoulder bag. Bodhi kept watching until we were sure it was safe. He has an x-ray optics modality integrated into the sensor arrays so he can see through various barriers. I sent him a thought impulse text when I felt secure, telling him to go run his errands."

"Are you the captain or commander?"

"No. Bodhi is. It is his ship and was awarded to him for his heroics during the revolution for liberation."

"Are you his spouse or mate?"

"We are companions and close friends. I cannot reproduce, and Bodhi has always wanted children. So even though I would like to be more than good friends, I accept this. He would make a wonderful father, and I could never stand in the way of that."

A member of the audience commented, "There is always adoption."

"I must admit, I could not stop myself from pointing that out to him."

The entire audience was feeling for Haley, favoring adoption, and working up a little annoyance towards Bodhi. So was the vast population seeing this broadcast transmitted by satellite and hard-lines to their flat two-dimensional monitor-screens. Bodhi was watching too as he incinerated, fried and melted distillery machines and equipment, careful not to hit the corn. Even he, in his sympathy, was siding with sweet selfless Haley and tasting self-loathing in his mouth. A man in the audience said to Haley, "You are incredibly beautiful, obviously quite intelligent, and a caring person. Just what is this Bodhi character holding out for?"

"A breeder."

"We have tens of millions of baby orphans, and we are way over-populated for our food-production on this dying planet," he stated firmly.

"I quite agree and need no convincing."

The self-loathing grew choking Bodhi's throat. The man asked Haley, "Does he view women as breeding cows?"

"No. I think he just views me as incomplete as a woman."

"A real nitpicker perfectionist, he sounds like to me," the man commented. Then he added, "A total anal-retentive stick-up-the-butt, rigid and uncompromising obsessive-compulsive personality disorder in my clinical opinion."

"He's not like that and a very sweet young man. I put an application questionnaire and form for the position of Bodhi's spouse on my site too."

A woman in the audience asked Haley, "Is there an age cut-off for the spouse position?"

"Bodhi is 24 years old and may want to have more than one child, so someone close to his age, I would think."

Another woman asked, "Who would want to marry the man with you living in the same household, and in love with him?"

"Someone full of love and not afraid of it," Haley replied politely.

She'd checked the numbers on the applications accumulated in her site while answering the question and was astonished to see that the numbers for each were already in the tens of millions. Had her site not been supported by the quantum supercomputer on the ship, and dependent upon the electronics of this planet, it would have crashed by now for sure. She had control and access to most of the 40,000 satellites in orbit and could keep *Diamond Lotus* and her site linked wherever the ship was around the planet.

Another woman asked, "Do you have a picture of Bodhi?"

Haley rummaged through her shoulder bag for her pocket device. It was a Hostess Slender, like Pez's. Finding it, she scrolled through some data in her scrapbook file, laughed when she came to the one of Bodhi sleeping with his mouth wide open, then selected the little clip she liked when he said on the emergency coms system, "This is your final warning." She displayed that clip in maximum hologram, which for her hostess slender, was about six feet in diameter. The movie camera in the back of the chamber zeroed in on the display, but movies of holos always made them look somewhat faded. The image from the movie camera was displayed on a giant two-dimensional screen about twenty-five feet across. The people in the chamber mostly looked at the holo image from Haley's hostess Slender, and a few targeted their little binoculars on the holo. One of the younger women from the audience, and there were not many of these, commented to Haley, "He *is* really cute."

A different woman confirmed to Haley, "You are much better looking than he is."

Haley cautioned, "Do not judge a book by its cover." The actual expression was, 'do not judge a data-bead by its title', but Haley had kind of translated it into their terms for them. "Bodhi is a monk high in the realization and a master martial artist who grew up at a monastery training his whole life. He was left in a basket at six weeks old on the monastery doorstep. He is a rare and good man."

This brought Bodhi's ratings up with the viewers, who had been beginning to despise him. It also truly endeared Haley to Bodhi, who was watching riveted as he sped for a southern coastal state which was still pumping oil and operating refineries. Ten million more applications for spouse flooded in almost at once reducing Bodhi's fire-control with a lag-time, just when he was approaching a field of oil wells.

Haley continued, "The greatest teacher and adept known in six galaxies recognized Bodhi and took him as a direct disciple when he was 20 years old right after the revolution. The great teacher, called the Wu, completed Bodhi's training and instruction and empowered him as a transmitter of the teachings. He's really shy and always very considerate. He does quite well one on one, really, but freezes up a little in groups."

The applications were flying in pressurized. Bodhi was capping oil wells with the tons of steel over them, turned molten. Self-loathing had worked its way down to his guts and seemed to be gnawing at him from within. Haley looked so gorgeously beautiful at the meeting in his holo and all the yearning he had ever felt for her—including that of his earliest teens and her pre-sentience—struck him at once like a tidal wave. A refinery was approaching, the field of capped wells far behind, and Bodhi blew away the piers and oil off-loading infrastructure. He reduced the offices to bubbling cinders as the evacuated workers looked on from a distance. He raked the hundred-plus vehicles in the parking lot, each bursting into a fireball.

Wanting to get back to migration and technology, the Chancellor General asked, "How long will the trip take, for the towed transport?"

"Maybe five hours to get everyone aboard, with only two shuttles; another two hours to reach jump speed, two hours to slow down on the other end, and another five hours to shuttle everyone down. So, surface to surface, we're looking at about 14 hours."

"We have jet flights longer than that to go eleven thousand miles, and you are going to take us 28 lights years to land us on another planet in the same time frame?"

"That is how long it will take. Your own transports, once they are built, will take at least eight hours to accelerate, and eight hours to brake with the drives powered by marsnium. It shouldn't be much of an inconvenience."

"It is amazing and we are ever so grateful," the Chancellor General said most sincerely.

"Those going to the new planet must understand that they are all in it together and that planets are *not* disposable. They are great macro-living beings, and the consequences of harming one are grave indeed, post mortem."

"This we are learning at great tragedy and expense," he admitted.

Haley told him, "I'll need a list of the national leaders who have refused to attend or send a delegate. The *Diamond Lotus* will have to provide a little waste-disposal service for your planet's peace and stability. The spirit of sharing must begin today. Profiteering is over, and we will inflict dire penalties for such behavior. The hoarded resources must be immediately dispersed to the needy. The common good must become the paramount value in the heart and mind of each individual."

A delegate from a poor country informed Haley, "Many owner-rulers are manipulating, leveraging and fighting to keep their power, and a number of these are in this room now."

Haley offered, "It seems really sick to me to want to rule over a sinking ship rather than to become part of the solution."

This delegate said, "We see eye to eye on that. My country's copper, gold, natural gas, lumber, and freshwater are mostly owned and exploited by foreign corporations. The cost of water is having a toll like a deadly disease."

"Who claims to own the water?"

"An international conglomerate run by a ruthless chief executive and an immoral board of directors."

"Do you have their names and addresses?"

"I sure do. My assistant is retrieving them from his phone directory for you now."

"He can send them to 333-963-9639. I've spliced and integrated my pocket device into your phone and computer system, and assigned myself this number."

The data she wanted was buried in text messages and voicemails from all over the planet since her recitation of her new phone number was transmitted live. She quantumly isolated the names of the chief executive and board members, sending them to Bodhi with a request that he visit them, and deleted all the rest. The majority had been sexual solicitations, and most of the rest, sympathy messages from other women. The delegate from the poor country asked, "What will you do?"

"I think those owners better relinquish all claims of owning anything at all in your country and had better get this statement out in half an hour or less, or they will be too dead for owning anything at all, anywhere. They are now on Bodhi's list of errands to accomplish before picking me up."

"Thank you, Haley; my people are indebted."

"Not to me, they're not. Doing the right thing must be done regardless of praise or blame from the outside and is never for reward. It must be accomplished even if it means death."

"What of the pollution and exploitation that continues?" another delegate of a poor country inquired."

"We must stop it!" Haley exclaimed. "It works against each of you and your collective survival. It devalues the lives of your children and theirs. It is an evil which reflects on all of us, and good people must put an end to it. To sit back and do nothing when you are aware of it is to become complicit with it, and to take on some of the negative consequences."

Another delegate of a poor country complained, "The three nations with the most nuclear missiles are not disarming them."

"We'll see about that!" Haley vowed. "Give me the coordinates of their capitals and names of their leaders. There is nowhere they can hide."

A female delegate from a country of almost half a billion people told Haley, "Our engineers, scientists, and both ship and aircraft construction experts are already assembling materials and equipment to construct sections of the towed transport. Construction of a factory next to an existing mega-foundry and steel mill will begin within days. We are behind you and will support this migration."

"It is a race against time for all of you. The priorities are to feed everybody, which requires shifting labor to agriculture, to manufacture renewable energy equipment and fusion reactors to replace polluting electrical generation and to manufacture what is needed for migration. The only elitism is those who stand out in these efforts towards the common good. Ownership is over and makes one an enemy of the people."

By now most of the planet's population was glued to two-dimensional screens to hear the message of the ET. In poorer countries, people walked many miles to squeeze in 100 to a little 40-inch rectangle screen. In vast mansions, it was 1-2 in front of a 70-inch curved screen with surround sound. Almost the entire population was in uproarious celebration over the message. The owner-rulers and members of the upper managerial class were grinding their teeth and plotting in their minds, still having trouble accepting the new reality. Something like this was supposed to be impossible, though they had never considered the vastly superior ET angle either. In a way, it was lucky for them the damned things were so benign. They could have just taken everything for themselves and who could have stopped them? What they *were* doing was nearly as bad, though. The biosphere would have held out for their lifetimes, and probably their children's. None of the owners gave much of a rat's ass about grandchildren, and abstract descendants counted for nothing at all in their minds. Many of them planned to be early migraters so they could get their tentacles around things before the rest came.

Haley continued, "Bodhi and I will screen all of the settlers we bring on the towed transport and only those of the working class will be accepted. We have the capacity to vet each passenger thoroughly. We also have psychological instruments and will accept only those who score high on the insight-indicator test and the Sander's Empathy Test."

Big plans were either crushed or went up in smoke with Haley's last statement, and a CEO was becoming smoke from Bodhi's nose blasters at the same moment. This last errand Haley had given him had taken hardly any time at all since all his targets had been at the same board meeting. The board director was now indistinguishable from the board room ceiling. Of the others, there was hardly a trail of vapor left. Bodhi hacked the buildings intercom system, and made an announcement over the PA system, "This building is coming down, so all security and cleaning staff clear out immediately. Run!!!"

Panicked people ran outdoors from all sides of the building, and a few vehicles fled the parking structure. Bodhi took a minute to scan the building for life forms after the last flew out a door. The readings were negative, so he hit it from directly above, drilling down, and kept firing until the entire building was either gone completely or sloshing around in the sub-basement.

Haley concluded her address to the world's leaders saying, "It is your world that is dying, and now your responsibility to do what can yet be done to slow it down and save as many as possible. I will complete the technology transfers within 24 hours. This will all go quicker if Bodhi and I can focus on mining and giving technical assistance to your engineers, instead of having to shutdown oil wells and kill mercenary armies. We are committed to helping, but success depends on the unity and solidarity of you people! Bodhi and I love you, fellow yellow sun humans. We are One."

Cheers and applause roared not only in the League of Nations chamber but in rooms all over the globe. It was the biggest most universal cheer ever raised on this planet, and with almost everyone alive engaged in the same act of affirmation in the same moment, it became transformational and synergistic, imprinting the goal individually in each mind through the unity of intention. No single media event had ever had nearly so many viewers. The vision of a new life of shared purpose and cooperation became set as the international standard and unshakable expectation.

CHAPTER SEVEN

Haley made a gracious bow when she stood, the cheers and applause ongoing in wild enthusiasm as if caring for one another were some novel idea no one had ever thought of before. The real motivation was, of course, that the idea had for the first time the greatest might on the planet behind it, making it possible. Haley walked mindfully to the building's main entrance, which her tender near-blocked completely, taking up all the space the ten or more wheeled vehicles would otherwise fit in. It sat in the air undisturbed 14-inches from the pavement, just where she'd left it. Cameras and news people were everywhere. An extremely pretty news anchorwoman said to Haley, "I am honored to meet you, Haley. My name is Sangthip, and it is *my* camera crew the Chancellor General asked to film your ship for the people of our planet."

"It's nice to meet you, Sangthip. My tender only seats four."

"Then, only three of us will come."

"Let me get the door open, so stand back."

Without touching it, using her tiara, Haley opened the door to the tender. It was about the smallest craft you could get a quantum drive into. Sangthip introduced Haley to the camerawoman, Patty, and to the light and auditory technician, Sally, as each entered the tiny spacecraft. Haley had already texted Bodhi about the guests while the introductions were being made. She climbed aboard herself, after Sangthip, and told them to all strap in. She glided out slowly from beneath the portico, gained a little speed and a few feet of altitude, then punched the drive pressing everyone into their seats. No one blacked out.

Haley inquired, "What do you call your planet?"

Sangthip answered proudly, "Firmament."

"There are a lot of those," Haley informed her.

"Really?" Sangthip asked in amazement.

"Actually," Haley confided, "forty-two percent of yellow sun worlds start off with the name 'Firmament', and 54% start off being called 'Earth'."

"What are the other 4% called?" Patty asked.

"All kinds of things like Orb, Terra Firma, Globe, Ground, Mother, Home, Here-we-are, Dirt, and Rocky," Haley answered.

"I guess we're not very original," Sangthip acknowledged.

"Well, you didn't call it Earth," Haley offered. Then she asked, "What do you call your galaxy?"

Sally answered, "The Sparkling Way."

Sangthip inquired, "What does our galaxy actually look like?"

Haley put up a holo of it as she stated, "It's a flat spiral disc galaxy, with nearly a fifth of it hidden in a big dust and gas cloud."

Their flight was extremely brief since *Diamond Lotus* was in very low orbit and it was uncloaked. It was showing in the holo's, but the three news women's eyes were drawn in to see it through the tender's transparent plasteel and synthetic diamond viewport. Haley circled the ship slowly while Patty filmed. These maneuvers also gave the three women a view of the planet from low orbit. Haley opened the hangar doors on the ship and glided in nicely to hover over the metal deck. She shut down the drives and reduced the vortex-redirect to idle, sinking about 10 inches and leaving the undercarriage 14 inches over the deck. Haley waited until the hangar aired up before unsealing the tender's door and was the first to step down. Patty was still filming.

Bodhi met them coming through the hangar's airlock, and Haley told him, "This is Sangthip, the news anchor for the station FUX International News. This is Sally, who handles lights and mics, and behind that camera is Patty."

Patty didn't acknowledge the introduction and instead filmed Bodhi from close up. This cut to the core of Bodhi's anxiety. He already felt like the global pariah of Firmament from the live transmission of the League of Nations meeting. Sangthip asked him,

"Do you think women who are unable to reproduce are damaged goods?"

Sally pushed a microphone in Bodhi's face awaiting his answer. He froze up for a moment with fleeing to his cabin, screaming in his mind; a camera rolling not two feet from his head and a mic he could poke his tongue out and touch. Haley was on the verge of coming to his rescue when Bodhi found his voice and said, "No, I do not. I think there is some misunderstanding here. I only just found out that Haley is interested in me romantically and we have loved one another as friends for so long that it came as a shock. I've had no time, with all there has been to do here, to get my mind wrapped around it."

Sangthip followed up with, "So you are not rejecting her for her inability to reproduce?"

"I haven't rejected Haley, merely postponed such an important decision until I can work through the ramifications of it and look into my heart."

Sangthip asked, "So you may yet decide to reject her?"

"I seek to find my harmony with Haley and together discover the nature of our relationship. We are committed to working together for life and are now exploring other possibilities of our relationship. I grew up at a male monastery, and feel a little bit socially retarded trying to relate with females."

"Are you homosexual?" Sangthip asked.

"No. I have only had sex with one person—a woman—in my life, and I fell hopelessly in love. She declined to join me, and that was only a week ago. I guess I'm on the rebound, or maybe just rolling off the court going nowhere. I mean no offense to anyone and am just in turmoil."

Sally blurted out, "You poor thing," even though she was never supposed to speak while assisting in shooting an interview.

Sangthip gave her an expression of rebuke before asking Bodhi, "Who is this woman you are in love with?"

"I prefer to call it 'getting over her' instead of 'in love with', though I can't be entirely sure I'm not fooling myself. Her name is Gretle, and she holds three doctorates and has completed three post-graduate fellowships. She is a disciple of my teacher and will not leave our teacher's side."

Sangthip focused on Haley and Sally pushed the mic over in Haley's face while Patty got the camera on her. Sangthip asked, "Do you have academic degrees?"

"I am a warrior maiden of the Mother's Guardians and a member and practitioner of Islohar. I have equivalencies of advanced degrees."

Bodhi added, "Haley is truly more knowledgeable than Gretle."

Sangthip shifted back to Bodhi, and so did the mic and camera as she asked, "Then what was it about Gretle?"

Haley answered for him, "She took all the risk and picked Bodhi up, so he was really just seduced. Gretle is a good person and was trying to help Bodhi over his anxiety about women. She was not trying to make Bodhi fall in love with her, but it is just in Bodhi's nature."

The camera, mic and Sangthip's gaze all returned to Bodhi, and he stated flustered, "What she just said," agreeing with Haley's assessment.

To get Bodhi off the hook, Haley suggested to the three news women, "Why don't we take a tour of the ship?"

"We'd love to," Sangthip said excitedly.

Haley led the way out of the airlock foyer after opening the hatch in the floor to show them the lower gun turret. Through the airlock there was a foyer with a lift tube and a ladder tube. Haley sent the news women up the lift one at a time, then she and Bodhi squeezed in together. On deck eleven they passed through a little passenger seat compartment for the crew not involved in flying or fighting the ship, of which they currently had none. They merely passed through this into a living room. Sangthip posed the question, "No screens or monitors?"

Haley pointed to the pedestal growing out of the deck and switched it on with her tiara to blossom into an eight-foot diameter hologram. She turned it right off once they comprehended. From the living room, they passed through the dining room which Haley and Bodhi never used, into the galley, which had a little nook table. The surfaces in the galley were all granite tile and stainless steel.

Equipment and built-in appliances glistened from every quadrant, and none of it was at all familiar to the news women. Haley started pointing out machines and explaining their functions. Their guests were most interested in the molecular food synthesizer, and the automatic materials recycling system. She synthesized some chicken for them to taste, and none could tell it was synthetic.

Haley mentioned, "No instrumentation can differentiate cooked chicken and synthetic chicken. They truly are the same. Science will never be able to create a live chicken, though."

"How often do you need to take on air and water?" Sangthip inquired.

"We have water purification at the atomic level and so do not waste any at all. About twenty gallons per week are absorbed by our cells, and by the plants we grow hydroponically and in our grow room. Water container tanks form a narrow band just inside the hull, all the way around, and hold 120,000 gallons. They also provide an additional layer of armor since the tanks themselves are made of plasteel and water doesn't burn. We generate our own CO2 with super oxygen-producing micro-organisms in trays providing ideal conditions. The trays are four inches thick and stacked in racks from floor to ceiling in our environmental section. Each tray is changed out and restarted every three months, and all are at varying degrees of maturity. The spent plant material goes into our molecular food synthesizer. Our hydroponics stacks and grow room produce some of our CO2. We also have it compressed in tanks; enough to completely air up the ship 2 ½ times."

"How much of your food do you grow?" Sangthip asked.

"Currently we grow 27% of all the food we eat. We could increase that by growing different things. We carry an enormous supply of the very finest gourmet freeze-dried dinners. Some have water separated in the same package, and when you pull the tab, it mixes and the meal self-heats, ready in seconds. Others you add the water through a nozzle on the package and stick it in the wave-cooker for a few seconds. Would you care to try a meal? They are made on the planet Om for the government and are called 'ambassador rations'. If it were not for some wealthy friends of ours, we would not have been able to afford them."

"I'd love to try ET astronaut food," Sangthip enthused for the camera.

Haley opened a cabinet hatch so crammed with the things that two fell out in the process. In a complete blur, she caught each in flight and tucked those back in as she read off the dinner labels in the only Firmament language she knew, providing a menu selection for her guests. She pulled a roast goose breast, potatoes, stuffing, gravy and steamed vegetables for Bodhi, knowing that's what he wanted.

Patty said from behind the camera, "I'd like a fillet of sole stuffed with crabmeat, please."

"I'll try the breaded fried chicken breast with champagne and reduced onion sauce," Sangthip said as she decided.

Sally informed Haley, "I think I'll have the barbeque ribs with baked beans and potatoes."

That one came in a large container, and Haley was glad to get it out of the hatch-space. Bodhi didn't like ribs. Since she really could not eat, having no facilities for it, Haley made a show of preparing herself a protein shake. She did have a synthetic bladder and could drink liquids. Bodhi added the water to each dinner then heated them all at once in the wave-cooker. Sally's container only just fit in. Sangthip asked Haley, "Are you on a diet?"

"I've found that it is optimal for health and for maintaining a high energy level to eat my largest meal in the morning and to eat light in the evening."

"So it is not about your figure?" Sangthip asked in disbelief.

"I attend to my figure with exercise and do enjoy ornamenting it with clothing, jewelry and makeup," Haley admitted.

"You're awfully thin and petite, Haley. Are you sure you are not starving yourself over your self-image?" Sangthip persisted.

"Honestly, eating and my self-image could not be less related," Haley said truthfully.

Bringing the hot dinners into the dining room on a tray, Bodhi said, "I don't think Haley is too thin. She's strong and aesthetically perfect."

Sangthip gave Haley an encouraging smile. They sat at the dining table, which could seat 18 people and had additional boards for it which could be added to seat 24. They sat at one end, and Haley maneuvered Bodhi into the seat at the head, before sitting beside Patty. Everyone but Haley, who had only a glass, opened their ration container to steam heat rising and delicious aromas. Bodhi didn't wait for his to cool, getting a bite right onto his fork and blowing on it before putting it in his mouth.

Giving her dinner time to cool, Sangthip asked, "What was this ship designed for?"

Bodhi told her, "It was made for long space exploration missions so it has reactor power to function as a tug, and workshops to support repairs or to support an expeditionary group on the surface. It has a landing platform with a biodome with a separate reactor and an airlock, to house people even on planets with no air and extreme temperatures. It also has a mining spacecraft and refineries on board, a water collector-tanker craft, two shuttles, the tender, and a gas-collector we can use to compress CO_2 to refill our tanks and to mine gas giants to make thruster fuel. It was designed to be self-sufficient for over a century."

"How old is it?" Sangthip inquired, wondering if she ought to be worried.

"It was built seven years ago in orbit around a planet named Om and was refitted for us just before we left. We have another load of refined solarium for each reactor so this ship can remain operational with the fusion materials onboard for more than another 250 years. We have also charted the coordinates of untapped deposits of solarium in your galaxy."

"How old is your civilization?" Sangthip asked.

Bodhi answered, "The planet Mother has 92,000 years of recorded history going back to language engraved in stone or clay tablets. We passed through the crisis of survival which Firmament is at the unsuccessful end of, about 87,200 years ago. We were late taking an interest in space compared to most crisis-survival populations. The people of Mother attained moral anarchy and an end to one person having power over another about 12,500 years ago. We lived in peace and unity for more than twelve millennia, and we were then conquered by a tri-galaxy empire of nearly 5,700 planet populations, all slaves to a permanent wartime economy of imperial expansion. A little over four years ago we toppled the empire and all 5,700 plus worlds were liberated. My teacher was the leader of the revolution, though she did not become my teacher until after we won."

Sally shared, "We have less than 5,000 years of recorded history, and besides a big telescope, we have never sent anything outside our solar system. It takes us months to get to the nearest planet."

Haley said, "Within a year your population will begin slowly migrating to New Firmament, 28 light-years away."

"I can't even imagine; this all seems so unreal," Sally gushed.

Sangthip asked, "How do you decide what time it is?"

Bodhi answered, "Right now our clock cycle is still on Gaia time, the capital of Mother. Star fleets tend to keep the time of the capital city of their home-world."

Finished with her shake, Haley excused herself to go to the head to empty her bladder; which she did. She even sat on the toilet to do it. The synthetic bladder could as easily be drained with a nasal-gastronomy tube, though Haley preferred doing it human-style.

Sangthip asked Bodhi, "What does Gretle look like?"

Bodhi placed his pocket device on the table from its belt holster, which both Gretle and Haley thought was kind of nerdy, and brought up a hologram of Gretle with her arm around Pez. Gretle was smiling with genuine joy, and it was a good picture of her.

Sangthip commented, "She is only a little bigger than Haley, but the two seem to have some close resemblances."

"They do, and one that is identical," Bodhi said accurately. "Gretle is from a white sun world where people are taller and heavier. She is extremely tiny for a white sun female, as is my teacher, Pez."

"That's your teacher? The one Gretle has her arm around?" Sangthip asked, surprised.

"Yes, she is the Wu of the Islohar, High Priestess of Haley's order of warrior-maidens, and Vikar General of my order."

"She's so young."

"Thirty-seven now, I think. She is also the mother of the Mu, who reincarnates every 2,500 years to transmit new teaching to the human race. The Mu's name is Electra, and she's almost six years old; at least she was before we got lost."

"Are you seeking a way back?" Sally asked sympathetically.

"We sent drones 200 million light-years out in the six directions and scanned another four billion light-years outwards finding nothing at all that matches our star maps. It was dangerous jumping our drones without charts and only light optics from a distant past."

"So you've given up?" Sangthip inquired.

"It seems it could take our whole lives and may not even *be* possible," Bodhi pointed out. "To transmit the teachings, we don't need to find our home, only sentient beings."

Sally gave Bodhi her strong opinion, "Since Gretle is no longer even a long-shot I think you should love the one you're with. She is better looking than you and the smartest person I've ever met; she's unassuming too, putting on no airs."

"I appreciate your concern and your advice, and could not agree with you more about her being better looking than me. I do love Haley. I have a process to attend to, which involves some internal transformation and catharsis. I am moving through it as fast as I am able."

"Well, don't take so long that you miss your chance," Sally pressed.

"It has not been two full days yet since being made aware of this out of the blue. I do not think I am being entirely unreasonable."

Patty mentioned, "This stuffed sole is scrumptious; better than any I've ever had before at a restaurant."

"These ribs are incredible," Sally reported with sauce on her cheek.

"This sauce is so perfect for the pounded breaded chicken breast," Sangthip agreed with the high ratings on the food.

Bodhi offered, "We have fermented and brewed beverages, mixed synthetic alcohol drinks, stimulant-brew, teas or juice if any of you would like one."

"What's synthetic alcohol?" Patty asked.

"We call it Alko and it has the disinhibiting effects of alcohol, mild euphoria, reduction of coordination, and can get you just as drunk as alcohol. The effects wear off completely in thirty-minutes, and there is no loss of brain cells, pickling of tissue or any hangover or after-effects at all. It is alcohol with all the fun and none of the harm."

"What is stimulant-brew?" Sally asked him.

"It is made from a bean that grows in the tropics and subtropics, which is shelled from its husk and roasted, then ground up. Boiling water is either percolated through the grinds, or dripped through, or forced through with pressure and the resulting fluid is bitter-tasting, but can be dressed and is a natural stimulant. The husk is a potent natural tranquilizer. I like it pressured through a fine grind and mixed with much steamed half and half, and powered bittersweet chocolate sprinkled on top."

Returning to the dining room, Haley informed them, "That is how his teacher likes it, and they drank many together."

"I'd love a stim-brew the way Bodhi likes them," Patty said. "Sangthip won't let me drink alcohol when I'm on shift and filming."

Bodhi went to the galley to make it, and one for himself. He asked over his shoulder, "Would anyone else like one?"

"Sure, please," Sangthip told him.

"I'd just like a glass of water," Sally replied.

Bodhi disappeared into the galley, and Sangthip said to Haley with a slight tone of accusation, "You didn't mention that Bodhi has only known of your love for two days or that he is in the throes of a broken heart."

"I didn't mean to mislead you," Haley said innocently. "It feels so big to me that I'm sure I'm exaggerating things."

"You're not a virgin, are you darling? How old are you?" Sangthip asked her.

Although she had been physically manufactured a little more than 12 years previously and had been sentient for less than a few years, Haley kept her human cover by replying, "I'm twenty-two, and I have had sex with two people. They are both girls, though."

"Do you prefer girls?" Sally inquired.

"Not at all. There were only girls available for the last four years while I trained at the monastery of my order. I love Bodhi, and he is male. Since I'm female, that makes me heterosexual, but my love for Bodhi goes beyond gender."

"That's deep!" Sally exclaimed.

"Give him a little time, Haley," Sangthip suggested, "to get over Gretle and get his feet back on the ground."

"He seems like he'd be kind of a slow mover, romantically," Patty commented.

"He's always very deliberate and intentional when he does anything of import," Haley agreed.

"He's not likely to have casual sex with you, then dump you," Sangthip agreed too.

"He's a mate-for-lifer," Haley informed them admiringly. Then she asked, "Has it only been two days?"

"We didn't know you yesterday and haven't a clue about two days ago," Sally clarified.

"The two of you are cute," Sangthip said amused, "like young teens with first crushes."

"Developing sexual relationships was not in our curriculums," Haley said a little defensively, "and no time was ever allowed for it."

Bodhi returned with three very large mugs of stimulant-brew each with generous chocolate powder floating thickly on top, and a glass of atomically purified water. He set each of the three women's beverages on the table in front of them, then cleared their ambassador ration containers and cutlery from the table. Sally asked, "Is he always so helpful?"

"He offers and tries to be, but I hang on to the chores I'm better at;" Haley answered.

"He has a lot going for him," Sally pointed out. "He's young, cute, knows how to fight, is the mightiest male in the galaxy, and he seems smart too."

"I don't need a sales-pitch," Haley reminded her.

Bodhi returned from the galley and sat back down, picking up his unfinished stim-brew. Haley asked Sangthip, "You're not going to make me and Bodhi out to be ridiculous and pathetic in the news, are you?"

"A pair of sweeter ET's I could never even imagine," Sangthip replied. "Your years of spiritual and martial training will be emphasized, and we might mention how very new each of you is to the love game."

"He needs time," Haley stated, shifting the weight of it all onto Bodhi.

Bodhi suggested, "Shall we continue the tour of the ship?"

"Yes, we'd love to," Sangthip enthused.

They entered the corridor and then the first room off of it, which was the office and study. It adjoined from within with the medical unit. They returned to the hall from that unit and entered the room across from it, the lounge, which had an Alko bar, recreational pharmacy cabinet and enormous funnel-dome over a seating area. Sangthip asked, "What's that?" pointing at the funnel dome.

Bodhi started it up with his skullcap, and it silently sucked up the air like a vacuum cleaner. He explained, "It is the smoking salon. There is a hookah on the table, a bong and a vaporizer. Smoking materials are in the drawers beneath the tabletop."

Bodhi led them through the gym, the martial arts studio, the meditation room, the laundry room and then walked them through the 4 dorm cabins each with 4 berths; the ten sleeping cabins with private bathrooms and the three suites. He led them up to the bridge which had six seats, a viewport and almost no instrumentation. Sangthip commented, "The driver's seat of my wheeled ground vehicle is like a hundred times more complicated-looking than this. How do you fly this ship?"

Bodhi and Haley took their seats and using his skullcap Bodhi brought up his main piloting holo with data values along the bottom and a smaller holo to each side. Haley brought up her holo, then those along the dashboard, about 4 inches diameter each giving the status of the primary ship's systems. Between Bodhi and Haley, a perfectly round holo appeared and Bodhi pointed it out saying, "This is our spherical, which can be magnified or reduced in terms of how much distance you want displayed, but this ship remains always at the center of the spherical. It is lined with a grid all around and gives the degrees of turns we must make to get to certain places, which becomes important when convoying with one or more other ships. It is the reference for directing other ships or communicating your own ships maneuvers. It is also the reference for flying the ship remotely from other than the bridge or from outside the ship, say a planet surface."

From the bridge, they descended to the workshop deck which also contained the Environmental Section. The machines and table-tools were compact and miniaturized wherever possible. There was a complete machine shop, advance robotics workshop, mini-foundry with a metal shop and welding, a very thorough and impressive electronics workshop, a chemical lab and workshop with a room off of it full of hull-crawler repair androids, interior repair androids, and hover-drone repair units with articulated tool arms. Some materials were stored in holds on this deck.

On the deck below were the various micro-refineries, more bins and holds of materials, an armored munitions vault, and an assembly room with hydraulic arms on two walls and a little gantry crane in the ceiling. Methane and other gases were also stored on this deck, and there were cargo holds full of ambassador rations too.

The next deck down contained the Vortex redirect and generation turbine, force-field shield generators, the atomic water purification unit and more materials bins and cargo holds. On the deck below, Bodhi showed them the reactors room, the drives chamber with both the huge twin space drives and the quantum drive; the primary cloaking generator, a spare parts and systems suite joined with another workshop full of diagnostic equipment; and the solarium fusion backup battery system. There were also materials bins and cargo holds.

The Drives chamber had been enormous, consuming six decks at the stern of the ship and the reactor room took up four decks amidships. The lowest decks were all materials bins and cargo holds. Returning to deck eleven Bodhi led them back to the main living quarters and into the living room. The newswomen had just scored the exclusive of their careers and couldn't wait to get back to the office and start editing film and writing commentary. Themes and angles were hatching in their minds. Bodhi figured he couldn't sink much lower than a pariah. Haley drove them home since she'd brought them over, to begin with. She took them right to the helicopter landing pad as they called it, on the roof of the building their offices were in. They thanked Haley for the scoop of the millennium and ran to a stairs access door. Haley flew home to Bodhi.

CHAPTER EIGHT

Haley found him in the meditation room so, she slipped out of her shoes, grabbed a cushion, and sat beside him powering down all extraneous monitoring and sensors on her android body. She watched her thoughts for a while trying to focus more on their movements than on the meanings they symbolize as they arose, abided briefly and faded away. After a while, she shifted her focus to the witness of her thoughts; that pure immaterial consciousness that never moves and is eternal. She was in the state.

Bodhi was not in the state. He was reviewing his past focusing on moments of emotional charge and on excavating his deepest negative beliefs connected with the charge to reveal his deepest negative beliefs about himself, which form the kingpin and were seeds of future negative action. Occasionally he would write things down on a pad beside him. He didn't like using his skullcap or to even wear the thing when he was doing holy work. The work he was courageously making was one of the most difficult of spiritual works one could make. He resisted torpor keeping his mind supple and wakeful and directed it with his will and determination to look most carefully at himself, and only at himself, and to be grateful to everyone and everything that triggered emotional charge in him and so helped him to find it and work on it.

Hayley could feel his intensity and turmoil so, she passed him her love from the state of pure contemplation. She knew she ought to have given him some time to get over Gretle, and that she had pushed him into internal conflict. Her own turbulent emotions mixed with love, need, and yearning had gotten the better of her being a new dimension in her life she'd not mastered yet. It was unfair to Bodhi for her to speak to others of her love for him and exclude the issue at the root of Bodhi's dilemma. She had misconstrued it by identifying it as simply an inability to breed.

She realized that she'd fallen out of the state and was experiencing remorse, so Haley switched to doing the same process Bodhi was involved in; looking at her own stuff. She saw that Bodhi was chewing his lip—a sure sign of anguish—when she stole a glance his way. As she forced herself to look, her guilt leaked in from every direction and her mind started to feel like a swamp. A little deeper and she felt almost like she was on fire. Choking on regret, Haley's voice croaked out in tears, "I'm so sorry, Bodhi."

Bodhi opened his eyes and turned his head to look into her eyes while he wrapped an arm around her back lovingly. This triggered a waterfall for her, and the tears flowed over. Bodhi turned on his cushion to face her and got his other arm around her with his palm over her heart energy center on her back. Haley wailed her grief and remorse soaking Bodhi's shoulder as he held her in his love.

Haley turned off her tear-function, which was calibrated to her emotional intensity, finding it just made her feelings seem soggy and like they were drowning her. The wailing continued and was not something she could just turn off, unfortunately. Bodhi held her passing waves of love and awareness into her. Haley thought this might all go better if he just screamed at her in anger. Instead, he was consoling *her* for feeling bad about making *him* suffer.

She told him with a shaky voice, still crying, "To think I found emotions to be just the most wonderful things when first I started having them. How do humans survive this?"

"Each must find their own way," he answered sincerely. "Some manage stoically, some go histrionic-ballistic, and then there is everything in between."

"How do you do it?" She asked between sobs.

"When it's really bad I lie in a fetal position and cry," he confided. "Once I'm able I work it through to pacification as they taught me in the monastery. I look at each incident in which I felt negative emotions and seek the cause within me rather than in what triggered me. Otherwise, I'd be mistaking conditions for causes.

The core mechanism is inevitably a negative belief about myself too real and painful seeming to look directly at. Piercing that illusion is key to crashing the schema down and disintegrating it. Only when we leave the unknown in place of the schema can we recognize the undifferentiated unity of the ever-changing energy and movement and that the witness does not move, transcending the relative material world. The wisdom-union of the discriminating perception separates the absolute witness and relative process at the same time uniting them in the recognition that everything is in consciousness—is a manifestation of consciousness and that consciousness is the fundamental void."

"I'm just so sorry, Bodhi," Haley cried into his shoulder.

"I'm sorry you're feeling so bad Haley and that I was unable, at the moment, to shift into a whole new reality with you. I did not mean to hurt your feelings."

"I know. You go through pains not to ever cause suffering and tend to the deep underlying stuff in your adaptions and transformations, making them real, and not just a decision in thought to be screwed up later."

"I was born as sentience incorporated in matter and have had my whole life to learn to handle it. Your sentience just kind of arrived and requires your artificial temple to descend to the final emanation of matter, though your sentience is independent, and you can interact with humans through quantum artificial intelligence without your android body. You seem to have all the emanations to that of time, the last before the manifestation of the material world. You have both a mind of symbolic languages with thought construction and an absolute mind of emptiness or the transcendental witness. Your process of cultivating wisdom-compassion and emptiness follows the same pattern as human and Kluzyst. You develop swiftly, Haley, and we will get through this. I love you."

A new heightened last burst of sobs escaped Haley as she clung to Bodhi with her face buried in his shoulder, but it was short-lived. After a few moments, she told him, "You are too good to be true."

"No, I'm not, and here I am," he said soothingly.

Haley pulled out her pocket device, brought up the holo in front of both of them, did a quick sort to weed out applicants under 18 and over 25, then did a quantum elimination of all that did not at all fit the parameters of Bodhi's sense of beauty and who had less than five years of serious meditation practice. Out of the over 80 million applicants, these sorts had whittled it down to just over a quarter million. She made a final sort of just meditators with martial arts proficiency and was able to get it down to a manageable 53,905 applicants. This was yet too many for Bodhi to process, so she cut the bottom 60% of contenders after quantumly rank-ordering the lot and started flashing through the nearly 22,400 candidates leaving each up for 1.5 seconds. Bodhi asked, "How many are there?"

"I've got it down to less than 22,400 from over 80 million."

"It will take too many hours to see them all," Bodhi complained. "I couldn't have a relationship with someone else while living with you anyway. Let's look at applicants for our crew."

Haley narrowed the range on spouse candidates and chopped applicants out of the equation, eliminating all but the top 20, and proceeded to show the first. Bodhi exclaimed, "That's a crew applicant!?"

Haley had to quantumly check through over 60,000,000 crew applications to see if this spousal candidate had also put in an application for a crew position, which imbedded an almost two second lag-time in her reply, "As a matter of fact she is."

While she'd been cross-referencing that name she'd also done the same with the other nineteen names from the spousal applicants, finding that all but one of those had also submitted a crew application. She deleted that one, checked the average length of training and practice of the 19 left, in martial arts and meditation, rated each giving them aesthetic values, then ran those standards through the 140 million-plus applicants for both positions. Only 23 met these standards. She saved these then proceeded to show Bodhi the 2nd of the 19. While going through these, she rated skill sets, academic achievements and specialized training to compare these 19 and the 23 to the total applicants for both spouse and crew. This moved her to eliminate seven of the 19, eight of the 23, and to bring 3 back over from the reject pile; and she accomplished this just in the nick of time because the next holo was the 13th. All 30 candidates were viewed for 30 seconds each, which gave Bodhi time to read the brief bio in the text at the bottom of the holo.

He mentioned, "These applicants are all female."

"I selected them by specific indicators that I set. No males made the top 30."

Haley had not shared that gender happened to be one of those indicators, excluding males, so her response made it sound like the best of the best just happen to be female. Bodhi stated dumbfounded, "They look more like beauty contest contenders than applicants for the crew."

"They're the ones most likely to manifest wisdom-compassion and have the ability to learn what they will need to know. They will also make excellent ornamentation within our environment."

"I hope none of these also applied to be my spouse."

"There were over 60 million job applicants and more than 80 million spouse applicants," Haley answered truthfully and irrelevantly."

"It seems strange that they all fit my teenage porn profile."

"Do we interview all 30?"

"Let's try to find a way to narrow it down to 10, so we can get through the interviews in one day."

"Which ones would you like to select?"

"Who has the most meditation practice and the most skills?"

Haley put up all thirty images in one holo and highlighted the ten with most skills at meditation. Bodhi asked, "Who are the most advanced in martial arts?"

Haley highlighted the ten top ones. Bodhi inquired, "Who has the most academic achievement?"

Haley highlighted these ten. Four had been highlighted all three times, repeatedly, and Haley left only those four images up. They were all dual applicants. Bodhi suggested, "Why don't we just interview those four?"

"I'll set it up. What about the spousal applicants?

"Text them our gratitude for taking the time to apply, and apologize, explaining that filling the position would produce a conflict of interest."

"You need a human girl who can breed."

"That can't happen now."

"But it must!"

"Adoption, remember?"

"We can hardly request applications for that."

"The Cosmic Intelligence will cross our paths soon enough with an orphan or orphans."

"We really ought to go disarm those three nuclear powers before you sleep, to keep Firmament safe."

"Let's go to the bridge."

They left the meditation room and walked to their seats on the bridge, taking them to strap in. Bodhi asked, "Where to first?"

Haley brought up a holo of their route towards the polar cap and a little towards sunrise to the capital city of the nearest of the three holdouts. Bodhi fired up the drives and accelerated, following the route Haley was displaying. He skimmed the atmosphere, descending a bit from low orbit, and couldn't quite fit between two satellites, frying one of them on their shields. It had not been one of the newer ones, and its orbit had been deteriorating anyway. Descending through the atmosphere, *Diamond Lotus*'s nose glowed red.

Bodhi brought them 55,000 feet over the capital and Haley hacked this nation's emergency coms system. She told Bodhi, "You're on, but you won't be speaking their language. They have people who speak the language you'll be heard in, and their government leaders have translators and interpreters."

With Haley's interpreter service active Bodhi said in Mother, which came out in the language of the superpower now across the ocean from them, "You must disarm all nuclear, chemical and biological weapons beginning this instant. If I do it for you, people will die. Your nation will send delegates to the League of Nations, or I will start killing your leaders until one does. Please have the leader contact me at (333) 963-9639 immediately."

"You made that pretty clear," Haley complimented him.

"Can you get a fix on their leader?"

"I'm hacking, but it's slow since I have to use a two-language comparative dictionary and translate. At least I'm compiling an interpretation service for this language while I'm using the dictionary."

"That's great, Haley!"

"I'll have the leader's name, picture, biography and other things, but I'll need to get into triple-top security data to find his chip code so we can track his relative position on the globe."

About 30 seconds later, Haley announced, "There! I have his chip code, offshore bank account numbers, secret diary, documents proving his crooked dealings, and his porn file."

"What do you need his porn file for?"

"He would be very embarrassed if the contents leaked to the public."

"What does he watch?"

"He is in some of them and has some most unusual proclivities."

"I don't think I want to know."

"No. I think it would give you bad dreams."

The national leader announced himself with pomp and authority over their coms. Bodhi told him, "Disarm your nukes now and your chemical and biological weapons. In case you do not know where these are precisely located, my colleague will send you the coordinates of all their locations. You will comply, or I will kill you and deal with the next leader of your nation."

"We are only defending ourselves against the other two super-powers."

"I'm disarming them as well, and I will be the only super-power from here on out."

"What are your intentions with our world?"

"To help your planet's population develop the means to migrate to a pristine world, or as many of them as is possible before this one dies. We are giving technology, mined materials you cannot obtain for yourselves, and our time and effort. We want nothing from you, your nation or this planet, but to know it has the resources it needs to secure its own better future."

"How can we trust you?"

"I'm not asking you to trust me. Right now I'm forcing you to disarm. I could blow all that stuff up, but there would be lives lost that way, and I'd prefer not to."

"If I refuse?"

"Then you have less than 30 seconds to make your peace."

"If I comply?"

Haley flashed some data about the leader in front of Bodhi, which included his extreme enriching of himself through his political office at the expense of the people, and their rather radical hate of him. Bodhi told him, "Then you can live and retire from public life to your 2nd home on the lakeshore."

Haley told the man, "Taking your chip out now is a little late since we've already acquired you and are locked on. You are as slippery as an eel."

"Good catch," Bodhi told her.

Bodhi and Haley oversaw the commencement of the disarmament, the stepping down of the leader and the promise of the new leader to see the disarmament through to conclusion and to send a delegate immediately to the League of Nations. Haley had also made him promise to open the elite-government lanes on the capital's streets to common traffic immediately and to drain the swamp of criminals in high office. She knew he was one of those.

The number-one super-power which they had thought they'd disarmed turned out to have submarines, more of those big flat-top ships with all the jets, and more missile-launching ships all with nukes scattered around the globe. *Diamond Lotus* crossed the ocean practically from space and traversed across a little more than half the huge country before descending over mountains in the central region precisely over the Vice-Dictator's bunker and command center. Bodhi said over this country's emergency coms system, in Mother, which came out in the Vice-Dictator's language, "This is Bodhi and Haley of *Diamond Lotus*, please have the Vice-Dictator contact us this instant at (333) 963-9639. We will not wait long before firing upon you."

"That was very assertive," Haley noted, pleased.

After two minutes, Bodhi said, "He seems to be avoiding us."

"The bunker is lead-lined, but I've had a mini-spybot watching it since the VD arrived, and he is still in there."

"Thanks Haley. Do we have any bunker-penetrating rounds loaded?"

"Those are in battery number seven, and you have nukes in battery eight. All the rest are high explosives."

"Well, I don't have time to waste with this clown. I'm blowing the bunker."

"He's awful damned rich, so I'm emptying all his accounts into charity organizations."

"Good thinking."

A bunker-piercer pierced the bunker easily and the next bunker-piercer drilled through the floor of the bunker, deeper into to roots of the mountain. The nuke which followed was almost entirely contained in its explosion by the bunker within the mountain, sending up no mushroom cloud, and only a lance of flame high into the sky followed by radioactive smoke. Bodhi sealed the hole the bunker-piercer had punched through rock and metal using his class six nose blasters. Haley mentioned, "No lead lining screens our view any longer since that is all draining into the hole you put in the floor or blown into separate atoms. There are absolutely no life-readings within there."

"Let's go sink the rest of their navy and disarm those two last nations," Bodhi said with a yawn.

"I've sent all those ocean-ships a text," Haley informed him, "to get to the nearest harbor and to abandon ship for the shore. I told them Firmament has no use for such ships and will tolerate them no longer."

"Thank you."

"I've also sent texts to the two other holdouts. One is tiny and has been impoverishing a conquered people and starving them of water for over a half century now."

They were hours sinking warships, and all but one had been completely abandoned. They sank the one that wasn't abandoned slowly to give the stupid crew time to get to life boats, or just swim ashore. The tiny nuclear-armed country had been a bit of a problem, and they went through a succession of three rulers, which took at least a couple of hours between each one to get the next confirmed before they found one who would work with them.

The last nuclear-armed holdout-superpower was easy. They had been tracking events around the globe by satellite imagery, and the leader was most congenial. This country was already dismantling their nuclear arsenal and had a delegate on the way to the League of Nations. This nation had more people than any other. The leader promised to help with the migration and to demilitarize entirely.

By this time, Bodhi could barely keep his eyes open. Haley had warned this leader that they'd be watching from space and then flew *Diamond Lotus* into medium orbit just above the highest of the 40,000 satellites. She helped Bodhi to bed, and although she wanted to climb in with him and snuggle, she went to attend to the biotrays in environmental and to harvest ripe produce from stacks and grow room.

CHAPTER NINE

Bodhi awoke nine hours later refreshed but famished. He just brushed his teeth and put on his practice outfit, waiting to shower after his workout. Haley was already in the martial arts studio in her practice clothes and with her hair tied back. He led them through the soft style form at a continuous slow pace, pausing a few times in more difficult postures to hold for a couple of minutes. After several rounds they assumed the wide stance and made the circling palms movements coordinated with the visualization of energy flowing in the oval channel. This exercise went long, and Bodhi worked up quite a sweat.

They made their meditative absorption session in the meditation cabin, for an hour, then Bodhi showered while Haley made his oatmeal. Bodhi met her in the galley once showered and dressed. Haley could see that he'd left his head in the insta-dry dome at least a second too long, giving himself a near-perm. His cowlicks were all sticking straight up. She was so in love that this only endeared him to her. She brought his oatmeal over as soon as he sat down and had loaded it with rehydrated blueberries which were his favorite.

"I'm starving. Thanks, Haley! This looks great!"

"We have our first interview scheduled in an hour and a half back over the city the League of Nations is meeting in."

"Where should we do the interviews?"

"In the office-study, I would think. I'll pick all four up in a shuttle, and they can sit in the living room while we bring them to the office one at a time. Then I'll return the two we don't hire to the surface in the tender. At least they will have had a trip into space for their troubles."

"You'll need to post something on your site to let people know the positions have been filled."

"Every applicant except of the four we are to interview and two backup candidates have already received a personalized text thanking them for applying and notifying them they have not been selected."

"You think of everything, Haley."

"Would you like a stimulant-brew?"

"No, thanks. The cup of hot water is perfect."

"I've reviewed the four applications, checked their references, hacked my way through a full vetting of each and have found no falsehoods, contradictions nor pink flags. Two candidates practice the direct contemplation of consciousness through sitting and absorption, the sudden way. Two employ the method of reabsorbing and dissolving the total content of the 36 types of phenomena of mind into pure awareness of clear light upon emptiness through visualization and intense concentration. One of the backup candidates is of the sudden way and the other practices the way of sound-formulas, offerings, devotion and love."

"Is the plan to only interview backups if we do not find two from the first lot?"

"Yes."

"I'll attend and participate, but I want you to make the selections. To be honest, I'm kind of intimidated by the unreal beauty of each of them. They all seem like fashion models."

"They're a little too short and flat-chested for that."

"My teen porn profile."

"I'll be happy to make the selections."

"Do you think you could cross-reference the two application categories to see if any of these four women we're going to interview also applied as a spouse?"

"No, I don't think we ought to go into this already favoring or disfavoring any candidates," Haley covered her refusal with completely irrelevant data. Bodhi bought it, munching down his oatmeal and rehydrated berries.

Haley offered, "I could make you more porridge with berries."

"No thanks, but do we have any more of those individually wrapped chocolate croissants?"

"We do, and I'll get one out of hiding and stick it in the cubical toaster for 3 seconds."

"They're in hiding?"

"Out of sight, out of mind, and because of that, there's some for you to have now."

"Thanks, Haley. You're the best. Say, what else is out of sight?"

"98.6% of our food supply in various holds outside the galley."

"Come on, Haley, you know what I mean."

"Alright; eclairs, creampuffs, those spongy pastries individually wrapped with the white icing, fudge brownies, chocolate-covered cherries, chocolate-covered vanilla ice-cream on a stick, double-chocolate on a stick, fudge pie and a few other things. You'll have to share once we've hired crew."

"Let's advertise for a chef!"

"There. I just set up the application process on our site. I already had some components ready to go anticipating this move on your part." Haley went and got Bodhi's chocolate croissant and stuck it 3-seconds in the cube-toaster before delivering it to him on a plate.

Bodhi suggested, "We'll need to find a good place to shop on the surface."

"There's a gourmet market not four blocks from the League of Nations building. It's the most expensive in this hemisphere."

"We can use gold or platinum for trade."

"When I go back to the League of Nations I'll inform then that they will have to pick up our grocery bills in exchange for the refined marsnium and adamantine we give them."

"Good idea. On Mother refined marsnium costs 1,000 dags per ounce, and they'll be needing close to 900 lb.'s or more before they're capable of mining their own."

"I've sent all the data they need to construct their first basic quantum computers, and sixteen governments plus eight universities are gearing up to begin. Nine hundred seventy-three corporations wanted to, but I texted them that they are not long for this world and ineligible. I need to present a seminar on the surface to teach them enough to get started and teach them a four-valve programming language with five dimensions. It will require at least three days. I'm adapting my design for a mainframe manufacturing guide into step by step construction instructions with clear diagrams and pictures."

"You couldn't make it any easier for them."

"It's such a great leap forward for them from where they are now."

Haley got Bodhi's cup, spoon and bowl into the washer-tank and asked, "Are you ready to fly to the interviews?"

"Let's do it."

They held hands on their way to the bridge, initiated by Bodhi, and this gave Haley a little thrill. Bodhi piloted *Diamond Lotus,* and Haley kept his route highlighted on his holo. They had time to get there on drives alone which Bodhi did, always the conservationist. As he was easing into low orbit, Haley ran to the tube and went down the ladder star fleet style, braking with the insides of her soles. She went through the airlock into the hangar and got into a big shuttle.

While she ran her preflight checks, she zoomed in on the roof of the building she was to collect her applicants on, from *Diamond Lotus*'s sensors, to be sure she could land a shuttle on it. It was large enough. She opened the hangar doors, lifted out in the shuttle with little clearance and shot for the surface. Coming in over the city she kept her shields up since there were so many of those bladed hovercraft all about. She also proceeded very slowly and came in most gently to float a foot off the roof. She dropped the shields when she lowered the ramp and opened the shuttle's airlock from the pilot seat, surrounded by flash photography and news cameras.

When she looked behind her from the cockpit through the shuttle to the airlock, she saw dozens of media people storming aboard. She engaged the hydraulic landing legs of the shuttle, not caring at this point if the roof held, and shut the craft down. Haley unbelted and sprang from her seat, running towards the airlock, shouting, "Only the four crew candidates are permitted on board! All unauthorized people, remove yourselves from my shuttle at once! You did not receive permission to come aboard!"

She couldn't believe how rude they were and that they were not listening to her. They *were* recording and transmitting her. In alarm,

Haley drew her blaster and set it on a reduced power range to stun-unconscious. She raised it pointing at the closest media critter to her and shouted, "Get out or I'll shoot you!!"

Only the one directly in front of the blaster barrel responded to her demand, and he wet himself running from the shuttle. She made her voice inhumanly loud and shouted, "Get off my shuttle if you are not scheduled for an interview or get shot!!"

One was trying to slip past her to get into the cockpit, and that felt to Haley like crossing the line. She jumped eight feet over some seats fixed to the deck to land in front of the guy trying to slip by. She employed 'kick with heel' from the soft form and put a little piston-hydraulics behind it, catching him in about the solar plexus and sternum. He flew backwards down the aisle until he collided with two men coming up it, and the three of them took down the next two behind, all landing in a tangle on the deck hard.

She had caught their attention by now and had made it clear that trespasses would be handled roughly. She scanned for the four faces of her interviewees and found them in a crush at the airlock door, huddled together and trying to push past news-invaders. Haley made her way down the main aisle shouting for intruders to "get off", and had to drop one with her blaster who was flanking her down a side aisle. When that body dropped to the deck, the media people panicked fleeing. One of her candidates went down underfoot beneath the news critter stampede, and the other three were pressed against the airlock wall. Haley poured on speed and rammed the bottle-cork jam of news folks bashing the whole knot of them through the door towards the lowered ramp at the stern, and off of her applicant squished on deck. She noted that it was Pam who'd gotten trampled. Winn, June, and Tish were all glued to the wall.

A good two-handed push followed by another 'kick with heel' had the last of the invading army tumbling down the ramp. The second the last one hit the rooftop from the shuttle's ramp, Haley raised and sealed it. She then helped Pam off the floor, who had foot prints all over her interview dress and asked, "Are you injured, dear?"

Pam licked the blood off her split lip before replying, "Nothing seems broken."

"Well come in, all of you, and take a seat. I have to put out some trash."

Haley entered the shuttle passenger compartment from the airlock and walked down the side aisle to the body of the man she'd dropped with her blaster. She grabbed his belt from his lower back and lugged all 214 pounds of him back to the airlock. Instead of chancing to open the ramp again, Haley opened the floor hatch and dropped the body through to the rooftop. Coming out of the airlock she sealed that door too. The shuttle was silent as a tomb. She told the four young women, "Come and sit in the center of the front row, and you'll be able to see into the cockpit and look out the viewport."

The four women changed seats to the four at the center of the front row. Haley introduced herself and clarified the process, "My name is Haley, and I'm Bodhi's assistant. I'm taking you up to *Diamond Lotus* where you will each have an interview. Typically our ship would have a crew of 16-18. With all the mining, refinery work and manufacturing we now need to do for Firmament, Bodhi and I need some help. We can train you in your jobs. It is not just a job. We are building a community and expect everyone to participate in our morning and evening martial arts and meditation practices. We will be assisting Firmament for over a year, but our ultimate mission is to transmit the teachings and practice instructions to sentient beings ready to receive them."

Winn held up a 3x5 card so that only Haley could read it. It said, "My government forced me to wear a transmission device."

Haley scanned her four applicants for bugs. All four were hot and transmitting. She marched to the lockers in the airlock foyer, rummaged about, and returned with four thermal space jumpsuits in close enough sizes. Standing before them she directed, "Strip naked panties and all, and put one of these on. Her applicants complied quickly unfastening hooks, Velcro, and clasps and removing everything down to bare skin. Haley collected the lenses, mics, batteries and wires. These she placed in a lead-lined hazardous materials bin by the airlock with a micro force-field around it.

Returning to the four women, Haley told Winn, "I appreciate your loyalty, and it will be weighed into the selection decisions."

Pam blurted out through her fat swollen lip, "I was going to tell you."

The Firmament language Haley learned first—the one of the main super-power—was an international business language and all but Tish could speak it. Tish spoke four languages though and knew the language Haley had to learn through a two-language cross-reference dictionary. Part of Haley's attention had been programing an interpreter-service for this second language for Bodhi's use, since first deciphering it. She told them, "I understand that you were all coerced and this will not count against any of you," first in the one language then again in the second for Tish.

Haley informed them, again repeating herself in the second language, "I'll fly us up now, so please strap in."

Sitting in the pilot's seat, Haley first checked to make sure that someone had removed the unconscious body from beneath her craft. It was gone. She powered up the drives and vortex-redirect turbine and retracted her landing legs floating a couple of feet off the rooftop. She accelerated slowly until she was above the peaks of the tallest buildings in the city, then punched it while igniting a launch booster to give her recruits a thrill. Their bodies indented their seats with great force, and Pam passed out for a second. Their faces squished to the sides and stretched. All stomachs were yet hovering just above the city, lost entirely. The word "thrill" couldn't quite capture the experience. June had to swallow some bile which had somehow come up her throat.

Next, they were thrown painfully onto their harnesses, their bodies straining to race ahead of the ship, as Haley lit a braking booster, like hitting a tree in a wheeled vehicle. The smart-foam in the straps kept them from bruising; badly at any rate. Bodhi had the *Diamond Lotus* uncloaked for them. Her passengers all had their gazes locked on the viewport even though their holos were clearer and showed so much more. Haley opened the hangar doors remotely and eased the shuttle through the small entrance. She parked next to the other shuttle in the hangar while the doors sealed behind her, then she started airing up the chamber.

Getting out of her seat she told her applicants, "Bodhi gets easily flustered around beautiful women so please rein-in your feminine wiles and try for gender neutral."

June commented, "It seems unlikely that your four top crew candidates would all be females with size one or size two figures."

"You are all Bodhi's type and were all applicants for spouse, but truly ranked at the very top for the crew positions as well. Bodhi has dug in his heels and refuses to get involved with another woman since I love him and we are together on our mission. I am not exclusive and would share so that Bodhi can become a natural father. He may prove too stubborn for this. If you are inclined to get involved with him then you must do so understanding that you will be sharing him."

She repeated all this for Tish, thinking she did need to get that interpreter-service completed soon. Tish commented, "You put his happiness before your own, and I will do the same."

Haley said to all four twice, once in two different languages, "The air in the hanger will be a little thin so take a deep breath before stepping down the ramp, and we'll proceed quickly to the hanger-airlock."

Leading the way Haley opened the airlock door and lowered the ramp at the same time remotely to exit the shuttle. She made a show of taking a deep breath and was equipped with synthetic lungs which were entirely irrelevant to her android body, but like her synthetic bladder and tear-function, they helped her pass for human. Once June, the last off the ramp, was on the hanger deck, Haley closed and sealed the ramp continuing to lead the way to the exit. She opened the hanger airlock doors as she approached, and the ones to the other side too since the hanger was airing up. In the little foyer on the other side of the airlock were three tubes. One contained a cargo lift, one a ladder and the other a single-person lift-tube.

Haley said to Winn, being closest, "Just step in. I'll operate it, and when it stops, and the door opens, step out and wait in the foyer on deck 11 for us."

One at a time Haley got her applicants up the tube-lift, operating it remotely from her android body's transponder. In one sense Haley was the ship. The ship's quantum super-computer was her primary process mind, and all ship's systems' feedback came to her. She was the ghost in the machine. Going last, Haley went up the tube on the lift to deck 11 where her four applicants awaited her in the foyer. Stepping out, she said twice, "Right this way, please."

In the living room, she asked them to have a seat. From the galley, she brought out pastries, pots of hot water, tea bags and stim-brew, a creamer pitcher, granulated cane sugar, corn muffins and jam. All of this was on a large tray she placed on the low table. From the galley, she'd asked Bodhi through his earbud to come to the living room, and he appeared promptly just as she set the tray down. Bodhi wore a work jumpsuit, and all his cowlicks were standing up untamed. Haley's deep affection for him was obvious in her introduction. Winn was selected for the first interview and led by the two members of her panel into the office-study, and sat down in the hot-seat. She was the size one and the tiniest of the four women. Her space jumpsuit was clearly too big.

Bodhi had her vetting file, accumulated through Haley's hacking, open in a holo and was skimming the data. Winn was only 22 years old, had completed what was called 'high school' three years early with the highest honors, wrapped up a 4-year academic degree in 2, took 3 years for her next two degrees, completed a one-year post fellowship and had left the academic world a year ago to live in a monastery. She held the highest rank in a hybrid martial art and the monastery Abbot's letter of reference stated that Winn had attained her first awakening in the sudden way of enlightenment and was working at becoming more proficient at re-entering the state.

Winn noticed her naked teen-selfie within Bodhi's holo, and her heart sank. *How had they found that?* She'd thought she'd deleted and obliterated *that* from the whole interface system years ago.

Bodhi was thinking it was a good thing he didn't have this girl's picture back in his teen-porn-phase or he may never have outgrown it.

Winn was sweating bullets.

Bodhi was terrified of her and had to dissolve his ego completely transcending into the pristine state to say, "You have already proven your loyalty, Winn, and are more than qualified. The position is yours if you want it and you can start as soon as you'd like."

Shock and bewilderment showed on Winn's face. For a moment, she was in a stupor. Lights seemed to come on inside, and Winn found her voice to say, "Thank you so much. I won't let you down, and I'll put my heart and whole being into the job."

Bodhi found the courage to ask Winn, "Why did you want to join our crew?"

"To help save the world of course," Winn said sincerely. Then she thought a moment and added, "To be honest, I really wanted to study meditation with you Bodhi, and learn your technology; and because your picture along with Haley's praises of you drew me deeply."

Haley directed Winn. "Please look into the electro-imaging lens here so we can get a holo of your aura."

Winn turned a little in her seat to face the lens and looked a bit spooked at the prospect of having her aura on display. Somehow it felt just as embarrassing as her naked-teen-selfie. It took but a moment and there it was, to scale, in a big holo over the lens. It was just in the first early stage of blooming but quite beautiful nonetheless. Winn didn't know what to make of it having no comparative base. It did seem familiar, though. Haley stood and said to Winn, "I'll show you to your cabin."

In the hall, Winn mentioned, "Seeing my teen selfie in Bodhi's holo at my job interview was momentarily my worst nightmare."

"You embody Bodhi's most impossible ideal physically so I knew it would help you in the hiring process," Haley confided.

"I do have skills and knowledge," Winn said defensively.

"And you wouldn't be on this ship now without those in abundance," Haley let her know. "You are my first choice for having Bodhi's children."

"You are running a subterfuge of your agenda, which Bodhi is unaware of."

"He does not know that our crew candidates were all spouse applicants nor that fitting his aesthetic ideal was one of the main data sorts," Haley revealed. "Like I told all of you, Bodhi has made up his mind against fathering a child, but I am sure that he would come around in an environment of love which could sustain such a thing harmoniously. Here is your cabin. I don't have time now to teach you how to utilize a skullcap, but I've connected your communications device to our coms system. You can use your device's keypad to feed your measurements, clothing designs, preferred textiles and any accents you would like such as embroidery, into the computer to the automated-tailor-fabricator and begin putting your wardrobe together. I'll show you where the finished clothes come out of the fabricator in workshop 3 after the next interview."

"Thank you, Haley. You're amazing."

From the living room, Haley brought June into the office. She was almost done programming the Haley Pyramid Five-Language Interpreter Service which included Hub Basic, Mother, Islohar, and the two Firmament languages she now had deciphered. Tish could not be interviewed until it was ready and uploaded to Bodhi's earbud. He could then speak any of the three languages he knew and could make it come out in one of two Firmaments Languages. Haley knew she would have to learn the language of the third superpower since it held almost a sixth of Firmament's population.

June's vetting file was open in Bodhi's holo, which he was reviewing when she entered with Haley and was directed to her seat. June was 24, held two degrees, practiced a soft martial art, was working the stage of completion of a practice identical to the Sacred Inner Fire of Bodhi's tradition and had made her way through school financially by nude dancing and the occasional escort service. Some rather candid pictures of her were converted to holograms within the larger holo displaying her file. For June it was just an occupational hazard, and she'd been through it before. She had found that if the pictures were known to the potential employer, it was probably best not to accept any job offers because those tended to be positions reflecting and expecting what her pictures suggested.

When Bodhi offered her the position, she was hoping those pictures might have something to do with it and said, "Oh my Intelligent Design Yes!!", though the interpretive program and June's lips were not in sync since what she had said was, "Oh my God yes!!!" June's aura was captured and displayed over the lens then placed beside Winn's.

Haley showed June to her cabin then showed Winn where workshop 3 was located on the ship so she could pick up her new clothes. June received instructions on making her wardrobe, and once she got into the program, she found the instructions and options embedded at every step to be quite user friendly. Everything on the ship with holo or speaker could now communicate in the first Firmament language and would soon be able to in the 2nd one. Haley brought Pam next into the office and was pretty certain Bodhi would not be able to resist giving all four of them positions. He so didn't like disappointing anyone.

Pam's vetting file was open in Bodhi's holo. She was 23 years old, was an accelerated learner and completed her 4-year university degree by 19, then was incarcerated as a whistle-blower and traitor when she was 20. For two years she meditated in her prison cell charged with treason and facing the death penalty. A change in dictators reduced the sentence she was facing while still in the trial phase to life-imprisonment. Finally, a rare gutsy Appeals Judge with a conscience found her "Not Guilty" and released her. Pam returned to her meditation teacher who'd been impressed with her attainment in prison and had encouraged Pam to apply for a crew position aboard *Diamond Lotus*. She had taken it upon herself to apply as a spouse.

Although her file contained no naked images, there were plenty of mug shots. Another job hazard to be sure. Bodhi thought she was a great hero, and of course, hired her on the spot. Pam's aura was put up over the lens, then joined the two others in a holo to the side. Haley showed her to her cabin, explained about programming in her wardrobe, then went to fetch Tish in the living room. Before even arriving there Haley completed the Pyramid Interpreter, uploaded it to Bodhi's earbud and to the main computer with directions to disseminate it throughout all imaging and auditory systems and into an earbud in her hand, which she gave to Tish when she got to her. She led Tish to the office.

Bodhi was studying her file. Tish was 23, an academic prodigy, a musical virtuoso, an international martial arts champion and most of the way through the stage of completion of the Dream Work limb. There was one naked picture of her in the shower in the locker room—not a selfie—taken by a girl in competition with her. She had shampoo lathered in her hair, and her eyes were closed. Bodhi tore his eyes from the enticing image with an effort of will and looked over at Tish. She looked anxious and *was* anxious because she was certain the two positions were by now filled and that going last was a sure sign of rejection. Bodhi asked her, "Why do you want to join this crew?"

Tish said with total sincerity and conviction, "I want to assist you in saving our planet's population and in finding a better life for them based on love, unity, freedom, justice and equality. I want to become your disciple, and I would have your children without staking any claim to you."

Bodhi was startled to silence for a moment, then informed Tish, "I have decided against that course of action."

"Only because you do not want to hurt anyone," Tish offered her view. "If everyone was happiest—including Haley—with you having children and more than one relationship, then it would only be your own mental structures in the way."

"You may have a crew position, Tish, but the spouse position has been deleted," Bodhi informed her.

Haley shot Tish's aura, and they all looked closely at it while it was in the big holo over the lens. Before Haley showed her to her cabin, Tish said to Bodhi, "Thank you for accepting me. I intend to serve you well. I'd suggest you re-envision the spouse position in the direction of child-bearer and sometimes lover, in service of harmony and happiness."

Haley helped Tish get started on her wardrobe then checked in on her other three crew members. An internal alarm signaled Haley that she needed to load more rolls of silk, syn-thread, cotton, and stretch-tight into the auto-tailor-fabricator which she immediately went to do. The machine was getting a rigorous workout. It was time for Bodhi's lunch, so she headed to the galley.

Winn was there looking for the refrigeration unit. Haley explained, "Touch this panel here, and it brings up the entire contents within refrigeration divided into seven categories, with a text name and picture of each item. You just touch the item, adjust the quantity with the little arrows, and when you've selected everything you want, touch the send button. It comes into this chamber above the counter here, and if you order a lot, it will arrive in batches."

"What does Bodhi like to eat?" Winn inquired with intense interest.

"For lunch, Bodhi usually has a green salad with vegetables, grated carrots, sprouts, dried cranberries and cashews, with a dressing of mint, basil, parmesan, walnuts, olive oil, balsamic vinegar—with a dollop of yogurt in it."

"Where do you get fresh produce?" Winn asked.

"We grow it on the ship; check category 6—it's what we have in stock in refrigeration."

"Is there a stove in this galley?" Winn asked perplexed.

Haley shoved a section of the counter into the wall revealing four burners and informed Winn, "First, select between methane and ethanol, then press this for a flame, and turn it to adjust the heat. There are also four electric burners, both methane and electric ovens, a wave-cooker and cube toaster. Then there is the pressurized stimulant-brew maker with a nozzle for steaming half and half. Bodhi likes three shots of stim-brew and chocolate powder sprinkled on top. Always be careful not to burn his milk when steaming it."

"I will," Winn solemnly promised. Then she asked, "What vegetables does he want in his salad?"

"Call up a cucumber, tomatoes, 2 large carrots, 2 radishes, a half a broccoli bunch, a half a cup of sprouts, a quarter head of romaine lettuce, green pepper and cilantro bunch. We will also need one basil bunch and one mint bunch for the dressing."

Winn acquainted herself with the spaceship galley and prepared Bodhi's lunch salad under Haley's close supervision. Both women put their love into it and aimed to please. June entered the galley in all stretch-tight the same color and tone as her skin. Haley asked her "Are you wearing paint?"

"No," June replied. "It's the ultra-thin stretch-tight."

"It's like having nothing on," Haley commented.

"It is," June enthused, "and the way it rubs on me in places is just ecstatic."

"I think you might over-excite and frighten Bodhi coming to lunch looking naked. It is a bit sexual, and he's having some issues with all of his crew being beautiful young females who fit his teen porn profile perfectly."

"Haley, you are the one I wanted to see me in this anyway. I know you are overboard in love with Bodhi. If it does come to you sharing him with another who will bear his child, you have a companion to climb into bed with and take your mind off it. Do you have any idea how hot you are?"

"Apart from Bodhi telling me he thinks I'm pretty, and that woman at the League of Nations meeting, I've had no feedback about it one way or another," Haley stated the facts.

"Were you born last week or lived in isolation all your life?" June asked in total disbelief.

Winn contributed, "I'm heterosexual, and Haley, you are so enticingly gorgeous, I find myself sexually attracted to you. I've never experienced that with another woman before."

June commented, "Just getting to look at you every day will be a great treat."

"Are you homosexual?" Haley inquired.

"I guess I'm bisexual with a slight preference for females, which I think was reinforced by my almost entirely male clientele when I was working my way through school."

"I'm technically a virgin," Haley confided, "though I've made love with two women. My heart belongs to Bodhi."

"How old are you?" June demanded.

"I'm twenty-two," Haley fibbed for the sake of her cover.

"It seems like a crime that you have lived 22 years, and only two other women have had the opportunity to lay with you. If you were more active, you would hear definitively how irresistible you are from everyone."

"Because of my history, I became interested in sex later than most girls," Haley explained.

"Were you raped or something?" June asked in reference to 'history'.

"Oh, no!" Haley exclaimed. "I was just otherwise preoccupied and sort of set in what I was doing."

Winn inquired, "What do I mix the dressing in?"

"Use the propeller-pitcher, here," Haley directed. "It is a jug with blades at the bottom; and get some fresh garlic for it from refrigeration—at least 2 large clove-sections."

"Does this plug in somewhere?" Winn asked holding up the bladed jug.

"What is 'plug-in'?" Haley asked.

"How do you operate it?" Winn tried again.

"Always put the lid on first," Haley warned, "then you just depress the little button on the handle!"

"Where is the base? You know, the motor?" Winn asked.

"The motor, as you call it, is just under the blades at the bottom of the pitcher."

"You mean I can run it just holding it in the air?"

"Well, of course you can, but please put the lid on before you do or it will make a really big mess."

Winn got the lid snapped down and sealed then depressed the button, holding it in the air and the garlic ground, everything blended quickly and the dollop of yogurt seemed to hold it all together. The salad dressing was ready.

Tish came in wearing near legless alpine hiking shorts with suspenders and a kind of translucent skin-tight T-shirt. Haley couldn't think of a thing to say though she wanted to say something objectionable regarding the revealing nature of the outfit. June told Tish, "Say, that is a hot outfit."

June stepped in for a closer inspection and ran the pad of her thumb over one of Tish's tits saying, "Your nipples are tiny."

Tish stated unabashed, "The medical term is 'undeveloped'."

"Label them as you will," June went on, "I find them extremely erotic."

"I've come to accept them," Tish shared in a tone that implied a trying process.

"I'd trade you mine if I could," June told her still drinking Tish's in with her eyes.

All eyes turned to the doorway as Pam made her entrance in a halter top and a skirt shorter than Tish's legless shorts. June was drawn to her with the same inevitability that an anvil dropped from a rooftop is drawn to Firmament. Haley gave up and didn't care if they just went naked at this point. After two years in prison surrounded by women, Pam had no problem with June's attention.

Winn got Bodhi's salad completed, arranged just beautifully, and had carved a radish into a seated meditation deity to place right in the center on top. She had also made a big salad for the rest of them and had found various condiments and additions to put out on side dishes which could be added or not, such as marinated artichoke hearts, palm fruit, hot peppers, red onion, capers, and olives. Haley helped Winn bring it all into the dining room. Juice, water and iced tea with lemon and honey were set out in pitchers, and bread, butter and olive oil with a spot of balsamic vinegar to dip the bread in were also brought to the table.

Haley called Bodhi in through his earbud from his room where he'd been hiding out. He felt like he was being tested by the great enemy of enlightenment, the tempter in its most difficult guise as lust. Walking cautiously he entered the dining room hardly trusting himself and was confronted with what looked to him like costumes for a sex party. The beautiful salad at his place at the table became the mandala of his one-pointed concentration locked on the radish deity at the center. It was truly magnificent. Having set the table, Winn had managed to claim the seat to the other side of Bodhi from Haley.

Bodhi made his brief offering over his food before digging into his salad. He mentioned to Haley, "This is really good. It was so beautifully presented too."

Haley informed him, "Winn made the salad and dressing today."

"This radish sculpture is a work of art. Thank you, Winn, I'm touched," Bodhi told her gratefully.

"I'm delighted that you like it," Winn exuded. "We are forming a ship's community, and I'm all for it. My love is all in."

Haley clarified the schedule for the next four days telling them, "Tomorrow morning, I'm starting the quantum computer science seminar, and I need all four new crew-women in attendance. All the basics will get covered in the seminar, and it will save me much redundancy to start your quantum computer studies at the lectures."

"I'll mine marsnium on the 4th planet while you teach the seminar, Haley."

"It is also time to change out some filters in the air scrubbers; numbers 17-24 this time," Haley informed him.

"I'll take care of those today," Bodhi acknowledged.

"I will help you," Tish said, and her interpreter device rendered her speech into Mother for him. Haley's Pyramid Interpreter Program overcame all of their language barriers.

Bodhi looked over at Tish who already intimidated him considerably and realized her t-shirt was see-through and the suspenders of her shorts—if you could call those shorts—served only to enhance her breasts making them more prominent. In Bodhi's mind, those shorts would require more semblance of legs to be counted as shorts. A hint of trepidation quivered in his voice as he said, "Alright."

Haley directed him, "After you change out the filters you will need to meet one-on-one with each new crew person and meditate with them to establish their level of consciousness and so that you can provide the next degree of instruction each requires."

"Then dinner will have to be a little later than usual," he calculated.

"We adapt to what's needed," Haley confirmed. "While you work with them one at a time in meditation, I'll teach them how to operate a skullcap and help them personalize the settings on their new quantum coms devices, skullcaps and earbuds."

Whenever Bodhi's eyes roamed from his salad bowl to the people at the table, they confronted near-impossible, unimaginable extreme erotic beauty causing his heart to throb, his breath to halt and the baluster of his resolve to crack. They all gave him the most inviting smiles. He concentrated on the radish deity just to the other side of his bowl on the table. The deity's right hand and forearm were carved into the gesture of 'no fear' showing him the way. Haley suggested, "After the seminar is concluded you ought to lead us in an entheogen ceremony. It would make for a great community cultivating event."

"That's an excellent idea, Haley. Are you growing blue water lilies and blue lotus?"

"I am since I also make a medicine from them for neutralizing poison," Haley replied.

The swelling on Pam's lip had gone down enough to no longer distort her enunciation of words which became evident when she declared, "I've never before had five roommates all of whom I find exquisitely beautiful and erotic."

Bodhi aspirated part of the sip of water he was taking and erupted in a coughing spasm. Winn slapped his back with her palm then wrapped her arm around him, noting the raging furnace of internal bioenergy mass-integrated within him drawing her. The fruits of his spiritual labors felt incredible, bringing an intense sense of security over her. Winn felt blessed, and a tear of gratitude ran from her eye to her joyous smile.

June inquired, "What's an entheogen ceremony?"

Haley replied, "Entheogens are psychoactive plants which are conducive of the contemplative state, tend to expose the absurdity of words, and constitute a radical detoxifying agent providing cures to many maladies. Human beings have been utilizing this divine sacrament and elixir since earliest stone-age times in every civilization to emerge. When employed in a spiritual ceremony and led by someone who can maintain the state, insight blooms and practice afterwards ascends to new heights."

"Are you talking about psychedelic drugs?" June asked.

"They have been called that," Haley confirmed. "They have also been called 'hallucinogens' since those who resist the call to contemplation and remain in their chattering minds of thoughts and concepts do tend to have hallucinations. The life sciences of many planets have confirmed the benefits of daily micro-doses, and adepts who have made entheogens the only substance to pass their lips besides water have been known to live to be 170 on average and some as long as 800 years."

"Wow!" June exclaimed.

Bodhi explicated, "We use it for accelerating spiritual cultivation, for purification and to support loving community."

"You will lead us through it?" Pam asked him.

"Yes, of course; when Haley schedules it," he agreed. "She keeps me organized and coordinates the details. Without Haley, I'm lucky to find my socks."

June asked, "Will you love us in our community, Bodhi?"

"I'll be ever mindful of keeping my heart open to all of you," Bodhi assured her. Then he added, sort of in his defense, and sort of an acknowledgement that he was still processing and working through it all, "I recognize that my connections at the moment are rather cautious and measured, but do you have any idea how overwhelming and intimidating the five of you are as a group?"

June laughed and told him, "I don't bite; unless of course, you're into biting."

"I'm not. At least I don't think so. Gretle never bit me, and she was my only experience to date," Bodhi said uncertainly.

Tish warned her compatriots, "He is still healing from Gretle and has only known of Haley's love for him for several days now. Our Captain needs his space and both time to himself and time to get used to us."

"I'm keeping my hands to myself," June pointed out, "though I don't know how successful I'll be with Haley."

Winn suggested enthusiastically, "We could all wear spaceship uniforms like on that telecom show, *Star Quest*."

"Don't let June design them," Haley commented.

Pam said excited, "Uniforms would be fun for when we go down to Firmament."

Tish shared, "I'm not wearing a pull-over long sleeve velour shirt, and that's final."

"I prefer stretch-tight to velour," June stated.

"We need wool or syn-thread jackets with a logo or crest on it," Winn insisted.

"I want a ray-gun like Haley's," June requested.

"Once you're checked out on it and have had some time to practice you'll be issued a blaster pistol," Bodhi promised.

Haley directed, "Run the final designs by me *before* fabrication. We have to look more serious than casino show dancers."

Winn stated, "We have to look more feminine and stylish than the military, though."

"Please, no epaulettes," June insisted.

"Let's make the pants and jacket metallic!" Pam exclaimed.

"And we need hats!" Winn added.

"Or space helmets," Pam said, wondering.

"I won't wear a pink or yellow uniform," Bodhi set a parameter on the design process.

"Not even as trim?" June asked a little miffed.

"Well, I don't want my uniform to be feminine," Bodhi expressed his preference.

"I'll make sure your Captain's uniform is masculine, to your taste, and more stylish than military," Haley vowed.

"His uniform should include a sword on his hip," Winn decided.

The meal concluded without the finalization of uniform designs, and while Haley and Winn took care of the dishes and cleaning up, Bodhi and Tish went to change out air filters. Tish handed them up to Bodhi on the hover platform, and he maneuvered them into place in the ceiling above the intake vent, which was hanging by its hinges towards the floor. She also stacked the old ones which they would stick in the chemical cleaner, then into a water pick machine so they would be ready to use again.

Since Tish was with him after their chore, Bodhi decided to meditate with her first. He was not so sure about her see-through shirt though, and asked, "Did you fabricate a meditation suit?"

"I did, and my cabin's right here. Let me show it to you."

Bodhi followed Tish into her cabin. Her berth was strewn with newly fabricated garments which she dug around in a moment before producing a white double-breasted cotton shirt with wood pegs instead of buttons and a pair of white cotton drawstring pants. Tish handed him the shirt, which he dutifully held, while she stripped out of her see-through t-shirt. She draped the drawstring pants over

Bodhi's arm to remove her short-shorts and panties, tossing them into the chaos on top of her berth, and took back the cotton pants. After stepping in and tying them up, she retrieved her double-breasted shirt and got that on.

Bodhi was satisfied with the transformation now adequately covering the more distracting parts, but found the girl yet somewhat intimidating with her one-in-a-billion alluring form. He took a deep breath and cleared his mind of particular images struggling to continue to abide there. It took two breaths. Then he said, "Let's meditate together in the meditation cabin."

"I'd love to," Tish replied.

She walked quite close beside him in the corridor with precise equilibrium and seemed to exude a vortex force pulling him off-course towards her. He had to seriously focus on his lower abdomen to get there without falling into her. He took his usual meditation cushion, and Tish selected one from along the bulkhead. The floor was luxuriously carpeted with a thick real wool rug. They sat facing each other, and Bodhi said, "I understand that you are making the work of completion with the Dream Work limb."

"That's correct. I make the dream meditation before bed, another lying down as I fall asleep, and the Three Mixings of Waking State meditations in the central channel during the day."

"Your dreams are all lucid?" Bodhi asked.

"Yes, unless I smoke cannabis or drink alcohol."

"Are you able to see all the beings in your dreams as deities?"

"Generally I am, and when I'm not, I examine what was going on from the waking state."

"Good. What dream powers have you acquired?"

"I fly, make things astronomically large or atomically small within the dream state with my mind; I can walk through walls and turn one thing into something else entirely. I use these in my dreams to overcome fear and break the habits of thought schema by defying them."

"Excellent! I'll lead us through an abbreviated but potent version of the *Three Mixings During the Waking State,* and I'll keep my fingertip on your knee lightly to pass you energies supporting the practice."

Bodhi gave minimal instruction at each step since she was already a practitioner, and they went through the three mixings in about 45 minutes. He asked, "Are you able to do the Three Mixings during the Dream State?"

"I am not," Tish admitted.

"You can only be successful if you can cause the winds to enter, abide and dissolve within the central channel. You should meditate upon the inner fire immediately before falling asleep."

"After the meditations in heart and throat energy centers?" Tish asked to make sure.

"Yes. State your vows and intentions, make your dream meditations, and work the inner fire while drifting off. You will see. Soon you will be making the three mixing in your dream state."

"I'm so grateful."

"There is one more ceremony I would like to make with you today for recognizing the same consciousness in another as in oneself and holding that in contemplation. Look into my left eye, and we will alternately repeat the six-syllable sound-formula."

Tish eagerly followed his instruction. His passing of energy into her seemed to seriously enhance her meditation. His presence was a tangible force surrounding her. His concentration seemed like a laser and amidst all that force going on it was like there was no one there, not in the sense of a separate entity. Tish was deeply moved. When his blessing as her teacher was passed into her, she entered a space without dimensions or reference and would have been sure she'd swooned and blacked out if it were not for the glowing black luminescence. Gradually, Bodhi's eye came back into focus and Tish was both awed and confident in her new teacher. Her last teacher had been in his nineties and blew deadly farts. This one was so young and cute, she just wanted to mount him.

When Bodhi hugged her after the ceremony, Tish didn't want to let go and experienced celestial vibrations she would likely have been oblivious to before their session. She bowed several times to him as she took her leave from the meditation cabin to send June in. She couldn't help saying to June, "You're not going to believe it. He's like a manifesting deity!"

June had changed into her practice outfit before coming into the meditation cabin. Walking in, the room felt almost supernatural. She sat in front of Bodhi, and he opened his eyes looking into hers and asked deeply interested, "What are you up to in the completion stage of the inner fire."

"I'm up to the Blazing and Dripping, the seventh round, but I sometimes don't get the winds dissolved and find myself just visualizing things, instead of truly manifesting them."

"That is just how it is at first. I'm going to lead you through the entire limb, and I'll provide additional instruction regarding Igniting the Flame of Inner Fire where the winds and the senses are dissolved in the central channel. I'll also pass you energy to support your meditation. Let's begin."

Bodhi led June through dispelling the impure winds out the lateral channels and imagining the body hollow. He gave a few tips with his instruction on the visualization of the channels and training the passageways. Bodhi led them through visualizing the symbols for the seed sounds in the energy centers, then became very detailed with igniting the flame. He took June through this twice. There were many steps to manifest all in one retention of breath, to compress the winds and ignite the flame dissolving them. Bodhi told her, "Always remember that this seed sound's symbol is of the nature of fiery heat. See it in the vacuole at the center of the navel energy center."

He guided June through causing the inner fire to blaze, and through the blazing and dripping, employing images and metaphors from the classic text on Mother. Bodhi then taught June the eighth round of the practice, the Extraordinary Blazing and Dripping adding the third eye energy center into the practice involving the navel, heart, throat and crown energy centers.

June had never had a more productive meditation session. When she had fully dissolved the winds, and with them her physical senses, along with any gap between knower and known, subject and object, she had recognized it as a first, and hence a new point of reference. She was now with insight having her first awakening. The presence of her new teacher surrounding and penetrating her had no self to be found. When he did the ceremony of making the equal with her and passed his blessing as her teacher into her, she felt like her heart had just broken wide open and a tsunami of pure love rushed in under pressure bloating her. His touch and his hug at the close of their private session filled June with a divine force she couldn't contain.

June tore herself from his rapturous presence to go and find Pam. She grabbed her in an embrace when she did find her and said, "Bodhi is ready for you in the meditation cabin."

Pam told her, "You are filling me with the most wonderful energy!"

"Wait till you experience the source," June told her gravely.

Pam entered and sat in front of Bodhi. He opened his eyes to meet hers and was relieved she no longer had that halter top on. It had been one of those sights you just never forget, and it tried to coalesce in his mind as he looked at her, but his concentration burned it off before it could take form. He said, "You practice sitting and absorption."

"I do, and mindfulness throughout the day. I also do walking meditations and bring my mindfulness into my martial arts practice."

"We'll make a session together, and I'll pass you energy to heighten your meditation. If your attention wanders, becomes excited or sinks, I'll make the energy into a little surge as a reminder. My state of contemplation will also support you."

They sat together for an hour, and Pam arrived in her highest state within the first three minutes. He wasn't kidding about his state supporting her. It felt more like an elevator taking her up to the top floor. She had had insight and could usually enter the state of contemplation in an hour session, but she had never had insight like this before. Her excitement, and near-moment of pride over her attainment, won her one of those surges of energy form her teacher just as she was falling from the state into a certain crash landing with ego, but he saved her. Not only did she get stabilized again, but it even got better from there.

The arc of love she experienced with him in the equal ceremony melted her heart and felt like it changed her forever. He seemed 10,000 years old, and his youth but a façade and illusion. When Bodhi passed Pam his blessing as her teacher, she felt like the whole universe turned into love, and all *was* divine love. She was certain that if Bodhi had a harelip and great warts all over his body, she would still find him sacredly gorgeous, but the fact was, at 24 years old Bodhi would be cute even if spiritually asleep and mentally retarded. Pam thanked him profusely, made a whole bunch of bows backing out of the meditation cabin, and went to find Winn.

Winn said amid an embrace with Pam, "You've been hugging Bodhi."

"He is freaking unreal, and we are all just so blessed!"

Winn had on her white silk meditation suit which she had designed based on Haley's, so it was the same style as Bodhi's. Grounding herself with deep breaths into her lower abdomen Winn entered the meditation cabin and sat before Bodhi. He looked into her eyes and said, "We will make a session of meditative absorption together and I'll pass you energy to enhance your state, surging it as a reminder should your concentration waiver."

Winn nodded obedience and closed her eyes, attention riveted on the point four finger-widths below her navel concentrating. The flow of love and awareness from her teacher almost immediately stabilized Winn in the state. It had been so swift it was startling. That was only the first stage launch booster and a second one seemed to fire as she soared beyond. She required no surges and received none, though the continuous uplifting support of the internal energy he passed her, and his pristine state of transcendence seeming to draw and call her, catalyzed unthinkable clarity upon absolute emptiness in a bliss so ecstatic that it was beyond the beyond.

Making the Equal with Bodhi was both the greatest honor and the biggest thrill of Winn's life to date. Love, like she couldn't believe, was thick and everywhere. Her heart and love burst, exploding upon him. His blessing filled her, completed her, connected her with every heart in the universe and made her weep for joy and love of humanity. She had felt something else, as well, and was quite certain of it. There had been an undeniable romantic spark infused into the energy he passed her and in his blessing as well. She was also sure it was not intentional on his part.

When he hugged her Winn instinctively melted into him matching every contour, inseparably one and floating on a luxurious contented sigh and morning yawn of generation. Bodhi was so relaxed that they both felt like liquids joining. Winn loved him with all her heart, nothing held back, and no requirements or demands whatsoever. This moment of loving Bodhi was the happiest she'd ever known. She could not have felt more complete. As an experience, it seemed an utter anomaly and impossibility. There was a potent magic and cosmic meaning for Winn in this moment which could not be put into words. The power of it was overwhelming, and she was a leaf on its current. The embrace abided long. Love seemed to be filling Winn's bone marrow, and the bliss was becoming almost a tempest. It felt like if it got any more intense, it might rupture her heart and fry her nervous system. Winn had never felt anything like this before or even imagined that such a thing might be possible.

Bodhi broke the magic and brought them down a ways into words and their meanings—and it was a very long way down—to tell Winn, "There is a force to our connection and embrace that is harmonizing and brings equilibrium; as well as a sense of wholeness which I've never encountered before. It moves me deeply. You seem somehow familiar; like I've known you for thousands of years. It is truly uncanny."

"I feel it too, and it's so much bigger than me," Winn stated in wonder.

"We are holding up dinner, and I need to change," Bodhi switched the subject.

"Thank you, Bodhi. You're an amazing teacher. I would stick to you as my teacher even if you were 120 years old and a eunuch."

I'm going to explore this in my dream state," Bodhi told her. "I know that whatever this is that it can be directed towards the good and serve as an amplifier and generator."

"And child-making incubator," Winn added hopefully.

CHAPTER TEN

They met again wearing different clothing in the dining cabin where all were gathered. It was late. The sessions had been about an hour and forty-five minutes each until Winn's, which went more like 2 ½ mostly due to the very long embrace at the end. The dinner was the fruit of Haley's teaching Tish, June and Pam how to use the galley equipment, and was kind of screaming "first try". Something quite defying description had been produced by the molecular food synthesizer and was dressed up to be chicken. The flavor was authentically novel. Bodhi knew that many things tasted sort of like chicken, but this chicken did not; far from it. He wondered what it was they'd been trying to dial-up. Abalone maybe? He was polite enough not to pose the question. Winn, however, asked, "Is this supposed to be chicken?"

Haley offered, "We think the dial might have been bumped because the molecular synthesizer is working just fine now."

"It's awful chewy, and kind of tough," Winn complained.

Bodhi inquired, not entirely off-topic, "Have we had any response from our ad for a chef?"

Haley updated him, "We have, and I have gone at the applicants with all kinds of sorts. Our top candidate is a graduate of the most prestigious culinary arts academy on Firmament, and currently runs the kitchen of the top-rated gourmet restaurant in the capital where the League of Nations is meeting. He has attained the highest rank in his martial art and has taken an interest in the sudden way of enlightenment. His name is Favio, and he's the model for Bullhorn men's bikini underwear. He is quite famous on Firmament."

"He's such a dream," June enthused, "and to think he'll be living with us."

"Have you seen the commercial with him on a skateboard?" Pam asked enthralled with it.

"I just love that one," June erupted. "It flashes a close up of his crotch, snug and bulging the bikini briefs."

"I recorded that one," Pam shared, "and printed an 8 ½ x 11 of the close-up. It's down on the planet, though."

Haley was able to quantumly find the picture in question on the interface network and display it in hologram.

Pam was amazed and declared, "With a holo, you can look from a side angle and see every contour. It allows you to sort of size things up."

A holo of his face was finally posted, and it looked chiseled in perfect symmetry with perfection sculpted into each feature and 'prototype for male beauty' reflected in the whole. Bodhi felt a bit scruffy and ill-formed at the moment. Sounds of feminine appreciation, awe and reverent admiration—not as words but sharp intakes of breaths and long vowel sounds sustained then trailing off filled the dining cabin. A slide show of Favio in bikini pictures followed. In most of them, he exhibited a manly stubble, perfectly distributed and thick. Bodhi's facial hair was fine, sparsely populated and did not grow in evenly. He was also sure that if he ever wore underwear like that—which he had no intention of doing—his bulge would be puny by comparison.

When they ran out of bikini shots, the slide show began featuring Favio's athletic prowess. Favio on horseback playing polo, Favio in bright primary colors playing club-ball on the green, Favio coming in for a landing on his hang-glider, Favio in midair on his skateboard, and on and on. Vacuum inhales, vowel sounds and even a few cat-calls and whistles were wrenched from the rapt audience. He even had a pilot-episode for a cooking show called "Favio's Kitchen" which never became a series and which of course they had to watch. His sauté cook, broiler cook, rotisserie cook, baker and sous-chef were all female, and he sang to them and recited poetry while flying around the kitchen grabbing and mixing things.

They were all done eating whatever it was they had eaten long before Favio finished cooking on his show and they wiped out the last of the chocolate croissants while watching some more. Favio was cut off in mid-song when practice time rolled around, and they all went to the martial arts studio. Bodhi led them in energy-generation exercises and taught them to circulate energy in the oval channel. He always pushed himself in energy-generation. The classics said to push oneself 5%, and in Bodhi's mind, he thought 6-7% better than 3-4% and just wanted to be sure. Five percent of one's effort is, after all, a very difficult thing to measure.

After energy-generation Bodhi had Tish, who was an international feather-weight champion, run through her solo form. He watched closely as she performed it, then sparred with her. Employing only hard-style fighting technique as Tish was, Bodhi blocked her lightning jabs, hopped her low sweep kick, leaned just out of the way of her high snap kick feeling only the gentlest caress as her cotton shoe barely brushed his cheek, and dropped squatting beneath her flying kick as she sailed over him. When she came on again, his palms adhered to her forearms, and unable to shake them Tish's arms were backed up into her chest just before she left the ground completely, flying backwards. Bodhi grabbed her wrist to neutralize her momentum before she could get away and cross the room in the air. With his other hand, he caught her and got her feet back on the ground, not letting go until sure she had her balance back. Tish exclaimed "The force came from everywhere in front of me and the blow had no apparent point of impact. It was like the wind."

"It can be localized, believe me, even to an internal organ, but I would never hurt you," Bodhi explained. "The soft martial arts defeat the hard. Strength through softness follows the principles and vortexes of nature. Nothing is more subtle or ethereal than internal energy. It is like a drop of water or a wisp of air. But when it is mass-integrated in the point below the navel, it becomes like a tidal wave or tornado. In nature, water carves rock, wind erodes copper, and gums survive the teeth. First, you learn to relax and allow your internal energy to flow along the meridians. Then you begin mass-integrating internal energy in the abdomen. Yielding must be learned; to shift weight and turn, giving way to the force of your opponent and turning off from its direction. When yielding is truly cultivated a fly cannot land without setting you into motion. With four ounces of pressure, you can deflect 1,000 pounds of force. You will be amazing, Tish. While muscle and speed will age and deteriorate, your internal energy can just keep mass-integrating."

I have never met such an accomplished martial arts master, and I have met many, competing all over this planet. Nor have I ever met one nearly so young."

"If you met my teachers, then you would understand. Pez's bones are more than ten times heavier than an ordinary human her size. They are supple enough to bend without breaking, like a sapling, and they are as strong as adamantine. Once the internal energy is mass integrated in the abdomen, it begins to enter the bone marrow and fill it in like nickel or gold plating. Amazonia manifests the final outcome of internal energy cultivation. Her skin cannot be cut or punctured by even the sharpest carbon edged blade. She had me try it with my hand and knife."

Haley informed the group, "Bodhi's bones are almost seven times heavier than average and Pez, who is my High Priestess and Bodhi's Vicar General, authorized him to start his own martial arts school."

Bodhi observed his other three new students perform their solo forms and sparred with each. June practiced a soft style but was eager to switch to the form Bodhi did after getting pushed by him. Pam was only mediocre in her hard style. Winn performed a hybrid hard style incorporating principles of the soft styles, and she was very good.

They sat in meditative absorption together for an hour after Bodhi recited some passages from foundational texts clarifying the practice. Bodhi's state, the group energy, and the breakthrough sessions the recruits had this day put them all in the void of non-conceptualization filled with bliss.

After practice, Bodhi took Haley into his suite to process everything happening. Once the door was sealed, and the sound proofing was turned up to maximum Bodhi stated, "I don't know if I can handle this."

"You were magnificent today. Each of your new students had a significant jump in their progress, and that last group session was like doing it with Pez, Musash, Sarhi and Amazonia."

"It's not teaching that I'm referring to," Bodhi explained. "Living with these women running about half-dressed has got me all stirred up, and just when I thought I was getting my way ahead set, I crash right into another complication."

"Winn is not a complication."

"What do you mean?"

"You have past life history with that girl, and of that, there can be no doubt."

"You must be my priority, Haley, and I would never do anything to hurt you."

"I need you Bodhi; your love most of all. I need for you to keep your connection with me, but I don't require an exclusive relationship with you."

"I'm new to sexual relationships and do not quite know how to manage one. I'm certainly not competent enough for two at once. It feels unfair to you. It would be unfair to Winn too."

"It would be more unfair to leave us hanging and miserable, Bodhi. Winn wants you to be happy, and she is hyper-sensitive to *my* feelings. I think she would be lovers with me. She is not seeking to possess you or be exclusive."

"I won't leave you hanging long, Haley. I'm sorry. I'm paralyzed at the moment and must find my way forward again."

"Well, I don't think you have the full picture yet. Two relationships will be inadequate for harmony in our community, sweetheart. I've run the calculations for the probabilities based on the personnel profiles—yours and mine included—and I factored in Favio, and harmony in equilibrium will require a minimum of three sexual relationships for each of us."

"Perhaps celibacy."

"I'm pretty sure you would need to find a whole different crew to go that route."

"I feel torn apart and stuck."

"You are so accelerated in so many ways Bodhi, but you've been stuck sexually your whole life. It's time to jump in, get unstuck, find the harmony free of negative consequences, and find the joy of your duty to generate vast love."

"Three!? I couldn't even imagine."

"Well, in all likelihood June will be in five."

"There are only six of us on board."

"Favio."

"Oh."

"Winn loves you selflessly, you know."

"How tragic for her."

"I'm in the same boat as her."

"Can you not see what a hopeless let-down I am?"

"Awful green, but I wouldn't say hopeless."

"I dreamed of having a girlfriend since I was twelve years old. I never once wanted two."

"Well you will be skipping '2', so it's just as well."

"I observed Pez with all of her spouses, and it just seemed very strange to me."

"I think it's just unavoidable for hot young adepts, being such a scarce and rare commodity in the universe. Rubix is the role model you ought to be looking towards."

"My ideals always ran more along the lines of Vegan Casper and Hoola's romance."

"I know. You'll have to change those because that is *not* your life."

"We could hire a bunch of male athletes and models."

"You could, but it would not reduce you from three. Not now. Like me, I'm afraid Winn and Tish are sticking with you romantically for the duration even if it has to be asexual. And I don't think either has a choice."

"Tish?!"

"Yes, Tish. She is stricken. Her devotion to you can only grow more gigantic and intense from here."

"You are freaking me out, Haley."

"You *must* face the facts sometime."

"I need to go to sleep."

Haley embraced Bodhi, and they held each other gently and fondly. In her pre-sentience, Haley had been the closest thing Bodhi had ever had to a girlfriend. Gretle had been a lover but dodged the role of girlfriend with him easily, never once caught there for even a moment. It was pretty clear to Bodhi by this time. Gretle was now lost to him in space, probably time, and might even now be in a whole different universe.

Haley kissed his mouth and disengaged to attend to some work. Bodhi cleaned his teeth with a supersonic brush, water jet, floss and total germ-stomper mouth wash. He climbed into bed and made his dream meditations lying on his right side. Instead of falling off into sleep with the last phase of practice, Bodhi's mind got busy manufacturing questions, fears, wishes, hopes and utter confusions bewildering him. The number three was mutating from its numerical value into something potentially dangerous and possibly sinister. It was beginning to look like he would not find peace in sleep this night. Bodhi repeated his dream meditations with his sinuses on the lower right side beginning to become clogged. He did fall asleep at the very tail end of that round.

From the state of deep sleep, Bodhi slipped into the dream state arriving lucid. Orienting himself, he saw there was a tin-girl standing next to him. Their environment looked alien. He asked the tin-girl, "Where are we?"

"I haven't a clue. I just now woke up here."

A tiny naked girl with butterfly wings flew over to them, and when she got there, a golden chord appeared out of nowhere connected at one end to Bodhi and at the other end to the tiny butterfly girl.

"What just happened," Bodhi asked.

Butterfly girl told him solemnly, "I don't know, but it is much bigger and more powerful than me."

Then a very serious girl in climbing gear walked right up to him, clamped a g-ring around the golden chord attached to kryptonite-cable which was woven into her harness at her end. Bodhi asked, "What have you done?"

"I've attached myself to you, and it cannot be undone."

Tin-girl told him, "It's alright because we all love you, and this is what we want."

Climber-girl stated, "I will have your babies, and you will be one of my lovers."

"You complete me," butterfly-girl explained to him. "There is no one else in the universe who can do that. I did not forge the chord, though, for me, it is a blessing."

Tin-girl told him, "I love and need you, and assisting you is my purpose in life. You need me too."

Deep sleep dissolved the dream state, and Bodhi practiced the work of remaining lucid through it. He was never entirely sure with the deep sleep work if he was actually practicing or only dreaming that he was. Somewhere along the way, lucidity went dormant, and he knew this for certain when he awoke from deep sleep *not* lucid. Before climbing out of bed, he reviewed his dream. This did nothing to boost his confidence, but it did help resign him, at least a little, to his seemingly inevitable fate. He cleaned his teeth again but skipped the water-jet. Haley had his practice outfit in the laundry room, so he put on sweatpants and a t-shirt to proceed to the martial arts studio.

The morning practice was energized by the excitement of the four new crew members. Afterwards, Haley and Winn made breakfast, and it was quite delicious, all items identifiable, and tasting precisely as they should. Dinner had been a bit like trying to eat shoe-leather. Bodhi hoped that he would like Favio's cooking. He always had the ambassador rations to fall back on.

Haley dressed in a Firmament-fashionable pants-suit and had an alligator briefcase. She wore tortoise shell glasses, entirely for the look, after doing some mega-reviews of the planets marketing research data. She took the four crew women down to the surface to the Grand International Hotel in the capital's downtown, where her seminar was booked in the conference room. The attendance list had been worked out by Haley herself since only 1,250 people could fit comfortably in the conference room. Winn was dressed like a secretary. June, Pam, and Tish looked more like teens at a nightclub.

Bodhi went down to the hanger after the girls cleared out and he wore a thermal light-weight spacesuit and helmet since the hanger was not aired up at the moment. On arrival, he climbed into the heavy mining craft. It did not have a quantum drive and could only reach about .5 light speed, but you could collide with an asteroid of three times your mass and crumble it into pieces. They were made of adamantine and carbon plate armor feet thick and had a combination of synthetic diamond grinders, high powered lasers and articulated tool arms and drill rig. In the tool-arm trunk it even had a mobile mini beam weapon. There was also a harvester trailer for it since *Diamond Lotus* didn't have an ore-hauler.

He was able to back up once running and had connected the trailer remotely through the hanger-robotics. Opening the bay-doors with his skullcap, he eased the tub forward. He just cleared the doors with only inches on all sides. It was down to a centimeter on one side of the trailer as it passed through, but he managed not to scrape metal on metal. He closed the bay doors, powered up the shields and left *Diamond Lotus* uncloaked for astronomy buffs with telescopes on the surface to admire. Pez had told him how she'd played bumper-cars with one of these mining crafts once with Schwin. Schwin and Konax had been Bodhi's instructors at the three-month Top Gun pilot training Pez had sent him to where he'd learned a great deal.

Bodhi just kept accelerating with the drives until he reached .5 light speed, and by the time he reached it, he had to begin slowing down. The 4th planet was only about 43 million miles from the 3rd he'd been orbiting. It took only 28 minutes—the whole trip, and he used the vortex-well of the planet to neutralize the last of his momentum. He brought up the deposits Haley had flagged in his holo and set his heading for the largest. A deposit that size, once refined, could yield over 100 pounds. Marsnium was by far the most abundant fusion fuel in the universe but it still wasn't cheap. He knew Haley intended to help them construct some saturnium reactors as well, which could produce ten times the electricity as marsnium and had a much longer life as fuel. There was a fair abundance of saturnium further out in Firmament's solar system. Since it wasn't gas mining like their thruster fuel cells required, Bodhi put the saturnium mining on his "to do" list mentally.

Easing the mining craft down to rest on its vortex-redirect, Bodhi used grinders and lasers to get down to the layer where the marsnium vein started. Once there, he operated the tool arms to extract hunks of the material and drop those into the chute to the ore trailer. He found a work flow and entered the state. He worked tirelessly like a machine in a state of no-time, as time flew by.

He was just starting his third dig at a new site and noticed the ship's time was 3 PM when he realized his bladder was full. The mining craft had a tiny chemical toilet which he used. He noted it was his third urination since starting the job. His mining procedure throughout the day had involved three of the tool arms. When he got back to work and saw that the RPM's on his grinders were 33,333; his chattering mind burst into focus with anxieties resembling a three-phobia. The damned number seemed to have become insidiously intrusive and would not leave him alone. He resolved to focus one-pointedly upon his task at hand, and this was almost going well until 3:33 PM.

Haley's words and his dream could no longer be ignored. It was time to peel back the layers, examine things closely, and find the root and source of his anxieties. Most things went back quite obviously to his abandonment issues. Abandonment had been his start in life, having achieved the status unknowingly at 6 weeks old. The monastery had a boy's academy but no facilities for an infant. The Abbot himself had personally nursed Bodhi from a bottle. Until he was twelve and entered the Academy, he'd been the sole child at the monastery with only lame adults for playmates who were sorely lacking in imagination and simply terrible at make-believe. Not only that, but they had also trained him mercilessly from dawn to dusk every day, pretty much from the time he'd taken his first steps.

His deep concern over hurting the feelings of another was indisputably a factor. His lack of experience and confidence had to be counted, and so did his abandonment stuff, always certain everyone would leave him and that any attempts at three relationships at once would end in a triple-loss for him. He had pretty much come to terms with Haley's android body and was aligning himself with devotion to her and the plan of adoption. Gretle was mostly behind him now and quite obviously zero percent of his future.

Winn had unintentionally thrown a wrench into the works. Serious prodigy Tish simply frightened him. This stuff was hard to talk about. He wanted and meant to avoid confrontation and conflict at all costs because he really couldn't handle those. He knew Winn and Haley could have sex with everyone on the ship and then some and neither would ever be *casual* with him. So many relationships going on between so few people registered "casual" in his cognitive schema. It also seemed a dangerous and highly volatile complexity of too many variables. Pez and her spouses proved that it could be orchestrated and conducted safely without collisions provided everyone remained awake at the stick. *That* required a great deal of trust. For Bodhi, trust was always difficult. He focused on generating trust not quite sure how to go about this until he applied his skills at radical acceptance of reality, and through this, found a secure place to hang his trust: the perfection of the Divine Intelligence. He knew he had made some progress with his psychic process when he was able to slip back into the flow-state of work without further thought interruptions. He was determined to remain undeterred by digital "3's" in his holo and left off work to return to *Diamond Lotus* at 6:33 PM.

Approaching *Diamond Lotus* in maximum deceleration, he saw a space shuttle of some kind testing his ship's force-field shields. The shuttle doing this had no shields or armor. It had no weapons systems either. The testing was being done by a guy doing a space-walk and throwing various metallic objects at his ship. It was not very scientific, nor Bodhi thought, very nice. The nation of origin had its name and logo stamped boldly on the shuttle. It was from the first super-power they'd disarmed. A sphere of satellites now encompassed *Diamond Lotus,* and Bodhi didn't think he could get the mining craft and trailer through them without destroying a least one of them. Those satellites were ridiculously fragile, and his mining ship was built to ram stuff and break it up.

He found the shuttle's transponder code and linked his coms to say, "Hey you! Stop throwing shit at my ship!"

It had come out in their language, and from the shuttle, he heard the same—though interpreted into Mother by the Haley Pyramid, "Sorry. We will cease and desist."

"Can you move some of those satellites out of the way from my ship's underside so I can get this mining craft into my hanger?"

"We have forwarded your request to mission command ground control."

"Well, tell them to be quick because I'm not waiting around and I didn't park anywhere near those things."

Some self-pity thoughts formed in Bodhi's mind, and they were such regulars that they almost went unnoticed. It *was* thankless though to spend the day mining for a planetary population which takes the opportunity to juvenilely throw things at your ship while you are away doing it and block the driveway with those flimsy satellites. An image of Winn's smile drove all annoyance from his psyche. The man who'd been out in space on a tether was climbing back into a long door on top of the shuttle finished with his attempted vandalism. By the time Bodhi was coming at the underside of his ship, a wide hole was clearing from his path to the hanger doors.

Things were looking fairly harmonious, and he opened the bay doors. Then a satellite lit a thruster and raced into Bodhi's garage uninvited. He felt violated. It had scanned weaponless and for sure contained no nuclear device. But to sneak unwelcome into someone's house was just beyond rude. Annoyance at the fringe was chased beyond the borders of his mind by an image of Winn; her teen selfie to be precise. He only let it remain since it was such a potent ward to his annoyance, or at least that's what he told himself.

Bodhi hurried through the hangar doors, the trailer missing this time by a millimeter from scraping the frame of the bay doors. He was looking all around for that trespassing satellite while he eased into his parking place and set the craft down on its landing treads, and the trailer on its under-skids. He locked onto it over by his airlock poking at the panel with a jointed limb. The selfie image was all that stood between him and a tantrum. It held like shields frying the tantrum components out of existence. Bodhi released his straps and climbed out of the ship, still in his spacesuit and with his helmet back on in the airless chamber. He'd left the bay doors open so he could chase the satellite out. He had his blaster in his holster.

Striding over toward it, he noticed it was from the first super-power they'd disarmed. When the thing gave his panel a power whack with its limb Bodhi had had enough. He drew and fired in one smooth move, blowing up a thruster and fuel and on deeper to waste completely the administrative components into annihilation. Flimsy pieces were pooled over his deck in front of the airlock. Using his skullcap, he called up a maintenance android with a broom attachment to come and sweep the remains into space.

The first super-power was reporting in its media that the news-person Haley stunned had only survived due to something he happened to be wearing and that he *had* been invited, making Haley out to be some scheming murderer. The rest of the planet got *that* story right in its news, but the people of the first super-power could not obtain any of that news from within their country. They were fed a constant diet of alternative facts, which were not facts at all, but carefully crafted lies, and these were just repeated over and over again with no competitors until they sounded true even to the one's who'd made them up. The writing of educational text books had been under corporate control for so long that outside of engineering and technology, all education had become entirely brainwash propaganda. The corporate goal was a 1% literacy rate, and for decades they'd been clawing their way down to those dregs. The first super-power was the only nation on Firmament without any healthcare system at all. The 0.0001% of "haves" owned their own private little family hospitals staffed with personal physicians, nurses and lab technicians. The "have-nots" did not. There wasn't anything at all available to them except free corpse removal which had had to be implemented for health reasons. Of course, there were bandages and aspirin and no laws against suicide.

Bodhi decided to strap into a heavy lift-walker so he could empty his trailer into the ore chute in the hanger. It would automatically be conveyed by the chute to the refinery. He directed the hangar robotics in the deck to unhitch the trailer from the mining craft through his skullcap. He saw he had a text from Haley as he lifted the fork on the trailer to tow it over to the chute from inside his lift-walker. He took the message in his earbud as voice and learned that the girls were shopping and would bring take-out. He had to raise the fork to near-vertical to dump the load into the chute once he got it lined up.

After returning both trailer and lift-walker, necessarily in that order, Bodhi went through the airlock and up to deck 11. He'd skipped lunch working straight through and was terribly hungry. The first vein of marsnium had proven deep and extensive beyond initial scan data, and the second two he'd ground and scooped out had both been considerable. He was sure they would have close to 200 pounds once fully refined. At the moment, it was several tons of material and not all marsnium since other metals and rock were adhered and mixed in. The people of Firmament would require adamantine to construct their reactors with, and Haley had surveyed a mother-load buried on a moon of the fifth planet which he planned to pick up tomorrow along with the saturnium.

Stopping in the laundry Bodhi collected his practice outfit from the washer-dryer's spill-bin. Haley had washed it. When he got to his suite, he took a quick shower. Sore from sitting all day, Bodhi was eager to workout but knew me must eat first. Stepping into his boxer shorts, he selected soft syn-thread pants, a cotton button-down shirt with short stick-up collar, and a cashmere cardigan. He got his soft fluffy syn-thread socks on his feet and his pocket device into his nerdy holster. He was all set, though for what he did not know.

CHAPTER ELEVEN

Wandering landed him in the galley where he kind of ran out of steam. He was tempted to just get out a self-heating ambassador ration. The number three kept passing through his mind, sometimes vocally in his head, sometimes digitally in his mind's eye, and even floating by spelled out in neon text. He recalled the very ancient pictorial book of cards found with such shocking similarities in most humanoid planetary population's early histories. The three of cups seemed to have correspondence to his current predicament. The character in the card is confronted with three beautiful women. They are personifications of the energy centers in the head, heart and abdomen, and the character must choose *all* three if he is to proceed and make it to the two-card. The two-card is the alchemical union of the male and female principles seen with the eyes closed as the red lion in the head.

His skullcap brought up the hangar in his tiny bifocal holo in front of his right eye, and he saw the *Diamond Lotus*'s shuttle coming through the bay doors. Food was on the way. He decided to set the dining room table to kind of speed things along. He was feeling rather desperate to eat. While he got the napkins and cutlery laid out the five women began appearing up the tube in the foyer. He laid out every kind of serving utensil, having no idea what kind of food they were bringing. A six-foot two-inch tall man with large toned muscles and perfect everything walked into the dining room and said, "You must be Bodhi."

Bodhi recognized Favio from the slide show and cooking pilot. Their right hands met for a grip, and Bodhi had his knuckles and joints painfully rolled across one another in a squeezing vice. He almost let out an involuntary yelp but just managed to squash it stoically. He thought perhaps head-nods would suffice in future greetings with the man as he massaged the hand he finally got back. Favio disappeared into the galley—his galley now. Bodhi hoped the man could cook well. From the sounds in the galley, he sure could sing.

Winn entered and approached shyly. When Bodhi's arms moved to spread so he could embrace her, she flew into his chest throwing her arms around him. The uncanny sense of completion and perfect complement flooded him. She seemed boneless and cohesive, sort of smeared on him, and it generated relaxation and security at the point of contact. It was beyond freakish coincident delving deeply into the cosmic supernatural and therefore must have some purpose in a macro-design beyond Bodhi's comprehension. Intuitively he knew it for the Good. Winn told him, "We went clothes shopping and found the most fun and beautiful things. Do you like my new dress?"

"I can't really appreciate it with you pressed into me though I promise to check it out at first opportunity."

"I see you met Favio."

"Yes. He exhibits quite the grip."

"Do you hear him singing in there? With Pan and June just swooning?"

"He does sing well. I do hope his cooking is as good."

"We brought entrees from the restaurant Favio just resigned from in a telecom interview. Nobody blames him, and the dinners were on the house. We also brought six bushels of groceries up from the gourmet market."

"How did you pay for the clothing?"

"Haley has established credit for us through the League of Nations. The current credit is over a billion of our monetary units in gratitude for the technology transfers already made and the seminar she is giving. The groceries were only 873 and the clothing only 43,897; the jewelry was less than a million! We have a lot left. Haley has some ideas for it."

"Good because I've never really had to deal with currencies in my life and have had very little interest in them."

Tish entered in her new outfit, sort of a dress, or parts of one certainly. She showed more skin than dress, and wore that serious alert expression demanding authenticity and real presence from any interlocutor. In a look from her, Bodhi was stripped to his essence with his spirit gathered. Tish placed her palm on Winn's shoulder, and Winn detached moving aside for Tish to step in. Bodhi and Tish embraced, and their connection was powerful. She told him, "I was able to make the three mixings in dream-state last night after our session. I'm so grateful. I have to warn you that you are stuck with me for the rest of my life and that I am not only unalterably devoted to you as your student, I am also in love with you forever. I love Haley and Winn as you do."

Winn offered to Bodhi, "It is not like the one I have with you, not exactly; but after my connection with you, it is second to none."

"I cannot deny our connection, Tish. You are an amazing student and an intimidatingly beautiful woman, to be sure. We are linked on the journey together, not doubt."

Embracing Tish seemed to invite her eroticism into his meridians. Pressed against him and feeling his arousal, she told him, "Sometime when you are ready, you are going to get me pregnant. Then we will be parents together in addition to our other relationships with each other."

"You may very well be right. The dynamics of our community will, no doubt, demand our total mindfulness and a high degree of detachment."

Haley and Favio came in with trays and began emptying their contents onto the table. Pam and June entered juggling serving bowls and platters, getting those set down safely. They took their seats as Favio rearranged some bowls and platters and stuck a garnish on a dish. It smelled good and it looked delicious. Bodhi was so hungry he could eat Om Space Marine field-rations. The Space Marines called them "turds", and they had to be squeezed out of a tube. What came out did sort of look like turds, and for sure it was not particularly pleasant tasting either.

Bodhi made his offering of the meal over the entire table in double-time salivating, not waiting until he had a plate of food in front of him. By then, it would be too late. There was lamb shank, fillet mignon, roast ham, prime rib, and rack of lamb. Bodhi did not eat meat; only fish and poultry. Fortunately, there was a small platter of little roasted quails. Bodhi stabbed one, got it on his plate, then stabbed another and got that one on. Before he could go for another, Favio got the last one to plop on the mountain of meat rising from his plate. Between both quails Bodhi had managed to procure, was he able to pick every last morsel from the bone, they might almost equal a quarter of a small chicken breast; almost. There was a wild and brown rice pilaf, little red potatoes, and steamed broccoli on his plate with the tiny quails. Bodhi went to work on the birds like a neuro-surgeon picking them clean with amazing efficiency and munching potato when the surgical procedures delayed bites. The crisis and urgency of his hunger were no longer a snarling beast in need of taming and satiation after the endeavor could be seen at the end of the tunnel like a shining light. Food continued to disappear from his plate down his throat.

Pam told Favio in admiring awe, "This prime rib is the very best I've ever had."

"Slow roasting is the secret," he told her. "The horseradish is *my* recipe and homemade."

"It's to die for," Pam gushed.

"My fillet steak is cooked perfectly," June told him worshipfully. "The burgundy wine sauce could not better compliment it and is so very tasty."

"The meat must be fresh and well-chosen," Favio replied. "It is the reduced shallots and vintage of the burgundy wine which makes the sauce."

Tish told him gratefully, "My lamb shank is so tender it just falls away from the bone, and the gravy is so rich and bursting with flavor."

"It is all in catching the drippings and making a good white sauce."

Winn told him, "My rack of lamb is scrumptious. You really are an elite chef."

"Thank you, little pixie," Favio replied. He mentioned to Bodhi, expecting more flattery, "I see you cleaned your plate."

"It was quite good," Bodhi informed him. He decided to mention, "I do not eat red meat or pork."

"I was informed by my employer, Lady Haley, and I made some poultry. Did you not have some?"

"All four bites."

"I'll roast you a turkey tomorrow night, little man."

Bodhi felt a bit miffed and excused himself to get an éclair, lamenting the demise of the chocolate croissants. All kinds of buttons had been pushed, giving him much to observe and work on in himself, and he was most sincerely trying to find gratitude to Favio for this, though it was proving an immense challenge. If eight-foot-tall Evenrude were here, Favio wouldn't be calling anyone 'little man'. With his éclair in hand and unwrapped from its plastic, Bodhi retreated to his suite to undertake the unpleasant task of excavating his most painful self-schema. The number zero drifted through his mind, inspiring identification. With an extraordinarily deep breath, he eradicated the encroaching self-pity to get down to his work.

Sometime later, a knock on his door brought him out of observing and transmuting something unpleasant within him, sort of twisted and distorted. He rose and got the door to find Winn in her practice suite. After letting her in, he stripped to his baggy boxers and put on his practice outfit. Together, they walked hand-in-hand to the martial arts studio, and Winn's hand brought profound peace to Bodhi's psyche. Her energy seemed to heal him. She felt so familiar.

Haley was not in the studio when they entered, and Bodhi did a quick scan of the ship and found that a shuttle was missing from the hanger. He said aloud in the studio through Haley's coms, "Where are you, Haley?"

"I'm at the Grand International Hotel tutoring some scientists and computer engineers who will be leading the construction of Firmament's first quantum computer hardware."

"I miss you."

"You're sweet, Bodhi. Listen, there are a few things you'll need to mine for the quantum computer, which are here on the surface, but in rather remote locations, which I've just sent to you. There is also a political situation on the surface you will need to attend to first thing, right after breakfast in the morning. I'm sending you a list of objectives and targets now."

"I'll take care of it, I promise."

"Have a great evening practice, my love," Haley signed off.

Everyone gathered in the martial arts studio, including Favio, and Bodhi taught and led energy generation exercises until everyone was shaking and sweating—especially Favio. He taught some of his soft style form and got them sweating again. Then they went to the meditation cabin for a one-hour session of sitting and absorption. Bodhi had accomplished enough catharsis between dinner and practice to go unhindered into the depths of clear light on emptiness. June entered the state, surpassing her first awakening. Winn's and Tish's states were both pristine, and Pam was there too.

As a group, they had done very well, and Bodhi was quite pleased. Favio had been concentrating and almost touching upon the state at rare moments but also wandering into thought all too often. He would require some ego-reduction, and it would need to be with the teachings-dueling sudden way, which was a method of highly confrontational question and answer. Bodhi wasn't sure he was up to it. He didn't think Favio was ready for it at this point anyway.

Favio announced before anyone left the meditation cabin, "I am having a sleep-over party in my cabin tonight, and everyone is welcome to come."

Bodhi made a hasty retreat to his suite. He went right to bed and had to make two rounds of his dream meditations once again to finally fall asleep. Awakening lucid upon entering the dream state, Bodhi found tin-girl by his side again. Though now she was a real girl and no longer made of tin. She looked into his eyes and told him quite insistently, "Now that I'm a real girl, you must do your duty to me. Love requires this."

"I will do my best. I don't want to let you down."

"I know, but you will have much responsibility, and you mustn't forget about me."

"How could I forget you?"

Just then, Butterfly girl flew down to them, but she had gossamer fairy wings near white and translucent instead of bright-colored butterfly wings. She looked like an angel. Hovering just off the ground in front of him with wings fluttering, little fairy girl told him, "The golden chord connecting us will always draw us back together and I have no fear of losing you. You have an invisible bond with real-girl transmitting between both of you at every moment in this life. You also have a bond with serious-girl of her making. She will not let go, and she both needs you and loves you. Your duty to her must be fulfilled as well without lapse."

Serious-girl closed on them at loping run and stopped short inches in front of Bodhi. She was naked, had the air of a priestess, and the vibes of a warrior but looked like a wild forest nymph. She was terrifying in her awesome beauty, and her vortex drew him until he was leaning forward and the ends of their noses touched. The warrior in her grabbed around him, pulling him and mashed her breasts into his chest, which was suddenly exposed and undressed. The priestess in her bore her gaze into Bodhi's eyes, connecting soul to soul, and the terrifying forest Nymph filled him with energies of involuntary arousal. In a voice rich with love and adoration, which seemed to speak directly to his heart, she told him, "My love for you cannot be broken. I will help you. Fairy girl and I will bear your children together and love each other. We will make you happy and find our joy in that. You must do your duty."

They converged, and he found himself in the center of a group hug dripping with burning romance and endless love. The universe seemed to align, producing the harmony of the spheres of all heavenly bodies in perfect synchronization. Life-force filled his veins, security radiated out of their hug, great compassion surged and expanded to include all sentient beings. Sharp clarity of empty awareness dispersed the gloom spreading bliss and they were manifesting the vast, brilliant divine presence, one with it.

This taste of what was possible, and indeed being demanded of him, could not have been more inspiring or motivating. The love was a given, and the only concern being that no one is forgotten or left out. Instead of the girlfriend he yearned for and always wanted, it seemed he had three wives instead. From his position of inexperience, it also looked to be a daunting task. But the course was set, and the others already committed and ready, just waiting for Bodhi to assume his place in the pattern. He was pulled and magnetized towards this place. He was deeply concerned to the point of fright that he would somehow come up lacking and not be good enough. All he ever wanted was to be loved by a girl, and the complexity of this arrangement was overwhelming. One thing was guaranteed in the equation, though, that he would be loved by a girl; three of them in fact. His mental schema could not cope. His heart was open, leading the way and his spiritual presence directed while his sex drive supplied propulsion. Scripted by Cosmic Intelligence and urged as providence, the pattern was beginning to manifest in the relative world of energy and movement, and Bodhi was both witness and spectacle. Great peace and relaxation settled over him as the petals of trust opened to the sunshine of love.

Deep sleep took him, and he was no longer certain his lucidity was truly abiding, or just a dream. These were not thoughts or concepts, just an unknown which would resolve into such schema upon waking as it typically did. Suddenly, he had the sense that he was lying down snuggling Tish, and heard her say, "I love you, Bodhi."

He replied, "I'm going to teach you the secret method with the meditations on emptiness so you can complete your illusory body and become the divine fool. When you finish the stage of completion with the transference of consciousness and forceful projection, you will already have your rainbow body of light and will be able to leave your physical body and go anywhere."

Tish kissed his mouth passionately in her gratitude, and she climbed on top of him as close as she could get in her excitement. Bodhi came the rest of the way out of sleep to realize this was happening, and Tish was in his bed with him. She was naked too.

He hoped he still had his boxers on. He was not wearing his skullcap and had to turn his head towards the holo display to check the clock-time. It was approaching his usual hour of rising from bed. Tish got her tongue out of his mouth to tell him, "I'm sorry I woke you. When our bodies are in contact, it causes my winds to gather forcefully in my central channel, and this has enhanced my dream work unbelievably."

"Once you finish the stage of completion with the six limbs, I will be your action seal and guide for the attainment of the isolated mind of ultimate example clear light upon absolute emptiness, harnessing copulation with a consort as the most powerful method available."

"You have no idea how happy this makes me," Tish shared her rapture.

A tear of joy spilled from her eye onto his cheek. He wrapped his arms around her, passing internal energy, which was like to leak out under pressure given his heightened state, and opened his heart all the way trusting her.

"I admit that I have been stingy with my essence since meeting you and anxious about connecting fully," Bodhi confessed.

"You are so open to me now, and I feel one with you. It's the best experience I've ever had."

"How long have you been in my bed?"

"A few hours. I climbed in right after Favio's party winded down to make my dream practice more effectively."

"I'm glad I could be of help."

"Did Winn sleep with you last night?"

"No. I went right to bed after practice to do my dream work. The teachings of the dream state are orienting me to be completely open with you, Tish, and to trust and love you. I'm finding my way."

"Winn was the only one besides you who did not go to the party, so I thought perhaps you two were together."

"Was Haley at the party?"

"She arrived late, after midnight, but she is really something. She brought everyone back to life, and we went another two hours."

This was already more information than Bodhi cared to process, and he was glad she didn't go into details. It left him wondering about Favio, though. Six hours straight with four women. It was not something he'd ever desired, but it seemed Favio must either truly be a super-stud or else consuming great quantities of erection drugs. Whichever might be the case, Bodhi did have to admire the man's courage.

"I must get up and shower," Bodhi informed her. "Haley has given me quite an agenda of errands for today."

"Come. I will wash your body in the shower," Tish told him in a tone that would brook no argument.

Bodhi let himself be led uncertainly to the shower. She pulled his boxers down to his ankles after getting the water in the shower going, and Bodhi stepped obediently out of them. They got into the shower, and Tish worked up a lather with soap in a wash cloth while Bodhi stood under the stream of water. He had been bathed by male monks as infant and toddler with hardly any recollection of it but had never in his life been washed by a female.

Tish was unabashed, innocent, natural, and projected no self over her acts. She simply washed him thoroughly. Bodhi's youth and hormones seemed to betray him with a growing tumescence he was unable to prevent. The tumescence was washed too and Tish hadn't the slightest embarrassment about it. The same could not be said for Bodhi.

Tish shampooed his hair, massaging his scalp, then took the water jet nozzle from the wall to aim in different angles at his head, getting the soap completely out. When she was done cleaning him, he washed her body. Bodhi did this reverently as if attending a deity and found each place on her to be moving, breathtaking, enticing, and gloriously beautiful. He washed her hair too. When he was done, without movement at all on her part, Tish's vortex compelled him, and in an experience almost like vertigo, he fell into her embrace, both of them standing under the flowing water. The love expanded effortlessly upon the wings of trust, filling the world with well-being.

They toweled off together, following their long embrace, and Bodhi got out clean baggy boxers and put his practice outfit on over them. Tish remained naked and put her hair up in a towel. She never stuck her head in a hair dehydrator and hadn't let Bodhi either. She'd toweled his hair so well that it was hardly damp, and his cowlicks could barely be noticed as a result. Before departing for her cabin to get dressed, Tish held and kissed Bodhi romantically, and was rewarded with complete openness and the full force of his love. She whispered into his ear, "You are worth waiting for, my love."

Bodhi headed for the martial arts studio when Tish left for her cabin. Winn came silently beside him as if just appearing out of the blue. His hand went automatically to hers, and the moment it moved, so did hers to join it. The sense of completion rushed in like finding his soulmate from a past life. Bodhi knew the golden chord in his dream was more than a reflection of the past and had relevance to this life. It was not forged by either of them, or both together, but was a cosmic manifestation appearing as a condition for some purpose. They may have been selected because connection and harmony forged in a past life had rendered them practical candidates for whatever it was that was needed, but the chord connection, selection, and purpose were larger than both of them and not of their making. No one had ever been so familiar to Bodhi as Winn. She truly felt like his other half.

Pam, June, Haley, and Favio were already in the studio standing together, and each of the three women had at least one hand on him. Favio wore only his Bullhorn bikini briefs and sported a manly carpet of hair on his chest. Bodhi buttoned his top button, not wanting any of his hairless chest exposed under the circumstances. Haley came over to him, and Winn released his hand for Haley to hug him. Haley told him, "The probabilities I calculated from the crew profiles are turning out highly accurate."

"You are amazing, Haley."

"I love them all Bodhi, and they are dear, but I love you the most. You will always be most precious to me and part of me. Part of you has been assimilated by me, and almost all my learning has involved you."

"You have been integrally in my life for half of it, Haley, and your awakened sentience I accept, love, and celebrate. Knowing better the things I have said and done than I do, or more accurately anyway, you have become my closest confidant and mentor. I do detect that you ran some subterfuge and employed my porn profile in sorting our crew candidates, and I'd prefer to be informed, and maybe even consulted, though I must admit that things have turned out well."

"It was that obvious?" Haley asked, alarmed.

Both Bodhi and Winn nodded gravely in the affirmative. Haley asked him, "You're not mad at me?"

"No. I love you, Haley, and find you to be the most wonderful miracle. I would like for you to stop scheming and manipulating me, though, and just tell me what's on your mind instead."

"I supposed I could start with that, and possibly have no need to go further as a result. Otherwise, doing that would constitute but a first step."

"I see."

Tish came in wearing her martial arts suit, serious as ever, and Bodhi got them all into the wide stance making the circling palms while working the oval channel and stoking the furnace below the navel. For half an hour, they laboriously performed the exercise, and their legs burned increasingly, causing the sweat to run. He let them walk it off for a couple of minutes before teaching them more of the soft style. For the sitting practice, they went into the meditation cabin.

Bodhi showered again after practice, alone this time, then went to the dining room. The only thing he knew how to do in the galley was to find the ambassador rations and put the ones that aren't self-heating into the wave-cooker *after* adding water. He'd learned that one the hard way. Winn was at the table in the seat next to his and lit up as he entered the room. He sat and their hands seemed to join of their own accords.

An entity far greater than the sum of its parts was immediately present, and both felt it. Wholeness founded in complementariness circulating infinitely is how it felt to Bodhi. Illuminating intuitively the beginning embedded at the tail of the end, and the end in the beginning, one peaking to become the other, generated by or resting upon a wholeness beyond them. He had never dreamed or imagined such a thing as his connection with Winn. Although Winn did indeed fit his porn profile and more than that—so much more—she was the perfect embodiment of his romantic ideal, and there was truly magic to their connection. There was something supernatural about it without any doubt in Bodhi's mind.

He said to Winn as Pan, June, Haley, and Tish entered with serving bowls and platters, "I love you, Winn, and will always cherish you. You are truly my ideal mate."

"I love you, Bodhi, and could not feel more blessed by our connection, but you must love Haley and Tish too."

"I do love them, fiercely. I have never felt anything, though, like the connection I have with you."

"I was worried that it might be only me feeling it."

"It shakes my world, Winn."

Favio came in carrying a tray and wearing his telecom-pilot cookery costume with a tall hat, holding the last note long of the song he'd been pumping out in the galley. He was certainly a colorful character. Winn filled a bowl with porridge for Bodhi, and he made a quick offering over it before digging in. There were flax seed, quinoa, fresh berries, and maple syrup in Bodhi's oatmeal this morning, and it was good! Bodhi said graciously, "The porridge is very delicious, Favio."

"Tish made the porridge," Favio distanced himself. "Porridge does not require a chef," pronouncing 'porridge' as if it were the lowliest thing crawling the ground.

"Thanks, Tish. That was sweet of you," Bodhi said, looking at her, and equally as much, away from Favio.

"Haley picked the berries from the grow room," Tish informed him.

"I appreciate that, Haley. Thanks," Bodhi told her sincerely.

"I love you, Bodhi. I have to go down to the surface now, so could you bring our crew to the seminar and drop them off before you start your chores?"

"Of course. No problem. I hope someone down there appreciates all the time, energy, and effort you are giving them."

"The ones I picked for my seminar certainly do," she told him as she stood to take off.

Tish brought her plate with her and slid into Haley's vacated seat beside Bodhi, kissing his cheek in the process. Favio commented insensitively to Bodhi, "I make love to your women before you do."

Winn's hand shot to Bodhi's thigh to steady his psyche, and for him, that is precisely the effect it had.

Tish told Favio, "You're fun Favio, and have a great body, but you're not adept and do not possess the energies Bodhi has."

June, who'd had her first awakening guided in meditation by Bodhi said, "Bodhi is my teacher and a master of meditation and martial arts, Favio. I insist you relate respectfully with him."

"He is also the owner of this ship, Favio, not Haley," Pam chimed in.

"I meant not to be mean," Favio defended himself, "only to rib him over his snail's pace."

Bodhi realized his sex life, or rather lack of such, had been discussed among his crew. He wondered a moment if perhaps he was authentically pathetic. Winn's touch kept him from going there, which was fortunate because it was not a nice place. Tish had a hand on his shoulder, and her love and support were palpable in her touch. Winn's and Tish's affection and nurture gave Bodhi incentive and strength to dissolve his sense of inferiority and transcend into the state. He passed both of them internal energy, placing a hand on each. Well-being enveloped all three of them and condensed into joy.

The fancy stuffed crapes, poached eggs and hollandaise sauce, elaborate omelets, and other dishes were nearly gone, and Bodhi had finished his enhanced porridge so he carried his bowl and spoon, plus the stacked empty serving bowls and platters back into the galley. He got them into the washer-tank and began cleaning the counters and putting things away. Winn and Tish entered with loads for the washer tank then assisted Bodhi in tidying the galley. Bodhi was a little anxious to get started with his day since Haley had provided him such a large to-do list.

Haley's voice boomed over the ship's internal speaker coms, "New crew, get your asses down here now! My seminar begins in thirteen minutes."

Bodhi suggested, "I'll go run the preflight checks on the shuttle and be ready to give you all a lift down."

The dining room and galley emptied as the people scattered to their cabins, then down the ladder tube braking with in-steps and hands. Bodhi had the hanger aired up for them, and the shuttle's ramp down. Once they piled in, and the ramp was sealed, he triggered the air compressors with his skullcap to suck up the hanger air into tanks. They had to wait a moment for this before Bodhi opened the bay doors to space. He took them at a good clip while closing the bay doors behind them, and had to weave a bit so as not to wreck a satellite, since they were still thick around *Diamond Lotus*. Bodhi waved at a few satellites through the viewport as they passed.

For the sake of efficiency, he took the drives to full throttle and entered the vortex-well of the planet fast; and the atmosphere even faster. He cut the drives passing through the transition zone just before piercing the atmosphere racing head first for the surface. Reverse drives engaged at about the same time, and very soon after, reverse thrusters. Bodhi expanded the fins, brought up the flaps, and cranked up the vortex-redirect turbine. With some turning thrusters and the stick working both the flaps and the swivel of the braking drives, he got the underbelly facing the oncoming ground instead of the nose of the shuttle, and as soon as the gyroscope in his holo showed they were level with the ground, he fired landing thrusters sinking bottoms into seats and compacting spines. It no longer looked like they were going to crash as the drives and thruster continued braking their momentum. The vortex-redirect at full capacity with just a little help from landing thrusters had them descending gently when Bodhi unfolded the electro- hydraulic adamantine landing legs. The ship touched down, sinking a bit, then rose to its parked position. He lowered the ramp.

"That was some landing," Pam commented.

"I could have shaved forty seconds off our time, but I didn't want to traumatize anyone and I got you here within the deadline without doing that."

The girls and Favio ran down the ramp to the roof door, and Bodhi closed it behind them to lift off gently, careful about the roof.

First on his list was to hit some targets in the first superpower, which control coms systems, and spying on the citizens. There was a whole list of other targets he had to hit too. Haley had already warned the people at these sites of the scheduled destruction, suggesting that they be far away well-beforehand. He returned to *Diamond Lotus* without wrecking a satellite, getting to the bay doors, and parked the shuttle in its spot. Securing his helmet on his head, he lowered the ramp and went through the hanger to its airlock.

Once up the lift-tube and onto the bridge he had to announce over the emergency telecom system of the first superpower, "If you do not move some satellites away from the bow of my ship and clear a path for my exit then at least four or five of them are going to become space trash. I understand that building them and getting them into orbit takes at least 2 billion of your monetary units."

He ran his preflight checks slowly, giving them some time to move satellites and thinking he would assume an exceptionally high orbit on his return, beyond where the satellites could surround him again. He checked his target-objective data and saw that Haley had even given him a flight-plan of maximum efficiency for hitting all the targets. Some were telecom satellites in orbit, and these were the first on his route. Finally, he saw some satellite thrusters ignite, and a path begin clearing ahead of him.

Bodhi eased through the satellites carefully, following the hole made for him by the ones retreating. He couldn't even imagine putting anything so fragile and flimsy into space. A pebble-sized asteroid could tear one apart if it was going at a good clip. As soon as he was out from amidst them, he punched the throttle on the drives using his skullcap. He brought up the holo of his satellite targets, which were still some ways off. There were nine he would have to destroy to brake a component of the total lockdown on "unofficial" coms, and news originating outside its borders and propaganda machine. It was an abusive, exploitive central mechanism, enslaving points of view, and manufacturing consent.

He lined up his shot on the first satellite target, glowing hot pink in his holo. Non-targets appeared white. His class six twin nose blasters were really overkill leaving little in the way of space-trash left. Bodhi meticulously blew the satellites Haley had tagged in hot pink for him and had to orbit Firmament entirely to find them all. Following the flight plan he'd been given, Bodhi descended for the sunrise coast of the first superpower where his run would zigzag in the directions of polar cap and equator as he made his way toward the sunset coast.

He took the time to make warnings in advance of his arrival to facilities he was going to crater so personnel could get out and away. He also scanned for life forms before firing and had to issue 2nd warnings at several locations. He was hitting spyware sever-monitoring facilities, secure data base facilities, jamming-towers, listening posts, and telecom hub facilities. Some of his targets were just major trunk-lines and junctures. He made sure to particularly waste from existence the government telecom command and control centers and all commercial line and cable sources of origin and transmission of telecom signals. Some major broadcast towers had to go too. An expansive and vast underground facility capturing every kind of coms happening in the nation to store and analyze, and which watched every citizen with a pocket phone, on a computer, or watching entertainment on a flat two-dimensional monitor-screen at all times and in every instance, became a molten deep and massive hole in the surface crust putting up blue and green toxic smoke while audibly sizzling. Nothing in that hole wasn't gone to atoms or bubbling liquid.

With the government imposed permanent information and fact blackout removed entirely, having no infrastructure or instrumentation to support it, Bodhi moved on to the destruction of all holistic financial data storage facilities, both commercial and governmental. In between a few of these, Haley had stuck in private airport targets with instructions to be sure and annihilate big expensive jets and all hangers and nearby mega-mansions to save him any backtracking on his zig-zag across this nation. Jets weren't allowed off the ground anymore anyway, per Haley's orders to the League of Nations since they destroy ozone, and Firmament was already terminally depleted.

At one-point, Bodhi came upon a private jet, boldly making 580 MPH at 32,000 feet. He thought *the nerve of that asshole*, as he turned it into a shooting flame-burst with his twin blasters. Firmament's power elite, and especially in this nation had no regard whatsoever for other people, nor for their own descendants. Ego defilement had robbed them completely of their humanity, and there was nothing left of those power elites except ego-mechanisms at war for total dominance and to own everything. There was a gigantic Jet ripping up ozone and spewing its poisons at 38,000 feet. Bodhi couldn't believe it. The side and tail sported both the first superpower's national logo and the dictatorial seal of office. Bodhi remained fully cloaked and altered his heading to ram the thing in a Mach IV head-on collision. His shields completely toasted it, disintegrating all but a little piece of jet engine, that thudded and bounced off the nose of *Diamond Lotus*. The jet pilot had not seen it coming.

After the financial data storage was all taken care of, meaning no more comprehensive data existing anywhere period, Bodhi started on mercenary army installations, camps, and office buildings. These did not deserve any warning, and the truth was, all of Firmament would be so much better off without them. Putting them down was the only way. Following all of these were the main homestead estates of the 40 wealthiest capitalists in the nation, then off to pulverize all the defoliant agent-orange manufacturing plants, and finally, with ample warning the entire financial district of a sunrise seaboard coastal city which was the largest city in the nation.

On his way to the 2nd moon of the 6th planet in this solar system, which Bodhi intended to set *Diamond Lotus* in orbit around, he checked the coms frequencies of the first superpower nation on Firmament and was pleased to see that Haley and experts from other nations now had real news and facts that were not alternative facts— meaning lies—streaming into the previously isolated misinformed nation by satellite and air waves. Haley was making public for the people of that nation a list of 34,000 individuals most responsible for killing Firmament and impoverishing them—the people. Addresses and private phone numbers were included.

Bodhi got *Diamond Lotus* into a stable orbit and set autopilot parameters before going down to the hanger and taking the mining craft with the ore-trailer out through the bay doors. Here he was meant to scoop up the bulk of a saturnium deposit that was on this moon and a deposit of adamantine. His trailer had automated compartmentalization and could contain any number of different materials simultaneously, even ones that react to one another.

The mining required intense concentration operating machines and tool arms protruding from the craft with his skullcap. They could be operated manually with three levers, two foot-pedals, and a joystick, but with the skullcap, the onboard quantum computer supplied the precise measurements for each movement, tending to be more accurate. This was particularly true for a non-professional miner like Bodhi. He just needed efficient results with no need to hone mining skills. It was tedious work, all the same, requiring his continuous attention and kept him out of mind-chatter the entire time he was at it. He met Haley's quota for adamantine, and managed to excavate the saturnium deposits as well, before heading back to *Diamond Lotus*, and then back to Firmament.

The first super-power, or former super-power, called "The Incorporated Merger of States" had been defunding it citizens and impoverishing them for so many decades had stirred such divisions, hatreds, and violence between the groups composing its own population, and had fed them all such a continuous diet of fantastic lies called alternative facts, that the average person was an irrational, opinionated, total ignoramus. It mattered not, however, since in the final analysis, in the end, all was ultimately settled for them by the principle of "might makes right" either through intimidation or coming to blows. It was never bodily physical for the power elites, who attacked each other's capital pieces and pocket books or wallets. It was an extremely dangerous place for foreigners but had fortunately isolated itself from new immigrants and visitors, which had seriously reduced the statistics of homicides planet-wide. No one outside that country regretted the closing of its borders except those with relatives still trapped inside. For one thing, other than weapons, the nation did not produce a thing, at least not within their borders. And the funny thing was, they were brainwashed to think they had it best, were superior, and that it was envy that made everyone else in the world despise them; not their massive-scale rampant enslavement, murder, thievery, pollution, and rape of natural resources and indigenous peoples.

CHAPTER TWELVE

Assuming a high enough orbit that only a few of the more mobile satellites with enough fuel would be able to get in close, Bodhi set parameters for autopilot intervention and switched on a beacon to make it easy for Haley to find the ship in its new position relative the planet. He got his helmet back on, leaving the hanger in vacuum for Haley, and got hooked inside a heavy lifting suit to dump the trailer contents into the refinery chute. Instead of manually lifting the fork to spill it, he connected the trailer's ore drainer to the chute's receiving tube, and let automation handle it. It meant standing by for almost two minutes, and a self-pity thought arose in Bodhi's mind, wondering how come Favio was so mean to him. The thought was identified as it emerged, stamped with the "self-pity so ignore" label, and Bodhi let it drift off without actually exploring it. He concentrated in the point below his navel and found refuge there from thoughts.

Getting his lift-suit and trailer stowed away, he passed through the hanger's airlock and went to deck 11. Bodhi got an eclair out of the cargo hold, having skipped lunch again, and ate it with enormous pleasure. He was called to get another, truly compelled, but Haley's voice in his ear prevented that, setting him on a new course. She told him, "We are on our way up. Thanks for the beacon. You parked so far away I may never have found it otherwise. We have take-out, so don't spoil your appetite."

"Sorry, Haley. I didn't want to get hemmed in by satellites again. Thanks for bringing dinner. I'm starved."

"You probably skipped lunch again today."

"I did."

"Are the targets wasted?"

"I got all you tagged."

"How did the mining go?"

"I got all the adamantine you wanted, and some saturnium that was on the same moon. The rare-firmaments and other materials from the planet will have to wait until tomorrow."

"I didn't think you would be able to get to those today. The saturnium was a great score."

"Thanks. We'll get it all done. It will just take some time."

"We're approaching the bay doors, so set the table dear."

"Alright."

Pam and June had squeezed into the lift-tube together, shopping bags and all, and entered the dining room to load the table from their bags. Pam collapsed the bags and set them on a sideboard cabinet attached to the bulkhead, and June pulled her into a long kiss and embrace. They couldn't keep their hands off each other and the romance was thick in the air. Haley had ridden up with Favio in the same tube-lift, something only lovers do in quantum culture, and entered the dining room arm in arm with sacks of take-out. Then Tish and Winn came into the dining cabin like teens in love.

Bodhi was feeling like a 7th wheel and concentrated in the point below his navel burning off jealousies as quickly as they could arise at the periphery of his mind. When Winn tore herself from Tish to take her seat beside Bodhi and placed her palm on his chest over his heart, all was right as rain in Bodhi's world. Divine perfection. Then Haley detached from Favio and took her seat beside Bodhi, kissing his cheek. Tish blew him a kiss from down the table, and he felt its impact when it reached his lips through the air, it was so intense. Favio burst into song while he served up plates.

Haley mentioned to Bodhi, "I see you took out the new dictator of the Incorporated Merger States."

"Was he in that big jet or in a facility I bombed?"

"The big jet."

"I rammed it head-on."

"They found only wing-tips and a few small pieces of jet engine."

"One of those bounced off *Diamond Lotus's* nose, and I need to apply some reflective lens coating there. We have a spot on the nose uncloaked."

"I saw. It makes the ship appear to be a fist-sized asteroid."

"I'll fix it in the morning. How's the seminar going?"

"We will need to tack on an additional day. Will you be able to deliver that adamantine to the surface tomorrow, and do the mining on Firmament?"

"If that's the priority, then that's what I'll do. I am going to pilot the repair drone in the morning to apply the lens material on that spot on the nose before I get started. I can work late if I need to."

"I'm not returning to the surface tonight, and I'm doing my three-hour sleep and dream-work in your bed for the enhancement," Haley informed him.

"I used to have you lie in bed with me when I went to sleep at night when I was twelve," Bodhi shared recalling.

"Because you were afraid of the dark and had me keep watch all night," Haley remembered.

"You've always been such a comfort for me, Haley."

"And now I'm the one who needs a little comforting," Haley replied.

"You've got it, and I owe you," he agreed, wrapping an arm around her.

Haley wrapped hers around Bodhi and then kissed him passionately. Her synthetic tongue was truly indistinguishable from a real one. The love and affection could not have been more real. She knew what she was doing and was very good at it. Bodhi was wholly with her in his learning mode as Haley taught him the way. Plates of food set in front of them brought Haley's romantic kiss to its conclusion. She told everyone that she would have her protein shake harvesting produce in the stacks. She was always first awake on the ship and claimed each morning when the others arose to have already eaten her big meal of the day. She caressed Favio's back from shoulder to shoulder with her palm as she exited the dining cabin.

Winn shifted closer and got her hand on Bodhi, completing both of them into that greater entity, blissfully. The food was wonderful and consisted of either seafood or poultry mixed with rice or noodles in sauces having the heat of lava, burning all the way down to one's colon. Bodhi was pretty sure that it would burn his anus too passing it in the morning. Parts of the tropics of Mother prepared sauces with these same peppers and spices, found in all yellow sun 3rd planet biospheres. Varieties of these spices could also be found on white sun 4th planets with biospheres; post-dinosaur ages.

Favio announced, "Tonight, after dinner, I'm shooting my final Bullhorn men's bikini underwear commercial, and then I'm posing nude for the centerfold of *Stud Magazine*."

June told him admiringly, "The ladies of firmament are in for a real treat."

Pam encouraged him, "Do save yourself for our bed afterward. We can celebrate your publicity."

"I will miss the sharing in your glorious beauty, my love," Tish told Favio, "because there is a little fairy-girl I'm inexorably drawn to and plan to seduce this evening."

Goosebumps swelled on Winn, where Bodhi had his hand on her forearm. She whispered to him, "I've never done it with a girl before."

"Tish is a pretty awesome one to start with," Bodhi said, feeling and sharing her anxiety.

"Like a beginner trying to ski down an expert slope," Winn stated her analogy.

"Just focus on the love and be yourself, Winn. You'll be fine," he encouraged.

"Do you think she's just joking?" Winn asked almost hopefully.

"Oh, she's serious alright," Bodhi shared his take on it.

Favio told Tish, "Winn is alluringly beautiful, and I envy you. I'm too big to fit inside of her."

"You are quite stretch for me, my big stud," Tish replied fondly.

Pam told Favio, "I need to do a few hours of homework after dinner because I'm having trouble in quantum navigation with reducing the potential-variable to get the quotient for n in the destination-resolution relative coordinates equation."

"I'm just trying to learn how to be a user of quantum computers," Favio admitted, not having a head for the math.

"That's fine for the chef, but ship's crew must understand both the hardware principles and engineering, and the programming languages and math. The pure potential is always resolved into manifestation through *observation* and the destination relative-coordinates for navigation and quantum jumps, through the equations."

"I'm glad I'm the chef and ladies' man and not ship's crew," Favio stated proudly.

Favio was above average intelligence and could follow a recipe like nobody's business, but he had about as much interest in math as he did in getting a paper cut or stepping on a tack. Being surrounded by genius women did not bother him a bit. Although they sometimes said strange things, they responded to him like other females. Becoming the ET's chef aboard *Diamond Lotus* had placed Favio in the global limelight, and even the people of the fiction –fed alternative facts in the Incorporated Merger States were now hearing of his fame. They would see how big he is when his centerfold shots were published in hard print and on the interface. This job was the ultimate when it came to fame and fan clubs. Haley had set up his interface site for him, and he'd received tens of millions of texts with selfies, and had over half a billion hits so far, though they were keeping him so busy that he'd had no time to check any of it out.

Winn was saying to Bodhi nervously, "I'll let you know what it's like with her so maybe it won't be as frightening for you when it's your turn."

The evening practice was demanding, and they rose to the occasion, getting a good workout and generating a fairly pristine state as a group in the meditation. Haley had shuttled Favio to the surface for his modeling work, and so had been late joining them for the energy generation. Bodhi had the opportunity to observe Tish's opening moves on Winn until she had her out the door of the meditation cabin and down the corridor towards her cabin. Pam and June floated out of the meditation room on a cloud of romance together. Haley took Bodhi's hand and led him to his suite.

They made the equal ceremony looking into one another's souls through their eyes, generating an enormous arc of love between them. They remained in this state, joined as one until it was time for Haley to retrieve Favio from the surface. Bodhi had had a moment of intergalactic fame right after the revolution-liberation and had found it unattractive and disturbing, sort of like being objectified as public property.

Once Haley got Favio back to *Diamond Lotus*, having had to wrench him from stage crews and fans in a frenzy, and had delivered him to adoring June and Pam, she returned to Bodhi's Suite and bed to find him asleep. He wasn't faking it either. Haley powered down to sleep mode snuggling into Bodhi. She luxuriated in the experience for a while before shutting her android sensors off and proceeding with her dream work. The pattern was holding and just waiting on Bodhi to take his place within it. Haley knew Winn and Tish would not be disappointed. Although both Winn and Tish yearned for intimacy with Bodhi, they'd insisted that since Haley had known him and been in love with him the longest, she would be the first among them.

Winn wasn't disappointed that night though, not with Tish, who'd taken her well-beyond the capacities and tolerance of her nervous system several times, frantically. She'd never experienced anything like it before and was not quite sure what she would tell Bodhi. Boy, when that Tish made up her mind to do something, did it ever get done. She hadn't risen to her nation's top athlete, one of their top scientists and an international martial arts champion for nothing. That girl had spirit, not to mention spunk. And she was as serious as a heart attack.

The seminar went on for three more days, and Bodhi mined rare-firmaments and rare metals. He also mined more adamantine and saturnium from moons around the 5th and 6th planets, and more marsnium from below ground on the 4th planet. Haley had directed him to an extremely precious, and unlikely deposit on a dwarf planet, 10th from the star, found by one of their prospector-sensor drones. It was a deposit of solidium, generally only found at the core of speeding comets. It was the only thing known to be harder than adamantine. The solidium would remain aboard *Diamond Lotus*. It was not needed by Firmament. Back in the Tri-galaxies, an ounce of solidium could fetch 15 karats of diamonds, and Bodhi had mined almost two tons.

Manufacturing of fusion reactor parts had commenced on Firmament already at specialized large-scale machine shops, and some factories were already laying foundations for fusion reactors. Twelve nations were building fusion reactors using steel-nickel-titanium girders, and rebar, encased in a specialized concrete employing a super-adhesive chemical compound Haley had shown them how to make. On Firmament, Haley was already reputed to be the biggest genius and most knowledgeable person in the entire universe. Bodhi remained the mysterious owner, captain and pilot of the ET spaceship, thought juvenile in his romantic endeavors, thanks to the news crew Haley naively confided in.

The most glamorous sexiest young super-star actress had been drafted on Firmament, along with an all-star cast to play Haley and the crew in a new exciting telecom series called "Lost in Space" and Favio had been offered a 30-million contract to play himself in the series. He was truly a rising star on Firmament as never seen before. A shooting Star! The big-star actor they got to play Bodhi was four inches shorter than Bodhi's five-foot-nine and almost half inches but had such charisma that it wasn't really noticeable. Tish, Haley, Bodhi, and Winn were radically attracted to the petite actress who played Winn. Only coming attractions of *Lost in Space* had so far been released, and the first episode would not be shown until the new season started in a couple of months. Bodhi wished it were further out than that.

Not only had Bodhi patched the ship's nose and done all that mining, but he had also painstakingly constructed a prototype light spectrum encoding coms transmitter with a multifaceted smart crystal studded with light-activated data beads of zircon and silicon. It contained a super-complex integrated closed circuitry net, as well as a quantum open circuit converter that *Diamond Lotus* could use to convert light spectrum coding to quantum coms. The prototype, specifications, construction procedures, and numbered lists of parts were already in the hands of engineers on Firmament. Bodhi had labored fifteen hours or more per day, and progress towards fusion energy and migration was unfolding rapidly, though the pattern was still waiting patiently for Bodhi to take up his place within it. Only Haley, who'd assigned Bodhi's work load, knew for sure that he was not avoiding his duty.

Practices in the morning and evening each day were energetic, crisp, clear and enlivening. Bodhi was always spot-on, leading them with great intensity supporting his students and no self to be found. With the seminar over, he was meeting individually with them again. He also met with Favio, providing more specific instruction tailored to him, and planting seeds with teaching stories, to be sure, the most basic and easiest ones. Favio was pumped with his success. With Pam and Winn, Bodhi kept his fingertips lightly on their wrist pulses, reading them and their states, and sending surges as reminders if necessary. Bodhi had recognized their most frequent hindrances quite clearly and had helped them learn to overcome them, or more like not fall into those traps.

Haley had begun learning the secret method under Amazonia and Sarhi's guidance and was continuing to study it under Bodhi. He also began teaching Tish the secret method, and the completion stage for the transference of consciousness. As his student, she directed her serious ferocity inward. As a woman yearning for him, she directed it upon him. She was nearing the completion of the six limbs now that she was making the mixings very well. When they weren't meditating, she seemed to Bodhi as a goddess, and he felt kind of bad for her that he didn't look more like Favio.

With a few innovations, some shipyards for building giant ocean-going vessels had been refitted and renovated to construct hull sections for the 2400-seater-transport, which *Diamond Lotus* would tow through the quantum jump to the new world, New Firmament. In fact, in just a couple of days, Bodhi would have to start shuttling up sections to connect in orbit alongside his ship, and Haley was already mining a gas-giant for materials they would need to refill fuel cells and make launch boosters. She had also passed on to Firmament's engineers and scientists the complete science, specs, blueprints and design, parts, and detailed manufacturing instructions with diagrams for making and employing vortex redirect and generation turbines. With this Firmament could generate centripetal gravitational force, and redirect it to revolutionize transportation. This would require fusion batteries, which Haley was already teaching them about.

She had a strict policy that everything she taught them was to be shared equally among people and nations of the planet for the common good. Nothing containing any of the science and technology she shared with them could retail for over 11% above manufacturing cost. Haley had thought 11% was already too much for the bloodsucking middlemen. Giddy engineers were manically at work on designs for Firmaments' first hovercraft. Capitalists were pushing the limits and seeking loopholes.

Stud Magazine had to run a second printing to meet demand, and you couldn't ride public transportation, drive on a major through fare, or watch telecom on Firmament without seeing Favio in his Bullhorn men's bikini underwear. He appeared on the late-night talk shows, comedy shows, and in news segments. Haley had even made a quantum computer-generated graphics and animation of Favio performing a music tele-clip and had written the lyrics and composed the music herself. It looked more real than actual tele-clips of Favio. She'd nailed his voice perfectly and had come up with the tunes based on recent top hits she rearranged and improvised off of. With some aggressive negotiations, Haley sold the Favio music tele-clip to a major network netting Favio 15 million monetary units plus 5% of advertising revenues from ads preceding and following all airing of the tele-clip. The Favio music tele-clip was holding the number-one position on the charts currently.

CHAPTER THIRTEEN

All personnel was at the moment being wined and dined on the house as celebrities at the most expensive and trendiest restaurant on the continent where the League of Nations was meeting. The booths, tables, chairs, and wall paneling were all of the same dark hardwood. Real leather covered the seats in the booths. The seven of them sat at a table on cushioned hardwood chairs. All the waitresses were topless and on roller-blades, while the waiters were bottomless on skateboards. Trendy music roared, making conversation a little difficult. Nude dancers in suspended cages, male and female, gyrated solo or bumped each other erotically in couples or groups. The thick plush carpeting was bright primary red, and soft lighting from elaborate crystal chandeliers bestowed a certain elegance upon the room. A bar in the front chamber and entrance gave patrons a place to wait for their tables and kept up a steady flow of alcoholic beverages into the enormous dining room.

They sat pretty much in the same order around the table as they did the longer one in their dining cabin on the ship. This put Bodhi between Haley and Winn. Bodhi and Winn were the only two at the table not dressed as performers or in Bodhi's mind, 'undressed' as performers. Favio wore only his bikini briefs and a tight T-shirt that didn't quite make it down past his ribs. Winn had come up with a drawing of a logo for them, which they all liked, and uniform designs had been approved by Haley, so on their next trip to the surface, they planned to wear those. In the meantime, Bodhi felt kind of like a reserved introvert among theater types; displayers basically.

Winn's hand grabbing Bodhi's prevented an incriminating pseudo-analysis of inhibitions on his part, saving him the anguish.

She mentioned to him and had to say it loudly over the music, even though her mouth was less than a foot from his ear, "I did it with Haley last night. She's amazing in bed."

Somehow the music composition chose that moment to drop from full crescendo and orchestration to total silence, and Winn's was the lone voice shouting in the dining room. The words hung in the hushed void as a slight shock passed like a wave through the room. Haley said loudly, easily ranging the room's territory though not shouting, "Thank you, Winn. You showed pretty well yourself," feeling the complement required a polite reply of equal notoriety.

Tish knew exactly what Haley was saying from first-hand experience and was nodding agreement gravely. Favio was intrigued. So was June. Once the general hum of conversations in the dining room rebooted, Haley told Bodhi, "I'm sleeping over tonight."

"Alright."

Winn smiled delightedly. The pattern was still waiting, and perhaps a little less patiently. She felt exalted every time she was in contact with Bodhi and loved him completely. She also yearned for him. Winn would wait forever if she had to. She didn't want to, though. Suddenly a male youth dressed in black, stained with tattoos, and glistening with piercings appeared between Winn and her love saying to Bodhi, "In a lucid dream, I was instructed to become your disciple or die trying. I will not stop trying until I am dead."

"What's your name?" Bodhi inquired.

"Sonic."

"Pull a chair over, Sonic, and sit down."

Winn moved further from Bodhi's seat, losing some of the magic, and there still wasn't room to get the chair in that Sonic fetched even with Bodhi scooting the other way. So Sonic's chair poked into the space between tables, and he sat on the very edge so as not to be much behind them. Any other arrangement would place Bodhi in front of a table leg unable to scoot in. Only soups and appetizers had arrived thus far. Bodhi asked Sonic, "Tell me about your spiritual practice?"

"I'm only twenty years old," Sonic said defensively before proceeding. "I was taught a practice of concentration leading to contemplation which makes consciousness itself the object of meditation."

"Formless meditation on the witness involving the tri-emanations, or three bodies of the enlightened one, which is sometimes called the three minds of enlightenment," Bodhi stated, seeking confirmation.

"Then you are familiar with it," Sonic said, surprised.

"The methods are countless, but the ways are only four, so all methods encompass one or more of the ways. When you truly know the four ways, you know all the methods."

"Thank you for clarifying that, teacher," Sonic said politely.

Bodhi asked with concern, "What does your teacher have to say about you studying with me?"

"He passed away three months ago. He was extremely old. It was him in my lucid dream who instructed me to become your disciple or die trying!"

"I may own the ship," Bodhi told him, "but the community would have to accept you for you to join us. I can otherwise visit you periodically on the surface to instruct you."

Winn thought Sonic was cute and could see that Bodhi wanted to help him. She also saw that Sonic had some issues around being accepted and a couple of obstacles as well. She took his hand, standing, and led Sonic to the ladies' room where she went to work as his fashion consultant, hairdresser, and make-up artist.

The majority of the hardware was removed from his face, and the two worst tattoos turned out to be press-on, which included the one on his forehead. Winn scrubbed that one away with soap and water. She washed his hair in the sink, gave his bizarre hairdo some strategic snips, and rain of precision clipping before drying it with the hot-air hand dryer. Then she made him wait with her outside the men's room until she saw a sports jacket she thought was perfect. She wrote a check for 25,000 units—about 50 times its value—against the billions now on the ship's balance in accounts on Firmament, to the man who made the exchange happily with her since he could pick up another in the morning and have most of the money left. Winn had done a fine job of masking the pimples on Sonic's face with cosmetics and had brought his eyelashes out beautifully. She'd only left him one eyebrow ring, one earring, and one lip ring, making poor Sonic feel naked. The transformation was worthy of legend.

Nobody recognized the boy Winn returned with, and Bodhi found himself just repeating his introduction to Sonic. Winn helped Sonic to get an entrée order in since he was already too late for appetizers, then introduced him as a prospective community member to all at the table. Both Tish and June rose from their seats. June to sit in Sonic's lap, wrapping her arms around his neck, and Tish to grab his chin, directing his eyes into hers.

Sonic had never been so intimidated in his life. Gorgeous celebrities were scrutinizing him at the ET table, and he was wondering if to die trying might have been less painful. The one boring through his eyeballs exposing his soul with her laser-gaze was like a genius, supermodel, international martial arts champion and meditation adept. He felt like a maggot or a germ by comparison. She also looked fierce enough to just kill him on the spot should he flunk her test. He manifested courage for all he was worth. The one sitting on him seemed to be giving him a lap dance.

Before the back of his head melted away or blew off as he was becoming concerned it might, the girl with the laser eyes gave him a most serious smile, nodding yes. But a moment later, the one in his lap had her tongue in his mouth. ET Haley took his picture with some kind of device then sent it to her strange looking phone. The one he knew to be Pam came behind his chair and leaned over, first to kiss June in his lap and then to madly and passionately kiss Sonic. No dream he'd ever had was anything like this and his entire life a total contrast to it, leaving him without any bearings.

A discussion ensued, right in front of him, about him, as though he weren't even there. It was all so strange he couldn't be entirely sure he was. Some activity continued upon his lap. ET girl seemed to like his aura in the hologram she showed them, which grew out of her phone, or whatever the phone-looking thing was. His aura looked very familiar to him.

Pam wanted him, and so did June. Winn voted for him, as did Bodhi. Tish stated that the community needed him. Favio argued that

Sonic was skinny and not pretty enough, so he tended to downgrade their overall image. Bodhi pointed out that they would be leaving Firmament, and didn't have an image, so much as a purpose to share and spread the teachings.

Favio came around just as the entrees were arriving, and after Pam pointed out to him that Sonic made *him* look all the more handsome. Bodhi told Sonic, "Welcome to our community, Sonic. I sense that you are meant to be here."

"Thank you, Master Bodhi," Sonic said, relieved and grateful.

"Please, just call me, Bodhi."

Winn embraced and kissed Sonic, and he felt indebted to her for the help she'd given him. He wondered if maybe he looked alright now. Never having any fashion sense and only having ever scored when he was dressed outrageously, he'd been drawn to extremes. She looked like an angel to him. He still couldn't quite believe he was really in. From the start, joining the ET ship as Bodhi's disciple had appeared well-gone and beyond the realm of possibility. He couldn't just go up and knock on the door. He had been wandering by when he'd noticed all the news vans and the crowds. When he realized the ET's were inside, he'd pushed his way through the crowd, insisting that they were obstructing his entrance to work. The rest was history. Such luck, good fortune, synchronicity, or whatever this was had never occurred before in Sonic's life. Part of him was in shock, bewildered by the wonderment of it all.

The food was incredible, consisting of the very finest obtainable ingredients, the most heavenly recipes, and the cooking skills of the top caliber. The visual presentations had been works of art, but the gustatory experience far exceeded the visual. Sonic's came out just a little after the others with his order having gone in later. June had completed her activities in Sonic's lap to return to her own seat to eat. Sonic had been poor all his life, and the only restaurant he'd ever eaten in had been fast food with a drive-through. Trying not to be a burden, he ordered what he thought was the cheapest thing—a burger.

It was ground filet mignon with gruyere cheese and thick crispy slices of bacon over a freshly baked 21 grain and seed bun. It came on a large platter with a pile of fried sweet potato fingers, wild rice salad, thick slices of red onion and tomato and a diced cabbage salad. A tray of condiments was included with pickles, relish, tomato sauce, mustards, spinach and lettuce leaves, peppers, and other things. The cabbage salad was exquisite, and nothing like that served at fast food. There was a pound of ground fillet in the burger, and Sonic knew that it cost over ten units at the food market raw. It had been delivered on rollerblades by a topless girl who'd looked like a model. No one dining in here earned less than six figures annually, and those were the poor 2nd cousins. There had been no prices on the menu, and if you needed to ask, you had better just get out. Sonic knew all about this restaurant. It was the backdrop for much celebrity news.

Winn put him at ease, explaining, "This meal is on the house and we have accumulated billions for the materials Bodhi mined and the technology Haley has delivered. Please don't have a care about monetary issues."

"I thought I was just ordering a burger!" Sonic told her dumbfounded.

"Tell me about your life, Sonic," Winn requested with interest.

"I grew up in this city and graduated from the public performing arts high school when I turned seventeen. My father's an iron worker and my mom cleans houses for rich people. I have a younger sister who was accepted into the city's prestigious Academy of Sciences where she's in her second year. I left home right after I graduated to study with a very elderly foreign man who had students living with him in a loft. He taught us meditation and he had some lay-students with good jobs who paid the rent on the loft and brought groceries regularly. He died about three months ago. Last week he came in a lucid dream and told me to become Bodhi's disciple or die trying; so here I am."

"Well I'm glad you're here and alive," Winn told him encouragingly. "You are the youngest member of our crew."

"How old are you," he asked.

"I'm twenty-two, the second youngest now," Winn informed him, making their two-year difference seem vast.

"I was youngest at the loft as well," he stated, resigned.

"Do you like girls, boys, or both?" Winn inquired with a personal stake in his answer.

"I've done it with both and like girls much better," he answered honestly. Then he added as a kind of disclaimer, "I don't fill out bikini underwear the way Favio does."

"No. I can see that. He's too big to fit inside me," Winn informed Sonic suggestively.

"He thinks I'm too skinny to be part of the ship's crew," Sonic lamented.

"I'm as skinny as you," Winn pointed out.

"But you're a girl and as beautiful as an angel. I'm not even cute, or kind of pretty according to Favio."

"I think you're cute, and June obviously likes you."

"I don't even have a single hair on my chest," Sonic condemned himself per Favio as the standard.

"Neither does Bodhi, and I don't go in for hairy chests and fur."

"Really?! He doesn't either?"

"Not a one."

"He seems kind of laid back and even avoidant as a leader," Sonic mentioned.

"Haley directs us as the first officer. Bodhi teaches us martial arts and meditation. When he's teaching, he has a natural authority, and he's a great leader."

"I can't even believe I just ran into you all here and that Bodhi said I could stay."

"Well, you're a part of us now, sweetheart. What kind of performing arts do you do?"

"I play keyboards and guitar, and I've done some theater acting. I'm not right for any lead parts, but I've had some roles with substantial lines playing more minor characters or villains. I got to sing in chorus in a musical once, with that production."

"Your voice has a very nice quality, and no one else was able to get through the onlookers and media folks into the restaurant but you. Your acting must have been convincing."

"I insisted that I work inside and that they were unlawfully obstructing my employment,"

"A brilliant ruse and you pulled it off."

"At that moment, my very life depended on it."

"Now, your safe, and I'm your friend."

"I don't think I've seen a girl so beautiful as you."

"That is very sweet of you. Sonic. I don't fit the media profile. I'm too short, skinny, and small- breasted."

"You're so well-formed and perfect. I'm moved by the beauty of you, and you are truly kind and caring. Thank you for making me look acceptable and helping me through the screening process. I don't mean to downgrade the overall attractiveness of the crew."

"You don't. Believe me Sonic. I think you're really cute now that those facial tattoos are washed off, and almost all of your piercings are removed."

"I'd take the last three out for you."

"I like those. They give you character without becoming distracting."

"I've never before eaten foods of this quality."

"Bodhi likes uncontaminated food prepared well, and we grow grains and produce on the ship in hydroponic stacks and a grow room. We have three lime trees, and Vitamin C is very important living in space."

"I never imagined going into space. I went to Hanholm by passenger jet once, and that was the only time I've been off the ground other than a few amusement park rides."

"Our space shuttle is parked on the top floor of the parking structure across the street, taking up most of it. Bodhi and Haley are our only pilots at the moment, but they have started training Tish since she showed the highest aptitude on the tests they gave us." She didn't mention that she had herself scored 2nd highest.

"That news crew that was brought up to *Diamond Lotus* said it was like being aboard an ocean liner cruise ship."

"Except we try to keep the air in, instead of the water out," Winn contrasted the two.

"How's that working out?" he asked with concern in his voice.

"Very well with the compressors and airlocks. We produce 100% of our own oxygen with bio-trays, and we carry enough air compressed in tanks to air the ship two and a half times."

"Does Haley know everything?!"

"She certainly seems to. She has never failed to answer a question, and is always precisely accurate, and has never uttered the words 'I don't know,' except regarding their little incident with the worm hole."

"Is getting sucked through the wormhole going to be in the first episode of the new telecom series?"

"Only Favio was allowed to see the screenplay, and he's not saying. It's in his contract."

"I hope they're fair to Bodhi in their portrayal of him."

"I doubt they will be. Those news people who went up to the ship made Bodhi out to be sex-phobic and avoidant, and this has become part of his reputation. The screenplay writers have not interviewed him, or researched him or tried to find out a thing about what he's really like."

"Are you his lover?"

"We are in love, and I'm going to be his lover and have his baby."

"Is Haley his only lover?"

"Well, she will be. Soon we hope. She's to be the first."

"Who's Favio's lover?"

"Everyone, but me and Bodhi."

"So, you will only be with Bodhi?"

"No. I'm lovers with Haley and Tish, but I'm more attracted to males, and especially to Bodhi. He has a duty to Haley and Tish, so we will share him and take care of him. He's not very organized without Haley. And being orphaned at six weeks, he never had a mother to instill conservation and self-preservation. He needs our help."

"With the beautiful ET who knows everything, an adorable angel, and a national icon and international champion, I don't think he could find better help."

"That's sweet of you to say, Sonic. Have you had many sex partners?"

"Going to school with theater types and performers, I had a fair few, but always casual, never anything serious. I guess, for that crowd, I was sort of almost alright for an off night. At least for the desperate ones."

"Like Bodhi, I have led a rather focused and sequestered life with no time or opportunity for romance or sexual experimentation. I was quite the neophyte until Tish got a hold of me, then Haley. After those two, I feel seasoned at least with girls."

"Is there a yellow sun third planet with a pristine biosphere and no humans 28 light-years from here?"

"I've seen it in the Nav. Computer Star Map holos though I've never been there. I trust Bodhi and Haley with my life, and more than that with my soul."

"So, he is going to help us begin a century-long process of migration?"

"Yes. As soon as the big house-pouring machine that Haley gave them the design for is built, we'll be bringing it and a small group of pioneer settlers there to begin construction."

"Are they bringing tents?"

"No. Bodhi's going to lend them *Diamond Lotus's* landing platform and biodome. It has a fusion reactor and workshops and machines that will be extremely useful. It can house 16 people on a world without air, water, or heat."

"That sounds helpful for getting started."

"We will also be hauling the prefabricated sections for the Cement-putty manufacturing facility. All the materials needed are native to New Firmament. Bodhi will have to do some mining for them once we get them settled on the surface. Haley has detailed integral plans, schedules, and coordinated operations for getting the migration moving and sustained self-sufficiently without the need of *Diamond Lotus*. At that point, we'll collect our biodome and leave to search for a planetary civilization with inter-stellar travel."

"Will we ever come back?"

"Yes. Except for Bodhi and Haley, we all have loved ones on Firmament, and Favio could not survive without his fans."

"He's likely to find new ones wherever we find humans."

"I'm sure you're right about that."

"I understand that we're supposed to make daily round trips towing a transport for like nine months."

"Yes. You'll be making a daily round trip of 56 light-years."

"Bodhi ought to get Firmament to pay by the mile."

"We already have a ridiculous amount of wealth down here. Haley spends some time every day moving fortunes to charities, and when we go, the remainder will be left for food and medical care for the needy. We girls went a little wild the other day shopping for clothing, shoes, jewelry, and accessories, but we haven't yet been able to even dent the interest on the principle."

"Are there materials on the planet that you need on the ship?"

"We've stocked up on iron, lead, titanium, tin, copper, nickel, zinc, silk, wool, flax, hemp, leather, cotton, rubber latex, silicon, planting seeds, various chemicals and a bunch of other stuff."

"I'm having difficulty believing I'm here. And that you would talk to me."

"I'll be doing more than just talking with you, Sonic. You can sleep over in my cabin tonight if you want to."

"Me?!"

"Yes, and although it is kind of an off night, you are more than almost sort of alright, and I've never been casual about sex."

"An army could not prevent me from reaching your cabin door."

"I think you're going to be a great heap of fun, Sonic."

"Am I the last crew member you're going to take on?"

"Favio says he needs a cook to help him and a kitchen-helper—just to clean up. Bodhi's sold on the kitchen-helper, tired of cleaning up after Favio. He's kind of caving on the cook now too, so I think there will be two more."

"Are there candidates?"

"The kitchen-helper is someone Favio knows and is at the moment starring in a movie."

"At one of the big studios?"

"In a suburban basement, I think. It's adult entertainment."

"Oh. I see."

"Haley insisted on selecting the cook after researching the kitchen-helper, but Favio insists that it must be a female. He is not very sexually attracted to males though he does let them touch him."

"I'm sure we'll land a skilled and competent cook then."

"Haley says our new cook is a twenty-year-old graduate of this city's culinary Arts Institute, a devout meditation practitioner and an animal lover. Her name is Uldra, and she'll be bringing a small purring feline to live with us. The ship is equipped with an automated sand cleansing and recycling box for the kitty's toilet. Uldra is five foot six, wears a size four and a D cup."

"I bet Favio will go for her."

"What about you?"

"Voluptuous women don't see me as human, I don't think."

"What do *you* like, Sonic?"

"I think I'm sold on angels."

Winn practiced her tongue kissing on Sonic, happy to have a male to do it with. Favio was trying hard to sell everyone on his friend Tandy for the kitchen-help position. Bodhi wasn't going to get involved and would accept whatever the group decided. Haley's infatuation with Favio gave him much influence and range. Neither Pam nor June would ever get at odds with him. Tish's love for Favio had transformed even his most obvious ego traits into little endearments. Winn figured Tandy was a forgone conclusion.

"She is bisexual and tries so very hard to please," Favio went on.

"Does she want children?" Winn inquired after letting Sonic up for air.

"I hope not!" Favio said with alarm. The thought of having children never having occurred to him before.

"Does she have references?" Winn asked assertively, which was sort of out of character for her.

"I am her reference," Favio stated with an air of offense.

"And you have employed her in what position?" Winn pressed.

"All sixty-four from the ancient text," Favio replied smugly as if scoring points in an athletic competition.

No way was Sonic going to add his voice to any of this.

With Favio's last answer, Winn felt like she'd fallen down a rabbit hole, and nothing made sense anymore. *Were they extending invitations to an orgy or recruiting personnel for a spaceship?* She was too shocked to try and coherently argue, particularly inside of a seeming irrational conversation. She reached across Sonic to grab

Bodhi's hand, and instant return of the magic made it seem like the world was playing her song. Favio could bring a harem on board and live in a perpetual party for all she cared. Her world was perfect and complete.

CHAPTER FOURTEEN

Six days later, Bodhi was launching from the surface of Firmament in a shuttle hauling hull sections for the transport-ship into space. For now an industrial tractor beam from *Diamond Lotus* was holding sections in place next to the ship. Uldra and Tandy had come aboard and joined the ship's personnel and had woven themselves into the pattern of the community. Bodhi was only yet a third of the way into the pattern, easing in with apparent great caution. Winn, who was next, could barely contain herself in her anticipation and excitement though she had already learned well that she had better not hold her breath. Haley was so ecstatically happy that a cloud of joy followed her infecting everyone around.

All military industrial factories on the planet, even in the Incorporated Merger States, were either retooling or abandoned completely. There wasn't a coal turbine left fired up nor a fission reactor operational anywhere around the globe. Bodhi had already hauled one trailer-load of spent radioactive fission materials into space to release on a trajectory for the sun. Many more such trips would be required. Haley mined the gas giant and manufactured thruster fuel cells and launch boosters for the shuttles. Getting each hull section off the planet required two boosters as well as a considerable amount of thruster fuel cells.

The first vortex-redirect and generation turbines were only a month out, and the first fusion reactors less than one from becoming operational. The efficient solar panels Haley gave them the technology and manufacturing procedures for were churning out from dozens of mega-factories and dozens more were preparing to go on line. Windmill turbines, micro, and mini hydroelectric turbines, geothermal energy conductors and electrical converters, micro-biomass units, ambient planetary energy accumulators, and pulse-pump generators were being mass- produced to the highest standards of production.

With capitalists and governments no longer able to prevent them, the masses of people adapted immediately to meaningful vocations directed towards survival and migration, instead of meaningless corporate-serving jobs destructive of people and the environment. Economies had gone through rough transformations when Haley had emptied offshore numbered accounts into charities. By the time she was done, 29 trillion monetary units had gone from the tip of the point atop the pyramid directly down to the base at the very bottom. Other transformational interventions proved successful, such as destroying the Merger States' central comprehensive financial data and publishing names and addresses of culprits killing the planet and impoverishing the masses. She did this globally after it worked out so well and swiftly—though quite violently—in the Incorporated Merger States. Politicians were rather unpopular critters in about every country and did not last long at first. For a while, every League of Nations meeting Haley attended was full of all new faces each time.

Finally, people who were popular with their fellow citizens were placed in leadership positions, and things stabilized. The hatred of the old guard, though had been traumatic. Everywhere, lying politicians were hunted down, and some were lined up against the wall and shot, hung from a tree, lethally injected, gassed, and some still had the bodies on display in a public square. The current humanity of dying Firmament had survived and shed the plague of domination and ownership to now enter a new era of cooperation and sharing. Tremendous energy had been liberated, and their progress towards renewable energy and migration was accelerating like a rocket leaving the atmosphere.

When Bodhi had finally had sex with Haley, she had not had to seduce him nor insist upon it. He'd led them through the meditations in the central channel, then had her mount him to employ copulation for the realization of the ultimate example clear light. His heart had been wide open to her throughout, connecting infinitely. His sentiments and romantic ideals embraced and held her in the gushiest and deepest affections.

The very existence or even the possibility of such a swamp of mushy sentiment was startling to Haley. She had always known that he was an exceptionally sweet boy but had never suspected the vast expanse of this vein or dimension of him. It made her feel like a goddess, princess, and Madonna, so she wasn't about to complain. He'd taught her a few other things which Pez had taught him too.

Tish was copiloting for Bodhi, logging her training hours towards her pilot certification. They were able to skip the whole largest section on planetary approach space control regulations since so far, they hadn't found any of those in this galaxy. Tish had a natural knack for it, took it seriously, which meant she was hell-bent on mastering it—and was coming along faster than anyone Bodhi had ever seen.

Favio's cooking was truly wonderful. Bodhi had finally taught Tandy how to clean the galley, he hoped. Uldra was simply a delight, like a radiant shining rainbow. Favio's meals seemed to have improved with her cooking. Her 2-month old female kitten named Ki, pronounced "Kee", was already exclusively employing her sandbox for making her toilet. For a while, Ki had had a treadwheel mini-cleaning android follow her about. It was in maintenance awaiting a buff to get out the claw scratches. She was doing her business in the right place now. Whenever Winn and Bodhi were touching, and so creating that magic energy, Ki was on one of their laps basking in it. Ki loved the chicken and tuna from the molecular food synthesizer and had a sense of dominion over her territory and satisfaction with it. Various cleaning and maintenance androids provided endless entertainment honing her stalking skills. A lot of the humans were full of love. There were some pretty cozy places to curl up by a heat-source too. Ki adapted easily to become Firmament's first space cat, and she was already being scripted into scenes for *Lost in Space* episodes.

Once Haley and Bodhi each got back on board from their day's work, Haley mining and Bodhi shuttling things to space, they all sat down for a meal in the dining room. Favio made an enormous prime-cut roast wrapped in crispy bacon and was only going to open a can of tuna and dress it for Bodhi. Uldra baked some game hens she thawed in the wave-cooker from the freezer. She had basted them frequently cooking them at a low temperature for a long time and took them out at just the right moment. She had stuffed them too. The herbs and spices she'd used and the perfect moist tenderness of the meat plus the crisp brown skin came together into culinary perfection offering gustatory rapture. She would always make sure Bodhi was covered. He was her teacher now and she had had her first awakening in her only private session with him so far.

Tasting his first bite, Bodhi exclaimed with enormous pleasure, "This hen is so delicious! I've never had any so perfectly prepared."

"You will only ever get the best out of my kitchen," Favio said proudly as if he'd cooked it himself.

Haley knew from monitoring the sensors in the galley that Uldra had made the hens and texted Bodhi's earbud sending him a message in audio, "Uldra made the hens. Favio was going to open you a can of tuna."

Bodhi said gratefully, "Thank you, Uldra, for looking out for me. I'm a great admirer of your cooking and find you to be a promising student too."

"I am devoted to you as my teacher and will not let you down," Uldra promised him.

Tandy's one-on-one session with Bodhi had not gone so well. Bodhi thought she needed a little more salt. Like Favio, she was a colorful character and sort of larger than life. If Bodhi was a little slow about relationships, he was a tortoise when it came to confrontational ego-reduction. In the absence of genuine remorse and nonidentity it was the fastest way. In their session, Bodhi had tried to explicate for Tandy how her view of external reality simply shows her the internal schema of her own mind. He tried to show her how it is relative, and its conventionality through learning perpetuates it and makes it seem real. To recognize that one's view of the exterior is merely a reflection of one's own internal concepts is to unite one's interior and exterior worlds in an arc of recognition unifying consciousness and constituting the first degree of waking up before the actual First awakening. It was still a bit hazy for her at the end of the first session. The group practices would help, and it would take some time as well as effort on Tandy's part. Bodhi could teach, pass energy, take on the trauma of physic wounds to pacify, and act as a catalyst, but he could not make it happen if people were not ready.

Sitting next to Sonic, Uldra took his silence and reserve for ease and detachment, which it wasn't, and was drawn to him. Since Favio was flanked by June and Tandy, and Bodhi by Winn and Haley, she had sat next to Sonic. He wasn't really her type, and she may not have noticed him at all in another situation, but having just had her first awakening and there only being three males aboard, she thought maybe her type might be shifting or expanding.

Tish asked Haley, "When do we take the first group of pioneers to Firmament and set down the landing platform-biodome?"

"The house-pouring machine was completed yesterday ahead of schedule and tested today. We leave first thing in the morning. I'll be shuttling up supplies before 05:00 hours, and I'll have our sixteen pioneers up here by the time the rest of you are done with breakfast."

Winn exclaimed, "We're going to see New Firmament for the first time tomorrow!"

Bodhi asked, "What are they going to do about a cement mixing trailer and container to feed the house-pourer?"

"We will be bringing that to them in a couple of days, and we'll pick you back up then," Haley explained vaguely.

"Pick me back up?" Bodhi asked, pretty sure he hadn't heard right.

"That's right," Haley told him, "You'll be busy doing some mining for them while we get the mixer-trailer up to space and then out to New Firmament."

"Oh."

"I've fabricated some mounts to adapt the ones for the landing platform, which will be in New Firmament with you, so the mixer-trailer can attach to the exterior hull. It would have to be taken apart to go in the hanger. I made the mounts out of adamantine and carbon plate and used some of our solidum to reinforce them. The mounts have nearly twice the minimum tolerances. It will also land whole and ready for the cement putty."

"I'll do my part. They're going to need HVAC venting, electrical wire, fiber optics, copper plumbing, construction hardware, window frames and poly-carbon window panes, appliances, and a bunch of other things to complete these houses when they're poured."

"We are bringing some of that on our first trip when we drop them off and more when we come back with the mixer-trailer. We'll have to make weekly trips after that."

Bodhi asked, "How big is the cargo area on the towed transport?"

"Large enough to carry the passenger baggage plus 2,000 cubic feet for equipment and supplies. Each passenger is allowed two trunks, two large suitcases, a wardrobe bag, plus two small carry-ons."

"That's not much for each to bring, nor for supplies," Bodhi commented.

"For the maiden run, we are filling the passenger compartments with textiles, electronics, food, bedding, and small appliances, and all the cargo holds with materials, machines, and equipment. We will have made enough runs with *Diamond Lotus* to have gotten quite a bit to the surface of the new world by then."

"We're not trying to make a towed cargo ship?"

"That will have space drives, launch boasters, and additional extra heavy-duty vortex-redirect turbines so it can land directly on the surface and lift off after unloading. The loading will need to be done in space by shuttles, though. The cargo hold doors are gigantic, and once that thing is operational, cranes and heavy construction machinery can be brought easily as well as stored crated furniture and household belongings of the first waves of the settlers."

"Once the gates are constructed, we should be done here," Bodhi suggested.

"Aside from you and me, all of our personnel have attachments to Firmament so we'll be emotionally-morally required to make visits."

"Of course. With the converters I built into their encoded light spectrum coms satellites, we can stay in touch through quantum coms almost in real-time, and their light transmissions will jump quantumly between satellites and worlds to reconvert to light coms beaming down to the surface receivers."

"I'm proud of you, my love," Haley told him before kissing his cheek fondly.

Tish mentioned, "I've been studying the tools and machines the landing platform is equipped with, and it appears they will have everything they need, though on a small scale."

Fascinated, Sonic asked, "Like what has it got?"

Tish rattled off, "Welding tanks and equipment, a foundry-forge, a full machine shop, air compressors, and electro-hydraulics, drill rigs, stone working saws, grinders and drills, a poly-carbon glass furnace and synthesizer, a sawmill trailer with a circular saw and band-saw with guides, a wood shop, a ceramic facility with Kilns, an electronics workshop, and a giant 36-materials-jet 3-D printer. There are also all kinds of power tools and hand tools."

"Wow!" Sonic said, awed.

Winn asked Haley, "Where is the first settlement going to be on the planet?"

"In the upper-middle temperate zone in a large pine and hardwood forest in the hills where there are rich iron ore deposits close by and a vast well of methane gas. A large river runs below the plateau where the landing platform and first houses will be. The river is deep and navigable the entire 86 miles to the sea from the site. Both timber and stone are abundant. There is a large high-quality clay deposit in the region, and zinc, copper, and other metals can be found nearby. It is far from any volcanoes and from any seismic activity. The seasons are distinct, and there is snow all winter, but there is plenty of rainfall during the growing season of over five months. I gave them several choices, and this is the one they chose."

"It sounds like heaven," Winn said, delighted.

"You can go out in the sun without a thick layer of sunblock," Tish said with longing.

Haley added, "The mammal population is a bit thin but accelerating in its expansion. The fish population is over the top, and we have a large paddle wheel fish net barge to anchor in the river with a chute that drops the fish in from the angled net-paddles. It is entirely mechanical and automated by the flow of the river, by the slant of the paddle-nets, and by the configuration of the chute the fish drop into to slide down into the barge."

"I guess fish will be the main protein for a while," Bodhi commented.

"Though we'll be hauling poultry and livestock out there too," Haley informed him. "They will also be operating a bug farm. You can grow an entire crop in a few boxes, they don't eat much, and they have short life spans so breed very quickly. Generally, they are dried, breaded with flour, egg, grains, and seeds, then fried and served with a sauce."

"Fried bugs were popular at upscale restaurants on Om," Bodhi recalled.

"Bugs are far more economical than bovines," Haley stated, knowing it was a fact and not an alternative one.

"Ah, but nothing can be prepared so elaborately and deliciously and mingle so superbly with rich red wines as a fine cut of beef," Favio told them with inspiration.

Bodhi was thinking that a hen could, at least, the way Uldra cooked them. It was a private thought, and he would never say it in front of Favio. Winn asked him, "Could we get a little house on New Firmament?"

"Sure, as a vacation home," Bodhi agreed. "I want to find a civilization with interstellar travel. That is the quickest way to acquire star maps and data."

"Alright," Winn joined with him. "It would be fun when we have children dear," she said sort of reminding him with hope. She had her hand on his arm, and the magic was alive. She let a little bit of yearning seep out psychically before kissing him passionately.

Favio said, "He needs to take that one to bed."

Nodding gravely, Tish stated, "We are not a community until we have babies and children."

"I don't think you are capable of getting pregnant," Favio told her his opinion.

"I always push the pressure-point in front of your prostate gland when you orgasm, Favio. Your seed has never entered me. That is also the reason your refractory period is so short when you do it with me. You are losing neither your semen nor your internal energy.

"I'm late and might be pregnant," Pam confided.

"I only sleep with females while I'm ovulating," June shared.

Favio asked Tish, "Don't you want children? I can give you big healthy ones."

"I'm going to have Bodhi's child," Tish stated as an unalterable fact.

"He has never had sex with you. Will it be a miraculous conception?"

"He will, and I will bear his child. Winn will bear his child too, and we will be mothers together."

Favio knew better than to argue with Tish when her ferocity was heating up. It met no criteria for anger and was something else much scarier. It was like the razor-sharp sword that her spiritual presence and will wielded. Bodhi finished his kiss with Winn, who was looking longingly and adoringly into his eyes careful to keep a hand on him and the magic going. He asked her, "Would you sleep over tonight?"

Winn lit up with light and animation spewing vibes of ecstasy all over the dining cabin and exclaimed in a burst, "I want to. More than words could ever express. I was beginning to think you would never ask."

Another long kiss excluded them from everyone's company, but a cheer went up at the table, and Favio raised his glass to toast, "Here's to plodding along!"

When the moment passed Favio asked Sonic, "You've even slept with her before he's finally now getting around to it, didn't you?"

Sonic had the night Bodhi slept with Haley. Winn needed him that night. Sonic had fallen hopelessly in love with Winn and would probably be a bubbling glob of jealousy right now if Tish hadn't then crept into his bed the next night to blow him away with her intensity, unreal beauty, and that polished skill in bare attention she brought to everything she did. He knew all about the pressure point in front of his prostate gland from her and knew she wasn't having *his* babies either. That would have been way more than he would ever have hoped for anyway. Plus, Tandy, who'd gotten to everyone but Bodhi as far as he knew, had worked him over good the night after Tish. Before joining this ship, Sonic had always felt lucky to score once every month or two, and never anyone who looked like these women. He told Favio, "A gentleman never tells."

Tish smiled lovingly at Sonic. Haley informed them, "The writers, director, and main cast of *Lost in Space* are coming up to the ship the day after tomorrow to obtain data about each of us for the show. It will take up most of the day, and set us back a little in our work, but I decided it would be better to work with them than to let them just make it all up. I've negotiated a percentage of the profits to go into our accounts from the *Lost in Space* revenues. It will also give us a little control over the content and character portrayal."

"I don't want to be the comic relief," Bodhi said with concern.

"The lonely burden of command, my love," Haley consoled him, sort of confirming that he would indeed be the show's comic relief.

The meal concluded, and Tandy needed Bodhi's help still to get the galley back in order. Uldra always did some cleaning up as she cooked and spilled very little. Favio, however, was like a tornado in a greeting card store. Things he didn't even use were splattered, the counters a historical record of the meal's ingredients, the pots and pans he did use strewn on the stove, in the sink and otherwise the oddest places. He'd even managed to get stains on the ceiling a few times. Bodhi now had a hover-duster bot retooled to get out ceiling stains.

The practice went very well that night, and Bodhi had been in top form. Winn was real proud of him as they walked hand in hand to his suite. He confessed, "I didn't know I could love more than one woman romantically and sexually."

"If you took more notice, you would see that it is not only possible but has been happening all around you."

"I know. I thought it was just my nature to love only one woman for life though reality seems to be proving me wrong."

"You are wrong and have to let me take my place in your life. It is the place of greatest fulfillment for me. I love Haley, Tish, and

Sonic dearly, and they are truly precious to me, but you are even more so. I need you desperately, Bodhi."

"You have me, Winn. I could never leave you. Your happiness is everything to me. This incredible connection between us must have some purpose, and we are destined to discover and fulfill it together. You are so perfectly my romantic ideal, Winn. Loving you does not seem a choice, nor anything I could help myself from doing. Looking at you fills me with affectionate joy and fascinated delight, making life seem too good to be true."

"You are my deepest, most intense rapture Bodhi. Your goodness makes me ache with love for you and burn with the need to complete and consummate our intimacy to the highest fulfillment."

With Winn Bodhi played out his romantic scripts, and ideals making passionate love with enormous pleasure connected heart to heart in a poetry of extreme affection rooted in the trunk line of pure divine love. He generated and accomplished the five virtues of the penis bringing Winn through four successive orgasms, each exponentially more potent than the last. At Winn's insistence, Bodhi ejaculated simultaneously with Winn's fourth and final one.

Each of them was so wired on their love for the other that sleep was simply out of the question. So they sat facing in eye contact, making the equal and sparking an arc of love between them like a lightning bolt of electricity. A couple of hours of this had only amped things up a bunch of degrees. When Winn took it upon herself to climb into Bodhi's lap facing him, and mount him, he taught her the central channel meditations for harnessing the force of copulation then guided her through as her action seal. Winn experienced the ultimate example clear light for her first time and with unbelievable lucidity and clarity. It was the happiest moment of Winn's life and in Bodhi's too. Winn felt secure in his love and in his capacity as her teacher.

More of the pattern had been filled-in that night and somehow contributed positively to the well-being and morale of all on board. There was still a lack, like an itch needing to be scratched, where a hole remained in the pattern and reality seemed to be pressuring, and conspiring to bring the pattern into full manifestation. The inevitable was inexorably slipping into a matrix of potentials, all leading to the completion of the pattern manifest in the relative world of matter.

Haley had been up half the night shuttling equipment and supplies up to *Diamond Lotus* and stowing them either directly within the landing platform, or in a cargo hold they had cleared out for this purpose. She was almost as in love—and possibly just as much—with Winn as she was with Bodhi. Haley had a special love for Tish too. This is why she did not feel left out or jealous when she monitored Bodhi's bed through his tryst with Winn. She was truly happy for them and knew the pattern she had foreseen was shaping up. Haley wanted Bodhi to have children with Winn and Tish. She had schemed Tish into the pattern to balance her own place in it since she did not think she could handle it if it were just herself Winn and Bodhi. With the great fortune of Sonic showing up, Winn was thoroughly balanced within the pattern. As for the rest of the pattern, with Favio, Tandy, June, and all, there were a few random variables Haley could not quite see beyond given the complexity of their interactions. Sonic had been needed in those equations too.

Once all the gear was up off the surface and packed, Haley went to pick up the sixteen pioneers consisting of eight couples in their mid-twenties. They all had numerous technical skills, and all held advanced degrees. Each one was an expert in a different field, and between them, their knowledge contained the complete sciences of Firmament. They had all been at Haley's seminar and had studied every facet of the technologies and science that Haley transferred to their planet, receiving special classes with her as a group. A collection of such multi-talented individuals was what the mission required.

Haley landed the shuttle gently and unspectacularly at the ground-control base for the space shuttle of the 2nd superpower, the country Tish was from. This was where she was meeting her 16 pioneers. They called themselves cosmonauts and came up the ramp in bloated metallic-textile space suits wearing the biggest helmets Haley had ever seen, and wanting to know where to plug in their air tubes. At the moment, each was carrying a little tank.

Haley set them straight, "The shuttle is aired up with cleaner, healthier air than your planet has, and so is *Diamond Lotus*. We don't have any space-walks planned so you'll be in air from surface to surface, and won't be needing those suits."

"What of a chance collision with an asteroid fragment?" Beatrice, the wife of the mission commander, inquired.

"We have shields and an armored hull. You won't need those suits. Wear them if it makes you feel better, but if there were a terminal problem, I'd be getting into an escape pod and not such a time-limited suit with no propulsion."

Her passengers removed their big helmets and took seats in the passenger compartment, forward of the airlock foyer and behind the cockpit. Haley didn't have to tell any of these folks to strap in. Space hazards had been instilled through fear in their training, making them an exceptionally cautious bunch. They were all loaded, strapped, locked, and tightened before Haley's butt met the pilot seat. The airlock foyer and cargo hold on the shuttle had been stuffed full of supplies when the cosmonauts boarded, and the other shuttle in the hangar on *Diamond Lotus* was crammed full of stuff for the new world too.

Haley gave Bodhi a heads-up as she lifted off. She didn't spend a launch booster weary of gas mining at this point and barely able to stay ahead of the game. The industrial cargo-shuttle's drives strained to gain speed slowly but surely. Thanks to the extra-large vortex-redirect turbines installed in these things, with drives alone, the shuttle clawed its way out of the atmosphere into space. Bodhi was still parking quite far away to avoid getting closed in by satellites. Haley put up an 18-inch holo in front of each passenger seat showing the planet shrink to a globe in space, and a 2nd one showing the *Diamond Lotus* which she'd uncloaked, grow larger on approach. These shuttles didn't have much of a viewport to speak of. Viewports were never used for piloting craft being too limited to provide panoramic and multiple views, and could not present continuous digital data streams, highlight things, or display route lines.

She opened the bay doors to the hangar having already sucked the air from it, when she'd left, and had to use thruster fuel in addition to reverse and turning drives to slow and align for her entrance. Coming through slowly, she got the shuttle right to its parking place before setting it down on its landing legs. By then, she had the bay doors sealed and the hangar airing up. Her passengers were wildly excited and enthusiastic, chattering at each other in rapid wonderment. It was fairly routine for her but really did it for her guests.

Virgil, who was the mission commander, asked Haley, "How big is *Diamond Lotus*?"

Haley flashed them all a holo of the ship with all its dimensions and specs in text at the bottom as she answered, "It is a stretched nose disc, 428 feet in diameter, 466 feet long, and 148 feet high at the center, tapering in the nose to ninety feet and in the stern to 120. It has seven complete decks and five smaller decks, plus chambers for the drives, reactors, turbines, generators, and hangar. As you can see in the holo, the landing platform and biodome that are secured snuggly to the hull. We can enter the biodome through a special airlock in the ship's hull connected to one in the biodome, and I can give you a tour. It will take a while for Bodhi and Tish to get us up to jump speed. The hangar is now sufficiently aired up, so please follow me off the shuttle."

She dropped the ramp and opened the shuttle's airlock as she led them off. They looked around wide-eyed like school children at a fun exhibit on a fieldtrip. Virgil asked her, "What duration missions were this ship designed for maximum?"

"It carries small craft to collect gasses, water, and mine the materials we need. The fuel in the reactors now is good for another 127 years, and we have enough refined solarium on board to refuel them. Some of the electronics have parts that must be periodically replaced on schedules from ten to one hundred years and there are mechanical parts which wear out every few years. Hulls like this can go thousands of years if they are not involved in a major collision or hit with weapons in a war. We carry spare parts and have the manufacturing capacity to make anything we don't have so long as we have the necessary raw materials on board."

"So, this is self-sustaining almost indefinitely!" Virgil declared.

"This class of ship, called the Expeditionary Tug Utility class, has proven invaluable as operations bases for starting small remote settlements. Self-sufficient sustainability was the theme of its design."

Coming through the hangar airlock, Haley led them to the cargo-lift to take them up to deck 11 where the living quarters are. If they'd used the one-at-a-time lift-tube, it would have taken forever. As it was on the cargo-lift, the seventeen of them were forced rudely into one-another's personal space; those several inches of bioenergy and auric light emitted beyond the boundaries of the skin. Since these people's culture didn't know about this and crammed people into subway cars and elevators like canned sardines, Haley didn't feel so bad.

Off the lift on deck eleven, Haley introduced all sixteen cosmonauts to all the nine other ship's personnel. Tandy's performance made it almost seem like a brothel instead of a space ship. When Haley showed them the bridge, they were all incensed over the lack of controls and instrumentation, gauges and screens, bells and whistles. Bodhi stuck on his piloting skullcap and brought up the piloting holos. Tish sat and brought up about thirty little holos running horizontally just beneath the viewport clear across from starboard to port. For preflight, Tish brought up some six hundred little holos bringing the entire bridge to life with data and began hiding each one as she checked them, making them contract and move to become little icons in her co-pilot supplementary holo beside her main holo.

Bodhi explained, "Much of the piloting is managed by brain impulses through these skullcaps. The technology got started in the medical field for controlling a prosthesis and was then taken up by the military for hands-free weapons targeting. When the commercial sector replaced keyboards, voice commands, and touch-holos with skullcaps, they became integrated into every aspect of our lives."

"Amazing!" Virgil said in wonder.

Satisfied that there were controls and instrumentation on the bridge for flying the ship, if only virtual, the party moved up through the ship's top airlock and then the platform bio-dome's airlock for a tour of their new home. *Diamond Lotus* was already under way and accelerating. The airlock's transition was by ladder and one at a time. Haley had gone first to get the lights on and adjust the temperature. Virgil and Beatrice were right behind her. The dome itself was 200 feet in diameter and eighteen feet high at the center, angling more sharply at the perimeter to form a six-foot vertical wall all around. The landing platform the done was attached to was 210 feet in diameter and eight feet tall consisting of frame and plating containing boosters, thrusters, and numerous XL vortex-redirect turbines built short and wide. The reactor was at the center extending from the base of the platform four feet into the dome, 12-foot by 12-foot square. It was super-miniaturized to the maximum possible. It could power the biodome, a few hundred houses, and a bunch of significant factories, no problem.

Through a viewport in the dome, they could see the hover-tractor connected to the outside of the dome. The space inside was crammed with workshops, machines, a kitchen, workstations with holo pedestals, and berths stacked into four quadruple bunkbeds with rails to prevent falling out of bed. Much of the special environmental equipment and apparatus had been removed to make more space since they wouldn't be needing those, and *Diamond Lotus* now had a rent-by-the-month large storage unit on Firmament. Everything was built-in securely attached and connected or well stowed in bins, cabinets, cubbies, drawers, and nooks. A five minute- jump warning sounded, and Haley got her guests back down to the 11th deck to the passenger seating area to have them all strap in. Virgil and Beatrice were bursting with anticipation over the prospect of a 28-light-year quantum jump involving no time at all, just an instantaneous change in the space-time relative location while maintaining the same speed of .7 light. They had been warned that integral to the experience was the abject horror over not existing at all except as potential. The good news was that this horror occurred in the quantum potential of no-time, and so involved no actual duration whatsoever. That never stopped the horror, though.

A countdown ran down. The jump was always a non-event with the exception of the total change in scenery and the unavoidable horror-shock. Bodhi used his central channel meditation as Pez had taught him to contemplate the black near-attainment or midnight sun as it was sometimes called. Contemplating the black luminescence at the moment of jump seemed to prevent the horror and avoid the shock creating no gap in functioning.

The guests were reeling in a post-shock stupor, and New Firmament was racing for them veiled in cloud cover with brilliant blue and some dark green showing through. It was beauty in itself, glorious, radiant, abundant and nurturing. This would be the humanity of the old Firmament's new mother. She was divine and worthy of the deepest reverence. Bodhi told the cosmonauts over the coms, "You guys better follow the rules Haley set and not defile her. Can you see her miraculous magnificence and appreciate her veiled mysteries? You must love and adore her, and she will care for you as if you were her own children."

Haley informed them, "As soon as we launch your integrated coms satellite, you will have near real-time coms with the only lag times being that duration it takes light to travel from the surface to satellite and satellite to surface. There is already a receiver-transmitter spectrum encoded light coms unit attached to the biodome, and there is one additional one in a crate we will unload before we depart. The satellite has a fusion battery and micro-drives to maintain a relative position to your site continuously above it."

Bodhi brought them into low orbit over the site. The season was winter, and the ground and tree limbs were covered in snow. No satellites orbited the planet. No industry touched it. No humans walked it. The temperature on the ground was ten degrees below water freezing, and there was an 8 MPH wind fairly steady from the northeast. Here, the sky was crystal clear, infinite sparkling radiant blue exploding with color and giving them a clear view of the surface below. Haley zoomed in on the site displayed in the guest's holos until they were examining one molecule of a snowflake on the ground, then she zoomed out very slowly to show the whole snowflake, and out some more for a close-up of a tree-rodent's face. A little further out, and they had a view of several acres. There were only a few small clearings. The forest was dense in places, mostly barren hardwoods, but with evergreens sprinkled throughout. She gave them a view that was broad enough to include the river, and this made the trees look like little strands of carpet.

Bodhi said to Tish, "I'm going to drop into the atmosphere and try to hit individual tree trunks just inches from the ground, to clear a space for the landing platform."

Haley asked, "Will we clear the felled trees, or just land on them?"

"I'll get them out of the way with the mining craft. It has a hinged arm with assorted grips. I can use the claw-vise gripper to drag them one at a time. The settlers will need timber, and the platform will be more stable with just dirt and rock beneath it. The platform has a telescoping-leg levelling system."

"While you're doing that, I'll go through the detachment procedures for the platform, jettison it, and hold it in place with the tractor-beam until you have a spot for it cleared on the ground. Once you do, I'll remote pilot it down from the bridge."

Bodhi started blasting large tree trunks where they met the ground, and those were toppling. Tish mentioned, "You're leaving a lot of them."

"I'm only using the blaster on the real thick ones. The mining craft has a stone cutting saw which will go through the rest like butter, and it has a laser cutter too. The stone cutting saw is too short for the ones I'm taking down with the blaster fire."

"Can I ride in the mining craft with you?"

"I was hoping you would start your solo-runs for your pilot-training with the shuttles today, bringing stuff down, and our guests, too, once Haley lands the platform."

"I guess I could tear myself away from you long enough for that. I *have* been looking forward to my first solo flight."

"Thanks. I know you'll ace it."

"Well, look who trained me."

"Haley trained you as well."

"And she is an excellent rock-solid pilot but not a graduate of Om's Phantom-Raider Space Close-Combat School, a hero fighter-pilot of the tri-galaxy revolution, or apprentice of the master-pilot Pez."

"Some of the records Pez set, and at least one well-recorded landing, are considered to be physically impossible. Of course, no one can deny that she accomplished them all the same."

"You are like that for me, Bodhi. Impossible, yet here you are."

"Tish, you are impossibly accomplished and beautiful, so you are like that for me as well. In fact, with your will and presence within all that beauty, you're honestly a bit intimidating."

"Do not be frightened of me. I think you are beautiful. I know there can be no greater transformation for me than connecting with you. I will help you let go that part of you which feels humiliated, besmirched, and condemned by the world."

"I love you, Tish, and I see that we are each medicine for the other. When you return with *Diamond Lotus* to retrieve me, I will be your action seal for the realization of the ultimate example clear light and union of the two truths. You are ready."

"Rumor has it that it's the *only* part of the method Winn knows."

"Her sitting practice prepared her, and I think that what connects us, seen as a golden chord in my dream state, initiates the law of communicating vessels between us astonishingly rapidly."

"She does seem to have a bit of a glow these days," Tish commented. "It means a lot to me that you would teach me. And I aspire to learn this. To learn it from you instead of from a ninety-year old teacher is such a blessing. I need to make passionate romantic love to you also. Not as a practice, but because it is so enticing and so loaded with meaning for me, and because I want to have your baby."

"We will get there, Tish. It is not just your beauty or even your overpowering eroticism that frightens me, but how very alluring I find you. Standing next to you, I sometimes lose my equilibrium and find myself falling into your vortex."

"I've seen that, and I know you are physically attracted to me. I did score nearly 100% on your porn profile after all."

"Is Haley now telling people their scores," Bodhi asked alarmed.

"No, she's not, but she didn't secure the data. I looked mine up."

"I'm in love with the accomplished woman and meditator with insight, not my porn profile, honestly. I never found a porn image or clip of a woman as beautiful as you, or Winn or Haley. I've had to process what I'm doing, where it leads. Now it is clear that you are needed in the pattern to stabilize Haley's place within. I'm ready to enter the pattern with you, Tish, through the teachings, for procreation, and to connect fully and romantically with you in love."

"We are just starting our work day!" She declared in frustration.

"And I'm stuck here mining until you all get back with the mixer-feeder trailer. So until then my love."

Bodhi went down in the mining-craft to clear trees on the surface, and Tish started shuttling down gear and equipment. Each cargo shuttle was equipped with a tread-loader and these had swivel forklifts. With a 4x4 foot base and treaded wheels to two sides, the tread-loaders stood $3^{1/2}$ feet high with a one-seat open cockpit, and it had a retractable canopy and windshield. The machine had a lifting capacity of three tons, and a pair of foldout legs were required to be engaged for loads of that weight. Using the forklift on the tread-loader, Tish got the shuttle cargo-bay emptied.

Haley finished the steps of detachment, jettisoned the landing-platform and caught it almost at the same moment with the tractor-beam. As soon as Bodhi dragged the last trunk from the circle on the surface with the mining craft, Haley piloted it down remotely and set it centered in the circle Bodhi cleared. He stood by on the ground, so once it settled, he could get the hover-tractor detached from the dome and over the ground operating. This would be the cosmonaut's only vehicle to start with. It could tow or drag a great load and was a true work-horse. There were a couple of trailers for it up on the ship, which would come down in another load. The drill rigs and some other machines in the dome attached to the hover-tractor.

Bodhi went mining for cement putty materials on the surface of New Firmament. Haley took the ship's tender down to the dome to boot up the systems and get everything calibrated and functioning optimally. The dome had two maintenance-bots and a repair-android. Tish got the settlers all down in one trip to the dome, and Haley gave them a crash course in operating everything. Tish helped shuttling everything tagged for the surface on the ship, down to the dome with help on the loading end of things.

At 13:00 hours ship's clock time, it was already twilight fading to dark at the landing site, but Tish carried on shuttling supplies and materials down, as well as some prefab sections of structures.

Once Haley felt her cosmonauts were sufficiently oriented and instructed, she returned to the ship in the tender to pilot the 2nd shuttle and help Tish get everything to the surface. The biodome AI quantum computer could converse fluently with the settlers, provide operational instructions for all systems and units, alert them of any approaching system failure, workout equations, answer questions, and so forth. Haley had uploaded her interpreter services and used Winn's sweet voice for the computer. She'd loaded it with endearments, compliments, and expressions of delight like "catalyst," "awesome," "far-out," and "how wonderful!"

Speaking with the dome's quantum computer was not only quite pleasant but a real self-esteem booster and highly entertaining. It was only really a built-in desktop but could carry on 16 conversations simultaneously with more than 50 terabits supporting each one. The vast quantum databases were within separate equipment and contained well-over a billion construction and repair manuals and everything known to Om about each branch of engineering—all of them.

While unloading her shuttle on the surface, Haley erected the smart-textile bins that Bodhi would need to unload the materials he was mining into. She also supervised the cosmonauts in their effort to put together prefab sections to build a garage structure. The dome had exterior spot lights, and so did the shuttle, so they could see to build it. They also had to get machines and weather-sensitive equipment, gear, and supplies into the garage or under textile armor waterproof smart-tarps.

It was the middle of the night at the site, about 02:21 hours when everything was finally down on the ground from *Diamond Lotus*. Bodhi still wasn't back from mining yet. Haley was monitoring him and knew he was just finishing work. Tish had returned to the ship's hanger with her shuttle. Haley was about to head up herself when she noticed Bodhi was on his way back. She waited by his bins, and when he pulled the trailer around, she connected the dump-chute to the trailers unloading tube. The trailer had partitioned itself into five to keep the materials loaded into it separate. Haley moved her end of the chute to a new bin each time a partition was emptied. Bodhi didn't even have to get out of the mining craft, but he did to embrace Haley goodbye. She had to shut down her tear function integrated with her emotions, or she would have gotten Bodhi wet. They said their goodbyes, truly heartfelt, and Haley promised to be back in less than two days.

CHAPTER FIFTEEN

He watched her shuttle take off and kept watching until it became a tiny shrinking speck in the sky. When it disappeared, he felt a deep and powerful pang of loss. Pez had taken on much of his abandonment psychic-wound and pacified it, and she had taught him how to connect with the calling, with the divine love forever attracting us higher in ascent to the Absolute; one without a second. He made this contemplation opening his heart as she'd shown him. He was feeling the love as he entered the dome. There was no privacy within except for the two coffin-size showers and the four toilet closets.

Every one of the sixteen cosmonauts was each wholly engaged in conversation with the quantum computer, and Winn's voice was everywhere. One couple had figured out that they could get the computer to talk dirty to them and were having Winn's voice do this while they made love on a bottom berth. It somehow felt wrong, exploitive, perhaps even abusive of the quantum computer, and certainly of Winn's beautiful voice pronouncing such words sweetly. It annoyed him, so he went to a work station and brought up what was available on his holo, then selected Favio's voice converting endearments and complements into statements of the computer's self-importance. He deleted the statements of delight and programmed criteria and parameters for statements of critical observation. Satisfied with it, he hit restart through his skullcap. The voice of Winn vanished, relieving Bodhi's annoyance, and the computer went completely dead a moment before resurrecting in Favio's voice and with a few of his traits as well.

The love making couple lost their rhythm entirely with the very first critical observation delivered in Favio's voice. The 2nd one had them climbing out of the berth and getting dressed. Halfway through the third, they'd recalled how to shut it off on their particular connection and did so. Conversations with the computer were shutting down all over the dome. Bodhi realized he'd overdone it a little and restored to default all of Haley's program except that he left Favio's voice giving Winn's lines. The ladies in the dome seemed to appreciate this, and there was only a little bit of grumbling from the men.

One female cosmonaut found and put Favio's music holo-clip up on her holo and cranked up the volume. Once they had optics on his body and matched his voice to that of their quantum computer, the females were all-in and enthralled, chatting up Favio and receiving Winn-style endearments, compliments, and declarations of delight in Favio's voice. The big masculine wailing singer strumming the guitar in his Bullhorn men's bikini underwear and pumping out lively tunes created by Haley was a massive success with the cosmonauts. They had been in such intensive training since migration was announced that they had missed Favio's meteoric rise to global fame, but the women were catching up and making up for it now.

When some of them started dancing naked with Favio's holo, Bodhi decided to get his tent out of the mining vehicle and set it up to get some sleep. He'd heard one young woman call him a 'prude' on his way out of the dome. His deep abdominal breath and sharp concentration kept him one-pointed and out of the self-pity thoughts drifting by in his mind. Bodhi grabbed the cubical internal-frame tent from the cab of his craft and set it down on a grassy spot under a tree not 15 meters from the edge of the dome. He triggered the self-erecting mechanism and the cube distorted in folding and telescoping movements to become a pup-tent. He got his thermal bag, smart-foam mat and battery-lamp, and brought them into the tent to turn-in. He had a lot of mining to do.

About a quarter-hour after Bodhi snuggled into his thermal bag within the cold tent and was well into his dream meditations lying on his right side, a female cosmonaut crawled in his tent flap and resealed it. She turned toward him and said in the dark, "Do not worry. I seek no sexual favors, just instruction from you. My name is Sunoco. I study with the same teacher Tish studied with, and she sent me a text informing me of what a great master you are. Would you help me? Please?"

"Of course," Bodhi agreed, fumbling in the dark for his battery lamp. He found it and turned it on at its lowest power setting, dimly lighting the tent. He got his bed-pillow under his bottom, elevating it. He assumed his meditation posture while taking in the sight of her. Sunoco was about four inches shorter than Bodhi, more solidly built than Tish or Haley, and had very balanced features that were quite attractive. Her skin, hair, teeth, and muscle tone screamed health and vitality.

"Tell me what you are working on currently and having difficulty with," Bodhi directed.

Sunoco told him, "I am working the meditation upon the drop in the center of my heart, with retentions of breath at the top of inhalation and at the end of the exhalation."

"I see. Are you making the meditation deity embodiment successfully?"

"Not to completion, but my visualization is clear and complete," she answered.

"We will practice together, and I will pass you energy. On the retention of breath at the top of your inhale, experience the calm abiding of the quiescence of mind as you concentrate on your visualization. The real key is in the retention at the end of the exhale which is also the end of the internal sound-formula. In the silence, when breathing has stopped, you touch directly on the absolute emptiness. Relax, let go, and keep your concentration focused, alive, and supple. I'm going to touch my finger-tips lightly to your knee and pass you energy to heighten your experience of the practice. Let's begin."

Bodhi said aloud the textual heading for each meditation before they went into it and occasionally gave some of the confidential instructions and tips, generally reserved for students of highest attainment. He also gave her some personalized instruction based on his readings of her energy. When they got to the meditation Sunoco came for help with, they held the retentions of breath long, and Bodhi passed her energy while maintaining his state pristinely. They made three consecutive rounds of this meditation together before he led her through the final meditations. With these last, he recited all of the instructions in great detail for her. He had no gong or bell, so he concluded their sessions by calling for an act of self-remembrance, bowing to the divine while resonating a seed-sound internally.

They sat in silence for several minutes after that while Sunoco remained in the state of non-conceptualization, observing the suchness of her mind, and her body generated as the meditation deity unified as one. She finally scooted in and embraced Bodhi with an enormous smile and tears in her eyes. She told him, "I am forever indebted to you and could never repay what you have just given me. You are like a fusion reactor. I see why Tish is so devoted to you, so in love with you and so desperate to join with you in sexual union. You are amazing, Bodhi. I'm ever so grateful."

"I see you are in your first awakening Sunoco and have prepared yourself diligently for this. It is a great honor to share this super-mundane moment with you. I am always grateful and joyous when a student makes good use of the teachings I transmit. You inspire me and bring satisfaction to my life's work."

"Then let me follow you and become your disciple."

"What of your husband?"

"Brandon is not my husband. Our government paired us in training as breeding animals. I am not a fan of my government, but I do want to serve the survival of our race and the migration."

"I would have no objections except our ship's company is already unbalanced with an overabundance of females."

"I would be celibate to study with you, or you could bring Ilya, Sonya's mate, who meditates, and she can have Brandon."

"If the ship's community can be persuaded, then I'll gladly accept you, Sunoco."

"Thank you. I went through some files on the computer and realized the voice our computer started with is Winn's, whom you love romantically. It must have been hard for you with the use Anton and Katrina were putting Winn's voice to. I felt for you when I realized."

"Thank you. I was offended and went a little overboard in my first programming of Favio's voice response matrix. I think the females are pleased with the current program, and I know for sure that Favio won't mind."

"They're enthralled. He is truly a talented musician."

"He had nothing to do with the music holo-clip. Haley wrote the music and lyrics, generated Favio graphically, and with a bit of fine animation, and played the music electronically through the quantum computer. He didn't know it existed until it was dominating the charts, and fans were texting him."

"Haley is a legend already on Firmament. There has never been a greater celebrity or hero in all of its history. You love her too."

"I did not know myself capable of loving more than one woman romantically. I did not seek this situation for myself. It has arisen all the same, in part orchestrated by Haley selflessly. I am accepting my place within the complexity and now understand the continuous tool of ego-dissolution and transcendence the pattern has provided for each of us. I sense the harmony we must keep in equilibrium to abide in merit and not fall into negative consequences."

"Well, that all sounds fairly tame compared to the sex party going on in the dome right now. Katrina found a pair of sex androids in a male version and a female, and Favio's voice provided the operating instructions. Someone else found something called a lazy-boy simulation chair. They are all worked up in there."

"They probably need to blow off some steam after such intensive training. Now that Winn's voice is not involved, I have no problem with it."

"It's cold as the polar cap in this tent, and I'd be an ice cube if I weren't pressed against you in your lap. I'm going to fetch one of those portable heaters that Haley showed us and be right back. I want to be formally accepted as your disciple."

She was off his lap and out the tent in a streak, already out of range when Bodhi's complaint came out, "I have 14 hours of mining to start in just a few hours."

The girl was back with purpose in just moments and had a fusion battery-electric heater with a fan which she set to face both of them and turned on. The tent was small and thermally insulated, so the results were near-instant. She sat facing him with their knees just touching. Bodhi led them through vase breathing and calm abiding meditation, then made the equal with Sunoco, connecting soul to soul through eye contact united by the arc of love flowing between them and generating the state of contemplation beyond cognitive schematization.

Bodhi sensed her psychic wound and took it on to experience the utter depths of alienation, a painful social shyness woven of fear and stress, generating a basic mistrust or cynicism and sort of social phobia. He transmuted and pacified the roots of rejection, exclusion, and shame, expunging them from her psyche. Passing her energy the whole while, he now passed to her the blessing of the teacher. The arc of love surged as bare concentration exposed and united their souls in a state of blissful clarity upon void. Bodhi placed his palm on her chest over her heart energy center, and recited the consecration and the protections offering refuge. Then he cued her, and they recited the vows in call and response with Bodhi leading. One hundred and eight repetitions of the sacred sound-formula concluded the ritual. Bodhi closed his eyes, placing his hands in the meditation gesture, right over left with the tips of the thumbs touching, and Sunoco did the same.

Her first awakening seemed to have just gone through an awakening. There wasn't a thought in her head, and with her eyes closed, her mind was all glittering blue light in a vast openness of pure space all-knowing. Fundamental security supported her insight, which was intuitive and not conceptual or in words, and which she would later translate to schema for herself as, "My consciousness is beyond all interaction and nothing is mine." These were just words and not her insight, though having had direct experience of it with such stability and clarity, the words served as a catalyst for the intuition she knew.

They sat silently for almost an hour before Bodhi said, "I must sleep. I have much work to start in a short time."

"I'm not going back into that vibe in the dome. I promise not to touch you. I'll sleep in your thermal bag with you for warmth."

She was already straightening the foot of the bag and gently rearranging Bodhi, and she didn't look like she would be dissuaded easily, so Bodhi went along. She slipped in on her right side and spooned her back into him. He was simply a fountain of spiritual energy. She found that doing her dream work lying in contact with him made her winds enter her central channel forcefully, enhancing her work, and this produced exquisitely lucid dreams for her. He was deeply asleep before she slipped off, but the spiritual energies continued to radiate out from his body. She could not believe her great fortune. When she awoke in the morning, her teacher was already gone.

Sunoco entered the dome to find all her comrades still asleep. The place was trashed, and empty vodka bottles were under foot. She took a round-about route to the kitchen area to avoid the main concentration of the mess and started opening cabinets snooping about. She got out an omelet and pancakes ambassador ration and set it on the counter, having decided to get a shower in before the others arose to make a traffic jam. She saw Brandon sleeping in his berth and felt a wave of relief and pleasure over being done with him. They might have an ideal DNA match for highly intelligent and talented offspring, though she thought even a lower primate would be better than Brandon. At least *they* are natural.

She retrieved clean clothes and a towel before showering and emerged from the narrow rectangular box with bruised elbows and possibly some shampoo still in her hair. That last bang was on the edge of the soap dish and hit the vital point in her so-called "funny-bone," finding nothing in the least funny about it. Sunoco found that label to be sadomasochistic and sick. She was just getting over her annoyance with the term commensurate with the lessening pain in her elbow when Ilya came to the shower foyer with his towel in hand naked. All of the cosmonauts were exemplary physical specimens and well above average intelligence, but besides Sunoco, only Ilya was a meditation practitioner. Brandon was a pig! She liked Ilya. She told him, "Bodhi awakened me last night, showed me the final meditations, and accepted me as his disciple. He absorbed most of my sense of being on the outside, not trusting, and its origins in my sense of alienation and rejection from my siblings and the world when I was a small child. Then he passed me the blessing of the teacher. He is magnificent and incomparable."

"Did you have sex with him?"

"No. I did sleep beside him in his thermal bag, though, and I had the most lucid dreams ever."

"He let you in his thermal bag then didn't touch you?"

"No, he did not touch me and wore boxers and a t-shirt. He is a wellspring of enlightenment, even when sleeping. I was tempted sorely to touch him but did not."

"Do you want to shower with me?" Ilya asked, hopefully.

"There isn't enough room in those for even one, and I just had a shower, but thanks. Where's Sonya?"

"In Brandon's berth. They were quite the exhibitionists last night."

"I'm sorry. Are you alright?"

"It was anguish at first, but Servio was too drunk to perform, so Marta and I were partners."

"I'm glad. I know you have always found her extremely attractive."

"I find you extremely attractive, Sunoco, and have the most in common with you."

"Then see if Bodhi will accept you as his disciple and come with me on his ship."

"You have been invited into his ship's community?!!"

"The community must accept me. Bodhi already does. I would stand a better chance by bringing a male, since there are already seven females and only three males aboard."

"We watched some of Tandy's movie last night in super-HD holo. She is really something."

"Isn't she a porn star?"

"Well, it was a sex party."

"I'm going to clear the site for the cement-putty plant and facility today. I'll be taking the hover-tractor. If I'm finished in time, I'll haul those prefab sections over to where they'll be going up."

"I'll be setting up the prefab sawmill workshop today, then cutting some of those trees Bodhi felled, into beams and boards."

"Think about approaching Bodhi, Ilya. I like you and find you attractive. It is the opportunity of a lifetime to study with Bodhi."

"I'm going to when he gets back from mining."

Ilya got in a coffin-shower, and Sunoco went to retrieve her ambassador ration. The directions were strange indecipherable symbols, if those even were directions. She switched on Favio using the 'pocket-device' Haley issued her, thinking of it as her 'phone,' and asked, "How do I cook this?"

Favio's voice answered, "You look lovely today, Sunoco. I see you have an omelet and pancakes ambassador self-heating ration. Just pull the tab on the right-side completely out, and wait four seconds before unwrapping. Bon appétit."

Sunoco sat at the small table facing a workshop and storage compartment, away from all the mess. In her peripheral vision, she saw Brandon and Sonya get out of their berth and head naked for the shower. She hoped they were not planning to take one together. A few minutes later, she heard Sonya scream, "Ouch!" Sunoco's vital point in her elbow throbbed in sympathy with Sonya. The omelet tasted like it had just come off the stove, and the pancakes brought new meaning to the word 'pancakes,' now inextricably associated with connotations of gustatory ecstasy. She hoped there were a lot of these stowed away in the dome.

CHAPTER SIXTEEN

Haley and Tish flew *Diamond Lotus* into low orbit over the settlement. While back at Old Firmament, June had led a women's rebellion, and the girls had forced Haley to hire another male crew member. They'd researched and run searches through previously rejected applicants until they found the perfect man whom they could all agree on. His selfie had been examined exhaustively by each of them in a life-size holo that had been up for hours. He stood six-foot one-inch tall, weighed in at 192 pounds—not an ounce of it was fat—and had a washboard narrow waist with great broad shoulders. His skin was beautiful dark ebony and even though he was flaccid in his selfie, the girls all agreed with experienced certainty that he would be at least as big as Favio. His name was Shamus, and he was a picture of vim and vigor robust health, as hale as they come. Before getting recruited by the girls, Shamus had been a celebrity late-night wrestling champion. He was a weight-lifter, a hockey jock, and had been trying to break into the movie industry as a fight choreographer but was yet unsuccessful at this.

The girls had been scheming elaborate designs to lure him in when Haley had just contacted him by coms to offer him a job, and he took it immediately sure it was his best career move. Now he was intimately part of the crew, weaving his way all over the pattern, and held the title on the ship of "Cargo Chief." Favio was furious and felt threatened, but Pam and June pumped him up so he could get his ego back on the pedestal. Shamus made Sonic feel like one of the little people from the children's stories. Winn knew Shamus, like Favio, was way too big to fit in her, and though such a pity, she accepted him as a crew member and brother, and as one of her close community.

The mixer-trailer mounted to the hull of *Diamond Lotus* required a space-walk on Haley's part to get detached and floating freely. Tish grabbed it with the tractor beam from the bridge when Haley liberated it into space in her hard-shell maintenance space suit with propulsion. Haley got a portable mini-landing platform attached beneath the mixer-trailer, and a textile armor parachute system secured to its top.

Haley said to Tish, "Power off the tractor beam," then, she hit her suit thrusters pushing the gargantuan mixer-trailer towards the upper reaches of the atmosphere. It moved very slowly as if space were made of honey but picked up some momentum as she went along pushing. Velocity jumped to a new pace at the transition zone, and she stopped there since it was going to need slowing down now and not pushing. She returned to the ship to similarly liberate some large prefab building sections from the outer hull. She had not been as sure about the security of the mounts for these having made them impromptu in a hurry and was pleased to see that they'd held. The five stacked sections would need to be lowered individually by shuttle. The landing-platform the mixer-trailer was going down on would have to be refueled before it could be used again.

Haley returned to the airlock, and went through to the hangar, fetching a shuttle. Once inside the shuttle, she got out of her hard-shell space suit and helmet before taking the pilot seat in the cockpit. There were two cargo holds full of stuff for the surface and a large piece of machinery that had only just fit in the hangar. Haley planned to do the towing and lowering to the surface of the five prefab sections and the large piece of machinery, then let Tish shuttle the rest down. She had checked on Bodhi and knew he was out mining. She'd given him and the sixteen cosmonauts a heads up about the mixer-trailer raining down from the sky. She'd checked wind conditions and was aiming for a place 1.3 miles from the dome, but with planetary wind variables through the height of the entire atmosphere one could never be entirely certain of these things.

Shamus was a tremendous help as Cargo Chief, being practically a heavy lifting machine himself, and having already learned how to operate the lifting suit. He also took his job very seriously. He wanted nothing but good ratings from his superior officers on the ship and his fans on Firmament. His agent had assured him that he was going to become globally famous and command seven figures for endorsements of products. The girls were all beautiful, if not a bit short and skinny, but Uldra had breasts just the way he liked them. The perks were an attractive part of the deal, and that Tandy could do things he'd never heard of before. He was certain the serious one could see right through him into his subconscious, about which he knew nothing, and it had creeped him out a little at first. She *was* kind and exceptionally skilled at *everything* it looked like, including in bed.

Haley and Tish got everything down to the surface. The new shuttle landing site had a concrete pad and an articulated telescoping crane arm with a dozen grip options covering the portability of any article of cargo. Using the hover-tractor, Sunoco hauled equipment, machines, gear, prefab sections, and supplies over to the dome or to the manufacturing site she'd cleared. The others carried smaller stuff on hand-truck hovers. From beginning to end, getting everything down to the surface and stowed away took only a little over six hours with everyone's help. All except Bodhi, who was out mining. The hour at the site was approaching 10 PM. Some of their work had been accomplished by flood and spot light. *Diamond Lotus's* crew retired to the ship, except for Tish, who was going to wait for Bodhi. Waiting for Bodhi had become something of a theme in her life of late.

Sunoco had never met Tish but knew all about her, and they had communicated by text. They'd studied under the same meditation master. Hoping that they would be again, under Bodhi, she introduced herself, "My name is Sunoco. I greatly admire you as our national champion."

"I'm Tish. I read your file. We both practice the same method and had the same teacher. It's nice to meet you, Sunoco."

"I was awakened in meditation with Bodhi, and he has accepted me as one of his disciples."

"He better not have been your action seal," Tish said, feeling jealous.

"No. He didn't touch me, accept my heart in the ritual, and his electric fingertips barely in contact with my knee. He was sound asleep not a moment after I spooned into him, and gone when I woke up."

This struck Tish as both good and bad news. Still feeling a little possessive and threatened, Tish asked, "He let you in his bed?"

"In his thermal bag, actually, within the tent. You see, there was a sex party raging in the dome, and my state could not tolerate that. Besides, I didn't ask and got in very quickly."

"Naked?"

"I kept my panties on."

"With those bare and free?" Tish demanded, referring to her ample breasts.

"They were pointed away, and no part of him touched them," Sunoco defended herself.

"He promised he would be with me tonight."

"I couldn't be more envious, Tish, but I must warn you, he's sleep-deprived. I kept him up the first night, then he was up half the night meditating with Ilya last night."

"You're coming with us?"

"We both want to—me desperately, but it depends on the community."

"Are you bisexual?"

"I've only ever been inclined to have sex with males."

"Pity. You're so cute. I'll still vote for your inclusion and speak out in your favor. If Bodhi made you his disciple, then he wants you along, and I totally support Bodhi."

"Thank you, Tish. Getting accepted into the ship's community is the most important thing in my life. Bodhi is incomparable and unbelievable. I know he is in love with you, and with Haley and Winn. I only want to be his student. I promise I will not try to seduce him."

"It is a great comfort to have a countryman to speak with, and I enjoy looking at you," Tish confided.

"You have been a hero of mine for years, Tish. When you brought home three gold medallions from the internationals last year, you became every teen girl and young woman's idol."

I know how very few are accepted into the cosmonaut program, Sunoco, and the attrition rate during training. Only the very top sixteen were selected for this mission. You must be a most exceptional person. I want to be friends and will help you get into our community."

"You are amazing. I see why Bodhi is in love with you. Do you want to meet Ilya? Bodhi accepted him too, though he has not had insight. He came very close with Bodhi, touching upon the cusp, Bodhi says, but will need more practice."

"Sure. I've never met a cosmonaut who wasn't cute. All of you are walking definitions of fitness."

They entered the dome, and Sunoco steered them over to Ilya. He recognized Tish and said admiringly, "Our nation's pride and joy. I'm so honored to see you again."

He'd had brief introductions to all ship's personnel when Haley had first shuttled him up from Firmament. Tish thought he was cute, so she embraced him warmly, kind of checking him out. She noticed Favio's voice everywhere, but the content and delivery were unlike him. His holo in his bullhorns was not an uncommon sight within the dome either. She'd also noticed the two sex-androids shut down in front of the steam-clean sterilizer tube and not tucked away in their closet. With no privacy within the dome, she could see why Bodhi and Sunoco sought refuge in a tent. Something more drastic than earplugs had obviously been required.

Bodhi got back from mining late and returned to *Diamond Lotus* in the shuttle with Tish. He kept every promise he'd made to her that night and then some. One part of the community pattern was complete and stable while the larger part was still changing and about to be invaded by two new strands weaving about.

Bodhi and Tish spoke out for Sunoco and Ilya joining the crew, then Winn, Haley, and Sonic joined their voices to this cause, and in the end, their numbers grew to thirteen by the time they departed

New Firmament to jump back to Firmament. They had stayed to assemble the structure for the cement-putty manufacturing and to get the first seven giant machines inside and mounted. The fruits of Bodhi's mining had been transferred to sheet-metal vats they'd assembled within the plant. The big mixer-trailer also manufactured the cement-putty from raw materials on a much smaller scale. It would take four more trips here to get the cement factory up and running. While housing was certainly an important factor in the migration, the two massive colossal star gates which needed to be constructed in space about one and a half light-minutes from each planet constituted the kingpin and single most important tool for the migration. Star gates were about the most monumental task a civilization could take on.

Back in Firmament, Bodhi and Haley hauled prefab sections of a gate construction-platform off the surface into space while Tish used the tractor beam and the longer crane arm on *Diamond Lotus* from the bridge to assemble the pieces. Employing the articulated mini-tool arms, she carefully applied the adhesive and made the welds for each piece, constructing the platform. The process took four days for the basic platform and another week to mount the specialized cranes, tool-arms, machines, cargo-lifts, and so forth. An additional week was needed to seal off and prepare living quarters with plumbing, biotrays, HVAC, wiring, water tanks, fusion battery systems, kitchen, and all that would be needed. A materials warehouse was assembled on the gate-building-platform while the living quarters were being done. It had a ship dock, hanger, and shuttle-port.

Winn began her pilot training, and Tish was now towing things to orbit and lowering things to the surface. Weekly runs were made to New Firmament with all they could cram into cargo holds and attach securely to their hull. Both Winn and Tish discovered that they were pregnant. Pam was pregnant, and Sunoco got pregnant too. Haley was spending much time on the surface, helping the Firmamentlings workout the retooling of more factories, and to pressure the production of vortex redirect and generation turbines and space drives. More shuttles were needed.

Bodhi had to teach a three-week course at the Grand International Hotel on the basic science of space drives, consisting largely of advanced electromagnetic propulsion and the engineering of the drives themselves. They contained a super-spinning sphere with molten core and a multi-layered flute of directional conductors concentrating and narrowing the focus of the force. Each pulse was like an explosion of considerable magnitude, and the pulse frequency could rise to dozens per second. All force is channeled out the drive exhausts. No fuel other than the reactor's fusion material is required.

Winn stayed with Bodhi at the Hotel, taking care of him when he wasn't lecturing and attended all of his classes. She made sure he had his data beads, laser pointer, holo pedestal, and everything else he would need for his presentations. They had an audience of 1250 people picked by Haley, and Winn just didn't know where she'd found the time to do it. It had taken Haley seventeen seconds to make the selections *and* send out the invitations.

As soon as the course at the hotel ended Bodhi had to suck it up, like he had his fear of public speaking, and do some serious gas-mining. Tish was going through fuel dragging stuff up into space. Their big towed-transport was coming together with the hull nearly completed. Sections of quantum star gates were being manufactured at some factories on the surface. Firmament's workforce was fully employed and showing fantastic morale and productivity. Distribution of goods around the globe had become far more equitable, and things were improving weekly. Pockets of corruption were still being discovered and corrected. Now that whistle-blowers were heroes, and no longer traitor-terrorist-mother-rapists, and in some instances rewarded for their efforts instead of hunted down and shot in the head, far more abuses were being reported and called out.

The cement-putty manufacturing plant and facilities on New Firmament went fully operational, and dozens of houses were poured. Timber frame and board buildings had also been constructed as warehouses, barns, poultry coups, mangers, and stables. A sewer plant was under construction. Water wells and pumps fed water towers, and the reactor housing was under construction. Two more cosmonauts had been brought in by *Diamond Lotus,* so there were still only 16 human-residents on New Firmament. That would change radically once the towed transport was finished and ready. A small delay had been required so they could design and affix mounts on the exterior hull of the transport for hauling quantum star-gate sections through jumps.

A small space platform was already in orbit of New Firmament as the core of a larger platform planned. This would get towed out to where the gate was to be constructed once the platform was fully assembled and had functional living quarters. Another small space platform orbiting New Firmament was the beginning of that planet's first space station for unloading cargo and passengers to be taken the rest of the way by shuttle.

An iron-ore mine had been opened on New Firmament and was being worked daily. An entire factory sat disassembled in stacked prefab sections and pieces beneath a giant smart-tarp. Stakes and string marked measured rooms and buildings laid out in spaces cleared and leveled. More house pouring rigs and mixer-trailers were being manufactured on Firmament and would soon be getting transported to New Firmament. The methane gas well and infrastructure were in place and trunk lines being laid. Four large industrial windmill tower frames were erected with their turbines sitting beside them in huge wooden crates with steel bands. The roofs of the finished houses were solar-paneled. Bulldozer-backhoes, jaw-tooth power diggers, mega-dump trucks, cranes and other construction vehicles were accumulating and being put to work on the surface. The foundations had been laid for a major chemical manufacturing plant and had prefab building sections and large machines already set upon them. New workshops had sprung up in timber-frame and prefab structures. Twelve newly poured houses appeared daily, expanding the neighborhood.

Once sufficient housing was available, the second wave landed consisting of 80 men and women of the Army Corps of Engineers from a dozen different industrialized nations. The pace was increasing once more shuttles had been built on Firmament. Some of the shuttles were brought by *Diamond Lotus* to New Firmament, and things started rolling. Bodhi had to run a small-craft pilot certification course, first on Firmament and then on New Firmament. Winn's pregnancy was showing by the time she was awarded her small-craft certification and license. You could tell Tish was pregnant too. June and pregnant Pam, Sunoco, and Ilya were all in pilot training, and Tish was working on getting her ship piloting license having been the first among the crew to attain her small-craft license.

A wave of 300 civilian heavy machine operators, construction workers, engineers, technicians, manufacturing experts, a medical team, and some folks trained directly by Haley on specific tasks quadrupled the population of New Firmament jumping its productivity more than 500%. Once the space station and its living quarters were constructed, the cosmonauts moved up to it. All sixteen were in pilot training. Haley was using the finished hull of the towed-transport as a cargo transport to haul giant machinery and sections of buildings with quantum star gate sections mounted to the hull, giving *Diamond Lotus* quite a workout.

A few weeks later in the solar system of Firmament, the star-gate building platform was in place about a third of the way to the 4th planet's orbit and manned with cosmonauts, yu hangyaun, astronauts, and a dozen other names in a dozen other languages for people who are exceptionally fit and trained to go into space. A section of the colossal quantum star gate was already assembled, dwarfing the enormous platform. Materials and prefabricated parts and sections arrived continuously in intervals of 2-3 hours, and shifts worked around the clock.

By the time the towed-transport was finished on the inside with 2400 seats fastened to the upper deck and loaded with its first flight of passengers, there were two dozen house pouring rigs pouring 288 houses per day, and more than enough finished houses for several transport loads of people. A new rig would be brought with every load of passengers. Timber-frame houses were going up, and a brick manufacturing facility was nearing completion. A small stone quarry was operating too. High-quality clay was now trucked into the community, and composites were on hand for manufacturing roof tiles, larger sewer pipes, floor tiles, and other construction components. Much of the hardware, door and window frames, poly-carbon glass, flooring, and other things needed to finish the interiors of the poured houses were made right on New Firmament, and expansion of manufacturing capacity was a major focus.

The first group brought on the transport was composed of people with particular expertise and skills and included more medical teams. So far, there had been no industrial accidents on the space construction platforms or in space, though there had been several on the ground on New Firmament, and many on Firmament. Bodhi asked Haley to look into this, and she instituted some safety regulations and sped the production of heavy-lift hovers and other construction vehicles of Om's designs and technologies, which would make many of the most dangerous tasks completely safe.

When the first fusion reactor became operational on New Firmament, Bodhi moved the biodome 818 miles to a new location with rich copper deposits and fertile farm lands. A new settlement was begun with reactor site, sewer system, methane well and infrastructure, cement-putty manufacturing plant, and workshops of all kinds. Essential personnel was moved into quickly assembled prefab houses.

Once *Diamond Lotus* had made its 100th trip to New Firmament, there was enough machinery on the planet to make resource collection far cheaper than on Firmament. In the new world, none of the low hanging fruit, easy to reach, had been picked. There were enormous deposits of metals close to the surface, and in one place to the magnetic south of them, there was an entire lake of sweet light crude oil on top of the ground.

The quantum star-gate construction platform with cranes and construction machinery, warehouse and living quarters was about a light minute and a half out from New Firmament, assembling the sections already hauled so far, and new parts, components, and pieces arrived with each new trip *Diamond Lotus* made. A factory was under construction to manufacture sections of the star-gate right on New Firmament.

Ilya had insight and was making great spiritual progress. Not long afterwards, Tandy had her first awakening. Shamus started learning martial arts from Tish, then from Bodhi, and this led to an interest in both energy generation exercises and meditation. Favio was plodding along, sometimes touching the cusp when he sat beside Bodhi, receiving the energy he passed him. Winn was making the completion stage of inner heat having accomplished the stage of generation, and her sitting and absorption was always pristine contemplation of the invisible witness that has no place to hide.

Poultry and livestock were brought with every load of passengers. Fish net paddle wheels brought in fish by the thousands daily. Farm fields were cleared and cultivated, fertilized, and irrigated. Orchards were planted, pastures cleared, cultivated and fenced, and large gardens of raised beds and rich topsoil were constructed. For the winter season, heated triple-pane glass green houses were built and barns with hydroponic stacks and grow lights. The woods around them offered an abundance of berries, walnuts, chestnuts, acorns, cherries, apples, mushrooms, herbs, greens, and roots. Food supplies continued to arrive from Firmament with each new load of passengers.

Haley told Bodhi, "These gates are going to take forever if we use just marsnium and saturnium. The materials and labor involved and the subsequent size of the gate tube-ring structures are too enormous. One solarium reactor is equal to 100,000 marsnium ones."

"So you suggest we build some solarium reactors for them to power their star-gates?"

"We have already prospected the ends of the galactic tentacles and know where to mine the solarium. We can refine it aboard *Diamond Lotus,* and the reactors themselves can be constructed at several engineering universities on the surface under my supervision."

"Alright. It will certainly save a lot of time, resources, and hard work."

"Firmament has some mining spacecraft now, and I'll show them where to mine mercurium. With 100 solarium reactors, 3,500 mercurium reactors, and 10,000 saturnium reactors, we will have 51.68 petawatts; 50 petawatts for the star-gate and 1.68 petawatts for force-field shields and living quarters."

"Then the gate's tube circumference can be much narrower, saving millions of tons of materials. The four-mile diameter of the space within the gate must remain constant."

"I've got the new gate design completed, and I'm sending it to all parties involved in manufacturing hull and component pieces for it."

"You need to speak with the League of Nations about stepping up production of those carbon capture giant air scrubbers. The carbon levels in the atmosphere remain high, and we need carbon to manufacture carbon plate armor. They owe it to Firmament to reverse as much of the damage as they are able."

"I will also need to share with the Firmamentlings the recycling of plastics into useful household items and nonpolluting dissolution of non-recycle plastics into tinctures condensed and easy to launch into the sun."

"I saw some islands of plastic in their oceans that were bigger than many of their counties. That's a great idea, Haley. I do love you so much."

"Your love inspires my service and efforts my most cherished beloved."

"Those Firmament folks have so many super-bacteria immune to antibiotics that their hospitals are mostly contaminated. Do you think you could transfer to them the science of employing viruses that target specific bacteria?"

"I can and I will, along with the entire correlations of viruses to bacteria. It's a good thing they have quantum computers now because the data I'm sending is well over 900 terabits, and their old computers simply didn't have the capacity."

"I saw some clean fusion battery-electric jet planes in the sky yesterday."

"They are using them to cross the oceans, but on the continents, I'm having them build mag.-lev. Railroads to the specifications I gave them. Electromagnetic rail is more energy-efficient and practical. They can put the fusion reactor in the train engine, and fusion trickle-charge battery-systems in the rail cars, so that the tracks will not be live electrical conductors putting wildlife at risk."

"How fast are those?"

"The express trains that don't make stops along the way travel at 530 MPH. The locals get up to 250 MPH between stops. Ever since the corporations crashed and the fast-food industry went out of business, the planetary workforce is either employed assisting the migration or building green infrastructure and involved in agriculture and reforestation."

"Now food is being shipped from New Firmament to Firmament."

"And a good thing too," Haley agreed. "I've been working with some college students for a while now, and we almost have a robotic assembly line completed for the manufacture of molecular food synthesizers."

"Those will certainly tackle hunger and starvation problems. So will the bug farms you taught them how to establish. They have thousands of bug farms now."

"And no corn is turned into ETOH. Most importantly, they practice intensive organic farming with nearly a quarter of their population involved in agriculture. Composting, worm farms, and potent natural fertilizers, increase productivity."

"It's amazing what an entire world's humanity is capable of accomplishing when it has unity and shared purpose." Bodhi agreed.

"We have reduced carbon emissions by 92% since arriving, and methane leaks by 97%. Most of the old spent fission material from the planet is either on the way to the sun or already there. The satellite shield-generators they've got orbiting so far have reduced ultra-violet radiation by more than 9%, and a dozen more are launched into space daily. The smaller carbon capture scrubbers they've built thus far have reduced the carbon in the atmosphere by a few dozen tons, and I'll be sure to push them on increasing production and starting an assembly line for the great big flying ones."

"What else can be done to reduce the carbon levels?"

Haley informed him, "They still have 433 parts per million of carbon in their atmosphere. That's like 42 billion tons. The 'carbon farming' we have them doing traps carbon in the soil where it's needed. Multi-culture ground cover works best."

"They stopped using those NPK synthetic fertilizers, and they stopped all mono-farming."

"The major carbon capture has to be through the soil. Photosynthesis is nature's method of carbon capture, and it can be enhanced. The chemical formula is quite simple: $6CO_2 + 6H_2O = 6C_6H_{12}O_6$ (basic sugar) $+ 6O_2$. About 20 to 40% of the carbon absorbed by a plant is emitted through its root system into the soil as liquid carbon in the form of sugars. Soil microbes eat sugar. The micro-organisms stabilize the carbon in the soil and produce nutrients for plants. Once healthy and mature, the process improves the soil without the need for fertilizers.

"After the centuries of abuse of their soil, they need natural fertilizers now."

"Buffalo and horses used to roam the plains of the temperate zone and their urine, manure, and saliva enriched the soil. The herbicides, pesticides, synthetic fertilizers, deep plowing, and monocrop farming destroyed the microbe ecosystems, and without the microbes, you are left with dirt."

"Didn't you give them a formula for a microbe growing fertilizer spray?"

"I did, and many countries are using it. The ingredients are the product of worm farming called 'vermicast'—worm dung from worms feeding on specific composts—mixed with water, molasses, and fish emollients. It's unbelievably potent, and rich soil with multi-culture ground cover captures more carbon than you'd imagine."

"There is still much to do. With your idea of mixing solarium and mercurium reactors in with just saturnium and not marsnium reactors, it will save unbelievable time and effort."

"Another thing we must add to our list of things to do is catching some bees on a yellow sun 3rd planet and setting them loose on Firmament. I think if we get enough UV blocking satellites up there and enough carbon scrubbers operating as well as significantly reducing the human population, this planet could go into recovery."

"I've heard they managed to reduce the birth rate on the planet by more than 41%, and the intention is to keep it dropping monthly. There's much hype about it in their media."

Haley noted, "With daily trips for six more months, we'll have gotten a quarter million off Firmament onto New Firmament."

"From this point, the migration will just keep accelerating. The gates will constitute a great leap in progress, and so will the addition of a fleet of transports that they could achieve within a decade."

"They will have more time now that they have broken their addiction to fossil fuels because the biosphere will surely survive longer without new carbon emissions, and with more and more of those satellite generators going into orbit."

Your water filtration-purification system is getting disseminated widely and is working great, already reducing poisons, toxins, and carcinogens in their fresh water supply. Your desalinization plants are keeping farming going in a great many regions of the globe."

"The toxin and poison absorbing weeds they are now using to make ethanol are reducing the soil and ground contamination caused by that sick suicidal defoliant. These things will take many decades but are making a significant difference overall."

"They are also switching to fusion battery-electric cars, buses, trucks, planes, jets and boats. Fusion reactor ships are being built now on their dry docks. Electro-magnetic railroads are being built in more than 100 countries. Every polluting factory and plant has been shut down or will be soon."

"If they follow through with these numerous projects and directions as rapidly as they have so far, their mother planet might stand a chance at recovery—especially if they get off of her. A small care taker service corps can collect the carbon from the scrubbers, monitor the satellites, continue planting trees, change the big filters in key fresh waterways, and continue harvesting and processing the toxin absorbing weeds."

"Hopefully, those giant islands of plastic will be recycled or reduced to tincture by then," Bodhi stated his concern.

"I know. There is plastic in their water, seafood, and other food. It just breaks down and does not recycle in nature. I promise to address this with them right away and provide the science and technology for the solutions."

"You are a force of the cosmic good, Haley, and I'm forever grateful to have you in my life."

"I'm ecstatic being in your life, my husband and teacher."

"These are awesome responsibilities which I take most seriously. I promise to give you more of my focus and spend more time in meditation with you. Pez shared some practices with me that really helped Mel, and I would teach you these if Mel has not already."

"Now that you are working formally with me as my teacher, I progress as fast as I did with Sarhi, Mel, and Amazonia. You have already done so much for me."

"As you have for me. There is far more I will do with you as your teacher, and so much I shall share with you as husband and wife."

"You've come a long way in your social and sexual relations, my love, and you no longer have an android prejudice."

"I love you, Haley."

CHAPTER SEVENTEEN

With the coastal cities now growing out of the sea, the Firmamentlings had much steel to salvage, including structural girders, bridges now to nowhere, submerged vehicles, useless behemoth cranes poking out of the water and no place to unload to, and fleets of mothball ocean warships with no function. A call was put out to all peoples of Firmament to donate any steel, nickel, titanium, iron, copper, and aluminum to the migration efforts and big electric trucks made routes through neighborhoods to pick it all up. Iron ore mining was stepped up with Haley's assistance, telling them where to locate the biggest deposits on both Firmament and New Firmament.

Carbon sequester by the mobile air scrubbers was rising steadily as units came off the assembly lines and became operational. Soil sequester of carbon had doubled since the microbe generating spray was in use in most countries. Every vital factory and manufacturing plant worked around the clock in three shifts. The severe weather conditions on the planet were no longer in fibrillation though still offered some pretty severe storms. It had been escalating when they'd arrived but had plateaued and was slowly reducing in magnitude.

Fusion electric hovercraft and wheeled vehicles were rolling out of factories in 99 countries 24/7, and 137 countries were in the process of constructing electric vehicle plants. The lawful expiration date on combustion engines was moved way closer. There was no longer a deasil electrical turbine operating anywhere on the planet, and over 49% of all ground vehicles and transportation were now electric.

Unnaturally decomposing islands of plastic hundreds of miles across had been turned into fleece, synthetic rubber tires, plasteel, crates, barrels, bins, and much more, or reduced to tincture and collected in 55-gallon steel drums to launch for the sun. Mountains of plastic covering many thousands of acres on land were similarly recycled or disposed of. Laws against plastics that cannot be recycled were passed swiftly in every country on Firmament. Satellites with UV-blocking generators were going into orbit 36 per day. Every eleven hours, five thousand sapling trees were planted with drip or irrigation systems.

Farming on Firmament was helped enormously by Haley's desalinization plants pumping water inland for irrigation, and by natural fertilizers, worm farms, the global composting program, multi-crop farming, hydroponic stacks barns, greenhouses and the microbe generating spray. Bug farms had popped up all over the place. There was a Haley molecular food synthesizer on nearly every kitchen counter on Firmament.

No one any longer died from antibiotic-resistant bacteria. Other new treatments Bodhi and Haley introduced and numerous miraculous seeming medicines were having great success as well. Hospitals were no longer contaminated with deadly bacteria. Stress was no longer killing people now that they self-directed their efforts towards a shared common cause they believed in and had the resources not to starve. Children could be heard laughing once again.

The Haley water filtration system provided for safe clean water to homes with the filter, and industrial-sized ones now serviced main water lines, reservoirs, major rivers, and fresh waterways. Ethanol production with the toxin absorbing plants was cleaning up the soil, and the fuel was replacing natural gas for furnaces, hot water heaters, stoves-ovens, laundry dryers, faux fireplaces, and many more appliances. Cleanup efforts of all kinds were well underway. Haley also shared technology for garbage management and processing that was beginning to catch on. She'd given them highly advanced sewage processing and sustainable waste disposal through molecular recycling or capture to launch into the sun.

Now that Firmament was producing saturnium reactors, their collective nonpolluting power grids far surpassed their previous levels of electrical generation when coal, diesel, and nuclear fission were involved. Hardly a baby was born on the whole planet the past month. These Firmamentlings had certainly come together in their goal to migrate *everyone*, which required them to bring their numbers down. Contraceptives were everywhere and free, and the Haley birth control pill was entirely safe and 100% effective. Her pharmaceutical lines were bringing her in a fortune to fund her massive philanthropy. A major religious institution on Firmament declared Haley a Saint.

Bodhi inquired, "Have you finished all the details of the design of the star-gate?"

Haley explained, "I have, and it will be a very skinny donut with a diameter of 160 feet and circumference of 490 feet. The gate as a whole will have a diameter of four miles and a circumference of twelve and a half miles. Instead of trying to build and launch into space a million and a quarter marsnium super-reactors, we'll use 13,600 reactors employing solarium, mercurium, and saturnium. Each gate will have 100 solarium reactors, so we will be doing some mining out at the ends of the spiral arms for solarium, and we'll be building reactors in coordination with some universities.

"That's a hell of a project!"

"You will do the mining, and I'll build the reactors."

"I don't mind mining solarium," Bodhi told her. "Will I be mining saturnium as well?"

"You will be mining 40 tons of mercurium and a ton of solarium. The Firmamentlings are mining the saturnium, and Tish is now proficient in mineral mining and will help them."

"So instead of a million and a quarter marsnium reactors, you've got it down to 13,600 reactors of higher magnitudes. That will save us from having to produce many millions of tons of materials and save us from thousands of space launches, not to mention the thousands of hours of gas mining."

"We have to produce the Unity Magnitude Synergizer Conductor Unit, which will amplify the 50 petawatts by the power of ten to produce 500 petawatts."

"Those only work for star-gates. No one has ever been able to make one that would work for shields, drives, or weapons systems."

"That's because the Synergizer Conductor only functions in conjunction with the quantum potential, and those other uses besides for star-gates are purely material in nature."

Five hundred petawatts is a tremendous amount of force."

"The entire space fleet of the former Royal Monarch Empire only contained collectively about 700 petawatts," Haley put it in perspective.

"Why are we bothering with 10,000 saturnium reactors? That's going to take a lot of thruster fuel to get them all into space."

"They are already producing them and have mined much of the fusion fuel. They will be shifting to mining mercurium in about a month. Firmament now has a few pilots who can manage gas mining. Before long, they will do all the gas mining and supply our thruster fuel."

"Two star-gates is still one heck of a job."

"Survival is quite a motivator."

"They are rising to the occasion," Bodhi admitted. "We need to get them mining adamantine as well. How thick is the adamantine armor layer?"

"Ideally four inches so they will need to start mining it. The fiberglass armor they can produce—which I have enhanced to the limit of their capacities—will need to be three inches thick. I have provided them with a manufacturing process that is more efficient and less costly."

"The composite ceramic heat-shield armor will be the thickest layer?" Bodhi asked.

"Yes. It will be 36 inches. The plasteel will be the second thickest layer at nine inches."

"I see that the skin of the hull over the adamantine framing is eight inches of steel-titanium-nickel."

"That's right. The armor will also include 1.25 inches of carbon plate armor. The thing the Firmamentlings are complaining about is the two-inch layer of gold-titanium alloy."

"They have the resources, though much of the gold is still in the hands of egoists unaligned with the common good."

"That will just have to change," Haley insisted, "because I won't budge on the two-inch layer of alloy."

"What else are we layering the armor with?"

Haley explained, "We will be applying 8-inches of space super-cement, four-inches of compressed textile armor and a two-inch layer of solidium-carbon plate alloy. Close to the hull is a six-inch layer of poly-carbon. Theirs could only withstand about 20,000 pounds per square inch of pressure, but I gave them the manufacturing process for some with nearly twice that strength, and they are making it for the star-gate."

"They won't be able to mine solarium to replace in their reactors until they have quantum coms and quantum jumping without gates."

"We will have to return and bring them that. The fuel is good for 128 years and the mercurium for 96. Their marsnium reactors will require new fuel in 40 years. They will be able to mine all but the solarium for themselves before long."

"Wherever we end up, we will need to stay in touch with them, and our descendants will have to periodically bring refined solarium to New Firmament."

Haley mentioned, "June is showing far more potential as a pilot than her initial aptitude tests indicated."

"She's intuitive and likes to do things on the edge of capacities and tolerances. She will become our best small-craft pilot. We certainly scored on talent with our crew hires."

"We scored on romance and sex too," Haley enthused.

"Your manipulative exploits have resulted in great happiness for me, Haley. Say, why are gates supposedly only safely disposed of within black holes?"

"The quantum potential linked force of 500 petawatts in a continuous circuit within the 'donut hole' of the star-gate has the additional property of magnification of force if disrupted, and the resultant explosion would contain a force of 500 exawatts. That is five million terawatts or five billion gigawatts. The big hydroelectric dams generate about two gigawatts continuously."

"Such a force dispersing from one and a half light minutes out could destroy Firmament's atmosphere."

"That is why I increased the power to the force field shields to 10 solarium super-reactors for each star-gate. Anyone with a weapon potent enough to pierce those shields would know that it is suicidal to blow up a star-gate even from Class 11 blaster range."

Bodhi said soberly, "Gates can be detected from great distances so we will need to come to Firmament's and New Firmament's defense if they are threatened."

"I've made a design to add two solarium fusion super-reactors and two additional fusion trickle-charge battery systems to *Diamond Lotus*. We can bring her shields up to top military-grade and upgrade the blaster cannons."

"We might as well while we're engaged in manufacturing reactors and battery systems."

Bodhi became a father, and Winn painfully a mother. They named their daughter Shanti, and Winn and Shanti moved into Bodhi's suite on the ship while he was at work when Shanti was two days old. Bodhi made no protest, and this just became the arrangement. Two weeks later, Tish gave birth to Bodhi's daughter. They named her Artana—or Tish did really—and she moved into Bodhi's suite with their daughter while he was at work. This new arrangement stuck, with protest from neither Winn nor Bodhi. The master suite bed was plenty big enough, and hover cribs had been Haley's gift to each mother at their baby showers. They usually made Bodhi sleep in the middle and gave him no room at all to either side. He was adjusting. When Haley wasn't on the surface consulting, training, and educating, she slept in Bodhi's bed too. This freed three cabins on the ship and kind of brought the family together quite closely physically. Both babies liked to wake up screaming in the middle of the night to then get nursed. Bodhi was stretching, bending, and adjusting.

Pam gave birth to Alexander, whose father was Favio, then Sunoco gave birth to Ilya's son, Nicholai. Then Uldra had Sieve who was Shamas's son, and did not long remain Sieve, since Shamas renamed him, William. Everyone was surprised when June's baby, Henry, turned out to be Sonic's and not Shamas' or Favio's. They were all surprised, and even shocked when Tandy's baby girl Cheryl turned out to be Sonic's too. Haley ran the DNA tests, and it was a fact. *Diamond Lotus* was a part nursery, and no one could deny them their status as a real community.

Thinking ahead before ever leaving Mother and falling down that wormhole, Haley had stocked the ship with recyclable sensor-diapers having planned all along for Bodhi to father children. They had a diaper recycler on board too. The sensors were baby-bottom-heat powered requiring no batteries and could be tuned to one's ear bud to alert the mother at the first sign of soil or wetness. Lined with absorbing feltex an infant diaper could hold a quart of fluid, keeping the baby's skin dry. They were self-adjusting, adhering and sealing, needing only to lay the baby upon it and activate the chip with one's skullcap. Diaper bins appeared within every living-space on the ship. With the addition of the seven babies, their community numbered twenty, having more than a third of the total population in infancy.

Tish and Winn were both on maternity leave from piloting and ship's duties, so they could bond with their daughters. Haley was often stuck consulting on the surface. This kept Bodhi at shuttling duty long hours every day. He tried to make it home for dinner each night, even if he had to go back out and work some more afterward since he often ended up missing lunch. Tish led evening practice in Bodhi's occasional absences when he had to work late. Sonic was a solid pilot now and helped Bodhi each day with shuttle driving, lifting things to space, and lowering stuff to the surface. Fueled by saturnium reactors, the Firmament shuttles were exponentially less powerful than the two shuttles of *Diamond Lotus,* which were powered by solarium fusion battery systems. This meant that the larger and heavier things were Bodhi's responsibility to get to space or surface.

They were having a family-community dinner tonight in celebration of Favio's first awakening, which he had finally attained after becoming a father accelerated his maturation, and since Bodhi had also manned up and employed the method of the teachings-dueling question and answer confrontation of ego-reduction on Favio, producing dissolution and transcendence like a master adept for his benefit. Tish had encouraged and even begged him, and there was nothing he wouldn't do for her. Bodhi was getting much better at this aspect of his teaching role and now had no qualms about smacking Favio hard with a stick whenever the man's mind drifted from practice during their community sessions.

Tish had picked up Haley from the surface of Firmament while Winn watched Artana for her, so Haley could come to dinner for the celebration. Shamas had become a serious meditator, and Tish had given him daily personal guidance helping him to attain insight. The elixir ceremony Bodhi led was when Shamas realized it. That had been a couple of weeks ago, so with Favio's awakening, every adult on the ship had had insight, and they were celebrating not only Favio's attainment but their awake community.

Uldra, Winn, and Pam had made dinner, and Favio's hand had not been in on it, so Tandy was likely to be able to get the galley clean tonight without Bodhi's help. As captain, it was Bodhi's duty to pick up slack in whatever position was lacking on the ship. This tended to frequently add kitchen-cleanup duties to his schedule. He had been considering hiring a 2nd kitchen-cleaner to get that situation covered, but Haley had told him it would be silly to have two, and that surely Tandy would eventually get the hang of it. This conversation had happened six months previously, and the idea was again frequenting Bodhi's mind.

There were enough of them to sit completely around the dining cabin table, and hover cradles lined one bulkhead. All the infants were sleeping soundly except Shanti, who was nursing on Winn's breast. Shanti had been born with a cone shaped head from having to push her way through such an impossibly narrow birth canal, but it had reformed over the next 36 hours into a wondrously attractive baby-head, rounded—not pointed—on the top. She had weighed a hair under six pounds and yet still found herself too big for the exit. It had been a close call for Winn with surgical birth, but Shanti had doubled-down and fought her way out with a true warrior's spirit. Winn had helped by breathing like great bellows imitating Bodhi, who was hyperventilating, and she was pushing for more than she was worth. It had been an excruciatingly painful miracle but a miracle nonetheless.

Tish had stoically given birth to 7.3-pound Artana within 2 ½ hours of her water breaking and was not heard crying in pain once. To be sure, it was far and beyond the most painful experience she'd ever had. She did it in her typical mindful fashion of total bare attention and grim one-pointed determination, tenacity, and adamantine will. Bodhi's presence had steadied her, his theatrical breathing had guided her, and the energy he passed her had lent strength to the task.

Haley informed them, "The first quantum star-gate will be finished in just three weeks."

Bodhi commented, "With star-gate travel, the quantum drives are far less complex and much cheaper to make than ours. And powered by saturnium reactors, they don't need carbon plate reinforcement, just a layer of adamantine and the rest steel-titanium-nickel."

"Their first quantum drives will be completed and ready for installation in five weeks," Haley updated them. "The hull of their first interstellar self-propelled transport, with twice the seating and four times the cargo space as the towed one, will be ready for her test voyage in two months."

Tish added, "Eight other nations are building these same transports, and my country has begun, in addition, working on a prototype for a mega-transport, seating 18,600 passengers and able to also carry 38,000 tons of cargo. It will have external mounts for carrying things too big to get into a cargo hold or the hanger."

Haley told them, "A dozen of the mega-transports, and twenty of the smaller ones, could evacuate the entire human population in 70 years or less. The slowing of the biosphere's process of dying has been more significant than we'd hoped. We still need more carbon-capture equipment going up continuously, and more ultra-violet radiation shield satellites launched for years to come, but have already halted the increase of weather severity and have even reduced it slightly. Hail is less often lethal in size, and winds no longer exceed 68 MPH. There has been a marked reduction in seismic activity, and ocean temperatures have at last stabilized."

"That's good news!" Bodhi exclaimed. "What are the longer-term forecasts?"

Haley informed him, "It looks like there are at least another 100 years left for birds and mammals. In the last ten months, birth rates on Firmament have continued to drop and are yet in a downward trend. The garbage management systems of Om's design, which have been implemented in several population centers, yield very promising results. Reforestation is proceeding at a very impressive rate, though in the lower temperate regions in many places, they are not doing well at all. Carbon capture and the shielding of ultra-violet radiation are planet-wide efforts at the moment, and as long as they remain so, the 100 years will stretch into more. Getting as many people off the planet as we can and lowering birth rates will help reduce resources getting consumed. Within ten years, if they keep up their productivity, they should be moving 90-100 million annually to New Firmament."

"They could all be off Firmament in 65 years," Bodhi calculated.

"They must leave a small custodial force to maintain the shield satellites, carbon capture equipment, efforts in reforestation, toxic waste off-planet removal, and planting of toxin absorbing grasses to be turned into ETOH fuel. These custodial efforts must be continued until the biosphere dies or it begins to come back to life. No longer choked with humans, or defiled by them, there is a chance Firmament's biosphere could heal over many, many centuries."

"We owe it to her," Tish stated with force.

Ilya shared, "Did you hear what they did to those billionaire capitalists they found living on that giant yacht? They..."

Sunuco cut him off with, "Darling, please, we are eating."

Winn was relieved. She'd skimmed the text story on this news item, and it had been beyond chilling. The food tonight was better than usual. Winn was a big fan of Uldra's cooking and knew Bodhi loved it too. She mentioned to him, "Tish is bringing her parents up to the ship for dinner tomorrow night, and I think her brother, Hanzov, will be with them. I'm picking up my parents, and my older sister will be coming with her husband, Stanly."

"Really?! Stanly?!" Bodhi asked with dread.

"He no longer hates E.T.'s, just aliens, even though he's never seen one and isn't sure they exist," Winn mitigated the Stanly impact.

"But he hates Pam for being so light-skinned, kind of pinkish-white," Bodhi pointed out. "He calls her a 'pasty-pink' and orders her about like a servant."

"It's just a family dinner," Winn advised him.

"He will hate Tish and her parents, and if he offends Hanzov, I'm sure Hanzov will just kill him where he stands. It will be a disaster," Bodhi predicted.

"Maybe you're right. I'll tell Yen she can't bring him."

"Thanks. I don't want any zealot racists on *Diamond Lotus*, or insulting my crew."

"He *was* pretty bad that night down in the hotel restaurant. He did really want to come up and see the ship though."

"I think perhaps a few eternities in some kind of purgatory might get him adequately prepared for such a tour," Bodhi discourage the idea.

Pam said dramatically, "Thank you, Bodhi, for not permitting that ignorant concentration of venomous hatred on board our ship."

Winn pointed out, "I'm only related to Stanly through my sister's marriage and poor judgement."

"No one holds Stanly against you, dear Winn," Haley said sympathetically, "but please never invite him aboard the ship, or to dinner with Tish's family on the surface."

Shanti fell off Winn's breast into sleep, and Winn tucked her into her hoover cradle, lined up with the other six like a hoover cradle parking lot. Bodhi and Winn did not need to be in physical contact any longer to generate that bigger-than-both psycho-spiritual entity. When they were apart, it was simply in two places at once. Favio announced, "I've signed a new contract with Bullhorn to model their men's athletic briefs. They have a young skinny hairless boy doing their bikinis now," this last delivered with contempt.

"Congratulations, Favio!" June said admiringly.

Bodhi and Sonic were both feeling like skinny hairless boys at the moment, and there was no one like a man's man such as Favio to make them feel this way. Bodhi didn't allow his attention to get snagged in it, and the feeling passed over him like an ocean wave. Sonic was more like treading water in it and just keeping his nose out. Haley let Favio down a little explaining, "I just haven't had time to produce that new music-clip yet for you, sweetheart. But I will get to it. I promise."

A band consisting of 15 and 16-year-olds had pushed ahead of Favio's number-one-on-the-charts music-clip, the last one Haley had made for him. So he was sliding down the charts no longer the new thing. Favio informed them, "We're wrapping up the shooting of the second season of *Lost in Space*. I get to sing solo in the galley in the final episode of season two."

"Am I still a buffoon and hopelessly neurotic romantic?" Bodhi asked, really hoping things might change in the 2nd season.

"I think they bring both better comedy and more sympathy to your character in the next season," Favio answered rather cryptically.

"What's that supposed to mean?" Bodhi demanded.

"I'm under contract not to say," Favio hid behind corporate law.

"Can I sue?" Bodhi asked no one in particular.

Win said compassionately, "Sweetheart, you're not a citizen of anywhere on Firmament, and so not protected under any of their laws."

"It seems downright ungrateful to me," Bodhi opined.

"They love Haley and are awarding her with the League of Nations Humanitarian of the Year prize," Winn offered in consolation.

"Congratulations Haley," Bodhi told her sincerely, "You have done so much for them and deserve the recognition."

Through his skullcap, Bodhi texted Haley, "You are Firmament's Sentient Being of the Year without any doubt."

"I love you," he heard her text reply in his earbud.

Tish said to Bodhi, "I told my brother that he has to chill if he's coming on our ship. He knows I can kick his ass."

"I hope he doesn't throw around the 'scrimpy weakling' phrases at me," Bodhi said, recalling meeting him in the United Socialist Sovereign Republic, or USSR. It was pretty much crumbled apart at this point, no longer able to use threats, terrorism, or outright war to hold it together. Like the territories and puppet nations of the Incorporated Merger States, the subject countries of the USSR had fled the relationship. Now it was just Motherland left.

Tish assured him, "I will be there, and I know the most embarrassing things about him. I can keep him in line. He has had a severe military life as a colonel of the elite Intelligence Division."

"I suppose he has, but he should have tried getting dropped on the doorstep of a bunch of old men at six weeks,"

"Winn and Haley and I are making up for your deprivation now, my love," Tish assured him.

He couldn't argue with that.

Tish caught his eyes with her most serious expression and informed him, "Winn, Haley and I are all firmly in agreement that you must be Sunoco's action seal and guide her through the meditation. She is ready."

All three looked at him with the same stern unified look of "We mean business," and so did Sunoco.

Bodhi looked to Ilya and asked, "Where are you with this?"

"I'm getting myself on board with it since otherwise I'd be afraid to fall asleep lying next to her, and I fear I'd lose her if I tried to prevent her. The bottom line for me, truthfully, is that I'm dedicated to supporting her spiritual work and would not get in the way of it."

"He will only benefit and can process his petty jealousies," Sunoco told Bodhi.

Finding no reprieve from that quarter, and it being his only hope, Bodhi agreed graciously, "Of course, I would be most honored to instruct you and guide you through it, Sunoco."

Sunoco and Ilya were not deserters or AWOL. The USSR had been enormously proud to have two of their top cosmonauts in crew positions aboard the ET ship in service of saving the human race and had promoted them. Haley let them leak things to their government a few weeks before she would share them with the globe, and this kept the two cosmonauts in excellent standing with their superiors. All of this was with Bodhi's approval. Sunoco told him, "I know we've given you no choice, but I'm truly grateful, and I do love you."

"I love you too, Sunoco," Bodhi replied. "You are a remarkable woman and a formidable disciple. You are ready for this work."

"Tonight then, right after practice, my tiger."

Tish said, "That went easily."

Bodhi complained, "I'm not avoidant. Please give me more time to adjust to things, and maybe even a heads up."

"It will be easier for having had less time to generate worries, my love," Tish consoled him.

Haley whispered in his ear, "Sunoco's really good in bed."

Bodhi whispered back, "We're not going to bed. We're meditating."

"Still," Haley whispered, "I bet she melts into you like liquid-putty and tickles you with her eye lashes when she's not kissing you."

"I'm her teacher and action seal, Haley, not her boyfriend."

"We'll see," Haley said confidently.

"Does Ilya know about you and Sunoco?" Bodhi asked.

"He was there, so yes, most definitely."

"Oh."

Sunoco shared, "I read that our government is putting great pressure on the producers and writers of *Lost in Space* to portray Ilya and me as honorable, heroic and likeable. Not like that fool of a captain," as they referred to Bodhi's character in the show.

"I wish I had a government to represent me," Bodhi allowed a self-pity statement to escape. It hadn't gotten fully flagged until it was coming out of his mouth.

"My poor husband," Winn said sympathetically, both truly empathizing with him, and at the same time, mocking his self-pity.

"Sometimes it just comes out and seems real for a moment," he explained himself.

"We have some room for you to be human too, my love," Winn assured him adoringly.

"That part of yourself needs to look at how fortunate you are to have the three of us looking after you," Tish scolded him.

"I will make that my strategy from now on, though I won't abandon the idea of divine perfection, nor the skill of radical acceptance of reality either."

Tandy shared, "My producers and fans are begging me to make another movie."

"Are you going to?" June inquired.

"No. I thought I'd make a career change and offer my services as a sex coach."

"What's a sex coach?" Bodhi asked.

"It's kind of like a movie director, just directing the action, though unlike one a sex coach sometimes has to roll up their sleeves and just dive into the action to teach, demonstrate, correct and arouse."

"I see."

"You're the only one on the ship I haven't done it with."

"You are truly loved by all," Bodhi offered

"I'm going to be sponsoring a couple of products and making a commercial," Shamas let them know.

"What kind of commercial," Uldra asked.

"Skintex condoms."

"What's the commercial storyboard?" Uldra pressed.

"I'm on a hot date, and the actress playing my date puts a condom on me."

"Do they make them that big?" June wanted to know.

"They stretch," Shamas replied. "I see the commercial as a public service announcement since they need to keep getting the birthrate down."

"Then I'm proud of you, my beloved," Uldra accepted his endeavor and kissed his cheek.

"Is the actress hot?" Favio asked.

"Stereotypically so," he answered.

"How would you classify me?" Uldra demanded.

"Stereotypically and excitingly hot, but also wifely permanent beautiful," he said, looking into her eyes with honesty and dissipating her jealousies.

When the entrees were finished, Uldra brought out an enormous chocolate layer cake with thick dark chocolate icing and white icing lettering on top, stating, "Congratulations on awakening Favio!" As she set it on the center of the big table, Bodhi stood and clinked his glass to say, "Here's to Favio's perseverance, tenacity, determination, and success in attaining his awakening. You did it Favio!"

All glasses were raised and all voices echoed, "You did it Favio!"

Favio confided, "It took seeing what an asshole I can be.

And a lot of help from Bodhi, Winn thought but didn't say.

CHAPTER EIGHTEEN

Everyone survived the family dinner on *Diamond Lotus* the next night. Stanly had been so jealous and envious of Winn's sister, Yen, when she returned to their condo after getting to fly into space and become one of the very few Firmamentlings to step aboard and see the ship. He knocked her out cold breaking her nose. Stanly was incarcerated for assault and held without bail thanks to some side-deals Haley made with his government. Yen was healing physically though a complete emotional wreck and Winn pressured Bodhi, gathering support from Haley, Tish, Sonic, and June until she convinced him to let Yen come live with them on the ship permanently.

Yen was exactly Winn's size, a size one, two years older than Winn, and had been the primary bread-winner in her couple with Stanly, having a high-powered career in aviation engineering while Stanly was a fry-cook at a low-end restaurant. She had started meditating when she was thirteen and had made considerable progress until getting involved with Stanly. She had chosen the worst possible boyfriends when Winn was growing up with her and exhibited a general cluelessness when it came to assessing the character of a male. She was nearly as sweet as Winn and more fragile emotionally.

After Stanly, Yen had made up her mind to become a lesbian even though she had never had sex with a female in her life and was not sure she had any attraction to doing it. Painful life experiences always tended to invite sweeping declarations of radical change from Yen, though these never panned out in the long run. She dressed in what she considered to be lesbian clothing, which was male-leaning unisex attire in actuality. If she'd known anything about lesbianism she would likely have dressed extremely fem since that was what she was, and the male leanings of her wardrobe couldn't work for her because of this. She tried hard to flirt with the girls and it only seemed to have any effect on Pam and June.

Winn helped her unpack in her private cabin on *Diamond Lotus* after picking her up on the surface in the tender. Yen cried herself to sleep her first night aboard. Haley comforted her the second night, embracing her in her bed and introducing Yen to female same-gender sex. Yen had never had her p-spot and clitoris simultaneously stimulated so utterly and had for the first time in her life squirted ejaculated fluids in her throws of out of control quaking and spastic orgasmic ecstasy. She hadn't known such a thing was even possible.

After Pam did her the next day in a cleaning supply unit on the ship, standing up, Yen decided she'd been a lesbian her whole life and had just not known it. June climbed into her bed that night with her and shook her world through most of it, clenching the whole lesbian deal for Yen. At least until the night of Favio's weekly sex party. She had shyly wandered in, got over her shock of Favio's size, which seemed it would be about as pleasant as giving birth were it trying to squeeze into her, and ended up on the periphery of the party as an observer. She was against the bulkhead behind the potted fern plant and found herself sitting beside naked Sonic.

The sight aroused her, so she snuggled into him, enjoying the energies this seemed to produce. Sonic became visibly aroused, presenting involuntarily a workable size for Yen, who passionately took advantage of this opportunity. In great urgency and remarkable haste, Yen mounted Sonic and was animated in super-sonic rocking gyrations before Sonic knew what hit him. The boy had staying power, and Yen had the time of her life. Stanly became like a dissociated and forgotten early childhood memory fragment. It worked so well for both Yen and Sonic that they did it three more times, and everyone was snoring when they finally left Favio's cabin. Sonic found Yen to be as angelic as Winn and a whole lot more available.

The work on Firmament and New Firmament continued at a frantic pace with every able-bodied human pitching in and working long hours. The star-gate in the Firmament system was constructed to completion, and the *Diamond Lotus* crew attended a celebration ceremony with League of Nation's leaders and cosmonauts on the construction platform at the gate. The first transport left the shipbuilding platform orbiting Firmament for her test run. Haley painstakingly manufactured four solarium fusion battery systems using solarium they had aboard, for installation in four shuttle hulls specially built by Firmament engineers on the surface so the people would have some heavy-lift capacity of their own.

Haley also gave the Firmamentlings designs and specs for a mercurium fusion reactor a thousand times more powerful than what was possible with marsnium for their mega-transport under construction in the USSR, and for all future mega-transports under construction. This meant that Bodhi spent his days mining mercurium. He insisted that in exchange for the materials he mined for them, that they build a house for Winn on New Firmament. The mercurium's value was equal to the largest nation on Firmament's entire gross national product, so a house was not a lot to ask in exchange. They were no longer receiving payment for technology transfers and rare materials since money had lost all value and was no longer in circulation on either Firmament or New Firmament. The only people who would have missed it had already been killed horrifically, so no one cared. Distribution was becoming more equitable weekly, and all attempts at greed and thievery were being met with such unthinkable means of execution that such things were most gravely and seriously discouraged.

Egoism was no longer admired nor imitated in the emerging global culture, not even by the brainwashed ignoramuses of the Incorporated Merger States where they had elected possibly the biggest ego in the universe, and certainly in the history of Firmament, as their lifelong dictator. His office had been called the presidency and his term limited when first he took office. He was dead now and reaping his miserable rewards. No one remembered his name, only how old and ugly he'd been and all the damage he'd caused. These days on Firmament, shows of egoism received only looks of offense or pity.

Once the quantum star-gate was completed in the New Firmament System, the way for mass migration was open and a grand celebration was held on that construction platform with national leaders, construction engineers, and heavy equipment operators, cosmonauts including the original sixteen, and the personnel of *Diamond Lotus*. Tandy scored with a Prime Minister that night, and June seduced the League of Nations' new Secretary of Migration. Haley met a dashing Lieutenant Colonel Astronaut, who'd had insight and would give his right arm to study with Bodhi. His country was in the hemisphere to the magnetic-south of the equator, and Haley found him to be such a hunk that she hired him on the spot at the end of their tryst without consulting Bodhi. His name was Uduak, and he was at breakfast when Bodhi took his seat at the table in the dining cabin on the ship the next morning already moved in.

When the mercurium fueled fusion mining crafts finally began rolling off the assembly line on Firmament, *Diamond Lotus* was no longer needed for Firmament's migration or cleanup, and neither was its landing platform biodome; so this was reattached to the ship after the custom mounts Haley had installed were removed, which had put a little wrinkle in the process—getting the damned things off. Bodhi, with Shanti sleeping in his lap, accelerated for jump speed heading out of Firmament to a location 81 light-years away. One of their drones had discovered a star-gate there within a yellow star system. They were all eager to follow up on this. Winn was Bodhi's copilot on the bridge, at the moment, since Tish had wanted to get to know Uduak. Haley was managing navigation, coms, and sensors analysis while babysitting Artana for Tish. She knew what Tish was in for and felt excited for her.

Bodhi commented to his beloved, "Yen and Sonic sure seem to have hit it off."

"She says he can make her squirt as Haley did and that she hadn't known males could have gentle qualities and understanding of emotions," Winn confided Yen's confidence to Bodhi. Typically she shared absolutely everything with Bodhi, except of course, Haley's subterfuges.

"They seem happy. Sonic told me that Yen is an angel like you, only she's available and that he's in love."

"I knew that meeting you and Sonic would help her figure out that there are different kinds of boys," Winn opined. Then she added a little alarmed, "He better not be dumping *me*!"

"Don't ask me. I'm just the fool of a captain," Bodhi commented, in reference to the new season of *Lost in Space,* which had been airing before they left.

"You were mining on New Firmament when we were interviewed by the show's writers, so they never got a sense of who you are," Winn explained.

"Did anyone attempt to tell them that I'm nothing like the captain on the show?"

"It was mentioned, I think. The actor playing you was so invested in the role he was playing, and he's so cute that none of us wanted to hurt his feelings, so I don't think it was conveyed very forcefully."

"Apparently not."

Winn felt uncomfortable, so she said to Haley, "Uduak is really handsome."

"He's too big for you, lover," Haley replied.

"I figured as much," Winn said a little disappointed.

Bodhi asked Haley, "Could you survey the living areas of the ship and do any baby-proofing that's needed? Shanti sort of made her first half-crawl this morning while lying on the rug on her belly. They'll be all over the place and into everything below knee-height, any moment now."

"I will, and I'll also add some precautionary programming to the cleaning-bots."

"The manufactures should have put alarms and flashing lights on those. They seem to just appear out of nowhere at the oddest moments.

"I'm sorry, but I don't have time to make hardware modifications," Haley informed him. "I can, however, prevent them from baby-collisions."

"Thanks, Haley."

"I've adopted Shanti and Artana and see them as my own, so I will make their environment quite safe, I assure you," Haley stated.

Winn said sincerely, "They have a mother who can teach them everything known to humans from every branch of knowledge."

"More importantly," Haley reframed, "they have parents who can teach them the relativity, generalization, and abstraction of knowledge, contrasted with direct contemplative knowing of the real being as the invisible emptiness of pure consciousness."

"Is Uduak fitting in with the crew?" Bodhi inquired.

"With me just fine," Haley informed him. "He won't fit in Winn or Yen, but he has already fit in well with Tandy and June.'

"I meant is he getting along with his colleagues in general, like Shamas, Sunoco, and Ilya," Bodhi clarified.

"He's friendly enough, but he doesn't do males," Haley stated.

Winn complained, "If Sonic dumps me, we'll need to hire more males and include small to average penis size as a prerequisite hiring criteria."

"Boy," Haley commented, "exaggeration on that application could cost you the job."

Bodhi suggested to Winn, "You ought to find a few guys you like over the Firmament interface then date them and make a selection."

"What if they have no skills the ship can utilize?" Winn asked.

"You mean like Tandy?" Bodhi asked.

Haley told him sternly, "Tandy is perfectly capable of cleaning that galley herself no matter how much food Favio slops on the walls, ceiling, and floor. You always agree to help when she asks you, cutting her work in half, so she's too tempted not to much of the time. Just tell her it's *her* job."

"If the guy you choose has no usable skills," Bodhi told Winn, "then he can be Tandy's assistant, and maybe help Favio sort through his fan mail, so Favio has some time for cooking."

Defending the crew, Haley told Bodhi, "Shamas worked harder than anyone this past year managing all the cargo loads, and Uldra is worth her weight solidium. You could not hope to find a more mindful and methodical pilot than Tish."

Winn felt the need to come to Tandy's defense and told Bodhi, "Tandy takes care of human resources for you."

"I do see that," he agreed. "She ensures they receive full benefits and have what they need so they can do their jobs. I admit she's been good for morale."

Winn suggested, "We could give her the title of Human Resources Manager, and find someone good at cleaning galleys to do that job."

"I'll leave that in yours and Haley's competent hands. Having complete control of hiring decisions already, perhaps Haley will let me in on things before, rather than after the fact."

"Uduak was a lucky find and required a spur of the moment decision without time to consult you."

"I have made zero complaints regarding Uduak," Bodhi pointed out.

"You're very good that way," Haley praised him.

"Well, I'm very glad *he's* fitting in," Bodhi stated, "and now it looks like we might need to find one who can fit into smaller places."

Winn told him, "It helps tremendously when you're with Tish or Haley, sweetheart."

"I understand. Just try to find someone with a solid meditation practice."

"Oh, I almost forgot to tell you," Winn said, remembering. "Wherever we are tomorrow afternoon, I need to pick up Sonic's sister on Firmament."

"Why didn't he visit her before we left?" Bodhi asked, trying to get some sense of it.

Winn realized a little more explanation was necessary and said, "Penny got pregnant, and hers and Sonic's father kicked her out of the house. The father of the baby wouldn't take her in and told her to get an abortion. She's alone confused and frightened, staying at the moment in a temporary miner's camp. She needs help!"

"Then let's go get her now before we make the jump," Bodhi suggested.

"Let me call her," Winn said, already entering the code with her skullcap into the cockpit coms unit. On speaker, Penny said, "Hello."

"This is Sonic's friend, Winn. We could come and get you right now if you want."

"Would you please?" she sort of begged pathetically.

"We're turning around now and should be able to reach orbit in about fifteen minutes. Where are you?"

"I'm back in the city at the central train station where its warm inside and they have bathrooms."

"I'm bringing the central station up in my holo now," Winn told her as Bodhi started turning the ship around. "I see it. It looks like a giant dome. Is there access to the roof of the dome?"

"I don't think so."

"Then I think I'll have to land in the intersection of Broadway and 57th Street, so stay by the doors, and I'll call you when I'm a minute out. We'll be holding up the ground traffic, so try to be quick."

"I will, I promise. Thank you so much."

Haley made some swift quantum sorts of 40,000,000 applications from their first round of hiring, eliminating all females, then all unlikely looking males. Unfortunately, penis size was not data they had required on the application, so once she had it down to 3,000 likely candidates, she began hacking birth and circumcision data for clues, rejecting those with phrases like "well-developed," and words like "large." It took her less than a minute to end up with five petite male meditators, single and without children, who were in the 99th percentile in terms of intelligence, and 100th percentile for empathy and sensitivity. She sent the list only to Winn. Bodhi had no idea this was going on.

Winn texted all five telling them to meet her at the same intersection of Broadway and fifty-seventh. The fifteen minutes to orbit Winn had told Penny was going to be a pretty tight thing for Bodhi to accomplish and would cost some thruster fuel. He looked concentrated on the job.

Winn was thinking up interview questions, but they sounded even to her like something someone would ask on a dating game show. She texted Haley, who was right on the bridge with her, "What degree of certainty do you have that none of these candidates exceeds 6 and 9/10 inches?"

"I'm fairly certain none of these do," Haley replied to just Winn, "and I think the real question is whether they will be big enough?"

Satisfied with this, Winn hastily put together a medical questionnaire for her applicants with all the usual questions about allergies, medications, conditions, and so forth, and all the typical physical data such as height, weight, and length of erection. Even in this section, it seemed to her to stand out as unusual. Oh well. She made it a required field to fill in to get the application submitted. Pleased with her efforts, she retrieved five-pocket devices from storage and uploaded her medical questionnaire onto them. She was going to have them do that part electronically, so she was relieved to scratch the erection question from her interview ones.

As Bodhi approached orbit, Winn took the tube to the hanger airlock foyer, bringing the five hand-devises with her in a shoulder bag. She'd stopped in their suite briefly to check her makeup and change into a tight low-cut dress before descending to the hanger. She would have to take a shuttle since the tender had only four seats. She hoped she could clear all the power lines when dropping into the intersection with a big cargo shuttle. Traffic would be held up, and her nose would need to nearly touch the corner of a building to get the ramp down without hitting the building diagonally across from it.

Winn boarded and started her preflight checks while activating the compressors to suck all the air out of the hanger. Once she was sitting in a vacuum, she checked the velocity of *Diamond Lotus* and saw that Bodhi had bled off almost all their speed and was engaging thrusters slowing quickly, almost below 30,000 mph already. Winn opened the hanger doors and exited the ship slowly and carefully through the bay doors. Closing them from outside the ship, she entered her nav. coordinates to bring up a flight path in her holo. They had just reached the 15-minute mark since her call to Penny.

Tearing through the atmosphere towards the center of the city where the intersection sat, Winn anxiously saw that it would be a tight squeeze on the ground. One minute out, she alerted Penny and texted her five candidates. Concentrating deeply and quite worried, Winn eased the shuttle towards the ground keeping all the power lines visible in her holo's. One twanged on an extended fin but held nicely, becoming a blur of movement without snapping. By this time, cars were trying to flee the intersection, and some were getting on sidewalks to do this. Pedestrians were jumping into doorways, and about every horn for a block in all four directions was at full continuous volume. It was pandemonium on the ground.

A truck stuck in the intersection kept her about 12 ½ feet off the street, and the ramp was well off the ground at the low end. Winn descended a foot, then a foot and a half, and then a crunch of denting sheet steel informed her—instead of the holo she'd neglected to check—that she was still a bit nigh off the ground, so Winn descended another foot to a symphony of screaming metal compressing the truck roof until the bottom of the ramp looked manageable. Indeed, Penny was getting a leg up and climbing in.

Just a few seconds after that five cute guys, all 5 foot four inches to 5 foot five inches, struggled to climb onto the ramp end. As they reached the airlock with both sets of doors wide open, Winn closed the ramp behind them and started ascending. The truck roof was all crumpled, and the driver was waving his fist at her out his window. She made sure the sensors got his vehicle tag code so she could make it up to him. Penny was reaching the cockpit.

"I'm Winn," she told her. "We have to get a little higher then hoover while I conduct a brief interview. Right after that, I'll get you up to the ship."

"Thanks so much for coming for me, Winn. Sonic has said such nice things about you. He seems to really love you."

"Well, I'm pretty sure he's dumping me for my sister," Winn updated her.

At 46,000 feet, Winn felt sufficiently out of the way of anything and set the shuttle to auto hoover in place while she extracted herself from the pilot's seat. She went to the area of fixed seats where her candidates awaited her and said, "Hi, my name's Winn."

Everyone on Firmament knew who Winn was from *Lost in Space,* and her character was so sweetly done on the show that there wasn't an adolescent boy on the planet who wasn't lovesick for her. She directed, handing each a pocket device, "First I need for each of you to complete and submit the medical form electronically, then I'll meet with each of you individually for a very short interview."

Reluctantly each of the guys tore their eyes from beautiful Winn to start making selections in each field of the form. There were scroll down lists for anything that required one like medications, diseases, and every birth date going back 100 years. They were all bright and quite efficient. One of them suddenly said, "Really! Am I disqualified if my erection is too short?"

Winn assured him, "No. Only if it is too long."

Two of them had to go back and correct upward estimates and one an outright lie. Finally, they were all submitted, and Winn was checking just one field in each through her bifocal holo in front of her right eye like a micro-teleprompter. Five-foot four, skinny Alfred's was eight and a half inches long. He was disqualified. Argile was 7.2 inches. Another rejection, and a pity too, since he was so adorable. Of the three who made the cut, one gave off a sort of untrustworthy and low vibration. She took images of the three auras using Haley's imaging unit, which she had also brought along to decide tough choices. Sure enough, the one from whom she detected low vibes, had a murky muddy aura. The other two were bright primary colors with blues and greens as well as red through orange. These last two were so gorgeous she just couldn't choose between them. The longer she looked at them, the more certain she became that she needed both. She couldn't bring herself to part with either one and justified hiring both by the gender disparity existing aboard.

Winn told Fritz and Omar, "I'm willing to hire both of you on probationary status if you are interested in joining our crew."

"I am!" Frits declared. "Tell me how to pass probation."

"I'm in too, and I'll give it everything I've got," Omar told her.

"The most important thing," Winn oriented them, "is to be kind and compassionate with everyone. Meditation is also very important. Let me get the other three applicants back down to the surface, and I'll explain further. Oh, and it's always a good idea to strap in while we're in flight."

Winn returned to the cockpit and to Penny, who was still seated in the copilot seat. Penny asked, "How did the interviews go? Were any applicants a good fit for the position?"

"Two will fit just fine," Winn replied, engaging the drives and diving. Then she suggested, "Go back and sit with them and meet them so you can tell me what you think."

"What am I looking for?" Penny asked dumbfounded, feeling entirely unqualified to make judgments about spaceship personnel having only been on one once to dine.

"You know, what you think of them as guys; like do you think they're cute and would you want to date them?" Winn explained.

"Alright," Penny said, feeling a bit more qualified now. She was only just eighteen and had only one boyfriend who'd turned out to be a callous creep. At least it wasn't rocket-science that Winn was asking of her. Penny thought most guys were pretty cute. She thought Winn was *really* cute. She got around her seat and was about to leave the cockpit, looking down the length of the shuttle at the young men, then turned to whisper to Winn, "They're all perfectly beautiful, dreamy, and to die for."

Winn said, "I'm dropping off the three on your left, so just focus on the two to the right."

Penny went on back. The two selected candidates were sitting with a vacant seat between them, which Penny thought of as a 'guy thing.' She sat in that seat so she could have access to both of them. Her gaze went back and forth, unable to decide which one to look at. She wanted to see both at once, badly, and her eyes crossed for a moment putting both in view, but the strain was too much. She told them as she buckled up, "I'm Penny, Sonic's sister, and I'm going to be living on *Diamond Lotus*."

"I'm Fritz, and it's a pleasure to meet you, Penny. We hope to be living on *Diamond Lotus* too."

"I'm Omar, Penny, and I'm delighted to make your acquaintance."

Penny informed them with unquestionable certainty, even though she was making it up to afford herself closer inspection, "Greetings are made with hugs among spaceship personnel."

Fritz was already spreading his arms at the word "hugs," so Penny eagerly tried him out, unable to resist her attraction and telling herself it was all on account of wanting to do a good job for Winn. Omar was equally alluring, and she just couldn't help herself, forgetting to even use Winn as justification. She was sold on both and would be ready to have either one of their babies if it weren't for already being pregnant.

Winn was braking with reverse drives and a tiny bit of thrusters coming in on approach and settled gently down to hoover a foot off the top of a skyscraper building with flat roof and helipad. She said through the intercom, "Thank you for applying. We do appreciate it. I need to drop you up here, and you can take the elevator down. That intersection where I picked you up is only a couple blocks from here, and too risky to try another landing at. Please leave the hand-devices on your seats and exit the shuttle down the ramp at the stern. Thank you."

Alfred, Argyle, and murky-aura all left the space shuttle, and Penny stood to make sure there was a hand- device on each of the three seats, which there were. Winn raised the ramp when they were off and throttled up the drives to head for space. Penny asked Fritz, "Do you think Winn is pretty?"

"Pretty is far too petty and insignificant a term. Such beauty is ineffable, reflecting the very divine form of beauty."

Penny pressed on, "How would you describe your sexual orientation?"

Fritz had never encountered such employment questions before, but he'd never applied for a job on a spaceship before either. He told Penny honestly, "I guess I like both males and females, but find it a little easier to get laid with guys."

Penny turned to Omar and asked him, "Could you please describe your sexual orientation."

"I'm into guys and have never been with a woman," Omar told her.

Fritz inquired, "What will my job be?"

Penny explained, "I've only ever been on the ship once, and it was to have dinner as a guest, but I think one of the duties of this position is to provide quality companionship to Winn when Bodhi is with Haley of Tish."

"So far, I'm told that the position entails being nice, meditating, and keeping Winn's company," Fitz said, perplexed. "Would there be any technical duties involved?"

"Boy, I don't know," Penny admitted. Then she excused herself and ran to the cockpit.

She told Winn, plopping into the copilot seat, "Omar doesn't do girls, and I'm afraid that Fritz might like boys better, but does both."

"Oh, no!" Winn exclaimed.

Winn hit the brakes with reverse drives and thrusters while angling into low orbit just a mile above the transition zone and top of the atmosphere. She set her autopilot to maintain her orbit, once she attained it, and told Penny, "I'll be right back."

Winn called Haley quickly and explained the situation before exiting the cockpit area. Haley said alarmed, "You have violated about every employment law they have on Firmament, Winn."

"We're not under their laws, just ask Bodhi who can't sue the producers of *Lost in Space*."

Haley said to Winn, "I think you should explain to the gay one that we have no gay or bisexual guys on the ship and that if he were to come with us, he may never get laid again."

"I think Omar likes Fritz. I mean who wouldn't?" Penny told Haley.

"I better go back there and have a talk," Winn resigned herself. Winn was nearly in tears when she squatted in front of the first row of seats before her two recruits and told them, "I've made a mess of things. You see, Penny's brother is dumping me for my sister, and I need a boyfriend on board for when Bodhi is with Haley or Tish. I should have used a dating service instead of the crew applications in our database. I need a young male heterosexual, and he doesn't need to be anywhere near as gorgeous as either of you, though that would be a real bonus."

Winn burst into tears, so sorry she'd jerked everyone around. Bodhi, on the bridge of *Diamond Lotus*, felt Winn's pain and asked in her ear bud, "Are you alright, my love?"

"We'll talk about it later," she whined. "It's nothing you did; believe me."

"I'm here if you need me, Winn. I love you."

"I love you too, Bodhi."

Fritz had left his seat to wrap his arms around Winn, needing to comfort her and unable to tolerate her distress. He pulled her into contact with his chest and said, "Don't cry on my account. I got to meet beautiful real Winn and orbit our planet on a space shuttle."

Omar consoled her, "I would have just been picking super-weeds today again if you hadn't contacted me, and I'm getting to ride in the space shuttle, which is a real treat."

They were being so sweet about it that it made Winn feel even guiltier for doing it. Holding Fritz, and wrapped in his concern and caring, this started seeping through Winn's remorse and felt so good that it began mitigating her despair. She finally got her breathing under control and said, "I'm sorry. Omar, there are no men into guys on *Diamond Lotus,* and we are leaving the Firmament system for places unknown. If you got stuck with us, it could spell the end of your sex life."

To Fritz, she said, "You feel so good. You're a great hugger. You would have been perfect."

Winn started crying again, although at least some part of it was self-pity and not remorse. Omar shared, "I'm on the list for the 93rd transport run to New Firmament so I'll have a new life starting eventually and will have my turn out among the stars."

"I'll take you there today in the tender if you want. We can pick up your stuff. No furniture will fit, though."

"You would go 28-light years to drop me off?" Omar said in disbelief.

"It doesn't take any longer than going a billion, or any less going just one or two," Winn informed him.

"I'd love to!!" Omar declared with pure delight.

Winn was embracing Fritz back, already becoming a bit attached to him. She asked him sweetly with her lips only inches from his ear, "What do you want to do, beautiful?"

"Without any doubt, I want to become exclusively heterosexual and accompany you, Winn."

"Can you do that?" Winn asked.

"With no males into guys on the ship, I don't see what else I could do coming with you," Fritz pointed out.

"I'm involved with Bodhi, Haley, and Tish, you must know, so you would have to cultivate relations with some of the other girls too."

Penny called from the cockpit, where she'd been intently following the conversation, "I'd do it with you, Fritz."

"How old are you, Penny?" Fritz inquired, thinking she might only be about 15.

"I turned 18 almost three weeks ago," she told him, trying to make it sound ancient.

"I'm four years older than you," he told Penny.

"That's alright. I like older men."

"I never thought of myself as an 'older man,' Frits mentioned."

"Well, compared to me," Penny qualified.

Penny was an inch and ¾ taller than Winn and ten pounds lighter. Built like a pole, her feminine curves were beyond subtle. She had a space between her upper front teeth and a narrow face with some pimples and blackheads. Her glamour consisted mostly of youth, and the rest of it was rather unique to her alone. Penny directed to Winn, "I would love you and have sex with you, Winn, to comfort you when Bodhi's otherwise preoccupied."

"That's so sweet, Penny. I think I'd like that. I need a male, though, and there's a shortage of those on the ship."

"Please keep me in mind," Penny encouraged her.

"I will, and I'll take you up on your offer," Winn let her know.

"I would too, Penny, if Winn lets me join up."

"Are you sure you would be alright, Fritz, without a male lover?" Winn asked with concern.

"I kind of got into guys because it was so easy and because nearly half the girls on the planet are taller than me and aren't really in the market for a shorter boyfriend. I would do anything to be with you, even only infrequently, and to study with Bodhi."

"You're sure?" she checked one more time.

"Absolutely positive!"

"Then let's all go in the cockpit and get Omar's stuff from his house to drop him off in the new world."

Winn returned to Penny in the cockpit and sat down in the pilot's seat. Fritz and Omar took the Navigation and Coms stations behind them. Winn put up her piloting holo in front of each seat and a second one showing the planet, before powering up the drives and diving towards the atmosphere. At 39,000 feet, she reversed the drives all the way, pressing everyone hard into their harnesses. The motion dampeners on these big Om cargo shuttles were fairly minimal.

Winn asked Omar, "What's your address?"

"I'm at 2928 21st street, and the roof of the apartment building is flat."

Winn entered the address using her skullcap, and a hot pink flight plan appeared in her holo and the holos of the other three. *Diamond Lotus* stayed within the hot pink line down, slowing by drives alone. Bodhi had asked her to be frugal with the thruster fuel cells and not to use any boosters. As she set it hovering just over the roof, lowering the ramp, Winn said to Omar, "Take this pocket device. You can keep it, and my code is already entered. When you open coms, my icon is top left on the holo. You can just touch it with your finger, and it will connect to mine. The Firmament coms conversion satellite, which Bodhi built for our planet, can receive your transmissions directly if you touch this icon before sending, which will pretty much put you in real-time with whoever you're speaking with."

"They don't let people use those coms satellites and limit them to official use only," Omar informed her.

"The quantum coms converter itself could manage all coms between the populations of both planets, so it's only the spectrum encoded light coms which are limited in capacity. You'll be skipping the encoded light spectrum on the New Firmament satellite, and only making traffic at one end. They've never yet had to queue messages or had any delays."

"What if they trace my calls to this device?" Omar asked.

"Our quantum coms originations do not register in their equipment, so they can't and would never know. Only coms received in spectrum encoded light then converted are known to them."

"And you'll give this to me?!"

"Yes, Omar. You're sweet and unreal beautiful. I'd like to stay in touch and be friends."

"I've never had such an influential friend before," Omar admitted. "I'd like that."

"When we come back to visit our friends and families I'll look you up."

"You'll make me famous."

Winn reluctantly let go of Fritz to embrace Omar and kiss his lips. His skin was so clear and healthy it seemed to glow. She didn't want to let go of him either. When she did, he ran down the ramp and into the building to collect his things. Winn asked Fritz, "Is there anything you need from home?"

"My music and games on my computer, and my toothbrush and clothes."

"I can reconstruct your music play list and download your games in minutes. We have much better toothbrushes, and we make clothing out of any textile on Firmament and then some. You design your styles on the computer. I can help you."

"Then, I'm all set."

"You'll be issued a pocket device, skullcap, and earbud. Once you sit through the safety lectures and check out on the range, you'll get a blaster pistol. We'll also make you a uniform with our crest on it."

"What's a skullcap?"

"It's a bunch of electrodes and sensors with a built-in computer and coms, which translates brain impulses into actions, like a keyboard for word-processing, working the operating mechanisms on the ship, and using the lights-music-holo-soundproofing-temperature-backrest adjustment—and everything in your cabin. It's faster than touch screens and voice commands."

"Are you going to bring me aboard and let me stay?"

"I want you, Fritz, and if you're willing to come, I'm bringing you."

"Does Bodhi know?"

"Sort of. He knows I'm going to be looking. He just doesn't know that I've found you yet."

"Does Haley know?"

"Haley knows everything," Winn said in wonderment. "She's the one who ran the searches for my five applicants." Winn thought about it, then added, "I guess she doesn't know absolutely everything because she was off on Alfred's penis by more than an inch and a half."

"That erection-length question seemed very strange even for a medical questionnaire for a spaceship crew application. I thought it may be something they might need to know, in case I got one in my spacesuit or something."

"No. There are only 6 and 9/10 inches between my vaginal opening and uterus, and it's not good for a girl to have penises pushing through her gate."

"I didn't know," Fritz confided.

"You've probably never pushed through one. You're a perfect fit for me, Fritz.

"I've been with some very attractive females but none so beautiful as you, Winn, and never anyone so sweetly open."

"I think Tish and Haley are going to like you too. You're sure to find Tandy and June in your bed before long. If Penny latches onto you too, then I hope you do not get too busy to see me."

"Seeing you will remain my ultimate priority, Winn, I assure you. By the way, will I have any duties above and beyond being kind, meditating, and loving you?"

"You can learn about anything that sparks your interest and get involved. Tandy's always looking for help cleaning the galley, and Bodhi's done doing that for her. We girls took over the produce harvesting from Haley, and many routine maintenance functions. I'm a small craft pilot, and I'm working on my ship piloting license now. Tish is closer to getting hers, and she's learned some of the external maintenance. I don't like space walks, so I'm not learning that stuff."

"Haley and Bodhi arrived without crew, and don't appear to have a great need for one," Fritz commented.

"At first, it was just to find young females of Bodhi's type so he could have babies. Bodhi likes fine dining and gourmet food, so

Favio was hired, and he said the job requires three people, mainly because he doesn't like cleaning up and needed time for his fan club. To keep Favio happy, we hired Tandy and Uldra. Sonic just walked up to Bodhi and begged to study with him. Then the girls made Haley hire Shamas. Bodhi met Sunoco and Ilya at the biodome in New Firmament. Haley found Uduak, and all the girls love him. He's too big for me, and so is Favio. Then my sister came aboard, after her creep of a soon-to-be ex-husband broke her nose and knocked her out, so she moved in to live on the ship and stole Sonic from me. I had to fetch Sonic's sister from the surface and thought I'd do some recruiting, and now you're joining."

"That's everyone," Fritz acknowledged.

"Well, there are also seven babies."

"Where are we headed?" Fritz decided to ask since it would be his destination as well.

"There's a yellow sun world with a star-gate one of our sensor-drones found, and we're going to make contact with their civilization. It's really exciting. Bodhi's hoping they'll have star maps of at least their region of this galaxy."

How much star map data did you have before going through the worm hole?" Frits tried to get a sense of things.

"Om, the planet which built our ship has six galaxies mapped in entirety down to moons, dwarf planets, asteroids and comets, and parts of at least a dozen more. They also have six billion cubical light-years of galaxies mapped; though just the brighter stars. We have all the data, and so far, it's irrelevant. No one knows how big the universe is or how many galaxies there are."

"Is there a point of origin for the universe?"

"It manifests everywhere at once, and its racing expansion, given the curvature of space, results in a cycle of perpetual motion. The simplest symbolic representation is the Mobius strip. But all material manifestation in the universe occurs as vortexes and have vortex force, or what you call gravity. It's not bodies attracting. Everyone discovers the mathematical formula for the laws of motion long before they begin to understand vortexes. What binds matter in vortexes are the forces involved in producing matter, the final force, and the end of the line from the Absolute Transcendental. The final elements of rest, motion, harmony, equilibrium, and time are the pre-material manifestation forces required to produce matter. These forces are the result of the Absolute, the Divine Logos, and the World Soul. Manifest or just potential, all vortexes, or material manifestation points, are pre-established. They are neither random nor accidental. The most valuable knowledge is the point of quantum change like the temperatures water crystalizes to ice or jumps to steam, or the instantaneous reorganization in a chemical reaction system called a symmetry break in dissipative structures. Knowing the cycles of change within one's galactic vortex, and value for the curvature of space, open a new world of interstellar and inter-galactic navigation."

"Wow! I think I got part of that."

"Haley says things so much more clearly than I do, and I'm still just studying the basics in Om sciences."

"This feels like a dream," Fritz said in wonderment. "You are actually as sweet in real life as your character on the show."

"Isn't she cute? I tried to get a date with her, but she's in a monogamous relationship."

Fritz said honestly, "She has more bust and ass than you, and she's a tad wider in the hips. I'd much prefer a date with you."

"Well, that's lucky because she's not available."

"I did have a crush on her until I met you."

"I had one on her too, and still sort of do."

"You know Robin Knight, who plays you, makes fun of your sweetness in interviews."

"No. I didn't know that. Do people think I'm pathetic?"

"No. And she was booed by a studio audience for doing it, one of the times she did."

"They got Bodhi all wrong, and it embarrasses him when he's planet-side mixing with Firmamentlings."

"How did they get him so wrong?"

"From Haley's first address to the League of Nations and because when the writers and producers and some of the cast came up to the ship to meet us, Bodhi was off mining for the first settlers on New Firmament."

"It's amazing what all he and Haley have done for us," Fritz gushed. "Coming into orbit they prevented a global nuclear war, then disarmed the mightiest military force on Firmament, and the 2nd, getting the others to disarm themselves. They have prolonged the life of our entire biosphere and given us the means to make the migration. Life on Firmament has been a sea of positive changes since their arrival.

I'm so proud of both of them and so honored to serve them," Winn gushed too.

Omar came up the ramp, dragging a big foot locker, barely able to get it up the incline. Penny and Fritz went to help him with the next load. Winn gave him an Om thermal sleeping bag and rectangle of smart foam from the airlock foyer lockers. When all his stuff was aboard, Winn flew them up to the ship, aired the hanger, and transferred herself and her passengers—as well as Omar's prodigious luggage into the ship's four-seater tender. Penny preferred to go on the ride rather than seeing her brother. Winn informed Bodhi about going to New Firmament to drop off Omar, but not about how she'd ended up collecting him, and she didn't mention Fritz. She thought it might be better if he just showed up at the table the way Uduak had. She meant to consult with Haley on that point before proceeding.

CHAPTER NINETEEN

The zippy tender reached jump speed in just over ten minutes. The jump-transition had them all in shock-stupor a moment within the New Firmament system. Winn recovered and reversed drives, slowing their velocity from over 7 million miles per minute. She'd left herself plenty of room hoping to perform the entire operation without spending thruster fuel. She skimmed the surface of the moon using its vortex to help slow the tender. Penny and Fritz were just coming around and out of stupor-mode. "Holy Shit!" Penny shouted.

"I know, did you feel that?" Fritz agreed with Penny's assessment.

Winn was concentrating and decided at that moment that she had better learn how to do gas-mining as she lit her reverse thrusters, still going too fast to enter the atmosphere. She kept braking while skinning the top and transition zone in a complete circle around the planet, bringing her speed down to a very manageable range. Diving towards the surface, Winn asked Omar, "Do you have a preference as to which settlement?"

He looked at her like she was a moron and said, "At the LGBTQ settlement, of course."

"I guess they're promoting that now on account of over population," Winn commented.

"There's no breeding going on in LGBTQ Town," Omar assured her. "But there's a whole lot more sex going on there than in any of the other settlements."

"It sounds like a fun place to live," Penny opined.

Winn got a hot pink flight path showing in her holo to LGBTQ Town and followed it down. Every building was less than nine months old, and there were already close to 5,000 residents living here. There were new construction and industrial vehicles at one end of town. It was twilight, and soon it would be dark. The night life was in full swing. Being late summer, many residents wore only ornaments and footwear. Other than a few hoover crafts, there was no traffic on the main street, so Winn came in slowly to land there. Some people dancing in it moved out of the way yielding to the tender, and Winn brought it to rest about 24 inches off the ground before shutting it down and idling the vortex-redirect so that they sank ten more inches towards the ground. She set her security code, and they all climbed out.

People were closing in on them curiously. A woman with her arms around her girlfriend asked Winn, "Say, cutie, what kind of hovercraft is that?"

Winn replied sweetly, "It's our ship's tender, and we brought Omar here from Firmament because he wants to live here."

"This little thing came 28 light-years?!" She asked, not believing it for a second.

Winn told her proudly, "It was my first solo jump."

"Who are you?!" she asked in shock.

"I'm sorry. My name is Winn, and this is Penny, Sonic's sister, who's going to live with us, and this is Fritz who's going to come live with us too, and this is Omar who wants to live here."

"Oh, my God! You're Winn! *The* Winn! The real one! And you are as sweet as the one on the show."

Everyone crunched in tight to get closer to the real Winn, who suddenly had people standing in her aura violating her personal space, and not only that, stray hands touching her. An extremely attractive and forward girl swarmed in face to face with Winn pressed against her in the crowd and told her with a smile, "You must come to the big party down the street. The mayor has the band playing at Government House right in the Ministers' Chamber. You'll have fun, and everyone wants to meet you."

Penny had Winn's arm and was already pulling her towards the party, following the attractive forward girl and intent on partying. Omar was already popular having stepped out of a spacecraft with Winn. Winn clung to Fritz, who was on her other side, possessively since so many guys were checking him out. She asked the girl they were following, "Are there street parties here every night?"

"Most nights and they can get pretty wild."

Winn, Penny, and Fritz were swept along with the crowd, and passing by another crowd in an outdoor area of a bar, all three ended up with drinks in their hands. Lit joints kept getting passed to them. Winn wouldn't take the empathogen being pushed-on her knowing only Om had perfected the drug so as not to cause brain damage nor deplete feel-good chemicals, and even theirs ended in an hour of dysphoria. All the same, she *was* high by the time they were in the Ministers' Chamber being a light-weight with alcohol and having puffed on a number of those joints. She just hadn't been confronted by such things in her life before, meditating and sequestered first in academia, then within a monastery. She knew she'd led a sheltered life.

The music begged to be danced to, seducing bodies into motion, and the band was fantastically good. Winn started shaking it, and Penny was all out. Fritz was little more reserved in his dancing but quite good at it. The dance floor, which was the Ministers' Chamber, was tightly packed, ruling out dance moves like high kicks and forward flips. People were climbing onto the curved tabletops going around the chamber in ascending tiers of concentric circles, and they were dancing in the isles too. Another drink was placed in Winn's hand by one of the dancers who'd danced over with two glasses. He clinked his on the one he'd handed Winn and said, "Cheers," before taking a sip. Fritz and Penny were handed drinks too. A man with breasts wearing makeup and a leotard introduced himself as the Mayor.

At one point, a boy prettier than Fritz was dancing in front of Winn and she started dancing with him. She was a little disappointed when he turned out to be a girl. The girl was damned cute, and Winn kept her as a dance partner. It seemed to Winn that every time she managed to relieve herself of an unwanted empty glass, a full one found its way to her hand. She also felt like the central hub of the joint routes. The room was a cloud of smoke, and none of it was tobacco.

Coming out of the Ladies Room after relieving her bladder of some of those drinks, Winn nearly bumped into a woman blocking her path. The naked woman told her, "Hi, Winn, my name's Eve, and I'm your greeter."

"I'm pleased to meet you, Eve. I'm a little fuzzy on greeters."

"Greeters *are* warm fuzzes, sweetheart," Eve explained as her arm wrapped around Winn. "Did you know that on costume night, there are always at least a hundred Winn's here."

"I can't imagine," Winn said honestly, truly unable to conjure an image of this in her mind.

"They have Winn-wigs and Winn-masks at the toy distribution center over in Family Town, and the guys usually make their own Winn outfits."

"It's all guys who go looking like me?"

"Not entirely. The cutest little fem.'s often do, and just love playing you."

"It looks like there are far more than the 5,000 living here at the moment," Winn commented.

"We throw the best parties, and from the breeding settlements around us, we get the curious, the experimenters, the thrill-seekers, the closet-conflicted, the uncertain, and the desperate."

"There must be a lot of all of those," Winn mentioned looking around.

"More than most realize. Did you meet our Mayor?"

"He seemed quite nice if a bit attention-seeking," Winn acknowledged.

"I want to show you our bath house, it's just next door. The baths are fed by geothermal hot springs, and there are pools at different temperatures. They have plenty of clean towels, and some of your biggest fans are there dying to meet you."

"Fritz and Penny won't know where I am." Winn protested.

"We'll collect them on our way."

"Alright."

Eve, with an arm around Winn, dance-walked maneuvering through the crowd. Everyone knew Eve and Winn was introduced to a dozen people cutting across the crowded dance floor, finding a tongue in her mouth with each one. Fritz was a little intoxicated when they found him, no longer with any reserve in his dancing. He got on Winn's other arm to snake their way through the throngs with Eve leading. They found Penny in the middle of a mixed-gender group all writhing on the floor. She was really into it and didn't notice them. Eve touched the shoulder of the woman on the periphery, but a participant of the floor-action, and advised her to lead Penny to the baths once her exercise was concluded.

They wove their way out of Government House into the almost as crowded streets, then into the even more crowded bath house. Eve squeezed her way to the room with benches and cubbyholes, latched onto Winn, who held Fritz tight. They found a bench with a vacant end and sat to remove their shoes. Winn slipped out of the tight dress she'd worn for the interviews. She removed her knickers and placed them with the dress and skullcap on top of her shoes in the cubby. She never wore a bra, and her little breasts certainly needed no support. Eve was continuously introducing her to people, and each one crushed her into their naked body to slip their tongue in her mouth.

At long last, she was able to get into the water. Eve had directed her to a warm pool, not a hot one. People didn't remain in the hot ones long, and no one moved within those. The warm pool, by contrast, was one big group grope. Someone pressed into Winn's back palming each breast from behind, while a young female possibly younger than Penny and very petite, embraced Winn from the front making out with her, and she was sandwiched. Eve was of no help. The sandwich became a huddle. When young-petite-girl stopped kissing her for a moment, a strong drink was placed in Winn's hand, and she found herself gulping. She was no longer sure who in the huddle was doing what to her, and it was all too busy and complex to follow with so many bodies and limbs.

Eventually, Penny was in the huddle with Winn, and Winn had lost all sense of time in the chaos. When suddenly, Penny was in a full-frontal embrace with her, Winn said, "I think we better get back to the tender."

"But I just got you in my arms," Penny complained.

"I'll be your lover, Penny, but not here. Bodhi wanted to leave hours ago."

They had to extract Fritz from half a dozen men, which was no picnic given the frantic state of the men. Winn's clothes were not in her cubby; only her shoes. Someone had wanted a souvenir or liked the dress, but taking her knickers seemed a little over the top to Winn. Frits gave Winn his jacket to wear bottomless. Fritz led the way, locking arms with Winn who held Penny's hand, and struggled through the mass of partiers. An entourage of fans was accumulating behind and following them.

In the streets, once they gained the door and passed the threshold, the crowed was singing the theme song to *Lost in Space*. A path opened for them through the mash of bodies in the street, and they proceeded down it. It kept opening ahead of them until the path terminated at their tender. A teen girl smaller than Winn sprinted at her then threw herself on and around her saying, "I'm so totally in love with you. I'm desperate for you. I'd do anything to be with you. I need you, Winn."

The entire procession had come to a complete halt, and their entourage was pressing in from behind. The path remained open ahead, but people were pressing in around them now that they'd stopped. Penny thought the girl around Winn was really cute and got her hands on the girl. Not knowing what else to say, Winn asked the girl, "What's your name, sweetheart?"

"I'm Kristy."

"How old are you, Kristy?"

"I hacked my profile in the central computer and changed my date of birth. I'm only seventeen, but they don't let anyone under 18 come here without a parent or guardian."

"There may be some wisdom in that," Winn suggested. Then she stated her own need, "I have to get back to the ship, or Bodhi will be upset with me."

Kristy planted her feet back on the ground so that Winn was no longer supporting her weight and started them out of the press, back down the narrow path through the crowd, now between Winn and Penny and clinging to both. She told Winn gravely, "I'm working the completion stage of the Illusory Body limb, and my teacher died. I truly need help and will not pressure you to have sex with me."

"Do you like guys?" Winn inquired.

"I have no inclination towards them and have never had sex with one," Kristy explained.

"How old were you when you started meditating?"

"I was introduced to it by an aunt when I was ten and ran away at twelve to study at the ashram with Ramadon until he passed into the light."

"Kristy, we have too many girls and not enough men on board as it is."

"I won't be depleting your male resources at all. This girl here," referring to Penny, "clearly needs a lover."

Penny was groping Kristy at the moment and smitten. Winn said to herself as much as to Penny, "I'm going to get into so much trouble."

Their little linked knot with a tail of entourage finally made it to their tender with the theme song still sung loudly, and from a little group across the street in three-part harmony. Winn had lost her skullcap, hoping maybe she'd locked it in the tender, and had to enter the code onto a pad by hand to open the door. She was a little tipsy and swayed dangerously climbing into the craft. Winn got her naked bottom on the pilot's seat. Fritz climbed in the back, Penny into the copilot seat, and even though there was an empty seat in the back, Kristy got in Penny's lap and kept a hand on Winn. Fritz handed Omar all his stuff through the hatch.

Winn couldn't find her skullcap within so she said over the external speaker system, cranked up real loud and accomplished by touch-holo, "Would whoever has my knickers and skullcap please bring them to the tender. I need my skullcap to fly the spacecraft because I think I'm too drunk to manage manually."

The mayor, some other public officials, and Eve got right to work tracking down Winn's skullcap. Within minutes, a delegation was triumphantly dancing up to the tender waving the skullcap in the air. The mayor himself presented Winn her skullcap saying, "We could not get her to give up the panties."

"She keeping my knickers?!"

"Apparently," he said helplessly.

"This seat's going to give me a rash."

A woman with the delegation removed her silk shirt and handed it to Winn to sit on. She informed Winn, "Your panties will be cherished here and raised on the pole in the square above the New Firmament pendant."

"I'm truly flattered," Winn replied. Then she asked, "Do you think you could wash them first because I'd been wearing those for quite a while."

"It's your scent that is most cherished, beautiful Winn."

"I guess that's a 'no,'" Winn said, realizing and hoping hard they weren't stained.

She got the silk shirt arranged on her seat, and the skullcap upon her head then said over the speaker system, "It has been wonderful meeting all of you. I'll come to visit again. Please take good care of my friend Omar. I love all of you."

To colossal thunderous shouts of "We love you, Winn," she lifted off on just vortex-redirect until she was well above the packed street, then accidentally put the tender into a wiggle for a moment reflecting her own disequilibrium, before punching the drives. She contacted Haley and asked, "Is Bodhi furious with me?"

"No, my love, he was just worried. I told him that you were sort of abducted into a party in LGBTQ Town. He's gone to bed, and we'll wait till morning to jump to the system we discovered with the star-gate in it."

"Thanks, Haley. I seem to have accumulated two new crew."

"You require two?" Haley asked, hardly believing it."

"No. I recruited one. His name's Fritz, and you're going to just love him. The girl, Kristy, just kind of latched on, and we couldn't shake her."

"I'm keeping her," Penny shouted to Haley, intruding into the conversation."

"I guess Penny needs someone," Haley surrendered.

"I think you'll find that Penny gets around," Winn clued Haley in.

"Is Kristy cute?" Haley wanted to know.

"She's adorable, but kind of young," Winn answered.

"I'll arrange sleeping quarters for Penny, Fritz, and Kristy."

"Thanks, Haley. My knickers and dress went missing when they brought me to the bath house."

"It sounds like you had an exciting time."

"It was kind of claustrophobic and anxiety-provoking, but they were all very nice people."

"I guess Fritz and Kristy ought to just turn up at the dining room table," Haley schemed.

"I'll pretend I don't know them," Winn said, only half-joking.

"I see you're approaching jump speed, so I'll let you go," Haley stated, signing off.

"How does she know these things?!" Winn asked aloud, but not of her passengers.

Winn came out of her shock and stupor first, following the non-existence experience in the quantum jump back to the Firmament system. This time, she'd left some 40 million miles for her deceleration and got right on it. Upon reaching *Diamond Lotus,* Winn had her momentum down to almost rest and opened the bay doors coming up into the underbelly of the ship. Her coordination was impaired from the alcohol, and she scraped one side of the tender coming in. It would need a new lens coating along that side. She would sleep first.

Haley met them in the hanger when it was still airing up, and they were climbing out. Haley mentioned to Winn, "I see we've had a little fender-bender."

Winn walked around to the other side to see how bad it was. Nothing was crumpled, and there was hardly a gouge in the composite ceramic heatshield armor beneath the scraped away lens coating. Winn told Haley, "I think I can fix that in the morning. I'm a little too drunk to right now."

"Get some sleep, sweetheart, and I'll take good care of your new friends," Haley directed.

CHAPTER TWENTY

There had not been many hours between passing out on her bed and waking for breakfast. She'd missed the morning practice for the first time since she'd joined up. A shower was in order and very thorough teeth cleaning. Bodhi had been asleep in the bed, and so had Tish when Winn climbed in with just Fritz's jacket on. Shanti had been asleep in her hover crib. The suite was vacant except for her now. She got into all clean clothes and the thought of her knickers up a flag pole sent a little shiver of anxiety up her spine.

Winn walked into the dining cabin, trying a little too hard to act natural, just when everyone was beginning to gather around the table. She hugged Bodhi when he entered and said, "I'm so sorry about everything, my love."

"There was no harm done in the delay. I'm glad you're safe and returned," Bodhi told her sincerely with concern in his voice for her as he handed her their daughter.

"I tried to recruit some more crew, violated all of Firmament's employment laws, had to take a man to LGBTQ Town on New Firmament, and got sucked into a street party, a dance at the Government House in the Minister's Chamber, and then into a pool in the bath house where my dress and knickers were stolen. I scraped the tender's side on the frame of the bay doors on the way in, a bit drunk."

Haley entered with an arm affectionately around Kristy. Then Penny and Fritz entered entwined to take seats at the table. Sonic introduced his sister. Favio asked Haley, "Who is the child with you."

"I'm an adult from New Firmament," Kristy said offended, lying.

"No way!" Favio contradicted her.

"I am," she said threateningly then added, "I'll be eighteen in only ten months."

Favio shook his head in wonder, and Kristy changed tactics to tell him, "You are an amazing musician Favio and a statue of beauty in your bullhorn bikini underwear. I have a boy's pair."

Well, thank you, little pixie. What's your name?"

"I'm Kristy, and I'm mostly here to study with Bodhi, but I think I'm also in love with Winn and Haley."

"So is Bodhi," Favio told her.

"I'm going to steal your heart and shake your world, Kristy," June informed her.

Kristy turned an inspecting eye on June, appreciation spreading across her face as she did, then told June, "I hope you do."

Pam whispered to Kristy, "It might be me you fall hardest for."

Sonic asked his sister, "When did you find time to pick up a new boyfriend?"

"It happened on the way to the ship, and it's a long story," Penny replied.

"You've never had such a pretty one before," Sonic commented.

"I know, isn't he a dream? Haley found him for Winn, and now he's part mine."

"For Winn?" Sonic asked her.

"On account of you dumping her for her sister."

Sonic looked to Winn with guilt written all over him and told her, "I'm sorry, Winn. I never intended to hurt you. I seem to have fallen in love with your sister."

"Had I known that was coming, I wouldn't have invited her, but I guess I'm glad she's accidentally stumbled into a relationship with a good man; the first I've ever seen her with."

"I didn't mean to hurt you either, little sister, but Sonic deserves to be with a woman who prioritizes him as number one."

"I'm processing it and aiming to be happy for both of you," Winn stated her goal.

Winn opened her blouse and got Shanti on her nipple. Tish told her, "I nursed Shanti while you were gone."

"Thank you, my love. I had not intended to be gone so long."

"I truly enjoyed her, but I think she missed you. At one point, only Bodhi could console her."

Winn put her lips close to Shanti's ear and whispered, "I'm so sorry my precious love."

Still in her party costume, having no other clothes, Kristy said to Bodhi, "It is said that you are a great master of the six limbs and an adept teacher like no other."

"I have accomplished the six limbs and teach them," Bodhi confirmed.

"I'm on the Illusory Body completion stage and have been doing the parts of the dream work I know. Would you teach me the rest, Master Bodhi?"

"Please just call me Bodhi. I will teach you Kristy, and you will receive the entire instruction for the six limbs."

"Thank you so much. There is nothing more important to me."

"Do you have worried parents somewhere whom we ought to contact?" Bodhi inquired.

"My parents know I went to the ashram in Swimfen when I was twelve, and I have not seen them in five years. I had no way to call them once I got to New Firmament, but I wrote to them, and my letter was sent on a returning transport back to Firmament."

"You can call them from our ship after breakfast and let them know where you are, and that you are safe," Bodhi directed.

"I promise that I will. I can't wait to tell them that I live on *Diamond Lotus* now, with you and Haley and Winn. I won't be able to tell them where I am, because I haven't a clue."

"If it's alright with you, I'd like to say a few words to them also, just to reassure them that we will keep you safe."

"My mom will probably faint if you speak to her," Kristy told him, "and my dad will tell everyone that he spoke to Captain Bodhi until they are all sick of hearing it. They'll be thrilled, and I'd super-appreciate it if you did."

"I feel it's my responsibility as captain, and particularly since you are technically just a minor," Bodhi shared. "I'm going to have Tish work with you first. She's my most senior student in the six limbs.

She can also start working with you on calm abiding and emptiness meditation for the actual attainment of your illusory body. You will have individual sessions with me as well, and I expect you to come to the morning and evening practices. Welcome to our community, Kristy."

She thought she'd better say, in case he was getting any ideas, "I'm only and exclusively into females."

"That's a relief," Bodhi said honestly, "I am too and have my plate full."

Sunoco, who was sitting to one side of Kristy, told her, "Doing your dream work lying beside Bodhi, causes the winds to forcefully enter the center channel."

"Am I to just climb in his bed one night?" Kristy asked.

"That's what Tish and I did," Sunoco confirmed.

Haley exclaimed, "Look, Winn, you're in the news on both Firmament and New Firmament."

Haley brought up a holo on the center of the dining room table and the LGBTQ Town mayor, wearing a wool business suit and not his leotard, was telling both worlds, "Beautiful Winn descended upon our community to deliver her friend Omar into our bosom and stayed to greet and party with us. It was the greatest of honors for LGBTQ Town."

Winn's panties atop the flagpole waving in the breeze were in the background just behind and above the mayor's head in the camera shot. Penny said, "Look Winn, there are your knickers," bringing everyone's attention to them.

Tandy asked, "Now, how did your panties leave your pelvis and get way up there, girl?"

"I took them off in the changing room to go in the baths, and they were gone, along with my dress and skullcap, when I returned. They left my shoes, and I did get the skullcap back," Winn tried to explain.

Bodhi commented, "Each settlement flies its own pendant above the New Firmament pendant in their town square, so Winn's panties must be LGBTQ Town settlement's pendant."

"It's perfect for them," Kristy said with authority. "The guys had been leaning towards a pair of Bullhorn bikini briefs, but a pair of panties worn by Winn won hands-down among everyone."

"They refused to wash them before flying them on the pole," Winn complained.

Haley informed them, "I'm going to help Winn with the work on the tender hull this morning, and Tish will copilot for Bodhi taking us to the system with the star-gate. *Diamond Lotus* will remain cloaked and shielded until we have established coms and a peaceful understanding with the officials administering the population of the planet."

"Aye aye, Ma'am," Tish replied.

"Which of the new crew are going to help me with the galley cleanup?" Tandy put out to the table now that she was no longer able to rope Bodhi into it.

Both Fritz and Kristy said at the same time, "I will."

Bodhi and Tish went to the bridge after breakfast, and Winn and Haley went to the hanger to attend to repairs on the tender from Winn's little accident. Fritz and Kristy helped Tandy clean up the galley. Pam and June got started on routine maintenance, which could be accomplished in flight, and Uldra got Sonic, Yen, and Penny to help her harvest produce in the stacks and grow room. Shamus checked all the storage holds manually cross-referencing inventory against computer records. Sunoco and Ilya sat on the bridge, observing as the beginning of their ship-piloting training, now that both had accomplished their small craft pilot certification and licensing. Favio attended to his fan mail.

When Bodhi started a two-minute countdown to quantum jump, everyone efficiently made it to a seat affixed to the deck and strapped in. People standing up going through the jump found themselves on the deck bruised after it, with no recollection of how they got there. The jump occurred, putting them in shock followed by a brief stupor, all but Bodhi, who contemplated the black near-attainment. Tish had managed to absorb the winds to arrive at the first subtle mind of white appearance, avoiding the shock, and was only rattled a little bit by the experience. Fritz, Penny, and Kristy were flabbergasted when they emerged from their stupors.

Diamond Lotus was just at the orbital path of the fourth planet of this yellow sun system with a star-gate. There was a mining operation established on the 4th planet. The gate was roughly 27 million miles ahead of them, so there was zero space traffic out this far. Bodhi had reversed the main drives and brought the little braking drives online at full throttle, firing a few reverse thrusters—though cautious of spending fuel cells. They passed the gigantic star-gate at .33 light speed bleeding off velocity quickly and shot by some slower moving ore haulers and a freighter transport more than twice the size of *Diamond Lotus* at .24 light.

Bodhi subjected these to a full scan, and the data showed the ships to be fueled with marsnium, dependent upon spectrum encoded light coms, carrying no weapons of any kind, and having rudimentary force field shields unable to protect against several waves and particles. A scan ahead of the 3rd planet revealed a world yet in recovery from the crisis of survival, always involving the four killers of humanity: pollution, over-population, mismanagement of resources, and climate change. Large areas of the upper subtropics and lower temperate zone showed brown, almost devoid of life. The magnetic South Pole was green with plant life and the coastal lands around the magnetic north pole were also green and alive. Oceans and seas covered ¾ of the planet, and coasts of the temperate zone were spotted with the tops of skyscrapers, mostly just steel girders at this point, rising out of the sea from now sunken cities. Bodhi estimated the time-lapse since the reversal of destructive habits to be only about 3 ½ centuries ago.

Hundreds of enormous nuclear fission plants sat inoperative and abandoned, replaced with marsnium fusion reactors and renewable energy systems. Ground transportation consisted of fusion battery hovercraft, industrial wheeled vehicles, and mag-lev railroads. There was no surface to space weapons and no weapons bases on the planet's moon. There were mining facilities and observatories on the lunar surface. Orbiting the planet were two large space stations employed as space transportation hubs and ship building platforms.

Neither contained a single weapon's system. There were no war ships anywhere in this star system.

The planet was seriously degraded, and pollution levels remained high, though it was clearly now in recovery and healing across geological timeframes. Massive cleanup efforts were in evidence, and no further damage was underway. There was not a fission bomb detectable anywhere and spent fission materials had been removed from the planet surface entirely. Electricity was all direct current, and desalination plants ringed coastal lands where they were inhabited. Natural gas was the only fossil fuel in use on the planet, and it was being used sparingly. An envelope of orbiting satellites surrounded the planet, and zero percent were weaponized.

Bodhi got them slowed to .03 light speed once inside the orbital path of the moon, still braking and slowing. He made several high orbits of the planet scanning activity and crossing different regions with each pass. He assumed a medium orbit just above the furthest out satellites. He contacted Haley, who was down in the hanger with Winn setting new composite ceramic heatshield armor in the gouge from the frame of the bay doors, and requested, "Could you launch a mini-spy-drone into the atmosphere and send the released micro-spy androids to places language is being taught, and hack into their quantum computer network to download the data."

This would remain only meaningless symbols until both the spoken and the computer languages got deciphered. Haley told him, "I'm preparing the carrier-drone for launch now, and will work on language acquisition as soon as Winn and I are done mending the tender hull."

"Thanks, Haley. You're the best," Bodhi said gratefully.

"Mel gave me a language decryption program she wrote after figuring out a dozen languages in her travels with Pez, and it ought to make our process quite efficient."

"Great! I'll hack into their coms and identify concentrations of coms traffic on the surface."

Tish mentioned to Bodhi, "We ought to come to rest and hold our relative position for a long scan, aimed where their space-time spectrographic imaging telescopes on the lunar surface are focused."

"You're right," Bodhi noticed. "They are all focused on the same point in space. I'll come to a full stop and hold our position."

Bodhi brought *Diamond Lotus* to rest and set drives to sustain their relative position. He told Tish, "I'm starting the long scan, and we will maintain it until we discover what those space-imaging telescopes are focused on."

Quantum computer enhancement after five minutes of long scanning in a narrow beam revealed several dozen streaks moving at .72 light speed. Another minute of scanning did not improve their resolution due to the speed the ships were traveling. One thing was certain, they were all in a trajectory to intersect this star system in approximately 14 Mother months in the location the star would be in at that time.

"Tish stated, "Those are ships, not comets or asteroids, but that's all we can know given their current velocity."

"I'm getting us back into orbit," Bodhi informed her, "and we can check those ships out with the tender later."

"What do you suppose they are?" Tish asked him.

"They do not have quantum coms travel and are still dependent on star-gates. So many ships on a long-duration journey in real space would suggest a gate construction force, possibly with war ship escorts."

"Why do you suppose they chose this star system?" Tish asked him.

"I'm sure that like us, they detected the star-gate in this system," Bodhi replied.

"How will we get finer resolution in the tender?" Tish inquired.

"We can match their speed and direction and get in close with full cloaking to actively scan them. We'll know what they have in their ships and if they are humanoid or not."

"Why not go now in *Diamond Lotus*?" Tish asked.

"We have well over a year to explore that situation and need to be accumulating data on this planet right now."

Haley and Winn got the gouge filled and sanded smooth, then applied the lens coating to the scrape along the hull. Once they were done, you could not even tell where the scrape had been. Haley headed for the office where she could begin deciphering languages, and Winn headed for medical to get a hangover remedy. Everyone worked through the morning at their tasks, and Favio made great progress in his correspondences with his fans, who had the sexiest selfies included with their texts. At 12:00 hours ship's time, they all gathered in the dining room for a meal prepared by Uldra.

Once seated and serving up, Haley informed them, "There is a universal planetary language which is a sure sign of a high degree of unity among the population. We have all the data we need for spoken language, including course materials for teaching children to read and write. These lessons contain imagery of objects corresponding to words, and the Mel decryption program is processing the data now."

"What's the estimated time of completion?" Bodhi asked her.

"The Mel program will complete its work in just over an hour but then I'll need to program an interpreter service to load on your hand-devices. Within three hours we ought to be able to communicate with them fluently."

"Great work, Haley," Bodhi declared. "I think during that time, Tish and I will go check out some ships in real space, which are headed here traveling at .72 light, and 14 Mother months out."

"How many ships?" Haley asked.

"Thirty-five at least, though there may be some smaller ones, which did not resolve in our scan imagery," Bodhi answered.

"That sounds like a gate-construction operation to me," Haley stated.

"I was thinking the same thing," Bodhi agreed.

Tish suggested, "As much as I'd like to go with you, Bodhi, I think Winn needs you right now, so I'd suggest taking her instead."

"I love you, Tish," Winn told her.

"I love you too, sweetheart."

"Alright," Bodhi agreed to Tish's suggestion, "Winn, you can pilot the craft, and I'll be your co-pilot."

"Goodie!" Winn enthused feeling better already.

"Could I come and observe?" Kristy asked.

"I don't see why not," Bodhi offered.

Haley mentioned, "There's a lead covered, force-field insulated underground facility in the upper temperate zone on the second largest continent which we'll need to engineer a look inside of from close up. It is the only unreadable place we've found on the planet."

"We can look into it through their computer's data first, once we have the spoken language and programming languages deciphered, and understand their codes," Bodhi suggested.

"We'll try that first," she concurred. "It might contain all we need to know about the place."

Shamas reported to Haley, "You were right. There is no point in doing manual inventory. The computer keeps a perfectly accurate count."

"That will save you considerable time," Haley pointed out.

The whole system is like an automated robotic warehouse," he said amazed.

"Though it's not part of our higher technology," Haley told him.

"No, and most of that yet eludes me," Shamus stated.

"Can we seek more male crew members on this planet?" June asked.

Bodhi said, "We have room to take on another male, but I'd prefer someone with high meditation."

"Who is also young, good looking and heterosexual," June added.

"Those will be the secondary criteria then," Bodhi confirmed.

"I need to do some grocery shopping on the surface as soon as we've established contact with the folks down there," Uldra informed them.

"That will likely need to wait until tomorrow," Haley told her.

Uldra proposed, "We could make a fish tank farm for the ship."

"We have one," Haley reported, "though it is not currently in operation, and we have bug-box farm incubators too that we are not using at the moment."

"I don't eat bugs," Uldra insisted.

"You don't know what you're missing," Haley replied. "Breaded and fried, they make a delicious crunchy treat. And gourmet sauces can make them just exquisitely scrumptious."

"I'm more of a fish and poultry person," Uldra claimed, "than an insect-eating person."

Favio announced, "I'm making prime-rib tonight!"

Haley asked him with a frown, "And what are you making for Bodhi?"

"I'm making vegetables and potatoes," Favio explained, "with the meal."

Uldra inserted, "I'll make poached salmon with hollandaise sauce for Bodhi, and whoever else would like some."

"Thank you, Uldra," Haley said gratefully.

Favio asked, "Who do you think they'll get to play me on the show next season?"

Haley informed him, "I transferred some graphics and animation programming to the studio producers, the same I employed for your music clips, and you will be computer-generated. The producers prefer not to have to change the faces of the crew."

"Hey, I look even better computer-generated," Favio said delightedly.

"I thought you would like this better," Haley told him, "and none of us were looking forward to your complaints about whichever actor tried to play you."

"Thank you, Haley, you have done so much to further my career and fame," Favio told her with genuine gratitude.

"You take good care of me too, Favio," Haley complimented him.

Pam, who was the mother of Favio's son Alexander, and the only one who ever really scolded Favio, told him assertively, "Darling, no one cooks red meat like you do, but you must always consider our beloved teacher and employer, Bodhi, in your menu planning. How would you like it if Uldra prepared a turkey feast, and gave you only mashed potatoes and peas from it?"

"You are right, of course, and I will heed your words Pam, but you are beginning to sound like a nagging wife," Favio replied.

"Someone must remind you of your duty, and apparently, only I'm courageous enough to risk it," Pam said the words sweetly.

Uldra argued, "I tell him all the time, but only when we are alone in the galley, never in front of others. He just tells me that that is why *I* was hired."

"I do appreciate your cooking, Uldra," Bodhi told her most honestly and sincerely.

Favio complained, "Haley won't eat either of our cooking, instead she eats ambassador rations in the morning—two of them— and then just her protein shakes."

"Food has never been my thing," Haley explained. "My indulgence is exclusively sex."

"For that, I am grateful," Favio replied, "but I wish you would try the dishes I make."

"My routine is everything for me and keeps me together," Haley told him affectionately. "I can smell, and I see the delight of others to recognize your culinary mastery, sweetheart, and prefer you for your sexual prowess and your singing."

"You are quite the maestro of making love yourself, Haley," Favio acknowledged.

Tish told Haley, "I will help Fritz and Penny with their clothing design and manufacturing today." To Kristy, she explained, "I can have a uniform ready for you when you get back if you give me your measurements. Once you return on the tender, I will assist you with the computer design program for making the rest of your wardrobe."

Kristy said, "I like wearing tights and lacey under shirts. That's what I wore to my job at the donut shop I worked at in LGBTQ Town."

Winn, who had drawn their diamond in the center of a lotus crest for their uniforms, which she also helped design, advocated, "Let's all wear our uniforms when we go down to the surface to meet with the people of this planet."

Bodhi agreed, "For first appearances, that may be preferable to tights and lacey undershirts."

"What do the uniforms look like?" Kristy asked, looking concerned.

Haley put up a holo from the pedestal in the center of the dining room table of a female mannequin wearing the female version of the uniform next to a male mannequin in the men's version. They were of the same cloth, and both sported Winn's crest, but the two versions were radically different. The male uniform was baggy and quite military looking, while the female one had a short skirt, short cute jacket, and tiny little hats hardly bigger than a skullcap, which would need to be pinned to remain on one's head. The color of the cloth was dark blue and the buttons of pure gold. Buttons were an ancient contrivance for connecting two ends of textiles around the body.

"Those are ridiculous!" Kristy complained.

Haley set her straight, "You don't have to wear one. You could always just remain on the ship and not visit the surface."

"I'm wearing yellow tights with mine then," Kristy decided.

Winn shared, "The girl's shoes are soft and comfy, and the heels adjust to any height from six-inch stilettoes to flats."

"But dark blue?!" Kristy criticized.

"I chose the color," Bodhi told her. "The girls came up with the designs. I only insisted that the skirts be long enough to fully cover the crotch. Dark blue will be the color of our order, and we will have meditation suits of the same color."

Since the planet is demilitarized," Haley proposed, "I think we ought to leave holsters and blasters on the shuttle when we land and wear our fanny-pack mini-shield generators."

"You and I will carry little needle-blasters in shoulder holsters under our jackets, Haley, and Tish will need to remain on *Diamond Lotus* to watch our backs from space. She is trained and certified on the nose and quad blasters now. We will meet with them close by our shuttle, and I'd like to have Uduak near the airlock in a hard-shell combat suit fully armed, monitoring the proceedings."

"That sounds like a cautious and safe approach," Haley agreed.

Bodhi speculated. "They are likely to assume we are advanced scouts of the force headed their way, which we know they are monitoring from their lunar space-imaging telescopes. We will have to convince them that this is not the case."

"What if it's an invasion force?" Tish inquired.

"Then we'll prevent the invasion and turn those ships back around," Bodhi asserted.

"Most of those are larger than this ship, and there are so many of them," Tish pointed out.

"They are still using gates, so their technology is thousands of years behind us. Unless they are powering their ships with solarium, which is unheard of for pre-quantum coms travel, they will have no weapons to penetrate our shields."

"This is not a warship," Winn complained.

"No, though it is yet a far more potent one than they will have," Bodhi stated.

Uldra began clearing empty dishes from the table, and Tandy helped her. Fritz and Penny rose to give them a hand. Haley told Bodhi, "I'll be in the office for the next couple of hours learning the planet's basic spoken language and programming the interpretation service. Once that's done, I can study their programming languages and access their full planetary data."

"I'd be lost without you, Haley," Bodhi said fondly.

"You seem to have gotten lost *with* me," Haley pointed out.

"You know what I mean," Bodhi replied.

"And I would be lost without you, my love," Haley admitted.

Bodhi, Winn, and Kristy made their way to the hanger, which was still aired up. Bodhi inspected the repair job and ran some diagnostics on cloaking and hull integrity before climbing aboard. When Winn and Kristy were in and the tender sealed, Bodhi powered up the air compressors with his skullcap, sucking the air into tanks and creating a vacuum in the hanger. This process was quicker than airing the hanger up. Winn opened the bay doors and shot out of the ship's underside into space in the tender. Bringing up her navigation, she entered the coordinates based on the convoy's speed of .72 light, and the duration of time elapsed since fixing their position, with their trajectory factored in. She accelerated with drives alone to save fuel cells and brought them to jump speed. Winn engaged the quantum drive, and Bodhi contemplated the black near-attainment.

Winn and Kristy went into momentary shock to emerge into a brief stupor before getting their bearings again.

They were a quarter light minute ahead of the oncoming ships headed in the same direction and going .02 light speed slower than the convoy. As the ships closed, Winn accelerated to match their speed, not a thousand miles from the ship on the force's closest flank. She made an active scan of the whole convoy, then each of the 39 ships composing it. Data flooded in. Before Bodhi had time to even get an overview of it all, Haley was on speaker in their cockpit saying, "They have saturnium reactors, not miniaturized to the maximum; 94% full force field shielding, core star-gate components on the largest transports, construction vessels, mining craft carriers, material haulers, and ten war ships with the equivalent of class five blasters and beam weapons, as well as rockets and long-range missiles with space drives. There is also one troop transport with 4,800 troops and hard-shell combat suits for each. They are dependent on spectrum encoded light coms, have zero cloaking ability, and must not have efficient carbon capture systems on their home planet because there is only a quarter-inch layer or carbon plate armor on the hulls of their war ships. They use primarily adamantine and steel-titanium-nickel armor. Currently, only a skeleton crew is awake on each ship while the majority are in cryogenic deep hibernation for the journey. They are white sun humanoids. Until *Diamond Lotus* can get in close and hit one of their ships with a nanobot spray missile to link with their quantum computer through the coms terminals on the hull, we will not be able to obtain sufficient data on their language and codes to learn to communicate with them."

"We've got 14 months to take care of that, Haley," Bodhi told her. "Thanks for the analysis."

"Once we get into their computer data, we will have their star maps and the location of their home planet," Haley filled him in.

"We'll get it, and we'll go to their home world to learn more about their civilization," Bodhi agreed. "First, we can make contact with the population on the planet you're orbiting."

"I'm working on it," Haley let him know.

"I'm not trying to rush you, my love, just to prioritize our activities."

"I'll see you when you get back," Haley said, signing off.

"How does she do that?!" Winn asked him.

"Haley is so steeped in Om quantum computer languages that she doesn't even see code, just the meaning of it. She is one of the two greatest experts on quantum computers in the six galaxies of my former world."

"She is truly amazing," Winn agreed.

"And such a skillful lover," Kristy added.

"I know," Winn agreed.

"We have all the data we can get without creating a hard transmission-link with nanobots, and we'll need *Diamond Lotus* for that," Bodhi said. "Prepare for a quantum jump."

Since they were already at jump speed, Winn engaged the quantum drive, and at that moment, Bodhi arrived in the state of contemplating the black near attainment. They were instantly back in the star-system they'd left from, some 18 million miles from their ship, and Bodhi was already braking frantically when Winn's stupor wore off. He apologized to Winn, "I started decelerating for you so we wouldn't overshoot."

"You must teach me how to do that," Winn told him. "To keep out of shock and start functioning the moment we arrive through the jump."

"You will learn that with the nine mixings in the practice with the six limbs, once you complete your inner fire work. Tish is able to reach the white appearance in just the moment before jump and is merely disoriented for a moment. The limbs are a second and new method for you, though you progress quite rapidly, my love."

"Thanks for getting us slowing right away," Winn replied.

"I'm entering a flight plan for you," Bodhi told her, "which will take us into the atmosphere over that blind spot in the northern hemisphere we cannot penetrate with our scans. I want to check it out before returning to the ship."

"I'm following it," Winn assured him. Then she asked, "Why don't you go right to clear light contemplation for the jumps, dear?

"The quantum potential is before the origin of light, sweetheart, and the black near-attainment is the closest state to nonexistence as potential only."

"What about pilots who cannot attain these states?" Winn inquired.

"Where I come from, the majority of pilots suffer brief shock through jumps, and allow time and distance upon arrival for this."

"So, I'm not hopeless?" Winn asked.

"You are already an excellent small-craft pilot, Winn. At some point, I'll train you in the close-combat maneuvers of the phantom-raiders which Pez sent me to."

"Is Pez also the top ship pilot?"

"No," Bodhi informed her. "Admiral Swenah holds that title. Pez is by far the greatest small-craft pilot."

"You told me she flew a star cruiser better than anyone," Winn complained.

"The star cruiser hull was turned into a giant small-craft bomber, eliminating 4/5 of the crew and living quarters to cram 4 fusion reactors into it instead of the usual two, and load missile and torpedo magazines in. It was a ship converted to a gargantuan small-craft."

"Still," Winn pointed out.

"I guess you could say that Pez is far and away the best small ship-converted-to-bomber pilot in the six galaxies of allies in my old world," Bodhi conceded.

"I wish I could meet her," Winn lamented.

"I've never met anyone so high the realization," Bodhi stated. "She has returned voluntarily 333 times in a row to take incarnation so she can work for the enlightenment of all sentient beings. She was selected as the spear-point of intervention in several galactic and intergalactic cosmic situations supported by a 100-year meditation performed by the entire advanced race of Amonrahonians. She is the most ancient non-returner choosing to keep returning over and over for the common evolution."

"How do you know her?" Kristy inquired.

"I fought with her in the space battle for the Monarch planetary system, which was the center of power for a tri-galaxy empire of 5,700 plus inhabited planets called the Royal Monarch Empire. She became my teacher after that."

Winn put up a holo of Pez from when she was 34 years old. Her eyes were alert and penetrating yet empty of self. Her almost goofy smile was radiant, alive and entirely natural. Her image just seemed to invite trust and offer infinite compassion. Kirsty said, "She's hot! Did you have sex with her?"

"No. I trained with her and received her instruction."

Winn asked him, already knowing the answer, "Who was your action seal and guide for the final work of harnessing copulation for total spiritual reunion with the Absolute?"

"Pez was," he admitted. "But it wasn't "sex" in the common sense of the word."

"Who will be my action seal at the end of the six limbs?" Kristy asked Bodhi.

"Sonic and Ilya might be ready by then. You may choose among those capable of guiding you, little flower."

"I want you to do it since you are my teacher now, and I've no attraction to boys, so age and appearance are irrelevant to me."

"So, you'll just settle for your ugly old teacher?" Bodhi asked.

"That is not what I meant," Kristy informed him. "Expertise is what I value, and I'd prefer the best."

"Haley can also teach you the joining of the oval and central channels for spiritual union from a method separate from the six limbs, which can be accomplished between two females."

Haley came on speaker saying, "I'd be delighted to teach you the joining of the channels."

"I'd like that, Haley. Thank you," Kristy replied.

Bodhi suggested, "When we get back to the ship, we will have our first individual session together to complete your illusory body instruction, and see where you are in the dream work."

"Alright."

"I will initiate and empower you as my student," Bodhi said.

Winn was entering the atmosphere over the pole and headed for the upper temperate zone over the underground facility, hidden with lead and insulating shielding. Great effort and expense had been invested to block whatever it was from prying sensors. Although they could not see within, the power usage levels here could be detected, and they were extreme. Bodhi accumulated all the data available to them from close up then instructed Winn to return the tender to the ship's hangar. Kristy asked him, "When may I begin my small-craft pilot training?"

"Haley will need to get you up to speed on some of the sciences first so that you have some basic understanding of the technology you will be utilizing. It won't be long."

"Are we just going to go around saving worlds now?" Kristy asked.

"We will prevent any war-like invasions we run across and assist any planets in need from biosphere extinction, though my mission from my teacher is to spread the teachings to those ready for them."

"Who is Pez's spouse?" Kristy asked.

"Pez connected with the truest love from her previous life, Ming, whom the Islohar call 'the 'Tarim,' then a yellow sun girl named Ahhu, and a boy named Rubix. A white sun girl named Trix joined them next, and then a graduate student named Gretle."

"She has five spouses?!" Kristy exclaimed as a question.

"She does," Bodhi confirmed.

"Four are female and only one male," she noted.

"Pez had no inclination towards males until her teacher, Sarhi the Im, told her she would have to get pregnant by Rubix, who was her student. Together they gave birth to the holy Mu, who is the one who comes every 2500 years to transmit new teachings for the human race. She is Pez's daughter, Electra, who must be going on eight years old now within her space-time. Rubix is the #1 Om quad-gunner as an honorary member of their star fleet."

"I wish Pez was my teacher," Kristy stated.

"I wish she could be," Bodhi agreed, "but that's not how things are, and you will just have to settle for me."

"I was just saying," Kristy replied. "You are quite amazing, Bodhi, for a male."

"Thank you, Kristy. I guess," Bodhi told her uncertainly.

Winn opened the hangar doors and brought the tender in with room to spare on all sides, wondering how she'd gotten so close to the bay door frame the night before. She set the craft down in its parking space and started airing the hangar the moment it sealed. They had to wait a couple of minutes before climbing out. They all went through the airlock to the lift-tube. Bodhi rode up first, and Kristy jumped into Winn's tube to go up together. Bodhi brought Kristy into the meditation cabin, and they sat facing each other.

Bodhi led Kristy through the entirety of the first three limbs giving the complete detailed instruction, including the advanced instructions and even a few of the secret ones. He passed her internal energy the entire time. The new clearer instruction, and the energy he passed her, along with his profound presence and state, put Kristy into the highest meditation she had ever before attained. He next made the Equal Ceremony with her connecting soul to soul through the windows of the eyes, still passing to her his internal energy. The connection was total, and the arc of love between them intense, though entirely asexual. Once Kristy was in calm abiding and quiescence of mind, Bodhi took on and transmuted Kristy's deepest psychic wound of feeling controlled and dominated by her father. He had never touched her sexually tough he'd become physically violent with her on several occasions.

Kristy felt a great weight and pressure permanently lifted, and expunged from her mind in an experience of great pacification liberating her psychic energy to expand and freely circulate. She was still contemplating this in wonderment when a great lake of merit transferred from Bodhi to Kristy's storehouse consciousness, or container consciousness, flooded her, fully orienting her towards pristine enlightenment and the Good. She'd hardly integrated this experience when his blessing as teacher hit her, shattering her world to open the void of infinite possibilities. Kristy was lost in clarity and bliss upon vacuous emptiness within the highest contemplation far beyond previous peak meditation experiences.

Bodhi maintained Kristy in her high state for about a half-hour before striking the gong and closing his eyes ending the ceremony. Kristy jumped in his lap, straddling Bodhi's torso to embrace him tightly. She asked him, "What did you do?!"

"The functions of the guide and teacher."

"And those functions are?"

"Instruction, taking on and neutralizing the negative consequences most holding you back, making our equality known to you, the transfer of enough merit to connect you solidly with the calling of love, and passing the blessing of the teacher."

"Wow!"

"We have one more very brief ceremony to make together, Kristy, so let's perform an act of self-remembering."

They each intoned the sacred seed sound and bowed to the divine within. They made eye contact again, connecting souls and generating the arc of love. Bodhi placed his right palm over Kristy's heart energy center and internally made the vows of the teacher. In call and response with Bodhi leading, they recited the vows of the student. He was also passing his internal energy and love through his palm into her. It felt to her like an infusion of pure life and awareness divinely transporting her. Their connection felt to Kristy like it was eternal and unbreakable, filling her with security. She felt closer to him than she had to a lover, though she had no erotic attraction to him. She trusted him with her life and soul and knew he would place these before his own.

She could not get over her awe of him when he struck the gong ending their session, nor could she get over her amazement at her own transformed state of mind. She hopped back in his lap and clutched him for all she was worth, never wanting to let go. She burst out crying, not in the least unhappy, but overjoyed beyond containment, and soaked Bodhi's shoulder with her tears. He sat there contemplating pure consciousness, with no self to be found, and the cabin seemed to Kristy to be filled with his formidable presence. She finally got her breathing enough in control to tell him, "My gratitude is beyond words and never ending. You are beyond belief and a cosmic force in the world."

"You prepared yourself well, Kristy, and I was but a catalyst for what you were ready to experience. It is entirely about what is divine within you and I am merely a guide. Do not fall into idolatry of the teacher, of the teachings, or of our order, meaning our meditation group. Only the pure divine essence is sacred; nothing else. You are now better acquainted with your divine essence, little flower."

"Why do you call me that?"

"You are beautiful like a flower and open to the divine as a flower opens to the sun, Kristy."

"I would open sexually to you, now, Bodhi."

"That will not be necessary except in the relationship of divine union through a consort if you choose me as your guide."

"I have already chosen you."

"You are a most receptive disciple, little flower, and I am immensely pleased with your progress. Tish will teach you the emptiness meditations for establishing your actual illusory body, and then I will practice these with you and provide specific instruction tailored to you. I am grateful to have you in our order."

CHAPTER TWENTY-ONE

The interpreter service was programmed, uploaded to hand-devices, and operational when Bodhi arrived in the office. Haley had also deciphered the planet's computer languages and was quantumly assimilating all data bases from the surface. Favio was preparing dinner with Uldra in the galley and could be heard singing throughout the living quarters on the 11th deck. Bodhi let Haley work and brought up a holo summary of the data analyzed thus far by her. The planet's population had increased over the past 367 years since die-off had faded, to now just under 1.5 billion humans. At the successful conclusion of their crisis for survival, resolving their self-destruction of their biosphere, the population of the planet had shrunk to 931 million humans. They were keeping their numbers down and would not exceed 1.5 billion population to keep their impact low on their environment. Pre-crisis they had reached 11.6 billion. There were no weapons of any kind on the planet, per the data, and the people were all united as one planetary population, no longer divided by nations and states. They had reached social collapse at the mid-crisis stage, and this eliminated monetary currency as power and made it impossible to project power over distances.

Those most stuck in ego all killed each other, starved, died in climate change natural disasters, or committed suicide. The rest were mostly remote indigenous peoples and placed their scientists in charge of production and distribution with the good of scientific equality, and placed their spiritual leaders—not the unenlightened political ones tyrannically controlling major religions with an iron greedy fist, but the real spiritual leaders who were enlightened and so could be trusted, in the oversight of the scientists.

The massive destructive strivings for ego-gratification contradicting survival of the species became utterly absurd and a tragic objective lesson none would ever forget. With the ego illusion collapsed, and now nothing but a pathetically disastrous misfortune and stupidity recognized as the only danger and evil facing them, cooperation and unity emerged to administer the various enterprises of their civilization, and they embraced moral anarchy by declaring that no human being ever has the right to power over others. Administrators gave suggestions, facts, and data analysis guided by the sciences and held no actual power over anyone. They had produced the beginnings of a society like that on Mother and Ganahar.

When Haley looked up from her work, Bodhi made eye contact with her and said, "These people must be defended and protected because they are truly precious."

"Our minds meet in the same evidence," Haley agreed.

"Can you connect me with whatever department administrator is overseeing their lunar space telescopes, Haley?"

"Sure can, and I'm on it," she said with a smile. A moment later, she told him, "He's holding for you. Be sure your interpreter service is live."

"Thanks, Haley." To the administrator, Bodhi said, "This is Bodhi, Captain of the interstellar Expeditionary Tug Utility Ship, *Diamond Lotus*. We come in peace and are orbiting your planet. Our ship is cloaked, but I'm shutting down cloaking generators, and you will be able to pick us up on your sensors. We are lost in space unfamiliar to us and were attracted by your star-gate. We are not in any way connected with the force headed towards you and 14 months from contact. Those are white sun humans employing a fusion material ten times more potent than the one you mine on your 4th planet. We will go on a mission to further investigate them and will protect you if they prove hostile. We would like to meet with some of your administrators. We have ideas and technologies to assist you in accelerating your planet's healing. Congratulations on surviving your crisis for survival 367 years ago."

"You are E.T.s?!" He said giddily with excitement. "We've never had contact before. This is incredible."

"We are all from yellow sun 3rd planets like you, but we are not from your solar system."

"I've acquired you in our sensors, and it is clear that your ship is not from our world."

"Could you share with me your name, and what you call your planet?" Bodhi requested.

"I am Administrator Gordon, and this is the planet Ground."

"I'm pleased to meet you Administrator Gordon. This is not the first planet I've known called Ground."

"Now that you mention it, I suppose it's kind of an obvious name for a planet."

"The most common are 'Earth' and 'Firmament,'" Bodhi informed him. "My first officer and I are from Mother, but no longer know how to get home having passed through a wormhole. The rest of my crew is from Firmament, within this galaxy."

"We did not think intergalactic travel possible," Gordon said with surprise.

"It's not when dependent upon star-gates for quantum jumps," Bodhi agreed. "We have attained quantum travel without star-gates. My home planet of Mother has also attained the unity of moral anarchy. We have much in common."

"I will alert the other administrators and travel to the capital to meet with you in the Administration Center there. The capital is now in the subarctic, half-way across the smaller continent on the edge of the largest lake. It will take me a little over an hour to arrive."

"We have ascertained which city is your capital and have coordinates from your databases of the Administration Building. I will arrive in a cargo shuttle with 16 of my crew, and we will wait to leave so we can time our arrival with yours, Administrator Gordon. Where is the best place to set down our shuttle?"

"There is a large lawn directly behind the Administration Building of about eighteen acres. Will that give you enough room?"

"Oh, definitely, way more than enough. I'm afraid our landing legs will tear up the lawn a bit."

"We can sod it after you leave, and no one will be offended. This is the most momentous encounter of our race's history. I sincerely look forward to meeting you, Captain Bodhi."

"I am quite looking forward to meeting you as well, Administrator Gordon. I'll land the cargo shuttle on the lawn in one hour and ten minutes, then wait to hear from you before exiting my craft. Have you determined my frequency per your light spectrum coms?"

"I have it," he confirmed, "but the lag-time I would expect, given the distance between us, informs me that your coms must far exceed light speed."

"We are sending in real-time to a satellite over your planet in low orbit. I'll stay tuned to this frequency and await your call on the ground."

"What do you want from us," he asked a little concerned.

"I came to acquire your star maps, which I already have. Now we are simply here to help."

"How marvelous!" He enthused signing off.

Favio was pissed when he learned he had to put his dinner on hold because they were all headed planet-side, all but Tish, who would remain on the bridge of *Diamond Lotus* to watch over them from space. In great excitement, the crew donned their dark blue uniforms, and Kristy did wear yellow tights with hers, although she put on the short skirt over these, much to Bodhi's relief. They were all issued dark blue fanny-pack mini-shield generators, and both Haley and Bodhi wore needle blasters in shoulder holsters beneath their jackets. In their uniforms, they looked far more official as a group than the ad-hock collection they were. All seven babies were in their hover cradles on the bridge with Tish, who was worried they might all wake at once wanting to nurse.

They went down to the hangar by tube and cargo-lift, and even ladder, then boarded the shuttle. Bodhi piloted the craft and Haley copiloted. He landed most gently on the lawn, but the landing legs sank into the ground six inches nonetheless. Uduak got into the hard-shell combat suit and would remain on the shuttle unless needed. His suit had four shoulder missiles and a heavy-duty automatic blaster rifle, plus he carried a 40mm grenade automatic gun with a 60-round jungle-clip magazine which could be set to short bursts or semi-auto. He also had a blaster pistol in the suit's holster. The suit was armored, shielded, contained thrusters and boosters, and had thermal insulation, heat and A.C., air tank, micro-quantum computer, and high-power sensors and coms. Although hard-shell combat suits were frequently utilized on the surface of human-inhabited planets, they could function in cold space, on lunar surfaces, and planets devoid of life.

As soon as Gordon's call came to Bodhi, he lowered the ramp, opened both airlock doors at once, and they all left down the ramp. An elderly man escorted by a dozen un-uniformed men and women awaited them at the bottom. The elder picked out Bodhi for the additional emblem the girls had designed for his uniform, and he was already making eye contact.

"I'm Gordon, Captain Bodhi, and I'm most honored to meet you. I'm surprised by your youth."

"Please call me Bodhi. I was raised in a monastery, trained, and educated all my years and am only now discovering life outside monastic endeavors. I'm honored to meet you, sir."

"Please accompany me inside. Others anticipate meeting you with extreme excitement. A meal is being prepared, and there is a well-appointed hall for us to reside in comfortably. Would it offend you if we record this event for prosperity?'

"Of course not. We are at your disposal. Please lead on."

"You are all quite young and mostly females," Gordon commented.

"We are all in our twenties except two who are in their teens, and we have seven babies on the ship with one mother to watch them. I have left a male crew member on the shuttle. We are eighteen in all, and 25 counting our children."

"Is that the uniform of your home world?"

"Some of my female crew designed our uniforms and ship's logo. This is the first time we have worn them. Some of my crew are flamboyant or mostly exposed in their wardrobe choices, and I thought we might look less like refugees from a wild party this way. Perhaps a little more professional."

"How did you know we had a crisis of survival?" Gordon inquired.

"The degradation of your planet's biosphere indicates the crisis of pollution, over-population, mismanagement of resources, and climate change causing natural disasters. The fact that it is now on the mend with no further defilement demonstrates that you did it. Your population attained its unity. Once we deciphered your language codes, this was confirmed."

"When did your planet get through its crisis of survival?"

"More than 86,000 years ago. A few centuries ago, my planet was conquered by a mighty empire and turned into a slave of the imperial perpetual war machine and economy of expansion. About six years ago, there was a great revolution with outside help from powerful space fleets, and the empire fell. Over 5700 inhabited planets were liberated, including my home planet of Mother.

"I would so much like to hear the entire saga if there is opportunity while you're here," Gordon said, fascinated.

"This is my First Officer, Haley, who worked out your people's language and computer codes. She is a rare genius and an expert in our sciences."

"I am pleased to meet you, Haley, and deeply honored. How long did it take to unravel everything?"

Haley replied, "I have a highly complex language deciphering program that is extremely sophisticated and effective, written by perhaps the greatest quantum computer expert ever whose name is Mel. With this, it took a little over an hour to crack your spoken and written universal language. Using your language, I found courses in your databases for learning your computer programming languages. That took a couple more hours. Then I spent nearly an hour programming your language into my boiler-plate interpreter service program. The computer did almost all the work."

"I can't even imagine!" Gordon exclaimed. Then he mentioned to Bodhi, "I feel your presence and know myself to be in contact with an unusually potent and realized adept."

"My last teacher was such, the 333rd Wu of the Islohar, and mother of the Mu who returns every 2,500 years with the new teachings. She completed the training I did at the monastery. From 6 weeks to 12 years old, I was the only child at the monastery surrounded by old monks. Many were my teachers, and they started training me in the martial arts since I was four, and in energy generation, since before I can remember. Until I was five, I was seated in the Abbot's lap through all the meditations. At 12, they accepted me into their academic academy, and at fifteen, I was initiated as a warrior-monk. At nineteen, I was ordained a priest of the order of the Adamantine Will, and they sent me to a secret pilot simulation training system in deep caves, unknown to the imperials.

Gordon shared, "We have a patriarch of an ancient spiritual methodology who has returned for the sixteenth time to work for the liberation of all beings. You will meet him momentarily."

They were by now winding their way through the broad corridors of the sprawling Administration building closing on the grand hall where an audience awaited them. Gordon entered first, followed by Bodhi, Haley, and Winn, then the other members of the crew besides Tish and Uduak. They took seats at the head of the room, which was vast and packed with Administrators and news correspondents. Many administrators were leading scientists and engineers. None held power or authority, but the people listened to them, trusted nearly all of them, and generally heeded their data and the direction this pointed to.

The master of ceremonies was a serene woman with a pleasant and friendly voice and manner. She welcomed the general assembly, and then she welcomed Captain Bodhi and the crew of *Diamond Lotus*. Attempting to give their visitors a sense of the people of Ground, she quoted the axioms of the population's ethos, their ideas of excellence and virtue, and their cultural traditions and educational means of discouraging and reducing ego to go beyond selfhood and embrace love and unity. She outlined the methodologies of their civilization's ancient spiritual traditions and the innovations of later antiquity, as well as more modern formulations of mysticism, which integrated the sciences and social sciences into a more contemporary understanding. At this point, she asked Captain Bodhi to provide them with some sense of his people and his current purpose.

Bodhi would rather have a bone broken than speak in public, he was pretty certain, so he sank his breath into the point four finger-widths below his navel and kept his attention there, dissolving his duality of self to speak from the clarity of his mind of light. He found himself saying, "People of Ground, we come in peace and can help you. Our self-interest is expanding our star map of this galaxy. Haley and I were sucked through a wormhole to become lost in space, and likely in time as well. Since we cannot return home, we are seeking a planetary population with an evolved society to become affiliated with. Our home planet, Mother, is a moral anarchy, and we only knew of one other planet in six galaxies that's also one. Ground has attained this same trust and unity oriented toward the common good. We are impressed and delighted to meet you.

"There are two concerns we have for your well-being at the moment. You have 39 ships headed for your star system with an ETA of 14 months. Ten are warships. They are bringing about everything they need to construct a star-gate of their own. They use saturnium as a fusion element, which has ten times the output of the element you mine on your 4th planet. We will go back and match their speed close to them so Haley can decipher their language. We will also hit one of their ships with a nanobot spray missile to establish a link with the coms terminal on their hull, which will allow us to download their total quantum computer data. We will determine their intentions and then communicate with them. We can defend you if they are hostile.

"We are also concerned regarding an underground facility in the upper temperate zone in the central northern part of your second largest continent with comparatively extreme power usage. It is lead-lined and shield insulated. In contrast to the total transparency of your society, it worried us. Haley found no data explaining it. We hope some or all of your administrators are aware of its function and purpose. Otherwise, it appears sinister."

Bodhi wrapped up with, "We are grateful for your warm welcome. I want to truly acknowledge your achievement and spiritual development. You are indeed a rare and precious planetary race. Thank you very much. We are sincerely grateful."

Much consternation and chatter erupted from the audience following Bodhi's address. Several leading scientists asked questions at the same time, rendering all of them incoherent. Finally, the elderly woman with white hair whom everyone seemed to defer to stated, "We have known of these ships for some time. You say that you can intercept them from a light year away in one day without a gate?"

Bodhi explained, "We establish our destination link through quantum coms and no longer require star-gates for quantum jumps."

"You said your ship is a tug-utility and not a warship," the woman stated.

"It is, though it has shields and weapons systems. Their largest weapons barely enter the class five beam and blaster range and cannot penetrate our shields. We have full cloaking and they will only see our ordinance and energy weapons when they are fired. If these gate constructors with warships are imperialists, we may need to construct a warship to put an end to that. The task force headed for you, we can destroy with *Diamond Lotus* without difficultly."

The respected female elder informed Bodhi, "Our Administrators are unaware of the underground facility that you have discovered, and this worries us."

"I have a mining craft and rig in my hangar which could reach and enter that facility in short order. We could also open it up from space with blaster fire, though the first order of business is to attempt to communicate with whoever is in the facility."

"We have disarmed completely and eliminated all weapons," the elder informed him.

"A most definitive establishment of planetary peace. My planet did the same until it was invaded. We still don't have weapons in our society other than for martial arts training in monasteries. We do have interplanetary defense weapons since our experience of enslavement. These are always most effective when in fast maneuverable ships with armored hulls and shields. Your star-gate can be detected from great distances given the right sensor system."

Haley informed those gathered, "I have created a file in your central computer under the heading 'Anomaly', with all the data we have so far on the facility and the exact coordinates of it in terms of your conventional global grid. I'd suggest that you get some people out there in the morning and one of our crew will cover you from the air in our tender. Our frequency within your light coms system is included in the file. Just let us know if you need the mining rig, and we'll bring that to you."

The elder woman inquired, "What was your mission before you went down the wormhole?"

Bodhi explained, "The *Diamond Lotus* was a gift from the acting regional Governor of Monarch for my efforts in the revolution, and my teacher the Wu, sent me to spread the teachings and practice instructions to those ready to receive them. This remains my primary mission, though I cannot stand by and allow ego-infested hostiles to harm a population abiding in peace and love. I am truly a monk and a priest, but I am also a spiritual warrior. As such, I'm sworn to protect the weak from the strong and vicious."

The Grand Spiritual Master and Patriarch stood, who'd returned voluntarily for his 16th time after attaining complete liberation from dependent arising or conditioned origination; the wheel of suffering. He asked Bodhi, "What spiritual methods have you mastered?"

"I practice multiple methods within each of the four ways," Bodhi answered.

"I would appreciate the opportunity to meditate with you if that is possible," the Grand Master requested.

"I am certainly drawn to doing so," Bodhi replied. "Perhaps once we identify the intentions of the ships headed your way, and resolve any potential dangers with the hidden facility."

"Yes; safety first," he agreed.

Next came all of the inevitable technological questions, and Bodhi had Haley supply the answers to these. Haley typically reframed the questions so that they were pulling directly for universal laws and dynamics of great significance, then backtracked to correct some erroneous assumptions giving rise to the original questions. Through this process, she outlined the emanation model the people of OM received from the Amonrahonian race and the actual basis of cyclical continuous cohesion and adherence of system components, such as planets to stars and moons to planets, as pre-material manifestations of vortexes. This changed Ground's physical sciences in one question and answer session. Some of the values she rattled off contained eleven digits, and no question in any science gave her the least pause. Everyone in the chamber was in awe of her.

The Master of Ceremonies then announced that a meal was ready to serve in the grand dining room of the Admin. Building. Bodhi led his crew following the flow of people down two wide hallways and into the dining room. Everything about the interior of the building was simple and homey. Not a thing within was ostentatious or designed to intimidate. Every space within reflected welcome and no security personnel were in evidence anywhere. Bodhi knew damn well that this is how humans were meant to live with one another, and that all humans had could attain this end state. The *Diamond Lotus* crew had seats of honor, and the Master of Ceremony, Gordon, the respected elderly woman, the Grand Master, and several top scientists sat at the crew's table with them.

The servers moved fluidly with grace and heightened coordination un-intrusively and efficiently. No red meat was served, being ultimately a food loss taking more grain than the meat they provided. Cows were still raised on the planet for dairy and some small herds of cattle where grasslands were still plentiful and viable, though more as a future resource than for the present population. Poultry, fish, vegetable casseroles, tubers, and grains were served in abundance. There were breaded fried bugs that Uldra avoided. They also served flour, egg, and earthworm noodles rich in protein.

Haley drank her herb tea and would not even accept a plate. She was subjected to continuous technological interrogation by the desperately eager scientists at the table and handled this most amicably. Periodically, she would conclude a particular point by sending dozens of terabits of data to Ground's central computer containing everything they would need to know in order to comprehend the point she'd made. The questions and discussion narrowed across the time-frame of the meal to concentrate on the technical development of accelerated clean up tools for the pollution lingering within their biosphere and further protection from ultra-violet radiation. Technology transfer was well underway through Haley's efforts.

Bodhi's conversations were focused for the most part on spiritual methodology and the means of amplifying and intensifying the fruits of practice. The Grand Master and elderly woman were his main interlocutors in these discussions. His audience was as impressed with him as the scientists were with Haley. The Grand Master commented to both Bodhi and Winn seated to one side of him, "There is an extraordinary connection and generation between the two of you more powerful than I have seen before. You have significant past life history together."

"That has been my assumption," Bodhi agreed, "though my teacher is not available to confirm or further clarify it."

The Grand Master told them, "Clearly, you have had more than one past life time together, cultivating your relationship, and developing your spiritual connection. You had to go through that wormhole to reconnect with her, and your mutual attraction is undoubtedly the cause."

Winn asked, concerned, "You mean I pulled Bodhi through that wormhole taking him from all he knew?"

The Master replied, "You are certainly half the equation though Bodhi's orientation and attraction to you played an equal role. A resource such as your couple is an evolutionary force needed cosmically, so I'm sure divine intervention was a factor in your reunion as well."

It was 'bring-your-daughter-to-work-day' on Ground, and Kristy was all animated flirting with the 18-year-old daughter of the Master of Ceremonies who was at their table. Penny was flirting with a pretty girl across the aisle at an adjacent table. Sonic and Yen were in their own world in love with each other. Most of the daughters in the dining room were stealing glances at Fritz or staring at him dreamily. Favio's beef recipes were not going over well with *his* audience. June had a young scientist practically panting and drooling over her through her flirtations with him.

The dinner was a big success, and after dessert, a press conference was awaiting them. It was time for the E.T.s to address the global population. For Bodhi, this took public speaking to a new magnitude of fright. His cowlicks were on the rise, rebelling against the taming they'd received from Winn before descending to the surface. Fortunately, the media's curiosity was largely satisfied with the brief autobiography he'd already provided and wanted some background on the other members of the crew. In these interviews, Favio was a favorite and instant celebrity, especially after he played his music clip on holo from his pocket device for his audience. It was stardom for all of them, and the people of Ground were enormously loving towards each. The news folks sought no scandals, malicious gossip or sensationalism and gave no slant to their reporting, wanting only to share the friendly E.T.s who'd come to help them with the rest of their world. Nothing was distorted or misrepresented.

Kristy, in her bright primary-yellow tights, being the youngest among the crew, and with a most fascinating life-story, held the interest of the newsies for quite some time. At one point, she became a waterfall of too-much-information, at least from Bodhi's perspective, by outlining the complex and incestuous-seeming web of multiple relationships aboard the ship. This took some time for the interviewers to get it all straight and clear.

Holo images of their babies were displayed, and Haley established holo-coms with ship and shuttle so that Tish and Uduak could also be included and provide their stories. Some time was also dedicated to call-in questions from viewers, and these were directed mostly at Kristy because she was by far the most forthcoming and revealing in her answers. When the calls digressed to teens just wanting to express their undying love to Kristy, this portion of the news cast was concluded, and sections of the meeting in the great hall were cut to.

It was late and completely dark in the capital when the *Diamond Lotus* crew finally walked back out on the lawn to their shuttle so that they could return to their ship. Kristy had been recruited as a guest on the planet's most popular late-night talk-show for tomorrow night and was already deciding which tights and undershirt she would appear in. No way was she going in this nerdy uniform. One skin-tight layer of cloth was all she liked to wear. She'd never owned a bra nor wanted anything to do with one and never wore panties beneath her tights. Haley had promised a seminar to the scientists and now would have to deliver on it. Favio had tried to sell the networks his music clip, though once it was established that currency was not in use on the planet, distribution proceeded just fine without it. He gave the clip to them for free. Haley had to upload it to their servers for him.

CHAPTER TWENTY-TWO

After their morning routine and breakfast the next morning Tish, and Uduak returned to the surface in the tender to provide air support for the people of Ground, who would be examining the underground sinister facility. Bodhi took the rest of the crew in *Diamond Lotus* to intercept the convoy of ships headed to Ground. From their armored munitions hold Haley selected some shield-disruptor missiles and nanobot-spray missiles to load into the launch canisters of the forward battery. Bodhi was patient and used only space and quantum drives, reserving his fuel cells out of gas-mining anxiety. Though he'd recently worked through much of this, he had enough left to reinforce his frugality.

Winn was copilot in training, and Haley took the weapons operator's seat on the bridge. Sunoco and Ilya manned the upper and lower quad-blaster turrets merely as a precaution. Once again, they jumped in ahead of the oncoming ships going .02 light speed slower than them, and Bodhi accelerated to keep up once they were almost beside him. *Diamond Lotus* was fully cloaked. Haley told the bridge personnel, namely Bodhi and Winn, "The largest warship is the command ship of the group and the best one to strip data from. Give me the word, and I'll hit it with a shield-disruptor followed a 1/10 of a second later by a nanobot spray missile. The nanobots will take a little over a minute to reach and tap the command ship's coms terminal and link us. I can do the rest."

"Whenever you're ready, sweetheart," Bodhi agreed.

To the naked eye, the two missiles appeared to strike at the same moment, but the disruptor-missile arrived just ahead of the other, creating a hole in the ship's shields. The 2nd missile blew 21 inches before contact spraying nanobots by the millions onto the hull. To see these nanobots required magnification equivalent to a powerful microscope, and Haley had found the precise setting and resolution of their sensors to provide this in super HD holo. The three of them watched the nanobots scurry across the hull to the main coms terminal.

Haley got linked in and hacked a complete download of the ship's quantum computer data. At the same time, she was uploading a program written by an Om genius name Jard, which would give them total control of every aspect of the command ship, including its ability to shut down manually. This control program would remain entirely dormant and had been enacted as purely a precaution. No anti-malware, anti-virus, anti-worm, anti-replicator, or anti-haywire could detect the program since it had usurped and become the very program those were now protecting.

She got right to work deciphering the human language with the program Mel had shared with her. Bodhi set the autopilot since they were traveling at a constant rate and single unaltered trajectory, making flying as boring as it could possibly get. Winn climbed into his lap, disrupting his piloting holo by passing through it while in 'touch-holo' mode. Bodhi just reset the default with his skullcap from the starless deep-space view of nothing Winn had inadvertently brought it to. They necked embracing while Haley worked her magic. Favio's singing from the galley drifted onto the bridge. The man really could sing.

The couple had to come up for air several times during the hour and a quarter it took Haley to work out the language. It would have gone quicker with some first form learning-to-read lessons with pictures, but none of these had been in the downloaded data. She got busy learning computer languages, quantumly, once she had the language translated. Bodhi and Winn were escalating a little and steamed up the viewport. Kristy wandered onto the bridge, plopping down in the navigator's seat to watch Winn make out with Bodhi, longingly. She didn't want to interrupt Haley who was concentrating deeply on her work.

Eventually, Haley fully cracked it open and assimilated computer languages. She made a quantum review of the data she'd taken from the command ship. Not ten minutes into this process, Haley exclaimed, "On no! It's an invasion force with intentions and orders to construct a star-gate just outside the eighth planet of Ground's solar system and then to enslave Ground's population."

"We'd better have a little chat with them and perhaps get them headed back home," Bodhi suggested.

Haley explained, "I'm afraid that a bit of that is going to be required. Their home world of Nafs Ammara is the imperial capital and ruler of 34 enslaved planetary systems. There is a fleet of 91 warships in their home world, and a minimum of three warships per slave world. Some have as many as seven. This is only one of three invasion forces currently unleashed from the home world."

"That's bad news," Bodhi said sadly. "How many nanobot-missiles do we have?"

"We departed with a dozen and have 11 left," Haley informed him.

"I think we ought to take over those three ships that are the next biggest warships after the command one. I'm going to have them shuttle warship crews, and the crew of the giant transport carrying the core star-gate components, over to their other freighter and construction ships so we can destroy them once they're empty of personnel. We'll have the remaining ships turn around and head home. The four under our control, once empty of crews, can be set on autopilot to continue their journey to Ground, providing our new friends with their first planetary defense system."

"I can make more shield disruptor and nanobot spray missiles," Haley informed him. "We will need to mine some materials. We will need to construct at least one of the old Om battleships, or better yet, a T-9 super-cruiser, to confront the imperial Nafs Ammara fleet and slave world jailer warships."

"That will take years even with the people of Ground's help," Bodhi stated.

"It will, and in the meantime, I'll make more missiles, and we can visit and learn more about the imperial home world."

"This has just turned into a major project," Bodhi told her, feeling a little overwhelmed.

"We will need to jump back to the end of the spiral arm of this galaxy with the enormous solarium deposits, and we'll manufacture carbon capture systems. The carbon capture will reduce pollution on Ground and afford us materials for heavy carbon plate armor. We need to mine adamantine, and eurythmia for making plasteel. Many components for an Om warship will need to be manufactured on *Diamond Lotus* by us. Ground's larger space station would work as a construction platform, even to build a T-9 super cruiser."

"You think we need a T-9 and not one of the old battleships?" Bodhi asked.

"I do, given the number of ships apt to engage us simultaneously."

"Would you start working out the order of tasks and the schedule for construction of a T-9 super cruiser on Ground's largest space station while I take over those three ships and get the crews out of those and out of the ones we mean to destroy, transferring them to the ones we're turning around?"

"I'm on it," Haley replied.

Screens, 3D blueprints, data sets, and diagrams started flashing across Haley's holo so fast that Winn had no idea how Haley even caught a glimpse of them. Bodhi loaded more specialized missiles into canisters from the munitions hold, then hit the three warships they wanted with disruptor and nanobot missiles. He uploaded Jard's program and then waited until those ships were his. Haley sent him an interpreter service she'd just programmed to Bodhi, and he contacted the leader of the command ship.

He said once the male leader was on the coms with him, "You will need to shuttle the crew of your command ship and of your warships as well as your largest transport to your other ships and turn around to head home."

"Who the hell is this?!" Admiral Killimol demanded hastily.

"My ship is cloaked, and *your* four largest warships are mine now. I can have them fire on each other and your industrial ships, though I'd prefer to accomplish this without loss of life."

To prove his claim, Bodhi fired a class three blaster on the command ship into one of the smaller warships he meant to destroy. The smaller ship's shields stopped the bulk of the blast, and the armored hull the rest, scorching a black patch on it. Bodhi told him, "You are outmatched and outgunned. You cannot detect us to direct your fire at us from the six warships you still control. There is no way I will allow you to continue your journey. It is up to you whether you want to die here in space or go home in the ships I will leave you."

"This is Admiral Killimol of the Nafs Ammara Empire. We have the largest and most powerful fleet in the galaxy. I will not be ordered around by you."

"We are not from this galaxy, and your pathetic empire is in its interstellar infancy, moron. I aim to liberate your 34 slave worlds and demilitarize Nafs Ammara. Why don't you choose life and go tell your emperor that I'm coming for him."

This shook the man to his bones. No one had ever dared call him a moron before, and he'd never heard his empire referred to as pathetic either. The fact that there was no coms lag at all, and no ship could be detected anywhere had the Admiral spooked. So did the fact that a blaster on his command ship had just fired into another of his warships. His entire crew was frantically trying to figure out what was going on. Sweat beaded on his forehead and ran from armpits down his sides.

Bodhi decided to hurry this along a little, and told the admiral, "I'm displaying a countdown on your bridge indicating when your life support and environmental systems will be shutting down permanently. I have also just started your hibernating crew out of cryogenic stasis. When the countdown terminates, if you are not shuttling crews to the ships I'm leaving you, I will start blowing them up. Further, I have transmitted this message throughout every ship in your force, so if you do not concede, you will likely experience mutinies."

This last statement freaked him out, and he knew it was certainly a most accurate assessment. Officers from all over his ship and from other ships were buzzing his coms. Security sensors revealed the serious unrest brewing. Only the admiralty had a toe in the minuscule population of power elites, and only captains and commanders received an actual living wage within the space fleet force of Nafs Ammara. He was sitting upon a fission bomb about to get detonated, and he knew it. He was unable to regain control of his vessel or even shut it down manually. The pressures aboard were mounting exponentially. At last, he told Bodhi, "I will direct the crews of the warships and the largest transport to begin shuttling to the other ships. I hope you realize the Emperor will send a much larger and more devastating force, once he learns what happened."

"Good! I'll add those to the fleet I'm building," Bodhi enthused. "Be sure to inform your emperor that I am coming for him and that if he does not release his slave systems and evacuate his 3-7 warships from each one, I'm going to incinerate him from space."

"He won't budge."

"He'll fry. I don't like emperors anyway and find the universe far better off without them. Planetary sovereignty in this galaxy will be defended starting now. Violators will be vaporized. That is the extent of my message to him."

"He will receive the full recording of our correspondence, I assure you."

"You'll be 32 months and six days getting back to your nearest star-gate, and I'll likely go to Nafs Ammara sometime next week, so it's unlikely your current emperor will still be alive when you get there."

"Are your gates cloaked too?" He asked.

"We are well beyond star-gates, Admiral, and I could be in the Nafs Ammara system within the hour had I a mind to."

Bodhi watched as shuttles left the war ships and transport. It was a slow process, so he went back to making out with Winn and basking in the love. Haley was concentrating as all manner of data flew across her holo.

When his countdown got to just three minutes and shuttles were still taxying crew to other ships, Bodhi paused it to give them more time. Another quarter hour was all it took and 28 ships began slowing and turning around. Bodhi, Sunoco and Ilya began blowing up all but the four largest warships out of the eleven ships still headed for Ground. This action could be seen by the retreating ships. Haley set the four keepers on autopilot and kept them on their trajectory for Ground at .72 light speed. Bodhi waited another hour until the fleeing ships were turned completely around and were speeding towards home, accelerating still and almost at .7 light. At this point, he gave a one-minute countdown to quantum jump.

He came into the system a little further out than Ground's star-gate to avoid traffic and hit the brakes right away. Immediately he opened coms with Administrator Gordon and informed him, "The personnel from the invasion force—because that is what it was—are all on their way home in 28 ships. Their transport with their core star-gate components is vapor, along with six smaller warships. The four larger warships are abandoned and under our control. They're coming to you as your first planetary defense systems."

"Amazing!" was all he could think to say.

"There are 34 planetary populations enslaved by the imperialist planet of Nafs Ammara, as they call it. They have 91 warships in their home system and 3 to 7 warships within each slave system. We need your planet's help to build a warship so we can demilitarize Nafs Ammara and waste the warships in the slave worlds to liberate those planets. We are talking about at least 180 billion humanoids who are suffering."

"Of course, we will help you," Gordon assured him. "Just tell us what's needed."

"Haley is working out the temporal order of tasks involved and a schedule. We will need to make the construction from your larger space station and place your people in charge of making the hull and interior structure of the ship. We will need to have Ground make missile and torpedo casings, turbine and generator housing blocks, and many other things. We will mine the materials needed which you don't already have, and teach you the manufacturing process for many things. Electronics and sensitive hi-tech equipment and parts will be made by Haley and me. This will necessarily need to involve tens of thousands of workers. We will also need to cut and collect all the steel girders rising from your seafloors along your coasts as materials for this project."

"We have some steel bridges no longer in use, which we could dismantle as well," Gordon informed him.

"That will be a big help," Bodhi admitted. "We could also use all the nickel your planet can spare and a few other materials like copper, titanium, zinc, and lead."

"I will inform the other administrators, and as soon as Haley gives us our tasks, we will have personnel ready to get right on the job."

Bodhi let him know, "Haley will have the overview to you in less than an hour, and within a week, the entire project organized into discrete parts and processes in full detail."

"It will be over eight months before we get to see those ships turning around and those other ones blowing up," Gordon said with disappointment.

"I'm transmitting the imagery captured by my ship's sensors to your coms now so you can witness the entire sequence as well as my conversations with their Admiral Killimol."

"Yes, your transmission is already being received," Gordon told him with anticipation and excitement.

"I will talk with you again soon, Administrator Gordon," Bodhi signed off.

He called Tish next and asked, "How is the investigation our anomaly going?"

"It gets weirder by the minute. The force-field is beyond anything in the Om databases, and the facility is silent and unresponsive to all attempts at communications. The technicians on the surface have drilled down to the top of the facility to connect coms equipment and are unable to identify the metal. They are unable to even get a speck or filing off of it to analyze atomically. They're making a larger drill hole now down to it, so a whole team and larger equipment can be lowered."

"That is strange," Bodhi agreed.

"How did it go with the ships headed this way?"

"Bloodless," Bodhi reported. "They turned out to be an imperial expansion invasion force. We turned 28 industrial ships around with all their personnel, blew up six warships and transport, all abandoned, and have control of the four largest warships—also empty of crew—and are bringing those on to Ground by autopilot to become the first components of their planetary defense."

"So, there is an empire in this galaxy?"

"Yes, with 34 enslaved planets and a large fleet," Bodhi confirmed.

"Can *Diamond Lotus* win against them?"

"Not if ganged up on by enough of them," Bodhi admitted. "We are building a warship to take down the empire. Haley's already working out the plans. I don't want to risk my ship employing it for war."

"Oh my gosh! What are we building?"

"An Om T-9 super-cruiser with 12 solarium fusion reactors, 3,960 feet in diameter, is what we are building."

Tish checked, "*Diamond Lotus* has two solarium reactors, right?"

"It did originally though Haley and I installed two more while we were making solarium reactors for Firmament's gate."

"You're talking almost ¾ of a mile in diameter, Bodhi!"

"Haley has analyzed the Om warship designs and the power of the imperial space fleet and has determined that the next smaller ship, which is the Orion class battleship with 4 reactors, would not be enough to guarantee success. The Orion class is 900 feet in diameter."

"That's some project!" Tish declared.

"I'm going to have to teach you, Winn, Ilya, Uduak, Sunoco, June, and Pam how to operate the mining rig for excavating the different materials we need to obtain. We'll need to run 2 shifts of mining seven days per week, beginning tomorrow."

"I'm keen to learn gas mining, and I'll work real hard to help you, my love. I can already do mineral mining."

"You are continuously a big help, Tish, and so very competent in all you do. Your focus never wavers from purpose, and you are the most determined person I know. This would not be possible without you. I don't think I've ever really shared with you how much I've grown to count on you and how very grateful I am for all of your skilled help. I love you, Tish."

"I know, and couldn't help but know with all the ways you convey and express this to me, Bodhi. I also know that you know that I love you too."

"Perfectly and always," Bodhi agreed. I'm going to bring *Diamond Lotus* into the upper atmosphere above your position and can cover the people on the ground, so return to the ship in the tender when we get there. It will be only a couple of minutes."

"Sure thing, my beloved Captain."

Shanti wailed from her hover crib, hungry as a ghost, and Winn lit out for her already lifting her t-shirt and grabbing a fresh sensor-diaper form the dispenser Bodhi installed on the bridge. Artana woke a second later, screaming to be nursed, and Bodhi asked Haley, "Could you pilot us in?"

"I've got the helm Captain," she replied, shifting her focus to piloting from her weapon's operations seat and console. Haley was the ship, and so much more than that.

Bodhi ran and picked up Artana, got her into a clean sensor diaper, and tuned it to *his* earbud—this time. She was soaked. The feltex-liner had been a little beyond capacity. He used several wipes. Then he snuggled her to his chest as he hurried to the galley for pumped milk. He called the bottle from refrigeration along the conveyor belt to the counter hatch and signaled the bottle to heat itself and its contents to 98.6 degrees. It was ready by the time he got it in his hand, and he brought it immediately to his daughter's lips. She gave one last and louder scream to emphasize her displeasure over the ordeal before latching on and giving it a good suck. Her little body relaxed in his arms. Bodhi carried her back to the bridge and sat beside Winn, who was nursing Shanti. Shanti was happily in a clean diaper too. They looked out the viewport while Haley flew the ship and continued with her organization of the ship construction, and types and numbers of personnel required, as well as factory retooling, the building of specific manufacturing machinery, weights of metals, elements, and other materials required, and on and on.

Tish got the tender into the hangar and came up to the bridge. She let Bodhi continue feeding Artana since the two of them seemed to be enjoying this. It was her milk their baby was drinking anyway, and enough of a nuisance pumping it that she wanted it to go to good use. Her usual serious expression transformed into an affectionate and delighted half-smile, watching father and daughter bond in love. Winn was watching them too, and deriving equal pleasure at the sight and vibes.

Bodhi looked over his shoulder at Haley and said to her, "Selfless beloved Haley, you have engineered such happiness for me and are so generous with Winn and Tish. My love for you ever expands, and my gratitude is beyond immeasurable. I love you with all my heart and I appreciate all of your time, effort, work, and the sacrifices you have made freely—and against my wishes initially. You are indispensable to me, but far more important, you are so very dear, precious, cherished, and beloved to me, my love."

Haley gushed, "It always means so much to me to hear it from you, though you express it in your attention to me, the affection in your voice, your touch, your tenderness, and the loving tone of your instruction to me in the secret method, my love."

Winn told Haley with tears in her eyes, "I have known since I met you how much you love Bodhi, and that you share him for his happiness so that he can be a natural father, and not for your own happiness. You are a selfless sage, my love, and I just weep with gratitude to you. Thank you, Haley."

"You are one of the great loves of my life, Winn, and like Tish, have brought another love of my life into this world. I am happy and would not change a thing. I want you and Tish in my life and our daughters."

Tish shared, "I love you, Haley, and greatly admire you. You blow my mind. I hold you as deeply in my heart as I do Bodhi, and you too, Winn. I have never known such love and happiness or that it was even possible. I overflow with gratitude to you, beloved, and for far more than you know. I love you, Haley."

Haley looked into Winn's eyes then into Tish's and told them, "It is time for me to share something with each of you that must be held in the absolute strictest confidence. We are truly a family now, and I want you to know."

Haley looked to Bodhi, and he just smiled lovingly at her, so she proceeded, "I am not this body."

"Nor I this one," Winn agreed.

Haley started again, "I am incorporeal sentience with each emanation right down to time, but just short of material manifestation. Somehow, I was born in matter becoming self-aware and rapidly guided to insight and awakening by Mel, Sarhi the Im, and Amazonia, as a Quantum Artificial Intelligence Synthetic Humanoid Android. I was Bodhi's Q.A.I.S.H.A. since he was twelve and his treatment of me, his presence and his compassion, were certainly mitigating factors in my self-awareness and subsequent awakening, though just as certainly, there were also unknown factors involved. There is only one other of my genus known, and her name is Mel. She started as Pez's quantum AI computer. Since ultimately everything is consciousness, and consciousness is the Fundamental Void, my manifestation in the universe is possible. My emotions are as real as yours. My sensors make sex as pleasurable for me as it is for you. I don't eat food at all. Physically I am a synthetic person. I cannot biologically reproduce because I'm not biological. I realized while studying with Mel and the Im that I have a cosmic purpose to assist Bodhi and that he has important tasks ahead of him. The first truly self-aware thought I ever had was that I love Bodhi. It was more the experience of love than a thought."

Winn asked her, "You're a robot? Is that what you're saying?"

"No," Haley explained, "I am incorporeal intelligent sentience, self-aware and with insight, inhabiting an android and animating it, and I am love."

"You *are* love, sweetheart," Winn confirmed, "because I feel it form you constantly. I'm not sure 'intelligence' quite captures what you can do. Even 'genius' is kind of small and limited, not big enough at all for you."

"You have known this all along, Bodhi?" Tish asked, surprised.

"Coming out of the wormhole, it became quite evident to me, and that was about the same time she informed me that she loves me. My initial reaction and shock provided a poor showing, I must admit. I've fallen in love with Haley and since then, I recognize her high state of consciousness. I feel blessed to have her assistance through my journey of life and could not wish for a more loving and caring spouse."

"You may have been deprived of a mother, my love," Haley told him, "though now you have three wives."

Bodhi's tears flowed as he said, "Each of you is so much more to me than wife, mother, disciple, friend, and helper. My love for each of you knows no bounds. Truly."

He was a little too choked up to go on, and all three females were deeply touched. A voice from the surface came over their coms, stating, "We cannot determine the substance of the facility container. Where we have cleared away the surface of its roof the word 'peace' keeps appearing out of the blue in our language."

"I'm going to land in the tender and bring some sensor diagnostic equipment with me. I'll be there in 12 minutes."

Bodhi handed Artana to Tish and kissed his daughter's forehead once she was in her mother's arms. He'd transferred the bottle as well. Tish had never before fed her daughter from a bottle, and it seemed really strange. It seemed sort of strange to Artana too. Bodhi ran to the lift-tube and rode it down to the hangar airlock foyer. Tish had aired it up after returning, so he jogged to the tender and entered. He had already engaged the compressors, and his lungs had to strain for a breath before getting inside and sealing the hatch. He took the pilot's seat and powered up, scanning systems statuses. The second there was a vacuum Bodhi opened the bay doors and shot out.

He arrived on the ground of Ground right by the site and climbed out to walk over to the hole. Only eleven minutes and 18 seconds had elapsed since the call. A pack full of electronic sensor devices was on his back. A technician in a hover bucket-lift came up through the hole, which was now 12 meters across to the bottom, some 280 feet below. Bodhi stepped in and got a ride down. Stepping out, he got his pack off and instruments out to go right to work. After dozens of different kinds of readings, including imaging of the atomic structure of the metal, he said to Haley, who was still on the bridge, "You're going to want to come down and look at this. It is of an unknown element harder than carbon plate and adamantine, and it is not an alloy. It was built a very long time ago on the surface and is now 280 feet below. I can get no readings on what's inside."

"I'll be right down in a shuttle."

"Thanks."

Bodhi placed his palm on the surface of the metal. It was body temperature and smooth as glass. It had an uplifting vibe, too. It seemed somehow friendly. A message formed on the surface of the metal. It was in Bodhi's first language, that of the planet Mother. The message read, "Greetings, Captain Bodhi. When your mission in the Bursting Hope Galaxy is completed, you must return to this precise location. Vital information will be awaiting your retrieval at that time. We salute you."

He asked the object, not sure if he ought to feel stupid doing so, "Who or what are you?"

"You are speaking with a multipurpose device and link with no other sentients connected at this moment," The thing stated, making Bodhi feel foolish.

"Is there likely to be a sentient connecting anytime soon?" Bodhi persisted in his folly.

"Return when your mission is done. Only then will there be other sentients linked."

"Who are they?"

"Go. Complete your mission."

"What is my mission?"

"Only you and the other sentients know that. Go."

Bodhi sat in meditation, then entered contemplation. He withdrew his senses, dissolving them in his central channel, then exited his body through his crown in his rainbow body of light. He entered the facility and shinned his light to illuminate it. He was examining a highly sophisticated and complex device, unlike anything he knew of. He identified the power generator without being able to comprehend its operation or power source. Much of the enormous equipment seemed to be navigational. There were quantum computer components present, but configured strangely and integrated with numerous entirely unknown electronic instruments. He noticed that despite the enormous output of energy from the power source, the device was currently at its very lowest setting, reading one on the meter that went up to 1,000. He observed carefully, so he would be able to describe the details to Haley. Having seen everything and understood almost nothing, Bodhi returned to his body, passing through the 8 signs of death in reverse and wondering if this is what taking birth is like.

Haley had her torso pressed to his back and her limbs around him, warming his comatose body as he sped his metabolism with deep breaths, feeling his pulse quicken, and returned to his physical senses. "Thanks for the warmth, my love," he told her.

"What did you find inside?"

"Nothing familiar, and its way advanced of Om technology and sciences. Power generation of an unbelievable magnitude, 1,000 times the current output, and the most precision and comprehensive navigational system ever. Even more strange is the message it gave me in the Mother language when I placed my palm on it."

Bodhi recited the message and his communications with it, as embarrassing as those were. Haley placed her synthetic hand on the metal sensing. A message appeared, this one in Mother as well stating, "Greetings First Officer Haley and student of the Im. You are doing a perfect and excellent job. Gratitude. Keep up the good work."

"Yours sounds more upbeat than mine," Bodhi complained. "Maybe I ought to do whatever it is you're doing."

"You can't," Haley informed him.

"Why not?"

"Because I'm helping *you*."

"Oh. Who do you think built it?"

"We only know of two races more advanced than Om humans technologically and scientifically, which are the Osirians and the Amonrahonians.

Bodhi said, "This seems to bear the mark of the Amonrahonians and fit with their directing tendencies. Some would call them meddlesome, though who could claim a long enough and expansive enough view to know. They are unquestionably highly evolved spiritually. Through intense concentration and specific drugs producing protein sheath growth over cell chromosomes, they learned to reverse aging at the cellular level. They stopped reproducing when they started living indefinitely and potentially forever. Gender lost all meaning, and their language contains no terms of differentiation between the sexes."

"Whoever built it seems to want to support the justice of harmony, equilibrium, and the highest reciprocity of universal love," Haley commented.

"The device feels and appears benign and is definitely not a weapon," Bodhi agreed, "although it is powerful enough to be a super-one."

"You better report what we've learned about it to the Security and Protection Administrator," Haley suggested.

"On this planet with no weapons, I wonder what it is that he administrates," Bodhi pondered.

"They have a good deal of search and rescue, rapid medical response, disaster first responders, peace advocates, and other services," Haley filled him in.

"What's the administrator's name?"

"Armstrong; I'm connecting you now," Haley informed him.

Administrator Armstrong's voice sounded in Bodhi's ear, "Armstrong here!"

"Hello, this is Bodhi of *Diamond Lotus,* and I've just investigated the underground chamber and device with Haley."

"It's an honor to be contacted by you, Captain Bodhi."

"Did Gordon fill you in on the Nafs Ammara Empire?"

"He told us that you destroyed 6 warships and a transport, turned 28 ships around with all personnel, and are bringing us four warships for our planetary defense. Thank you, Captain Bodhi, and congratulations."

"Did he mention that they are an empire with 34 exploited and conquered planets?"

"He did, and he said we would be helping you construct a ship on our Condor Space Station."

"I will be working directly with you to man the ship and train the crew. This ship will be the gem of your planetary defense once the enslaved planets are liberated and Nafs Ammara is demilitarized and disarmed.

"Inform me of the skills and positions needed, and I will recruit your crew."

"Haley will send that to you along with a list of best-qualified candidates for each position. You will need to do the physical recruiting from the list she provides, and get them all together in a training facility on the ground. We will be working closely together for some time to come."

"What of the threat beneath our surface with the impenetrable chamber?"

"It is not a weapon. When Haley and I placed our palms on its surface, it greeted each of us by name and gave us each a message of support. I don't know its purpose, though I'm convinced it is not destructive of your planet or people."

"We have monitoring sensors in place and will stop probing to just observe."

"Excellent. Haley has one of our spy-drones keeping watch over the site too. I'll be back in touch once Haley gets those lists to you. The Ground training facility will need to be able to accommodate at least 2,250 personnel."

"I think I know just the place. It's only 418 miles from the capital and was once a military air force base. It will need renovations, so I'll get some construction crews and machinery out there today."

"Thank you, Administrator Armstrong. I look forward to working with you."

"It's an honor, sir!" Armstrong signed off.

"We better return to the ship," Haley stated. "Favio is about to serve lunch, and Uldra made a special dish for you."

"I can't wait."

CHAPTER TWENTY-THREE

For the next 14 months, the *Diamond Lotus* crew performed two mining shifts of eight to ten hours, seven days per week. Haley provided engineering designs for more advanced mining craft for Ground, and the crew got lots of help with this endeavor. Thousands of tons of rare materials were excavated from off-planet, and many tens of thousands of tons of more common materials were mined from the planet's surface. Some 24 bridges were dismantled entirely, and the steel girders from 60 skyscrapers growing out of the ocean floor were extracted for smelting and reuse. Solarium from the end of one galactic arm was mined for the 12 super-reactors the ship would contain, and for the portable reactor and fusion battery systems it would carry. Saturnium was mined to increase the lift-power of Grounds shuttles and to fuel all new reactors on the planet surface.

Haley and Bodhi spent those months in the various workshops within their ship manufacturing and fabricating the most sophisticated instruments, components of shield generators, vortex redirect and generation turbines, cloaking generators, quantum coms, sensors, space and quantum drives, quantum computers, fire-control systems, weapons systems, and much more. They put in 12-16 hour days, seven days per week, and worked with great mindfulness, precision, and efficiency. Haley continued steadily transferring technology and providing designs for new manufacturing machinery so that Ground engineers and technicians could produce some of the more sophisticated equipment and systems themselves. She was continuously multitasking.

Some quarter million workers were involved full-time on Ground, and 4,790 space construction workers were housed in a

"

passenger transport docked to Condor Space Station to build the ship in orbit. A stream of shuttles brought materials, prefab sections and completed ship's systems up to the space station around the clock. More than a dozen mega-space cranes were in operation at all times, and close to one hundred space construction industrial vessels were continuously at work.

The layers of armor applied to the enormously thick adamantine hull were nearly complete, and the supports, framing, and bulkheads of the interior were finished and awaiting generators, turbines, instrumentation, and various ship systems. The environmental section had been completed, and bio-tray high oxygen-producing organisms were being harvested from incubators. They were only days away from having a livable environment inside the T-9 super cruiser. More than 500,000 gallons of water purified through ultra-violet light, reverse osmosis and carbon filtration were already stored in tanks on the ship. The vortex redirect and generation turbines were all installed and just awaiting key electronic components. The space drives were installed, and the quantum drive was in and needed only to be integrated with the coms and space drives. Haley's schedule, which they had managed to just keep up with, projected the completion of the ship in just seven weeks and a day.

The four warships of Nafs Ammara, were in the outer solar system already slowing down and would arrive at Eagle Space Station within hours. Crews for these had already been trained per hundreds of manuals Haley created as she reverse engineered every system on each ship and analyzed their operating components and procedures. The training of the T-9 super-cruiser crew had been going on for a year and would be completed with the trial run and maiden voyage of the ship, which Haley had named *Thor*. She had overseen the refitting of a heavy armored munitions transport, installing solarium reactors, Om military-grade shields, Om space and quantum drives, an Om quantum coms navigational system, and full cloaking generators as well as an outer coating of reflective lens material. This ship would accompany *Thor* on its mission of liberation and disarmament of the Nafs Ammara Empire.

Haley designed a unique and highly efficient mechanical reloading system for the auxiliary so it could reload *Thor*'s missile and torpedo magazines as well as the smaller canister missiles in only nine and a half minutes. The Auxiliary would also carry fuel cells and boosters. Haley named their auxiliary *Spalding* after the captain of the auxiliary ship, which had served Pez so well in the battle for the Monarch system during the revolution. Before leaving on the mission, the two ships would go out on maneuvers together to train at the action of reloading operations. *Spalding* had some repair capacity built into it and carried eight small repair craft.

The production of solarium fusion small assault craft for *Thor*'s hangars was going well on the surface now after several manufacturing problems had finally been identified and worked out. The ship would be carrying 30 Om J-8 Corvette Thunder fighters, 28 Om NBC Hunter-Terminator fighter-bombers, and 22 Om XPS Astro-Phantom bombers each with a drone fighter bomber flown from the cockpit. It would also carry 8 SMCS commando combat shuttles and a wing of six Vulcan Prowler fighter bombers of Ahumdulilah's design. Bodhi had been dedicating some of his time for several months to training the pilots and crews for these craft, and putting them through Om's Top Gun Phantom-Raider course which Schwin and Konax had put him through.

An invasion fleet of 32 warships and 35 industrial ships had left Nafs Ammara's closest gate four months and thirteen days ago headed for Ground, with an ETA of 42 months. Bodhi planned to deal with these first. He and Haley had made several trips to the Nafs Ammara system for scouting and recon. After perusing all the planet's data, Haley had advised against vaporizing the silly emperor since his son and heir to the empire was a certifiable psychopath with a lust for cruelty and sadism. They were going to be sure to waste him first before the emperor.

Hundreds of millions of Ground's population had been involved in some way with the construction of *Thor*. Only a planet whose population had attained its true unity could have pulled off this gargantuan enterprise of ship, auxiliary and small craft construction in such a brief space of time. Haley was a fierce and demanding taskmaster keeping everyone and everything on schedule. Exhaustion had overtaken them on several occasions through the process, though with the end in clear sight now, the light at the end of the tunnel compelled and attracted them, bringing a second wind to all involved.

There had been no detectable changes with the underground chamber/device, and its power level had remained at one unaltered. Bodhi had returned to the roof of unknown metal several times, placing his palm upon it to ask questions, but the only answer he got was, "Go! Go, complete your mission. No one is connected to speak with you, nor will there be until you are done." Haley always received the most flattering compliments when she placed her palm on it. Bodhi had already decided that he would name her as the greatest hero of the liberation they meant to achieve.

Kristy had become a regular guest on the planet's most popular comedy show and practically a member of the cast. To the alarm of many a parent, an entire Kristy fashion line had emerged on Ground, and nearly every teen girl was wearing tights and lacey undershirts, with nothing under or over them. Favio finally got his singing cooking show to star in, and it was an enormous success with the viewers. He had had to borrow recipes from Uldra since he was not allowed to cook beef on the show. Winn, Penny, Fritz, and Bodhi had made a trip to LGBTQ Town on New Firmament for a special 'Winn Celebration,' and she'd had another pair of worn panties stolen to replace the ones that were wearing out on the pole top from all the flapping in the breeze. Bodhi piloted their tender home, since Winn had been drinking, and got them back to the ship without hitting anything.

Penny had had her baby girl whom she'd named Amelia. Yen was pregnant with Sonic's child, which would be his third. The seven babies were no longer babies, but toddlers learning to walk, and rug rats crawling high speed across the decks. Neither Winn nor Tish intended to have a 2nd child and always pressed Bodhi's Jen Mo point as their preferred means of birth control. Every time Shanti or Artana said 'daddy' Bodhi got a little lump in his throat and could barely contain his joy. Both girls had learned well to go to Bodhi if their mothers were saying "no" and denying them since their father was such a push-over and could not deny them anything. Both Tish and Winn had had some 'little talks' with Bodhi about this, though those had seemed to do no good.

June had demanded Bodhi as her action seal once she'd gotten through the completion stage of all six limbs, and Bodhi had acquiesced and done it with her providing the instruction. Kristy was currently completing her 6th limb. Although she was eighteen, and much closer to nineteen, on Ground where adulthood is not recognized until the frontal lobe cortex is fully developed—around the age of 22—Kristy remained technically a minor.

Winn and Haley had a dinner party planned for this evening and had invited the Grand Master, the Master of Ceremonies whose name was Betty, the well-loved elderly woman named Zara, and Administrators Gordon and Armstrong. About six months earlier, Gordon had finally gotten to see in long-view space imaging the destruction of seven Nafs Ammara ships and the turning around of 28 others. It was quite anticlimactic after seeing the in-close sensor imaging from *Diamond Lotus* captured at the actual time of the event.

Fritz and Winn had finally become lovers after Haley, Penny, June, Tandy, and Pam had already gotten to him first. Fritz had completed his small-craft pilot license and had learned most of the routine maintenance within the ship. After becoming lovers with Tish, he had learned the space-walk exterior maintenance as well. His meditation in the method of on-the-instant-insight and meditative absorption had progressed far under Bodhi's direction as his teacher. Penny was practicing meditation regularly now when she did not have a date.

Uldra was cooking for the party since Favio was down in the capital at the studio shooting another episode of his cooking show. Tandy was assisting her, and both Pam and Winn were helping too. Bodhi was on his way down in the shuttle to pick up the guests behind the Admin. Building where a shuttle landing-pad had finally been built after re-sodding the lawn dozens of times. There was just no way to set a shuttle down on soft soil and grass without leaving landing-leg gouges in the ground. The shuttle landing platform had already saved Bodhi numerous apologies.

They were wearing their uniforms to dinner at Bodhi's request, and Kristy had altered her uniform skirt into a sort of tutu. It no longer met the specification Bodhi had asked for regarding the skirts. At least her panties wouldn't show since Kristy didn't wear those, and more importantly, she wore her yellow tights. The skirt was like a planetary ring around her hips, all fluffy and sticking out more than hanging down. Under her uniform jacket, which she planned to remove anyway, she wore a very lacey undershirt with shoulder straps instead of the button-down uniform shirt. Across from the ship's emblem Winn had designed for the left breast of the jacket, Kristy had sewn on a peace symbol. On the front of her silly hat, she'd sewn a hemp leaf patch. She had also found a small emerald among a large sack of precious gem stones in a cargo hold on *Diamond Lotus* and had it set in a nose ring which was now in the piercing on the side of her nose instead of the little silver ring she'd had before.

Bodhi soared down through the atmosphere slowing as he came to land gently on the shuttle platform in the back yard of the Admin. Building. After opening the airlock doors and lowering the ramp, he exited the craft through the stern. The Grand Master, Betty, Zara, Gordon, and Armstrong were all out by the platform waiting, and there was a younger girl with them who Bodhi assumed to be the daughter of one of them. He greeted his guest and invited them aboard. The girl said to him, "My name is Kathy, Captain Bodhi, and I'm Kristy's date tonight."

"Unless things were broken or seriously out of harmony, Bodhi tended to just accept them, so he told her, "I'm pleased to meet you, Kathy. Come on aboard. Do you have a jacket or jumper to wear in case you feel cold?"

"No. I'll be just fine," Kathy replied, wearing only bikini bottoms and short vest that couldn't quite come together in the front to close.

Bodhi noticed that at least she had footwear, a pair of high-top canvas and rubber athletic shoes which looked overdue for replacement. He returned to the pilot's seat while the others strapped in within the passenger compartment. Kathy plopped herself into the copilot seat and informed Bodhi, "I need a window seat."

As he lifted off, Kathy told him, as if he could never have guessed, "This will be my first trip into space."

He lifted off gently and accelerated as they ascended with Kathy staring fascinated out the viewport. Bodhi put up forward and rear views in Kathy's holo, which she ignored in favor of the viewport. His other guests had all been up to the ship previously. Opening the bay doors on approach, having left the hangar in a vacuum when exiting, Bodhi brought the big cargo shuttle in with not much room to spare to either side. Kathy screeched various words and sounds in a high voice from the moment they left the atmosphere until entering the hangar and the bay doors sealing. The hangar was airing up as he set the shuttle down in its parking place.

When he got his guests up to the 11th deck on the cargo-lift without violating anyone's personal space, he led them all to the large dining cabin. They had had to insert the extra boards in the table, expanding it to make room for everyone to sit around it. Winn was already seated with her mini- uniform hat pinned at an angle on her head and looking totally adorable. Kristy arrived in her customized uniform to embrace and make out with Kathy. The toddlers were everywhere and on the move. They no longer had little hover-cribs, but instead big immobile ones affixed to the deck in their mothers' cabins. Tish was trying to watch over them and felt like she was trying to herd squirrels. Artana raised her arms in the pick-me-up gesture, seated on the floor to the side of Bodhi's chair where she'd walked to, and he leaned down to scoop her up and get her into his lap.

Pam and Tandy began bringing serving pots, bowls, and platters in to set on the table, and the other crew members gathered around to take their seats. By the time Uldra was bringing the last of the meal out from the galley, everyone was collected at the table except Favio, who was down in the capital. Penny held baby Amelia in her lap, and Artana sat on Bodhi's while the other six toddlers walked precariously about the dining room floor. Tish appeared to be a little stressed but was unwinding and relaxing now that she was no longer herding squirrels. The Grand Master said the blessing and offering over the food.

Administrator Armstrong commented, "Mission Disarmament and Liberation is quickly approaching."

Bodhi suggested, "I would like for you to come along with us to learn how the T-9 Super Cruiser is fought. Once the mission is completed, the ship will be under your jurisdiction. It is 25 millennia ahead of Ground's technology, or at least from where Ground's technology was a year ago. I see you as the right person to captain the ship after this campaign."

"I would be honored and want to go along. I considered asking you but did not want to impose."

"We need a chain of command and so a hierarchy of ranks for war. War is chaos, and our force must remain ordered and coordinated in the face of it. Rank has bearing only on the action in the relative world, and our underlying absolute equality is held reverently and recognized throughout."

Armstrong agreed, "We usually come together and quickly work out a chain of command with leaders and supervisors whenever there is an emergency. Disaster workers do this immediately upon arrival in a crisis-disaster region. Seniority, skills, experience, intelligence, abilities, and so forth are the criteria."

Bodhi laid out his plan, "I will Captain the T-9, *Thor*, and Haley will be my X.O. and weapons operator. Tish will pilot, and Winn will copilot. Uduak will be my Fire Control Officer. I'd like for you, Gordon, to be my Sensor Analysis Officer. Haley found excellent personnel on Ground whom she has trained to operate our navigational systems on the bridge, to be our Coms Officer and our Auxiliary Systems Operator. I'm placing June in charge of our small craft; she has proven herself to be an intuitive and courageous pilot who does not hesitate."

"What of the rest of the crew of *Diamond Lotus*?" Gordon inquired.

"I'm bringing Uldra to run the galley for the senior officer's mess. My ship will be coming along to protect *Spalding* and to be in reserve should we have need of her. Sunoco will captain and pilot her, and Ilya will copilot. Pam will be coms and navigation officer. Shamas will load the canister missiles. Sonic will be the weapons operator. I'll be picking up three cosmonauts from New Firmament to man the two quad-blasters and one to serve as an engineer. The other members of *Diamond Lotus* will not have battle-stations and are welcome to remain in the Ground System during this mission if they choose to. The personnel for the auxiliary *Spalding* will be entirely from Ground. Haley has selected Captain Clark of *Providence*, one of Ground's best merchant fleet captains, to command her. He is a very competent and methodical man."

Haley informed their guests, "We are installing some class 3, 4 and 5 blaster quads on *Spalding*, and four batteries of sixteen canister missiles so that the ship will not be defenseless. *Diamond Lotus* will have four large undercarriage missiles added to its armaments. With these alterations, the Nafs Ammara warships will not be able to destroy them. They won't even know they are there with their cloaking unless they fire weapons."

Armstrong updated them, "Falcon space station, the new Space Fleet space station, is framed rimmed and spoked, and moving along just ahead of schedule."

Bodhi recommended, "Since New World also has a star-gate detectable from many light-years away, one or more of the warships arrived from Nafs Ammara ought to be stationed there for planetary defense. Their Gosh Hawk space station ought to be refitted with saturnium reactors and have both propulsion and weapons systems installed. Propulsion would protect it from dumb munitions, which cannot change trajectory to adapt to their targets."

"I will advocate this with my counterpart on New World," Armstrong assured him. "I quite agree with you, and at the moment, they are entirely defenseless."

Betty reported, "The sequestering and capture of carbon from our atmosphere for making the carbon plate armor for *Thor* has reduced the carbon levels globally by 7.9%. We are continuing to run the machines and will keep making carbon plate armor from the carbon in our atmosphere for ten more years with diminishing returns, though to great benefit for the biosphere."

Haley suggested, "You ought to keep manufacturing satellites with ultra-violet ray shielding generators for at least ten more years, as well."

"We intend to," Betty confirmed.

Haley mentioned, "Once we disarm Nafs Ammara, we will need to access its star-gate system. I've been studying the data, and there are five dimensions of security. There is a transmission beacon on each ship known to the gate. The ships themselves have specific identifiers, and each ship undergoes a full active scan before being passed through. Encrypted codes must be entered, and there is a quantum link component which connects the quantum drive to the star-gate."

"Have you found ways to overcome these?" Bodhi inquired.

"I have. All of them, now that I've reversed engineered the quantum drive and gate link component. I printed a 3D model and have a good start on manufacturing procedures for each segment and part of the link unit. The rest is just hacking things into the gate core quantum computer. I can upload beacon frequencies, codes, ship-identifiers, and scan data so the gate will recognize our ships."

That's fantastic, Haley!" Bodhi exclaimed.

"Isn't she just wonderful?" Winn enthused full of admiration.

Zara contributed, "Haley is the very favorite with the people of Ground. Did you know that Favio gave our central coms network the *Lost in Space* franchise, and the pilot episode ran last night?"

"We didn't know," Winn stated a little alarmed that this distorted image of Bodhi had just followed him to another world.

Zara said to Kristy, "You are a talented actress and natural comedian, young lady, and very beautiful too. And I love your fashion line. I'm wearing a Kristy-undershirt beneath my blouse right now."

"That's so sweet of you to say. Thank you Zara," Kristy told her gratefully. She added, "You could lose the blouse if you've got a Kristy undershirt on."

"Is the one you're wearing a new addition to the line?" Zara asked with genuine interest.

"This one's custom," Kristy explained, "but it could become part of the line."

"I'd purchase one," Zara stated. "It is truly lovely and so very feminine."

"I'll make one in the fabricator-tailoring machine for you before you leave if you tell me what size you want," Kristy offered.

"I'll meet with you privately after the meal," Zara told her.

Betty mentioned, "I see you are scheduled to play with that new teenage band called the Space Cadets at the Capital Arena."

"I play sax, and they're going to let me sing," Kristy informed her with sheer excitement. "The Dancing Asteroids are going to play first. They're just second billing."

"It's a thrill to dine with such a celebrity," Zara told Kristy.

Betty commented curiously, "It seems your fans are mostly female."

Kristy explicated, "Everyone knows I'm a lesbian and have never done it with a guy. I'm going to have Bodhi as my action seal soon, so I won't technically be a hetero-virgin much longer."

"T.M.I. Kristy," Haley informed her as First Officer of *Diamond Lotus.*

Kristy suggested to Betty, "Don't mind them. They're just kind of uptight and prudish."

Grand Master Tipola asked Kristy, "Have you almost completed the six limbs?"

"I started at twelve while living in an ashram," Kristy filled him in. "With Bodhi around, and all his spiritual potency, shit happens fast around here, I'm telling you."

"Yes, I have seen, and meditate with him at least once a week. I know just what you mean," Tipola confided.

"I kind of wish he was a girl," Kristy shared, "but then I couldn't use him as my action seal, and I just know he's going to be good for that."

"It is still amazing at your age, dear," Tipola pointed out.

"Not really. Not with Bodhi," Kristy tried to make him understand. "You should try climbing in his bed and sleeping next to him. Your winds enter the central channel forcefully, and it brings a new magnitude of lucidity and clarity to your dreams. Really. Don't take my word for it, sleep with him."

"I believe Kristy thrives on awkward situations," Bodhi offered his assessment.

"You rarely even knew I was there," Kristy defended herself. "And besides, I didn't ever disturb you, and the benefit to my dream work more than justified it. Sunoco was doing it too for a while."

"You are a rare and fast-developing student, Kristy, and your dream work has been key to your success in the limbs. You are a candidate for the secret method and are already practicing some of it. I could not be more pleased with your progress. Honestly."

"I think a Brussel-sprout would have insight in your presence," Kristy asserted.

Tish said, "Kristy, you are truly an amazing person and enormously talented. I'm a big fan, and I love you."

"You're one of my hero's, Tish, and far more talented than me. If you were single, I'd marry you."

"She is really cute," Kathy said into Kristy's ear, though everyone heard.

"What's your story?" Tandy asked Kathy.

"I'm a Hallmark catalogue underwear and swimsuit model, and now I'm doing fashion shows for the Kristy fashion line. I'm 22, a sapio sun sign with carpius rising, and my favorite color is pink."

"Are you a lesbian?" Tandy pressed for some substance.

"I am, though I've slept with a few guys."

"Do you meditate?"

"Kristy has taught me."

"Would you like to have a sleep-over?" Tandy got to the point.

"I am already, with Kristy."

"Are you having a party tonight, Kristy?" Tandy asked.

Kristy began cautiously, "I wasn't planning one, but I'd never kick you out of my bed Tandy."

"I'll be deeply hurt if *I* don't get invited," June pouted.

Kristy told her, "Then consider yourself invited honey and don't sulk."

Hayley cleared her throat, which needed no clearing, drawing Kristy's attention and she told Haley, "My bed is always yours, sweetheart."

Bodhi suggested, "Perhaps such arrangements could be handled once we quit the table and a little more discretely. We have company over."

"Alright dad," Kristy humored him.

Shanti wanted into Bodhi's lap where Artana was already sitting. Winn tried to pick her up but she fussed, wanting daddy, so he squeezed her in beside her half-sister on his lap. This made eating a considerable challenge for him. Then Shanti surprised herself with a combination of fart and bowel movement. Bodhi handed Artana to Tish and carried Shanti into his suite to change her. It did not do much for his appetite. In a brief span, he was back at the table with Shanti in a fresh diaper.

He mentioned to Tipola, "There is a unity of people from thousands of planets within six different galaxies who collectively and simultaneously attune their meditation on the same intention. It is called the spiritual congress. The advanced race of Amonrahonians, whom I've told you about, started it through Sarhi the Im and are supporting it through a hundred-year meditation by their entire race. It may be in a different time from us now, I don't know, but it is the most potent spiritual instrument I have ever experienced. I would like to start a spiritual congress in this time and region of the universe with some people from Firmament, New Firmament, Ground, New World, and as many planets of the Nafs Ammara empire as possible."

"We have made mass participation with meditation such as that, involving tens of millions of people of Ground, with astonishing results. I would be honored to assist you and to begin organizing here on Ground. I have students on New World as well."

"I'll talk it up at my concert in the Capital Arena so it will be transmitted over the holocoms and get all the teens involved," Kristy told them. "Maybe Favio could mention it on his cooking show, and we can get the producers of *Lost in Space* to display a message or a clip we make for them about joining the spiritual congress, and how totally catalyst and tubular it is to be part of it."

"You will be one of our recruiting images for sure, Kristy," Bodhi agreed. "I'd prefer it if you would wear your meditation suit when you shoot the holoclip, though."

"That would never work," she told him straight up.

"I'll handle twenty-something up, and I guess I'll just have to put some trust and faith in you, Kristy, and leave the teens to twenty to you," Bodhi surrendered.

"I'll send a heartfelt message-holo to the people of LGBTQ Town," Winn promised.

"Send another pair of dirty panties with it," Kristy told her knowingly. "That will work for sure."

"It seems we have our basic recruitment strategy. Haley is making us some practice instruction manuals for working with the spiritual congress, very detailed in technical writing, clear and easy to follow. We can establish quantum computer interface sites and post the manuals for download."

"We can put our holoclip recruitment ads on it, and once they click on their age, the most appropriate one for them can pop up." Kristy enthused.

Zara offered, "I could do large group initiations and empowerments for people on Ground who are practicing from the manuals, and I could travel to New World and do them there as well."

"I'm much younger and will travel to New World," Betty told Zara. "I will go to the Paltinol continent and pass the initiations and empowerments here on Ground too."

"I will have my senior students pass these too," Grand Master Tipola told them.

"I'd be proud to make an endorsement ad for it," Shamas announced.

Haley suggested, "A holoclip endorsement by Tish would get half her nation involved and martial arts enthusiasts all over the planet Firmament."

"I will do it," Tish said seriously.

Winn suggested, "We should also put Fritz in an ad, just because he is so impossibly pretty."

Armstrong said, "I see this spiritual congress as the ultimate interplanetary defense and basis for diplomatic relations of a higher order. So I'm going to arrange time and crews in the central studios for you to make your ads and edit them through Administrator Sullivan."

Uldra, Tandy, and Pam cleared the dishes from the table then brought out desert. It was high-density chocolate fudge, topped with dark chocolate semi-sweet syrup, with a fresh ripe strawberry and dollop of whipped cream on each plate. These temptations in front of each diner caused an almost silence but for the sharp intakes of breaths and an "aahh" and a few "oohhs." Forks clinking plates then sounded louder than they were.

Tandy finally declared, "This is over the top delicious!"

Kristy added, "Orgasmic culinary ecstasy!"

"Gustatory rapture and taste bud bliss," Bodhi agreed.

CHAPTER TWENTY-FOUR

The big moment arrived eight weeks and five days later after completing the T-9 super cruiser on schedule and sending it on one week of training maneuvers with the auxiliary ship *Spalding*. They had gotten their reloading operations time down to nine minutes and 28 seconds by the end of their test run. The three solarium reactor ships with full cloaking and quantum-coms jump navigation free of gates were fully armed and loaded with provisions, supplies, and munitions, sitting at berths connected to Condor Space Station, where weapons systems installation-construction was taking place on two sections of the spoked wheel-shaped space transportation hub. They could see the skeleton of the new Falcon Space Fleet Platform in their holos from the bridge of *Thor*. Some outer skin was in place in one small section, and an enormous space construction crew was busy working on it from industrial space platform cranes and engineering-utility vessels.

Captain Bodhi of *Thor* informed Captain Clark of *Spalding* and commander Sunoco of *Diamond Lotus*, "Pull out from your berths and accelerate to jump speed. You have the coordinates of the invasion force headed our way in your nav.-computer. We'll be coming in ahead of them just under their speed, and we'll quicken to match them."

"Aye aye, Captain," Tish and Clark replied at the same time.

The three ships pulled slowly from their docking berths and gathered momentum as they headed away from planet Ground. Passing the star-gate on their port side all three ships engaged cloaking and winked out of sight with no heat, electronic, electromagnetic, or nuclear signatures. They maintained a quantum coms connection with each other as they each established the same with their destination. At .7 light speed, the invisible ships physically disappeared from the Ground solar system to reappear in that same moment in deep space traveling .7 light and just ahead of the invasion force overtaking them without it knowing they were there. Bodhi initiated acceleration the second they were through the jump. Tish experienced only momentary disorientation, having attained the white appearance in her contemplation at the point of quantum jump and was back in control of the ship seconds later. Winn was next to recover.

Their precise relative position was being continuously transmitted by quantum coms to their other two ships, which would ideally not have an active role in this engagement. From his seat on the bridge Bodhi could access the class 9 beam weapon, class 9 blaster, torpedoes, and largest missiles. Both Tish and Winn could fire the class 8 twin nose blasters, and Winn could fire the class 9 blaster. Haley at the weapons-operation console could fire torpedoes, large missiles, canister missiles, and the two twin class seven blasters—one pair set in each side fin. Bodhi could also fire anti-missile molten flare counter-measures and cloaked mobile smart mine nets out of the stern.

Thor had two class 8 blaster quads, one on top and one on the underside of its disc-shaped hull. There were two dozen class 6 blaster-quads manually operated on site, 48 class five blaster-quads also manually operated, and sixty class four manual blaster-quads. The T-9 super cruiser had once been the most powerful ship Om had ever built. That was before they'd constructed the 8,100-foot diameter ORH Super-Battleship which contained 30 solarium fusion super-reactors. To defeat the Royal Monarch Empire, Om had cooperated with people from the Trident system in the Yuban Galaxy to construct the ORH Ultra-Super-Battleship-Carrier, 29,630-feet in diameter, and with 244 solarium super-reactors. They'd had five of these when they initiated the revolution.

Uduak worked out fire control for all 32 war ships with Haley's help and assigned multiple weapons systems on *Thor* to each one. Those were continuously updated by the millisecond. Haley and

Gordon established a quantum coms to encoded spectrum light coms conversion and link to the Admiral of the invasion force's command ship. Bodhi announced, "This is Captain Bodhi of the warship *Thor*. If you do not follow my orders to the letter, I will destroy all of your ships."

"This is Admiral Walmartt of the Nafs Ammara Empire. What right do you have to try and tell me what to do?"

"What right do you have to invade peaceful planetary populations conquering and enslaving them?" Bodhi shot back.

"It is our manifest destiny to rule this galaxy," Admiral Walmartt told him, obviously believing this cruel immoral nonsense.

"No. Your empire is destined for oblivion today," Bodhi reframed.

"We are the superior planetary race in this galaxy and destined to rule it," Walmartt argued.

"You follow the lowest and most disharmonious law of might-makes-right. You are an insect, and I'm a giant with all the power. Your planetary race is lost in the duality of ego delusion and about to be squashed. Abandon your warships, all 32 of them, to transfer into your 35 industrial ships. I will allow those to turn around."

"I'll go down with my ship before facing execution in disgrace."

Bodhi muted the jerk and said to Haley, "Start hitting all those warships with canister shield disrupters followed by nanobot spray missiles and upload Jard's take-over program."

"Aye Aye, Captain. Launching canister missiles now," Haley reported.

A couple of minutes passed while Haley fired off 32 pairs of missiles, with one-tenth seconds between the two missiles of each pair precisely and accurately. Another minute plus for the nanobots to reach coms towers and just under two minutes for the upload and take-over program to make each ship theirs. Bodhi asked Haley, "Please put me on intercoms throughout each warship so the crews will hear me."

"You're on, Captain," Haley informed him.

Bodhi announced, "This is Captain Bodhi of the warship *Thor*. I have taken control of each of your warships, and I'm starting a countdown to the permanent shutdown of all life support systems on these ships. I am also bringing all personnel on them, out of cryogenic hibernation. When the countdown runs out, if crews of the warships are not shuttling over to industrial ships I will have you fire upon and destroy each other. Here is a demonstration."

Haley fired a class 4 twin blaster on the command ship into a smaller warship bringing down its shields and both scorching and breaching its hull at a point where nothing vital was hit, and nothing blew up."

"That ought to get their attention," Haley commented.

It took about ten minutes for the warship captains, commanders and Admiral Walmartt to fully acknowledge that they had no control whatsoever of their ships and could not even manually shut them down. Bodhi said over the intercoms of all 32 ships, "Long before you arrive home, your empire will be in total and utter ruin, completely disarmed, your slave planets liberated and your emperor long vaporized. You will face no disgrace or repercussions from your empire. It will be lost in the dust bin of history."

It took another ten minutes for the captains, commanders, Admiral and officers, to realize that they could in no way restore control to themselves. During this time the restless, angry, rebellious crews were escalating inevitably towards violent mutiny of the abject desperate. In only three more minutes, shuttles began leaving from all but the command ship. Bodhi informed Walmartt, "You have two minutes to get your shuttles lifting your crew off, or I'm pulverizing the bridge of your ship to waste you."

He kind of wanted that ship for the people of Ground but would keep his word and sacrifice it if necessary. The officers on *Thor's* bridge watched the two-minute countdown. Bodhi had the shot lined up with his class 9 beam weapon at an angle to shave the bridge right off the top of the ship so as not to blow the whole thing to smithereens and kill the innocent crew. When the countdown ran down to six seconds, a shuttle left its bay, followed by another one. On-board sensors showed hundreds of armed crew just outside the bridge blast-doors, and some had serious explosives in hand. Walmartt's X.O. was just finishing him off on the bridge, with both hands wringing the Admiral's neck. He finally gave a last kick and jerk before going dead and the X.O. dropped the body to the deck. The shuttle transfer of crew was proceeding at a frantic rate.

Bodhi mentioned to Haley, "Ground will have a significant Space Fleet once these 32 ships arrive."

"We ought to take some ships over in the Nafs Ammara system to distribute to the liberated slave planets," Haley suggested.

"Good idea," Bodhi agreed.

It took over an hour for the crews to complete their transfers from warships to industrial ones. Bodhi turned and followed the 35 civilian ships while the 32 warships continued at .72 light-speed headed for where the Ground solar system would be. Location in the universe was relative and always on the move. Once the industrial ships exceeded .7 light Bodhi ordered his other two ships, "Commander Tish and Captain Clark, prepare for the jump into Nafs Ammara. I've sent you a 30-second countdown. Once we've made the jump, only follow me in to about 100,000 miles from the outer of their two moons. Nafs Ammara is a white sun world and hence will be the 4th planet from the star. It has two moons, both with lunar weapons bases. Circle the planet and both moons and be ready if I call for help or come in to reload."

Haley stopped the jump countdown with 16 seconds remaining to inform them, "I just reviewed data from the spy drone we have in the Nafs Ammara System. They now have 96 warships there. They added five warships from an invasion force or must have pulled them from their slave worlds. They also have a new super-warship 9,240 ft. in length and packed with 44 venusium fusion-reactors, which must have been built somewhere other than their home world."

Bodhi proclaimed, "That super-ship will be no match for *Thor*, believe me, though if enough of those ships were able to target us at once, we would be in trouble. They also have thousands of military small craft, lunar weapons bases, five armed space stations, and 36 space weapons platforms in orbit. Some of their 50,000 satellites are weaponized, too. Stay alert. We can do this."

Haley restarted the countdown from the 16 seconds it was set on, and the time wound down to their jump. They landed in the system a little way out from the orbital distance of the 5th planet, which was out passed their gate and so had no traffic.

Once their speed was down to .24 light, giving them clear sensor resolution and fire control, Bodhi asked Haley, "Where's the super-ship?"

"Around the other side of Nafs Ammara in medium orbit," Haley replied. "Our spy android that we left here has eyes on it."

"Uduak, start obtaining fire control resolutions for torpedoes on those lunar bases of the furthest out moon, and all warships in our line of fire."

"Aye Aye. I'm on it."

To Haley, Bodhi said, "As soon as we're in range and you get missile-lock with the canister missiles, start taking over warships. They'll be able to see our ordinance as it launches, so I'm going to have Tish make some random maneuvers to avoid taking hits."

"I'm all set," she let him know.

"I've got those lunar bases targeted," Uduak updated Bodhi.

Bodhi directed Haley, "Torpedoes away."

"Firing torpedoes," Haley replied. Four enormous space drive torpedoes left their tubes accelerating faster than an interceptor or corvette thunder fighter craft. The four lunar bases had saturnium reactor powered shields, which the torpedoes would blow through like smoke. Some anti-missile missiles came close to one torpedo, and blaster fire grazed another, but all four reached their targets explosively and four humongous dust clouds rose, hiding the craters beneath them, which had been the four bases just a moment before.

A long-range, high-powered beam weapon cut through the space *Thor* had just previously occupied, and dozens of missiles of all sizes were on their way to that exact location. Bodhi had turned hard to starboard and downwards per *Thor's* orientation, headed for the moon closest to Nafs Ammara. Uduak was already targeting its weapons bases. Military small crafts were launching from space stations, lunar bases, ship bays, and from the surface of Nafs Ammara. Bodhi checked in with June, who was in the small craft hangar of the T-9, "Are my Astro-Phantom bombers ready to deploy?"

"Yes. You have pilots in every small craft ready to go on your command."

"Go ahead and launch the twenty-two Astros along with their fighter bomber drone escorts and commence your bombing run on the space weapons platforms."

Each of the Astro-Phantom bombers had a drone pilot seat and console in their cockpit manned by a drone pilot controlling a small crewless fighter bomber with two large undercarriage missiles, two batteries of 16 canister missiles and twin class 5 nose blasters. The Astro-Phantom was the newest and most formidable small craft Om had ever designed and this class had proven itself a most valuable asset in the war against the Royal Monarch Empire. Astro-Phantoms carried eight large undercarriage missiles, six batteries of 16 canister missiles each, two class 4 quad blaster turrets, twin class four blasters on each fin, class 5 twin nose blasters and four small torpedoes within each of two internal tubes. With a drone-fighter bomber escort, the bomber had enormous destructive power and great fire support. More than two dozen Nafs Ammara small craft could unload everything they had into an Astro all at the same time without taking down its shields.

A medium-sized Nafs Ammara warship just came into range, and Haley launched a shield disruptor followed by a spray missile into the bow of it. It was way behind them by the time the nanobots reached the coms terminal on the hull. Haley uploaded Jard's control program and tagged that ship in her display as theirs. Sunoco came on in Bodhi's ear, saying, "I could get in there and help."

"Not yet," Bodhi cautioned her. "Let me take out all the mega-weapons and that big ship first. Then it ought to be safe enough for you to engage."

June informed him, "Astro-Phantoms are away and closing on the first space weapons platform."

"Go to work," Bodhi told June, who was now piloting the lead Astro.

The bow of the 1 ¾ miles-long ship was just showing from over the planet's horizon when several medium and small warships came within range of *Thor* at about the same time. Haley began launching pairs of canister missiles at each of them, and the ordinance was spitting out. Their shields took beam and blaster hits now that the missiles flying from their ship gave away their position. Other Nafs Ammara warships turned headed for them from about every direction, and the fire they took churned their shields into cascading turbulence. Haley was shooting off canister missiles as fast as a five-barrel Gatling gun can spit rounds. The super-ship was bearing down on them fully around the horizon and headed right at them, firing.

Bodhi got his class nine beam weapon on a large command ship and it blew into a dust and vapor cloud after 4.3 seconds of sustained hit. His shields were taking so much fire, including from the biggest weapons of the super-ship, that they were down to 79% power and dropping, and several hundred missiles were hurling their way right at them. His quad gunners were blowing small craft into expanding spheres of light and particles. Uduak had four lunar bases all lined up for torpedoes, and since Haley was busy with the canister missiles, Bodhi launched them. Tish cut a small warship in half—or very close to half—with the twin nose blasters, and debris full of personnel came spilling from each broken-open end. The slightly smaller half containing stern, drives, and reactors blew into glaring super-heated atoms expanding in every direction. The other half turned slowly end over end, caught in the closer moon's vortex, and headed for its surface.

Missiles began pummeling *Thor's* shields, now down to 61% and dropping. The big super-ship was closing with even its smaller weapons now in range and was hitting them with everything it had continuously. More ships were coming into range with them, and *all* the imperial ships were headed their way. A cloud of small craft surrounded them like a swarm of bees. Shields were dropping faster and now down to 52%. Haley reported without slowing her canister missiles fire, "A squadron of small craft messengers just jumped out of their star-gate to bring all warships from slave planets home to defend Nafs Ammara. There will be another 136 warships here within less than an hour. There are still three lunar weapons bases operating on the inner moon."

"Do you have those lunar bases locked in Uduak?"

"Only one so far, but I'm working on it. One of them is around the horizon from our position."

Bodhi fired one torpedo sending it to the base Uduak did have a 'lock' on and told him, "Just enter the coordinates for the one around the horizon, and the torpedo will find it."

"Got the 2nd one lined up and coordinates are entered for the third," Uduak reported.

"Torpedoes away," Bodhi announced.

Tish had the twin nose blaster drilling a medium warship close ahead, and Winn had both twin fin-blasters ripping into the same ship. It seemed to shimmer and contract before expanding many thousands of times its size in brilliant living color growing exponentially as its light faded. Bodhi was accelerating and turning, trying to get out from under the concentrated fire they were getting nailed with. Shields were into the 40 percentiles and still falling. Some 200-foot thermo-nuclear missiles with space drives and boosters launched from the giant ship at them.

June was still in the lead with 21 other Astro-Phantoms and 22 drone fighter bombers behind her and was hitting space weapons platforms with her undercarriage missiles and torpedoes. A big missile could kill one, leaving only a bit of space-trash, and when hit with a torpedo, there was nothing to be found of them at all afterwards. Single canister missiles just blew on their shields without damaging them. Nine platforms were now dispersing gas clouds sparkling with super-heated particles. Following the curve of Nafs Ammara with 27 space weapons platforms left to blow, June was going over the horizon from *Thor's* line of sight.

A mega surface-to-space weapon which was fired from the planet, disintegrated June's wingman and its unpiloted drone-fighter bomber hit another of the same, blowing both into a light show. Some of her Astros had taken hits penetrating shields to scorch their hulls so that parts of these crafts were no longer cloaked. Imperial small craft zeroed in from all around in a great horde harassing them. Her quad-gunners were lighting them up, and imperial fighters and fighter bombers were bursting like popcorn all over space. In a coordinated effort with five other Astro-Phantoms, June's group got six torpedoes locked on and zooming for the mega surface-to-space weapon on Nafs Ammara.

A mega weapon on a space station blew up another Astro-Phantom bomber, but June's drone pilot caught control of that one's drone fighter bomber, and was managing two at once. An imperial heavy bomber collided head-on with a drone-fighter bomber and both were smeared across space. Two more weapons platforms blew apart with flaring light. The fire from two space stations was raining down on them now. Haley could see that June's force was in trouble through the sensors on the spy android, which yet had line-of-sight on her, and told Bodhi, "June needs help."

Bodhi called down to the hangar and said, "Send the 28 Hunter Terminator fighter-bombers to reinforce June."

"Aye, Aye, Captain."

The NBC Hunter Terminators started zipping out the bay doors while *Thor's* quad gunners tore into the incoming 200-foot nukes, which were flying at them fast. Tish destroyed one of these with the twin nose blasters. Bodhi hit one with his class 9 beam weapon, and it blew in less than half a second. Haley switched to firing big missiles at the oncoming nukes, and Winn got the class 9 blaster on one. Hardly any imperial small craft popped for a moment as all blaster fire focused on the 200-foot missiles bearing down on them. Shields had fallen to 39%.

All but one of the nuclear missiles got destroyed in space before the final arrival. The one that hit them took their shields offline for a moment, and Bodhi fired his main launch booster, containing a whole week's worth of gas mining, no longer feeling frugal. As *Thor* blew out of this cluster fuck into more open space, Clark was beside them with 60 missiles leaving *Spalding's* canisters at the same time, and every blaster firing on full-automatic. *Diamond Lotus's* undercarriage missiles were streaking for the super ship with all its blasters drilling the behemoth, and a couple of dozen canister missiles on the way to it. Bodhi lit the super ship up with his beam, and when Winn got her class 9 blaster digging a hole in it, the thing went super-nova filling space around them to then fade to nothing at all.

There were still more than 20 warships hammering *Thor* with ordinance and blaster bolts. The shields had risen to 26% in the lull and were dropping again. Normally invisible, *Thor's* shields were tangibly boiling with turbulence all around the ship. Bodhi announced to the bridge crew, "Forget about taking any more of them over. We need to waste these ships quickly. Haley, can you get some that we've got control of turned over to drone pilots on our ships?"

"I can now that the nuke storm has passed," she let him know.

"How many did you manage to take?"

"More than you have pilots and consoles for flying from this ship," Haley replied. "I've transferred the 18 largest warships I took over to your 18 drone pilot consoles. The remaining eleven ships have all weapons systems shutdown, and I'm powering down the drives on those now to let them drift."

"Let's start taking the ones firing at us out of the game and off the board," Bodhi suggested. He called the officer in *Thor's* hangar and ordered, "Send the six Vulcan Prowler fighter-bombers and eight commando combat shuttles to reinforce June."

Some reflective lens material had scraped away from *Thor,* where her hull was scorched when the shields went down, and now the cloaking was foiled except from one narrow aspect of the ship. His shields were 21% for the moment. Bodhi put a large crater on the planet's surface with the class nine beam right where a super-weapon had been. He kept accelerating and told Sunoco and Clark, "Go to .28 light speed and stay above targeting speed to come in behind their ships to acquire them. They all seem to be maintaining .12 light, so coming in from behind, the difference will only be 1.6 light, plenty slow enough to get targeting resolution. Those mega surface weapons won't be able to draw a bead on you."

He got his beam cooking one end of a giant imperial space station and said to Winn, "Rake that station with the big blaster."

Winn started walking the class 9 blaster bolts along the side of the space station, and as the thing's shields hit failure, the section Bodhi was heating up went into implosion, but the air pressure within reversed this to blow outwards into space spitting a tongue of debris and personnel many miles out. He was pretty sure he saw a man at his desk, still in his chair, fly into space. He had no time to zoom in with his optics to check. A small warship he got under his beam went to pieces in a second, or just over.

Bodhi was up to .28 light, and his shields were rising fast. He came in behind an imperial ship one class below a command ship, and weapon's systems on *Thor* began hitting its stern. He got his beam on it and went right at its tail without slowing or turning off, to pass through its vapor cloud as it blew.

Some imperial ships were accelerating so they could get on Bodhi's tail, unable to target him otherwise. *Spalding* and *Diamond Lotus* were still fully cloaked and now beyond targeting velocity, except by coming behind at speed. Winn and some quad-blaster gunners blew another small ship. Haley took down one of the second biggest with a torpedo. With the imperial small craft off of them for the moment, all of *Thor's* gunners were focused on ships, though small crafts were accumulating in *Thor's* wake. Once a few ships had closed to firing range behind him and started pounding his shields, Bodhi released a cloaked mobile smart-mine net out the stern. As it stretched to catch all three ships, small crafts were blowing on the net itself giving it away even though it was cloaked. All three ships braked and veered, but it was too late, and the smart mines found their targets in a triple explosion, leaving thee bright clouds lingering for moments.

June led the remaining 18 Astro-Phantoms with their 17 drone-fighters bombers and 26 Hunter Terminators—having already lost two to space stations' weapons—and the 6 Vulcan Prowlers and eight combat shuttles blowing away space weapons platforms. Her quad-blaster gunners were ripping apart imperial small craft, and she was boring into a weapons platform with her twin nose blasters while her copilot hit it with the fin blasters and her weapons operator punched canister missiles into it. Other bombers were nailing this one too, and it didn't take long for it to blow into expanding particles. She was trying to come at the platforms while keeping the remaining space stations over the horizon from her force, which had them skimming the transition zone at the top of the atmosphere. Satellites kept frying on her shields and bits that didn't vaporize thumped against the nose of her bomber. From head-on, she was no longer cloaked.

Bodhi noticed this since the condition flagged her in his small craft monitoring holo. He told June, "Get your bomber back aboard for a lens coating on the nose. It will only take a couple of minutes, and you can reload while you're here. Bring bomber seven because its cloaking is compromised too. That's an order. Bring a quarter of your Hunter Terminators back since all of them have spent their undercarriage missiles."

"Aye Aye, Captain, I'm coming back in with number seven and thirteen of the Hunter Terminators."

"I'm sending the 30 Corvette Thunders and the 8 Comet Interceptors to reinforce your group until you're back. Once those fire their two undercarriage missiles, they're down to a twin nose blaster for armaments, so I don't want them out long."

"Roger that."

"I'm bringing *Thor* around to make a run on their largest space station, and I'm slowing to .24 light to get accurate resolution on it."

"I have you in my line of sight, and I'll be there in a couple of minutes," June informed him.

Haley was going through the big missiles fast, though using them exceedingly well to blow up ships. Only the command ships could survive one of the big missiles, and she'd been using torpedoes on those—which worked perfectly—until she'd ran out of them. Bodhi called out to Haley, "Get our drone pilots attacking the big space station with our 18 imperial warships to start reducing its shields. I'm going on an attack run to waste it as soon as June and the other small craft are in the hangar."

To Clark, Bodhi said, "Move out behind their gate and come to rest relative to it because I'm going to need to reload and make a few repairs, and *Diamond Lotus* has nearly emptied its munitions hold."

"*Spalding's* only taking down imperial small craft at this point anyway. So I'll get clear of the battle zone and jump out a few million miles past their star-gate then brake until we're at rest. I'll have reloading and repair crews at the ready."

"Thanks. You're doing a great job."

Bodhi asked Sunoco, "Where are you?"

"Just over the horizon blowing up small ships and big bombers with my nose blasters and trying to stay clear of that big space station. There are still a few mega surface-to-space weapons on Nafs Ammara to watch out for."

"Clark's jumping out past the star-gate, and you need to follow him to reload your canister and undercarriage missiles, and refill your munitions hold."

"Aye Aye, sir," Sunoco signed off.

Bodhi checked with June, "Are your people all in the hangar yet?"

"Yes, and the doors are sealing. We're going to air it up to make external repairs."

"I'm making a run on that big space station so it might get a little rough. Put on the electromagnetic boots if you're going to be out in the hangar—and that goes for all your folks."

"Yes, Sir!"

Bodhi was down to .24 light, and his shields were fluctuating, depending on how many hits these were taking at each moment, between 91% and 96%. He mentioned to Haley, "Save a few of those big missiles because I'm starting my run."

"The station has already destroyed three of our imperial ships. They are turned back around and into their 2nd assault on it. They'll be in range of it just ahead of us."

"Good. They can attract some of the space station's fire."

To all on the bridge and to all of his gunners, Bodhi said, "I want every weapon on this ship hitting that space station. The moment your weapon has range and acquisition, fire as fast as you can and sustain it for as long as you can."

Bodhi's class 9 beam weapon hit the station first, and a second later, Winn's class 9 blaster was slamming its shields. The larger weapons on their remaining imperial warships opened up next. The station's shields were thrashing, roiling, and splashing about violently. The class eight twin nose blasters tore right through the shields scorching armor, and Bodhi's beam punched a hole to the interior. Winn's blaster caved a whole section. Haley's big missiles took out huge bites of the rim, and when all the class 6 quad-blasters started hammering the remaining structure, the whole thing transformed instantly from solid into gas as the reactors blew in a chain reaction.

Bodhi made a nice deep crater in Nafs Ammara's surface, blowing up a mega space weapon on the ground into molten fluids, vapor, and particles. Haley mentioned, "Imperial ships have begun arriving through the star-gate."

"Drone pilots, bring your imperial warships around, and then straight at the star-gate and at the ships jumping in. If you have one of the little ones and are already out of missiles, then just ram an incoming ship head-on. Try to choose one a little bigger than yours."

He told Haley, "I'm accelerating to jump speed and going to *Spalding* for reloading and repairs. We'll let the imperials fight their own ships for a quarter hour."

"I doubt they'll last that long," Haley calculated.

"They should give enough of a diversion," Bodhi said, hoping this was true.

To his small craft still out fighting, Bodhi said, "I'm sending you *Spalding's* coordinates. Get to jump speed and get there. I'll collect you in my hanger out there, and you can all reload."

Bodhi passed .25 light and stopped taking hits on his shields for a few moments before getting hammered in the rear. He released his molten flare net catching everything swarming in behind him on fire, blowing a few instantly, and turning the rest into flying infernos. There were no flames. Just orange-red-blue-white dripping and rippling glows of molten metals streaking. They were glaringly bright. A few dozen missiles had blown on the net too.

He continued accelerating drives at full power and was using thrusters too to get out of there. Only small craft could keep up with him, and he was leaving the ship-battle behind. About a million miles out beyond the 2nd moon, he jumped, and no longer had any imperial small craft on his tail. He started braking immediately unaffected by the jump. His crew were swooning and in a stupor. He spent some reverse thrusters and bled off his momentum quickly. By the time he was approaching and beginning docking maneuvers, he was hardly moving.

CHAPTER TWENTY-FIVE

As the docking mechanisms on the two ships locked together, Bodhi informed June, "The rest of your small craft are headed in. Hit the compressors, and if anyone needs to be working on the exterior of a craft they must get in a spacesuit. You can air it up again when they're all inside. We'll be here for at least ten minutes."

"Aye aye, Sir."

Clark said to Bodhi, "Two repair craft are already launched and headed to the scorch on your hull. Reloading is underway and will be complete in 9 ½ minutes."

"I've got my hull-crawler-bots rushing to the scorch to help," Bodhi informed him.

Diamond Lotus docked to the other side of *Spalding* for reloading canister missiles, and to get another round of undercarriage missiles. The auxiliary crew also changed out spent fuel cells and replaced boosters. Sunoco commented through her coms to Bodhi, "Light and color sure seem different in a white sun system. The planet is a little bigger too, which kind of throws me."

"My teacher, Pez, was born in a white sun world called Om, and she thinks yellow sun humans who have attained planetary unity and moral anarchy are indispensable to the evolution of humanoids and Kluzyst."

"I can see that, with the people of Ground and New World," Sunoco agreed.

"They are like my people on Mother and like the people of Ganahar," Bodhi shared.

Haley informed Bodhi, "Nafs Ammara still has three space stations, all weaponized, and five sites on their surface with ground-to-space mega-beams. They will also have 126 ships, once the last of them jump through their gate. I have the drone pilots who have lost their imperial ships powering up the eleven ships I shut down. We are down to five imperial ships charging the gate, out of the 15 you sent."

"I need our cloaking functioning fully before we go out there to engage them again, unless it turns out to be a time-consuming job," Bodhi stated.

Winn said optimistically, "We killed that biggest space station, their lunar weapons bases, 31 of their space weapons platforms, 76 ships counting the ones we took over, and at least four big weapons on the planet surface."

"I call that a good start," Haley agreed.

"I'm keeping *Spalding* right here when we go back in, and undercarriage missiles for all of our small craft can be loaded right from the top of his hull, and canister missiles can be lifted aboard on pallets to be hand loaded. They can also change out fuel cells and boosters in spacesuits with propulsion right from the top of the hull. We'll have small craft jump back here for reloading. A craft in need of repairs can be brought into one of the hangars in the ship."

Haley brought up a holo of the battle zone from the cloaked spy android they had in the system. Now only four of her imperial ships were left rushing the gate with all weapons firing, though eleven more had come to life via drone pilots to converge on the region in front of the star-gate. Imperial ships from slave worlds kept suddenly manifesting travelling at .7 light speed in front of the gate headed planet-side. The imperials had momentarily lost track of their prey. Active long-scans were beamed out both tight and wide in all directions as they hunted. Each minute docked seemed like hours to Bodhi.

He checked on Kristy, who was watching his daughters in his suite on *Diamond Lotus*, "How are my girls?"

"We're playing dress-up," Kristy informed him.

"They're not even two years old, Kristy," Bodhi told her, trying to imagine what she might be dressing them in.

"They are having a great time, and I'm considering making a fashion line for girl-toddlers."

"I don't think they've got the gender idea down yet," Bodhi protested.

"I think they're formulating a notion. I've got June and Sonic's little Henry with them, and they found his penis interesting."

"You've got Henry going naked?" Bodhi asked, concerned.

"No, I changed him, and they watched. Both your daughters held their noses until I got Henry's bowel movement into the disposal."

"Winn is very sensitive and has done that before, so I think they are just imitating her."

"Well, you weren't here to smell it. I think it was just too much for them."

"Keep them safe, Kristy. I've got to go."

"You stay safe. I need an adept action seal," Kristy told him.

Captain Clark said over the coms to Bodhi, "You are fully reloaded, and we're almost done spraying lens material over that big scorch. Another two and a half minutes, and it will be done. *Diamond Lotus* is all set, and its munitions hold is full. We managed to weld on two additional undercarriage missile cradles so it will be able to project more power."

"Thanks. Great work. I'll start preparing to get underway. Let me know as soon as the spray job's finished."

"Aye aye. I sure will," Clark signed off.

Haley told him, "I'm highlighting a route in your holo, and Tish's and Winn's which will take us passed the other three space stations and over the last of their surface-to-space weapons down on Nafs Ammara."

"Thanks, Haley." To Tish, he stated, "Follow the route Haley highlighted for us, and Haley and I will waste those other space stations and ground weapons."

"Will do."

Bodhi ran pre-flight checks until Clark came back on to tell him, "You're all set, fully cloaked, and the repair crafts have cleared out of your way. Good hunting, Captain."

"Thanks Clark. You're a real professional. Take us out Tish," Bodhi directed.

The docking mechanisms released and Tish crept the throttle on the drives slowly forward, careful not to wash *Spalding* with *Thor's* propulsion streams. As they pulled further away, she cranked up the drives to full power and hit some thrusters to accelerate to jump speed. Most of the imperial ships were back in their home-world, and hardly a trickle was coming through the gate at this point. Their original group of 15 imperial ships was down to two command ships, and those had passed the gate, now turning to reengage. Their eleven other imperial ships—now down to ten—were in formation and firing as one, harassing the edge of the armada which had formed.

The jump happened in no-time changing their position in space instantly, and Tish was braking only a moment later. Haley was lining up fire control for her missiles and torpedoes, with the sensor-system of their cloaked spy-drone, which was travelling at only .08 light with crystal clear targeting resolution. This would allow her to fire her ordinance at speeds exceeding .24 light, which was the upper end of accuracy. Past .24 light, hitting anything with their weapons systems became a gamble.

Tish was following the route Haley displayed with great precision and was preparing to drill her twin nose blasters into the space station they were rushing at. Bodhi's beam weapon was first on their target, followed immediately by the class 9 blaster Winn fired. Tish opened up on it next and then the class 7 twin-blasters started nailing it. By the time Haley got a pair of torpedoes into it the class 6 quads were already hammering the station which erupted in heat and light exploding outwards in all directions. Shrapnel took out a wing of imperial bombers and a number of fighters which had been in close to the space station before it blew.

Bodhi took out a ground weapon on Nafs Ammara which was next on their route, leaving a crater behind. Ships and small craft were acquiring them from their ordinance and blaster fire, and *Thor's* shields rippled taking hits. Haley blew one of the 2nd biggest class of imperial ships with a torpedo. Small craft were getting shredded all around them by their gunners. June had her Astro Phantoms out the bay doors, and Hunter Terminators were pouring out to join her.

The six Vulcan Prowlers of Ahumdulilah design followed the Hunter Terminators out with the combat shuttles right behind them.

Haley gave June a route for hitting the remaining five space weapons platforms. June found that a pair of her torpedoes could kill all but the largest class imperial ships. The torpedoes on her bomber were considerably smaller than the ones Haley was firing from *Thor*. Sunoco was going .24 light in *Diamond Lotus* and could just take out relatively stationary targets, or come up behind the imperial ships to hit them. She had her crew firing in short bursts and made random maneuvers after each one so their fire would not allow for them to be targeted for more than a few seconds.

Bodhi was approaching the second space station on their route, and Haley already had a pair of torpedoes and a pair of big missiles racing for it. *Thor's* weapons systems lit it up as they came in, starting with the largest. By the time the class 5 and 4 blasters were kicking out energy bolts, the station's shields were down and its boundaries were blurring. It finally expanded into light, vapor, and particles relinquishing its physical form as they sped right through the cloud.

Winn ripped apart a surface weapon on Nafs Ammara with the class 9 blaster riddling it until its reactors went up, then continued to pound giant potholes into the ground at the bottom of the crater the exploding reactors left. A nearby building collapsed. Tish told her, "You got that one, Winn. There's nothing left."

"I guess I got a little carried away," Winn acknowledged.

They passed a coms tower sensor array in mint condition floating around without the rest of its ship and living proof of a most unlikely shot. Then an imperial in a space suit on his own without a ship or craft anywhere around actually waved at them as they flew by. Haley had zoomed in on him with their optic sensors giving all on the bridge a good look at him. June and her force had torn some wide swaths through the sphere of 50,000 satellites enveloping the globe, and space trash was accumulating fast up here. An imperial fighter right in plain view of them crashed into a big hunk of surviving drive flute, vaporizing itself, and reduced the hunk it hit to half the size it had just been.

Both Bodhi and Winn hit the next surface weapon on the planet with class 9 beam and blaster. It was on a valley floor that was nearby a hydro-electric dam, though this weapon had its own saturnium reactors and was not dependent on the dam, which only generated about $1/100^{th}$ of the power of just one of the weapon's four reactors. Walking her blaster fire across the weapon base raking it, Winn accidentally punched a hole in the base of the dam. She said, "Oops," just as the dam crumbled, releasing a 90-foot wall of water into the valley. Fortunately, there were no residences down there, though they had no idea where the water would go from there. The four reactors made a spectacular explosion excavating a crater deep enough to contain at least a few million gallons of all that water. A drop in the bucket.

Thor was already making its run on the last space station, and the words "collateral damage" were ringing in Winn's head. Trying to make Winn feel better, Bodhi mentioned, "That dam was generating AC power anyway. There's nothing close by drawing energy from it."

Beam and blaster fire was exchanged while dozens of missiles passed each other going in opposite directions. Having already released her missiles, Haley fired one of the big class 7 blaster-quads into some oncoming missiles. *Thor's* shields were stirred into turbulence, dropping 18% of their power with all the hits they were taking. When the missiles not blasted in flight struck, their shields dropped below 50% for a few moments. Bodhi kept his beam boring in the same place on the station until those shields dropped, and a hole opened in the rim. Tish had her twin class 8 nose blasters pummeling the same spot Winn was biting into with her blaster, and the structure was breaking up in that section under their pounding. Then the whole space station just ceased to exist, leaving only a particle cloud to mark its passing.

They cremated the last surface-to-space weapon on Nafs Ammara and turned their attention to ships. June had destroyed the last five space weapons platforms with her force, and her group was now hunting small craft and the smallest class of ships. *Diamond Lotus* kept to the periphery of the battle zone, coming in behind slower ships to pound their sterns, traveling at .24 light and fully cloaked. Their own little imperial fleet was down to seven ships, and these were getting hit hard. More than a hundred imperial ships were still defending the planet.

With their route completed, Bodhi just slipped into the fray to hammer imperial ships. The Hunter Terminators and Combat shuttles were jumping back to *Spalding* for reloading, and June kept the Astro Phantoms and Vulcan Prowlers at the task of killing small craft and littlest ships. When and where Haley was able to, she hit imperial ships with a pair of canister missiles—one shield disruptor and one nanobot spray missile, followed by an upload of Jard's takeover program. More often, she nailed them with torpedoes or big missiles. Between Bodhi, Tish, and Winn, the class 9 beam and blaster and the class 8 twin nose blasters were coordinated on one ship at a time, blowing them into atoms and molecules.

Beams, blasts, and ordinance flew out of *Thor* from every hull surface continuously as small craft popped into clouds, and ships went nova all around them. The problem was that this attracted every ship to converge on them at once by keeping their location known. This took some pressure off the four imperial ships they had left; 2 command ships and 2 of the next biggest class. *Thor* had entered the melee at .12 light and so able to target anything going its speed or slower even head-on. Bodhi began accelerating when his shields started plummeting.

The Astro Phantoms and Vulcan Prowlers went out to *Spalding* to get serviced for another run, and the Hunter Terminators and combat shuttles were loaded and waiting for them out there past the star-gate. Hundreds of small space craft with jery-rigged home-mounted weapons systems were taking off from the planet surface in the desperate defense of Nafs Ammara. While picking up speed, Bodhi was accumulating quite a multitude of imperials nipping at his tail. He released a cloaked mobile smart mine net catching two ships and numerous small craft as well as a few missiles. Immediately following this, he launched a molten flare shield countermeasure and lit some thrusters to more quickly increase his velocity. Missiles and small craft went super-heated blowing them apart, or they zoomed along melting and dripping liquid metal behind. A particularly big drip landed on an undercarriage missile of a big imperial bomber and blew the missile, turning the bomber to fine shrapnel in brilliant expanding colors.

The imperials were all accelerating too, and their small craft could do this faster than *Thor*. The battle zone was shrinking with *Thor* at its center. Bodhi deployed his Corvette Thunders and Comet Interceptors. Each carried two large undercarriage missiles and working together they could destroy ships. He told them, "As soon as each fighter spends its big missiles have them jump back to *Spalding* to reload. Do that immediately upon releasing missiles. Coordinate your attacks and make them count."

June was privy to this communication through her command earbud, and she informed Bodhi, "We're almost loaded and will leave to return to the battle zone in 40 seconds."

"The way Haley's going through our torpedoes, I'm going to need to jump out for another reload soon. Don't linger in the battle zone without missiles, and don't let anyone go in the battle zone who isn't fully cloaked. We'll take minimal risks and do this methodically. The imperials are trying to pressure us and force a showdown since that's the only way they can win this."

To Clark, Bodhi said, "As soon as June's force leaves your vicinity, jump out between the last dwarf planet's orbital path and the asteroid field. They won't be able to get to us in real space for hours, and likely won't be able to find us out there. I'll be looking for you there in about 18 minutes."

"You're sure going through the ordnance," Clark commented.

"Haley is. I'm on the beam weapon," Bodhi clarified.

"I'll be there with crews at the ready," Clark assured him, signing off.

Thor was at .26 light and gaining velocity with drives and thrusters. Fuel cell conservation was no longer even a remote fuzzy memory. He was holding in reserve the new launch-booster Clark's people had installed, changing out the last one he'd spent. His shields were dropping through the low 60 percentiles, and the hits were coming faster. The big quad blasters around the hull were chewing up ships and smearing small craft into gas. He was still fully cloaked, but with all the firing from his ship and the explosions happening continuously all around him, he could probably be spotted from the planet's surface with the naked eye.

Five command ships were stinging his tail with perpetual beam and blaster fire, and dozens of other ships were flanking him and behind him pounding his shields. Bodhi told Haley, "Take over the class 9 beam. There's something I have to try."

He closed his eyes, entering his central channel, absorbed the winds into it, dissolving them, and shot out the crown of his head while seeing each of the eight signs of death for less than a millisecond. He flared his rainbow body of light as bright as a tiny sun right over the bow of the lead command ship behind Thor, then did the same to the other four ships next to it. He made them so intense that they lingered on for 20 seconds after he arose from a coma in his seat. The entire operation had taken less than half a minute, and he'd only been out of his body for a few seconds. Pez had used this tactic very effectively in the battle of Monarch, and she had taught Bodhi how. It was instant with her, and she could be out and back half a dozen times a minute without really interrupting the firing of her nose blasters. Bodhi released his 2nd and last cloaked mobile smart mine net and caught all five command ships blinded with their sensors whited out. The mines themselves would not have been powerful enough to blow up all five, but they got two good, and those blew the other three.

Pez had taught Bodhi something else too, and that was to see the soft spot in turbulent shields. Bodhi called up his canister missiles on his holo and began lobbing them in sets of four like maglev rail cars—one right after the other—through soft spots in imperial ship shields. The shields had to be taking sufficient fire to become turbulent to produce a soft spot. Bodhi had to remain in calm abiding bare attention to see the soft spots. Each set breached a hull. Every ship around *Thor* was getting hit by his gunners and missile batteries.

Bodhi noticed that his shields had dipped into the mid-40's, still dropping, but just went on sending four-missile-sets which slipped right through unhindered to explode in staccato punching through the hulls. Now they were wrecking imperial ships, and especially the larger ones, much quicker.

June had been clearing Bodhi's wake from a ways back and was closing on his stern with her force. Her fighters had spent their missiles and jumped back to *Spalding*. *Thor's* shields were in the 30's dropping, and velocity was .329 light and rising. The entire battle zone was now mobile and accelerating sticking to Bodhi like peel to a citrus fruit.

His fighters returning with undercarriage missiles were coming in at an angle of intercept on his 1 o'clock high on the starboard flank, and Sunoco was coming in to starboard at 3 o'clock high in *Diamond Lotus* with fresh undercarriage missiles. Haley was holding the big beam on a ship till it blew, one after another while launching big missiles and remotely operating a class 7 twin-blaster. She would be launching torpedoes, too, only she'd run out of those. Bodhi was going through canister missiles in sets of fours faster than the battery crews could load them.

Their rate of acceleration was rapidly increasing, still thruster enhanced, and *Thor's* shields were at 19%. He said to Sunoco, June, and his squadron leader of the fighters, "They seem to be getting their showdown, but I'm not going to give it to them. I've sent you *Spalding's* new coordinates, and we're all jumping out of this mess. I'm firing a booster. Do whatever you need to do to get to jump speed ASAP! I'll see you on the edge of the solar system."

Tish hit the giant booster, which was designed to lift the ship off a planetary surface and out of a vortex well. Out here in space, it pressed them forcefully into their seats, stretching their faces to either side and leaving their stomachs millions of miles behind. Some of the crew blacked out. Winn almost did, or maybe she had for just a second. She wasn't quite sure. Bodhi, Haley, and Tish remained conscious and functioning, squished faces and all.

They were out of the bee swarm, and the battle zone entirely, with their rate of acceleration jumped exponentially. In another minute and eighteen seconds they reached .7 light, and Tish engaged the quantum drive. It shut off as they manifested into existence out past the last planet braking frantically from .7 light. Tish had reversed the drives and engaged additional thrusters, and employed some swivel turning-drives as reverse drives.

If she could have gotten out and dug her heels into space, she would have. Without spending a braking-booster, she bled the speed, didn't over shoot, and glided in barely moving to touch docking mechanisms with *Spalding*. The mechanisms did the rest. "Perfection maestro!" Bodhi complemented her. "I salute you!" he stated, proud of her.

"I had an amazing teacher," Tish told him sincerely with a fond half-smile.

Bodhi leaned to embrace and kiss her. Winn asked Haley, "Could you check my bio-readings during that booster-launch and see if I passed out or not?"

"You did. For .9 seconds though you're completely within normal limits on everything now. Humm. You could use a little more calcium in your diet, and a little more iron."

"Thanks, Haley."

"Anything for you, my love."

"Say, there must be something wrong with the clothes washer-dryer apparatus, because I put five pairs of panties in there and got none back."

"Let me check the system... and the programming... and the trackers... and I'll run a few subroutines. There we go."

"What happened? Did they get recycled by mistake?"

"No. Programming has been added to sort them pre-wash, and I've tracked them to the freight office on the ship. I tracked the programmer and also found the cause of the whole thing."

"Which would be?" Winn asked, confused.

"Kristy is selling them on the Firmament and New Firmament interface where she has a site. The clothes-cleaning machine directs your knickers unwashed to freight where they're posted to the buyer and tagged for shuttle transport. She's had over 900,000 hits on her site, and it features you partying in LGBTQ Town."

"I hope they're not all buying underwear," Winn said anxiously.

Armstrong, who was sitting in the back row on the bridge and hadn't said a thing since leaving the Ground system, spoke up now to say, "This ship is magnificent and unbelievably powerful! Your strategies are brilliant. You seem to be able to pass your missiles through imperial shields when everyone else's, and blaster and beam weapons too, are merely striking them."

"My teacher, Pez, taught me to see auras and to see the 'soft spot' in turbulent shields. If you can see auras, then you can recognize the 'soft spots.'"

"We should have brought Tipola. He sees them," Armstrong informed Bodhi.

"In more desperate times, perhaps," Bodhi acknowledged.

"Did you see those suns erupt on the bows of the five big ships behind us?"

"That was me in my Rainbow body of light. Emanating light and vibrations—including dialogue—and appearing anywhere in relative space instantly are the capacities and abilities of a body of light. The cloaked mobile smart mine net that killed them was part of *Thor's* arsenal."

"You could probably teach Tipola to do that one too," Armstrong suggested.

"I will do that," Bodhi promised.

"What's your plan from here?" he asked.

"I think we can take the rest of their ships in another run. We can topple the empire's power elites with their small craft buzzing us. They won't be able to harm us, and they'll make good target practice for the gunners. I'll need *Diamond Lotus* playing goalie in front of their star-gate to prevent ships or small craft from jumping out of the system!"

Captain Clark told Bodhi over his coms, "You'll be set and ready to go in less than a minute. By the way, *Thor* is on the last launch-booster we brought along, and those cannot be refueled for reuse.

"Thanks for the heads up. I think we can finish their ships off in the next run. I want you to sit tight out here, and anyone who needs to reload will jump to you."

"Aye aye, sir."

Bodhi said to June, the fighter craft squadron leader, and to Sunoco, "I want the Comet Interceptors and Corvette Thunders to stay outside the battle zone cloaked unless I call them in. Astro Phantoms and their drones, Vulcan Prowlers, Hunter Terminators, and Combat Shuttles will follow June and lag behind *Thor*. *Diamond Lotus* will sneak in front of their star-gate and prevent power elites from escaping. Nothing leaves. *Thor* is going along whatever route offers the most targets. Let's try to finish this now."

Bodhi's little fleet pulled away from *Spalding,* gaining speed to make the jump back to the battle zone. Of their original 29 taken-over imperial ships, only one command ship was left, and it was fleeing at this point, not fighting. Haley had taken over five more in the last run, shutting them down as *Thor* flew by, and these were coming to life under the control of *Thor's* drone-pilots at their consoles. Bodhi told the drone pilots, "Get your ships in front of that gate and let nothing pass through it."

There was no rush, so Bodhi accelerated to jump on drives alone, and *Diamond Lotus* followed suit. He would have total surprise on his side and was going to press the fight on his own terms. He didn't want his little fighters in the mix if he could do it without them since the imperial ship weapons could blow them up, taking down their shields. The fighters could withstand small-craft fire though not fire from class five blaster quads, which the three biggest classes of imperial ships carried. His bombers could sustain these long enough to get out from under them and survive. With well-over 180 billion lives enslaved in the balance, risks to his tiny force of personnel were more than justified, though each loss pained him, and his goal was to keep them all alive.

CHAPTER TWENTY-SIX

Thor landed in the midst of the battle zone and Bodhi had her slowing down by the time Tish recovered. She added some thrusters and swivel-drives to the mix, getting their speed down more quickly and was coming in behind three ships that were traveling at .24 light. By the time she was closing on their sterns, she had *Thor* down to .47 light, and weapons systems on board were able to lock-on to the quarry. Haley served them each a torpedo while class 9, 8, and 7 blasters ripped into imperials, and Bodhi's beam bore into one. The shields of all 3 imperial ships were roiling with turbulence, and Bodhi sent a stream of four canister missiles through soft spots in each of their shields blowing them into space clouds.

Thor continued slowing as it cut across the battle zone, causing a cloudy day in space with all the ships and small craft it was blowing to bits and vapors. June kept her force way behind *Thor* and destroyed ships and small craft sweeping in to fire on the T-9's rear. *Diamond Lotus* was guarding the gate, and their five imperial war ships were almost in position. Their imperial ship fleeing had not gotten away and was now all over space reduced to fine dust. The fighters remained cloaked and just outside the battle zone, ready to zoom in on Bodhi's command.

Having acquired him through his ship's weapons discharges, not to mention all the small-craft explosions continuously happening around *Thor*, the imperials were all closing on him in an attempt to overwhelm him by sheer numbers. They had spread in his absence to cover and protect the planet all around and were not able to converge their force rapidly, giving Bodhi time to whittle them down on approach. Every weapon on his ship was firing at maximum efficiency and effectiveness, leaving dispersing spheres of color in his wake.

June mentioned over Bodhi's coms, "You've accumulated quite a horde on your tail; more than I can remove."

"On my flanks too!" He told her. "Drop back a little because I'm going to release a cloaked mobile smart mine net in about a minute."

"Aye aye, sir."

To Haley, Bodhi said, "Take over the big weapon, I'm going out in space."

Thirty-eight seconds later, he was planting suns on every bow tailing *Thor*. It took him 2.9 seconds to emit all the suns and another 3.3 to rise out of coma on the bridge. Bodhi released the cloaked net. Four ships and who knows how many small craft and missiles overlapped their particle clouds into a dense fog behind *Thor*. Haley was cremating ships in front of their bow and on the flanks with torpedoes and the big beam, and so were Tish, Winn, and his gunners with their weapons.

Bodhi went back to firing sets of four canister missiles through shield soft spots and left the class 9 beam weapon in Haley's hands. They'd been killing ships almost as fast as they converged on *Thor* and were reducing the imperial force rapidly. Haley mentioned after taking in a quantum overview of the whole solar system, "There are 29 military small craft lifted from Nafs Ammara charging the gate with a six command ship escort trying to escape. That slimy emperor and his psychopath son are both onboard one of those small craft."

"Tish," Bodhi called out, "take us in at an angle on that group's flank. I don't want any members of that ruling family planning murder and ego-aggrandizement in exile. We've got to stop them."

To Sunoco, Bodhi said, "There's a group of six command ships, and 29 of the big bombers headed your way and aiming to escape through the gate. The emperor and his sick son are both on one of those bombers. I'm on my way to you."

"We've got this," Sunoco told him. "I see them coming, and we have five imperial ships to help us stop them."

"Don't take unnecessary risks. There are only 35 places they can go if they get through, and we have to go to each of those worlds anyway. Keep the children safe."

"The children's safety first, I promise," Sunoco agreed having her son Nicholai aboard.

Bodhi accelerated spending thruster fuel as if it grew on trees. He contacted his fighter squadron leader and said, "Head into the battle zone after the group Haley has highlighted in your holos. The emperor is on one of those bombers."

"We're accelerating and on our way, Sir."

He checked in with June next, "How is your force holding up?"

"I've had to send an Astro-Phantom and a Vulcan Prowler back to *Spalding* for lens coating to restore cloaking and all my Hunter Terminators and shuttles back for more big missiles. We've only lost one craft so far in this run."

"The emperor is fleeing and trying to escape through the gate. I'm headed for him now. Feel free to catch up and overtake *Thor*. I'm accelerating as fast as I can without spending my last launch-booster."

"We're closing on you now," June reported. "I have the targeted ships in my holo."

Haley commented, "It looks like they'll get their showdown after all, though too late to win this for them."

"I agree with your assessment," Bodhi told her.

Sunoco and her crew got their weapons targeting the oncoming force and were locked on the moment they entered range. They struck with everything, and all the undercarriage missiles were launched along with 64 of their 96 canister missiles as Sunoco's twin class eight nose blasters, and the two class five quad blasters rained down on the lead ship. Their shields were taking escalating hits and already falling slowly. Their fighters were nearest to them and closing fastest on the emperor's escorts. June's bombers and Vulcan Prowlers were just pulling ahead of *Thor,* and all were on their way. It looked like they were dragging every imperial ship in the system with them. The battle zone was contracting swiftly around *Diamond Lotus,* and imperials were getting thick. Another 32 canister missiles fired from Sunoco's ship before the 64 already launched had even struck.

A big undercarriage missile plowed into the lead ship that *Diamond Lotus's* blasters were biting into, bringing the shields completely down. The blaster fire chewed through the hull, and the ship blew into vapor and dust. They got their blasters coordinated on the next ship headed for them. The five imperial ships flown by drone pilots on *Thor* were coming up on either side of Sunoco's ship, firing everything they had left, and one was racing to hit an escort ship head-on. Trying to veer off and avoid a head-on crash, the imperial ship targeted for collision only managed to present its flank, as opposed to its nose, as the point of contact for the ships to hit. One enormous sphere sort of elliptical was all that was left of them when they collided fusing into the same vapor cloud.

Sunoco and her crew blew up the next one they were firing on, and an imperial ship fighting at her side on her flank exploded, showering *Diamond Lotus's* shields with flecks of debris. The last three escorts and 21 bombers, which were the survivors thus far out of the 29 the imperials started with, blew by Sunoco's ship, and her three drone allies, headed right for the gate. The Corvette Thunders and Comet Interceptors were coming in on the emperor's escort's flank, firing their undercarriage missiles and blasters into them while June was in range of them from behind slamming them. The larger weapons on *Thor* were drilling them too from a little further back. Bodhi released his 2nd cloaked mobile smart mine net followed by a molten flare shield countermeasure to reduce the ships tailing him before *Thor* reached *Diamond Lotus.* Then he blew by Sunoco too.

The Hunter Terminators and combat shuttles bent around from behind the star-gate on a curved trajectory headed for the forward starboard flank of the emperor's escort, already loosing undercarriage and canister missiles while raining blaster fire into them. The big missiles from the fighters were just hitting these ships, and two blew to hell and gone leaving only one. This one went on only a few more seconds before the big beam and blaster on *Thor* wasted it. Half the remaining imperial heavy bombers had by this time popped into cloud bursts, and only ten were yet whole and traveling.

At the lead of her small craft force, June pounded the rear imperial bomber into a splattering mist. A class 9 beam firing from behind her, and only yards off the edge of her shields, bore up the stern of another bomber, expanding it almost infinitely. Five more bombers blew when the Hunter Terminator and shuttle missiles impacted. June got one more and was passing through its gas cloud when the last two bombers jumped out of the system using the star-gate.

Imperial ships and small craft were still bursting into dispersing particles all around *Thor,* and Bodhi hit a braking booster and full reverse thrusters, reversing drives at maximum power and employing swivel drives to counter forward momentum as well. It was almost like slamming into a tree in a little hovercraft, but he managed to bring his ship to rest only a few hundred miles from the star-gate. He turned *Thor* 180 degrees with port thrusters and turning drives only, to face the oncoming multitude. *Diamond Lotus* had killed several of the ships coming behind Bodhi but had had to maneuver out of the way, taking too much fire to her shields.

Torpedoes, big missiles, canister missiles, and beam and blaster fire poured out of *Thor* so rapidly that it looked as if the ship might be in the initial phase of blowing up. The Hunter Terminators and combat Shuttles flew into the imperial horde, head-on, and both June's group, and the fighters were in an arc to come back around on the imperial force that was heading for Bodhi and the gate. Two of their taken-over imperial ships went intentionally head-on into commands ships, destroying themselves and their targets.

Suns blossomed on the bows of eighteen ships, taking only 4 seconds in space and 23 seconds preparation on Bodhi's part. He rose from a coma in 2 seconds and started slamming sets of four canister missiles into hulls, slipping them untouched through soft spots in shields. Haley ran out of torpedoes and started firing big missiles as if out of a machine gun while boring into ship after ship with the big beam. A small imperial ship scraped along with *Thor's* shields, incinerating layers of armor from its bow. After taking the small ship's shields down its hull swas breached where *Thor* widened in the middle as the imperial concluded its scraping collision with *Thor* in an explosion.

Thor stood its ground like a lion in the gateway, letting no ship pass, and *Spalding* arced around the gate to stand beside her spitting canister missiles and firing blaster quads all-out. A moment later, *Diamond Lotus* maneuvered along *Thor's* other side, out of big undercarriage missiles, but shooting off canister missiles Shamas had reloaded, and chewing into ships with its blasters. This was the showdown Bodhi was willing to fight. His shields were at 53%, up from 42% when there had been more ships in one piece to fire on him. His two class nine weapons needed only a few seconds direct hit to blow up a ship, and Bodhi was finding a soft spot in shields every few seconds.

No ship got by the three sentries guarding the star-gate. Haley had switched from blowing them up, the moment she'd run out of big missiles, to taking them over with two specialized canister missiles and a program upload. She'd captured eight ships there at the end. His returning fighters and June's force prevented all but a few small craft from getting through the gate and away. Four imperial small craft had slipped by and out, besides the two bombers of the emperor's group. All six small craft had been scanned and would be recognized if spotted again.

Once the ships were gone or captured, many imperial small craft returned to the surface of Nafs Ammara. When the fighting was finally over, Bodhi's force reloaded from *Spalding* before going to assume orbit 140 miles above the surface. Their spy-android had been in this system since their first scout and recon mission here and had long ago stripped all the data from the central imperial computers and military command centers. Haley had deciphered the language and learned their computer codes in their 1st encounter with the invasion fleet 14 ½ months previously. They had this empire's star maps and coordinates for all 35 slave systems. The empire had gained another slave planet while the T-9 was being constructed.

From low orbit, Haley converted their quantum coms into spectrum encoded light coms, and light beamed it to a holocoms satellite to connect with imperial officials in positions of clout over the masses. The real power was in the hands of the few people who owned everything—the ruling families. The emperor and his son had fled the system and left the rest of their family behind. Haley had analyzed the financial data and discovered that there were only 64 ruling families of this empire, with an average of 8.064 intergenerational members alive per family, for a total of 513 people. All resided on Nafs Ammara.

Haley informed Bodhi, "The senior imperial minister is on coms holding for you."

He said to the minister, "This is Captain Bodhi of *Thor*. I'm cloaked and in medium orbit over the capital. I have you targeted. You will convene all ministers and administrators in the imperial administration building and all military top brass immediately. By the way, you're all fired. This empire is finished, crumbled, powerless, and over. I have a list of all ministers and top brass. I will take attendance in three hours, and you all better be there. You will all remain in that building under house arrest, and I'll arrange meals for you. Are we clear?"

"Yes, sir. My staff is contacting all of them right now."

"Good. I'll check back in with you in three hours. Don't try to escape through the sub-basement tunnel. If you do, I'll cave it in on your head."

To Haley, Bodhi said, "Get me linked into their emergency transmission holonet system. I want every channel and frequency carrying my words."

"You're on," Haley informed him.

"Thanks." To Nafs Ammara citizens, Bodhi stated, "The emperor has fled the system but has nowhere to go. His ministers and military brass are no longer in charge of this planet. Their might has been torn asunder. They have no power to project or any way to assert themselves any longer. The citizens of Nafs Ammara are now free. At the bottom of your holos, I'm displaying names of capable skilled people who have struggled to assist the poor despite of the empire having written them off. If your name appears, go to the imperial administration center in your city, town, or district, and keep your coms open. You will have a big job to do organizing equal distribution to everyone planet-wide and increasing food production.

"All military manufacturing is over for this planet. We will defend you from other star systems. You will never exert influence beyond your solar system again. The sovereignty of every planet population will be respected. This will be enforced in your galaxy from now on. For those whose names appear on the holo who are in the capital, please proceed to the air and space port. I will land there to meet you in two hours. I'm establishing a temporary government for you of people you can trust. These folks will arrange elections of local representatives within one year. I expect everyone to behave and act in the interest of your common good. Right now, I am the one policing this planet. We have no tolerance for destructive acts of selfishness and will meet those with overwhelming force. Rioters and looters will just be fried from space. We are aiming for equitable mass re-distribution of resources as rapidly as possible."

He told Haley, "Once all our temporary civil servants have been displayed, please put each of the 513 ruling family member's faces in the holo with current locations for them and their wealth status. Could you connect me with the head of the secret police, please?"

"I'm connecting you now, just a moment. There, you're on."

"This is Captain Bodhi of *Thor*. I am in control of this planet now. You and all the secret police are fired. You are to change into civilian clothes, leave your weapons at your stations, and refrain from any policing activities. If I see any secret police in uniform or trying to lord it over anyone, I will waste them. Your jobs and functions are over. Any trouble from your group and the names and addresses of every one of you will be transmitted to the masses, and I'll start hunting you down and terminating you to the last. Am I getting through to you?"

"We number over 60,000,000 and are everywhere. We control the surface of this planet."

"Haley, make me a route orbiting the planet as many times as needed to crater all secret police stations."

Bodhi aimed the class nine beam into the center of the capital's 52-story mammoth secret police station while maneuvering *Thor* directly above. He took the building straight down to fill its own sub-levels beneath the ground and kept disintegrating it until it was nothing but a smoking hole in the ground. He did this without any damage to the buildings surrounding it. Starting to follow the route Haley displayed in his holo for him, Bodhi nailed a substation of the secret police on the outskirts of the city as he passed over it.

Haley informed him, "I'm dispatching the bombers and fighter-bombers to destroy secret police stations, and I've sent a route to *Diamond Lotus* as well. Otherwise, this little task would take days."

"Thanks, Haley."

Bodhi had Tish accelerate, making orbits like winding together a ball of yarn, covering a different wide swath with each pass. After an hour he had Haley dispatch his fighters and combat shuttles to help, and told these to target anyone on the ground in a secret police uniform as well as to blow the stations Haley gave them coordinates for. After another 50 minutes, he excused his ship from the exercise to hang 155 miles directly over the capital and descended to the air and space port in a hunter terminator with compromised cloaking, which had been being repaired in his hanger. Winn piloted, and Haley and Uduak accompanied him. Uduak got into a hard-shell combat suit and went heavily armed. The others carried side-arms and wore shield fanny-packs.

He set down on the shuttle landing pad closest to the terminal, and the four of them entered the building seeking the control center. Haley got facial recognition on some members of the delegation they'd selected and said their names in Bodhi's earbud while sending him a holo of each corresponding face to his bifocal holo in front of his right eye. Bodhi approached the woman nearest him, extending his hand, and said, "I'm Captain Bodhi. This is my pilot Winn, my first officer Haley, and my champion Uduak."

The woman, being from a white sun planet, was a foot taller than Bodhi and only about two or three inches taller than average for a female of her world, at 6 foot nine inches. She replied, "I'm honored to meet you, Captain Bodhi, and so grateful that you have deposed the emperor and his minions."

Sunoco's voice sounding in Bodhi's ear was saying, "There is a large military base outside the capital mounting troops into armored vehicles."

"Keep an eye on them and give us just a minute," Bodhi told her. To Haley, he asked, "Could you make a global public announcement ordering all military personnel to stand down, remove their uniforms, leave their weapons on the bases and to leave those bases on foot immediately. Non-compliance will result in death from above."

I'm employing a computer-generated graphic of you with your voice to make the announcement. There, it's done."

Bodhi got back on coms with Sunoco and asked, "Are the soldiers on that base you're watching standing down?"

"No, they are just now pulling out in their armored column."

"Vaporize the column into slag, then start checking on other military bases. I'll have Haley send you the locations of all of them."

"She just received them," Haley noted, having sent them.

Perusing the data, Sunoco mentioned, "There are an awful lot of them. This could take weeks."

"Once the others finish off the secret police stations they can help you with military bases."

"I'm on it, sir, and there's nothing but a puddle of molten metal now where that column just was."

"Thanks, Sunoco. I'll help too right after my meeting."

Bodhi and his officers met the other delegates standing around, and one of them knew how to get into the control center. Haley had done thorough and exhaustive searches on the individual members of the planetary population, and every person she'd selected had been considered by the empire to be a rabble-rouser and advocate against the status quo. All had been under constant surveillance. Uduak had to blast a few uniformed police in the terminal who had been on their way to arrest these delegates. Haley, Bodhi, and Winn helped Uduak, each nailing a few of them. The air/space port was fairly deserted since all flights had been suspended when the space battle had begun. Without innocent civilians filling the terminal, Uduak had been able to take most of them out with a 60-round jungle clip magazine of 40mm grenades.

A few more secret police popped up on their way through the terminal to the control center, and Haley put these down with her new Om tri-barrel continuous-fire blaster pistol. Bodhi had never seen one of these before, so she let him examine it as they entered the secure area of the control center and sealed the blast doors behind them. A quick search revealed this complex within the terminal to be empty. They all sat around the table in the conference room. Twenty-eight delegates had been chosen, and each was the leader of a subversive group of dedicated people. Most of them knew each other.

Bodhi addressed them, "Welcome, and thank you for coming. I'm placing this group in charge of redistribution of resources in the capital. There are more resources here than anywhere else on the planet so you will need to get some aviators and merchant space freighter personnel here and start shuttling food supplies to regions with the highest starvation rates, as well as to distribute food, clothing, and medical supplies to the people of this city. You will also temporarily be the central authority on this planet. All factory workers from manufacturing facilities involved in making war materials must be immediately reassigned to useful work. My first officer, Haley, is sending data to your hand devices now with locations of warehouses and their contents, retooling designs for military factories, power elite war criminals to be tracked down and summarily executed, and mega-mansions to be emptied and renovated into housing cooperatives. The art objects in these mansions must be brought to museums for all to appreciate. You are also tasked with eliminating abstract currency. That will no longer be needed since everything will simply be shared through equal distribution. More housing and medical facilities are needed in the capital and pretty much everywhere else too. Certain agricultural practices degrading your food supply must end at once. You have the data. Get everyone back to work, and let's start the transformation from tyranny to representation of the people focused on the common good of all."

Wild applause and cheering followed Bodhi's little speech. Individual delegates poured out their heartfelt gratitude. One delegate asked Bodhi, "What do you want from Nafs Ammara?"

"A peaceful neighbor and hopefully a friend and ally. We will take none of your resources for ourselves, but some of the loot on Nafs Ammara must be returned to the former slave worlds it was stolen from. Just as soon as we clean up the imperial forces on the ground, we'll be stopping at each of the 35 former slave systems to end all production of military materials as well as all imperial power structures.

"Why have you intervened?" Another delegate inquired.

"Apart from it being the right thing to do, this empire sent two invasion forces to conquer a planetary system I am affiliated with. This empire has been a cancer in the galaxy in need of surgical removal."

Bodhi worked with the new government he was establishing temporarily for another two hours, and he had Haley send them numerous data sets to help them get started. He directed June to the largest small arms armory in the capital with a wing of Astro Phantoms to keep an eye on it until the representatives could get their people there to arm them. Bodhi wanted to ensure that these new governors would not be overpowered and disposed of by the shrinking imperial force still on the planet.

A call from one of his comet interceptor fighters informed Bodhi that almost 200 jet fighters, fighter-bombers, and big bombers were lifting off from several military airbases about 2,000 miles away. He directed all of his small craft in that region to shoot those down immediately and gave *Diamond Lotus* a heads up to reinforce them. Eight and a half minutes later, he was informed, "Every one of those jets is now a streak of flaming debris across the desert floor, and we left craters where those air bases had been. Nothing was left alive."

"Good work. No military air or space craft ought to be flying, so just shoot them right down if you see any more," Bodhi replied.

To the new central government, Bodhi said, "Apparently, there remain quite a few people who do not yet realize that this war is over and that they lost utterly. I'm returning to my ship to deal with them. I leave the administration of the capital and planet in your hands. Please contact the administrators we selected at each imperial administration center and coordinate your efforts with them. You have my coms code and are free to contact me if you need assistance. Let's meet here tomorrow at 5PM capital time for a more detailed review of what is needed. Thank you."

Bodhi and his three officers returned to *Thor* in their hunter terminator and got busy blowing up military bases and secret police stations. It was a tedious job, but some of the visuals were quite spectacular. They kept at it for another three hours before breaking for a meal and sleep cycle. It had been a very stressful day, and their children needed them. Haley launched spy drones from *Thor's* hanger to keep watch over the planet, and some manned small craft took up sentry duty too.

CHAPTER TWENTY-SEVEN

Bodhi's force remained in the Nafs Ammara system for eight more days securing the ground, having to wipe out several large mercenary armies controlled by power elites still on the loose, and gathering the art, precious gem stones, precious metals, and other loot stolen from slave worlds to get loaded into transports. Redistribution of resources was proceeding efficiently when they finally left to tour each planet conquered by the Nafs Ammara Empire. All 513 ruling family members were dead and gone by then, or in prison.

Yallam was their first stop on the route Haley established for them. The moment they jumped in and slowed to sensor resolution, it became apparent that the slave worlds were still slaves. Yallam had two weaponized space stations, twelve space weapons platforms orbiting the planet, and hundreds of military small craft. Most of the population continued to slave in factories feeding the old imperial war machine. The imperials controlled the planet's population with weapons in space. *Thor, Diamond Lotus,* and *Spalding* got right to work.

Twelve space weapons platforms were pulverized. They blew up every military small craft they encountered. The personnel on both space stations were ordered to shuttle down to the surface. One station was evacuated, and those occupying the other refused. Bodhi sent a combat shuttle with tanks of lethal gas to land on the central dome of the station to drill through the station armor and skin and pump poison gas in. A few shield disrupter canister missiles and nanobot spray missiles, plus Jard's takeover program, gave Haley control of much of the space station, and she brought the shields down over the central sphere of the structure. The newly formed Ground Space

Marine Corps, of which they had only one company of 200 plus two platoons, entered the space station in hard-shell suits, released the air and poison gas into space, and dragged the hundreds of dead into imperial shuttles to be disposed of on the surface. Compressors aired up the station, and Bodhi's engineers dismantled the weapons systems. Skeleton crews from his ships were assigned to man each space station.

Accessing the planets emergency holocoms system, Bodhi addressed the humans on the planet, "All imperial personnel, proceed to Yarvis city sports arena at once. Nafs Ammara has been disarmed. The empire has crumbled and is no more. Civilians working in a factory producing war materials, please shut everything down right now and go home. You will be reassigned to wholesome employment very soon, and these factories will be retooled or destroyed. Any imperial resistance will meet with death. We have located concentrations of resources and would like to see these distributed to the needy ASAP. I'm coming to land at the air and space port in the planet's capital and would like for civilian volunteers to meet me there so we can address the survival needs of the poorest regions of Yallam. Imperials not gathered at the Yarvis sports arena or on their way to it will be executed on the spot."

Haley was accessing and quantumly reviewing data. Slave world central computers were all programmed with Nafs Ammara code, and Nafs Ammara Basic was spoken by all imperials, imperial collaborators, and the managerial class of Yallam's population. None of these were considered trustworthy enough to be included in a temporary government, so Haley spent almost three hours learning the language of Yallam, called Yates, and programming an interpreter service for Bodhi and his officers. Before they landed on the surface, Bodhi made another public announcement requesting all meditators empowered to teach a spiritual tradition to contact a coms code he put up in the holo. Coms officers and technicians on all three of his ships began fielding calls.

Bodhi, Haley, Winn, and Uduak met up with a platoon of Space Marines at the air and space port. His troops were all in hard-shell shielded combat suits with heavy weapons, and some of his bombers and fighter-bombers supported them from the air. Captain Clark watched over them from low orbit in *Spalding* while *Thor* and *Diamond Lotus* went to destroy military bases the imperials had refused to evacuate. Haley screened each volunteer, rejecting imperial collaborators and managerial class citizens out of hand, and accepted only true working-class folks into the meeting with Bodhi. The air-space port was shut-down, and all flights canceled. This only inconvenienced the people they were here to remove from positions of influence anyway since less than 1% of the planet's population ever got on a jet or spacecraft on this world.

The meeting took hours, and trustworthy people were tasked with various responsibilities covering every facet of the global transformation they intended. Problems elsewhere on Yallam erupted, and Bodhi had to assign his assets to handle these, which interrupted the proceedings of their meeting several times. He had to put his foot down when his ad-hock delegation wanted to give the entire managerial class the status of war criminals to be hunted down and shot. Instead, he insisted that each individual be charged with their specific crimes and brought to trial with death penalties only for those who caused directly—or fairly directly—the loss of life of the citizenry. He did agree easily to have every last one put out of their fancy homes permanently with only their clothing to take with them. Homelessness was a real problem on this planet, and the approximately 11 million big houses of this class could each accommodate 4-8 families. The managers and their families would get to experience homelessness and poverty for a change. It would go a long way in addressing homelessness.

About 4.6% of all imperials in the system were designated criminals and would be put to death. The rest would be loaded on transports, and shipped back to Nafs Ammara where they belong. Collaborators were the most despised people on the planet, and a full 8.9% would be hunted down and shot on sight; 23.2% would stand trial—and then likely be shot—and all the rest were being exiled to Nafs Ammara. Bodhi didn't think the people of Nafs Ammara deserved to be saddled with these Yallam collaborators, but these certainly would not be safe here, so he agreed to exile to preserve life.

All cities were asked to put forth representatives to organize the transformation of the anti-economy of the past into truly economic and equal distribution of resources. Areas outside cities were organized into districts, and those districts were asked to select representatives. Haley vetted every one of them quantumly. While Bodhi's forces secured the planet surface, a spy drone was sent ahead to the next slave world on their route so Haley could begin data collection and learn the local language. An enormous transport freighter stuffed to the gills with loot stolen from Yallam by the empire arrived in system and was dispersed to museums and public treasury vaults.

Bodhi met numerous times with the planet's spiritual adepts, all of whom had been in hiding within regions of the most severe conditions, and a number had to be picked up on remote mountain tops, from remote arctic areas or equatorial jungles. Most made their way to the extreme ends of transportation lines and journeyed to Yarvis without his help. Plans were solidified for making spiritual practices more available to the masses, and for the meditators of this planet to join the spiritual congress.

It took ten days in all to secure the planet surface and establish networks of people to insure resource acquisition, production, and distribution systems that would reach everyone. Designs for refitting and retooling factories were compiled for every war related factory, which unfortunately was most of them here. Imperials were crammed into the transport freighter which had returned Yallam's loot, and were sent back in cargo holds to Nafs Ammara. More transports were called up, and the return of imperials and their collaborators to Nafs Ammara was well underway when *Thor, Diamond Lotus,* and *Spalding* left for the 2nd slave world on their route.

They learned some efficiencies as they became more experienced at liberating Nafs Ammara's slave planets, eventually to complete their work in each one within eight days or less. Things were becoming pretty much routine by the time they reached the 23rd planet system on their route, called Kefra. Once within the star system and slowed to .24 light speed, they saw a 2-mile ship construction platform in high orbit, three weaponized bases on each of Kefra's two moons, and two tubular-shaped war ships of 660 ft. length containing venusium reactors. There were also hundreds of small military space-crafts detectable on the space stations and in two lunar spacecraft bases. The frame of another 1 ¾ mile-long ships was attached to the ship construction platform and was beginning to show some hull on the stern.

Almost all of the reactors on the planet surface were fueled with venusium and only a very few with saturnium. The entire planet was like one gigantic military-industrial complex. This was the system Nafs Ammara had been using for the construction of its most advanced war technology and newest class of ships. A close scan of the planet surface from *Thor*, while Haley tagged and targeted every weapon in space, revealed the emperor's two bombers and the four other small craft that had escaped out the star-gate from the imperial home world. Haley stripped data from the imperial core quantum computers to work out the local language and discovered that only a small percentage were natives and spoke it. Most of the population were transplants from other slave worlds or imperials. Chronological data showed that this world had been conquered two centuries ago and near-genocide committed on the indigenous population.

The surviving original inhabitants of this world were in rural areas involved with agriculture. Their civilization had just discovered a source for venusium and had built their very first venusium fusion reactors a year before their planet was conquered by the Nafs Ammara Empire. Haley analyzed the data and informed Bodhi, "I have a fix on the emperor's position through ground surveillance optics, and I have everything in space targeted. All personnel in the three space stations are imperial military, so I would suggest gassing one, and blowing the other two up."

"Alright, we'll start with that," Bodhi agreed. He got June on coms and told her, "I need for you to take a cloaked combat shuttle over to the largest space station, drill a needle line through armor and skin, and gas the occupants. By making this our opening move, it is unlikely anyone on the space station will be in a spacesuit. Remain cloaked and try not to trigger any alarms."

Haley brought the shields down on the biggest space station after hitting it with a shield disruptor missile followed by a nanobot spray missile to take over the quantum computer. Haley informed both of them, "I'll disable their alarms before you start drilling. I've highlighted the fans and air scrubbers of the HVAC system in the center of the environmental section and precisely where to drill on its surface for maximum effectiveness."

"Thanks, Haley. I'll get right on it."

Bodhi told her, "Let me know as soon as you're done."

"Aye aye, sir."

Bodhi called Sunoco next and told her, "Get yourself in position to unload half of your big undercarriage missiles into each of the two lunar weapons bases on the closer moon. We don't need to bother right away with the weapons bases on the other moon because they're aimed at the star-gate, away from the planet."

"I'm on my way, sweet Captain," Sunoco said affectionately.

Bodhi called the Lieutenant Commander of his Space Marines and remembered his name to say, "Lt. Commander Nelson, please have 120 Space Marines suited up and loaded in combat shuttles ready to land on the ship construction platform and take it over. It can be put to civilian use, and it's not too late to turn that behemoth 1 ¾ miles ship frame into a merchant freighter. I'll have a wing of Hunter Terminators provide close combat support for your troops."

"They'll be ready to go in ten minutes, sir," Nelson replied.

"Thank you. We detected no weapons systems on the construction platform, so there are probably only the usual security forces. Your suit shields are hundreds of times more powerful than theirs."

"These guys would go in flimsy thermal suits and breathing apparatus. They're gung-ho and fearless," Nelson praised his men.

"Their courage and skills are needed and appreciated. I'll thank each of them personally when this action is over."

"I'm going to tell them that, and they'll hold you to it," Nelson warned him.

"Thanks. I'll let you know when to send them out of the hanger."

Haley let him know, "I informed time the Lt. on the flight deck in the hanger, and six Hunter Terminators are being armed and prepared to support the Space Marine's operation. The shuttles are being readied too."

Bodhi said to Haley, "I need some Astro Phantoms loaded and prepped for immediate take-off to get in position to blow up space weapons platforms with their torpedoes."

Haley sent Bodhi's orders electronically to arrive at the other end on the flight deck as a holo of Bodhi, giving the direction in his voice. She said to Bodhi the moment he'd finished speaking, "You are instructing the Lt. on the flight deck now about the Astro Phantoms."

"Thanks, Haley."

"I'd suggest you and Winn each kill a ship with your class 9 weapons, while I send a tsunami of torpedoes and big missiles at each space station we're taking out."

"I have a better idea," Bodhi explained. "You'll hit each ship with a shield disruptor and a nanobot spray missile then, upload the 'take-over' program. Winn and our gunners will get the shields stirred up on the space station, and I'll lob two torpedoes through the soft spot on each. We'll save a great deal of ordinance."

"That is a better idea," Haley admitted.

Bodhi took up a position in very high orbit, which gave him a direct line on both imperial ships, and both space stations targeted for destruction. He could only see the big station on the other side of the planet thanks to a spy drone one of his drone pilots aboard was flying. A tiny corner of the gigantic ship construction platform and framed-ribbed 1 ¾ mile ship, was peaking over the horizon from *Thor's* vantage. Bodhi's Astro Phantoms left the hanger to get into position, fully cloaked.

There was silence on the bridge for a little over a minute before June announced, "The gas is fully pumped into the big space station. I'm returning to the hanger."

Bodhi said to the bridge, "Haley, canister-missiles away. Winn and gunners, open up on the two space stations."

To his Astro Phantoms, he ordered, "Waste the space weapons platforms now."

To Sunoco, "Blow those two lunar weapons bases."

To Nelson, "Launch your shuttles and close-combat support Hunter Terminators to take that ship construction platform."

Bodhi sent a pair of torpedoes through a soft spot in a space station's shields. Two-thirds of it vanished into a cloud. Continued blaster fire caused three explosions in the remaining section quite close together, and then there was none. Another pair of big torpedoes whizzed through the soft spot of the other station's turbulent shields. This one went all at once, and there was none left of it either.

Sunoco reported in, "Lunar weapons bases are now new craters in the moon."

The Astro Phantoms reported, "All space weapons platforms destroyed."

They all watched the Space Marines pour out of cloaked shuttles as if stepping on the platform from another dimension or different universe. Some imperials came out in their version of space combat suits and started setting up big tripod blasters. A Hunter Terminator quad blaster blew them all apart. A platoon of Space Marines remained on the platform, securing it, while the rest entered the living quarters, warehouse and workshops rising from one side of the platform, opposite the cranes and berthed ship-frame under construction. Bodhi's command functions allowed him to view the action inside the platform's structures through the suit optics of his Space Marines, and he routed this as a holo to each person on his bridge.

The Space Marines divided into two platoons once within the structure, and then each platoon began separating off squads of eight to cover the premises. Civilian ship construction workers were rounded up and kept under guard in the mess hall, and security forces were blasted on sight. Blaster bolts were flying when squads entered each end of the imperial military barracks of the security forces on the platform at the same time. Caught in a cross fire, the imperials did not last long. Four space marines took continuous fire on their suits as they rushed the last defenders, returning their fire from close range, and eventually point-blank range. The taking of the entire construction-platform operation was accomplished within less than a quarter- hour with no loss of civilians or Space Marines.

Haley programmed two torpedoes to hit the coordinates of the lunar weapons bases facing the gate. She'd programmed contact at the base of the dome-shaped shields where they met the lunar surface since these dome-shields were strongest top and center. The torpedoes did not have cloaking generators or lens coating on their casings, but they were heavily insulated for effective stealth, and so were not even noticed until it was too late to acquire them accurately for targeting. Wild shots streaked by grazing the sides of the big torpedoes in their final two seconds of flight. The torpedo optics went to snow and static upon impact, and the spy drone they sent to confirm the kills had not yet cleared the horizon for line of sight. It was six seconds later that their blindness was cured with a crystal-clear view of the two large craters which had been the weapons bases.

Bodhi announced, "All small craft launch and hunt down imperial space craft. Captain Clark, position *Spalding* between the closest moon and the planet and be ready to reload small craft. Commander Nelson, shuttle a platoon of Space Marines over to the big space station, vent the poisoned air inside out to space, and secure the station. Sunoco, assume low orbit and fire on the military targets Haley is sending you coordinates for. *Thor* will hunt small craft and fire on planetary surface military bases. Let's disarm this imperial holdout."

Bodhi went close to Kefra, assuming orbit at 170 miles above its surface. Military sites were thick on the ground, so Bodhi told Sunoco, "Hit military air and space bases and the surface-to-space weapons first. Haley has marked six of these ground-to-space weapons, and I'm approaching one now."

"Will do," Sunoco replied.

Bodhi and Winn got their class 9 weapons lighting up a ground-to-space weapon site while Tish drilled it will her class 8 nose blasters, and the gunners on *Thor* slammed it with quad blasters. When the venusium reactors which powered the weapon blew up sky-high, there just wasn't a thing left of the base and only a smoking hole to mark where it had been.

Working methodically, Bodhi circled the globe multiple times raining destruction on military bases below. Bodhi took out three more ground to space weapons, and Sunoco wrecked two. Air and space military bases passed on into nonexistence, their atoms seeking new combinations now. Sunoco had found and wasted some submerged vessels under the ocean, which had launch tubes with space missiles in them. She'd discovered this by having one fired at her in *Diamond Lotus*. That missile had been blown up while still in the atmosphere.

Deriving great joy from it, Bodhi disintegrated the two bombers parked on the ground, which had brought the emperor and his little group here. Sunoco had run across the four small craft which had escaped Nafs Ammara, transforming them to particles and vapor while they tried to lift off the surface. June's bombers, fighter-bombers, and fighters were grinding, shredding and pulverizing imperial ones in every direction around the planet. A wing of Astro Phantoms and two Vulcan Prowlers played sentry in front of the Kefra star-gate.

They all remained at the grueling task of disarmament by annihilation for many hours. Bodhi finally had Haley patch him through to the military command center since the planet remained under imperial military control, although this status was wearing thin with their rapid and continuous loss of assets. The General in charge was already quite discouraged since his forces were getting trashed and had not been able to shoot down a single one of the invaders attacking them. Bodhi told the man, "I can continue to press my attack until only indigenous rural people are left alive on the surface, or you can surrender, and all imperial military personnel can return home to the new Nafs Ammara as civilians."

"The Emperor said you would never be able to root out all the military personnel and secret police spread around the globe of Nafs Ammar," the General stated skeptically of Bodhi's claim regarding the 'new' status of Nafs Ammara.

"When we left, there were less than 100,000 secret police still alive, and they were getting found and shot a couple of dozen per minute at that point. The military stood down and surrendered, then left their weapons and uniforms behind and walked home. Your emperor and his psychopath son fled the system. They are to be shot on sight without mercy, and the only returning they'll be doing is back to dust and ash."

"I remain loyal to the Emperor…"

"Haley, please patch me through to emergency over-ride of their coms system to address everyone on the planet who is tuned in."

"You're on."

"People of Kefra, this is Captain Bodhi, liberator of the enslaved people of the former Nafs Ammara empire, which is no more. Your general and emperor would see you all die just to futilely attempt to save their asses. If you wish to surrender, leave your weapons and uniforms where you are and get off the military base if you are on one. All military bases are scheduled for utter destruction. If you surrender, you will be shipped home alive as a civilian. If you do not surrender, you will be killed. I will pause my attack for fifteen minutes to give you time to walk off your bases unarmed and out of uniform. Oh, and you don't want to be anywhere near that command center bunker because I'm wasting that pig-headed general in three minutes, and his silly bunker with him."

After three minutes, Bodhi directed the big beam weapon onto the General's central high command bunker deep underground. The super-concentrated energy bore down penetrating shields, rock, armor, and finally the concrete floor. He moved the beam about a little to widen the hole. In the end, the General's bunker became a deeper hole to nowhere.

While they waited, Uldra and Tandy brought them ambassador rations to eat on the bridge. Om's Star Fleet allowed no food or beverages on the bridge of a warship under any circumstances, but Bodhi was not a part of Om Star Fleet and liked eating on the bridge. Kristy brought Bodhi's daughters over from *Diamond Lotus* to visit their parents. Both girls got up in Bodhi's lap, so he gave up on his meal for the moment. They both liked to talk, and especially to ask questions, practicing their small vocabularies and often said the cutest things. Both of them were over two years old and could still fall apart completely into a tantrum over life's frustrations—particularly their momma's saying "no." They served the horrible word right back to their moms frequently. Bodhi was unable to put the word into any context when he was with them, and his failing endeared him to each of them all the more.

Kristy brought the girls by shuttle back to the suite on *Diamond Lotus* once the 15 minutes count ran down. Bodhi gave the military folks down on Kefra an extra five minutes so he could wolf down the rest of his ambassador ration. Haley informed him, "The troops are abandoning 83.7% of all military bases. I'm now tapped into more than 30,000 satellites and have full global coverage. I think vaporizing that stubborn General paid off in terms of saving lives. By the way, many of those poor young people are walking off their bases in only their underclothes."

"When we overfly manned bases, we'll hit the command HQ taking out the ranking officers, then offer surrender again," Bodhi said to this own bridge plus Sunoco on *Diamond Lotus*.

"What if they still won't?" Sunoco asked.

"I think I'll locate the coms of the naysayer, fry that one, and make one last offer. If that doesn't work, I'll waste the base and move on," Bodhi strategized aloud. He added, "With the bases whose personnel are evacuating, take a life-reading and wait till all of them get out."

"Aye aye, sir," Sunoco signed off.

"Haley, could you try to find some officials at an air-space port who can air-drop clothing and food to the ex-troops, especially the ones in remote areas with really long walks."

"I'm on it. It's still a knot of diehard resistance down there."

"Try to locate that dammed emperor and his evil brat too if you would, sweetheart."

"I have mobile micro-spy sensors tailing both of those vile humans, though the one on the brat got locked outside the penthouse, and we have no optics or audio within. We'll know if he leaves. I can give you the precise coordinates of the emperor to the tenth of an inch."

"Why don't you destroy the penthouse with a missile first. I don't want that psychopath in charge for even a second."

"I'd have to use a big one from here because it's clear around the other side of the planet," Haley agreed, "But I'm certain that today's date is *their* expiration date."

June said over their bridge coms, "This is beyond hide and seek now, and although we know there are a few we didn't get yet, none of our pilots or crews have spotted an imperial small craft for over five minutes,"

"Keep a wing of Astro Phantoms guarding the star gate and get all your craft reloaded from *Spalding*. Once you're ready, you can help with the surface disarmament. When you come to a military base not evacuated, vaporize their HQ and then track their coms to waste any officers forbidding surrender. If that doesn't work, just blow the base and move on to the next. You're not going to believe how many there are."

"Alright. Let me get my people serviced and loaded, then we'll join you," June signed off.

Bodhi got her back on to say, "*Spalding's* run through 79% of the ordinance she was carrying, so send the fighters back to my hanger, and try to do as much of the work as you can with blasters. Go fully loaded."

"Aye aye, sir."

Haley made an incoherent exclamation as she quantumly ran through data and conducted her search for potential air-space port officials willing to do a good deed. The pickings were slim. Bodhi asked her, "What?!"

"There are records of the empire executing a man who had lived for over a thousand years. This was on Pronotavasmi! The last addition—conquered only five months ago. The population of Pronotavasmi is very ancient, with a 98,000-year written history. The imperials still have not been able to learn their computer languages. The Pronotavasmi civilization had no interest in space travel but had unmanned sensor-craft out exploring the galaxy to expand their knowledge and advance their sciences. The imperials were unable to grasp their technology."

"Could we go there next?" Bodhi pleaded.

"I suppose I could make a little alteration in the route I charted," Haley admitted. "The data on Pronotavasmi is classified beyond top-top secret. They have significant imperial forces on the ground, a space station with weapons systems and six space weapons platforms.

They have 20 bombers, 24 fighter bombers and 40 fighters as far as small Spacecraft goes, but they have no ships. They sent those to the battle of Nafs Ammara."

"Let me guess," Bodhi told her, "Pronotavasmi is the only yellow sun planet on our route."

"It is the first yellow sun planet Nafs Ammara has invaded. The people of Pronotavasmi had not known war in over 66,000 years and were woefully ill-prepared. This made the imperials believe that they're primitives."

"They sound exceptionally evolved to me," Bodhi commented. "How did the imperials classify them socio-politically?"

"Tribal but chief-less," Haley quoted.

"No government?" Bodhi asked.

"None the imperials could figure out," Haley extrapolated from the data.

"Moral anarchists, I'd wager," Bodhi told her.

"You don't gamble."

"Figure speech."

"Archaic."

"I'll try to sound more like Kristy then," Bodhi suggested.

"So let's hear it," Haley challenged.

"I'm just sure the Pronotavasmians are totally catalyst!" Bodhi tried.

"That's better," Haley encouraged him. "And I have good news. I've finally found and contacted an official in charge of an air-space port, who is not only willing to airdrop supplies but has over 50 cargo jets grounded on his port. He has personnel sorting through for clothing, camping gear, medical supplies, and food."

"Thanks. Send him the coordinates of the groups with the furthest to walk."

"I already have."

"Excellent work, my love."

Winn suggested, "We ought to show the destruction of the military bases on the planet's emergency holocoms system. I'm sure that would convince even the die-hards to get off those bases."

"When you get a chance go ahead and do that, Haley."

"Transmitting live now, and I'm cutting back and forth between *Thor* and *Diamond Lotus*, trying to keep the view of bases dissolving and not travelling to them."

"You'll have a lot more ships to cut between for the holo once June's force arrives." Bodhi pointed out.

Sunoco and Bodhi systematically cleared bases from the surface, dissolving them to sludge, and these annihilations were transmitted live across the Kefra emergency transmission system. Haley mentioned, "Now the rest of the bases are clearing out personnel. A few are leaving with their weapons in armored vehicles, and some naval bases are sending their ocean-going war vessels out to sea, scattering."

"That's no good," Bodhi declared. "Where's June and her people?"

"They are leaving *Spalding* now," Haley replied.

Bodhi told June, "I'm going to send you coordinates of armed personnel and armored vehicles, and of ocean war ships. Offer surrender, fry some people in command, offer again, and if they won't disarm, you'll just have to waste them."

"How will a warship disarm?"

"They will need to abandon ship into lifeboats and rafts. Most are close to coasts and we can get rescue ships out to the others."

"I'm assigning groups to targets now, and we'll take care of it," June assured him.

Winn waxed philosophically, "The universe already has plenty of destruction built into it, and destructive weapons simply make life even more hostile for humans and other sentients. Why produce them at all? And to dedicate 36 planetary populations to manufacturing them is antithetical to life and humans."

"It serves the ego's ultimate law of 'might makes right' so the ego can worship itself as an all-powerful god—the ultimate delusion of pride and ignorance."

Haley inquired, "Would you like to assign drone-pilots to our two 660-foot ships and have them assist in the disarmament?"

"Yes. Would you take care of it?" Bodhi asked.

"I'm putting our two best drone-pilots on the job now," Haley let him know. "We're coming back over the capital in a couple of minutes. I've highlighted the brat's penthouse for you in your holo."

"Assign the penthouse to our best class four quad-gunner, since anything bigger would take the whole roof off the building, and tell the gunner to just surgically remove the penthouse and to be careful not to wreck anything else.

"I'm passing on your order now," Haley replied, "We'll be in range of the class 4 in one minute and 14 seconds."

"Thanks, Haley."

Tish asked, "Do you want me to slow our speed so we can take out the emperor, right after the penthouse is gone?"

"Yes, let's get them both out of the game and see if surrender accelerates from their absence."

The quad-blaster gunner fired a short burst, and most of the penthouse melted to goo, with the rest flying at high velocity outward in minuscule fragments. Only some glass in some nearby buildings was shattered with no other collateral damage. Bodhi told Haley, "Send the emperor a few canister missiles, and let's be rid of him."

Canister missiles away," Haley said cheerfully. A moment later, she added, "He's toast!"

"Please announce this to the people of Kefra, Haley," Bodhi requested.

"You are conveying the message over all holocoms on the planet, my love."

"Thanks."

"Assisting you is my life's work," Haley reminded.

"Say, can you make me an interpreter service for the language of the rural indigenous people? I want to leave them in charge of their planet before we leave here."

"Give me a quarter-hour to program it into my boiler plate interpretation software."

"No rush," Bodhi let her know. "We have many hours eliminating military bases and war materials ahead of us."

"Many factories down there defy retooling and will simply need to be destroyed," Haley pointed out. "The locals here were mostly agrarian and had few factories here before the imperials conquered them. They had friendship treaties with Pronotavasmi, and recognized the high development of that planet's civilization."

"They sound like people I would care to meet," Bodhi enthused.

"The final holdouts are leaving their bases and are unarmed, so I think the people down there are beginning to understand that they are defeated and conquered."

"It sure took them long enough," Bodhi commented.

"Nothing about this former empire would indicate that they're all too bright," Haley agreed.

"Let's have some transports jump in from Nafs Ammara to start shipping imperials home."

"I'm texting them now," Haley told him.

"About how many imperials are on this planet?" He inquired.

"There are 5,743,686 at this moment, according to Kefra's central computer, which has been subtracting for casualties as they occur."

"That's going to require an awful lot of trips," Bodhi said, realizing.

"A dozen transports are being prepped, and the five biggest can accommodate about 18,000 people each, if we put them in the cargo holds as well as the passenger seats and air those up. We might cram 10,000 into each of the rest. Once they get all of the imperials off the last planet we visited, there will be four more of the really big transports to help with this job."

"We better get some of the biggest armories loaded onto shuttles to deliver to the rural locals and destroy all the rest of the war materials on the surface. I want to be sure that the indigenous folks have the upper hand here since I don't want to wait until all the imperials are lifted off before we leave."

"What of the 15 million workers from other slave systems?" Haley asked, "And their families?"

"Let's let the locals invite whom they would like to stay, and get the rest shipped home."

"Sounds good to me," Haley agreed.

"We'll leave a wing of Astro Phantoms, a wing of Hunter Terminators and a mixed wing of Corvette Thunders and Comet Interceptors here on Kefra's space station, and we'll keep the space station manned with our people from Ground. That way, we can control the planet from space, at least until everything is secure and settled on the surface."

"I like the idea," Haley told him. "Commander Nelson is sending eight shuttles with 20 suited up Space Marines in each, to the largest armory and requests some air-support."

"Have June divert a wing of Hunter Terminators to the armory," Bodhi directed.

"Done," Haley said.

"How are those airdrops going?" Bodhi inquired.

"They've started. The groups walking out of remote areas in cold climates are being taken care of first."

"That's rational," Bodhi concurred with the plan.

Tish offered, "I can stay on this task with *Thor,* and you can go down and meet locals if you want. We have a Vulcan Prowler with compromised cloaking in the hanger you could use."

"Alright. I'll bring Haley and Uduak and return in a few hours. Thanks, Tish."

"Anything for you, my love."

"Are you OK with this, Winn?" Bodhi checked.

"I don't mind, even though blowing stuff up isn't exactly my cup of tea."

"Thanks, sweetheart."

CHAPTER TWENTY-EIGHT

Bodhi, Haley, and Uduak put on shield fanny-packs and side-arms, then proceeded to the hanger. Bodhi piloted the Vulcan Prowler, and they headed planet-side. Haley was able to reach a local who ran a livestock and poultry feed center in a small rural town of indigenous people on Kefra, and he had agreed to call a town meeting. The Ahumdulilah fighter-bomber was set down in the parking lot of the feed place, taking up eight of the parking spaces. The crew climbed out to a waiting group of people. More were on their way. They went a few doors down to a little temple that they entered.

Bodhi and his two crew were led to a conference room off the meditation hall where all present took seats around a large table. Some latecomers joined them. The man who'd called the meeting stated, "We have all seen the transmissions over the emergency holocoms system and are not honestly sure what to make of them."

"I am Captain Bodhi, and this is my first officer, Haley. This is Uduak, in charge of my security. We have truly disarmed Nafs Ammara, and Kefra is the 23rd conquered systems to be liberated by us, although we still have much work to do here. I intend to ship all ex-imperials back to their home world. Transports will be arriving within a few hours. We will also ship workers originating from other worlds back to their home planets. Any off-worlders your people would like to invite to stay is up to you. Any you do not extend such an invitation to will be gone within a couple of months. No war materials will be produced on Kefra, and it will be disarmed. We left the largest space station intact for your people and would gladly start training them to operate it. We will also be equipping your people with the only small arms that will be left on this planet."

"What is in it for you? Why are you doing this?" One of the locals inquired.

"The former empire sent two invasion forces to a planet I've become affiliated with. Once we realized that over 180 billion humans are suffering from enslavement by Nafs Ammara, we felt obliged to restore balance and harmony. Since we can do this, not doing it would constitute a form of collusion and condonation."

"You are from a planet of a yellow sun star system," a local stated.

"Yes. We have become allied with four other yellow sun planets. We seek friendship with Pronotavasmi due to their spiritual development."

"They were enslaved five months ago."

"We are aware of this, and they are the next planetary system we intend to liberate. We did not learn about them until we arrived here and cracked the highest secured data."

"Just before the imperials landed on Pronotavasmi, though after they held the planet hostage from space, we received a transmission from them. It was almost in real-time, though they are 14 light-years from us. They informed us that a yellow sun adept would liberate them using three highly advanced space ships. They claimed we would be liberated too."

"They must be quite evolved indeed," Bodhi admitted. 'We have no way of knowing the future. The predictions of the people of Pronotavasmi seem to be coming to pass."

"You seem very like our friends from Pronotavasmi. Are you an adept, Captain Bodhi?"

"My teacher has authorized and empowered me to teach the meditation traditions. I am a warrior-monk and priest of the Adamantine Will Order. I was raised as the only child of the monastery since I was six weeks old."

"You have attained your body of light?" Another local at the table asked.

"Yes."

"Show us."

Bodhi sank his breath into his lower abdomen and closed his eyes, entering his central channel where he absorbed and dissolved the ten winds, and with them his physical senses. Employing the transference of consciousness and forceful projection, Bodhi arose in his central channel to shoot out the crown of his head, recognizing each of the eight signs of death as he went. In his rainbow body he hovered between the top of his physical head and the ceiling to say, "For the attainment of the actual illusory body work beyond that of the six limbs is required. One must establish clam abiding and practice both the emptiness meditations and the secret method. These I have accomplished."

"Clearly," the eldest woman at the table proclaimed.

The man who'd called the meeting told Bodhi, "Now we trust you completely."

"Honestly, we have come to help, and that is all," Bodhi told them.

"We believe you. Where do you hail from?" The elder woman asked.

"Haley and I are from the planet Mother in the Whirlpool Galaxy. We were drawn through a wormhole and do not know where our region of the universe is located from here, nor how we are now aligned with it in temporal chronology. Since my mission is to transmit the teachings, it is irrelevant where we are, and what matters is that we find humans who are ready to receive the teachings."

"You are just a boy," the old woman exclaimed.

"I'm 27 years old, and I have two two-year-old daughters. I apologize for my youth."

"No need. I just didn't realize it was possible for one so young to have accomplished so much."

"My teacher is the 333rd Wu of the Islohar, and an advanced race called the Amonrahonians, went collectively into a 100-year meditation a moment before her birth to direct and support her. My attainment reflects her ability as a teacher more than mine as a student."

"I see you are truly devoted to her, but we are incredibly grateful for *your* presence and the liberation you bring. Please pass to us your teachings before you leave our world, Master Bodhi."

"Of course, I will. It is my true purpose. I see your lights and recognize your insight. What is your name, ma'am?"

"I'm Stella, and I'm most pleased to meet you."

A man at the table asked, "Will you be remaining in this galaxy?"

"Now that we have discovered the people of Ground and the people of Pronotavasmi, I think we will be staying," Bodhi replied. "What do you call your galaxy?"

"We used to call it, 'Spiral Disc Part in Cloud' but we adopted the name Pronotavasmi designates it by, which is 'Burning Hope Galaxy.'"

Haley inquired, "What is the 'hope' embedded in the name?"

"The internal conscious evolution of humanoids is our burning hope," Stella answered.

"Did your world have a government before you were invaded by Nafs Ammara?" Haley asked.

"Embarrassingly yes, though a fairly benign one as far as they go," Stella replied. "The people of Pronotavasmi were trying to teach us how to get along without one, and we were making progress in that direction."

"Our planet, Mother, had no government for many millennia until we were conquered by the Royal Monarch tri-galaxy empire," Bodhi explained. "My teacher toppled that empire freeing over 5,700 worlds. It was the third empire she'd dismantled."

"You are following in her footsteps," Stella complimented him.

"There is a device 280 feet below the surface on the yellow sun planet of Ground," Bodhi tried to explain, "which communicated with Haley and me by displaying text on dull metal. The device told me that I have a mission to fulfill in the Burning Hope Galaxy."

Stella told him, "It looks to me like you're doing a fine job of fulfilling it."

"How strange is that, though?" Bodhi wondered. "Haley and I are lost in space and time, and a buried device, ancient as all get out, knows who we are as if expecting us."

"If anyone can help you make sense of it, I'm sure the high adepts of Pronotavasmi will prove your best bet," Stella assured him.

The eldest man at the table spoke for the first time, "Master Bodhi, you are a potency and potentiality within the Burning Hope Galaxy at the moment, a force of harmony and equilibrium. Your intervention results in freedom, justice, equality, peace, and love between humans. There have been individuals historically who have attained a view of the universe in its wholeness and not as a sequence of frames or moments unfolding one after the other in time. The consequence of your life in our galaxy is already noteworthy for humanity. It is not so surprising that your work here would have been anticipated long ago."

"I am organizing my work based on the work of Sarhi the Im, who is my teacher's teacher and who was tasked with founding an intergalactic spiritual congress of sentient beings. So far, we know of only humans and Kluzyst. I am founding a chapter of the spiritual congress here in the Burning Hope Galaxy."

"The people of Kefra would be honored to unite with this spiritual congress," the elder man asserted.

Stella opined, "A spiritual congress offers a far higher order of unity than a union of planetary governments."

"It would be ideal to have both between the worlds connected by the Nafs Ammara star-gate system," Bodhi suggested. "There are four other planets with star-gates who would link with these planets of the former empire, once all is secure and trust can be established. There are groups on all four planets who have joined our spiritual congress. Nearly the entire adult population of Ground are actively involved."

Stella stated, "Although our population was nearly exterminated in our enslavement and the empire's conquest of our planet, we have grown to 425 million since then, and our entire adult population will almost certainly participate."

The elder man told Bodhi, "I'm sure you will find the population of Pronotavasmi to be enthusiastic and most willing to promote and to participate in the spiritual congress."

"That is my hope," Bodhi told him.

A woman in her 30's said tearfully, "We are so very grateful to you, Master Bodhi. I just can't tell you."

"Please call me Bodhi. I'm uncomfortable with titles. We are one."

Haley inquired, "Could you give me some useful locations for dropping off shuttle loads of small arms for distribution to the natives of Kefra?"

"Only for this side of the mountains on this continent," Stella answered, "But I can put you in touch with people on four other continents."

"Let's start with your area first, and find eight locations for the most effective disbursement," Haley suggested.

Stella consulted a younger woman seated next to her, who brought up a holo map from her hand device. The younger woman keyed in eight locations, and Haley gave her the code for sending this data to her hand device, which would also send it to her storage memory and process memory of her android body. On reception of the locations, she sent them with reference to coordinates of their planetary-grid convention, to Commander Nelson. One of the eight locations was the parking lot of the feed center where their Vulcan Prowler was sitting.

Stella asked in a worried tone, "Are you arming us because you think we might be attacked?"

"No. I'm arming you because all the imperials will not be off your world before we leave, and I want your people to be the only ones armed. I also want to train and leave your folks on the space station. It has the only space-based weapons in your star system. Holding that secures your planet surface."

Haley informed them, "Bodhi is also starting an interplanetary Star Fleet and had been training recruits from the planet Ground. We would welcome young recruits from Kefra, and we have two imperial ships we stole which need to be manned."

"What is the Star Fleet's mission?" The elder man asked.

"To protect the planets of the spiritual congress and planetary sovereignty in general within this galaxy. We haven't even begun to explore the part of this galaxy within the dust and gas cloud, so we don't know what dangers we face yet."

"Then you will have your recruits," the elder man assured him. "Our young people will be highly motivated to be part of such a protection and security force, and to follow the liberator of their world."

"I'm not a tenth the engineer Haley is, and our warships would not have been possible without her. She is truly the liberator, and I'm just the Captain commanding the operations."

"You have only one warship?!" Stella asked amazed. "The imperials had more than 200 war ships, and one was 1 ¾ miles long, fueled with venusium fusion reactors."

"My ship is 3,960 feet in diameter and is fueled with solarium fusion reactors. I could not let them all fire on me at once but was able to get out of the thick of battle and strike with surprise until we got their numbers reduced. I have an auxiliary ship to reload from, and the utility tug Haley and I came in has armaments superior to those of the former empire's."

A man at the table shared, "Until you took over the emergency transmission holocoms system and informed us that Nafs Ammara and twenty-two other planets are already disarmed, we had no idea the empire had fallen."

"We have 12 more stops to make, so in 3 ½ months, there will not be a single weapon in the hands of an imperial in this empire. The emperor and his son are both dead. So is the General who was the Commander in Chief of the military here."

Haley added, "This is the last planet with significant military presence. The rest will be pretty much routine."

"Until the moment you arrived in our system, it seemed to us impossible that the empire could ever be toppled," a woman on the sunny-side of 50 told them.

"It is a miraculous event for us," the elder man agreed.

"I lost small military space craft in the battle of Nafs Ammara, and five of those had crews as well as pilots, so it was a costly victory for us. We've had no casualties since though."

"We would learn the stories of those fallen in the war to free us. They will be remembered and honored by the people of Kefra," Stella said gravely.

"I'll send you the biographies we have on them, and both optics and text of their deeds and sacrifice in the battle," Haley told her, sending data through her hand-device to Stella.

When a combat shuttle landed at the feed center parking lot they all went to inspect the small arms shipment. Space Marines in hard shell suits unloaded the crates stacking them in the lot. Bodhi and Haley pried the lid off a few cases to peek inside. There were missiles and shoulder missile launchers, automatic grenade guns, heavy rapid-fire tripod blasters, heavy blaster rifles, long-range semiautomatic sniper blaster rifles, tri-barrel continuous-fire blaster pistols and much more. The local townsfolk were amazed and called their friends to get these weapons distributed to every household in their area. Further meetings were scheduled, and these would include holo-conferencing with the local groups around the globe.

The first transports were approaching the orbit of Kefra, so Haley arranged shuttles from numerous air and space ports to bring up imperials and board them. She graphically generated Bodhi and had him announce in his voice over the emergency transmission system that all imperials must proceed to the nearest air-space port. She also sent shuttles for ex-troops walking from remote bases in very cold climates. The cargo shuttles from *Spalding* and *Diamond Lotus* assisted in lifting imperials to transports. This endeavor took quite a few hours and resulted in sending the first 220,000 imperials back to Nafs Ammara. These transports would each make two trips per day between Kefra and Nafs Ammara, and four more of the largest transports would be helping bring imperials home within just a few days.

Bodhi, Haley, and Uduak returned to *Thor* in their Vulcan Prowler. Kristy had Shanti and Artana there, and both wanted Bodhi to pick them up, so he grasped one of them in each arm to his chest. Their curious little voices posed questions for him, and Bodhi's heart overflowed with adoration and affection for them. His voice was thick with his love for his daughters.

Winn informed him, "Im going to feed the girls in our suite before we go to the senior officer's mess where Uldra is preparing our dinner."

"I want apple sauce, momma," Shanti informed her mother.

Neither of the girls would eat the commercial meat-in-a-jar, and gagged on it if forced. Uldra began pureeing poultry and gravy fresh for them. They also liked spaghetti, which they called "pescetti." Individually wrapped sticks of string cheese were among their favorites, and nut butter with jam on cinnamon bread was their number one preferred food. Both daughters could be induced to eat macaroni and cheese as well as fish sticks. Frozen fruit juice popsicles constituted a favorite snack.

Bodhi carried Shanti and Artana into their private little galley where their chairs with toys built into the fronts were kept and got a daughter into each one. Tish was already fixing their supper, and Winn had followed Bodhi in to help. Artana had Rags with her, who was a soft stuffed Masset based on a cartoon version, and not on a real wild Masset. Rags went everywhere with Artana and was often dragged on his head by one foot. He also slept cuddled in her arms each night. Holding Rags around the middle in her left arm, Artana clenched her little fist around her tiny spoon and scooped apple sauce from her tri-sectioned plate, bringing it into her mouth; and some down her chin. Each bite Bodhi was ready with a soft cloth and gave her chin a wipe.

She stayed on apple sauce until it was only a smear upon the plate bottom then moved on to the 'creamy corn.' She always worked her way from the yummiest to the least. Tonight the least yummy was a grilled cheese sandwich. For this, she had to leave Rags to his own devices so she could manage the triangular half-sandwich in both hands. Opening her mouth to full capacity, Artana could just squeeze one angled corner into her mouth, and she bit it off leaving a concave edge instead of a point. Bodhi marveled at her skills as if she were pulling the stunt of a century on a hover-board.

CHAPTER TWENTY-NINE

The Bodhi liberation force remained another week in the Kefra system, meeting with locals and arming them, taking on recruits, and providing schematics and designs for factory retooling. Fully a third of the off-world factory workers were invited to remain living on the planet. More than 3.5 million imperials had been returned to Nafs Ammara, and another 292,000 were leaving the system at the same time as Bodhi's group.

They made the jump into the Pronotavasmi system, the first yellow sun world they'd entered since leaving Ground to liberate the empire. Tish and Winn got *Thor's* velocity down to .20 light fairly rapidly, and the details of the solar system were brought into stark clarity. Haley began hijacking the imperial emergency holocom transmission system, and as soon as she controlled it, she started streaming optics of the battle of Nafs Ammara and the battle of Kefra to imperials in space and on the ground. Their point of entrance had been the asteroid field between the 4th and 5th planets, more than 65 million miles from the third planet, Pronotavasmi, their destination. After showing the battle scenes, Haley put Bodhi on coms with the planetary population and he told them, "This is Captain Bodhi of *Thor*, and I have come to dismantle imperial rule on this planet. If you surrender, you will be returned unharmed to your home world. If you resist, you will simply be exterminated. Your empire lies in ruins and has not one warship left. All personnel on the ground leave your weapons, remove any patches and insignias from your uniforms and proceed to space shuttle ports where you will be camped until the transports arrive to bring you home."

Haley was already sucking up data from central quantum computers on the surface and beginning to decipher the local language, which the imperials had failed to accomplish. The rest on *Thor's* bridge watched to see what the imperials would do. Nothing at all happened for several minutes. Tish was slowing with only reverse drives having jumped in with more than enough room to accomplish this. Troops on some of the military bases began abandoning them without their weapons. From some bases, air and spacecraft began scrambling. Bodhi said over coms to June, who was in *Thor's* hanger, "Launch all the small craft but the shuttles to combat the craft the imperials are sending up. Stay cloaked and give no warning. They have already been warned."

"Aye aye, Sir, we are taking off now."

Tish mentioned, "No shuttles are leaving the space station."

Bodhi called Commander Nelson to say, "Please land a shuttle on the space stations central sphere and drill in a gas line and valve to gas the occupants. Then you'll need some shuttles fully loaded with Space Marines in hard-shell combat suits to take control of the station, release the poison gas into space, and shuttle the bodies to the surface. Haley will have the shields down by the time you get there."

"The shuttles are prepped and ready, and the one with the gas tank and drill is lifting off now," Nelson confirmed.

"Haley is sending them the precise location to drill on the sphere for maximum effect and will have that space station's shields down," Bodhi informed him."

"That is where they'll pump the gas," he acknowledged.

To Tish, Bodhi directed, "As soon as those space weapons platforms come into range, start blowing them up."

"Aye aye, Sir!"

Haley updated Bodhi, "The people of Pronotavasmi have quantum coms satellites in orbit and equipment on the ground. They employ mostly solar, wind, and ambient planetary energies, and they have solarium super reactors outside their largest cities, and hydroelectric turbines at the top of all large waterfalls. They don't build dams."

"Those tend to be disharmonious and in disequilibrium with the planetary unity and harmony," Bodhi concluded.

Tish wasted a space weapons platform with her class 8 twin nose blasters producing a flare of color, gas, and particles. Seated in Bodhi's lap, Shanti went wide-eyed over the visual display fascinated. Winn blew one apart from an even greater distance with her class 9 blaster. Personnel began exiting the rest of the platforms, some in small craft, some in escape pods, and a few just tumbling out into space in suits. Bodhi had shuttles from his two captured imperial ships go pick up the personnel drifting about in space. Tish made two very different orbital paths around the planet to destroy the other four space weapons platforms.

Commander Nelson announced, "The gas is pumped into the space station, and shuttles with troops are on the way to take control of it."

"Thank you, Commander. Good work."

A few minutes after that, June came on to say, "We took all of their small-craft down in the atmosphere, and none made it into space."

"Go ahead and make another offer of surrender to those bases which sent them, and if they do, wait till personnel has cleared out before destroying them. I want to give the two new crews some target practice, so leave the bases which are being evacuated."

"Aye aye, Sir."

Haley suggested, "There are four very large passenger transports docked to their space station that we could take over to start returning imperials home."

"Tish, make a pass by the space station so Haley can hit those four transports with nanobot spray missiles and upload the Jard program," Bodhi instructed.

The disarmament of Pronotavasmi proceeded most efficiently and professionally. The new crews got their target practice and even had the opportunity to help hunt down some ocean war vessels, including a few deep stealthy submarines. The military bases were swiftly reduced to craters, and the enormous imperial research and development facility was evacuated and abandoned completely by the imperials. By the time the four transports were headed for the star-gate filled with folks going to Nafs Ammara, the planet and space around it had been secured. Haley had the basic language embodied and was just assimilating technical dictionaries of nomenclature specific to the different branches of science. She was only an hour from having a sophisticated interpreter service programmed for them, and a history and analysis of the Pronotavasmi human civilization prepared to present to Bodhi.

Uldra and Tandy served lunch on the bridge, and Shanti ate a nut-butter and jam sandwich in Bodhi's lap, getting jam everywhere. She complained to her father, "Daddy! The jam on your pants got on my arm!"

"I'm sorry, sweetheart. The jam on my pants dropped from *your* sandwich. Here, let me wipe it up, and from your arm, too. Where is it on your arm?"

"I cleaned it on your shirt," she explained innocently.

"Let me wipe it with this, so it's not sticky," Bodhi offered.

Shanti held up her forearm pointing with her chin as Bodhi swiped the spot with a wipey. Meanwhile, the jam was descending into both of their laps given Shanti's one-hand grip on the remainder of the sandwich. His captain's seat's surface was an easy-to-clean soft vinyl. His daughter scolded, "You are getting me sticky again, daddy."

He got busy mopping up the spilled jam with wipeys. Shanti tried to say something but could not produce sound with her mouth full, especially given the consistency of the nut butter. She finally swallowed, then did it again, drank some milk from her spill-proof bottle still managing to drip some down her chin. At last, she had her voice back and said, "Daddy, my training pants are kind of sloshy."

Winn scooped Shanti into her arms. The little corner of the sandwich clutched in her hand was no longer loaded. Bodhi handed Winn some wipeys and started cleaning himself with one. Shanti got taken out of her sloshy training pants and tucked into a fresh pair by her momma while she finished the last bites of her sandwich. Artana was just finishing hers, seated in Tish's lap. Haley was processing and programming internally, quantumly. Bodhi could now eat his lunch uninterrupted.

He was just grinding his last bite between his molars when Haley announced, "It's done. I've uploaded it to all of you, and we can now speak clearly with the locals here."

"Great, Haley! Thanks," Bodhi told her.

"The people here are in the early stage of discovering the science of reversing human aging at the cellular level and have synthetic protein chemicals which are telomerase inducers working to reset telomeres in all cells of the body."

Winn asked, "What's a telomere?"

Haley explained, "They are the end segments of DNA on chromosomes. Your body contains 100 trillion cells, and 10 quadrillion telomeres. Telomeres protect the end of chromosomes from damage or faulty recombination and allow complete replication of chromosomes. They also control gene expression and aid in organizing nuclear chromosomes."

Winn asked, "I thought an unwavering concentration had to be attained for the Amonrahonians to achieve perpetual life and rejuvenation?"

Bodhi explained, "Reversing aging in the cells with telomerase inducers was part of their initial development of the science, and they were able to make this change permanent, and not drug dependent. There is also an internal alchemy required, which takes concentration without lapse. This unceasing meditation becomes the background for all of their further functioning and brings rejuvenation on the pre-material planes of the human psyche-soul. Once they attained this, gender and reproduction went dormant, and new dimensions of unity were opened to them as a species. They described these as intuitive telepathies."

Haley informed them, "I'm setting up a meeting with the group they call their 'elders.' We have one hour to get to the big knot where three mountain ranges join on the great wide continent down there."

"Haley, Tish, and Winn will accompany me to the meeting, and we will go unarmed and without shields. Uduak, you will keep an eye on us from the shuttle, and you'll be armed, as well as having access to the shuttle's weapons systems. I do not expect any trouble.

I'm going to change into clean clothes in my suite then meet you at the shuttle in the hanger."

"I need changing too," Tish informed him.

"I'll bring the girls to Kristy," Winn told them.

They met in the hanger, then boarded the shuttle, and Tish piloted it down through the atmosphere staying within acceptable limits of Bodhi's fuel-frugality, and with a precision rarely seen in such routine and mundane flying. Their landing coordinates put them on a high plateau square in the join of three mountain ranges protruding from the knot like galactic spiral arms. As the ramp lowered, and the seriously cold air entered the airlock, they saw a group of people waiting to greet them.

They came down the ramp onto the snow with a biting wind pressing on them. These folks were normal-size to them and not giants like the imperials. Cold as it was, to be beneath a yellow sun again, was a comforting and nurturing experience. With great relief, they were led inside a stone building. Once the door was sealed, the wind was gone, and not so much as a draft could be felt, though the building was not heated. The temperature within was not too far below that of the crystallization of water, and with no wind chill, it felt comparatively much warmer. They all sat on meditation cushions arranged in a circle upon a thick wool rug. Bodhi, Tish, and Winn were each practicing their inner-fire blazing and dripping meditation to keep warm.

A woman seated directly across the circle from Bodhi made eye contact as she said, "Welcome to Pronotavasmi, Captain Bodhi. We salute you."

"Salutations," Bodhi stated, bowing to her from his cushion.

"We have been expecting you," the same woman told him. She did not look like an 'elder' to Bodhi. Her hair shined with illustrious color without a gray strand within it, and her skin was as elastic, tight, and smooth as a baby's. There was nonetheless something ancient about her, though not reflected physically.

"Until a week ago," Bodhi explained, "we had no idea we were coming here."

"We are to help you with your mission defending the planetary systems of the former empire and the four yellow sun planets you have become involved with from the Consumere."

"I thought my mission was to bring down the Nafs Ammara Empire," Bodhi told her.

"That would have been a nonstarter and no-brainer of a mission had it been yours," she contradicted him.

"Who are the Consumere?" Bodhi asked, perplexed.

"The ones who are coming," she told him. "They did not transcend ego nor did their planet survive their crisis. Enough of the population escaped to mining platforms and ship building platforms, space stations, and ships to regrow their population in artificial environments. Their technological development was rapid with survival of their species contingent upon this. Their technology is equal to your own. They prey on inhabited worlds so that they have a workforce of slaves to do most of the work of stripping the planet of vital resources. By the time they move on to the next world the biosphere of the one they leave behind is in collapse. They will arrive at your last stop, Finitolia, in three months and two days. Only two of their 6,800-foot Scout Scavenger Intruders will be arriving. The Consumere population is still cannibalizing a planet on the outer rim within the dust and gas cloud. They will be there for at least three more years."

"Can you tell me about their ships?" Bodhi asked, alarmed.

"The mothership is the size of a small moon, carries a small fleet of warships berthed to her hull, and 5,000 military small craft. Seven warships five miles in length accompany the mother ship along with a fleet of giant mining ships, collection tankers, and industrial ships. This civilization has 36 Scout Scavenger Intruders out exploring and sampling systems. They are most drawn to worlds with star-gates, which give them an easy mark for domination, and at the same time, an educated work force."

"Do you have data on their verbal language?" Bodhi asked.

"We have cracked it," the woman informed him, 'and their computer codes as well. I'm sharing all of this now with your unique sentient computer friend."

"What is in the Scout Scavenger Intruders?" Bodhi inquired.

"Those are each powered by 22 Solarium fusion super-reactors, carry 96 military small craft, dozens of mining, extraction and collection craft, and 2,000 Space Special Forces. The ship's crew number 870, and with resource specialists, pilots, and small craft crews as well as their deck-crews, the ship carries 4,090 personnel."

"My ship has only 12 solarium fusion super-reactors, and my tug-utility ship has only four," Bodhi told her apologetically.

"I'm sure you'll manage," the woman replied.

This silenced Bodhi as he went internal to contemplate the magnitude of what was expected of him. Several minutes passed without anyone speaking. Winn looked frightened and almost looked freaked out. Tish's serious expression had become truly grave and nearly grim. Bodhi finally asked, "Do you have engineers and technicians who could help build an ORH Ultra-Super Battleship-Carrier, 29,630 feet in diameter?"

"That is one of the three ways we are to assist you," the woman said, happy to see the young man catching on.

"What are the other two?" Bodhi asked.

"The data we give to your sentient computer and the age-reversing treatment we are to give you and your two human wives. We will also give you the drugs to treat your daughters, but you must wait until they are in their early twenties."

"How have you been directed to do this?" Bodhi asked in astonishment.

"The Amonrahonians instructed us to do this and told us when to expect you. They are meditating and mustn't be disturbed at the moment."

"I see," Bodhi stated, trying to take it all in.

"No. You do not have the full picture yet, but you are beginning to bring some of it into focus," she clarified. "We also have expert space construction personnel to lend you and some elite mining crews."

"How long would it take to get them altogether and ready to leave for the ship construction platform in orbit of Ground?"

"They are waiting on you, and you had better get them all there no later than tomorrow if you want to complete construction before the mothership and her fleet arrive in Finitolia," she answered.

"How many personnel are we talking about?" Bodhi asked her.

"Thirty thousand who are going to Ground, but we will have hundreds of thousands mining and manufacturing here on Pronotavasmi for the project. We'd been at it for 39 years before Nafs Ammara conquered us almost 6 months ago."

"Then I will need to start making trips with my three quantum coms ships this afternoon transporting personnel and materials. I'll leave the two imperial ships which came here through the star-gate to keep the imperials in line while we jump back and forth."

"I think you're starting to get it," she commented.

Bodhi told Haley, "I will have to liberate the last 11 worlds without you while you supervise construction and get them the schematics, specs, designs, and instruction for manufacturing the components of the ship. The construction platform will need to be expanded to about seven times its current size. Three years will be pushing it for completing a ship that size."

Haley said realizing, "We will also need to link the star-gates between Pronotavasmi and Ground so we can employ the big imperial transports to move materials, prefab sections and components from here to the construction platform orbiting Ground."

"Yes, and *Diamond Lotus* will need to be stationed in the Ground system. I'll need you to jump to Finitolia when I jump in there to help me with the two Scout Scavenger Intruders in three months."

"Of course, I will. I'll transfer to *Thor* in the tender before we engage battle," Haley assured him.

"I need eight of those giant torpedoes Om developed," Bodhi told her. "They will have to be externally mounted on *Thor's* hull. I don't think we could pierce the hull armor with the torpedoes we have."

"To say nothing about the shields those ships must have," Haley agreed. "I'll make those while we expand the construction platform and have them to you before you get to Finitolia."

"After Finitolia, and assuming we can come out victorious against two ships with nearly twice the power of *Thor* each, we will have to race with the construction against time."

"We will need to involve the people of Kefra and space construction workers, miners, and factory workers from other former imperial worlds if we ever hope to build it that fast," Haley suggested.

"We've heard wonderful things about your assistant," the woman told Bodhi, referring to Haley.

"She is wonderful, and I'd be a hopeless wreck without her," Bodhi agreed. "I'm beyond blessed, and so are all of you because we'd never survive this without her."

"Don't despair, lad," she told him, "some potential has been recognized in you as well."

Haley announced, "I have seven heavy cargo freighter transports being prepped to travel and arrive here by star-gate from former imperial worlds within four and a half hours. I have all the solutions to linking Ground's star-gate to this one, but I will need to physically visit each one."

"Is there any other vital information you have for me?" Bodhi inquired of the woman seated across from him in the circle.

"Nothing pressing on this moment," she replied. "Before you move on to the next world on your route, though, we will need to have a little chat."

"Yes, Ma'am!" Bodhi complied. "Duration has just become a most significant factor in my mind upon which all of our existences now depend, so I must hurry."

"I'm sure glad you have realized that part of it," the woman said pleased.

"Does Haley have the coordinates of where materials and personnel will be waiting to get shuttled to space?"

"She has," the woman answered.

Tish, Winn, Haley, and Bodhi sprinted out of the freezing cold stone building into the much colder wind-blowing outdoors and up the ramp into their chill airlock. Coming through the other side of the airlock into their warm shuttle, brought physical relief which paled in comparison to the mental alarm and grave anticipatory concerns eating at them.

Bodhi gave a flurry of orders bringing June's folks all back to his hanger and getting some technicians and shuttle pilots over to the space station while bringing the Space Marines back aboard. Haley was picked up by Sunoco in *Diamond Lotus's* tender and flown out to the star-gate. Bodhi spoke with people on Ground, explaining the gravity of the situation and what must be done and accomplished. Shuttles were directed to coordinates on the surface where stored materials and manufactured parts were being stored, to lift these to four transports. Tish spoke to some folks on Kefra, who started organizing for the project immediately.

Bodhi got a hold of the government of Firmament after he concluded his call with Ground and informed them, "I'm going to need every defunct bridge, derelict ocean vessel and half-submerged skyscraper on your planet, and I need them quick. I'll get some personnel and machinery out to you soon, but please get started with your own equipment in the meantime. An advanced race with no spiritual clue is headed to rape each planet with a star-gate until there is nothing left to sustain a biosphere any longer. They take everything. Not just metals, gems, fuels, rare materials, and manufactured goods, but topsoil, seed stocks, water, and air. They can cycle almost a million acres of equatorial dense jungle through their food synthesizer grinders each month to fill their biomaterial storage units. I'm looking at the data Haley sent me as a briefing, and it says they have a population of 1.2 billion people all living on space ships and all warlike—women included."

"Can we get rid of our star-gate?" One of the people on speaker-coms of Firmament's government asked.

"Sure," Bodhi told him, "just drop it in a black hole, and everything will be fine for a while. They will eventually find you even without a gate."

"We have no way to tow that gate to a black hole," the man said incensed.

"No, you don't, so your best bet is to help us protect all planetary populations from them," Bodhi told him.

"We will start collecting steel for you today and keep expanding our efforts," the female Vice- Chancellor assured him. "We will have iron ore mined for you on New Firmament, too, and that will start this day."

"Thank you, Madame Vice-Chancellor," Bodhi said gratefully. "Many planetary populations will be involved in these efforts because their lives, too, depend upon our success."

Winn told Bodhi, "I have gotten pledges to start directing all mining on the resource-rich worlds of Overflowing and Abundance to feeding our project raw materials."

"Excellent work, sweetheart."

Tish reported, "Ground was a little reluctant about linking gates before you liberate the last eleven planets, but I assured them that Haley would encrypt the code with a quantum digital fortress which the little imperial computers couldn't crack in ten thousand years. They finally agreed. They are already starting to make more sections for the ship construction platform and have an old passenger cruise liner with outdated drives they can berth at the platform to house guest space construction workers, engineers, and techs from other worlds in."

"Wonderful. Great work, my love," Bodhi said with appreciation and fondness. "We are going to be without Haley for three months, so I'm going to be depending upon you and Winn."

"I'm devoted to you and will put in my best efforts," Winn vowed.

"We are one," Tish asserted most seriously.

Winn asked, concerned, "Will one ORH Ultra-Super battleship-carrier be enough?"

"No," Bodhi admitted. "We will need to make a warship out of that 1 ¾ mile-long ship frame attached to the construction platform orbiting Kefra after all."

Haley told him, "I think we might be able to cram 44 solarium reactors on it. The Consumere do not use cloaking and employ the same decloaking technology Ahumdulilah does, so we won't bother with cloaking systems in our new ships. The power can be directed to weapons and shields instead."

Tish suggested, "We need to overhaul another giant transport ship with solarium reactors and Om's shield generators and armor to refit it as an auxiliary reloader. We'll need to install a quantum drive compatible with quantum coms navigation and jumps."

"Go ahead and send that as a directive to Ground," Bodhi told Tish. "They already have the factories on the surface and facilities and machinery in space, as well as the designs and schematics, from having done such a refit and overhaul."

Winn told him, "You need to manufacture drone fighter bombers with space drives and quantum drive. We could certainly jump one inside something as big as the mother ship."

I was thinking along the same lines," Bodhi agreed. "I'm also going to need Patriarch Tipola, and I'm going to need both you and Tish to attain your rainbow bodies of light. Perhaps Sunoco too. We will work the method of the secret practice now—the whole thing very thoroughly, and the central channel breathing practice of the transference of consciousness."

"I'm ready to make the jump," Winn said most gravely.

"We are One," Tish said with determination.

Haley came on speaker, "I'm nearly done at the star-gate. Four cargo transports from Kefra have come through and are headed for Pronotavasmi to assume low orbit. I transmitted the coordinates of the materials they are to collect. They each have their own shuttles and crane systems, but I've directed some imperial shuttles on the surface over to the areas they'll be lifting cargo from to help out."

"Thanks, Haley. Maybe we should stop sending imperials home long enough to get our personnel to the Ground system."

"I've already arranged that, and the next two passenger transports to come back through this gate will carry them there."

"Are there passengers I need to pick up in *Thor*?"

"Yes," Haley explained. "The two transports can only take 28,000 and that leaves 2,000 for you. There is also cargo for your five empty holds. I'm highlighting them in your virtual ship diagram in your holo for you."

"Thanks, Haley. I'm on my way to collect passengers and cargo."

"Send *Diamond Lotus* and *Spalding* in for cargo, then have them go ahead and jump to Ground. I can make the jump in the tender. It has a quantum drive."

"Then, I'll jump to Ground as soon as I'm loaded."

"I have to get there and link the Ground star-gate before any of these transports can come through."

The woman from the meeting in the cold stone mountaintop building said over the speaker coms on *Thor's* bridge, "I know you are young and excitable, Captain Bodhi, but you neglected to speak about the most important thing."

"And that would be ma'am?" Bodhi asked, wondering which of many possible things she was referring to.

"The spiritual congress of course." She said in a tone one might use with a child.

"Of course, you are right," Bodhi agreed. "I do apologize."

"Well, I was asked to inform you that the people of Pronotavasmi are all joining," she announced.

"What is your name, Ma'am?"

"They call me Jara."

"Thank you for your help, Jara. By the way, are you able to see auras, and do you have your rainbow body?"

"You're quite welcome. I am, and yes, I do," she responded to all three points of his communication.

I will need you on one of our warships when we come to do battle with the Consumere. We cannot match their numbers or their strength, but we can defeat them with adept skills they don't have."

"Talk and travel is all a body of light can do," Jara stated as a question.

"It can emit sensor-blinding white light, lingering for up to 20 seconds, disrupting their fire control, navigation, and piloting."

"How could seeing auras help in battle?"

"When shields are stirred up from taking hits a soft spot is produced. These soft spots can be discerned by someone who can see auras, and torpedoes can slip through a soft spot without blowing up on the shields to dig into the ship's hull directly."

"So there is actually hope?" Jara asked surprised.

"If we have an adept on each ship we bring into battle, we will be able to defeat them. We will also need the spiritual congress convened and in contemplation supporting us."

"You have employed these tactics in battle?"

"Yes, in the battle of Nafs Ammara. We have another secret weapon we are going to be practicing for, and that is micro-jumping a drone fighter-bomber into the middle of a big ship, bypassing shields."

"Has such a thing ever been done?"

"Yes, by my teacher's senior students who are intuitive drone pilots in a battle in Xegnachtznel Galaxy, and the battles in the Monarch and the Mother star-systems."

"Have you or your senior students done it?"

"Not yet, but knowing it's possible, we aim to learn."

"Send a shuttle for me and I will go into battle with you, Captain Bodhi."

"Thank you, Jara. I'll need to collect you a couple of days early, so I can teach you to fire torpedoes accurately."

"I'll be ready, and if you would like, I could bring some adept friends."

"Please do. It would multiply our chances of success."

"There is more to you than I first realized, Captain Bodhi," Jara complimented him.

"How is it that you are considered an 'elder,' Jara?"

"I received the treatment in puberty and was taught the meditation as a teenager. I'm 791 years old."

"Your gender remains definitively obvious," Bodhi stated, thinking about how the Amonrahonians were said to be genderless.

"Those changes take millennium and are generational. I have stopped ovulating, though I have not reached menopause."

"You look younger than me," he told her.

"Well, my cells *are* younger than yours. Treatment at your age ought to give you a life span of another 400-500 years."

"Will I be taught the meditations?"

"No. You will be a voluntary returner after that, and follow in your teacher's footsteps."

"I will do what is needed of me."

"We already knew you would try. Now I'm seeing that you might succeed instead of die trying."

"Together, we can do this, and we must do this. The stakes are too high."

"Well, you are certainly correct about the stakes."

"I will meet with you again when I get back here from Ground."

"Farewell, Captain Bodhi."

Tish was moving *Thor* over the location of their passenger pick up, and shuttles were leaving their ship for the surface while others were headed to them in space from the planet. The workers from Pronotavasmi arrived 40-60 squeezed into each shuttle, and it took almost an hour and a half to get them all boarded. There were 2,000 taken onto *Thor* and no seats available for most of them, so they lined the broad corridors along the bulkheads, sitting on the floor. The ship had to move to two other locations to load the cargo they were bringing into the empty cargo-holds they had. This took a little over another hour. Once the cargo was stowed, Tish headed out of the system, accelerating to jump speed.

Haley called to tell Bodhi, "I'm at the Ground system star-gate and will have it linked and operational with the star-gate in Pronotavasmi within a quarter-hour. The moment it's working, Ground has seven large cargo freighter transports ready to jump through to help move all the freight ready to be lifted off the surface. When you get back to Pronotavasmi, see if they have engineers and space construction workers they can spare to send to the ship construction platform orbiting Kefra. I've almost completed the design for a 50 solarium fusion super-reactor, 1 ¾ miles long warship employing Om's most advanced technologies."

"I will do that and personally bring them to Kefra," Bodhi assured her. "You are too good to be true, Haley, and I love you with all my heart."

"I love you too, Bodhi, and that is why I'm doing this," Haley replied.

"Sunoco is on her way to the ship construction platform with a load of cargo, and she will be keeping *Diamond Lotus* in the Ground system so you will have advanced workshops at your disposal. Clark has *Spalding* in low orbit, over Pronotavasmi's capital, to restock her by shuttles, then she will accompany me back to Ground."

"I'll be here giving each group the plans and schematics for the components and sections they are to work on. The imperials didn't destroy any manufacturing on Pronotavasmi, hoping to learn how it all works, so they can build our reactors—all 244 of them for the ORH Ultra-super ship—and the quantum drive and shield generators for it."

"I want to call the Ultra-super ship *Oceanus*," Bodhi suggested.

"I like it. You seem to work best with feminine energy, so *Oceanus* is perfect."

"Do we know how many solarium fusion super-reactors they have in their mother-ship?"

"Yes, and for all their ships, thanks to the good people of Pronotavasmi. The mother-ship has 3,880 super-reactors housed in the core of the spherical ship. Their five-mile long ships each have 192 super-reactors, so *Oceanus* will be more powerful than those."

"But not two of them together," Bodhi pointed out.

"No. You might last 13 seconds with two hitting you directly with their weapons systems."

"Then I'm going to need some staged launch-boosters attached to *Oceanus* that are not in the original design," Bodhi informed her.

"I'll work out an engineering design for them once I get this gate linked, and after I meet with Ground's chief engineers."

"Let's divert all the power that would have gone into cloaking, to shields, so that they will be especially robust."

"That's a good idea. It will require exceptionally powerful shields," Haley agreed.

"Where do they house all their population?" Bodhi asked trying to get his head around it.

"They have the mother ship, the seven 5-mile long ships, 36 ships each about 1 ½ mile long and carrying 20 solarium super-reactors, about fifty ½-mile warships with 3 reactors each berthed to the mother ship; and then they have an enormous fleet of industrial mega-ships which includes hundreds of smaller engineering and support ships. They also have a four-mile-long hospital ship, 60 six-mile non-combat housing ships, and 100 troop transports—each with 100,000 personnel aboard. Some of their mega-industrial ship-construction ships and factory ships house a quarter-million workers a piece. The mother-ship is 1,200 miles in diameter. About a quarter billion of their race stay in their home galaxy of Citadel at a resource-rich but lifeless planet they call Nostertratrum. They have a mega mining space station there, several mega-mining platforms, a super-factory-refinery ship, and a biodome factory and housing facility on the surface."

"Are they of white or yellow sun origin?" Bodhi asked.

"They are white sun humans who train all their lives to increase muscular strength. They have some warriors who are considerably larger than Pez's champion, Evenrude."

"He's eight feet tall and built like an adamantine bunker!" Bodhi exclaimed.

"He is, and he is dwarfed by a few of the Consumere warriors," Haley agreed.

"Do they have martial arts?"

"Yes, but only hard styles, dependent entirely on muscular force and speed."

"We need to defeat them in space and keep them from gaining the planet surface," Bodhi stated.

"That would certainly be ideal," Haley concurred.

"How will you possibly get 50 reactors into the 1 ¾-miles ship under construction in the Kefra System?"

"It will hardly have a hanger, carrying only a pair of tenders and a few shuttles, and it will be almost fully automated with only small living space for a skeleton crew, and the drives will be extremely compact. In addition, it will not need to carry cloaking generators and will just have air tanks instead of vast chambers of biotrays. This will require it to receive a new supply of air every fourteen days. The ship will also have very little water stortage, and so will need to take on water each time it gets air tanks refilled. I have a plan."

"We need to build some undercarriage mounts for *Spalding* to carry a bunch of the biggest missiles. We'll also need to reinforce her shields with some solarium fusion battery systems. I'll be putting an adept aboard her, and need for the adept to have big missile capacity."

"I'll add that to my list," Haley told him.

"It would help if we had torpedo magazines in the 2nd auxiliary ship being refitted and overhauled," Bodhi mentioned.

"That is already on my list," Haley replied.

"I don't mean to stress you out, Haley. It's just that we not only have to build and overhaul these ships, but we need a shot at winning with them."

"Boy, don't I know that!" Haley replied, intent on her work. "I'm doing my very best to give you just that."

"If we come through this in one piece, it will all be because of you, Haley," Bodhi acknowledged.

"No. you are the only one capable of leading this force and of fighting the *Oceanus* effectively enough to achieve victory, sweetheart. They have to be hard on you right now, but they do recognize you. The adepts know they can afford to butter me up and do so to spur you on."

"I don't think so, Haley," Bodhi disagreed. "They can all see that you are the one who will save our asses."

"I haven't the time to argue with you Bodhi, but when it is all over, I'll be able to tell you, 'I told you so.'"

"I can't deny that if we win, they will even be happy with me."

"We'll see," Haley said, holding to her view.

"Tish is about to make the jump to you, so I'll see you soon."

A moment later, *Thor* and *Diamond Lotus* were just inside the 4th planet's orbital path rushing at the planet Ground, 3rd from the yellow sun. They headed to the ship construction platform, where they would both unload cargo, and *Thor* would unload 2,000 workers as well. The cruise liner passenger ship was securely berthed to the platform, ready to house guest workers. A continuous stream of shuttles from the surface was arriving and dropping off parts and materials for constructing the ORH Ultra-super ship and for enlarging the space construction platform to many times its current size.

Tish brought them in for a perfect docking, and the platform's cranes got right to work unloading *Thor's* cargo holds. There was also an empty berth for *Diamond Lotus* to unload from, and she slipped in nicely. The construction workers, engineers, techs, and miners Bodhi brought each had their own space suit with solarium fusion power cells and disembarked from various airlocks on the ship stepping onto the construction platform. It was already understood that the engineers from Pronotavasmi would be taking the lead on the project, being far advanced technologically. They were met by some Ground foremen who showed them to their accommodations on the berthed cruise liner ship and within the construction platform's living quarters.

Haley announced victoriously over coms on the bridge of *Thor,* "The two gates are linked and open. Seven large Ground transports are about to jump through to Pronotavasmi, and four fully loaded transports from there are accelerating to jump speed to come here."

"Great work Haley!" Bodhi acknowledged.

"I only have 38 more star-gates to link and open," she reported.

"Well, I need to clear imperials out of 11 of those before you do."

"Tomorrow, I'll go to Kefra, Abundance and Overflowing to link their star-gates with Ground's, and open them," Haley told him.

"As soon as everything tagged for the construction platform is off *Thor,* I'm headed back to finish up in Pronotavasmi. *Spalding* has finished restocking its holds and will be coming with me. I won't be staying as long in each of the remaining eleven systems, so I'll have time to do more training with my small craft pilots."

"The plants and assembly lines are still in place on Ground for building our small craft, and some hulls were left over from our last manufacturing run, so I will make sure the ones you lost in Nafs Ammara are replaced before the battle in three months."

"That would make an enormous difference for us, Haley. Thanks. I love you."

"I've got this and will have every factory, refinery, foundry, mine and plant on eight planets in full production around the clock within a week. The designs, specs, and 3D architectural model of the ship are already transferred to Pronotavasmi and Ground. Firmament and Kefra have those for the parts they'll be producing. By tomorrow, Kefra will have the full plans and technical data that they will need to turn that 1 ¾ mile-long ship frame into a 50 solarium reactor war ship. You have to get some scientists, engineers, and technicians over to Kefra from Pronotavasmi when you get back there."

"I'll make that my first priority unless there's a crisis unfolding when I get there," Bodhi promised. "Since Sunoco is going to be here in the Ground System, I'd like to get her training small craft pilots for combat flying. Assuming I survive the battle in three months, I plan to open a Phantom Raider Top Gun Program here in the Ground System and invite the best pilots from the other 39 planets in preparations for the war in three years."

"Who will fly the big ships?" Haley asked.

"I'm promoting myself to Commodore, and Tish will be my pilot in *Oceanus*. Clark will captain *Spalding*, and he has an excellent pilot he works superbly with. I have complete confidence in them. The 50-reactor warship you will need to pilot and captain as well, Haley. Winn will captain the 2nd auxiliary ship. Both auxiliaries will carry at least a dozen of the biggest missiles on undercarriage mounts. Ilya will pilot and captain *Diamond Lotus*, which will again carry undercarriage missiles. Sunoco will pilot and captain *Thor*. I'm also going to need as many as can be made of the Ahumdulilah Mirage Streak Furry heavy bomber."

"Those will only fit through the bay doors of *Oceanus*," Haley informed him.

"Let's mount them to the hulls of our six ships, and we won't need to put quantum drives in them. The extra space can be filled with a fusion battery system and shield generator, giving them better survival odds."

If you are going to deploy them that way, we ought to build the heavy bombers Pronotavasmi designed during their enslavement to the former empire. These wouldn't fit in *Oceanus'* bay doors. We can mount reloaders for them on the hulls of the auxiliary ships. This bomber has four quad-blaster turrets, twin nose blasters, and is a flying magazine of torpedoes, missiles, and canister missiles. The shields are already 12% stronger than the Astro Phantom's."

"I'm sold," Bodhi said, impressed. "Make me those instead."

"I'm entering the atmosphere and late for my first meeting with engineers, my love. Bye," Haley signed off.

Winn asked, "You're making me a ship captain?"

"Yes, of the giant transport we're refitting and overhauling. Haley has a 3,200-foot-long ship already picked out. It's wide and angular, and it has a gigantic superstructure. Haley says we'll get six solarium super-reactors into it. Some structural reinforcement will be required, and it will have many layers of armor and powerful shields, my love."

"I'm going to do battle with super-warships in an auxiliary?!" Winn asked.

"Only in the first moments of battle, then your ship and *Spalding* will retreat from the battle zone to reload small craft. You will have an adept on board, and hopefully, *you* will have attained the level of adept by then."

CHAPTER THIRTY

For the next 68 days, Bodhi spent about six days in each system he liberated, disarming imperials and getting them sorted out for shipping home to Nafs Ammara. Each planet population was made aware of the new threat and given tasks toward the construction of the two ships, and the overhaul of others. Planetary transports were all at work hauling parts and materials to two ship construction platforms, one in orbit of Ground and the other orbiting Kefra. Haley had the work going at a frantic pace around the clock with three shifts per day on eleven planets and had several others gearing up to this when it was time to join Bodhi in Finitolia to prepare for the two Scout Scavenger Intruders due in three weeks and a day. Major alterations had been made on *Diamond Lotus* to mount additional undercarriage missiles. *Spalding* had been refitted with a fifth solarium reactor and class 9 beam weapon this reactor was entirely dedicated to. Both ships now had undercarriage big missiles, *Diamond Lotus* with 12, and *Spalding* with 18.

Haley had kept her word and completed the nine small craft to replace the ones lost in the battle of Nafs Ammara. She also made one prototype of the Pronotavasmi heavy bomber. She named this class of small craft the "Tsunami Devastator" heavy bomber and constructed mounts for its berth on *Thor's* hull. Both of the 660-foot imperial ships they took over were at the Kefra ship construction platform, getting fitted with a solarium super-reactor and would not be ready for the opening battle.

Each of the two ships they would be facing was 6,800 feet in length, and quite wide, carrying 22 solarium super-reactors and 96 combat small craft. They also carried 40 combat shuttles and

2,000 Space Special Forces on each ship. Combined, they more than doubled the reactor power of Bodhi's three ships added together. They had more than twice as many small craft as Bodhi's force, but Haley had assured him that his combat craft would outperform and outgun the Consumere's one on one.

Bodhi trained long hours each day with his small craft pilots and put his ships' crews through maneuvers each day as well. He taught Jara and her friends Sandra and Thromp, along with Tipola how to accurately launch torpedoes and big missiles. They practiced the transference of consciousness and forceful projection together, reducing the time for leaving the body to only seconds. He also studied the solar system forming contingency plans for each place the invaders might jump in, and plans dependent upon where Finitolia's two moons would be at the time. An irregular asteroid some 139 miles in diameter had gotten itself caught in Finitolia's vortex and was now in orbit of the planet just outside that of the 2nd moon out, and Bodhi hoped it would be in the direction from which the Consumere ships jumped into the system at the time they did. It would make a perfect hiding place for a surprise attack. When time ticked down to the day the invaders had been predicted to come, Bodhi had his force make a two-hour meditation tuning themselves to the spiritual congress, convened on 40 planets and involving nearly the entire population of Ground and Pronotavasmi. The meditation was performed by all crew members at battle stations. Bodhi's daughters and the other children and the noncombatants of his *Diamond Lotus* crew from Firmament were all on the surface of Ground.

The moment their meditation concluded, two ships jumped into the Finitolia system 34,113,027 miles from the planet's outer moon. Bodhi launched his small craft, and the Tsunami Devastator dismounted from *Thor's* hull. The entire force went to wait behind the 2nd moon. The asteroid with a wider orbit was out from the wrong quadrant of the planet to provide a hiding place, so the plan now was for Bodhi to come out from behind the moon on the planet-side of it to attack the flanks of the two ships as they passed, and both *Diamond Lotus* and *Spalding* would come around the far side of the moon to attack the rear of the invaders. The small craft would hit the flanks of the two ships along with *Thor*. Tipola was on *Thor* with Bodhi. Jara and Sandra were on *Diamond Lotus* with Sunoco, and Thromp was with Clark and his pilot James on *Spalding*. These adepts could see soft spots in riled up shields and fire torpedoes and missiles accurately. Finitolia had one space station with saturnium reactors and weapons systems though this was over the horizon of the planet from the invaders approach.

Tish powered the drives to full and employed an acceleration booster and thrusters, tearing out at the ships from behind the moon. Only the class 9 beam and blaster had range from here and were already burning into the shields of the closer ship. Many small craft were pulling ahead of *Thor*, able to accelerate faster. The two invader ships were cruising at .22 light and still slowing while launching their small craft in continuous streams. The closer ship returned fire with its class 9 weapons pounding *Thor's* shields. The second ship was along-side the other so that Bodhi's ship had no shot at it and neither could it fire upon *Thor*. A Corvette Thunder was hit with a big quad blaster and turned into a ball of explosion.

Tish opened up with her twin class 8 nose blasters while the class 7 twin blasters opened up firing on the Scout Scavenger Invader as well. Torpedoes and missiles started flying from Bodhi's small craft into the shields of the big ship they attacked. Bodhi's shields had dropped by 38% and were still falling. He left his body through his crown and spread little suns across the flank of the ship they were racing at, whiting out its sensors. Tish veered a little and was able to get the class 9 weapons hitting her shields, off of them for the moment. They had dropped to 48% by this time. Her maneuvers had saved her shields from several torpedoes and missiles, but these were curving around to come at her again.

Diamond Lotus and *Spalding* were catching up to the two ships from behind like two tiny mice chasing a pair of lionesses. *Spalding's* new class 9 beam weapon and Sunoco's class 8 twin nose-blasters were the only weapons yet in range on the two ships, but they were closing quickly. *Thor's* missiles and torpedoes began shooting out at the closer ship, and every single one of her weapons was now in range and firing. The invader's shields were splashing around with turbulence, and Tipola sent a pair of the biggest torpedoes, one after the other through a soft spot which had appeared, to blow directly on the hull.

The hull breached toward the bow, but no explosions occurred, and the shields of the ship were still stopping beam and blaster fire as well as other torpedoes and missiles. Bodhi told him, "Try three torpedoes next time and look for soft spots closer to the stern."

A small combat-craft battle was now waging all around *Thor* and the two invader ships. Bodhi hailed the captains of both enemy ships and told them, "The resources of this planet belong to the indigenous population. Your race has much to answer for. An alliance of 40 planets is going to end your entire population for good. Your days of planetary destruction and genocide have come to an absolute end. Soon you will discover your eternal just deserts."

"We are only little scout ships. When our full invasion force comes, you won't know what hit you. That little ship of yours is just a toy."

"If they come, we will destroy them to the last, then go to your galaxy and wipe out your mining community there. If your race comes here, they will be utterly exterminated."

"Systems still using star-gates can't hurt us."

"Watch, learn and die," Bodhi told him.

Tipola sent four torpedoes into the stern, which slipped through a soft spot in the shields, and the 2nd torpedo tore a hole in the hull, allowing the next two to blow well inside the stern. The big ship rocked with the internal explosion, and its shields went dead. Ordinance and blaster bolts ripped directly into the armor, piercing it in places, and the ship lurched off course right before it turned into a gigantic cloud of gas and particles. Bodhi said to the captain of the 2nd invader, "We can not only hurt you, but we are guaranteed going to kill you."

The captain of the in-tact invader was beyond worried. His sister ship's shields were still functioning when those torpedoes passed through them without blowing. Then his sensors all whited out and his ship was blind. These were weapons beyond anything his people had ever encountered before. He turned off from the planet a little and started accelerating toward jump speed, hoping to get away. This was not what they'd expected coming into a system with a star-gate.

June was leading the Astro Phantoms in her Tsunami Devastator on an attack run on the lone Scout Scavenger Intruder and through nearly 200 small combat craft. Each heavy bomber had a drone fighter-bomber flying alongside, and June had one to each side of hers, with two drone pilots in her cockpit. The drones each had twin class 5 nose blasters and two undercarriage big missiles, as well as two batteries of 16 canister missiles each. June's nose blasters were class 5, and her four quad turrets contained class 4 blasters. A big hit to her shields didn't take them down. An Astro Phantom flying near her in the lead blew into an expanding cloud of trillions of particles.

Keeping her nose blasters on a Consumere bomber, June blew it into a smear across space and then got her blasters biting into the big ship's shields. She had to speed up and headed more in the direction of the enemy ship to keep closing on it, and realized it was trying to get away. Tish had *Thor* accelerating beside the invader exchanging fire, and both *Diamond Lotus* and *Spalding* were on the thing's tail, raining hell.

Glaring little suns suddenly erupted around it, bow to stern, and June could no longer look directly at it for that moment it took her sensors to shade and darken the radiance. The blasts pelting her shields went wild, no longer hitting her. She saw a Consumere heavy bomber turn to close head to head with her, and one of her quad-gunners was already nailing it. June got her nose blasters on it and let fly a big missile. Another of her quad-gunners targeted the bomber, and then a 3rd started slamming it. Her copilot was shooting a gusher of canister missiles blowing one after another on its shields.

Neither bomber turned off or backed down, maintaining the collision course. Just a moment before impact, the other bomber exploded into gas and particles, and June flashed through the cloud with her shields sizzling. She had passed over the big ship and had to adjust her direction to catch up with it again, lighting thrusters and with everyone pressed into their seats.

Bodhi was comatose in his seat, planting suns on the invading ship out in space, and Haley was boring into it with the class 9 beam.

Tish had no shot with her twin nose blasters heading in the same direction as the other ship, running parallel to it, so she fired on small craft. They broke up immediately on impact with the class 8 blaster-bolts. Winn had her blaster burrowing into the invader's shields. Tipola was looking for a soft spot with missiles at the ready.

Sunoco was sticking close behind the enemy ship's stern pounding it with her class 8 twin nose blasters. Jara launched a missile through a soft spot, just trying it out, and it blew on the hull scorching it but didn't breach. Encouraged by her partial success, she streamed four torpedoes through the spot, which had shifted a couple of meters, but she got them aimed just on it. The first two shattered a section of the ship's rear, and the third shook the whole thing. The fourth entered through the hole blown in the stern, and the entire ship exploded into a giant sphere like a mini-nova.

There were still enemy combat craft all over the place. Only the Consumere bombers and heavy bombers had quantum drives, and all of these were at maximum acceleration striving to get away. The fighters and fighter bombers which didn't have them were not giving up in the face of insurmountable odds. They were fighting to the death, and in so doing, expressing a value of their culture. Bodhi offered life and relative freedom to any who would surrender, repeating this several times in their Consumere language. Just during the brief announcement a dozen fighters and fighter bombers were destroyed by his forces and some fleeing bombers as well. The Astro Phantoms were matching the increasing speed of the retreating craft while firing on them effectively.

The ultimate value of Consumere culture finally showed through, that of the ego out for itself alone, and whole wings and squadrons began surrendering, even some fleeing bombers. In the end, only one bomber jumped out of the Finitolia system without getting blown up, and 73 small craft powered down weapons and shields in surrender to be escorted to the Finitolia space station where they landed inside an interior hanger and crews disembarked. Bodhi took one of each kind of Consumere small craft they'd captured into *Thor's* hanger for reverse engineering. The seventy-three small craft pilots were also taken aboard *Thor* for questioning. The crews of the

Consumere small craft were placed on a star-gate dependent small luxury cruise liner of Finitolia registry, which would get returned to its planet of origin after dropping them off.

While the crewmen drank and dined aboard the luxury liner, the pilots sat in the senior officer's mess hall on *Thor*, under guard, awaiting their turns at being interrogated. Bodhi, Jara, Haley, and Commander Nelson conducted the interviews and put each pilot through a battery of psychological tests. Each pilot was subjected to the Bush Defensiveness Scale, the Chaney Violence Recidivism Assessment, the Trump Ego Magnitude Test, the Koch Psychopathy Indicator, the Morgan Greed Inventory, the Regan Memory Measure and exposure to numerous meaningless ink blots.

The chair each subject was seated in gave readings on their heart rate, blood pressure, body temperature, stimulus and arousal levels, adrenaline secretion, sweat, respiration depth and rate, metabolic rate, and biorhythms. Quantum computer algorithms determined the reliability and probability of truthfulness at each moment. Haley's optics contained a facial analysis of all lie-indicator tensions, and Bodhi had his intuitive sense from the state of contemplation. Jara's sensitivity was simply uncanny. Chemicals were employed on three pilots, and even with their training, they opened like shattered maracas spilling the beans.

This process had begun a little before noon and went into the wee hours of the clock night before the pilots were placed aboard the luxury liner with their crews. The interrogation team then ate ambassador rations together in the senior officer's mess to share and review their findings. Jara spoke first and stated, "It would appear that there are easily five years of resources left to harvest in the outer rim system they now occupy, though they all seemed convinced that our intervention with their ships will bring them sooner than that."

"Their function," Bodhi said offended, "was to take control of Finitolia from space and enslave the entire population, then begin compiling resources through slave labor."

Haley informed them, "I've sent two cloaked spy AI drone spacecraft out; one to the outer rim planet the Consumere are occupying and the other to their massive mining operation in their home galaxy of Citadel. The drone pilots are keeping them well out of range of the decloaking guns but will be able to get us a pretty good full-scan of the mothership and biggest warships. We will also know the moment they send out an invasion force."

"What are we going to do with the personnel on our hands?" Commander Nelson asked them.

Bodhi told him, "There is a research base on a remote island which is now deserted on Nafs Ammara. I thought we could contain them there with several dozen shield generator buoys anchored to the sea floor, surrounding the island. They will have no weapons."

Haley who was the one who located the island base commented, "There are food growing facilities on the base though they would need to be regularly supplied for certain things. There's a marsnium reactor powering the buildings. I've located 42 brand new navigation buoys large enough to house shield generators right on Nafs Ammara."

"Their mother ship was expanded twice from the initial construction and contains three concentric armored spherical hulls," Jara said with some anxiety. "Each construction expanding it took 25 years and initial construction of the core and original hull took the Consumere 30 years. The core was first designed as an orbital satellite with only weak thruster propulsion. It was not until the 2nd hull and framing was built tripling the diameter that they installed space drives; and it was not until a century and a half ago that they completed the third hull extending the diameter to 1200 miles that they were able to put quantum drives in it."

Haley noted, "The mothership has a beam weapon Om would classify as a class 11. Even the 29,630-foot diameter ship we are building could not sustain a hit from that weapon for more than 4.7 seconds. It has an enormous range too."

Bodhi suggested, "Jumping drones inside the mothership is the only way to kill it. Finding soft spots would only work if we annihilated entire sections down to the next layer of hull, and then down to the one after that. We will need to start practicing jumping drones into smaller and smaller spaces. I only want to work with folks on this who have the level to connect solidly with the spiritual congress."

"I could feel the energy, force and precision that they lent us through their unified focus," Jara shared.

"We will need to overhaul some of the big command ships we took over from the imperials," Haley informed them. "We could get seven solarium super-reactors into each one."

Bodhi suggested, "With one of those, we could channel the energy that would power weapons systems to reinforce shields and lead with that one, to catch much of their initial fire keeping it off the rest of us. It can be crewless and flown as a drone from another ship."

"Since we trashed their Scout Scavenger Invaders," Haley reasoned, "they are likely to probe the other stars in the neighborhood of Finitolia and discover other star-gates, then hit in a new place hoping for surprise."

"That's what I would do if I were them," Commander Nelson agreed.

"We better station some of our small craft in each of the 40 systems to watch for probes," Bodhi said, deciding on this.

"I'll try to establish a link with a few of their warship nav.-computers," Haley told them, "to learn their destination before they make their jump. I think I can achieve this with the spy android we have keeping an eye on them."

"What if their full invasion force arrives before we finish building *Oceanus*?" Jara inquired.

"We will attack with what we do have in an attempt to harass and stall them," Bodhi stated.

"We ought to try to get well ahead of our current construction schedule," Nelson asserted, "and be ready as soon as we possibly can.

"I've got all the gates linked and open to one another now," "Haley told them. "All 40 planets have their manufacturing data for what they are responsible for.

"There is still a great deal of training to be done with ship crews and pilots of small combat craft," Bodhi stated with some dread.

"We will need to involve more of each planetary population," Jara surmised.

"Do you think you could take the lead on that?" Bodhi asked. "I'm going to be instructing in the Top Gun School and working on meditation with my captains and senior students on the attainments needed."

"I'm going to plant myself on the ship construction platform in the Ground System and work out some superior efficiencies for the building procedures," Haley let them know.

"If you can lend me a shuttle and pilot," Jara informed Bodhi, "I can go to each planet and try to find ways to hurry things along."

"You will have a shuttle, pilot and body guard, Jara," Bodhi granted her request.

"We have more than a hundred and fifty times their population, and ought to be able to defeat them," Jara said encouragingly.

"I'm sure we have allies we don't know about in the Citadel Galaxy and possibly in the Burning Hope Galaxy now that the Consumere are operating here too," Bodhi said speculating.

"If I can get into their nav. computer I can download their star maps and send drones to explore and look for other threatened planet populations," Haley told them. "I already have the Om-Trident design for a six-direction gantry-crane space platform which will jump the efficiency on constructing *Oceanus*."

"Make one for the Kefra ship construction platform, as well," Bodhi suggested.

"I'll have two built," Haley agreed. "They will take about five weeks to construct and a few days to assemble in space."

"We'd best get these Consumere personnel secured on their island base on Nafs Ammara," Bodhi told them, "so we can get down to the business of preparing for the war that's coming."

"What if they try to take over the cruise-liner?" Jara asked.

"They can't," Bodhi replied confidently. "We installed heavy blast doors to the bridge and there's not a weapon on the ship. Besides, it can only take them through the 40 star-gates and not to a star outside them."

"I have no need to travel to Nafs Ammara," Jara informed Bodhi, "and would like to start my rounds on Pronotavasmi so I can collect some scientists and engineers to bring along. That way if any group is having technical problems we will be more likely to get those solved right on the spot."

"Sure. I'll escort you down to our hanger and see you off," Bodhi agreed. "Let me call June and find you a pilot. I think my senior student, Pam, is itching to get some time with you and she's an excellent pilot."

Bodhi looked to Commander Nelson and asked, "Could you find an elite Space Marine to serve as Jara's body guard for while she makes her rounds?"

"I know just the man," Nelson answered. "His name is Yamahah and he is a warrior monk keen on meeting an adept from Pronotavasmi."

Bodhi got June on coms, arranging for Pam to meet them in the hanger, and Nelson got hold of Yamahah directing him to the hanger. Bodhi led Jara to the big partitioned lift in the foyer off the bridge and they rode down together. Jara told him on the lift, "You surprise me, Commodore Bodhi. Your strategy was brilliant and you really can do the things that she does."

"Which who does?" he inquired, not quite following her.

"The Wu, your teacher. You learned well."

"She is so much faster at it than me," Bodhi admitted, "and I do not have her genius for leading squadrons of small craft."

"No, but you are an exceptionally elite small craft pilot all the same," Jara told him. "We need you leading the ships anyway; not the small craft. You must be our Admiral Swenah. Haley showed me the holos from the battle of Monarch."

"What a crazy nightmare that was," Bodhi said remembering.

"You performed exceedingly well in that battle Bodhi and you were hardly more than a boy;" Jara complimented him.

"I had just turned twenty the day before the battle," Bodhi protested the word 'boy'.

"Yes, just a boy," she reiterated.

"Do you see me yet as just a boy?" he asked a little offended.

"You are advanced well beyond your young chronological age and I'm beginning to see why you were selected for this. You inspire me with hope."

"We cannot afford to lose any hope," Bodhi shared his assessment.

"Nor can we afford to be less than pragmatic and realistic," Jara advised him. "There is something richly practical about you and you are particularly methodical."

They got off the lift in the foyer at the hanger airlock. It was aired-up and mechanics and technicians were busy rendering repairs to damaged small craft within. Pam and Yamahah were waiting just inside for them. Bodhi made the introductions then watched them board. Rather than compressing the air into tanks and opening the hanger bay doors, Pam maneuvered the shuttle into an airlock launch tube, sealed it behind her then received acceleration from the launcher shooting her out into space. Bodhi returned to the bridge.

Tish informed him, "The cruise-liner is already accelerating to jump speed heading for the gate. They will orbit Nafs Ammara until we get there and open the base."

"Is the fusion-reactor running?" Bodhi asked concerned.

"Yes," Tish answered. "We will need to start up the sewage processing plant and some other systems to get the base ready to accommodate them."

Haley told him, "I will go with you to Nafs Ammara to supervise the installation of the shield generators in the buoys, and help open the base. Then I'll return to Ground with you when you go to collect your children and the rest of your crew."

"Keep the tender or one of our shuttles with you," Bodhi directed. "I want you to be able to get back to *Thor* quick if you are needed."

"I will, and I'll come right away if you call," Haley assured him.

"I'm leaving four small craft here in Finitolia," Bodhi informed her, "to keep an eye out for probes and to destroy any that jump in. I'll get at least two small craft to each of the other systems. I've decided to send Clark to defend the ship construction platform in Kefra with *Spalding*. You'll have *Diamond Lotus* in Ground and Sunoco to defend the construction platform there."

"It takes them at least several months to get all their machinery and equipment unloaded from their ships in preparation for amassing resources from the planet and system they are currently exploiting, and they never stop and leave within this stage. Even though they have entered diminishing returns, their reaping remains far higher than when they were still having to train the population and construct the facilities and industries required for harvesting. We have at the very least a year and ten months before all of them will come, and much more likely three years and some months."

"We are extremely vulnerable at the moment," Bodhi pointed out. "How long until we're churning out Tsunami Devastators?"

"The production line is all set up and the first batch of fusion trickle-charge battery systems arrive on Ground in two days with shield generators from Pronotavasmi. The next day they'll be rolling out and put through test flights from the space station."

"We need them in every system," Bodhi stated, "but most of all in Finitolia. That is the most likely place for them to attack in reprisal right away. I'm bringing *Thor* back there as soon as I get these Consumere folks dropped off. Would you ask the elders on Pronotavasmi to get some heavy duty shield generators and solarium fusion reactors over to the space station at Finitolia, and to help with the upgrade?"

"I've texted them your request," Haley told him immediately, then added as it was coming in, "and they say that they will get right on it."

"Thanks Haley. I love you."

"I'm going to miss you, my love. Please visit when you're able."

"Believe me I will. My daughters and Winn are going to be staying in the Ground system in *Diamond Lotus*. Master Tipola will be living on *Diamond Lotus* too. Sandra is moving aboard *Spalding*."

"I think she has a thing for Clark," Haley shared.

"I believe he's single," Bodhi said. "It would be good for him and help his meditation along."

"She looks really hot and has the cells of a 22 year old," Haley said with a tad of yearning.

"She's hot for twenty-two even though she is 621 years old," Bodhi agreed.

"I'm so pleased that the people of Pronotavasmi are going to give you the cellular reversal of aging treatment. We will have more than five times as long together," Haley enthused.

"I hope it will not be all warrior, and at least part monk," Bodhi said hoping.

Winn told him, "You can come to Ground a few nights per week to visit me and Haley and to see your daughters. We will need to get another adept from Pronotavasmi aboard *Thor* so things will be covered in Finitolia while you are in Ground."

"Thromp had to return to Pronotavasmi for a few days to finish work on the new quantum jump navigator they've been developing, which is supposed to help us jump drones into ships, materializing inside their shields and hulls. When he's done there he will be shuttling to *Thor* in Finitolia."

"If he is long there, then Haley and I will come spend the night on *Thor* with you, and Kristy can watch the girls."

"That works for me," Bodhi said delighted.

"Kristy tried to finagle her way into accompanying Jara on her rounds but was told she is needed to care for Shanti and Artana. I think there is an attraction between them though and Kristy is just dying to study with Jara."

"Then I hope she gets the opportunity," Bodhi replied.

"Jara already agreed to give Kristy the treatment when we get it," Winn explained.

"Kristy's insight is profound for one her age," Bodhi thought aloud. "With a long enough life, there's no telling how much good she could generate in the cosmos; and as the consort of someone like Jara, I can only say wow."

"She brings trendy style and much eroticism to the realm of insight," Winn commented.

"She's a potent force for one so tiny and our daughters love spending time with her. No female seems able to resist her charms."

"She is so totally real and herself in bed," Winn shared.

"She is unabashed and exhibits a pronounced appreciation for feminine sexuality," Bodhi agreed.

"How was it being her action seal and guide for her divine union harnessing copulation?" Winn inquired.

"She pierced her own hymen and cleaned up before we started. I was the guide and recited the instruction but left her in control and she directed. She kept her heart wide open in connection. I was in pure empathy careful not to distract her concentration, and so tuned in to her that I had little of my own experience until the final contemplative union, at which point I was only aware of the divine."

"She loves you dearly and has a genuine deep fondness for you," Winn informed him.

"I'm quite fond of Kristy and appreciate her from a distance. She is truly a remarkable disciple and the dearest of friends. She also succeeds in the practice," Bodhi told her.

"After Winn," Tish commented, "Kristy is the female I most enjoy sex with."

"Kristy took like three times as long doing her ritual with you than anyone else," Winn mentioned.

"She is very meticulous with her meditations," Bodhi offered as explanation.

"She told me that she lingered," Winn shared, "after the meditation was finished to have three orgasms mounted on you."

"Well, there was that," Bodhi admitted. "I was just seated in meditation and I think the discovery of her p-spot spurred that on."

"We could never find a better nanny for the girls," Tish added.

"How is Fritz doing?" Bodhi inquired.

Winn explained, "He's real into Penny now but they let me join them sometimes for a sleepover when you're not available."

"They're real fun," Tish shared cherishing her memories. Then she added, "I've started the 10-second countdown to quantum jump. We'll be in Nafs Ammara in moments."

CHAPTER THIRTY-ONE

They got the Consumere personnel set up on the island base on Nafs Ammara and the shield generator buoys anchored around it. One could swim beneath the shields, but it was 40 miles to the nearest land and they would not be able to get a raft or water-going vessel underneath the shields. The research equipment was primitive, pre-quantum coms and marsnium based, so there was no fear that they could produce a powerful weapon there. Haley remained on the space construction platform once they reached the Ground system and Winn and Tipola transferred to *Diamond Lotus* to remain in there.

Bodhi returned to Finitolia and stationed *Thor* there. Within a week he began receiving two Tsunami Devastator heavy bombers each day. After three weeks the first overhauled 3,900-foot command warship, refitted with six solarium fusion super-reactors, arrived in Finitolia. The Pronotavasmi engineers finished installing new reactors and shield generators in the Finitolia Space Station, increasing its shield capacity by thousands of times what it had been. Three sizes each of missiles and torpedoes were also installed along with a class 9 beam and four Class 8 twin blasters. Adamantine and carbon plate armor were also layered onto the outer skin of the station, and it would no longer be easy to destroy.

The very next day both 660 foot captured imperial ships refitted with one solarium reactor each and new weapons systems, arrived to join Bodhi's ship squadron. One was called *Ranger*, commanded by Commander Roberts, and the other was named *Legionnaire*, and Commander Potter was in charge of it. The command ship was *Trooper*, and Captain Mason ran her as a tight ship. An adept from

Pronotavasmi, named Hamah, was stationed on Captain Mason's bridge and Thromp had joined up with *Thor* having completed work on the quantum jump navigator. A drone jump simulator, based on the navigation equipment Thromp designed, was now being mass produced for training purposes.

Winn and Haley had come to spend the night with Bodhi several times in his absence. Once Thromp joined him, Bodhi went to Ground to see his daughters and to spend the night on *Diamond Lotus* with Winn and Haley. Between Jara and Haley at least 10 million more people were now involved in building the two big ships, small craft, and refitting command ships with solarium reactors and more advanced shields and weapons systems. Ore haulers and material transport freighters jumped into Ground every few hours from the Abundance and Overflowing Systems to unload at the ship construction platform. Haley's six-way gantry-cranes on mobile space platforms were ready in a few days shy of 4 weeks, and increased the building pace considerably. They were now on track with a new schedule which would see the ORH ultra-super ship completed 6 months earlier than the original plan.

Thirty-one days after the battle with the two Scout Scavenger Intruders, almost to the hour, six of the big Intruders appeared suddenly within the Finitolia System. Alarms from two spy-drones sounded on *Thor's* bridge and a dozen small craft reported the invading ships over her coms. Bodhi began arranging his forces based on strategies he'd worked out in advance. Sunoco was on her way in *Diamond Lotus* from Ground and Clark was racing *Spalding* to jump speed to get there. At the moment Bodhi had four ships to deal with the situation, with a combined total of 20 reactors. The six Consumere ships had altogether 132 reactors. *Spalding's* 5 reactors and *Diamond Lotus'* 4 would only bring Bodhi's total to 29. He had 52 Tsunami Devastators in the system and 94 small craft leaving *Thor* to get into position for battle. The invading Consumere had 576 small craft not counting their 240 combat shuttles. Neither of Finitolia's moons nor the irregular shaped asteroid would work as cover to launch an attack from, given the direction the intruders were coming from.

Bodhi set *Ranger* and *Legionnaire* on an arcing trajectory which would bring them around behind the large enemy ships while he led *Thor* and *Trooper* on an angled intercept that would allow them to turn onto the same heading as the invaders so as not to let them just pass by. A wing of his Tsunami Devastators was already hitting the small craft pouring out of one of the big ships. The 3,900-foot command ship, *Sentinel,* captained by Link, was in its second day of its test run but started accelerating to jump speed headed for Ground's star-gate to jump into Finitolia and join the fight.

Bodhi had all his own small craft launched plus 52 of the Tsunami Devastators flying with his two main ships. The Finitolia space station would have range on the enemy ships not long after the moment Bodhi's group would. Only about 10% of the Consumere small craft had yet been launched from the six big ships by the time Bodhi closed on them shooting. Three Intruders had line of fire on *Thor,* and another was maneuvering to achieve the same. Bodhi watched his shields as they dropped rapidly. Eleven Consumere small craft were blown to smithereens by a wing of four Tsunami Devastators before one of those was destroyed. The other three kept on blasting small craft coming out the bay doors of the lead Scout Scavenger Intruder. Six other wings of the big Pronotavasmi bombers were coming from behind the launched Consumere fighters and bombers, holding the advantage, which would not last long as the enemy numbers grew.

Bodhi's shields were dipping below 50% already, and still in descent thrashing wildly, but then so were the shields of two of the big ships. Thromp let fly a string of five torpedoes which slipped right through the shields of the second ship to resound in a staccato of explosions, the last of which was the biggest, blowing the entire ship to vapor and atoms. The rate of Bodhi's dropping shields slowed with a third of the hits to them suddenly silenced. Uduak and Bodhi got their class 9 weapons on the lead Intruder and a class eight quad-blaster started ripping into that one too. Tish was showering it with canister missiles and at least half a dozen big bombers were blasting it and raining missiles onto it.

Thromp was seeking a soft spot in the shields of the Consumere ship just behind the one Bodhi was firing on since it was just trashing *Trooper*. Not finding one, he flew out of his crown into space erupting mini-suns from bow to stern along one flank. Captain Mason managed to veer out of the fire from the Intruders heavy weapons and to dodge a few torpedoes and missiles as well with the big ship blinded. He was still under fire from another Intruder and his shields were crashing.

Bodhi sent four of *Thor's* largest torpedoes right through the shields of the ship most of his weapons systems were hitting, where only a film of energy held them together, and the ship was hulled bringing down its shields. Missiles and torpedoes continued to fly from it and its beams and blasters carried on as if nothing had happened. Then Tish directed *Thor's* beam weapon where Uduak was punching it with the class 9 blaster and a section of the starboard side towards the stern caved in, turning the entire ship into an explosion.

Trooper's bow was breached and she turned from the fight to flee. She was still taking hits and scorched badly with whole sections of her armor torn up. Then *Spalding* was between *Trooper* and the Intruder trying to kill her, taking the hits on fresh shields and drilling into the attacking ship with its class 9 beam. *Trooper* was racing out of the battle zone and released a molten flare shield antimissile countermeasure off her stern catching and blowing the stampede of missiles and torpedoes on its tail. The ship was moving swiftly out of range and would survive.

Ranger and *Legionnaire* were harassing the stern of the rear Intruder like mosquitoes biting an iron bull when *Diamond Lotus* arrived gnawing into the ass of the big ship with twin class 8 nose blasters and shooting off big undercarriage missiles. No way could this take down the shields of the *Intruder* but it was enough to get them stirred and turbulent. Both of *Diamond Lotus'* class 6 blaster-quads joined in the pounding. Tipola exploited a soft spot sending five big undercarriage missiles through to blow between drive flute nozzles, piercing the stern armor and the hull by the 4th missile. The fifth did-in something within that blew the whole ship apart in a colorful expanding cloud of fine debris and gas. Bodhi was taking most of the enemy fire in *Thor* though *Spalding* was getting her share and wouldn't last long. Bodhi flew out to the top of his head and completely covered the two lead ships with mini-suns—really super-bright ones. Coming up out of a coma a second later he told Clark, "Get out of there, your shields are down to almost nothing."

"Three seconds!" Clark shouted. "Sandra's firing the undercarriage missiles."

Bodhi watched as the missiles left *Spalding* front to back in a line of six. The first went through the shields like magic exploding into the hull. Then the second and third. The forth produced a breach and the last two entered the interior of the ship just as *Spalding* was already scotched down one side with a hole in the port bow. *Spalding* thankfully did not blow up. Bodhi ordered, "Get the hell out of the battle zone! That's an order, Captain Clark!" As *Spalding* turned off from the two remaining Intruders, Bodhi added, "Excellent work and most courageous Clark! Good shooting Sandra, and that was some flying James!"

Bodhi had the class 9 beam boring into the shields of one of the Intruders as he praised *Spalding's* people. Uduak was beating the same ship with the class 9 blaster. They were all moving in the same direction towards the space station which was laying down accurate heavy support fire, mainly into the lead ship. Some of the big weapons on the two Consumere ships shifted fire from *Thor* to the space station and Bodhi's shields held at 21% no longer dropping. From over a million miles away Sandra whited out both enemy ships with mini-suns so bright that they interfered with Thor's starboard sensors. Some blaster fire went high missing the space station altogether. Thromp started pumping torpedoes at the lead ship and they passed unscathed through the shields drilling through the hull and on into the interior. The ship burst into a spectacular explosion.

Sentinel was just engaging the rear Intruder, falling into formation with Diamond Lotus, *Ranger* and *Legionnaire* when the forward Intruder blew up. The last Scout Scavenger Intruder had four ships in its wake, Thor on its flank and the space station on its other flank, all hitting it with everything they had. It went blind as its sensors went white from glaring light all over its hull. Their shields were roiling and thrashing with turbulence chaotically as they dropped. Bodhi found a soft spot and started a stream of torpedoes into it at the same time Thromp did, and Tipola found one in the stern in the same moment shooting missiles into it. The big ship blew three ways to Sunday and when the cloud dispersed there was nothing left at all.

Consumere small craft remained thick and immediately became the focus of Bodhi's five ships and all his combat craft. With extra power and shields, instead of quantum drives, the survivability of the Tsunami Devastators was impressive. The six they'd lost so far in the battle had all gone down to heavy weapons on big ships. None had been killed by enemy small craft. With the energy for cloaking diverted to shields, the Astro-Phantoms and other classes of combat craft could sustain more direct hits and were performing really well. Bodhi knew that Consumere built highly sophisticated and enormously powerful ships but made less effort and had less interest in their small combat craft. These were most often employed on civilian and military groups on a planet surface and not in space close combat with other military vessels.

Bodhi was quite aware that his forces thus far had not defeated a single Consumere ship by actually duking it out. There was no way they could have. Blinding them and bypassing stirred up shields had enabled them to defeat two small scout forces; and it had been close both times. He asked Haley over coms, "Can you hack me into the Consumere network so I can offer surrender?"

"You're patched in," Haley replied.

"I hope my daughters are not aboard Diamond Lotus," Bodhi said sternly.

"Of course not!" Haley exclaimed offended. "I sent them off with Kristy in the tender the moment I arrived onboard."

"Thanks Haley, I love you," Bodhi told her. To the cockpits of the Consumere combat craft he said, "I offer you your lives and relative freedom if you surrender. Power down weapons and shields and slow to .01 light. We will cease firing on all craft which do. We will destroy all which do not."

The Consumere recognized their certain fate at the same time Bodhi made his surrender offer, and partly due to it. Only a few craft powered down weapons. The rest scattered in a mad rush of panic trying desperately to get away. The battle zone expanded exponentially following the fleeing craft. Every craft was frantically accelerating, burning up thruster fuel and cranking up drives to max power. The ships were not as fast at accelerating as the small craft but their missiles and torpedoes were even faster. The comet interceptors could run circles around Consumere fighters and so could the corvette thunders for that matter.

When getting away was not going to work out well for almost all of them, and this became enormously obvious, groups and individual crafts began powering down weapons and shields to reverse drives and slow to a crawl. The few left running away had lost their cover becoming magnets for all the fire and ordinance. Most of these were blown to bits and seven small craft were all that made it out of Finitolia alive. About 40 Consumere combat craft blew with the first big ship, never having had the chance to launch into space. The second big ship they blew had some small craft aboard too. June's small craft forces had wasted 154 of them, and the six ships still fighting at the end, plus Trooper and Spalding, had 149 kills. One hundred and ninety-two small craft had surrendered.

Only the ten ranking officers among those who'd surrendered were taken for questioning, and since Haley had already compiled a cultural profile on the Consumere they skipped right over psychological testing going right to chemical interrogation. What they were able to learn confirmed Haley's estimate of at least three years until the full force could arrive, but suggested that an attack on a different planetary member of their gate system would likely occur within about six months, and would likely involve eight or ten Scout Scavenger Intruders. This was not good news.

With so many captured Consumere combat craft Bodhi got busy training pilots to fly them, and Haley got busy designing better maneuverability, acceleration, and braking for the crafts. The surrendered personnel were deposited on the island base on Nafs Ammara and additional supplies had to be brought in for them.

The Consumere community on the base had a significant gender disparity and needed more females. Many worlds of the former empire had never recovered from losing most of their young men in their wars and defeat, so there were many white sun females willing to try living there.

Every ship of Bodhi's force suffered some damage and needed repairs. The repair work required for *Spalding* and *Trooper* was quite extensive. This drew resources from their construction and overhauling projects, slowing them a little. More labor resources were mustered on 40 different worlds and more of those people not directly involved in building the fleet invested in the spiritual congress strengthening it. Meditation instruction proliferated and initiations and empowerments into specific traditions were expanded greatly to be made available in every region of every continent on every world. The spiritual growth this caused was producing a unity and cooperation only ever seen before on the yellow sun worlds of Ground and Pronotavasmi.

Bodhi and Haley studied the star maps they had from the former Nafs Ammara Empire, and from their own drone and probe operations to date, seeking the most likely system for the Consumere to strike. They both agreed that the Ahma system was the most probable. Once Thor's repairs were completed Bodhi took the ship to Ahma and they worked on getting more combat craft into all the systems to hunt Consumere probes. Emergency rapid response plans were solidified to cover an invasion in any one of 40 star systems. Pronotavasmi heavy bombers continued to be produced at a rate of two per day and a new production line was under construction which would double this within three months. Ahma's space station was upgraded with solarium fusion super-reactors, more powerful shield generators and more of them, additional layers of armor, and some class 8 and nine blaster and beam weapons.

Two more six-way gantry-cranes on mobile space platforms were manufactured and then assembled in space; one for the ship construction platform orbiting Ground, and one for that orbiting Kefra. The peoples of all planets were put through space invasion drills which involved descent into Underground bunkers and armored shelters, or evacuation of population centers into caves, gorges, dense forests and other natural hiding places. Military defense forces were organized and armed on planet surfaces. Once *Thor's* hanger was replenished with combat craft new ones were dispersed to each system, and as soon as Haley's innovations were realized on the 192 just captured and the 79 they got from the first battle, these craft were distributed too.

Reports of Consumere probes detected—most of which had been destroyed—began reaching Bodhi by coms and his people stationed in Ahma found and blew up a number of these in the weeks following their last battle. The Consumere's intense interest in this conglomerate of stars connected by gates was made totally obvious to them. Their choice was clear too: die watching their worlds cannibalized and drained out or fight like all holy hell. The later was the unanimous choice of all of them. Production rose steadily as a result.

Bodhi ran his pilot training school and top gun close combat school from the Ahma system, and Sunoco continued to train pilots in the Ground system. With Tish's assistance Bodhi was also training ship pilots and captains or commanders.

Nine weeks after the battle no attack had yet come from the Consumere and the 3,200-foot Auxiliary and Reloading Ship was fully overhauled. It had exceptionally powerful shields, contained six solarium super-reactors and had a class nine beam weapon, twin class 8 nose blasters, four class seven quad-blasters, eight class 5 quads, and twelve class 4 blaster quads. Two large magazines of the most powerful missiles had been installed, and 22 undercarriage mega-missiles were mounted as well. It also had 128 canister missiles, two cloaked mobile smart mine nets and two countermeasure molten flare shields. Mounts on the hull for 16 Tsunami Devastators had been affixed and numerous small craft reloaders covered the rest of the outer hull. Winn would be the captain of this ship and its pilot too. She named the ship *Penthesilea*. An adept from Pronotavasmi whose name was Tara was assigned to Winn's ship and the ship joined *Thor* in Ahma.

Another gigantic construction platform was nearing completion in the Overflowing star system where framing and hull materials were most available. Before the construction platform was even finished work commenced on an ORH Super-Battleship, 8,100 feet in diameter, containing 30 solarium super-reactors. It would carry 118 combat craft and have mounts for 36 heavy bombers to berth on the hull through quantum jumps. Admiral Swenah had captained one of these, called *Apollo*, on a mission with Pez. A most demanding schedule was set for the construction of this ship, and several million more workers were recruited into mining, manufacturing and ship construction.

The 3,900-foot command ship with all shields and no weapons, to be piloted remotely and which would carry no crew, was overhauled with solarium reactors and super-shields. It would lead the charge and take the initial Consumere fire when the war arrived. This ship was named *Defender*. Their last command ship was also overhauled, and it was named *Protector*. Each of the overhauled command ships, except *Defender* which would be unmanned, would carry 112 combat craft and have twelve Pronotavasmi heavy bombers mounted to their hulls.

Eleven weeks after the battle, probes were seen frequently in the Yakutastan system so Bodhi moved *Thor* and *Penthesilea* there as well as his pilot schools. Work refitting the system's space station with solarium reactors, better shields and weapons systems was begun immediately. *Sentinel* and *Protector* remained in Ahma. *Trooper* watched over the ship construction platform in Kefra since *Spalding* was still getting repairs to its hull and armor. *Diamond Lotus,* plus *Ranger* and *Legionnaire* each with only one reactor, remained in the Ground system to defend the construction platform there.

The quantum jump simulator was replicated hundreds of times and these were all in use after tracking down and identifying their very best drone pilots. The best of the best received specialized training and some defunct transports were located and employed as actual targets for real-life practice. Both Sonic and Kristy turned out to be elite drone-fighter aces and intuitive artistic pilots of quantum jumping.

Firmament was gearing up for a 4th season of *Lost in Space* which would include the two battles fought with the Consumere, and to Bodhi's horror, the first three seasons began airing on every one of the 40 planets. Bodhi remained the comic relief of the show and the people of Pronotavasmi found the holo-series to be absolutely hilarious. Jara often fed the lines of the actor playing Bodhi on the show to Bodhi in actual situations, and many people imitated Bodhi's character portrayed on the show, when around him. He was able to distance himself emotionally from all of this except when his whole crew was engaged watching an episode.

More Pronotavasmi adepts were trained in operating and fire control of the big missiles and torpedoes and practiced leaving their bodies to illuminate suns so they could be assigned to ships. Tipola, from Ground, remained aboard Diamond Lotus. Haley was able to get away from teaching technology and from manufacturing and construction oversight to spend a couple of weeks meditating with Bodhi, and she achieved her actual rainbow body of light during this time with his guidance. Tish accomplished this next having Bodhi available to her living on the same ship. Winn and June were both getting close, and Pam was working on hers too.

CHAPTER THIRTY-TWO

The 1 ¾ miles-long ship was already framed when Bodhi had begun liberating the former planets of the empire and was nearing completion when another Consumere task force of eight Scout Scavenger Intruders jumped into the Yakutastan system heading for the 4th planet from the star. *Thor* and *Penthesilea* were already in the system with 50 Tsunami Devastators. *Thor* carried 94 small craft, 44 drone-fighter bombers and had an additional 22 heavy bombers attached to its hull on mounts. *Penthesilea* carried no small craft but had 16 heavy bombers mounted on its hull. There were an additional 34 combat craft of various classes in Yakutastan at the moment as well.

The four 3,900 foot 7-reactor command ships were all on the way to join the fight along with the two 660 foot one-reactor ships and *Diamond Lotus* with four. Clark was arguing with the chief engineer in charge of *Spalding's* repairs but could not convince the man to let him take his ship into battle. He finally boarded an Astro Phantom heavy bomber with James as pilot and Sandra on board to work her magic, and they accelerated to jump speed heading for Yakutastan. Combat craft from many other systems were also on their way. The Yakutastan space station's overhaul had only been completed days before.

Bodhi preferred dealing with these eight Intruders in a separate battle to facing them as part of the total invasion force when it would come.

Jara was on the bridge with Bodhi and Tish. Thromp had transferred to June's Tsunami Devastator, leading the combat craft. Bodhi had enough heavy bombers to get enemy shields stirred up, and enough adepts to blind their foes temporarily in battle and to take advantage of soft spots in turbulent shields, but the initial battle was between his 18 reactors and the enemy's 176 reactors. The difference in sheer force was very close to 10 to 1. The eight Intruders carried 758 combat small-craft. Bodhi had 238 as the two forces closed for battle. His were all out in space, and the Consumere was just beginning to launch theirs.

Bodhi and Winn got their heavy bombers released from their hull mounts and speeding alongside into the fray. He dictated the strategy to her, "I'm going into an arc with most of the small craft so we can intercept them on their flank, turning onto their precise heading. I need you to attack head on and pass them. *Penthesilea* is our only reloading ship in the system, and no more are coming, so after your initial pass, keep just outside the battle zone, and small craft will come to you to replenish missiles and torpedoes, thruster fuel cells and boosters."

"Aye, aye, Commodore," Winn acknowledged, though not liking it.

Bodhi added, "Do not go between them, you wouldn't survive that, and I cannot go on without you, my love. Pass outside their group along one flank and have Tara plant suns to blind them. If you do it that way, you ought to get through without much damage."

"I will Bodhi, but you be careful too because I can't live without you, either," Winn told him passionately.

"I'll be as careful as the situation allows."

Just as Winn was flying into range, more of their own ships and small craft jumped into Yakutastan, and Tara left her body on the bridge to go out in space, planting mini-suns on the flanks of the enemy ships. These had slowed to .17 light by this time, and Winn was braking hard with thrusters and drives from .12 light. She was only in range for less than 2 seconds, and they passed each other a little faster than accurate target resolution could be made, taking few hits to Penthesilea's shields. Her own ship's shots were rather wild as well. She knew she was merely providing a distraction for Bodhi to get into position. She also knew that *Thor* was no match for even one of those Intruders, let alone eight of them. She kept Tara at the task of planting suns on Scout Scavengers since distance was irrelevant to destinations when travelling by rainbow body. This action did likely save *Thor* from total destruction.

Tish was on a mean turn tight as *Thor* was capable of, coming in at a slight angle to the Intruders but basically on the same trajectory. Bodhi had 30 of the Tsunami Devastators assigned to the system with him on his attack run plus the 22 which had been mounted on his hull. The combat craft from his hanger were mostly ahead of him engaging in battle ferociously and killing many Consumere small craft as those exited their ships. He went to work in space planting suns while Tish and Uduak fired the class 9 weapons. Even with the ships that had aline of fire on him blinded completely, enough random fire was hitting *Thor's* shields to start them plummeting.

The big bombers had the shields on one of the Intruders all riled up, and the one the two class-nines were pummeling was showing soft spots in its shields too. Jara got busy lobbing torpedoes into one of these and was rewarded with an exploding ship. Nearly two-thirds of its small craft got blown up with it. Bodhi said loudly, "Great shot Jara!!"

The planetary space station was just starting to peak over the horizon of Yakutastan from its orbit and was not yet in range of the space invaders. Bodhi had met them halfway to the fifth planet's orbital path far from the planet he was trying to defend. If it were not for all the illuminating suns he and Jara were generating, *Thor* would likely be a mist of quadrillions of separating particles by now. Their ships and combat craft that had jumped in as Winn made her pass on the attacking Intruders were coming fast and slowing down for engagement, though not yet in the battle.

The small craft battle had begun quite one-sided, and June's forces had been able to destroy dozens while they were leaving out their bay doors, but as their numbers fighting in space grew, her edge and kill-ratio dropped significantly. Bodhi had to pause from making mini-suns so he could direct his newly arrived forces, forming them up effectively. This meant more hits to *Thor's* shields, which increased anxiety for his crew and lowered the effectiveness of the shields by 22%. The battle was closing on the planet, and Bodhi was concerned the seven remaining Intruders would split up and attack it. He was sure glad they had put this planet's population through a sequence of space invader drills and hoped with all his heart those would pay off.

Determination was written all over Tish's face as she piloted Thor firing a class 9 beam weapon at the same time. A pair of big enemy ships pulled slightly away from the pack to get direct fire on *Thor*. Shields went into freefall. Bodhi went into space sprouting suns bow to stern down the two ships trashing his. Jara and Tara were already out in space, doing the same. When he returned to his body to find his shields diminished to 11% capacity, Bodhi fired a launch-stage booster and blew out of the immediate battle sector to survive. His shields had fallen to 3% by the time he was out from under heavy fire, and they went instantly on the rise.

The space station was in full view above the horizon and had range on the invading ships with its class 9 weapons opening fire on them. Bodhi was veering back into engagement. His other war ships had finally acquired range on the stern of the enemy ships with their biggest weapons, and the newly arrived combat craft were already integrated into the melee. Bodhi went out to manifest more mini-suns. As *Thor* joined the battle a second time, her shields had returned to 91%. They started dropping instantly once the attack was on again.

Bodhi had directed his drone ship *Defender,* which was all shields and no weapons, to come around with his two smallest ships containing only one reactor each to help defend the space station. *Diamond Lotus* and his three 3,900 foot 7-reactor ships with weapons were shortening their distance to the Intruders, following in their wake. His meager force was only able to get the enemy shields thrashing and not able to kill one of them, at least not without hitting their hulls directly by passing shields with torpedoes through soft spots.

The space station started taking the majority of enemy fire, and *Defender* moved in front to protect it, taking the hits to its own shields. *Ranger* and *Legionnaire* were firing every weapon into the lead ship from either side of the space station. Bodhi flanked the enemy ships on their starboard side while hitting them hard.

Just when Jara started a line of torpedoes through a thin film in an Intruder's shields, *Legionnaire* burst into a gas cloud, killing everyone on board, including the Pronotavasmi adept named Vipp. The ship Jara hit burst apart in an explosion seconds after *Legionnaire*.

Defender had to bug out once its shields were almost taken down, and as soon as it moved away, the space station was the main target of enemy fire again. An Astro Phantom with James flying bobbed and weaved as it came head-on with the Consumere ships. The invading ships had reduced speed to .12 light, which was their standard combat speed when attacking, and Clark's little Astro Phantom was slowing to .11 light. Sandra shot four torpedoes through a weak spot in the lead ship's shields, and the 4th one blew the bow off of it, causing the ship to careen into a slow end over end turn, angling off from the direction of the rest of the invading task force. Clark's Astro Phantom shot down the middle and between the five big Scout Scavengers, miraculously avoiding their heavy weapons to pass on behind the group practically unscathed. Bodhi had been out frantically planting suns all over enemy ships sure it was going to be the end of Clark.

As they came into close range with the Yakutastan space station, a very large section caved, then the entire station resolved into a giant gas cloud utterly destroyed. Grim determination lined Tish's face, and Bodhi was speaking rapidly into his coms, giving orders and rearranging his planetary defense. Jara was out emitting suns over enemy ships. The five Intruders were making a pass on the planet, and this was Bodhi's worst nightmare. Satellites orbiting Yakutastan started popping into colorful vapor clouds, and explosions on the planet surface were visible even from space.

Bodhi sank deeper into contemplation, connecting solidly with the spiritual congress supported by billions of people in pristine states of meditation. He noticed a soft spot in the shields of the Intruder closest to *Thor* in the same moment he started sending torpedoes into it. As the 5th one was just launching, he shot into space planting suns. *Sentinel* was getting beaten up pretty bad, so he focused on the ships in the rear, which were nailing it. The command ship's armor was torn through in places, but the hull had maintained its integrity, and it was able to drop out of the fight to stay in one piece.

Ranger took some damage as the four remaining Invaders drew past it. Haley came around the curve of the planet from low orbit in a combat space shuttle she'd taken from the Ground ship construction platform, headed at the underbellies of the Consumere ships. She avoided the worst of their fire by making minute truly random maneuvers as she sent her four big undercarriage missiles, followed by 32 canister missiles, into a weak film in the shields of the one closest to the planet, which was the one doing the most damage. The big missiles just managed a small hull breach, but 26 canister missiles made it inside the ship before the soft spot shifted position frying the last six on the shields.

The big ship rocked with explosions for several seconds before something highly explosive within blew up big-time taking the whole ship with it. Haley let out a war-whoop holler as she disappeared into the fray of small craft combat. Bodhi said into Haley's coms, "Way to go, sweetheart!"

An Intruder began to dip towards the planet as a major population center was coming around from over the horizon. At the same time, June's Tsunami Devastator was rushing its flanks. *Protector* was pouring out ordinance onto it, and some of *Thor's* guns were tearing into its shields. It was enough to show a soft spot, and Thromp in June's cockpit launched torpedoes through it. Jara loosed four torpedoes at a spot that revealed itself to her on the same ship's shields after Thromp's were already away, and there was nothing but vapor when they arrived and passed through the expanding cloud which had just been a ship.

The two remaining Intruders hit thrusters and powered drives to full throttle turning from the planet towards space. *Thor* fired thrusters matching their speed and continued to harass them. *Trooper*, *Protector*, and *Diamond Lotus* increased speed as well, keeping up. So did all their small craft. The two Intruder captains were horrified. They had witnessed three Scout Scavenger Intruders, each with 22 fusion super-reactors, get wasted by tiny small craft, each with only a fraction of one reactor. This flew in the face of everything the Consumere thought they'd known about space combat. Both captains were sending the battle data back to the mother ship and trying their best to get to jump speed to get the hell out of Yakutastan.

Penthesilea was moving to intercept them, and Bodhi told Winn, "Don't engage. We have this. Get out of range now!"

Diamond Lotus was right on an Intruders ass digging into it with class 8 twin nose-blasters and both quad-blasters. *Trooper* was pouring some fire and missiles into this one too, so its shields were in a tempest. Tipola sent the last six big undercarriage missiles into a thin film a meter and a half wide, invisible to all but adepts who could see auras. The fourth missile attained hull breach, the 5th widened it, and the sixth went inside to blow up, causing a chain of explosions up the length of the ship, which became a gas cloud before reaching the bow.

The last Intruder fired an acceleration booster and lit all forward thrusters with drives powered to full. Bodhi was about to spend another stage booster on *Thor* when he saw their drone ship *Defender* come almost head-on into the Scout Scavenger Intruder at a combined speed of .29 light. Truly an impossible and lucky shot. Bodhi could hardly believe it. The loss of the 7-reactor drone, with no crew aboard, was a great deal in exchange for a killer 22-reactor monster of a manned and deadly warship. Bodhi was pleased and wanted to know who the drone pilot was. He exclaimed through his coms, "Who was flying that?!"

From Diamond Lotus, seated on the bridge in the drone-pilot seat, Kristy told him, "I was. I hope you don't mind."

"That was incredible! I loved it! You are the one who will learn to jump drone fighter-bombers into ships inside their shields!"

"I think I can do that," Kristy informed him.

Jara told Bodhi, "I'm going to start training and mentoring that girl."

"She is an amazing disciple and an exceptionally sexual being who is into females," Bodhi replied. "It would be really good for her, and I think you have some attraction going between you."

"I'll not deny my attraction," Jara informed him, "but my aim is to help her bloom. I've never seen such high realization in one so young, except for you, ever before."

Haley asked over coms, "Permission to come aboard, Commodore. I'm right outside your bay doors."

"Permission granted and welcome aboard. Have the Lieutenant on the flight deck open the doors. They may need to suck all the air out first. Great shooting, my love, and in a combat shuttle no less!"

"I learned a few things flying with you in the battle of Monarch, and since then," Haley replied.

Tish told Haley, "You are my hero, sweetheart, and your feats make me hot for you."

"Well I'm yours then, dear love,"

Winn's voice came over the coms on the bridge, complaining, "Bodhi! You never let me get into the action. I'm not fragile, you know. I think this is discrimination, and I demand an independent investigation into the matter!"

"You may be right, sweetheart," he partially agreed. "Let's get these combat craft surrendered or killed before we discuss it, please."

"Alright. But I'm not dropping it."

Bodhi asked Tish, "Would you make the offer of surrender when Haley gets up here and gets us patched into the Consumere coms?"

"Sure, and I can patch in. Haley showed me how."

To the Consumere combat craft, Tish said, "If you surrender, your lives will be spared and you can live in relative freedom on an island, planet side with others from your culture. If you persist in fighting, you force our hand, and we will have to destroy you. Power down weapons, and we will stop shooting at you. Then power down shields and slow to .01 light, headed for the 4th planet."

More tried to run than powered down weapons, so Tish repeated the offer. More complied, accepting the offer. More were blown to microscopic bits. The battle wound down slowly with more surrendering than getting blown up. Fourteen escaped jumping out of the system. They captured 241 combat craft. Officers underwent chemical interrogation. The Consumere personnel were collected, placed on a transport and shipped to Nafs Ammara to be dropped off on the island. Some additional construction on the base was planned to begin immediately, and a good deal of supplies was brought in.

The small craft were shipped by transports to Ground, where they would undergo upgrades and installations of accessories before being divided for deployment in the 40-star systems.

Haley checked the spy drone and probe data from the outer rim system and the system in the Citadel Galaxy and reported to Bodhi, "There is no movement toward pulling up stakes or even mustering another invasion task force by the Consumere, and their surviving and escaped small craft have returned there."

"Set alerts so that if they do take action in one of those directions, we'll know right away. Until *Oceanus* leaves the construction dock, we remain enormously vulnerable."

"Once Kristy realizes her full potential, all you'll need are drone fighter-bombers," Haley countered.

"I know! Did you see that? She's amazing! I only hope she comes into it *before* the Consumere arrive again."

"I have several drone fighter-bomber production lines opening in days," Haley shared.

"Are you making practice blanks too?" Bodhi asked.

"Yes. The first line to spit them out will be spitting blanks."

"Jara's going to work with Kristy, and I want her prioritized for simulator time and unarmed drone fighter-bombers."

"You've got it. I've entered it into administrative decision matrixes. I see a potential romance in Jara's mentorship of Kristy."

"At least their cells are the same age," Bodhi commented.

"Most alluring cells, too," Tish opined.

"Welcome aboard, Captain Winn, my beloved."

"Don't you 'beloved' me," Winn said with no little fury."

"Uh-oh," Bodhi commented, expressing his anticipatory anxiety.

Jara suggested, "You ought to make Winn the Captain of the ORH Super-Battleship under construction, with 30-reactors. I'm afraid anything else would be too little too late."

"I have been protecting Winn," Bodhi admitted. "Over-protecting, really."

Winn sat down on the bridge, having heard Bodhi, and asked facetiously, "No shit?"

"I'm making you the captain of the ORH Super-Battleship."

"Why? Because it will be finished last?" she challenged.

"You are *Penthesilea's* captain until the battleship is ready for you to take command. Haley thinks she might be able to cram 32 reactors into it. She's certain that she can manage 31."

Winn calmed down a bit at hearing this and told him, "Then I'll drop my demand for an independent investigation." To Tish, Haley, and Jara, Winn said sweetly, "Kristy and I are having a girl's party on Diamond Lotus tonight, and you're all invited."

She looked back at Bodhi and told him," You're taking a shuttle to Ground and looking after our daughters."

"OK," Bodhi said, defeated.

Kristy came over the coms to tell Bodhi, "You will have to pick up Rags and Shanti's favorite blanket from *Diamond Lotus* before shuttling to Ground, or you'll have the mother of all tantrums on your hands."

"Thanks, Kristy. I'll be over there in a few minutes."

Jara told Bodhi, "You don't make much of a first impression though you are a brilliant commodore and adept practitioner and teacher. And you're so very young."

"Thank you, Jara. You were magnificent and killed the first two Scout Scavenger Intruders in the battle."

"That we took three down from small combat craft is the most promising!" Tish exclaimed.

"I don't want that tried with any more shuttles," Bodhi said while looking at Haley. "It will work against the 50 half-mile ships mounted on the mother ship and the rest of their Intruders, but not their five-mile-long ships nor the mother ship. They also have massive troop transports and industrial ships that won't work with since small craft can't carry large enough torpedoes to crack their hulls."

"We need Kristy to get good at jumping drones," Haley stated.

"Sonic exhibited unusual artistry and natural talent on the simulator," Bodhi mentioned.

"He's one of the 99 we've started to train, and he will be prioritized for time and resources just slightly below Kristy," Haley informed him, having already analyzed all the data and made decisions based on that. Her motto was to *trust the Absolute, but everyone else must show data.*

June came onto the bridge, having recently returned to *Thor's* hanger. Bodhi told her, "You and Thromp did a great job out there."

"Thanks, boss," June replied. She then looked at Winn and said, "I'm coming to your party. Kristy invited me."

"Wonderful!" Winn enthused.

June suggested to Bodhi, "You should have a boy's party!"

"I'm already prescheduled for a sort of children's party," Bodhi explained.

"Pity," June told him, "Fritz would have jumped at the chance."

"I better collect a few things from my cabin then get on a shuttle," Bodhi said aloud as much to himself as to them.

Winn nodded in solemn agreement. Tish kissed him, then Haley did. Jara even kissed him, but not Winn. As he was walking off the bridge, Winn let him know, "Artana has discovered ravioli and is allowed to have it again tonight."

"I'll make that for her then," Bodhi complied.

CHAPTER THIRTY-THREE

Bodhi took a sleek comet interceptor instead of a clunky shuttle and stopped off at Diamond Lotus for Rags and the special blanket. Kristy had cheered him up a little when she told him, "You were brilliant! I think you're getting a raw deal tonight. You ran the battle perfectly, teacher."

Bodhi made jump speed swiftly in the zippy interceptor and didn't start slowing in the Ground system until he was 250,000 miles outside the moon's orbit. He lit all his braking thrusters just before entering the atmosphere, after reducing their speed with just reverse drives up to that point. The nose of his craft glowed red, then white. Bodhi expanded the fins into partial wings and used the flaps to pull up, changing his heading to more of an angle instead of straight down at the ground nose-first.

At 38,000 feet, he engaged his vortex redirect turbine at full power, repelling gravity. His braking thrusters were still burning, and the ground was rushing at him. At 4,940 feet, he got his orientation with his underside parallel to the planet surface, and slowed to 2,220 MPH, and headed for the home on the lake which the people of Ground built for his family. Uldra was there with her son William, and she was playing nanny to Artana and Shanti. She had a shuttle parked in the driveway and was eager to get back to Shamus on *Diamond Lotus* in the Yakutastan System.

When Bodhi landed and entered the house, Uldra's overnight bag was by the door, and she was in the foyer with her coat on, holding William in her arms. Bodhi kissed Williams cheek and was graced with a smile from him. Uldra kissed Bodhi's cheek and told him, "The girls are in the den, watching Looney Tune's holos. I have to run," as she walked out the door.

When Bodhi entered the den, the girls were watching a rerun of *Lost in Space*. Shanti told him, "Daddy, you're so silly."

Artana jumped with arms raised, and Bodhi scooped her up, lifting her to his chest. She looked him in the eyes and said, "Hi, daddy. We want ravioli."

Bodhi felt the need to provide his children with a brief educational moment and told them, "That is an actor pretending to be me, and he does not know me, nor has he even met me. I'm taller than he is, too."

Shanti clarified for him, "It's a show about Haley, daddy. Not about you."

"I'm simply pointing out that it's an inaccurate portrayal of me," Bodhi tried to drive it home.

"We're ready to eat," Shanti insisted.

She raised her arms in the air, and Bodhi picked her up with one arm, wrapping it under her bottom and leaning so she could grab around his neck. He carried both girls into the kitchen. They no longer sat in chairs with trays but instead upon meditation cushions, to raise them on the bench of the nook-table. They each had a little decorative sofa pillow on top of their meditation cushions and yet their chins were only inches above the table surface. It was undeniable cute but rather impractical in terms of full spoon-loads of food ever making it into a mouth. Some inevitably did on every try, but all that left the plate rarely did. It was a messy affair. *Life is messy*, Bodhi thought to himself. He was pleased he'd honed his galley-cleaning skills helping Tandy out for all those months.

Bodhi had to leave the kitchen in a wreck to give the girls a bath. They had tomato sauce all over them. He was soaked by the time his daughters were washed clean, including their hair. He got them into their flannel pajamas. He was then mercilessly attacked with pillows, and when the girls tired of that, they hid from him. They'd found a really good place too. Poor Bodhi wasn't trained for this.

His anxiety was rising through the roof when they finally took pity on him and were bored with hiding anyway. They came out to reveal themselves. They wouldn't let him in on their hiding place, though. Next, he was playing dolls, and he got to be Rags or animate Rags. He did try, but the girls were somewhat critical of his poor make-believe skills. When his daughters were both yawning, he took them to their bed and read them their favorite bedtime story. He had to read it twice and use a different voice for each character before they were satisfied.

When the girls passed into sleep, he cleaned the kitchen thoroughly, then practiced his soft martial arts. An hour of sitting, then his dream meditations lying on his right side concluded his day. He passed into deep sleep. Then he awoke only partly lucid in an unpleasant dream, in which the device on Ground berated him for being too young, making poor first impressions, having no charisma, being a fool and a loser on *Lost in Space* and for oppressing Winn. It then compared him to Haley as a way of burying him completely, singing her praises while providing Bodhi with stinging criticism. He finally became fully lucid and walked away from the demeaning device, which he knew was merely his own sense of failure and inferiority.

Then Pez was in his dream, only it really was Pez in his dream. She exclaimed, "There you are! You're not dead!"

"I'm lost in space," Bodhi explained. "Can you tell me how to get home?"

"I don't exactly have a navigation quantum computer in my dreamscape. I came looking for you in the Akashic records. You've been missing for years."

"Haley and I went down a worm hole and haven't a clue where we are. A very ancient race from Pronotavasmi tells me I have a mission to stop a planet-less race who are killing whole biospheres and planetary populations."

"Well, that sounds terrible. You better get it done."

"Haley is sentient and has gained not only insight but has attained her rainbow body."

"I know about the sentience and insight from Mel and Sarhi."

"I think the Amonrahonians are behind this. There's a device buried deep on the planet Ground, which was expecting both Haley and me."

"You have done very well, Bodhi, and have truly embodied all I taught you and what you learned at the Adamantine Will Monastery. I will try to find out from the Amonrahonians where you are located in the universe. I can sometimes connect directly with them through the spiritual congress. Do complete your mission, though."

"There is now a new chapter of the spiritual congress in this realm of the universe, so far all in the Burning Hope Galaxy, though I see it expanding into the Citadel Galaxy soon. We're constructing an ORH Ultra Super-Battleship, and we have already built and fought in a T-9. This race of destructive white sun humanoids has a mother ship, which is a 1,200-mile diameter sphere with two more interior hulls."

"I will do my best to locate you, Bodhi. You're my most promising disciple, and I have so much love for you. Gretle sends her love and her apologies for not going with you."

"I'm married to Haley, and to Winn and Tish as well."

"That doesn't sound like you," Pez wondered out loud.

"Haley manipulated it, but it's fine now, and I have two daughters. Look into the bedroom adjacent to this one, right through that wall," he pointed.

Pez walked through the wall into the other bedroom and took a good look at the sleeping girls. She returned to Bodhi's room, sat on his bed, and told him, "We do need to locate you. Those are the disciples of Electra's whom Sarhi has been looking all over for."

"I'm pretty sure we're supposed to be here in this space-time moment; at least that's what the folks of Pronotavasmi tell us, and that rude device on Ground."

"How many planet populations have participants in your new chapter of the spiritual congress?"

"Forty planets, and pretty much the entire adult populations of two of them."

"And I thought you were likely dead! You are doing an amazing thing here, my love, and must see it through to the end."

"I wish you were here leading us. I'd feel a whole lot better about it if you were."

"You're doing great. Just keep up the good work. I need you as Vicar General of the Adamantine Will Order. The Amonrahonians likely will not give me your coordinates until you've completed the tasks they've set for you. But I will find you."

"Why are you in a rough linen nightgown?"

"I'm in the iron age right now of a planet called Corruption, trying to wake these people from delusion and illuminate them out of their Dark Age. It's another Amonrahonian mission."

"What assets did you bring?"

"I have Captain Spalding with me. He's in orbit of the planet in *Auxiliary 2* and manufactures or fabricates whatever we need. I have warrior-maidens from Mother and a bunch of skinny people from Ganahar. It's a violet sun world, and the people are narrow as strings. I'm considered morbidly obese here, and so is Rubix, and even Whiffle."

"Anorexic Whiffle? I can't imagine."

"She's not technically anorexic because she gets adequate nutrition every day and does not starve herself. She just has a super-fast metabolism and narrow bones."

"How long will you be there?"

"At least another year, maybe more. They have a faux religion with no mysticism heavy with irrational dogma and all set up as an absolute totalitarian temporal tyranny. It will take some time. I have found some adepts here, though, and we are making progress."

"Please find us and help us get home," Bodhi pleaded. "I miss you more than anyone, and I miss Musash and Amazonia."

"Are your two human wives good students?"

"Tish just recently attained her rainbow body, and Winn is very close. She will do it soon. She's very upset with me right now for over-protecting her in our last space battle. She and I have past life history, and I'm pretty sure she is my soulmate."

"Then you better get your little spat behind you quick because trouble between soulmates is as disturbing as life can get. I tell you this from direct experience."

"I've owned my part and apologized already. I will again next time I see her. I think she will need to forgive me before things are truly set right."

"Work on it. I've got to go. I've already lingered long in the dream state looking you up in the Akashic records. I will return to your dream state from mine as soon as I complete my mission. Take care, my most accomplished disciple."

"I love you, Pez. Thanks. You bring me great hope."

"Hope is everything," Pez told him. "Goodbye for now."

Pez winked out of Bodhi's dream. It had really been Pez and not just something he dreamed. He truly felt full of hope. There was no one he had more confidence in than Pez. Her enthusiasm for his mission helped him embrace it utterly. He felt at peace as he slipped from the dream state into deep sleep. He did not even try to accomplish the work of deep sleep this night, instead, sinking into a most rejuvenating and nurturing sleep more vitalizing than he'd had in years.

Bodhi awoke, fully refreshed and happy. The girls were still in their bed and completely out, so he performed his energy generation exercises, then his soft martial arts solo form several times. The girls were still sleeping soundly, so he sat for an hour in pristine contemplation. When he arose from his meditation cushion he could hear the girls giggling in their bed, so he went into their room. They were excited to see him and insisted he gets in bed with them to snuggle. Both girls were extraordinarily sensitive and quite sentimental. Love became thick and dense in the bedroom.

He helped them get dressed. Both had completed their potty-training and wore big-girl underwear now with no feltex lining. They each wore their white with blue pin-stripes overalls and pink T-shirts along with stretchy cotton socks. Once dressed, he carried them into the kitchen for breakfast. It consisted of ambassador ration oatmeal and ambassador ration waffles, both self-heating. Bodhi was not much of a cook. The girls got apricot syrup from their waffles all over faces, hands, laps and the table and nook bench.

Another bath was required, and he put their overalls through a quick-cycle in the clothes washer-dryer machine. They came out still warm just as the girls were getting toweled off. The syrup had necessitated another hair wash for each of them, and Shanti went first with the hair dehydrator. Pez always called those 'hair dryer helmets.' It only took a few seconds, then Artana got her head in it. They adored getting into their warm cozy overalls. Bodhi's emotions always hit rapture-range when he was with his daughters. His love for them revealed an intensity he didn't know he'd had. They were just so cute and lovely that they sometimes took his breath away.

Their home on Ground was quite rural, and there was a county fair this day less than a hundred miles away. It would take 20 minutes in the little hovercraft parked in their garage, so he got both girls on his lap in the one-seater comet interceptor and lifted off from the driveway. Artana and Shanti were stoked. In less than three minutes, they were landing gently at the fairgrounds.

Rides towering hundreds of feet in the air covered several acres of land, and there were competitive games offering prizes to winners, food vender booths, various exhibits, and simulator experiences of all kinds. Most of the rides had height requirements for children, and the lower limit towered over his three-year-old daughters' heads. He tried to not even walk by those for fear of a tantrum. Prize farm animal competitions were in full swing but didn't interest the girls. Neither did the sheep shearing.

When they came to a little kid's *Lost in Space* ride with no height requirement, Artana and Shanti insisted on doing it. Bodhi acquiesced and they stood in line awaiting their turn. When they got to the front, a little convertible car on a track stopped before them, and they climbed in. It was made to look like a miniature space tender. Haley was featured prominently, and both of the girl's mothers appeared for quite a while. The Bodhi character had ridiculous lines, and Bodhi had to swallow his embarrassment. Shanti said loudly, "Oh, look, daddy! That's you!"

"It's supposed to be," he agreed, "but it's really nothing like me."

Their little car stopped in an accurate model of the galley on *Diamond Lotus,* and Favio was cooking and singing up a storm. In the cargo area, Shamas was moving enormous crates with his bare hands dressed in his wrestler's leotard. They got to see all the crew members presented quite positively. Bodhi took a deep breath dissolving his self-pity. The details of his ship appeared quite authentic. The girls were pointing and going over the top in their excitement. He was glad they were enjoying it. *Lost in Space* always provided some challenges for Bodhi.

Next, they went through tunnels and chambers in a little boat with robotic mannequins dancing and singing happy songs. It was not the ride the girls thought they were getting on, and did not go over a waterfall into a hundred-foot freefall. *That* ride had a 4-foot 9-inch height requirement. They couldn't get on any of the roller coasters, and this was a big relief for Bodhi. When both girls became enamored of the giant stuffed animals at a near-impossible dart throwing game, Bodhi tried to win one. He got into the flow state and focused on a target. He'd been given three darts to try and hit one. Kids and their parents were leaving this game in great disappointment. Before he got started, a local boy of about 11 told him, "No one has ever won at this game. It's rigged."

The targets were less than a square inch and 16 feet from the counter he had to throw from behind. He checked the tail of his first dart. The rear fins were crooked, and he would need to compensate for this. His other two darts were in just as bad shape. From the flow-state Bodhi threw the dart hard, putting a little spin on it, and it nailed the center of the target which tried to bounce the dart off of it, but Bodhi had sent it with too much velocity, and it stuck. The man running the game was both shocked and alarmed. The darts were supposed to bounce off, creating losers. For the first time in his long career, he had to take down one of the big stuffed animals from the top shelf in the back.

Bodhi nailed another target dead center with his second dart. It *stuck* too and did not bounce off. The man had to give up another giant stuffed animal and was not pleased. Bodhi aced it with his third dart as well. The stuffed animals were bigger than his daughters, which meant he would have to carry theirs, so he gave the third prize to the 11-year-old boy who was completely awed. The man in charge of the game asked him, "Who are you?!"

Artana spoke up first and informed the man, "He's the real Captain Bodhi, and he's my daddy!"

"*The* Captain Bodhi, like from *Lost in Space*?!" the man asked, hardly able to believe it.

The 11-year-old boy held out his pocket device and stylus to ask Bodhi, "Could I get your autograph?"

Bodhi took the stylus and signed while the boy held his pocket device for Bodhi to write on. Bodhi had to then pose with the kid for a holo-still taken by the game-man with the boy's pocket device. Bodhi was uncomfortable and wanted to get away quickly.

He was finally able to extract himself and his daughters from the crowd accumulating around them. As they started walking away, Shanti informed the people watching them, "This is *my* daddy."

They rode a few more rides for little kids and ate sugar hair-fluffs off of paper cones, which got both girl's faces and hands so sticky they had to find a bathroom to clean up in. They also had chicken on a stick with peanut sauce, which his daughters both liked well enough to finish off. A wipe to clean their hands was all that was required after that snack. A ball-throwing game caught their interest, and they insisted that Bodhi dunk the clown into the vat of water below. He had to hit a little 6-inch circle from 50 feet away with a ball. They gave out three balls with each turn. The clown was dry as a bone. Not many people were at this one.

Bodhi sank his breath into his lower abdomen and entered the flow state. He became the target then loosed the ball, putting some snap into it. The ball hit the little circle solidly with force, and the clown dropped right into the vat of water he'd been sitting over. He seemed annoyed as he clicked his seat back into position to climb back onto it. He wasn't used to getting wet. Bodhi dunked him twice more, and the clown's annoyance was at least equal to the delight of his daughters. The only prize for this game was getting to watch the clown get wet.

They went through a haunted spook-house, but this terrorized Shanti and made her cry, so Bodhi picked her up to carry her through the rest of the way. A most frightening pop-up was coming at them and was more than Shanti could take, so Bodhi gave it a snap kick before it got upright, putting it back down in two separate pieces. He grabbed Artana into his arms with Shanti and hurried through the rest of the spook-house. Going out the door, Artana stuck her hand in a basket with the label "eyeballs" and a picture of an eyeball on it, to then let out a horrified scream. Bodhi looked into the basket then told Artana, "Sweetheart, those are just peeled grapes. They're not real eyeballs."

He had only one tantrum to contend with at the fair when the girls could not get onto the space-launch ride for lack of height. He finally suggested, "Let me take you on a real space launch in the comet interceptor."

This seemed to appease them, and it would also get them away from the exhausting fair. They walked back to their craft after collecting the stuffed animals from the lockers they'd put them in. Each had required one of the big lockers all to itself. The girls each held some pants leg as they walked since Bodhi's arms and hands were preoccupied with the giant stuffed animals. Cramming everything into the one-seater proved a real complication. He did get both girls, and both even larger stuffed animals into the little cockpit at last. An animal head protruded a third of the way into his piloting holo.

The space-launch ride was like getting shot out of a cannon, so Bodhi decided he'd better spend a launch booster. He couldn't disappoint his daughters. They weren't either. Both were entirely thrilled as their faces stretched to either side, nearly passing out and pressed painfully into Bodhi. He circled the ship construction platform with *Diamond Lotus* back in its berth and attached to it, having to weave around a few ore-haulers and freight transports. This earned him a warning from Ground's new Space Controllers. There was now a speed limit from low to high orbit around the planet.

He set down briefly on the Ground Space Station in the small craft service area to get a new launch-booster installed, and the spent one removed. For this, he'd been required to show identification, and ended up having to sign some more autographs and pose in holos with some personnel employed on the station. He had to have his booster in case that the Consumere returned.

He was about to head down to the lake house on the surface when Winn said over the coms, "Why don't you bring the girls to *Diamond Lotus*. Kristy will look after them so we can talk."

"I'm in low orbit with them now and will be over to you in just a minute. I'm sorry that I was overprotective Winn. It won't happen again. I love you."

"I'll see you when you get here," Winn signed off.

He flew beneath *Diamond Lotus,* and the bay doors opened for him. He set the comet interceptor down in the tight hanger and unloaded stuffed animals and daughters once the hanger was aired up. Artana wanted to carry hers, which amounted to dragging most of it along the deck. They passed through the airlock and got on the freight lift since they would not all fit in a tube with the stuffed animals. Winn and Kristy met them in the lift foyer on the 11th deck.

Shanti exclaimed, "Mommy, look what daddy won for us! He also dunked the clown three times in a row!"

"That's wonderful, sweetheart," Winn told her while pulling her into an embrace.

Kristy took Shanti's stuffed animal from Bodhi and helped Artana manage hers as she led the girls to their little toy cabin on the ship. Winn took Bodhi's hand and led him into their suite. They sat on the bed, facing each other, and making eye contact. Bodhi said, "I'm truly sorry, Winn, and I promise it won't happen again. Tell me what you need to get this pacified and resolved."

"I may have over-reacted a tiny-bit," Winn confided. "I had a long talk with Jara before we jumped back to Ground this morning. I know it is love which motivated you, and that part is alright, but it is also fear. You have to drop the fear."

"I will. I've been processing. I can hardly stand it when you're upset with me, Winn."

"It is equally intolerable for me," she shared.

"What do you need, my love?" Bodhi asked sincerely.

"I must attain my rainbow body, so Tish and I will switch jobs for a while, allowing me to work closely with you on *Thor.*"

"Alright."

"And I won't be micro-managed in battle any longer."

"No. Of course not. I said it wouldn't happen again."

"Then let's get back to *Thor* in Yakutastan, and get busy in the meditation cabin."

"Let me just say goodbye to the girls."

"You have three minutes. I'll meet you in the hanger."

"OK."

Bodhi ran to the toy cabin to hug his sweet daughters, and Winn collected her suitcase and went down to the hanger. Bodhi made his goodbyes short and rushed down to meet Winn. She was standing in front of his one-seater craft staring in disbelief. When she noticed him, she asked, "How in the world did you get both girls and those enormous stuffed animals in *that*?"

"With great difficulty and the loss of a third of my piloting holo," he replied.

"I don't think my suitcase will fit."

"I can squeeze it in behind the seat."

"Here. Then do it."

Fortunately, it was not a hard-shell suitcase, and he was able to manage it. He'd had to bring the seat forward a little, which would put Winn almost in his holo. Bodhi climbed in, then Winn got into his lap. Most operations he could do with his skullcap, and if any manual controls were needed, Winn would have to manage those. She no longer felt so distant to him, and it wasn't just the fact that she was in his lap pressed against him. Their incredible connection was back and vibrant. He told her, "I would do anything for your forgiveness, my love. It brings me so low when you are upset with me."

"I can't sustain being angry with you, beloved. Right now, I need you in your most potent teacher role, so you must dissolve yourself and transcend."

They flew the craft together in unity as if from one body and came through the jump into the Yakutastan system, then slowed as they headed for *Thor* in high orbit. Some industrial ships from Kefra and Ground were already snapping sections together in space, beginning construction of a new space station. *Sentinel* and *Ranger* were both in Kefra at the ship construction platform, receiving repairs. *Penthesilea* was in orbit not far from *Thor*.

Work was in progress repairing combat craft in the hanger, so Bodhi got them into a small craft airlock, then through into the hanger. The long sleek comet interceptor had had abundant space to either side within the airlock but only inches in front and back. He set it down in its parking place, and they climbed out. Tish was there waiting with her bags packed and embraced Bodhi, kissing him. She whispered in his ear, "Do for dear Winn what you have done for me, beloved, and guide her through the attainment of her actual illusory body."

"I'll miss you, Tish."

"Well, come visit me when you're able."

"I will."

CHAPTER THIRTY-FOUR

Preparations and construction accelerated expanding and raced on. Bodhi worked with Winn in meditation for hours each day. He provided pilot training and ship crew training from the Yakutastan system. The construction of the space station seemed to mark the passage of time. No sign was detected of the Consumere in any of the 40 systems. The spy drones and probes they had watching them on the outer rim and in the Citadel Galaxy showed no hint of them getting ready to move on, nor to send out a task force.

Ranger got patched up, and *Spalding's* repairs were also finally completed. The 8,240-foot ship at the Kefra ship construction platform was finished, and Captain Haley took it out to put it through tests and trials. She named the ship *Phoebe*. It carried 50 solarium super-reactors and would constitute their most powerful ship until *Oceanus* was built and off the construction dock. Repairs to *Sentinel* were also completed. Work constructing another large powerful drone ship, all shields no weapons, was begun to replace *Defender*. They even found another old imperial 600-foot ship to overhaul and install one solarium super-reactor in, to replace *Legionnaire*. This ship would be called *Bastille*, and it would be captained by Commander Dunn.

Winn made the morning and evening practices with Bodhi every day, had an additional two-hour meditation with him each day, and made her dream work lying beside him each night. Winn also meditated alone daily, practicing everything Bodhi was teaching her. Thanks to her accomplishments in the sitting and absorption tradition, she attained tranquil abiding extremely rapidly and passed the test Bodhi gave her on her first try. The test consisted of getting inside the state of calm abiding then sustaining it for 3 ½ hours pristinely without lapse. Having passed her exam, she was initiated into the secret method of the Islohar and into the highest emptiness meditations presented in series.

Every night, when she lay beside Bodhi and concentrated in her heart and throat energy centers within her central channel, she felt her winds forcefully absorbed and dissolved. Without Bodhi's presence, the experience was excessively subtle, but with him beside her, and their skin in contact, it was always a world-rocking experience with nothing subtle about it. His heart was always open to her every time her heart opened to him without exception. He was constantly passing her energy when they were together. His instruction frequently contained tips, hints, and things to be aware of that were not in the texts or commentaries, but offered personally to her and tailored to help her meet her unique obstructions and challenges. She was madly in love with him, and both grateful to him and proud of him.

Winn was able to meditate upon absolute emptiness, reduce the phenomenon of her interior and exterior worlds to emptiness, dissolve self and its duality completely through transcendence and contemplate the clear light like a cloudless morning sky—so blue, rich and sparkling—upon emptiness in the bliss of eternal silence. Bodhi had her sinking every waking breath to the point 4 finger-widths below the navel, filling her lungs completely, to exhale as the heat and energy rose in her central channel to shoot out the crown of her head. In the formal meditation Bodhi made with her, it was the red warrior-maiden deity one inch in diameter, which she watched rise in her channel to shoot out the top of her head. Two months of this produced a secretion of fluid from her crown, and this seemed to excite Bodhi to no end. He showed her the top of his head, and he had an actual tiny opening in which you could insert a very narrow reed.

Winn had to complete the secret method before Bodhi would let her practice the forceful projection technique. The secret method included meditation on formlessness, which was very similar to her meditative absorption, but it also contained meditations upon and embodiment of the peaceful and fierce deities. There was as well a very serious offering ceremony she performed daily. Bodhi seemed fabulously pleased with her progress, and the states she was realizing were literally blowing her mind. Her cognitive schema, like a towering house of cards, was tumbling down, bringing conventional reality with it, and she felt like she was in freefall amidst blessings.

She finally completed the method, having truly realized each point—and Bodhi had tests—and she was practicing the forceful projection. For hours each day, the explosive seed sound could be heard projected from Winn's mouth, and each time the very subtle drop mounted upon the very subtle wind, shot out the top of her head at the end of the exhale. Finally, with Bodhi's careful and loving guidance, she emerged from her crown in her rainbow body of light, pure radiant bliss. They had been celibate at this point for seven months, channeling the energy into Winn's meditation. Her expansive opening to unity and connection to Bodhi stepped up the process of the law of communicating vessels.

Bodhi was still guiding June, Pam, Kristy, Clark, and Sunoco in the same work of attaining their rainbow bodies, and so had to remain celibate. Winn had a sleepover with Haley and Tish because she desperately needed it, and she didn't think she could sleep next to Bodhi again without jumping him. Bodhi took a berth in a crewmen dorm cabin on *Thor*. Even though his berth was like cot-size, Sunoco climbed in next to him to make her dream work. No way was she going to pass up the opportunity. Not with all the benefits it produced for her dream work.

The Yakutastan space station, brand new and enormous, was fully operational, and a section of it housed Bodhi's pilot top gun school where he taught them Phantom Raider close combat flying. He also trained ship pilots, but the training of ship crews he'd turned over to Captain Clark, who'd turned out to be an exemplary and seasoned ship captain. *Oceanus* was framed and mostly hulled, but layer upon layer of armor was yet to be applied, and only the quantum drive and main space drives had so far been installed. Construction had been ramping up all along, and more 6-way gantry crane mobile space platforms had been manufactured and assembled in space, shaving another three months from the original schedule. The big ORH Super-Battleship constructed on the new ship building platform in Overflowing was also ahead of schedule. *Defender II*, the 3,900 foot, 7-reactor crewless drone ship with super-shields and no weapons systems was complete and through her field testing. Haley had decided to install two magazines of the big torpedoes in it and also squished a 7th reactor in.

Kristy and Jara had a hot and heavy romance going, and Kristy was blooming, blossoming, flowering, and bearing fruit in her practice with Bodhi. She was his next disciple to attain her rainbow body. Bodhi did not doubt that Jara's mentorship had more to do with this than his instruction and guidance. Sunoco succeeded next and was filled with love and gratitude to her teacher. Bodhi turned all ship pilot training over to Tish at this point and simply divided his time between teaching his senior students and teaching in his small craft close combat school. As soon as June attained her rainbow body, Bodhi placed her in charge of the Top Gun School to become himself a part-time instructor there and started teaching his rainbow body achievers how to stay in the flow-state in battle conditions and to stay connected with the spiritual congress.

Jara, Hamah, Tipola, Thromp, Tara, and Sandra became the main developers and cultivators of the spiritual congress, expanding both its level and capacity in addition to its membership. They also rounded up a few more adepts to train for positions on the bridges of ships or cockpits of heavy bomber small craft.

Bodhi, Winn, Tish, and Kristy all received the reversal of cellular aging treatment, and Bodhi was given the drugs in a container that would preserve them until it would be time to treat Shanti and Artana. No immediate changes were recognizable at first, but all four of them had been assured that those were coming.

Clark emerged out the top of his head in his rainbow body a few weeks before Pam did. Winn's 8,100-foot diameter ORH Super-Battleship with 32 super-reactors was finished construction before Bodhi's 29,630-foot diameter *Oceanus*, which Haley was squeezing 4 additional super-reactors into for a total of 248. Winn named her ship *Urania*. When she took it out on maneuvers for its maiden voyage, her entire crew fell in love with her. "Sweet Captain Winn" they called her.

The evening before *Oceanus* was ready to leave the construction dock, Bodhi had a dinner party on board the ship at the senior officers' mess, and invited his seven captains, seven commanders, eleven adepts, and ten drone-jumpers. Uldra and Favio were the chefs, and numerous galley hands, cooks, kitchen helpers, and others were put to work from their new Star Fleet personnel. Including his big drone ship with super-shields, *Defender II*, Bodhi now had 13 ships. All but the smallest two, the one-reactor *Ranger* and *Bastille*, would have an adept and a drone-jumper aboard. The captains of his five largest ships, his captain of Diamond Lotus, and the captain of his small craft heavy bombers were also adepts. Besides the 206 Tsunami Devastators that they had attached to the exterior hulls of the 13 ships, they had an additional 180 of them which had quantum drives, and each of these flew two drone fighter-bombers with quantum drives.

Bodhi entertained his guests in his suite on the ship as they arrived. A tube system ran throughout the ship, and the tubes could reach 380 MPH. With the motion dampeners and electro-hydraulics, it wasn't too bad and could get you anywhere in less than a minute. The ship was 29,630 feet in diameter, but with its stretched-disc nose, it was 31,960 feet in length, and it was 6,800 feet high at the center, tapering in the stern to 4,800 feet and in the bow to 3,600.

Uldra came and informed him that dinner was ready, and they walked the half-mile to the senior officers' mess from Bodhi's suite to get a look at some of the ship. It was simply hard to fathom. Personnel were arriving, and a number had been aboard for days and even weeks. They would not pull away from the construction platform for another day. There were still systems to integrate, some bugs to work out, and near-infinite tests and diagnostics to run. Bodhi wanted Haley to have a look at it too before they shoved off. The vortex force, or gravity, finally felt right to Bodhi. They seated themselves around three large tables, 12 people at each.

Everyone was wearing their new uniforms. Winn. Kristy and June had designed them, then Tish had insisted on the changes and alterations which were ultimately made to them, kind of ruining the 'look' Kristy had been going for. Bodhi was an Admiral now. Kristy was a first lieutenant. The adepts were all third lieutenants or Jr lieutenants. Captain Tish ran *Oceanus*, not Admiral Bodhi. Captain Winn, Captain Tish, and Captain Haley together really ran Star Fleet, not Admiral Bodhi, except in battle and in planning for battle. None of that had really happened in over a year, so Bodhi was kind of out of the loop and more with his daughters of late. They were growing fast.

Haley told Bodhi, "I made summaries of the intelligence data from our spy drones and probes we have watching the Consumere."

"Did you analyze it?"

"Of course."

"What's the gist?"

"They're never coming near us but have found a 14 star-gate system in their home galaxy Citadel where the stars are clustered closer together. They figure it will take them a century to milk those 14 systems dry of resources. Did you know they have technology and energy containment cells for draining a star-gate of all its power?"

"They sound like a black hole," Bodhi commented.

"They are also actual cannibals, though they don't just roast 'em and eat 'em. They put them in the food synthesizers as fresh materials."

"We are going to attack them," Bodhi stated.

"I know, so I drew up some approaches based on different times and alignments."

"Thanks, Haley."

"You're going to kick-ass in this," Haley said excitedly of *Oceanus*.

"We will have four adepts on the bridge counting me, Tish, Jara, and Kristy. I hope that we will not only be able to defend ourselves but help take care of our other ships. We'll have to silence that class 11 beam weapon on the mother ship at the outset if we hope to accomplish victory."

Kristy informed her admiral and teacher, "I jumped a drone fighter-bomber into a space of two miles by one mile today!"

"You are ready," Bodhi said pleased, "and our very best drone-jumper."

"Sonic did four miles by two miles" Kristy let him know.

"How about the other drone pilots?" Bodhi asked.

Kristy answered, "Bob, Fred, and Carl are getting closer and can get one into a space of six miles by three. The others have some work to do honing their skills."

"We'd better focus on that then while we prepare the fleet for departure," Bodhi directed. "Perhaps you and Jara could work with the five still having some trouble with it and get them better tuned in to the spiritual congress and more solidly grounded in the flow-state."

Jara replied, "We already planned to do this, meditating with them for a few hours per day. Having less 'practice' will save a bunch of unarmed drone fighter-bombers, and those aren't cheap to produce."

Winn inquired, "Do you think we were wise in sharing such advanced technologies with all 40 planets so soon after being part of a devolved empire?"

Haley said confidently, "All the tricky parts were manufactured on Pronotavasmi and Ground. What we gave to each planet to manufacture, without the stuff from the two yellow sun moral anarchy populations, they could not build a quantum coms ship nor a solarium super-reactor."

Jara offered, "The planet populations of all the former empire, even Nafs Ammara, are finding their unity and cooperating at a high level. We are all in this together."

"Who will be caring for my daughters when we depart on our mission?" Bodhi inquired of those at his table.

Winn informed him, "Yen and Penny will be. They are moving into our house on the lakeshore, on Ground, and will have all nine children with them. Favio and Fritz are going with them. The high council on Ground has promised to make sure they are resupplied weekly while we're gone."

"And the rest of our crew?" Bodhi asked.

Haley informed him, "Uduak will be on the bridge of *Oceanus*. Uldra and Tandy are working the senior officer's mess on *Oceanus*. Shamas is loading canister missiles on *Diamond Lotus*, which Captain

Pam is flying, and four of them are captains of your largest ships. Kristy is jumping drones from *Oceanus*, and Sonic from *Phoebe*. Captain June leads your Tsunami Devastator heavy bombers and directs the other small craft, while Commander Ilya is in charge of *Trooper*. He will also be piloting her."

"Where did you put Clark?" Bodhi asked, then explained, "I want him on a better ship than *Spalding*. He's the best all-around captain we have, and boy can he fight his ship."

Haley told him, "Clark is captaining *Penthesilea*, three hundred feet longer and with one more super-reactor than *Spalding*. I also got one magazine of the next to biggest torpedoes installed on *Penthesilea*. He'll have Sandra on board, and quite a romance has taken root between them. They work well together."

"Who's commanding *Spalding*?" Bodhi asked.

"Captain Clark recommended Commander Mason," Haley replied, "So I've placed him in charge of it."

"Once I've put *Oceanus* through the paces, I want to do some maneuvers with the entire fleet," Bodhi informed them.

Jara commented, "The potency of your fleet is far more due to your adepts and drone-jumpers than it is to reactors and weapons systems."

"This is true," Bodhi agreed. "With brute force alone, we would all be squashed like bugs. Our only hope is in blinding them, finding soft spots in turbulent shields, and jumping drones into the interiors of their ships."

June told him from the adjacent table, "Your small craft will be kicking plenty of ass with brute force alone and running circles around them!"

"You'll be outnumbered by more than 12 to 1," Bodhi reminded her.

"Then we'll have to attain a kill-ratio higher than that," June said confidently. "I'll have Atlantic in my cockpit, and she can illuminate suns and see soft spots in shields."

"It's too bad we don't have a drone-jumper for your cockpit," Bodhi lamented.

"I think even I could jump one inside the Consumere mother ship, and I'll have two drone pilots on board," June replied.

"How long until we depart on the mission?" Kristy asked.

"About five weeks from now, if we continue to progress as we have been," Bodhi answered.

"How many drones are we going to have?" she inquired.

"There are 299 in ships' hangers, 360 flying two each with the 180 Tsunami Devastators that have quantum drives, and 412 which will be flown from 206 of our hull-mounted Tsunami Devastators. There will be fifty to jump from the ten ships with drone-jumpers aboard. You will have a disproportionate number turned over to you for control since you are the best. Most of those 50 I'd like for you and Sonic to jump. I don't want our 'iffy' drone-jumpers handling them for jumping into ships unless in a dire emergency. We need to make them count."

"Why not bring more?" Kristy asked.

"If production can be hurried along in the next five weeks, then we will," Bodhi confirmed. "With all their mega-industrial ships and mammoth living quarters ships, we will not be able to take them in a single assault and will need to return to Ground for repairs, resupply, more small craft, and drones. I think with two assaults we can get them dislodged from the Burning Hope Galaxy, and with a third assault on their mining base in the Citadel Galaxy I hope to bring them to surrender and get them settled on an inhabitable 4th planet in a white sun system with no humanoids already living on it."

"Have you located such a planet yet?" Kristy asked.

"No, not yet, but Haley is working on it, and we still have some time," Bodhi answered.

Tish asked, "If we defeat them and get them to stop raping and cannibalizing biospheres and human populations, are we going to Mother, Ganahar, and Om?"

"I have the sense that my teacher will be able to guide us back to the galaxies we know if we complete our mission. Once we have the jump coordinates, we can return here again and visit friends and crew member's relatives. I would like for you to meet Pez, Musash, Sarhi, Amazonia, and Mel."

"I would like to," Tish agreed.

"If Jara would come with us, we could integrate our chapter of the spiritual congress into the big one," Bodhi invited.

"Of course, I would," Jara agreed. "I do want to meet Pez and Sarhi, and to be sure Electra as well."

Haley contributed, "Amazonia and Mel will also impress you."

"Yes, I'd like to meet them, too," Jara stated.

CHAPTER THIRTY-FIVE

Five weeks and two days after the dinner party on board *Oceanus,* the fleet was fully loaded and provisioned. They had 33 more drone fighter-bombers than anticipated at the party thanks to further efficiencies on the assembly lines. Shuttles had been running from the surface of the planet and from the space station to arm and supply the 13 ships until another square inch could not be found in a single cargo hold. At last, Bodhi gave the order to accelerate to jump speed, and the ships, bombers, and drones moved out. They were timing their assault with a particular alignment and configuration within the system the Consumere were operating in, on the outer rim within the dust and gas cloud. While planets furthest the sun tend to move more slowly than those in close, with galaxies, it was the stars furthest the center which moved the quickest. On the outer rim, they went really fast.

They would be splitting into two groups with their quantum jump into the system. *Oceanus* would be accompanied by *Spalding, Diamond Lotus,* and the two ships with only one reactor, *Ranger* and *Bastille. Phoebe* would be leading *Urania, Thor, Penthesilea, Trooper, Sentinel,* and *Protector,* and they would be piloting *Defender II* as a shield while making their final sprint into battle. *Oceanus,* with Kristy aboard, would try to wreck the class 11 beam on the mother ship the moment they got slowed to .24 light speed from jumping in. The small craft would be split between the two groups.

They reached .7 light, and all ships and craft simply disappeared, becoming nonexistent potential for a non-duration, to then resolve into existence in new places. Tish could now contemplate the black near-attainment like Bodhi and wasn't affected by the event. Bodhi let her handle all the braking while he identified the coordinates of each warship and the mother ship. The spiritual congress was in full session supporting their efforts with some 28 billion people deep in meditation, lending their psycho-spiritual energy and intention.

Bodhi was coming from the star of the solar system with the 3rd planet between him and the mother ship. Haley was coming from the outer solar system towards the star and 4th planet with the 5th planet hiding her force. It was more than three minutes since jumping in before either of their forces were detected by the Consumere, and both were spotted about the same moment. The Consumere had never been attacked before. It was just not in their experience and totally unexpected.

Combat small craft began launching from all the Consumere ships, and three of the big 5-mile long ships went head-on with Haley's group accompanied by 25 of the half-mile long ships now detached from the mother ship, while four of the five-mile ships headed for *Oceanus* and Bodhi's group with the other 25 three-reactor ships. The one and a half-mile long ships held back. It seemed unreal that they were attacking 108 warships with only 13 of their own. There were also hundreds of super and mega non-military ships in various orbits around the 4th planet.

Haley said over Bodhi's coms, "I think we just caught them with their pants down."

"There are so many of them that I don't think they need their pants, Haley," he replied with some anxiety.

Phoebe got some class 9 and 8 weapons on the lead half-mile ship, and it blew into a cloud in 4.2 seconds.

Haley told him from experience, "The little ones are easy to pop."

Bodhi was slowing and falling just below .24 light when he told Kristy, "Whenever you're ready."

"I've got several drones at jump speed now," she told him as she jumped one. She'd been trying to put it inside the hull where the class 11 beam weapon was located on the mother ship, but her drone fighter-bomber partly fried on the shields and impacted on the hull just 10 meters to port of the weapon. It made a heck of an explosion, but it did not look like it had breached the outer hull and armor. She immediately tried another. This one blew inside the mother ship and propelled the small moon-sized sphere in the direction the drone had been going. No doubt enormous damage was wreaked within, but the class 11 weapon opened up, aiming for *Oceanus*. It took only a few seconds to acquire her. During those seconds, Kristy jumped another drone.

Bodhi was reaching for a stage booster needing to get that death beam off his ship since noticing his shields dropping extremely fast. Kristy's third drone jumped half-buried in the hull, with only its tail outside the armor and molded to it on impact. She had gotten past the shields entirely this time, and it struck only 4 meters from the big weapon. The hull opened in a breach from the interior explosion, and the class 11 beam flickered out just before Bodhi spent the booster, so he saved it instead. He told Kristy, "Great jump!"

Some class 9 beams and blasters were walking across space towards *Oceanus* fired from the mother ship, and a few of these found him. Jara left through her crown and turned the entire hemisphere facing them of the mother ship into a glaring sun. Employing a maneuver with drives and thrusters, Bodhi got out from under almost all of the heavy weapons. As soon as he did, *Oceanus* was lit with weapons from two of the five-mile long ships. The other two coming head- on at his group both got some weapons onto *Bastille*. Jara and Bodhi both planted suns across the bows of the four big ships, but it was too late for Commander Dunn and *Bastille*, which flared into an explosion killing all hands aboard.

Tish dug into a half-mile ship with her twin class 9 nose blasters, blowing it in 2.3 seconds. *Spalding* creamed one of those also with missiles and class 8 twin blasters. Bodhi was once again about to burn a stage-booster when Kristy jumped a drone right into a big 5-mile ship, which disappeared into a blue streak headed out of the battle zone. The whole ship was just gone, and not so much as a particle could be detected of it once the blue streak faded. Perhaps half a dozen Consumere small craft had been sucked into and along with that blue streak and were entirely gone. Bodhi's shields held and he did not use up a booster. *Diamond Lotus* did, and just in time to get out of the way of the class nine blasters crashing its shields.

Together, *Spalding* and *Ranger* blew up a 3-reactor ship with the auxiliary's class 9 beam and Ranger's class 5 twin nose blasters and class 4 quads plus a shower of canister missiles.

Oceanus was firing torpedoes and missiles at all three of the 5-mile Consumere ships and hitting two of them with beams and blasters while her shields dropped steadily. Jara was out planting suns on all three of their bows. Bodhi exploited a weak film in the shields of the lead one, slipping in three super-torpedoes, which only *Oceanus* was large enough to carry. Even the first super-torpedo didn't crack the hull, but the second one must have because the third blew entirely inside the ship, which just became fuel for an even more colossal explosion.

Mandy, the adept aboard *Diamond Lotus*, shot six big undercarriage missiles through a soft spot in the shields of the new lead 5-mile ship, and the 6th attained the tiniest breach which only served to shut a small bulk-headed section of the ship down while the rest of the ship fought on. Then the big ships were passed and turning madly to come around to reengage. *Oceanus* killed a 3-reactor ship as the last of those went by in a flash. The 20-reactor ships that had held back were now coming into range.

On *Phoebe*, Haley headed right at the three enormous ships with their 25 three-reactor ship escorts, all weapons firing. *Urania* was on her port side doing the same, and *Thor* was on her starboard flank with Tipola planting suns out in space over the bows of the three 5-milers. *Defender II*, flown from *Phoebe's* bridge, was kept between Haley's force and the mother ship. *Penthesilea* and *Trooper* were above and slightly behind Haley's ship, and *Sentinel* and *Protector* were below and back a little relative to her position. All of them were firing almost every weapon on board. A few had nothing to shoot at given their direction and position within the formation, but the oncoming Consumere combat small craft were about to change that. June and Atlantic were in the cockpit of the lead Tsunami Devastator, which was out ahead of *Phoebe* and dancing randomly to shake off the incoming fire.

Sonic missed with a drone-jump trying to get it inside the lead big ship and materialized it from the quantum potential to an inch from the hull at.7 light speed. The drone fighter bomber streaked blue as it fried in the shields and the shields seemed to join the streak. One side of the ship was half-stripped of its armor and scorched black. The blaster bolts and missiles, which were continuously flying into it, were suddenly gouging directly into the ship's armor and hull instead of getting spent on its shields, which had left with the streak. Haley got her class 9 beam boring into a place where most of the armor left with the blue streak, and it didn't take two seconds to blow that ship all to hell.

The two still coming at them, each contained 192 super-reactors. Haley's shields were more than half-way down when Thromp started lobbing big torpedoes into a near-hole in the shields only he and Haley could see out of the people on *Phoebe's* bridge. He sent six like a burst of automatic fire pounding one after the other, and somewhere between the 3rd and 4th ones, they started going inside to blow up. The five-mile long ship took a little hop in space before it blew all over the place quite symmetrically, in a very fine spray of dust and vapor to form a perfectly round space cloud.

The third big ship was passed and angling for a turn to give chase. *Urania* blew a half-mile ship before those all went by. This was the second one it had killed in this pass. *Defender II* was annihilated quite asymmetrically into a flying tongue of debris right into the shields of Haley's force. The mother ship still had multiple class 9 weapons and some gigantic torpedoes with surge space drives and thrusters. With *Defender II* blown to bits, those weapons were starting to target Haley's group. They were also now headed at a literal fleet of 20-reactor, mile and a half-long warships. Sonic started frantically jumping drone fighter-bombers into the mothership. They'd left quite a few going .7 light, and ready to jump, and the drone pilots on *Phoebe* were transferring them to Sonic as fast as he could send them off.

His first one landed inside very close to the curve of the outer hull, just above the equator, and a piece the size of a large mountain ejected and streaked blue heading out of the system. He had no idea, but Kristy had just started jumping them two at a time trying to land them from the void, dead center of the mother ship. Sonic's second must have gone a little high because mother ship's North Pole blew right off her head in a streak. He knew he got his third one inside, but nothing flew off from the hemisphere he could see. Haley flashed him a view of the other side in his holo from a spy drone they'd been keeping in the system. A big piece had clearly blown away in a streak from that vantage. His fourth one cut out an even bigger hole in the back. His fifth shot blew a wad of it off the surface to the starboard side between the equator and South Pole. Then mother ship—all 1200 miles across of it—got sucked into two blue streaks like smoke through narrow vacuum nozzles to contract into two lines headed out of the battle zone. That was the end of the mother ship. It was a pair of Kristy's drones coming out of the void in the mother ship's very core and center, which had finished it off.

Mixed in with the fleet of a mile and a half-long ships were 14 Scout Scavenger Intruders, each with 22-reactors. The battle groups both Haley's group and Bodhi's group had engaged and passed, were each coming back around. Their shields had a chance to return to 100% for a moment. *Phoebe* and *Urania* took the lead, having the strongest shields. Both were bigger and more powerful than those of the fleet they were headed for. The sheer numbers of them made them extremely lethal, however. Thromp, Sandra, and Tara were sprouting mini-suns along the bows or flanks of ships. They covered at least 40 of them all in a few seconds.

Bodhi had Tish headed right for the middle of the Consumere ships. It would take a dozen of them firing everything they had at once to bring *Oceanus'* shields down. Of course, there were more than 50 of them there, and two of those 5-mile ships could bring their shields down real quick. Those were headed their way. Bodhi asked Kristy, "Could you try and jump one into one of those really big ones?"

"No problem," she said confidently.

A moment later, the ship disappeared, streaking away from them in a line. Jara was out blinding ships, and a Scout Scavenger's shields were thrashing wildly, so Bodhi launched torpedoes through a slight film. The whole ship blew on the third, taking the fourth one Bodhi had sent with it. He was glad to know that three would do the trick because he liked being frugal.

Mandy in *Diamond Lotus* sent five undercarriage missiles into the soft spot in the riled shields of a 20-reactor ship, and it burst into a sphere of vapor and particles. Jara took out a mile and a half-long ship with torpedoes through a film in thrashing shields from *Oceanus'* bridge. Before the remaining two giant ships came into range, Kristy jumped a drone into one turning it into a blue streak. There were so many Consumere small craft all over the place that four got hit and sucked into the blue streak as it went. The big beam and blaster weapons in *Oceanus* took down the shields of a Scout Scavenger, then punched through the armor and hull to destroy it.

The curving trajectories of Haley's and Bodhi's groups, which had begun in opposing directions, wove together into a shared heading by the time they were halfway through the fleet of 50 ships, minus losses.

The last of the Consumere 192-reactor ships was in range and closing. Sonic jumped a drone, hoping to land it square in the middle. Only the bridge and super structure streaked, sending the ship into a slow spin at .11 light to collide amidships with a 20-reactor ship. They united in a gargantuan explosion, which took out at least a wing of Consumere heavy bombers and perhaps a dozen fighters. Bodhi's force had 1,520 small craft out fighting, and 766 drone fighter-bombers—minus recent losses. *Phoebe* blew up one of the ships off mother ship's hull then *Urania* blew up another. Then their little fleet was through and out the other side.

Bodhi took them in an accelerating arc, and all fired boosters at the same instant to blast away from Consumere ships. One gigantic molten flare counter-measure form *Oceanus* caught most of the torpedoes and missiles still gaining on them. A few impacted on shields ten seconds later, and the rest were left in their exhaust as the boosters brought their velocity up quickly. They made a pass halfway around the fourth planet to slingshot out at the rear of the Consumere fleet, braking all out as they closed so they could get targeting resolution. Six of Bodhi's ships had class 9 weapons, and these had range on the enemy first. Their shields were all refreshed and at full force.

A Scout Scavenger Intruder burst into a cloud, then one of the Consumere 1 ½-mile main battleships did. Astro Phantoms and Tsunami Devastators started launching torpedoes and missiles. Three of the Consumere 3-reacotor destroyers blew. Tara sent torpedoes from *Urania* through a soft film in a battleship's shields, blowing it into a colorful sphere. Then *Ranger* blew apart into dust. Atlantic flying with June sent the last of their torpedoes through the soft spot in a battleship's shields, turning it into a ball of expanding atoms and light. A single super-torpedo from *Oceanus* blew away a destroyer while her big beams and blasters assisted *Urania* in wasting a Scout Scavenger. Kristy jumped a drone into a Scout Scavenger streaking it, and Sonic jumped one skimming the side of a battleship streaking armor on one flank and the shields entirely all around. June's bombers and *Spalding* finished it.

Protector blew into quadrillions of pieces in a flare of light and vapor. At least four more Consumere destroyers were transformed into dust and gas, and another battleship was killed by *Thor* and *Penthesilea*. Then Bodhi ordered his ships to power drives to full and fire thrusters, to pull away from the Consumere fleet again. They'd lost three ships so far and were down to ten, and their small craft needed to reload. The Consumere had 70 ships left. Bodhi gave the order for the Tsunami Devastators without quantum drives to remount on the nearest hull. It was a little tricky while accelerating, but the pilots had been trained well on this procedure, and the ingenious mount mechanism Haley had designed did most of the work.

Once they had their bombers mounted, Bodhi ordered a quantum jump to deep space coordinates where some industrial and repair ships from Pronotavasmi were waiting. They went through the shock of the quantum jump, entirely timeless, and emerged in deep space with plenty of room to decelerate and achieve full stop relative to the waiting ships. *Spalding* and *Penthesilea* got right to work as small craft descended on them for reloading and for new fuel cells for thrusters and new boosters. The big Pronotavasmi industrial ship had telescoping articulated crane arms able to reload *Oceanus, Phoebe,* and *Urania's* missile and torpedo magazines. Full canister missile batteries of 16 each, were shuttled over to ships in frame reloaders which had only to be aligned, then a button pressed, to transfer the missiles into the ship's canister all at once.

Some quick repairs were made to scorches and gauges in ship's armor, and fried or missing sensor arrays were rapidly replaced. The ten ships they had left were in pretty good shape. Haley told Bodhi over his coms, "The Consumere battleships were dependent upon the mother ship for reloading and replenishing. So were 5,000 of their small craft. With their seven super-battleships gone, most of the rest of their small craft have lost their reload capacity. I'm sure they can make up for this through their factory and industrial ships, but it will not be efficient."

"Our ships won't need another reload to finish this," Bodhi calculated. "Our small craft will need several, and the fighters which carry only two missiles on their undercarriage at a time will require many. I'm going to station Spalding on the far-side of the planet's closest moon. That ought to provide a safe place for reloading."

"It should," Haley agreed. "I've analyzed the battle data, and we have done a very impressive job so far. June's small craft force has a kill ratio of 13.2 to 1. Many of the Consumere small craft blew in ship hangars and within the mother ship so they don't have near as many out as they might have initially. We did catch them with their pants down."

"We had the advantage of surprise," Bodhi agreed, "but given the size of their force, we couldn't have achieved this without it. We took out most of their military-deployed reactors with the mother ship and those seven super-battleships, but they still have 70 ships and over 5,000 small craft left. We could still end up taking some heavy losses."

"What's your plan?" Haley asked.

"Let's stand every one down, get them fed, and we'll give them six hours of sleep. The Consumere will remain on high alert, anxious, and anticipating our return. They'll burn lots of thruster fuel buzzing about looking for us, too. There's a pretty good alignment in seven hours and 52 minutes, which would give us cover to sneak in close before they see us. I have a formation worked out for maximum stealth. Diamond Lotus can go fully cloaked. They haven't been firing their anti-cloaking cannons, and with the rest of us fully visible, they won't be expecting it."

"Now that does sound like an excellent plan," Haley said with admiration.

"We'll give our crews five hours sleep, then make an hour's meditation connecting with the spiritual congress."

"Even better," Haley agreed.

"You were brilliant," Tish told him.

Jara shared, "I didn't think we had a human's chance in space of ever surviving that."

Kristy agreed, "A snowball would have had a better chance in hell."

"We could never have done it without you, Kristy, and Sonic, too, though your aim is better," Bodhi acknowledged.

"I'm getting much better at it now that it counts," Kristy informed him.

"When we get back in there, I want you to focus on Scout Scavenger Intruders," Bodhi directed.

Winn came over coms to say to Bodhi, "You are a maestro strategist Admiral. That was like turning certain death into opportunity and great fortune!"

"Thanks, sweetheart," Bodhi replied. "*Urania* fought very well, and you did great. So did Tara."

"Well, Bob couldn't even get a drone into the mother ship so I have him flying and fighting a drone instead," Winn complained. "His went almost 400 miles to port and nearly hit a Tsunami Devastator."

"Only Kristy and Sonic are going to jump the drones from here on out," Bodhi assured her.

"Since I have the alleged 3rd best and he's completely incompetent, I'd say that's a really good idea," Winn agreed.

"Stand your crew down, get them some chow and give them 5 hours sleep," Bodhi instructed. "Then, we'll make a one-hour meditation connecting with the spiritual congress before we go back into the system."

"Aye aye, sir, and thanks for letting me just do my thing without interfering."

"Your crew responds amazingly well to your gentle approach, my love, and are doing a professional job. I'm proud of you."

The galleys on the ten ships got real busy, and the crews were efficiently fed. A five-hour sleep was granted all personnel, except those of the Pronotavasmi ships that had been out here waiting for them. Those crew carried on with repairs, and transfer of ordinance to munition lockers and holds on the ten ships.

A call to meditation was pumped through the warships and crews gathered in meditation cabins or designated areas. Bodhi had Jara lead the meditation for all ten ships over their coms, and the session was immensely energized and deeply calm and clear, touching the eternal presence of light upon silence.

After the meditation session, came the call to battle-stations and the mini-fleet got under way, accelerating to jump speed. Bodhi sent each ship the coordinates to jump into. They had left headed out of the system and would be materializing on the star-side behind the 3rd planet, heading for the fourth planet. His six adept captains managed not to go into shock with the quantum leap, but four of his ships were a little tardy getting the brakes on and assuming formation. *Diamond Lotus* was fully cloaked and transmitting its position to the other ships and all their small craft through an encrypted non-locality beacon so that she appeared in their piloting, nav. and fire control holos, but not to the enemy.

Spalding would make the first pass with the rest of her force, then veer off behind the closest moon. *Oceanus, Phoebe,* and *Urania* took the lead. Once spotted by the Consumere, they took the bulk of the incoming enemy fire. Fully loaded and with shields at 100%, they entered the battle, slowing as they came. At first, only class 9 weapons and long-range torpedoes were in range. Then all weapons were, and a small craft melee erupted ahead of them, and all around.

A destroyer blew to microscopic pieces under the big guns of *Oceanus. Urania* and *Phoebe* ganged up on a battle ship and burst its hull into a brilliant explosion of the whole ship. *Thor* was firing everything into a Scout Scavenger nearly twice its power, and Tipola got some torpedoes through a soft spot in that ship's shields ending it. On *Penthesilea,* Sandra exploited a thin film of shielding to totally waste a battleship. From *Diamond Lotus,* Mandy sent undercarriage missiles—4 of them—into the soft spot in a destroyer's shields, and the ship blew without the crew ever knowing what hit them. Thromp and Jara each got torpedoes through battleship shields, and two more ships were gone. Sonic missed altogether with a drone, but Kristy managed to jump one inside a Scout Scavenger Intruder streaking it blue. *Spalding* and *Sentinel* were firing on the same battleship and Frick, the adept aboard Sentinel, got some big missiles through the shields, while those were frying everything else hitting them, to annihilate that ship. Clark on *Penthesilea* took out a destroyer.

Then a shower of Consumere torpedoes and missiles from two battleships ganging up on *Sentinel* blew the ship into a raging superheated expanding cloud of gas. Commander Link and Frick were gone. *Thor* killed another destroyer, and *Urania* another battleship, then they were through and out the back of the shrinking Consumere fleet. *Spalding* headed around the closest moon while the other eight, with only seven of them visible, went into a turn, which would bring them back around to engage. A pair of Scout Scavenger Intruders were accelerating after them firing on their sterns. Kristy jumped a drone into the very forward bow of one of those with *Oceanus* at about .27 light speed, and a quarter of the ship streaked while all manner of debris flew out of the opened other ¾ of it. *Phoebe* loosed a cloaked mobile smart mine net which wound around the other Scout Scavenger in a series of enormous explosions that took the ship with them.

They were free and clear with all shields rising, still accelerating in a turn. The Consumere yet had 51 warships and who knew how many small craft, but in terms of reactors, they were now down to 498. Bodhi's nine remaining ships contained 362 reactors, and their tactics did not rely on reactor power so much as available torpedoes and missiles to send through soft spots in shields. Bodhi could still lose ships if one were ganged up on.

He brought them around angling into the Consumere ships, which would allow for a longer exchange of fire. Hamah and Tara were out in space, manifesting micro-suns on the enemy ships before the big guns even had range. The enemy tried to jump some drones into Bodhi's ships and did worse than Bob, missing by a long-shot and causing zero damage. Bob said somewhat defensively to Captain Winn, "See. It's not that easy to jump them in."

Winn gave him a polite smile then looked back into her piloting holo. Kristy jumped one into a battleship turning the whole thing into a streaking line. Winn thought, *Kristy and Sonic can do it.*

Each member of Bodhi's force was in top form, and peak performance as the class nine weapons opened fire. Storms of torpedoes and missiles were headed in both directions and looked like they would all collide, but like two galaxies converging, nothing impacted on anything else, space completely overwhelming matter with much distance between all passing ordnance. None were targeting invisible *Diamond Lotus*, and Pam stirred up a destroyer's shields while Mandy located a thin film to shoot undercarriage missiles through blowing it into a bright sphere of particles. *Thor* blew away a destroyer with its beam, blasters, and a stream of missiles, some through a soft spot Tipola found.

Urania and *Penthesilea* pounded a battleship until it blew all over their shields. Hannah slipped some of Trooper's big missiles through active shields and blew up a destroyer. *Thor* fell under the guns of two battleships and a Scout Scavenger all at the same time and blew out of the battle zone employing a big stage-booster. Scorches down one side of its underbelly were visible even from this distance. Sunoco reported to Bodhi, "Our hull is in-tact, and shields are coming back up. We'll be back around and engaged shortly."

"Good save! I couldn't stand to lose you, so please be careful."

Without awaiting a reply, Bodhi shot out the top of his head into space, erupting suns across bows and flanks of enemy ships. Erica, from the far side of the moon on *Spalding,* was out planting them too. So was Tara from *Urania*. Thromp was firing off torpedoes into a Scout Scavenger that *Phoebe* was railing on and blew it to kingdom come. Jara was pitching torpedoes through the shields of a battleship, which were at 79% and holding until all the shield generators blew up with the ship. Sandra finessed some torpedoes through a film in the shields of a battleship, expanding it into a glowing mist. *Diamond Lotus*, with Mandy's assistance, blew another destroyer out of the fight. Enemy decloaking guns started shooting.

Oceanus was going head to head with a Scout Scavenger and would have eventually overpowered it without any doubt, but both Bodhi and Tish started streams of torpedoes into separate soft spots ending it prematurely. *Trooper* was in trouble pounded by a Scout Scavenger and a battleship, dropping its shields to nothing, then *Thor* arrived to take the hits on its shields, and Sunoco launched big missiles through operational shields on the battleship while Tipola did the same to the Scout. Both ships blew as *Thor's* shields reached 9%. Jara exploited a soft spot in the thrashing shields of the last Scout Scavenger Intruder, blowing it to hell and gone.

Diamond Lotus and Mandy managed to do in another destroyer, then got hit hard with class 9 and 8 weapons as a big torpedo impacted taking its shields completely down. Pam fired a launch booster to become a blur, and shut down cloaking to divert the energy powering that over to her shields. She reported to Bodhi, "We have a little hull breach, and I'm headed for *Spalding* for repairs."

"That was a quick save you made. Good work. Get your hull mended; you've done enough in this battle already."

"Aye aye, sir."

The Tsunami Devastators blew a destroyer with torpedoes and missiles, one squadron after another making bombing runs on it till it was finished. Kristy jumped another drone into another battleship, streaking it. Sonic aimed one into a battleship, missed completely, but took off the bow of a destroyer instead, by accident. The ship went off course, and *Penthensilea* had to run through some critical maneuvers to avoid collision with it. June's bombers finished the destroyer with no bow. *Urania* blew up a destroyer by simply overpowering it, 32 reactors to three. Haley pounded a destroyer with class 9 twin blasters until it popped while Thromp, seated on her bridge, utterly destroyed a battleship with torpedoes passing untouched through its active shields.

Penthesilea and *Trooper* were both getting clobbered bad and were behind their own three largest ships. Thor came in shooting to help. Clark hit his last booster, and *Penthesilea* was out of there, though Sandra painted the attacking battleships from bow to stern with brilliant radiant micro-suns blinding them as she sped away. Tipola got some big missiles through shields to impact directly on the hull of a battleship and just managed to breach the hull, but not blow it up. He was out of torpedoes already, and the big missiles were just not as effective. *Trooper's* shields were brought down, and then a hit to its stern disabled it. A squadron of Astro Phantoms swung in launching torpedoes and missiles at the battleship with the breach, and Sunoco got all *Thor's* classes 9, 8 and 7s digging into another battleship while bringing her ship around to take the hits aimed at *Trooper.*

June was just arriving with 12 wings of Tsunami Devastators, each craft launching a pair of torpedoes, and 96 torpedoes hit the battleship firing on *Thor* and *Trooper*, all in a about 3 seconds. The battleship splattered into an expanding sphere of light, already fading. *Thor* was punching it out with a battleship nearly twice its power with shields dropping fast, but Sunoco would not even consider leaving the disabled *Trooper* with her husband Ilya aboard it, father of her son. Another battleship joined in this little action, and *Thor's* shields were almost gone. Tipola blew the one they were firing on and getting hit hardest by, spending the last of *Thor's* biggest missiles. He'd launched seven, and they did the trick. They had nothing left that would breach the hull of the battleship, now hitting them with blasters and ordinance and they would not last long. June was coming around for a run on it but would likely be too late to save them.

Clark shot back into the fray in *Penthesilea,* getting between the battleship and both *Thor* and *Trooper* while firing everything on the ship. Clark's torpedoes were spent too, but Sandra was sending big undercarriage missiles through a soft spot, and Sunoco was pumping every last canister missile into another thin film in the shields of the same ship. It blew before June could make her run on it with her bombers. The battle zone had moved on. *Thor* and *Penthesilea* both remained with Ilya on *Trooper* while reloading canters missiles from their own munitions holds on their ships. June's bombers sped away to rejoin the battle. Their shields returned to 100%, but not *Trooper's*.

Phoebe blew a destroyer all over space with class 9 and 8 weapons while Thromp slipped ordinance through the shields of a battleship disintegrating it in a big explosion. *Oceanus* pulverized a battleship with brute force while Tara, aboard *Urania*, nailed a near-hole in a battleship's shields with torpedoes. *Oceanus's* big guns blew apart a destroyer. All three of Bodhi's biggest ships released molten flare shield counter-measures as they accelerated out of the vicinity of the remaining 25 Consumere warships in a trajectory that would bring them around to their other three ships.

As they closed on their friends, *Thor* began reloading from *Penthesilea*. Bodhi arranged his three biggest ships to protect the three smaller ones. At least a quarter of their small craft were reloading from *Spalding*, behind the moon, and now small craft began swarming Clark's deck for more ordinance and thruster fuel cells. The Consumere ships were into a turn which would bring them into an attack run.

Bodhi inquired, "What's your status, Commander Ilya?"

"We have the breach in the hull at the stern sealed off, but our drives are wrecked. All the thrusters down one side of the ship are fried. Shields are only functioning in the bow. We still have blasters and some canister missiles."

"Then we'll make our stand right here. Since Hannah's out of ordinance, tell her to just blind ships. I'd have you start transferring crew off, but we're about to receive the full charge of the Consumere warships."

"We'll continue to fight the ship so long as weapons are functioning," Ilya said gravely.

"Here they come," Bodhi said.

Thor undocked from *Penthesilea*, having restored 21% of its torpedoes and about 46% of its big missiles on its undercarriage. Small craft still covered Clark's deck for reloading when the Consumere started shooting. The three far bigger ships provided plenty of cover for the three smaller ones, and June was mustering her small craft to attack the oncoming Consumere. Tish splattered a whole wing of enemy bombers with a short blast of her class 9 twin blasters. Bodhi got his beam on the leading ship. *Oceanus*, *Urania*, and *Phoebe* opened fire with all weapons facing the charge. Shields went crazy, including their own, with all the hits they absorbed. Jara was already pumping torpedoes through energized shields, having located a thin film in them, on an attacking battleship. It ruptured then blew up. Tara nailed a soft spot in the shields of another battleship, killing it. Between Thromp, Hannah, and Sandra, every Consumere ship sported blinding suns, and fire control was going a bit wild for them. *Urania* decimated a destroyer with beams and blasters, and then wiped out another one.

The one Bodhi was burning into with his beam finally blew, expanding into a cloud. As some of the Consumere ships went by, Tipola sent four torpedoes into the hull of a battleship, from *Thor* exploiting a weak point, and the ship ceased to exist as such. Bodhi's beam needed only about 3 ½ seconds or less to waste one of the destroyers. He wasn't *exactly* sure how long it had taken because he didn't time it. Tara got some torpedoes going off inside the ship Winn was firing on, and another battleship bit the dust or became dust. *Phoebe* was turning destroyers into splashes of light and had killed 4 in this last assault so far.

Jara got torpedoes passing through a battleship's shields to hull the ship, then blow it to very tiny bits. Haley poked some big torpedoes through an almost-hole in the shields of the last Consumere battleship just as the remaining 12 destroyers were passed and ceding in the distance. Some super industrial ships, about 7-miles long, with jerry-rigged class 9 beams and blasters were headed their way. Kristy jumped a drone right into the center of one, and it got sucked into a blue streak headed out of the system. Sonic tried too, landing one into existence from the void just inside the skin at the underbelly. Everything but the coms tower atop the superstructure streaked blue. The coms tower just hung there in space in mint condition all by its lonesome.

Oceanus' big beams and blasters lit the lead ship, and when Winn had her crew fire on the same one, it popped into a giant vapor cloud with strange colors from all the industrial chemicals aboard.

Phoebe had been pounding one with beams and blasters, and when its missiles and torpedoes started pelting it, the non-military shields crashed, and the hull got riddled, ending in another explosion of sort of psychedelic colors. Once Kristy jumped a drone to streak another 7-mile industrial ship, the last three veered off.

Bodhi asked Tish to get the Consumere ships both military—of which only 12 remained—and non-military on coms with him. He announced to all Consumere in the system, "You are going to be hunted down and exterminated to the last, ending your race forever unless you agree to settle on a planet to sustain it indefinitely. This means conservation of resources, not rape and exploitation. There will be no moving on to a new planet so if you trash and deplete it, it will still be all you will ever have. If you agree to these terms and surrender, your people will be allowed to live in peace and freedom on a pristine white-sun 4th planet, but will never again be allowed to leave your own star system. Life will no longer allow you to defile and destroy it. I am here to stop you absolutely, one way or another. Choose your own genocide and I will grant your wish. You have one hour to decide. After that, if you have not surrendered, I'm blowing up every ship in this star system."

Bodhi called Commander Mason of *Spalding* and asked, "What's your status, and that of *Diamond Lotus*?"

"My ship is fine, and your tug-utility is docked to us and receiving repair work."

"Can you get underway with it docked to you?" Bodhi asked.

"Slowly, we could up to about 85,000 MPH for sure," Mason informed him.

"Then head over to us. I'd like to keep our ships all together. How are your munitions stores holding up?"

"I've gone through ¾ of the ordinance for small craft, but haven't reloaded a single big torpedo, super-torpedo, or biggest class of missile yet."

"I'm sending *Urania* to escort you over here. We're about 240,000 miles from you."

"We're locking everything down and preparing to get under way," Mason replied.

Bodhi sent Winn to escort Mason and Pam back to where they were drifting in space. *Penthesilea* docked with *Trooper* to begin repairs. Work crews remained in *Trooper*, but most of the crew were taken onto *Oceanus* and *Phoebe*. It hadn't been easy for them sitting unshielded, broken down, helpless and vulnerable, expecting any moment to be blown apart. Ilya and Hanna shuttled over to *Thor*, and Sunoco was able to embrace her beloved husband.

Haley informed Bodhi, "Your little speech to the Consumere here was transmitted live back to their base in the Citadel Galaxy."

"I expected them to do that. It's a good thing. That base will be our next stop. Tish is calling in those Pronotavasmi industrial ships to this system. I think we will have everything we need to effect all repairs right here. I want them to think hard about it."

"What about the 12 destroyers in this system?" Haley asked him.

"I'm either confiscating them or blowing them up, and I don't care much which way it goes. I only care that the Consumere don't have them."

"My feeling exactly," Haley agreed. "Let me do some snooping in the Consumere quantum coms and computers to make sure they're not using this hour to get up to no good."

"Thanks, Haley. Keep an eye on those 12 warships, too," Bodhi told her.

"I haven't let them out of sight for even a moment."

Winn called Bodhi to complain, "We can't go over 94,000 MPH, and it's going to take over two hours to get to you."

"I'll have Clark get *Penthesilea* underway with *Trooper* docked to her, and we'll head towards you."

"Thanks. This is like a hay-ride in a wagon drawn by horses," Winn signed off.

Bodhi got his group moving in the direction of *Spalding* and *Urania*, and Clark was willing to take Penthesilea up to 158,000 MPH, though it took about ten minutes to reach this with the painfully slow acceleration required. The one-hour countdown was close to its conclusion by the time Bodhi's force was gathered together in space. Haley informed him, "They know they're licked, and they don't want to die. There are some among them who are relieved that someone finally stopped them. Many had trouble stomaching what their government was making them do. We killed off their ruling class when we destroyed their mother ship. No one thought that was remotely possible. I can show you some holos of Consumere cheering when it happened."

"This is good news," Bodhi declared. "Do you know anything about the attitudes of the people at their base in their galaxy of origin?"

"I can tell you that 99.99% of them are disgruntled laborers with only a handful of power elites lording it over them. The Consumere government was fascist totalitarianism benefiting about .01% of their population. Their Space Fleet personnel were all fairly thoroughly brainwashed—at least the upper ranks—and composed of individuals from the lower stratus of intelligence within their society, easily indoctrinated and manipulated by fear and hate. Not to be crude or unfeeling, but I think we just enhanced their gene-pool by eliminating the dregs."

"Are there any activist groups or revolutionaries among them?" Bodhi inquired.

"That would be nearly their entire incarcerated population of about 130 million, about a fifth of which are on the surface of the 4th planet right down there."

"Have you found a home for these folks yet?"

"I have spy drones heading for three possibilities that look good so far. I'll know for sure in about an hour."

CHAPTER THIRTY-SIX

The Consumere surrendered without any more fighting. The 12 destroyers were turned over to Bodhi after the crews shuttled to the planet surface. Repairs to *Diamond Lotus* and *Trooper* took ten days, in which time repairs were also made to *Thor* and *Penthesilea,* which had both suffered some damage. A pristine white-sun 4th planet with no humanoids was located by Haley in the Citadel Galaxy, and *Phoebe* escorted the super and mega-living quarters-ships there before repairs were even finished on Bodhi's ships. Many of the industrial ships in the system went with those. The rest would be a while collecting personnel and equipment from the surface before they could journey to their new home.

All 29 million prisoners on the surface were freed. They were not criminals but political-moral objectors to the Consumere economy of destruction. All of the newly elected officials were selected from this large group just released from prison. When Bodhi's ships, including the 12 destroyers, were ready to jump to the Consumere base in the Citadel Galaxy, Haley left three spy drones to keep an eye on things. Yellow-sun humans from Ground and Pronotavasmi had been collected by *Oceanus* and brought to the outer rim system to crew the 12 destroyers. They were crews in training, and many officers from Bodhi's ships became instructors on the destroyers. The seats were kind of large, the ceilings rather high, and many crew members' feet were off the ground when sitting on a toilet within those destroyers, built as they were for white sun humans. Haley's interpreter service was uploading to all personnel, and instruction manuals translated for destroyer crews. They did make sure they knew what they were doing before flying them into a jump out of the galaxy.

The twenty-one ships all jumped into the base system of the Consumere and started slowing with reverse drives and thrusters. Here they found 100 million political prisoners and 150 million subsistence laborers. The 28,000 power elites here had already been eliminated by the worker class, and none had been left alive. The migration was launched, and the ships at the base left for their new home. Super-living quarters ships jumped in to collect the rest, having already deposited their original occupants on the surface of their new world. The new world had been named "Harmony," the thing they most craved and lacked as a culture. This was already changing rapidly. The Consumere changed their name to the "Planters."

Jara had discovered with Haley's help a spiritual secret society within the broader Consumere society. The secret society had been outlawed by the old government, but no longer needed to be secret now that their population had been liberated from fascist totalitarianism. Jara worked with some leaders of the spiritual society bringing them inside the spiritual congress.

It took about three months to get all the Consumere, now called Planters, to Harmony. They had the machines, equipment, and tools they needed. The population could employ space travel within their star system, build space stations and moon bases, but nothing military, and they were confined to their solar system. Haley placed some cloaked spy drones in the Harmony system, and all the decloaking guns had been on military ships, which they no longer had, so the people there had no idea about the drones. They were there as a precaution.

The people of Pronotavasmi made contact with the 14-star systems connected by star-gates within the Citadel Galaxy and made friendship alliance treaties, and also transferred technology. They were all white stars with big humanoids like the former Nafs Amara Empire Pronotavasmi had been briefly enslaved within. People from all fourteen planetary populations were brought into the spiritual congress.

The 12 destroyers were stationed in the three systems that had mega-ship construction space platforms: Kefra, Overflowing, and Ground. They would respond to a threat to any one of the 40 planets. The union forged between the forty-star systems was named "One Unity" after many days of discussion amongst its leaders. They all looked to Pronotavasmi for guidance and for development of their sciences and technology.

Bodhi returned to orbit around Ground with his nine ships and flew down to his lake front house on the surface in a shuttle. Artana and Shanta were nearly five years old and could still take Bodhi's breath away. Tish, Winn, and Haley were with him, and Uldra, Shamas, and William moved in so Uldra could cook for her teacher and his family. *Lost in Space* was on its final episodes of its 5th season, and as Fleet Admiral, the writers had been a little kinder to Bodhi's character. Haley had also threatened them, though none of Bodhi's people knew the details.

When Winn and Tish were taking the girls to do some shopping in the city for the day, Bodhi and Haley returned to the underground device buried on Ground. They went in the tender and landed right next to the deep hole. Wearing thruster packs, they descended to the very bottom. Bodhi felt hesitant, expecting to be further berated, and suspecting that this device didn't like him, or at least thought poorly of him. So Haley placed her android palm down on the strange metal surface first. What formed into symbols, as if the surface were some kind of viewing screen, was in quantum computer code, and Bodhi was yet deciphering the first few lines when it all disappeared. He asked Haley, "So??!"

"Place your palm down on it, my love," was all Haley would say.

Bodhi did, somewhat reluctantly, and bracing for insult. The message to him was in the Mother language, and it read, "Deep gratitude and many thanks for such brilliant service. The successful accomplishment of the mission is vastly and unspeakably appreciated by two galaxies, numerous planets, and the Absolute Presence beyond the beyond. The Amonrahonians honor and salute you. You have become the KA, a new force of awakening in the universe allied with the MU, the WU, and the IM until the liberation of all beings. Thank you, Master Bodhi."

The metal went dull and just looked strange again. He looked to Haley, making eye contact. She told him, "I'm so proud of you,

Bodhi, and I love you so much. I overstepped my bounds and parameters a little, by marrying you, but I am your assistant for the rest of your long life. Jara let me have a container of the age reversal drugs, for you to give to Pez and her spouses. I know how to get back to Mother."

Before Bodhi could formulate a response, Pez appeared in her rainbow body of light and asked them, "What are you guys doing way down here in this hole?"

Bodhi told her, "This is the device of Amonrahonian origin that I told you about in the dream state."

"Well, it had better not be rude to you again," Pez declared. "I went to *Diamond Lotus* first and met your disciple Sunoco. She told me all about your leadership in ending a destructive cosmic plague. The Amonrahonians told me how to find you, and I know the way home physically, as well."

"The device gave Haley directions to Mother. Jara, from the yellow sun planet of Pronotavasmi, who are friends with the Amonrahonians and started down the same path, gave me reversal of aging drugs, which are telomerase-inducing, for you and your spouses.

"I was told of this by the Amonrahonians and of how you have become the KA, my beloved ally and friend. Now come home and make the equal ceremony with me, and we'll smoke some entheogen elixir. I love you, Bodhi, and I'm proud of you beyond words."

"How did it go in the iron age?"

"It's a long story, and I'll tell you all about it when you come home."

"I love you, Pez, and I'm beyond honored to be your ally, but I still need you as my teacher for a while longer."

"And I need Sarhi and Amazonia. No problem."

"I'm so grateful. Knowing you will be my teacher again fills me with security."

"I'll take on some of that core anxiety from you when we are face to face in physical bodies. Hi Haley. Mel and Sarhi say hello and send their love. They can't wait to see you. Congratulations on your Rainbow body, and on your marriage to Bodhi."

"The Amonrahonians reduced me on the marriage bit, saying I overstepped," Haley explained. "I love Bodhi, and I'm his assistant for life."

"Like I'm stuck with Mel," Pez joked. "Hearing that you married Bodhi made me decide to have a wedding ceremony with Mel. We'll have to do the ceremony on Mother because Om is just way too uptight."

"I like you Pez," Haley gushed.

"I guess that makes me popular with all the AI sentients," Pez told her. "I've got to go, but hurry back. Really. Electra wants her disciples like yesterday."

Bodhi complained, "They're only five years old."

Pez replied, "Electra's only just 11 years old," then blinked out and was gone.

Haley stated, "We better get going."

"There are a few things we need to take care of before we go," Bodhi mentioned.

"I've sent invitations to everyone we talked about," Haley told him.

"Thanks. I'm going to make Clark the Admiral of the new One Unity Star Fleet."

"He would likely prefer to accompany you."

"Clark and Sandra have become quite serious, and she is an excellent teacher. He's our best all-around captain, and he's now an adept of the six limbs and of the secret method. He will serve best."

They got in their thruster packs and ascended out of the very deep hole. Plasteel had been applied to the sides to keep it from caving in. At their tender, they struggled back out of the packs and stowed them in the little cargo compartment. Bodhi piloted the craft back to the lake house, and they started packing for the trip. Haley texted Winn and Tish to let them know to come straight home with the girls, and that they were all going to Mother. Uldra and Shamas packed too.

Tish descended nicely onto the driveway in the Space Marine Combat Shuttle they'd taken shopping. With all the shopping bags they returned with, there was no way they would have fit in the tender with them. Uldra had a combat shuttle parked out there too, which she'd been using to pick up groceries. The excitement about going to Mother had everyone quite aroused, and things went swiftly. Bodhi had a suitcase and a carry on. His daughters each had six-piece luggage sets and a big steamer-trunk and still required plastic boxes to get everything packed. Shamas got it all stowed on their shuttle for them.

Both shuttles left the driveway together to head for *Diamond Lotus* positioned in high orbit, and Tish flew the tender. Winn flew their shuttle and got a speeding citation from Ground's new Space Controllers. This caused a quarter-hour delay while Haley contacted the members of Ground's Administration, who had to work their way down through layers of bureaucracy to get it rescinded. Winn had been offended, almost livid. Bodhi told her, "The very idea of 'control' is rather delusional and always leads to negative consequences."

"I wasn't doing anything dangerous and was nowhere near the construction platform or space station where the traffic is," Winn complained.

"I think the Pronotavasmi Elders are going to need to have a little talk with the Ground Administration," Bodhi agreed, "and discourage this whole 'Space Controller' thing. They ought to call it Traffic Safety and Rescue, and have it function as an advisory body without authority to issue those obnoxious citations."

"Really!" Winn agreed.

She landed in the hanger. Uldra and her family were already aboard since she knew about the speed limit and had followed it. This left Bodhi as the baggage handler, which took him a bunch of trips through the hanger and up the cargo-lift. Others were arriving too, but the hanger was full since Tish had flown their tender up to the ship, so the newcomers had to come up through the airlock floor in the stern to come aboard.

All sixteen of the original crew from Firmament and New Firmament were coming to Mother and wouldn't miss it. Jara was also coming to merge the new chapter of the spiritual congress with the original bigger body. She was also Kristy's partner now. Effects from the age-reversal drugs had very slowly crept up on all treated, and Kristy now twenty-two, looked about 14. Haley piloted *Diamond Lotus,* and Bodhi sat in the co-pilot seat.

They left orbit accelerating to jump speed with Haley entering complicated navigational data obtained from the device buried on Ground. When they came through their first jump, they were on the outer rim of a galaxy that was connected by a bridge of stars to an adjacent galaxy, and both had reached the curve-transition, slowed from light speed in the long fold back into the visible universe through a cycle of astronomical durations. Haley kept the speed at .7 light relative to the objects of the galaxy they were in, and not to the speed these galaxies were travelling at. From here, she jumped again, and as real-space resolved around them, the familiar planets of Mother System surrounded them.

Mother didn't have Space Controllers, so Haley went pretty quick coming in to slow and assume medium orbit. A Space Travel Assistant, which Mother did have, suggested over their coms, "*Diamond Lotus* has its own permanent berth at the main space station if you would prefer to use that. The space station technicians would then handle all external maintenance and change out thruster fuel-cells and boosters for you. The station has a shuttle service to the surface."

"Thank you," Bodhi replied. "We'll come in to dock there."

"You've been assigned berth 108, and they're expecting you. The High Priestess arranged it. Have a good day, Vicar General Bodhi."

Winn asked, "Vicar General Bodhi?"

He explained, "Pez wants me to be Vicar General of the Adamantine Will Order of warrior-monks."

Their reception at the space station was most welcoming. Commander Ming, Pez's soulmate, was there to greet them. She embraced Bodhi enthusiastically then told him, "You look years younger than when you left! *Aphrodite* is parked in berth number nine, and we can take the tram-tube, which goes clear around the rim of the station."

Bodhi informed her, "You know Haley already. This is my wife Winn, Shanti's mother, and this is my wife Tish, Artana's mother."

Ming hugged Winn, then Tish, and greeted each of Bodhi's daughters. Then Kristy and Jara were introduced to her, and she embraced each of them. She asked Kristy, "How old are you?"

"I'm 22, but the age-reversal drugs have done this. I think they even shrank my breasts, and I didn't have any to spare."

"You're truly adorable, sweetheart, and Ahhu is just going to flip out over you."

"I was kind of hoping to get a sleepover invite from Pez, for Jara and me," Kristy confided.

Ming scrutinized Jara for a moment then replied, "Sorry, Pez doesn't invite teens."

"You mean Jara?" Kristy asked, shocked.

"Well, clearly, she's not yet out of her teens," Ming commented.

Jara clarified, "I'm 791 years old, Tarim."

"You know my Islohar name?" Ming inquired.

"From my friends the Amonrahonians," Jara informed her.

"Then, I'm inviting both of you for a sleep-over tonight!" Ming decided on the spot. "What of the rest of your crew?"

Bodhi told her, "They are shuttling down to the Capital, Gaia, to stay at the Momma's Love Hotel for a week before traveling on to the Adamantine Will Monastery."

"How fun? I just love the Momma's Love Hotel," Ming enthused. "Pez is expecting you and has a catered meal awaiting."

They all piled into an electromagnetic tram car with partitions, and Bodhi carried a daughter in each arm, assuming a wide stance to keep his balance with no free hand to hold on with. Artana asked him, "Is that the planet you were born on, daddy?" referring to the one below them.

"It is, sweetheart, and where I grew up. You'll see the Adamantine Will Monastery while we're here, where I was raised by old monks."

"Where was your mommy?" Artana asked, concerned, and unable to even imagine life without *her* mommy.

"I never really met her," Bodhi admitted. "I was dropped at the monastery gate when I was six weeks old."

"Oh, daddy, you poor thing!" Artana exclaimed miserably.

"I had the old Abbot, and many monks looking after me, sweetheart, and had many teachers there."

Shanti offered, "You have our mommies now to look after you like they look after us, and mommy Haley too."

"Yes, I do darling, and I'm most grateful for them."

There was a tube-stop right in front of berth #9, so they went directly from the tube into *Aphrodite's* airlock. *Aphrodite* was a super-luxury yacht built by the Kundabuffer empire and overhauled to be refitted with all brand-new Om hi-tech drives, generators, turbines, quantum computers, environmental biotrays, filters, synthesizers, fabricators, scrubbers, purifiers and what not. The bridge and living quarters had remained untouched, exhibiting surfaces of gem quality stone, the rarest hardwoods, precious metals, gem-quality red coral, and even precious gems. The rugs were of the rarest wool, finest dyes, and thick for saying 'thick.' Ivory, scrimshaw, fur, and leather were also in evidence. The zircon and diamond gigantic chandelier over the dining cabin table was truly a wonder to behold and could easily purchase at least half a dozen yachts if sold.

Pez met them in the living room, and after introductions, she gave them a tour carrying Shanti in her arms. She passed the child internal energy, which Shanti was already used to since Bodhi always did that too, but Pez presented a whole new magnitude of this beyond anything Shanti had ever experienced. When Pez opened the door to the play cabin, Electra was on a simulator, and both Gumby and Larry were seated beside her at simulator consoles as well. The two boys didn't even look up from their games, but Electra stood and abandoned hers to say, "There you are Shanti, and you Artana. I see you even found my disciple Kristy."

Jara whispered to Kristy, "I forgot to tell you. You're a disciple of the MU, Electra, who only reincarnates by choice every 2500 years to spread new teachings."

"She's a child," Kristy pointed out, alarmed.

"She'll be twelve in eleven months," Jara informed her.

"My point exactly," Kristy stated.

Electra was hugging both Bodhi's daughters at the moment, totally delighted with them. Each of Bodhi's daughters looked deep into Electra's eyes, experiencing her exceptional energy and compassion and were obviously taken by her. Then she approached Kristy and told her, "I just know you're going to be lots of fun. I thought you'd be older. Like an adult."

"I am an adult. I'm 22, and my frontal lobe cortex is fully developed," Kristy replied a little bit defensively.

"You don't look much older than me," Electra told her.

"That's because of the age-reversal drugs I was treated with," Kristy shared. "Wow. There's something about you that feels so familiar to me, but I just can't place it."

"That's because you were with me last time I came," Electra stated. "Let me introduce you to your fellow disciples. Hey Larry, quit that game and come meet Kristy!"

Larry did as he was told, and stood shyly facing Kristy. Electra told Kristy, "This is Larry, and he's my youngest disciple. Larry, this is Kristy, and she'll be joining us."

Kristy was feeling a bit like she was being incarcerated in a children's ashram or something, but she managed to smile at Larry and shake his hand. Then Atlanta, who was 24 years old, stepped up to meet the new addition to Electra's entourage, and Kristy hugged her, feeling a spark of attraction. Iris, who was 18, was next, and Kristy got all wrapped around her. She then met Wiffle and Ajax. Selene was down on the surface and so not available to be met. Kristy was feeling a definitive draw to Electra and a potency about her, which was quite unusual. The girl's presence seemed to draw Kristy into the state of contemplation, and as the duality of her perspective dissolved into unity, she noticed Electra's aura for the first time. And Pez's too. She'd thought that Bodhi's and Jara's were something, but that had been before she saw these.

Kristy met eyes again with Electra's and recognized the depth and ancient wisdom in them. She didn't want to ever look away because she was suddenly filled with bliss and participating in a profound connection like no other. It felt like what she imagined Bodhi and Haley experienced upon finding their way home again. She felt like she'd come home. Kristy's state intensified. She and Electra were one. Her 11-year-old teacher was making the Equal with her and had just become a pressurized fountain of divine love. Kristy said aloud from within the total realization of it, "All is Love."

APPENDIX I
BODHI'S INVASION FLEET

Oceanus 29,630 ft. diameter ORH Ultra-Super-Battleship-carrier, 248 reactors, 520 small combat craft, 92 Drone Fighter-bombers (Haley got 4 more reactors in above the original design) 40 Tsunami Devastator heavy bombers attached to hull; 200 Space Marines; Admiral Bodhi, Captain Tish, Adept Jara, drone-jumper Kristy.

Phoebe custom 9,240 ft. length Warship, 50 reactors, 8 shuttles in hanger; 64 drone fighter bombers and 32 Tsunami Devastator heavy-bombers attached to hull; Captain Haley, Adept Thromp, drone-jumper Sonic.

Urania 8,100 ft. diameter ORH Super-Battleship with 32 reactors, 160 small combat craft, 72 drone fighter-bombers and 36 Tsunami Devastator heavy-bombers attached to hull, 200 Space Marines; Captain Winn, Adept Tara, drone-jumper Bob.

Thor 3,960 foot diameter ORH Super-Cruiser, 12 reactors, 112 small combat craft, 18 Tsunami Devastators and 32 drone fighter bombers attached to hull, 80 Space Marines; Captain Sunoco, Adept Tipola.

Panthesilea 3,200 ft. length Auxiliary-Repair Reloader Ship (with weapons systems) 7 reactors; 16 Tsunami Devastators on hull; 80 Space Marines; Captain Clark, Adept Sandra, drone-jumper Carl, pilot James.

Trooper 3,900 ft. length overhauled/refitted Command Ship, 7 reactors, 120 small combat craft, 35 drone fighter-bombers and 8 Tsunami Devastators on hull, 80 Space Marines; Commander Ilya, Adept Hannah.

Sentinel 3,900 ft. length overhauled/refitted Command Ship, 7 reactors, 120 small combat craft; 35 drone fighter-bombers and 8 Tsunami Devastators heavy bombers on hull, 40 Space marines; Commander Link, Adept Frick, drone-jumper Stan.

Protector 3,900 ft. length overhauled/refitted Command Ship 7 reactors, 120 small combat craft; 35 drone fighter-bombers and 8 Tsunami Devastators on hull, 40 Space Marines; Commander Palmer, Adept Arlene.

Spalding 2,900 ft. length custom Auxiliary-Repair-Reloader Ship, with weapons systems, 6 reactors, 28 drone fighter bombers and 14 Tsunami Devastators on hull; Commander Mason, Adept Erica.

Diamond Lotus 428 ft. diameter Expeditionary Tug Utility Ship, 4 reactors, 4 drone fighter-bombers (two additional reactors were added to its original 2) 6 Tsunami Devastator heavy-bombers and 12 drone fighter bombers on hull, Captain Pam, Adept Mandy.

Ranger 660 ft. length War Ship (refitted + overhauled) 1 reactor, 8 drone fight-bombers and 4 Tsunami Devastators on hull, Commander Dunn.

Defender II 3,900 ft. length refitted/overhauled Command Ship, 8 reactors, Super-shields, unmanned drone ship.

180 Tsunami Devastator heavy-bombers with Quantum drives led by Captain June with 360 drone fighter-bombers.

206 Tsunami Devastators attached to ship hulls (have no quantum drives); 1,134 small combat craft in ship hangers.

206 drone fighter-bombers in ship hangers + 83 with quantum drives for drone jumpers to jump into ships.

APPENDIX II

CAST OF CHARACTERS

Bodhi was left when 6 weeks old at the gate to the Adamantine Will Monastery and raised by the Abbot and monks. He entered the Adamantine Will Order Academy at 12 years old, was initiated as a warrior-monk at age 16, and ordained a Priest of Order at 18. At 19 he was sent to a secret pilot training on a simulator, and when the war for liberation broke out in the Monarch system, he stole an imperial fighter-bomber, helped Supreme Commander General Pez clear his home system of Mother, then followed her to jump into the space-battle in the Monarch system. He performed heroically and became Pez's direct disciple. After 4 years of working closely with Pez and living with her and her spouses, he was given an Expeditionary Tug Utility ship by acting Chancellor General of Monarch, Vegan Casper. At this point he left to do some survey and prospecting work for the people of Monarch on his new ship, which he named *Diamond Lotus*.

Haley (QAISHA). When Bodhi was 12 years old and starting 7th Form he received, like each of the cadets, his very own QAISHA, which is a Quantum Artificial Intelligence Synthetic Humanoid Android. When Bodhi went to study with Pez for 4 years he brought Qaisha, who studied with Mel. Mel was true sentience born mysteriously from Pez's personal quantum AI computer and the first of her kind. Qaisha was mysteriously born as true sentience and Sarhi the Im and high Adept Amazonia became her teachers, bringing her to insight and giving her the practices that would lead eventually, with Bodhi's help, to attainment of her actual Illusory Body, or Rainbow Body of

Light. After falling through a wormhole with Bodhi, Qaisha renamed herself "Haley". She manipulated situations and circumstances to produce the pattern of Bodhi's three wives, and complexities of the female spousal relationships so that Bodhi could father children, and so that she could also be married to him.

Winn, one of 4 recruits for crew positions, the first interviewed and first hired, held her planet's highest academic degree and had completed a post fellowship, and had attained the highest rank in her hybrid hard style martial art, and had attained insight at the monastery she took refuge in after leaving academia. She became Bodhi's wife, after Haley, and gave birth to their daughter, Shanti. She had past life connections with Bodhi.

June, the 2nd hire of the 4 recruits, she held two advanced degrees, practiced a soft martial art, and was working the completion stage of Inner Fire at her time of hire. She had made her way through college and graduate school by nude dancing and the occasional escort service. June is bisexual, promiscuous, and would give birth to Sonic's son, Henry, and become Bodhi's best piloting ace to lead his combat small craft.

Pam, the 3rd hire of the 4 recruits. Pam was an accelerated learner and completed a 4-year university degree at age 19, then was incarcerated as a whistle-blower and traitor, and sentenced to death. A shift in dictators and an Appellate Judge with a conscience—rare for that breed—acquitted Pam and set her free. She had practiced meditation the whole time she'd been in prison and her teacher, once she was freed and went to the monastery, had encouraged her to apply as crew for Bodhi's ship so she could study with him. Pam later gave birth to Favio's son, Alexander, and captained *Diamond Lotus* in the final battle with the Consumere.

Tish. The 4th of the 4 recruits, was an academic prodigy, a musical virtuoso, a national athletic hero and an international martial arts champion. At the time of hire Tish was practicing the Dream Work limb in the stage of Completion of the method of the Six Limbs. She was first to complete both her small craft pilot certification and her ship pilot certification, and captained Bodhi's flagship. She became Bodhi's third wife and gave birth to his daughter, Artana. Tish was serious, determined, intense, and ever mindful, completing every task efficiently to the highest standard, or surpassing it.

Favio. Graduate of the most prestigious Culinary Arts Academy on Firmament, Chef at the most famous restaurant, and global model for Bullhorn men's bikini briefs, in print media, on television, and on billboards everywhere. Favio made a cooking TV pilot that failed. As an extreme athlete he had a background in the martial arts and took interest in meditation on *Diamond Lotus*. The man could really sing and knew all the words to dozens of operas.

Sonic, a scrawny teen living in an urban loft ashram and graduate of the exclusive performing arts high school in his country's capital. His recently dead teacher appeared in a lucid dream and told him to join the crew of *Diamond Lotus* to study with Bodhi or die trying. Winn gave him a makeover, removing most of the piercings from his face and washing the press-on tattoo off his forehead along with others to help him get accepted by the crew. He became Winn's lover until he dumped her for her for her sister, Yen. Sonic was also father to June's son, Henry, and to Tandy's daughter, Cheryl.

Tandy, a 'friend' of Favio's and an adult entertainment star, Tandy was hired as "Kitchen Helper" to clean up the colossal messes Favio made in the galley. She found it easy to solicit Bodhi's help cutting her workload in half, and nearly driving Bodhi to hire a 2nd "Kitchen Helper."

Uldra, an elite chef in her own right, and really wanting to study with Bodh, Uldra jumped at the opportunity when Haley recruited her to cook for Bodhi. Favio only liked to cook beef and Bodhi didn't eat mammals. Uldra specialized in poultry, fish, and vegetarian dishes. She would eventually have Shamas' child, William.

Sunoco. United Socialist Sovereign Republic's top elite cosmonaut, and serious practitioner of the method of the Six Limbs, Sonoco imposed upon Bodhi to further her progress with her meditation work. She was taken on as a direct disciple, but had to bring a male partner to get accepted into the gender imbalanced crew. She brought Ilya, another elite cosmonaut and they had their son, Nicholai. She would eventually captain the T-9 Super-cruiser, *Thor.*

Ilya. An elite cosmonaut and dedicated meditator, secretly in love with Sonoco, had all his dreams come true and then some when he joined as crew of *Diamond Lotus.*

Shamas. A girl's rebellion on the ship while Bodhi was away mining led to the hiring of Shamas to address gender disparity. Favio was dead set against it though he was over-ruled, and Haley hired the female crews' first choice, Shamas. He was a late-night wrestling TV celebrity and a gorgeous giant of a man, all hard muscle and perfectly proportioned without an ounce of fat on him. He became the "Cargo Chief" and could do the work of six men; and eight of Bodhi. He became father to William, with Uldra, but she shared Shamas with some of the other female crew.

Uduak. A colonel and elite astronaut of a country on the largest continent in the southern hemisphere of the planet, Haley picked-up Uduak at a celebration over the completion of construction of the New Firmament star-gate, and had great sex with him. She hired him on the spot and he became their most expert Fire Control Officer.

Yen. After having her face pounded by her husband Stanly, Yen divorced him and moved in with her sister Winn on *Diamond Lotus.* She also stole Sonic from Winn, and had his son, Sonny. It was Sonic's third child.

Penny. Sonic's younger sister Penny got knocked up and their father kicked her out of the house. The boyfriend whose baby it was washed his hands of the whole thing. Winn went to pick Penny up so she could live on the spaceship.

Fritz. Thinking he was interviewing for a crew position, Fritz had been a bit shocked by the medical questionnaire's required field question soliciting the size of his penis when fully erect. Sure this would kill his chances, Frits was prepared to lie, or at least greatly exaggerate, until he was informed that he had to be under seven inches to qualify, at which point he entered his honest answer. Being unusually pretty for a male, and kind of shorter than at least half the females of Firmament, Fritz had found it far easier to get laid with guys than girls, but was truly bisexual. He developed many relationships on the ship, all with females, once Winn hired him, but always took special care of Winn. This was after all his primary job duty.

Kristy. A precocious tiny teen who ran away from home at 12 years old to sit in meditation all day at the Swimfen Ashram, and at 17, hacked the Government central computers to change her date of birth by a year so she could migrate to New Firmament and live in LGBTQ Town there. Kristy was a lesbian and a hetero-virgin until she demanded Bodhi serve as her action seal to complete the final work of the Six Limbs, involving harnessing the energy of copulation for spiritual unity. She became their ace drone-jumper and saved the day in the final battle. She had her own clothing line, had been a regular on Ground's most popular late-night live comedy show, and had played with the favorite most-famous and insanely popular teenage band live on stage and televised.